He Humiliated Her...
Wooed Her...
Deceived Her...
Then He Became Her Slave.

THIS OTHER EDEN

The story of
a love that became
an obsession

"Lusty . . . a smooth blend of the authentic
and the romantic . . . executed
with a stylistic panache and attention
to period details."
Publishers Weekly

THIS OTHER EDEN

MARILYN HARRIS

AVON
PUBLISHERS OF BARD, CAMELOT AND DISCUS BOOKS

AVON BOOKS
A division of
The Hearst Corporation
959 Eighth Avenue
New York, New York 10019

First Avon Printing, March, 1978

AVON TRADEMARK REG. U.S. PAT. OFF. AND IN
OTHER COUNTRIES, MARCA REGISTRADA,
HECHO EN U.S.A.

Printed in the U.S.A.

For Judge and Karen and John

Contents

The secret of the entire world is whispered
here at Eden Point in the tumultuous union of
sea and land, cliff and air. And for a very
brief space, every heart is touched and
melted with the sense of things divinely fair,
immeasurably great, immeasurably sad. . . .

—From the diary of
James Eden, First Baron
by tenure of Eden Castle,
written in 1232.

Eden Castle
North Devon,
England
1790

HE Public Whipping of Miss Marianne Locke, age sixteen, was scheduled to take place at seven in the morning on Friday, August the third, 1790, in the inner courtyard of Eden Castle, situated on the North Devon coast at the exact point where the Bristol Channel prepares to join the turbulence of the Atlantic Ocean.

The cliffs veered sharply southward from this point, fronting the unbroken force of the Atlantic winds and waves, and were shattered by them into a grim array of jutting points. Here the gales and ocean were supreme.

But atop the cliffs of Eden Point, supremacy resided in human hands, and the command for the Public Whipping, considered barbaric for the civilized late eighteenth century, had been issued by Thomas Eden himself, Thirteenth Baron and Fifth Earl. Thomas Eden possessed the power and had suffered the outrage, so on a hot humid Thursday afternoon he shouted at Ragland, his male servant, "Whip her!" As his anger showed no signs of abating, he added, "Publicly! And all those who fail to witness it may also find themselves in her unfortunate position!"

The whipping had been announced to all the tenants and fishermen of Mortemouth, the village that sat at sea level at the foot of Eden Castle. These people were totally

3

dependent upon the Lord of the Castle and his twenty thousand acres of rich sheep-grazing land.

The prisoner was led by Ragland into the Keep through the Norman doorway. She found herself imprisoned in a small, windowless room, barely able to breathe. She waited for Ragland to say something to her, acknowledging the many evenings he had shared a pint with her father in their cottage in Mortemouth.

But the old man refused to look at her. He kept his hand over his nose to shield against the poisonous vapors of the charnel house, and he kept his white head bowed. Only when he was closing the heavy door behind him did she hear him mutter, "Keep close to the floor, Marianne. There's life there. The breathing's easier."

The door closed, the bolts slid into place. In terror and despair, she hurled herself at the solid oak barrier. Slowly sensing her predicament, she sank to the floor, still struggling for breath.

A series of almost invisible shudders passed over her, over her mouth, and down into her shoulders and arms. A spasm of waking moved upward from some deep-shocked realm. She closed her eyes and then opened them. Instantly she tried to get to her feet, but fell back into a pose of annihilation.

From this stunned state, she observed her surroundings, a small room of solid stone. On the floor nearby was a pile of straw reeking with the odor of urine and feces. And there, in the far corner, the pit itself, the deep hole of the charnel well descending thirty feet to the level of the courtyard outside, the place where the rotting carcasses of cattle and sheep were thrown, from which the stench of putrefaction arose to asphyxiate any prisoner long held in the room.

Focusing on the hole, her face went rigid. The foul air burned her lungs, then her terror blended with a curious relief, since she had certain knowledge that she would never endure the pain and humiliation of the public whipping. She would not survive the night.

She pressed closer to the door, still keeping her eyes on the charnel well as though it were alive. She remembered —although she did not relish gossip—about three weeks prior, shortly after she had climbed the cliff staircase to take her place in service at Eden Castle, that she had been warned by the House Warden, Dolly Wisdom, to stay away from the Keep. The serving women in the Buttery had told her a Cornwellian, caught stealing sheep, had been thrown still alive down the charnel well, on top of the rotting carcasses. For a week thereafter, Marianne thought she had heard shrieks of death.

She watched her hand ascend to her mouth, as though both belonged to someone else. She felt a long, slow convulsion in the pit of her stomach. Only at the last moment, threatened with unconsciousness, did she remember old Ragland's advice—"Keep close to the floor. There's life there." In spite of her torture, she flattened herself against the stone floor, her nose pressed against the hairline crack beneath the heavy door. It was true. She found, coming from beneath the door, a brief respite. Thus she lay with no sense of time, her body pressed against the crack.

In an extreme act of will, she soothed herself. *If* the man had indeed been thrown into the well, he would blessedly be dead by now. The eyes in her back had nothing to worry about. But the flesh of her back did, for she had decided that she would survive the night, that at seven o'clock the following morning, she would still be there, that she would be led out into the inner courtyard to the whipping oak, would have her back bared, and would endure ten lashes and the greater pain of sober observance by people who had known her all her life.

Imagining the coming ordeal was more terrifying than the resurrection of the rotting Cornwellian. Suddenly she tasted blood on her lips, the natural stress of image becoming fact. She sent her thoughts elsewhere, to the headlands along the top of Eden Point where she had run as a child, taking bread and cheese to her father at sheepshearing time, to her roses which, by general consensus, were the prettiest in all of Mortemouth, to the grave of her dead mother in the tiny parish churchyard by the quay.

Such thoughts produced a surprising change in her expression. From behind the fair hair fallen over graceful shoulders and slender neck framed by a crude muslin collar looked a face that was quite astonishing, not only for its beauty, but also for the strange intensity in the eyes, an appeal so gently and almost courteously denied by the mouth's civilized half-smile. Yet there was uncertainty in the face, even tentativeness, a surprising and alarming force.

She longed for the comforting arms of her father. His agony was certainly as great as her own, as he blamed himself for her present ordeal. It had been his idea that she go into service at Eden Castle. "A good future for you, Marianne," he had said. "The only reasonable option for a young woman."

She groaned aloud and longed to comfort him, although she knew his comforters were all around him, that the low-ceilinged cottage fairly was bursting with commiserating friends and neighbors, all dreading the ordeal of the morning as much as she.

Her gentle features contorted. Quickly she reversed her last thought. No, not as much as she, for their backs would not be bared, nor their arms bound in tight embrace of the whipping oak. The flesh of their foreheads would not be ground into the tar-covered bark, nor their nerves and muscles resisting the cutting lash of the whip.

The full horror of the ordeal swept over her. She made a curious sound as though she had already sustained the blows of the whip. Her arms lifted over her head. Her fingers went forward, hesitated, and trembled as if they had found the comfort of a hand in the dark. Her crying mouth tasted the grit of the stone floor.

The tears continued for some time, a small indulgence, smaller comfort. Laboring under the weight of her own remorseless visualizations, she fell into a stupefied exhaustion. Outside she heard the faint deep voice of the night watchman calling, "All is well." Her tear-stained face now seemed possessed of a stubborn cataleptic calm. All was not well, not yet.

Abruptly she lifted herself upward, first drawing a deep breath of clean air from beneath the door. Then, slowly, she crawled forward on hands and knees, as though she were a supplicant suffering some inscrutable wish for salvation, stopping at last at the very edge of the charnel well.

She knelt, gasping for breath. The clean air from the door was depleted in her lungs. Still kneeling, she forced herself in the dying light to look over the edge and down. The features of her face set, as though convinced of this abrupt necessity. Something in her body commensurate with the weight in her mind where reason was inexact forced her to look down at the rotting liquid carcasses of cattle and sheep with stiffened legs, swollen, exploded bellies, entrails like red snakes in shimmering piles amid blood-encrusted hides. She forced herself to look closer until in the semidarkness she found it, a human hand, a human torso, a human head cradled in the burst brains of an animal, glassy eyes distended, mouth agape, frozen in a scream at the exact moment the poisonous air had suffocated him.

Drawing back from the edge, she closed her eyes. The Cornwellian was beyond her prayers, yet she prayed anyway and her prayer was monstrous because in it there was no margin of forgiveness. For the man walking somewhere in the upper regions of Eden Castle who had put her in this place, she felt no compassion. She prayed only for the Cornwellian and for herself.

After the prayer, she moved farther back from the edge of the charnel well. She felt a sharp pain in the pit of her stomach, the result of breathing the poisonous air. Shuddering in the double pain of poison and fury, she crawled back to the door.

For three or four minutes she lost herself. Where she had gone, she had no idea. When she came to, she was pressed against the crack beneath the door. She did not wonder what had happened.

She said aloud, "There is nothing in this place of which I need be afraid." For the rest of the night, she held her terror at bay with that gentle though misleading smile.

In 1790, on the West Coast of England, to speak of castles was to speak of Eden. Seen from the coastline below, it looked like some great fortress, hewn roughly out of natural rock. Nature was taking back to herself the masses of stone reared centuries earlier. The giant walls and mighty buttresses looked as if they had been carved by wind and weather out of a solid mass, rather than wrought by human handiwork. Historically Eden had served England well, and by the end of the eighteenth century there was no reason to believe that it would not endure into eternity.

On this sultry August evening, Thomas Eden, Thirteenth Baron and Fifth Earl, lay abed in his private chambers off the Morning Room, thinking not at all about the young

girl he had imprisoned that afternoon in the charnel house
cell. At forty, he was more his grandfather's son than his
father's, a tall man whose face and features bore the unmistakable imprint of genes gone awry. Both strains of the
unpredictable grandfather seemed to have been captured
simultaneously in one unruly personality. Instead of divid-
ing his life as his grandfather had done—forty years for
dissipation and thirty years for a puritanical God, this
Thomas Eden seemed to effect the change at the alarm-
ingly rapid rate of every other week.

In all fairness, he faced life unprepared. There had been
a dazzling older brother, James, a fair, noble-hearted boy
on whom both father and mother had placed their hopes
for the future. Then Fate cast a contrary eye on Eden.
James, in the throes of duty not only to Eden but also to
England, and as head of the Militiamen of North Devon,
went to fight in the unnecessary War of American Independence. He fought well and nobly, and died in the
Battle of Yorktown. He was buried there, along with the
hopes for the future of Eden Castle.

Grief-stricken, both parents soon followed James to the
grave. Thomas was left in a world he did not understand,
facing responsibilities that he was ill-prepared by nature
and training to meet.

Thomas walked with a slight bend to the head as though
anticipating future apprehensions. His face was a long lean
oval which on certain days suffered a laborious though
warranted melancholy. One feature alone spoke of the
Edens and that was the mouth, which though sensuous and
full, pressed too intimately close to the bony structure of
the teeth. His nose was straight and even, pure Anglo-
Saxon, as were his other features. But in the deep blue of
the eyes it seemed another sense than sight had taken its
stand beneath the flesh. On occasion and in certain in-
definable moods, there was no respite from that stare, as
though he had just awakened at sea without compass or
anchor.

Still, on good days, he was a kindly man, taking a considerable interest in his tenants and workers, mingling
with his sheep shearers and overseers as much as one can
mingle atop a white stallion. On occasion he even ventured down the side of the steep cliff to the village of
Mortemouth. His father before him had created and

launched a sizable fleet of fishing vessels, thus building the village's prosperity as well as his own. Those who did not work the land and tend the sheep put out to sea each morning in search of herring, grateful for their new wealth.

During these walks through the village, Thomas usually performed with grace. But on other days he could be arrogant and exacting, lashing out against the slightest offense. He was an amateur musician, a keen sportsman, and in his younger days a halfhearted soldier. Unhappily, the semiregal state in which he had passed the greater part of his life made few demands on his intelligence. When he visited London he made frequent company with the elder sons of George the Third, not on the whole uplifting companions. He was only vaguely aware of the world, for what mattered beyond Eden? There was some sort of trouble brewing in France, and taxes were climbing ever higher. The American conflict, which had taken the life of his older brother, eluded him altogether.

In short, there were those who, when asked to define his basic character, would say without hesitation that he was essentially weak and intensely selfish. The next man, asked the same question, would reply, "A good man, brave, the most generous of Lords."

In one area of his life, all were in firm agreement. His moral standards were rudimentary. During his twenties and thirties, an assortment of young women of mixed classes had been brought to the castle for his enjoyment. Not that he mistreated them. On the contrary, he treated them, one and all, like princesses, catering to their every whim, but finally tiring of them and sending them away, richer by several trunks of gowns and a few jewels.

This dissipation took a heavy toll. It was common knowledge that no decent family would consider him as a proper suitor for a marriageable daughter, in spite of his titles and great wealth. At forty, he was still a bachelor and seemed destined to remain one.

From the mixed passions that made up his past, out of the diversity of bloods, from the crux of almost eight hundred years of arrogant breeding, Thomas Eden had become the accumulated and single—Lord of Eden Castle.

He was alone and lonely, but this night he was awaiting important news that would lift his spirits. In a state of semirelaxation, he sat up, listening. There it was, old Ragland's step on the stairs. He'd been waiting all evening, waiting for word. Quickly he stood and drew the dressing gown tightly about him, stood at a position of attention as though he felt that the great past might mend a little if he bowed low enough, if he received even his manservant with humility and homage.

Truthfully, Ragland was more than a manservant. As a boy, the old man had served Thomas' father. He now occupied a place in Thomas' life somewhere between butler, aide, adviser, and confessor. In spite of his low birth, there was a dignity and honesty about him that pleased Thomas, although unfortunately the old man's honesty had gotten him into trouble on more than one occasion.

At the sound of a discreet knock at the door, Thomas called out in a slightly impatient voice, "Ragland? Come in," and stepped forward to receive him.

Ragland appeared, carrying a lantern aloft, something ferocious in his blue eyes. He knew too much to be cowed by Lord Eden. Indeed, he knew too much ever to be cowed by any mere man.

Thomas stepped forward to greet him, taking the lantern from his hand and motioning him toward a chair. The old man was breathing heavily from the long climb. At the exact moment that Thomas invited him to rest, he also commanded him, "Speak! Is there news?"

Ragland sat in the chair, nodded his head, and wiped the perspiration from his forehead. Something about the glinting in his eye delivered the message moments before the actual words, for Thomas was already grinning when Ragland said, "The ship's arrived, milord. It's anchored off the cove of Mortemouth."

Thomas smiled beatifically. He began waving his hands, saying, "Thank God, oh, sweet God," and abruptly he had a notion that he looked foolish in his dressing gown, shouting thank God. Now he waved his arms in distress and said, "Please, please," and stared at the floor, embarrassed.

Ragland endured the embarrassment with patience, as though he understood precisely how Thomas felt. It *was* good news.

Thomas drew up a chair opposite him, eager for more information. His face, only moments before cast in loneliness, now came alive with excitement. "And the cargo, Ragland? Give me news of the cargo."

Ragland fanned himself with his hand, thin, white, and blue-veined. "Intact, milord. Ninety gallons of rum, sixty pounds of tobacco, and eighty-four pounds of sugar."

"And no one saw?" Thomas pressed on.

The old man shook his head with satisfaction. "No one saw except the gulls and those who will profit from not seeing."

The two men stared at each other, then laughed openly at the success of the run. Thomas stood up abruptly and walked to the bedside. He looked back at Ragland, sitting in the light of the lantern. So! A man with a fleet of fishing boats had dual occupations. The obvious one, fishing. And the profitable one, smuggling. He paced now as though his excitement were generating more energy than his body could accommodate. Only a year ago, he had discovered Ragland's small operation and with a certain amount of gentle coercion had convinced the old man that he would be wise to tell all.

Ragland had told the story, sensing in Thomas an interest that went beyond mere moral indignation. The account had been beautiful in its simplicity. Using Eden's fishing fleet, a group of men in Mortemouth had contracted with French merchant vessels for a variety of goods. The exchange was made at sea, then the small fishing vessels came home to the cove off Mortemouth, loaded with duty-free mechandise to be sold at enormous profit, though still cheaper than the tax imposed on such items in normal trade.

Simple yet profitable for Ragland and the band of men from Mortemouth, and exciting for Thomas, who certainly did not need the money but clearly needed some form of sport with which to relieve his boredom. Then too, as most wealthy men, he had his own rhythm, an increasing, driving rhythm which demanded more and more until finally the acquisition of money became the sport itself.

A silence came over the room. Thomas bent forward, still eager. "When will it be brought ashore?"

"Before dawn," Ragland replied.

"Before dawn, yes," Thomas parroted, looking satisfied. He thought suddenly of the work being done beneath his castle, the narrow staircase being laboriously chipped out of stone which led down to sea level and the long tunnel which emptied directly out onto the beach at Mortemouth cove. How greatly they might expand their operation when that passage was completed! He had appointed Ragland overseer, and Ragland in turn had appointed several of his most trusted fellows to guard both the beginning of the staircase and the mouth of the tunnel, while inside, in the bowels of the cliff, over one hundred men worked on the project itself. The labor was a year old and going slowly. With revenue men all about, Thomas was eager for its completion. What a simple matter it would then be to carry the goods the few yards across the beach, then disappear into the tunnel to emerge in the safety and protection of the castle itself.

Of late, the work had slowed to a snail's pace. The need for secrecy was paramount, yet the job must be completed. They were fast exhausting their supply of trusted cottages and cottagers in the village in which they might stash their loot.

Again Thomas stepped forward, deprecatory and slightly annoyed. "The men must work faster," he ordered. "Double the shifts if necessary."

Ragland shook his head. "Too much traffic passing through the castle. Incidents like yesterday are bad."

Thomas glared at him, remembering the girl now imprisoned in the charnel house. "She knows?"

Ragland nodded. "Of course she knows."

Thomas crossed to the table where Ragland sat and slammed his fist down, causing the lantern to jump. "Damn it. Ragland," he protested. "The construction *could* be innocent. I do what I want here, and perhaps I wish for nothing more than easy access to the ocean."

"For what purpose?" Ragland smiled, a cordial Devil's advocate, a role he played well, a master by experience.

"For whatever purpose I wish!" Thomas thundered.

Ragland shook his head. "Not good enough, milord. Not when her brother reports weekly to the authorities in Exeter."

"They must prove their suspicions," Thomas protested, his anger subsiding slightly.

Again Ragland nodded, all-knowing. "Not very difficult with a quick-eyed, quick-witted girl in the Buttery, working directly above where the digging is going on."

Stymied by this logic, Thomas turned away, still angry, though now partially defeated. "Then I shall be rid of her," he muttered, gazing out the window across the darkened inner courtyard toward the Keep on the opposite side.

"Is that wise?" questioned Ragland, something in his manner which suggested that he was dealing with a stubborn child. Receiving no answer from the man at the window, Ragland went on, his voice smooth and soothing despite his almost seventy years. "To incur the wrath of a loyal brother and a devoted father over the mysterious disappearance of a beloved daughter is what I would call taking unnecessary risks." He shifted in the chair, pushed back the rough collar of his jacket, exposing withered neck flesh. "Better," he suggested, "to let the child go unharmed, give her tasks away from the lower floor. Instill in her the fear of God, but treat her with stern kindness." He smiled, revealing gaps between his teeth. "Dolly Wisdom will know what to do." He nodded again, as though he had just solved the problem. "Yes, trust her to Dolly."

Thomas looked sharply back from the window, looked at the old man at the table as if he were looking down his life, sighting it the way a man looks down the barrel of a gun for aim. He wouldn't trust the tail feathers of his weakest falcon with Dolly Wisdom, an addleheaded-old serving woman who had been his mother's maid and who had now somehow connived her way into the prestigious position of House Warden of Eden Castle.

Thomas looked back at Ragland with suspect calm. "There is one thing that has always troubled me. I've seen it happen among a few of my friends, that unfortunate turn of events when servants become masters."

Ragland looked as though a cleaver were being held over his head. Quickly he stood, sensing in his master's dulcet tones the beginning of a tirade. "I was only suggesting, milord, that—"

Then Thomas turned on him, steadily drove him back until he was pressed against the door. "I will have my way," he announced, "in all things. The girl shall not be released, not to Dolly or to you. If she survives the night, she will face the whipping oak in the morning and she will learn the lesson of silence at the instruction of the whip." He stepped closer, though mildly disgusted that he had to behave in such a manner. "Further, I suggest that you see to it that the staircase and tunnel are completed by the first of the year, or I shall take myself and my ships out of your little enterprise and incur the King's lasting favor by directing the revenue men myself to the band of smugglers who infest the coast of Devon." He stood directly before the old man, pinning him against the closed door. "Is it clear? Have you heard?" he demanded in a final thrust of authority.

Ragland heard. He lifted the collar of his jacket in a pitiful attempt to recover his dignity. Reaching behind him, his arthritic hand finally located the doorknob. "Yes, milord," he muttered, head bowed in a stance of true repentance. Yet there was something suspect about his manner, as though he were merely playing the role he had played all his ife.

Thomas called after him. "See to it, Ragland. Increase the number of termites working beneath my castle, or worse than stone will come down on your head."

Ragland bobbed in deference, exiting quickly through the Morning Room. Thomas smiled. The old man had forgotten his lantern. The passage going down the Grand Staircase would be dark. Thomas sincerely hoped that the man didn't fall and break his neck. He enjoyed playing smuggler with Ragland, enjoyed more the respite from his boredom, enjoyed even more the promise of greater riches.

He turned back into his bedchamber and stared for a long moment at the lantern left by Ragland on the table. He disliked venting his anger on the old man. He sat stiffly on the edge of the mussed bed and returned to his instincts, the enormous gamble he was taking. If he were ever discovered in his smuggling pursuits, his friends at court would do him no good. He could be ruined, stripped of his lands and titles, and led away to Plymouth to stand trial like a commoner. Yet it was these very risks that increased his appetite for the sport.

He was on the verge of becoming a smuggler, and only that thought was capable of bringing him a sense of life. No small operation, his. No waiting for unfortunate ships to run aground, then scavenging what was left of the booty. His would be organized, contracts signed with French vessels, night runs into Mortemouth Cove, transferring the goods to the mouth of the tunnel that led directly into the security of Eden itself. Who would suspect?

Again he closed his eyes, almost delirious with anticipation. What was he doing that was so wrong? Merely providing the overburdened and overtaxed Englishmen in his community with simple, duty-free pleasures; tobacco for their pipes, good brandy for their mugs. The King was wrong with his never-ending weight of taxes. Hadn't the recent follies in the colonies proven that? Yet still George persisted, as all men of vision could see, preparing for a prolonged engagement with the troublesome French across the Channel. Well, Thomas didn't give a damn about the French, or the rabble-rousers in the colonies. England was his one concern, his only concern, and since his island country had reached the last pinnacle of civilization, since every frontier of human endeavor had now been approached and conquered, what was a man of action to do to keep from dying of boredom?

A look of anger, intense and hurried, shadowed his face and drew his mouth down. It was his tragedy to have been born when the world was finished, when a sturdy coach could take a man from Exeter to London in less than three days, when a few shillings would buy the finest meal in London, when salons and drawing rooms could be made spectacles of warmth and comfort with imported tapestries and the finest silks, when the heavens had been charted, the movements of the tide marked down to the last degree, when the circlings of the sun itself were common knowledge, all mysteries solved, all Gods dead, reason in the saddle, spirit buried with superstition.

Such ease of living was its own reward, and punishment. What was there left to do? Then slowly a quiet joy radiated from his eyes. His first ship had landed. The booty, probably at this very moment was being carefully stashed in the mouth of the tunnel. Tomorrow, first thing, he would go down and take a look at it, calculate the profit, urge the men to greater speed in completion of the secret passageway. Distribution would not be easy. He needed specially trained horses. He would have to see to it. So much to do.

As his excitement grew, he started walking in the narrow room, stopping now and then to glance out the window down into the inner courtyard. The night was interminable. He cursed aloud. There was work to be done, yet here he stood, confined by night.

Without warning he remembered the girl again. He stopped abruptly by the window and stared bleakly down at the massive door of the Keep. Perhaps he had been harsh, but discovering her staring down the stone staircase, looking for all the world as though she had perceived the cause and purpose of such an excavation, turning toward him not with frightened eyes, but with accusatory ones, resisting first his offers of bribes, then his advances, finally striking his very person, a stupid, ignorant, lowborn female, disorderly in heart and head, with a brother whom he knew was in the pay of the revenue men in Exeter—

No! This "child" as Ragland has falsely called her was capable and perhaps eager to do him damage. Thomas knew all too well that his safety lay in secrecy. He would on the morrow order all servants to stay away from the lower floor. There was absolutely no reason for any of them to go near the excavation site, which made him even more suspect of the girl's prying. She had been in service less than three weeks. Perhaps the revenue men had gotten wind of his new enterprise.

The punishment would be carried out. If she survived the night, she would endure the whipping oak. And if she endured the whipping oak, she would be exiled. Her father and brother could come and take away what was left of her, a good object lesson for all who planned in the future to spy on him in his own castle. He was a peer of the realm, surrounded by senseless creatures who would do his bidding at all times, in all matters.

All matters. *All* matters. She could have obliged him, could have spared herself her present predicament. He looked quickly about; the room gave back evidence of his occupancy, looked as mauled as his present agony. It was close, hot, so hot.

Undoubtedly she was a virgin.

He threw off the dressing gown altogether, exposing his body. The night was a long journey and he was ill-prepared to make it. He extinguished the lantern and two candles beside his bed, then watched his hand in shadow, still poised from sniffing out the flame.

He would not humble himself, and he had no appetite

for force. Let her be. She would learn her lesson come morning, and that would be the end of it.

Now he stretched out on the bed, perspiring heavily. He would not sleep. He could not sleep.

But at least in the dark, he was the sole proprietor of an unknown land.

Hartlow Locke was a widower, a middle-aged man who had been married three times. Each wife had pushed forth a child and then died. He had been like a squirrel racing a wheel day and night in an endeavor to make the three children survive. Now he was tired.

He had a small head which was going bald and was covered with only a rim of coarse, gray-black hair. His body, large, flashy and robust, somehow made one associate him with a giant. The head and body did not go together. Only severed could any part of him be called "right." There was an occasional palsy in his wrists and fingers, the result of the inhuman strength required to hold sheep when they were in the process of being sheared. He also suffered from body vapors, excruciating pain rolling constantly in his gut, but ask him for help or assistance of any kind and he would be there with muslin shirt, handmade shoes, a loaf of bread, a ready ear.

He sat at the scarred table in his low-ceilinged cottage in a swelter of close air, surrounded by a half a dozen of his best fellows and three village women, with tears running down his face, hands clasped though trembling before him on the table.

No one spoke. What was there to say? Earlier, a few of the men, made brave by the light of day and several pints of ale, had talked of forming a militia, of taking the castle by storm and freeing the girl, the youngest and most beloved daughter of the wretched man.

But night had fallen and caused a judicious rise in their common sense. Hartlow had stumbled into the girl's bedroom and returned with a stuffed calico elephant, her favorite toy as a child. Now the sight of this giant of a man rocking back and forth in the chair, caressing a small stuffed elephant, had plunged all into silence.

The toy now lay beside the lantern, its small trunk limp from years of childhood stroking. Now and then, Hartlow's eyes fell on it and the tears increased. There seemed to be one horror predominant in his mind and he voiced it over and over again. "She won't last it. They'll kill her. She's too frail. She won't last it."

The other fellows, all strong, strapping, and hardy, looked embarrassed and turned away to dark corners where there were no eyes to stare back at them.

The women hovered, hands extended, ready to relieve the burgeoning agony. Jenny Toppinger, who had known all three dead wives and who had helped Hartlow raise the three children, spoke most often although her words were little more than angry expulsions of air.

All during the evening, Hartlow was not truly aware of what was going on around him. His mind was fixed on one horrible image, that of his daughter locked in the Keep, enduring the charnel well, facing worse. And of course the most agonizing question of all. Why? What for? What had been her crime? What possible mischief could a sixteen-year-old child cause to warrant a public whipping, a form of punishment usually reserved for thieves and poachers?

But there were no answers to his questions, only the horror itself. He pulled himself forward on the table, grasping the far edge with his long powerful hands as though he intended to lift it and hurl it through space.

Quickly Jenny stepped forward and stroked his arms, until at last he relaxed and drew back, touching the stuffed elephant, in passing as though deriving strength from it.

He lay limp on the table, his eyes staring sideways at the sparsely furnished cottage, a place where until three weeks ago Marianne had been both his light and his life, preparing his meals, reading to him in the evening. Reading was a talent which Jenny Toppinger herself had passed on to all three of his children. Marianne had been the most insatiable of all, reading her way through Jenny's books, treasures brought years ago from Bath where Jenny had served as tutor to the children of the aristocracy who came to take the warm medicinal waters.

Hartlow remembered, as though seeing it in the flesh, his daughter's beautiful face. He scowled through his tears. She had had no discipline, that was the trouble. She'd driven her sister, Jane, away to a life of God knew what in London. Jane was a practical girl who might have taught her some practical lessons. Then with Jane gone, four years ago, Marianne had ruled supreme over both her father and her brother.

Abruptly Hartlow raised his head. "Where's Russell?" he demanded. "Russell should be here. He can stop it. He knows—"

Then Jenny was there again, scolding him. "You sent Russell to Exeter, Hartlow. Remember? This afternoon you sent Russell to Exeter on Dan Trigg's fastest horse."

He remembered and sank back into the chair, relieved now by a thread of hope. Russell was a smart lad with well-heeled friends in Exeter. Perhaps he could manage a reprieve, if only he could get there and back in time. It was a thin hope, but it was all he had. That, and old Ragland's promise to try to intervene with Lord Eden.

"Ale, Jenny," he said weakly. "I'm dry."

The woman obliged, quickly filled a mug from the cask on the far wall, and delivered it to him with a loving scolding. "No wonder," she murmured with mock sternness. "You've shed enough tears to fill the estuary." She hugged him gently. "Drink, so you can shed more."

He took the mug and drained it to the bottom, looking as though he'd fallen into a trance. Memory, that fearful monster, was punishing him dreadfully. Slumped in his chair, he remembered the argument three weeks ago which had led to him forcing Marianne into service at Eden Castle. Impudent always, but more impudent on this particular evening, she had scorned the suit of Bobby Fishly, a decent lad, son of a good friend. He had come calling with a bouquet of posies, and Marianne had laughed at his earnest ardor and taunted him cruelly, calling him Fishly the Fishmonger. She had embarrassed the boy by accepting his posies with her fingers pressed against her nostrils, and had ultimately reduced him to complete mortification, causing him to flee the cottage with the echo of her laughter ringing in his ears.

Hartlow had exploded in a rage, smacking the insensitive girl twice across her face—the first time in his life he had ever lifted a hand to her. But she had merely smiled back at him, had reminded him that Bobby's suit had been his idea, not hers, an unbearable smile of arrogance that no father in his right mind could endure. The very next morning he had bundled her clothes together and dragged her up the cliff and deposited her in the stern, capable hands of Dolly Wisdom with the instructions that Dolly was to bring her to her senses through whatever means she saw fit.

Oh, God, how deeply those words cut now. He groaned and fell forward again, covering his head with his hands as though to ward off the blows of an assailant.

The women hovered, the men refilled their mugs, and there was no sound in the small hot cottage but the unendurable sobs coming from the man with his face pressed against the table. It could not be borne, the weight of memory and guilt. Without warning, like a madman, he rose from the table with such force that the chair clattered backward. Jenny screamed, "Stop him! He's left his senses!"

Upon this command all the men fell upon him, a screaming, spewing turmoil of violence, the strength of the six seemingly inadequate to the outrage of the one, a caldron of oaths and shouts and curses, boots upended, fists flailing. Jenny grabbed the lantern before the table was pushed over in a crescendo of rising fury, Hartlow dragging all of them to the floor in one screaming, writhing body of frustration and pain. Foaming at the mouth, his eyes resembled those of a frightened stallion.

A male voice shouted for rope. Jenny went flying out of the low rear door, returning a moment later with a long thick piece of hemp, dragging it awkwardly behind her, her sharp eyes taking in at once the damage that had been done to the cottage and the worse damage done to the man himself.

Hartlow lay pinned upon the floor, a man on each limb, his mouth still working, pleading with God to place His hands on her. He lay quite placidly as the men bound him, as though he wanted to be restrained. Starting at his massive shoulders, they wound the thick hemp around and around, weaving in an arm there, another here, the full-length of his body, twisting and knotting it finally about his ankles until he was trussed at last, unable to move.

He strained now and again against his bondage, but they were efforts of no great magnitude. At last his physical agony matched his inner agony, all the trappings of his soul and personality bound with misery.

Jenny made an attempt to communicate with the suffering man. She placed the lantern beside her and knelt down. "Hartlow," she whispered "you mustn't do this. Marianne will need your strength tomorrow."

At the sound of the name his eyes grew wide and rolled upward, leaving two white ovals as though he were examining something inside his skull. His lips moved. "Be quick, child," he whispered. "It's late. Time you were abed."

Jenny shook her head sadly. "He's gone," she murmured. The men stared, horrified, down at the man mumbling bedtime instructions to a nonexistent child. He was speaking aloud now, a firm voice command. "Marianne, I want my tea," his face suddenly and mysteriously at peace. Then incongruously he smiled. "Holy Mother of Mercy." His eyes fluttered as though a spectacularly dazzling vision had just appeared before him.

Jenny and the others watched and listened for as long as they could stand it. Drying her tears roughly with the back of her hand, Jenny ordered one of the women to fetch the small pillow from off Hartlow's bed. She gently lifted the small head and slipped the pillow beneath it. Slowly, as though moving in a trance, the men went about setting the cottage to rights, restoring the chairs and table, picking up a piece of tinware here, straightening a candlestick there.

Activity seemed to take their minds off the man lying in the center of the floor, although once or twice he laughed crazily and sang a little melody, drawing all eyes fearfully back to him.

They all seemed to be trying very hard to keep busy, reaching out again and again for tasks that had been completed. So busy were they in their mock duties that they failed to hear the footstep on the stoop. Jenny looked up first. "Ragland!" she gasped and rushed to embrace the old man who stood in the doorway, taking all in, his boots covered with dust from his rapid descent down the cliff walk.

"What's happened here?" he demanded, seeing his friend trussed and mumbling on the floor.

When no one seemed inclined to speak, he demanded again, "What happened?" and rushed to the man lying on the floor.

Jenny followed after him. "It's no use," she whispered.

As though to make a liar out of her, Hartlow raised up. His eyes opened, focused, seemed for a moment to respond to Ragland's presence. "Did I show you," he began with a weak smile, "the embroidery that Marianne completed yesterday?" He seemed to warm to his subject and again tried to raise up. Weakly he fell back, but continued to speak. "The image of a unicorn it is, as elegant as any you would ever want to see, with a garland of roses wrapped about his horn." The large man pushed his head backward against the floor, laughing heartily. "Roses wrapped around his horn! Can you imagine, Ragland?" Now he motioned with his head for Ragland to come closer as though to share a secret. "Don't make sport of it, in front of her, my friend. She has a man's temper and a woman's wiles." Now he wagged his head back and forth. "Can you imagine? Roses wrapped around a man's horn?" Then again spasms of silent laughter seized him. He rolled his head rapidly from side to side, then finally was still, although his lips moved continuously, silently forming the words "Marianne, Marianne."

Through it all, Ragland stared, disbelieving. "Dear God," he whispered.

Jenny tried to soften the realization. "Do you have news, Ragland?" she implored. "Good news might bring him to his senses."

Ragland brought the palms of his hands together, his expression that of a man gazing into a fresh grave. "My God," he whispered again, the full horror dawning on him. He stepped around the fallen man without a sound. He looked angrily at Jenny. "Could you not have prevented it?"

And she in turn displayed a small temper of her own. "Oh, yes," she snapped. "As soon as I stopped the tide, it was my intention to stem his madness."

Ragland shook his head as though to tell her he was sorry, then something tightened in his face. "Perhaps it's just as well," he said, turning his back on the fallen man. There was an air of authority about him now, like the bearer of bad tidings. He wasn't responsible for the content of the message. "It *will* take place," he announced, moving toward the door. "My plea went unheeded."

When his announcement brought no audible response from the others in the room, he turned back almost angry, quite defensive, "Her offense warrants it. I can assure you of that," he added. "She was given every opportunity to apologize and she refused."

The disbelief and condemnation of every eye in the room was on him now, an intolerable burden. He stepped quickly through the doorway as though to end the distasteful encounter. Then slowly he came back, a portion of his authority gone, replaced now by decent compassion. "I'm sorry, Jenny," he muttered. "I tried to convince him it would serve no purpose." He shook his head, recalling the futile encounter with Lord Eden. "I tried to tell him that Dolly Wisdom could—" He broke off and concluded simply with, "He refused. Everything."

A bleak silence fell over the room. In an attempt to lighten their burden as well as his own, he added, "It will be only ten strokes." He lowered his head, eyes closed. "She won't like it, but she'll survive it."

One woman mourned, "Sweet Jesus, she's only sixteen."

Ragland countered, "Her youth will be in her favor."

One of the men asked, "Who is to administer the punishment?"

Ragland looked sharply in the direction of the question. "The same as always," he said, annoyed. "Who else?"

Still there was no end to their misery. "The same as always" was as good as saying Satan himself. Indeed Satan was another word for Jack Spade, head overseer for the Eden estates, the man whose power outside the castle walls was equivalent to that which Ragland held inside the fortress, a highly trusted man known for his blind obedience to Lord Eden, with brute force in the breadth of his shoulders and a slightly vacant look in his red face, red eyebrows, long red hair, and thick red-splotched bull neck. The news that Jack Spade was to administer the punishment plunged them even deeper into gloom, until every occupant of the room looked as distracted and unseeing as Hartlow himself.

Jenny murmured, "He'll kill her."

"No," Ragland promised. "I'll be there."

It was a small comfort, but the best he could offer. Now it was clear that he'd had enough of the grim gathering. He retreated over the threshold. A clear look of pain crossed his face, as though this last message was perhaps the hardest. "Remember," he added in a weak voice, "it is to be public." He faltered, then went on. "It will go easier on her if you climb the cliff tomorrow. At seven."

All eyes in the room were on him, a new resistance in their expressions, something akin to hate, as though Ragland were not merely the emissary from the source of all authority, but the authority himself.

One man standing in shadows muttered angrily, "Has he gone yet? There is a stench in the room."

Ragland looked toward the voice, sorrow creasing his eyes, but still resolved through a total lack of options. His hands were trembling as he reached out through the opened doorway as though for support. "Hartlow, too," he called back, his voice breaking. "It's important that her father witness, and her brother—"

Apparently he could not finish. He muttered something and stumbled out into the hot night.

A dog barked somewhere in the distance. There was the continuous hum of the surf. Then, as though their constitutions had no more strength for endurance, the men began to drift toward the door. Jenny urged them on with considerate tones. "You go," she suggested, "all of you. I'll sit with him. He may come around."

One woman passing by the fallen Hartlow prayed, "Please God that he does not."

All understood the terse prayer. One by one Jenny bade them goodnight. No one offered to stay with her. They merely took their apprehension out in the night, the last one closing the door behind him as though in an effort to contain the misfortune which had this night descended upon one of the citizens of Mortemouth.

Alone, Jenny looked helplessly about. It was impossible to catalogue the precise fury in her brain. A good man had been run to the ground. In the morning a young girl would have to endure suffering and humiliation that would test a saint, a son had been sent off on a wild-goose chase over black moors rife with highwaymen to plead a lost cause to deaf ears. And there was nothing she could do, nothing she could do about any of it.

Her body gave slightly, a mere bowing of the head at first, then the softest of collapses at the side of the still grinning Hartlow. In his face with the tense expression of a man surviving in an alien element. For a moment she wished to join him. But unfortunately her own mind felt solid, specialized, and as polished as oak.

She remained bent over him for a moment, rebounding with waves of hope. But when he looked up at her with haunted eyes, spittle drooling in an uncontrollable stream down the side of his chin, and begged in childlike tones, "Fetch Marianne," all hope vanished. She pressed her head against his heaving chest and gave release to the grief within her.

Staring sideways through a residue of tears, she spied on the floor, in the shadows of the room, something white.

She tried to look more closely with failing vision made doubly weak by her weeping. What was it? She couldn't tell, although it lay only a few feet distant. Then she saw. It was the small stuffed elephant, Marianne's calico pet, its back broken open in the recent melee, spilling white cotton stuffing from the split seam of its back.

She rose laboriously to her feet and scooped up the injured toy. Quickly she found Marianne's sewing box. Drawing a chair close to the table, she bent over the lantern light, surveying the damage. It could be mended. It must be mended.

Seeing that Hartlow dozed, Jenny drew the chair even closer to the lantern. Like something once dormant, but now moved out of death's way, she carefully restored the stuffing through the crack in the spine.

At twenty-five, Russell Locke was normally a reliable eldest son. He was tall and lean, displaying the small head and potentially large frame of his father. He lacked only filling out and that would come in the middle years, and then he would be an exact duplication of Hartlow Locke—in every respect save one.

He had left Mortemouth at seven on Dan Trigg's fastest horse, Daybreak, a powerful tawny-colored stallion who could race the wind. He was keenly aware of the importance of his mission, to ride to Exeter and to return with the excise men who paid him handsomely to keep his eyes and ears opened and report to them any illegal operations which took place off the rugged North Devon coast. He had performed this questionable duty for three years, not through any sense of moral outrage. On the contrary, those who wanted to buy his silence could do so simply by leaving a six- or eight-gallon cask of rum behind the small cottage at Mortemouth. But after the "run," if no gift was left, the names of the offending parties were carried directly to Exeter to the excise men, and the culprits mysteriously found themselves on their way to Plymouth to elect to stand trial or join the Navy.

There was an enterprise to Russell which was respected in most quarters. He would always be paid by one end or the other, a simple, workable way for a young man always to have the assurance of guineas in his pocket.

As he urged Daybreak through the night, he felt almost overcome wth excitement. No small fisherman this. No petty seaman bringing in more than fish in his nets. His target now was Lord Thomas Eden.

As the powerful horse galloped easily, Russell Locke slid his whip into the slot alongside his saddle. His hair, black and full and long, lay plastered with sweat against the sides of his face. The road was deserted in all directions, a lonely stretch, leading to the even lonelier moors. He had The Hanging Man to look forward to a few miles ahead, the last public house before he crossed Exmoor. He would stop there for a quick pint to ease his parched throat and his doubts.

Daybreak snorted in confusion, bewildered that speed was no longer required of him. Russell let the reins go limp, gave the horse his head. Now sitting well back in the saddle, his mind returned to his unfortunate sister, locked up in the Keep like a common criminal, facing the whipping oak come morning.

A knot formed in his throat, not so much out of pity for Marianne, but rather suddenly seeing himself in her same predicament, feeling in his imagination his own arms being bound around the whipping oak, his back laid bare.

The reins fell from his hands. Engrossed in the coils of this new disquiet, he stared, unseeing into the night, unaware that Daybreak had wandered off the road in search of fresh young grass to nibble.

The self-induced fright gave him even greater pause for thought. He knew about the tunnel and the secret staircase. Was Lord Eden so foolish to think that a secret like that could be kept in a village the size of Mortemouth? He also knew its purpose and intent. Obviously Marianne had made the same discovery and had come to the same conclusion. He couldn't be held responsible for her stupidity. He was certain that Lord Eden had given her a chance to prove herself loyal. And obviously she had turned down that chance. He smiled weakly into the night. Perhaps the humiliation would do her good, bring her down from her great airs.

Still, she *was* his sister, favored of their father. He leaned forward until his forehead was resting against the neck of the horse. Oh, God, what to do? He longed for Jane, the middle sister who had been the closest comfort he'd ever known, simple Jane who had always sided with him against the favored Marianne, who, four years ago, no longer able to stand the unfair competition, had bid him a tearful good-bye and had gone off to London to make her own way in the world.

The main outline of his dilemma was this. He knew there was profit to be had by completing his journey to Exeter. But there might be greater profit by spending the night at The Hanging Man and returning to Mortemouth on the morning, dirty, exhausted, and empty-handed. His father would never forgive him, but then his father need never know. There would be ways of letting Lord Eden know of his abortive journey, and in anticipation of his future silence, the Lord of the Castle might find it within his power to be very generous.

These thoughts occupied him completely. Daybreak wandered father and farther afield, clearly enjoying the feast of tender grass. And Russell, in his own way, followed suit, slumped idly in the saddle, concentrating on nothing visible, rather seeing himself standing before a most grateful Lord Eden, receiving a full purse, lasting gratitude, and perhaps—and here his pulse quickened— a trusted position inside the castle.

He looked sharply at the night sky and laughed aloud. Oh, Jesus, what beautiful visions! Perhaps a horse of his own, decent and varied clothes, always a full belly, and an endless supply of coin.

With a kind of fury, his decision was forming. Divine justice perhaps. Even that! The spoiled arrogant younger sister, the pretty child who had chased off one sister and made life unbearable for a brother, who had had her way in all things since the day of her birth was now providing the opened door through which he might step into paradise.

At that moment the catastrophe was inevitable, though there was pain inside his chest, a fundamental frailty which prohibited him from being a totally good man or a totally bad one, the burgeoning weight of indecision, like a runner with lifted foot, but without the relief of the final command to bring the foot down.

He grew aware of his wayward horse straying into the night. He jerked on the reins with such force that the horse whinnied in pain. It was a good sound, a comforting sound. He pulled the animal's head about and dug his heels into the flesh of the underbelly. Eagerly he lifted the whip into the air and brought it down with a resounding slap across the broad rump. The horse shot forward under the duress of pain, reached the road with flying hooves, confused and angry by the whims of the young man who straddled him.

With a kind of delirium in his eyes, his cheeks drained of color, his long hair flying backward in the night, Russell urged the animal forward, searching the horizon for The Hanging Man, for respite, for relief from his agonizing doubts.

Even after the horse reached top speed, Russell forced him on, shouting, "Faster! Faster!" Out of the wind whistling by his head, he thought he heard a young girl's screams.

"Are you well?" Ragland whispered. He bent close to the bolted oak door, pressing a linen against his face to keep from gagging on the odor of rotting flesh.

Although he had wanted to go directly to his quarters and the sweet silent company of his charge, Elfie, he had stopped by the Keep on his way back from his disturbing visit to Mortemouth. A man *did* have responsibilities to his friends, duties. Stealthily he had let himself in through the outer door and now stood in total blackness. The odor was that of death itself.

Again he bent his head low and clamped the linen more closely about his nostrils. "Marianne? Can you hear me?"

No response. The primary source of his distress came from the fact that he knew Hartlow Locke and his daughter as intimately as family. Indeed on occasion, with the exception of his beloved little Elfie, he looked upon them as such, had spent many happy hours in their cottage.

Before now the prisoners he had locked up in this stinking place had been men, full-grown and brutish, whose crimes of theft, murder, and insubordination had been clear-cut and worthy of punishment. Then, too, most had been strangers.

Again he leaned close in apprehension. "Marianne?" He waited, listening, his ear cocked to one side. Asleep? Not likely. Dead? Pray God, no!

He looked quickly over his shoulder. What he was doing was in itself a crime. Those assigned to the charnel house were to be given no respite, no succor. Still he had to make sure she was well, a mere child who in the past had charmed him with her beauty, had charmed all for that matter.

Save one! Old Ragland glowered at the bolted door, a look of anger crossing his face. Generally he was completely loyal to Lord Eden, supportive to a fault. The present Lord Eden was not a bad man. He was weak perhaps, certainly bored, and arrogant. But not evil. That was why this extreme punishment was so out of character.

Again he called out "Marianne!" his voice still louder, throwing caution to the wind, realizing that if he didn't take care he would attract the attention of the nightwatchmen.

Still no answer. The small cell behind the locked door gave back only silence. Mother of God, what was he to do? He could not close his eyes tonight knowing what lay suffering behind this door. The poor child wasn't even aware that she'd lost her father to madness. His despair and guilt mounting, Ragland suddenly cried out, full-voiced, "Marianne. Answer me!"

Still there was no response. The old man thrust his chin forward, allowing the linen to fall to the floor. His hands were on the bolts, ready to slide them backward, when suddenly he heard a disturbance at the outer door. Quickly he fell back against the far wall, safe in darkness. The heavy outer door swung open, revealing a splash of lantern light and the hooded sleepy-eyed faces of two night watchmen.

"In here you say you heard it?" asked one, holding the lantern aloft.

"Here it was, a man's cry—" At that instant the stench reached their noses. Wildly they waved their hands before them as though such a simple gesture were capable of cleansing the air.

"My God," gasped one of them.

"Come on," said the one holding the lantern in an anguished voice. "Ain't nuthin' here but the dead Cornwellian and he ain't likely to be crying out. As for the girl—"

But the other persisted. "I swear I heard—" he began, then broke off in a choking tone.

"All you heard was her," the other scolded. "Gawd! The whipping oak will be paradise after this." Waving his hand in a gesture of desperation he added, "Back! Ain't no man alive in here."

With incredible swiftness they stumbled out of the door, closing it rapidly behind them.

Old Ragland, who had denied himself breath during the short interruption, turned his face to the wall, gasping. The beating of his heart increased. He realized how narrow had been his escape. He could not stay a moment longer. His own position was at stake. If she was dead, so be it. If she survived the night and the morning, he would assist her. And it wasn't as though she were truly alone. She still had her brother, Russell, a fine boy, who would go to any lengths to help her.

He found comfort in this thought, at least enough to enable him to walk past the bolted and silent door. He thought how much better his sleep would be if only he had received one brief reassurance from her.

But it was not to be, and he adjusted rapidly to its absence and moved quickly across the blackness to the outer door. Stealthily he opened it a crack, peered in both directions of the inner courtyard. He closed the door behind him and moved rapidly along the castle wall. Where the wall angled to accommodate the Great Hall, he spied the bobbing lantern of the watchman.

At the same moment the man spied Ragland. "Who passes?" he called out sharply, again lifting the lantern high above his head.

Ragland drew a deep breath and tried to give his voice an ease of manner. "A highwayman," he called back, in a feeble attempt at humor, "come to loot the castle."

The dull-witted watchman stopped in his tracks, as though he believed the absurd answer. Then, coming still closer and upon seeing Ragland, he laughed heartily in relief. "You're up and about late, sir," he scolded. "Gave me a start, you did."

Ragland greeted him with a cordial slap on the shoulder. "Just a breath of air, that's all. No sleeping on a night hot as this."

The man concurred. "Did you just pass the Keep, sir?" he asked.

Ragland shook his head.

The man grinned. "Not that I blame you." He stepped closer. "But I swear I heard a man's voice there."

Ragland dismissed the notion out of hand. "Not likely," he comforted. "The only man in that place has long since met his Maker. God rest his soul."

The watchman nodded in pious agreement, then grinned again in relief. "Well, then, on toward morning. Right?"

Ragland nodded. "Watch well," he called in parting.

The man assured him that he would, then hoisted the lantern aloft and continued his sentry through the night. Ragland watched him until he disappeared down the way near the Guardsmens Mess where, unless Ragland missed his guess, the man would stop in for ale to quench his thirst before he started his rounds again.

Alone in the night, Ragland looked back toward the Keep. He was not a praying man, knew Jesus only vaguely, scant knowledge picked up at his mother's knee before that poor woman had died of consumption when Ragland was a boy of four. He had grown up on the Eden estates, working in the fields and with the sheep at first, and then, because he had a way with animals, handling the hounds for the present Lord Eden's father. He had enjoyed that bland man's company, had in later years even hunted with him on occasion. To this day there was nothing capable of stirring greater emotion in his breast than the sight and sound of the hunt, the scarlet livery, the hounds yelping, the horses, white-eyed as though sensing the excitement.

Too old now. The curse of age was upon him. He was Master of Domestic Duties. "Is the butter churned properly?" "Lord Eden will take veal, not beef." "The beds require airing."

Standing in the dark on the steps leading up to the
Great Hall, his flesh ached like an ailing woman. And why
not? He had been assigned to women's chores. This castra-
tion had led to boredom, and the boredom, several years
ago, had led him back to male enterprise, the art, the
sport, the cunning pleasure of smuggling.

In spite of this momentary comfort, there was something in him that wanted to pray, some need for a heavenly promise that the girl in the Keep would be looked after,
supplied with fortitude and courage beyond her years. But
he knew no words, did not even know how to begin. In
his frustration he turned against her. Let her be!

At the top of the steps, he looked back across the vast
inner courtyard. The night sky was filled with scudding
clouds obscuring the moon. It had been so for several
weeks, promising a rain that had yet to come and break
the back of the present heat wave.

The moon resembled an eye shedding light on the center
of the courtyard, the place of punishment, the whipping
oak. Again he considered prayer. But he knew all too well
that God was what we made Him, and life didn't seem
to be getting any better. Since he was hot and restless and
couldn't sleep, his distraction dragged him back down the
stairs, his eyes riveted on the whipping oak.

He approached the center of the courtyard with a quick-
ening of breath. As he drew nearer, the oak grew larger,
a monstrous trunk, dragged over a century ago by a crew
of forty men across the Severn river from the Forest of
Dean to satisfy the whims of mad Charles, the present
Lord's grandfather, the man rumored to have impregnated
his own daughter.

Forty men! Ragland shuddered. Once here, they had
stripped the tree of small branches and had plunged it into
a deep hole, packing earth and clay around it until it
hardened, leaving the top exposed, a good twenty feet,
in width the size of four bushel baskets; no single man
could reach around it. The victim was always asked to
embrace it, then the wrists and ankles were secured with
a length of hemp, the shirt stripped, revealing a bare taut
back, forehead pressed against the rough bark, the hapless
soul awaiting the first sting of the whip.

The moon was cruelly cooperative now. Its light caught
the patina of black tar which had been splashed on the

oak over the years to resist the acid of human sweat and tears and blood and urine. Ragland had seen men beaten to death here. He had seen human flesh lacerated until the skin had turned a solid glistening red. He had heard men cry out for a pistol to be placed to their heads. He'd heard anguished cries for mother, for father, for lovers, for God. It was an evil place, this black finger surrounded by open courtyard.

The present Lord Eden's father, preferring the hunt, had considered taking it down. But at the last minute he had always changed his mind. Eden was an isolated outpost with little arms and ammunition. The nearest government troops were fifty miles away. There had to be, or so he had concluded, an awesome threat of authority. For over a hundred years the whipping oak had served that purpose.

The relentless moon shone on. Ragland appeared to be in a trance. He had seen much in this circle of pain. But he had never seen a woman here.

He tried to imagine the morning, Marianne being led, white and shaken out of the door, the eyes of the entire village upon her. Jack Spade's command for her to embrace the oak, her arms reaching only a scant distance around—

Ragland was no longer merely thinking of the scene. He stepped up to the oak as though under orders to do so. He pressed his face into the shiny black surface, then slowly raised his arms in embrace. He closed his eyes and discovered that in such a rigid position it was impossible to turn one's head without scraping the flesh. He thought he felt the hemp being twisted about his wrists, his ankles bound in the same fashion. Then as though his senses were suffering from indecent gluttony, as though he wanted to know all, he heard with perfect clarity the shirt being torn from his back, the penitent laying himself open to a peculiar kind of forgiveness, giving pardon to himself, mentally making the sign of the cross, hearing the crowd grow still, feeling a coolness of air on his bared back, hearing the heavy step of the man behind him, the practice lashes of the whip, small circlets of dust rising where the whip struck the ground. Then silence. Then the upward whir as the thongs were airborne, then—

Hanging there on the oak in non-existent bondage, old Ragland let out one sharp cry and wet himself. As the hot urine dripped down his legs, he pushed backward, slightly demented-appearing, embarrassed and in need of immediate privacy. . . .

On Friday, August the third, 1790, after five weeks of the worst heat wave the North Devon coast had ever suffered, exactly one hour before the scheduled public whipping of Marianne Locke, it rained.

The servants who staffed the castle were held prisoners in the quarters at the end of the wall by the driving downpour. Nothing stirred at Eden Castle but an angry nature and an almost half-dead girl who had strangely connived an angel to see her through the night and who had endured the pestilential room which in the past had killed strong men.

Not that she had taken the easy way out in sleep. She hadn't. She had remained awake and conscious throughout the whole night. She had heard old Ragland calling to her, the man having the gall to seek comfort from her. But she had held her tongue, and thus had left him to suffer a hell as bad, if not worse than her own.

She had charted every circle of the night watchmen, following the dot of their lantern light as though they were beacons, and again had strengthened herself against outcry, refusing to give them that satisfaction, then too fearful of attracting their attention, of reminding them that a female was in the charnel house this night.

She had lain pressed for most of the night against the small slit beneath the door, rising only when it was necessary to vomit, depositing her sickness in the pile of putrid straw, then returning, weakened, to the door.

She listened to the storm, giving in to the one thought which she'd held at bay all night, the remembrance of her father. Even now, such a thought made her weak. Instead she concentrated on Thomas Eden, deriving strength from hate. The thought of the man had a strange effect on her. She remembered his anger at the sight of her peering down into the excavation of the secret stairway. Of course she knew what it was for. But what did it matter? She had tried to convey this to him, but in his distracted state he had misinterpreted her manner for arrogance. It wasn't until he had approached her, viewing her as though she were nothing more than one of his London whores, that she had grown genuinely angry. She recalled the look on his face, as though he were a sorcerer who knew the power of his horn, approaching her as though she were merely a transaction, scarcely taking the time to identify her save for her female qualities, where to thrust the horn, the humbling position, the ancient stance of male superiority—

She shuddered, remembering, and new, reviving anger surfaced. She had run from him, a simple act, which apparently in his presence no female had ever done before. He had caught up with her and she had pushed his hands away, had brought her knee up in one sharp blow against his groin and had left him howling. Then she had raced up the steps and into a semicircle of guards who had been alerted by their master's cry.

Still remembering, she managed a smile, seeing him grasping his now bent horn as though mortally wounded. She sighed heavily and lay on her back. The sound of the rain was faint through the thick walls. It was impossible to chart the hour of the morning by the dim gray light slipping in through the high slit window.

No need for impatience. They would come for her soon enough and lead her forward. Firmly she gripped the folds of her dress and closed her eyes and for the first time during the night of her imprisonment she slipped into an easeful sleep, dreaming of her garden, of her father's kind face, and of her small calico-stuffed elephant.

No need for impatience. With furious breath they would come for her. They would put out their hands, as Thomas Eden had done and make everything dirty and tired and old.

In sleep she turned her face toward the slit beneath the door. In her dream she saw a girl child pick up a doll and hurl it to the floor, put her foot on it, crush her heel into it and, crying, she kicked its china head all in dust.

No need for haste. Soon they would come. . . .

And they did.

Shortly after ten o'clock the rains stopped, the skies cleared, and the inner courtyard was a steamy, blazing, water-soaked amphitheater already filled with over a hundred citizens. They stood in clustered knots, eyeing the whipping oak, then the heavens, then the locked door which led from the Keep.

Ragland awakened shortly after eight. His nose took note of his urine-soaked garments, the same ones he'd slept in. Then remembering all, he raced up to Lord Eden's chambers, hoping for a last-minute reprieve. For one cruel moment he thought he had it.

Upon the instant of awakening and upon being reminded what day it was and what was scheduled to take place, Lord Eden, obviously suffering a painful head, raised up from his pillow and hoarsely whispered, "Cancel it."

Ragland, in a burst of repressed joy, turned back to the door, only to be stopped by a sharp "No!"

Again he looked over his shoulder at Thomas Eden, now sitting upright in bed, naked, only a light coverlet over his legs. Then he heard a strangely soft, almost regrettable countercommand. "See it finished," was what he heard. When Ragland waited a moment longer to see if there would be yet another command, Lord Eden, still suffering from some unknown cause, raged at him, "I said see it finished!"

Disheartened, Ragland turned back to the door. But there was yet another command, a faint, almost plaintive order coming from the grand bed, "No knots, no spikes, Ragland. Tell Jack Spade to be easy."

Ragland nodded and for the third time started out of the door. For the third time Eden stopped him. "Any further news?" he asked, looking expectant now, though slightly ridiculous, his long dark hair about his face in a state of disarray, his fleshy, naked torso matted with black hair and glistening with perspiration. The rains had done nothing to ease the heat. The bedchamber was like an inverted stone bowl.

"News?" Ragland parroted, still struggling with the previous commands, dreading what was yet ahead of him.

Thomas Eden sat up straighter, his sleep-creased face darkening with impatience. "The ship, man," he scolded. "My God, have you forgotten? The ship!"

Sweet Jesus, he *had* forgotten. The ship was to have been unloaded last evening in Mortemouth Cove. He had intended to check on the progress after he had left Hartlow's cottage. But what he had seen there had caused him such distress that the activity at the cove had completely slipped his mind.

But he covered his omission with a finesse and artistry based on years of experience. " 'Tis done," he said, with a confident bob of his head, knowing that it probably *was* done, that the crew in charge were trustworthy.

This seemed to satisfy his Lordship. He lay back on the pillows in an obvious state of exhaustion. His hands pressed against his eyes as though to black out the bright sun. "Providence sent us rain, I see," he muttered.

Ragland nodded. "Yes, milord."

"When this thing is over, we'll go to the cove," Lord Eden added, his eyes still covered. "I want to see for myself."

Still a third nod from Ragland. Outside the window he heard the crowd gathering, the curious, the sympathetic, the vindictive, the bored for whom a public whipping was merely a morning's passable entertainment. Ragland shifted restlessly at the door. "Will you come down to the courtyard, milord?" he asked, his head bent forward in an air of deference.

Lord Eden looked sharply up at him. "I'll watch from my room," he muttered. "I can see all. Enough." Then he rolled to one side, plumping the pillow about his head, clearly closing the conversation.

There was nothing for Ragland to do but carry out the order. Softly he closed the door behind him. The handsome, thickly beamed ceiling of the Morning Room caught his eye, the rich red and green Brussels tapestries depicting the story of Isaac and Rebecca and Sodom and Gomorrah, the pewterware and silver lined in the lavishly carved wooden cask, the marble fireplace, a vision of luxury, like all his Lordship's personal chambers. For an additional moment, Ragland fed on the beauty, as though to fortify himself against what was to come. Ah, Jesus, the gulf between the two.

As he moved toward the staircase, he felt his joints fret with the morning dampness, a sharp pain in his left ankle, a catch in his back. He remembered with an acceleration of his heart his madness at the whipping oak th⸍ night before. He grasped the handrailing. He must ʰ taken leave of his senses, like poor Hartlow.

He moved quickly toward the bottom of the ⸍

saw Jack Spade standing there, hat in hand, obviously come to find him. The man looked up hopefully as Ragland descended the staircase. He was an enormous man, his leg muscles bulging beneath his hose, dressed quite grandly this morning in knee trousers and scarlet plaid as though for a fete, a custom of the whipman, a kind of homage to the victim. But his finery did nothing to mask the obvious distress in his face. "What's the word, Ragland?" he whispered, his normally dull eyes alive with apprehension.

Ragland had never seen him thus, this simple man who had whipped scores of men into bloody pulps, and whipped others into their graves. He was known to have the most powerful swing in all of Devon, plus the largest assortment of whips, singular beauties with hand-tooled leather handles of varying length, ten-thong, fifteen-thong, their slivers of leather bleached and hardened knife-sharp, some knotted to cause greater agony, others with miniature spikes tied carefully into each knot, capable of grating a man's back like a piece of Cheddar cheese.

But what made Jack Spade the premier whipman of the West Country was not his amazing collection of whips, but rather his apparent and insatiable appetite for his job, an appetite which Ragland saw now had clearly diminished.

At the bottom of the steps Ragland delivered a simple, terse message, "See it finished!" Then he pushed quickly past, not wanting to concentrate on the man's clear distress.

But Spade merely followed after him, protesting. "I have no urge to see it finished, Ragland!" he shouted. "I ain't never whipped a child before. Never whipped a woman. Something in me says no, I tell you. So I've no urge to see it finished." He almost danced from one side to the other, trying to keep up with Ragland, who was moving with great speed toward the inner courtyard. His thick face flushed as he added, hurriedly, "What's she ___ ___ ___ost plaintively added, "What's her crime?" ___ ___y Ragland swung around, his face hard. ___ of no concern to you," he said, sternly. ___g out the explicit command of Lord ___ecessary that you know more. Now, go ___e toy, no knots, no spikes, then deliver yourself of ten strokes across the main of her back and be done with it."

The big man faltered under the weight of Ragland's authority. He continuously creased and uncreased the soft-brimmed hat in his hand. He muttered a stubborn. " 'Tisn't right," and as Ragland stepped forward, still glowering, the man retreated, not contrite or resolved, simply trapped. He was fed, housed, and clothed to perform a certain duty, and perform he must.

Standing in the doorway, Ragland heard a hush fall over the waiting crowd at the sight of the whipman. They knew that at his appearance, the performance was about to start. Ragland lifted his hand to shield his eyes from the sun and surveyed the faces a distance away. Most of them were familiar. A few were not. On one side of the whipping oak stood the castle servants, keeping apart from the villagers as though they were elevated in rank. In their midst he saw the bulky figure of Dolly Wisdom, a piece of linen pressed against her mouth. He predicted to himself that at some point in the proceedings the linen would be covering her eyes.

There, in the front circle, he saw the grinning facsimile of Hartlow Locke, supported on one side by Parson Branscombe, and on the other by Digby Bell. Ragland stared fixedly at the poor man. Obviously the night had failed to have a medicinal effect on him. He looked mussed, soiled, like a child, clutching at something, a stuffed animal perhaps, although it was difficult to tell from that distance. Ragland noticed that both men kept a firm grip on his arms, while to one side Jenny Toppinger wept openly, a small female circle supporting her, trying in vain to comfort her.

Quickly Ragland pushed his vision on. He was like a man arming himself. There were threats and hazards everywhere, in the cluster of small children playing idly in the loose gravel, skimming stones over puddles left by the rain, in the unhappy faces of the women, the fortified faces of the men, the blank grin of Hartlow's face, and Jenny's endless supply of tears.

Ragland muttered, "God, let's get it over with." He lifted his hand in signal to the two guardsmen waiting nearby. On the command the two men turned smartly and marched in step toward the door of the Keep. At the same

moment Jack Spade appeared, coming up the small wind
from the Servants' Hall, a thin whip hanging limp at his
side, his hat squarely on his head.

A silence went over the inner courtyard. Parents hastily
gathered their young about them. A wind whistled over
the castle, the sea breeze that always played about the
edge of the high cliffs. There was no other sound save the
crunching of gravel as Jack Spade approached the whipping oak, standing at attention, clearly resigned to the duty
at hand.

As the two guards disappeared inside the Keep door,
all eyes focused in that direction. Ragland maintained his
position of authority on the central staircase. In the painful interim, he once more surveyed the crowd. Suddenly
he realized that Russell Locke was missing. The orders
had been clear. Father and brother both were due as witnesses. He looked sharply up toward the windows of Lord
Eden's chambers. No one in sight. With a surge of resentment, it occurred to Ragland that his Lordship probably
had gone back to sleep, his customary habit in the face
of unpleasantness.

So be it. The brother was missing and Ragland was
clearly in charge. He would not postpone the grim proceedings a moment longer. He felt stretched, his nerves resisting the terrifying memory of his charade at the whipping
oak. He looked quickly about. Where was Elfie? He did
not want Elfie to see this. He had given her instructions
to walk the beach this morning. As witless as she was, it
was difficult to know if she understood anything. Apparently she had understood his early morning command,
for she was no place in sight.

He gripped his unsteady hands together, closed his eyes
against the foul odor creeping out from the opened door
of the Keep. With his eyes closed, he felt dizzy and moved
to the hand railing, leaning against it for support.

When he opened his eyes, he saw a sea of white linen,
all the witnesses covering their noses against the odor
which completely conquered the rain smells left on the
air. The silence of the courtyard persisted, interrupted by
coughings as the poisonous air spread. But no one turned
their backs on the door of the Keep. Was she still alive?

What was taking them so long? Ragland squinted impatiently across at the Keep doorway. Again he glanced

up toward Lord Eden's window. He tried to look closer when suddenly a sharp gasp from the waiting crowd drew his attention back to the doorway.

There, hanging limp between the two guards, fairly collapsed on her knees, her long fair hair obscuring her face, the folds of her dress hanging loosely about her feet, was Marianne.

She *had* survived. There still was life. Perhaps God would be merciful and permit her to stay passed out. But he heard a sharp collective intake of breath like the wind rising and saw the girl standing erect, pulling away from the rough hands of her guards, her face upturned, the attitude of one preparing the audience for a miracle.

Erect and standing on her own strength, she led the way down the stairs. She did not smile, but there was something in her step which defied the occasion, a straightforwardness as though she knew precisely what she must do, and was now presenting herself to the spectators as a "picture" forever arranged.

Ragland watched with the others as she made the long walk, knowing with them that he was witnessing something unusual. He saw her approach the whipping oak as though it were little more than a Maypole and this was the most incredible of all—approach Jack Spade with a small white extended hand.

She spoke, her voice light as the breeze though carrying effortlessly in the enclosed courtyard. "Good morning, Jack. I hope you are well."

Under the duress of the moment, Ragland saw the large, greatly feared man turn away and throw his whip to the ground.

Then Spade must have seen something at the window of the upper bedchamber, for within the moment Ragland saw him straighten himself, retrieve his whip, and go about his business for which he was fed, clothed, and housed. . . .

In all her careful planning, she underestimated one small matter—the oceanic distance, under certain circumstances, between one and ten.

Everything else was exactly as she imagined it, precisely as she rehearsed it. She knew the sun, after the dark night's confinement, would be blinding. And it was. She knew that the first breath of clean air would be painful in her lungs.

And it was. She knew she probably would experience a moment of weakness. And she did. But she knew too that she would recover, and that in order to execute the long walk around the inner courtyard and the approach to the whipping oak, she would have to prevent her vision from making direct eye contact with anyone in the arena. And this she did by merely lifting her head and concentrating on the high stone wall finding in the stone the colors of potpourri, dried rose petals mixed with the gray of lavender. She knew she would greet Jack Spade and that the greeting would undo him, knew too that he would recover and go about his task with admirable dispatch.

She knew and thus was ready for the guards when they pressed her against the oak, obliged them readily when they ordered her to embrace it, was completely prepared when the hemp was twisted about her wrists, then her ankles. She turned her face to one side in the close bondage and could smell the pungent tar, could feel the bark cutting into her skin. But she had prepared herself for the smell of pitch and the scrape of bark and was in no way surprised or shocked.

Further, she knew that Jack Spade would feel badly about tearing her dress and baring her back, and she comforted him with a whispered, "It's all right. Do it quickly, a clean tear that can be mended." He obliged, as she knew he would, cursing beneath his breath, sniffing as though he were suffering a cold.

Thus too she had prepared herself for the coolness of air rushing over her flesh, the torn dress split to her waist and pushed backward by rough trembling hands. What she then said was merely the shortest way to a quick dismissal. "I forgive you, Jack." The big man groaned as though he were the one tied to the oak, and within the instant she heard him step back, heard the whip whistle upward into the air.

Then, number one. The leather struck her back and took her breath away, a sharp snap which left a burning sensation and drove her forward against the oak. Her eyes watered.

While she was still recovering from the first, the second came. The fingers of her bound hands clawed at the air. Reflexively her head turned into the oak, scraping her forehead. She was still in the process of catching her breath when the third came, bringing a new wave of pain. She cried out and pressed closer to the oak as if brought to movement by the blows themselves, her knees buckling, but her body still held rigid by her bondage.

She was unprepared for number four. Her breasts, caught in the press of her own body, felt raw. What was that sound? The whip lifting again? But she wasn't ready yet. Out of the corner of her watering eyes she saw Jack Spade angling his body into the descent, a whir, a snap, then—

Again she was driven forward, as though the whip were insisting she become a part of the oak. Her back burned as though someone were holding a torch to it. Again the breath caught in her throat and she gagged on her own saliva, her helpless hands clutching at nothing, looking back at the faces staring at her, looking safely, for all were a blur.

Only five? Dear God, help, not five more. She could not endure it. As she was contemplating her ability to endure, she suffered number six. Her head shot forward in a grinding collision with the oak. Her legs gave away. Her whole body shook. As from a great distance she heard a woman scream, "Enough!"

Then came seven, cruelly, for instead of pushing her over the edge into blessed unconsciousness, it seemed to revive her. She caught a shallow breath in her lungs and found the strength to stand on her feet, thus relieving the pressure on her arms. Her eyes cleared. She saw Jenny Toppinger collapsed in the arms of several women. The sight of the familiar face only added to the pain. She closed her eyes while her arms tried to move upward in a gesture of defense. But she could not alter in any way her vulnerability to the whip, which was lifting again, slicing downward through the air. Under its impact she jerked upward, her head fell backward, the small determined chin scraping bark, something cool and liquid running down her back.

Surely it was over. Why so vast a distance between seven and eight, a worldspan of time, of waiting, seeing, focusing on her left on a small boy grinning at her?

On the count of eight the whip caught in her long trailing hair and jerked her head further backward, and for a moment she was forced to stare straight upward into heaven. Her lips moved wordlessly as she struggled to digest the pain, the sensation of the skin being torn from her back. Her hands were numb, still grasping at air, her tongue slipping backward into her throat, threatening suffocation. She was in her extremity now, dangling there, counting the ages between seconds, hearing women crying all about her.

Someone was whispering in her ear, pushing her head gently forward. Her tongue rolled helplessly about her mouth. A man's gruff experienced voice suggested that she give in. "Don't fight it, Marianne. Let the oak take it." Then the tortured male voice moved back from its mindless advice and the whip lifted again, again came furiously down. The thickness of the tongue prohibited either speech or outcry. Her mind reeled under the damage being done to her back, the very bones of her spine felt exposed. A leaf of darkness had fallen across her eyes. Her fear of the whistling sound was as great as the lash itself. A high price for dignity, purchased with blood.

Her distracted mind lost count, drowned in grief that she had so hopelessly underestimated the oceanic distance between one and ten. At five, she might have endured, perhaps six. But beyond that there was only unendurance, an awful estrangement in her bowels, ribs pressing against flesh.

Tears ran openly down her face. One more. Number nine? The bright light of morning faded. The grinning child stepped closer, curious.

She was not aware of number ten. As the whip whistled upward, she felt her heart murdered, her body swung limp in its swing, and her mind swept into a still quiet place where it sat and prayed.

"Once I was. Now I can rest."

Safe in his upper bedchamber, in the confinement of a hot white nightshirt, Thomas Eden stood at the window and endured number five. Then he turned quickly away in search of brandy. Damn her! Damn the girl!

With trembling hands he lifted the goblet and welcomed the burning sensation in his throat. He resisted the urge to fling himself face downward into the comfort of his bed and forced himself to return to the window. There he focused on Jack Spade, a loyal fellow, performing his duty well in spite of its distasteful nature. He would have to reward him.

What count was it now? He'd lost track. Suddenly he noticed the crowd pull back. They seemed to have no appetite for this public whipping. In the past he'd known them to bring their cheese and loaves of bread, eating heartily while the victim's blood splattered about them.

But not now. Even from his high angle he could see the reflected horror in their faces, the women, most of them, crying openly, a few, like old Dolly Wisdom, obscuring her face with a square of white linen. And there, the girl's father, grinning like a magpie, obviously drunk or drugged in order to endure.

And the girl herself? Thomas looked more closely at the pinned, white, bleeding back. His eyes grew fearful at the sight of what he had done. Perhaps he had gone too far. He might in time have confirmed her loyalty, wooed and won her, and led her skillfully to his bed.

Now she would be ruined for all time, her back scarred, her virginity worse than useless. Even men who had been publicly whipped acquired an unrecorded look, as though they were being tried by the continuous blows of an unseen adversary. If they survived, they wore an unwilling set of features, they became old without reward, generally dying young.

Then what would it do to her? In a sudden agony he again felt compelled to turn away. Remorse invaded him. His eyes scanned the scene below him as he saw that it was blessedly over. Jack Spade dragged his whip through the air for the last time, then hurled it angrily into space and ran off down the narrow wind which led to the Servants' Hall. Thomas knew he would be drunk within the hour and well he deserved it.

He saw the crowd push farther back as though to put a safe distance between themselves and the poor creature hanging on the oak. From where he stood it was his guess that she had lost consciousness, her legs spread relaxedly about the oak, her entire body slipping down, the hair cascading over the damaged flesh of her back.

Why didn't someone go to her? In the name of God, why didn't someone—He saw old Ragland shooing the witnesses even further away, waving them back toward the castle gate, clearly disbanding them.

Only then did Thomas remember the customary conclusion of a public whipping, that the victim was to remain on display until sunset. No! Suddenly everything in him resisted the spectacle he would be forced to endure for the rest of the day. In a surge of anger, he stepped forward, flung open the window, and shouted, "Cut her down. Take her away!" His voice echoed across the inner courtyard, summoned all eyes to him. In an attempt to cut through their simpleminded bewilderment, he shouted again, "I said take her down. It's over. Remove her!"

Upon the second command, he saw Ragland designate two men and two women who quickly separated themselves from the crowd and moved back to the whipping oak. As one of the men cut the hemp from her wrists and ankles, she collapsed in a small heap, revealing bleeding breasts. Hurriedly one of the women draped a shawl about her shoulders. The men lifted her gingerly into their arms.

Thomas watched until the sad procession disappeared through the gate and continued to stare down on the courtyard, empty save for the guardsmen closing the gates. A wave of nausea rushed over him. He closed his eyes and sank to his knees beside his bed. He had gone too far, God have mercy, he had gone too far. His authority was still intact, but his soul was not faring so well. He would make reparation. He would pay for her dress, and when she healed, he would take her back into the castle, give her another chance, assign her some simple task, and give Dolly Wisdom stern orders to look after her, as though she were her own.

There the prayer stopped. But his conscience, newly revived, punished him mercilessly. Not *when* she healed. The question more accurately phrased was *if* she healed.

He bowed his head lower, groaning. Why was there not someone here to keep him from himself? He was not worthy of Eden, not fit to administer justice, certainly not fit to pass judgment.

His eyes narrowed, a plan evolving to relieve his misery. He would fast the whole day. Neither food nor drink would he take. He would imprison himself in this room, bare his flesh, refuse all succor, and spend the day in prayer and fasting. He had done so before and the discomfort had been good. Surely God understood. God would forgive him.

His ship could wait. Part of his self-imposed punishment would be to deny himself a firsthand look at his illegal treasure. His booty would wait, earth itself could wait. He must first purge himself of her blood.

He went to the door and bolted it, stripped off his night-shirt, and fell on his knees beside the bed. . . .

Carrying an apronful of medicines and a flask of brandy for revival, Dolly Wisdom ran as fast as her age and breakable cargo would permit after the sorrowful procession making its way down the side of the cliff. Her thoughts were as erratic as her steps as she bobbed this way and that, trying to avoid the puddles left by the morning rain. Clearly his Lordship had gone too far this time. She had never witnessed anything so barbaric in all her sixty-seven years, the public flogging of a sixteen-year-old child.

She spied the guardsman at the gate and hoped, for his sake, that he did not give her any trouble. He didn't. As she drew near, he hurled himself at the pullrope and dragged up the iron grille, permitting her ready passage. She noticed that it was old Dobber, an ancient guardsman who had been in service at Eden Castle almost as long as she. She saw his weathered face slightly pale as though he had not recovered from his close view of the wretched creature who had been carried out ahead of her.

As she scurried past, he called out mournfully, "She'll not live the night, Dolly." Dolly started to reply but decided to save her breath for the treacherous descent and not waste it on Doubting Thomas'.

Once outside the gate, she paused, glancing over the vast headlands, majestic green cliffs leading down to a white fringe of lapping water. "God's View," the natives called it.

The breeze was always good here and she lifted her chin for respite from the heat and the nightmare of the morning. Dolly was a spinster approaching old age. She had risen in service at Eden Castle from a scullery maid at twelve to the awesome position at sixty-seven of House Warden, a breathtaking climb for anyone, but an extraordinary ascent for a woman of low and questionable birth and no education.

She was admired and respected on both sides of the castle wall. She had a beaked head, a body fleshy and growing feeble, but still ferocious, that somehow made her resemble a plump gaming cock. While she frequently talked about everything being the "death of her," it was accurately assumed by all who knew her that she would survive intact forever, along with the ancient and sturdy cliffs upon which she was now standing.

As the sea wind blew through her prim black skirts, she listened to the surf below. Upon seeing again in her mind's eye the bloodied figure of Marianne Locke, she felt her emotions rise with unprecedented fury. There was no excuse, no excuse at all. This *was* 1790. She had thought that the English mind and sensibility had exhausted itself of such barbarism.

As she moved quickly toward the narrow path which led down the cliff, the movement of her head was as jerky as though a nerve had broken. She should have intervened on that day when it happened, should have insisted that Lord Eden give the girl over to her. She had been aware of the child's arrogance and airs. It wasn't that Marianne was a bad girl. Her indulgent father had simply given her her head too soon.

She grabbed up the ends of her apron and once again started downward, her shoulders drawn up around her neck, with renewed purpose in her step, a wish to arrive on the scene and assess the girl's chances for herself.

Several arduous minutes later, her head like a broken puppet, she felt the safer footing of cobblestones beneath her feet and started off down the wind in the direction of the Lockes' cottage. There still were clusters of quietly talking people standing about in front of the shops, idle fishermen who had been robbed of the day's catch, first by the early morning rain, then the public whipping. She knew them all, there Kerry, there Williams, and Wotten and Tim Clarke and Bob Duncan. She received the quiet bobs of their heads with dignity, considering that her own head was bobbing continuously. The medicines in her apron jangled together, a kind of melody proclaiming her arrival, the only medicinal expert this side of Exeter.

Ahead she heard someone calling to her. She looked up and saw Parson Branscombe running toward her, his fat little stockinged legs flying.

"Ah, Dolly," he cried. "I was just coming to fetch you. She needs more than my prayers. Hurry! Please hurry!"

She lifted her head in search of air. "I'm coming," she snapped, drawing away from the pudgy little fingers which reached out for her arm. "Can't a body stop for breath?"

With her mantle of authority clearly in place, she brushed past Parson Branscombe, holding her ladened apron aloft. As she caught her first sight of the Locke cottage, she stopped, appalled. She had passed perhaps a half a dozen people on her way here. Now it looked as though the other ninety-four inhabitants of Mortemouth were all pressing to get into the cottage, their appetites for suffering insatiable.

"My God," she cursed, impervious to Parson Branscombe still hovering at her elbow. "They must be cleared," she ordered.

Parson Branscombe, obviously grateful that someone else had arrived to take charge, ran ahead of her, shouting in a voice that resembled a woman's "Make way, please. Go back to your homes. Please, oh, please, make way!"

The people standing at the outer edges of the circle looked at him as though he were little more than a honey bee. From where Dolly stood, still a few yards removed, it was not apparent to her that anyone had even so much as shifted their feet.

A residue of anger left over from the entire miserable morning flared within her. She stepped closer to the edge of the garden, which was being trampled into oblivion, drew herself up to her full five feet, and shouted, "In the name of God, go home! The lot of you. This isn't Tyburn or Newgate. There will be no head on a pike to amuse you. Haven't you seen enough? If you want more, go home and beat your wives, or yourselves. It matters little to me. But clear this place. *Now!*"

A stillness fell over the faces, all turned in Dolly's direction. She took the weight of their stares and in spite of her furiously bobbing head, shouted again, "Go home, I say! The entertainment's over."

She began to move slowly through the parting crowd. At the door of the cottage she stood on the stoop, a helpful elevation of almost a foot, permitting her to look out over the faces. With a surge of emotion, she added, more softly, "Go home and pray. For Marianne, for her father, for Thomas Eden."

Parson Branscombe murmured, "Amen," and pushed through the crowd in an obvious attempt to align himself with Dolly.

But Dolly was in no mood to be aligned with anyone.

She took a last glance over her shoulder at the backs of the departing crowd. Then she stepped over the sill into the darkness of the tiny room, her failing vision temporarily rendered useless by the transition. Somewhere she heard weeping.

"Is that you, Jenny?" she called out, her eyesight beginning to clear. "Jenny," she ordered, recognizing the weeping. "That's enough. I need help." When the woman weeping in the corner could not or would not respond Dolly hastily emptied the contents of her apron out onto the table, and watched with dwindling patience as again the woman buried her face in her hands. Through this wet strangle, Dolly heard dreaded words. "She's gone, Dolly. She's passed."

Dolly struggled to digest the simple words. She blinked in the semi-darkness, her eyes focused on the weeping woman slumped on a low stool. Then as if by sheer dint of will she hoped to alter the flat pronouncement, she snapped, "Nonsense! She isn't dead!"

Leaving her medicines where they lay tumbled on the table, she tried to steady her furiously bobbing head. As she passed the door which led out into the garden, she spied Hartlow sitting placidly beneath a beech, holding the toy in his hands, an awesome vacancy in his face. Quickly she dismissed the grinning giant in the sundrenched garden and proceeded on through the low doorway to Marianne's room.

One small window on the back wall was the only source of illumination. But it was enough. What lay facedown on the bed scarcely resembled a human being. Still bared to the waist, her back a mass of glistening wet red, one arm, its wrist scraped and bleeding, her lovely face bruised from repeated contact with the whipping oak, was Marianne. Her eyes were closed, mouth opened, no sign of life.

Dolly moved toward the couch, and dropped laboriously to her knees. Without touching the girl she leaned her face close to the opened mouth, pressed her cheek against the lips caked with dried blood. In that awkward position she held perfectly still.

Nothing, not even the faintest hint of breath.

With an energy born of fury, Dolly pushed to her feet and bodily lifted the girl, turned her over onto her back, feeling the wet blood coat her hands. She pushed the blood-soaked hair away from the face and in rapid order delivered two stunning slaps to the sides of her face. The echo of the blows resounded through the still house.

She hesitated to see what response she had elicited and seeing none, she did it again.

A voice cried out behind her, "Stop it!" and she turned to see Jenny, clinging to the door, her face shocked.

But her attention was drawn back to the lifeless head on the pillow. It stirred. The chin tilted upward, the thin, purple lips parted. Dolly froze, afraid that her vision was playing tricks on her. But when the lips moved a second time, and when she leaned over the face and felt the softest of breath, she raised up, crying, "Jenny, she's alive!" Not waiting for the woman at the door, Dolly ran back into the front room, retrieved the flask of brandy, came hurriedly back, gently lifted the girl's head, and forced the liquid down her throat.

No matter that it came up again. The strong spirit had accomplished its purpose. Marianne's eyes fluttered open, then closed immediately, but at least they had opened and the soft breath was increasing along with a restlessness in her body as her nerves responded to the damage done to her back.

Again Dolly shouted for Jenny's assistance. The woman in the doorway looked up as though toward a miracle, then flew into action. While Jenny supported the limp head, Dolly forced the entire flask of brandy down Marianne's throat. Wise enough in the ways of medicine, Dolly knew that total inebriation was the girl's only hope. There was a vast amount of work to be done, repairing this body, and it would be best if Marianne suffered it all in a semiblissful state of complete drunkenness.

When the flask was emptied, Dolly ordered Jenny to find more, and a moment later, the now-smiling woman returned with Hartlow's full keg.

About three-quarters of an hour later Marianne lay back on the pillow, her eyes fluttering open, her lips moving wordlessly, a sufficiently glazed look on her face.

The two women worked steadily for over four hours. Dolly lost count of the number of times she sent Jenny for a bucket of fresh water, only to return it to her a few moments later blood red with orders to fetch more. She used an entire bed sheet of linen, tearing small strips, dabbing gently at the lacerated back, then applying a thin coat of camphor to staunch the bleeding.

It was approaching six o'clock when at last she stepped back from the couch, her work done. Marianne lay stripped on fresh linen, again on her stomach, her long hair freshly washed and pinned up on her head, clean bandages on her scraped wrists, her back a lacework of strips of camphor-soaked muslin, each following the contours of a single lash.

Dolly dragged a low stool close to the bed, and sat wearily. Jenny hovered behind her. Gently she patted the thin arm crooked about the silent face.

"Marianne?" she whispered.

There was no response. The wide blue eyes simply stared sideways out of their pain at the small room.

"Marianne?" Dolly tried again—"Can you hear me?"

Concerned, Jenny asked, "Why won't she speak?"

But Dolly lifted a finger and shushed her. Softly she ordered her to "Prepare some broth. Hot, Jenny, if you don't mind."

As soon as she was gone, Dolly again leaned close to the silent face. Carefully she moved her hand before the wide-awake eyes. They did not blink. Puzzled, she sat back. There was discernible rising and falling to the pitiful back. Breath was moving through her lungs. She *was* alive. And yet—

In the room beyond, Dolly heard voices, some neighbor no doubt, inquiring for the village. She heard Jenny's whispered reply, comforting, for Dolly had permitted Jenny to believe that all was well.

Dolly tried a third time. "Marianne?"

About ten minutes later, Jenny appeared with a steaming mug. Carefully the two women lifted Marianne, held her upright, trying to avoid reopening the cuts on her back. Jenny held her head while Dolly placed the mug to her lips. Marianne drank, not all of it, but enough, her head still dragging and heavy.

With tenderness they returned her to her stomach, arranged her arms beside her head, denied her a pillow for fear of suffocation, and throughout it all, the opened lips made no attempt to form words, the eyes mere shadows, recording nothing, revealing nothing.

Apparently Jenny could not tolerate the frightening emptiness. "Will she be all right, Dolly?" she whispered.

Dolly, experiencing a state not unlike total exhaustion, assured her that she would.

The interminable night began. Dolly stayed on, impervious to whatever duties might be awaiting her at Eden Castle. She lit candles and tried to avoid the vacant stare in Marianne's eyes. She agreed with Jenny that perhaps if Hartlow could see his daughter, the sight of her might bring him back to his senses.

While Dolly covered the girl with a light quilt, Jenny fetched the big man, who had passed the day and evening sitting in senseless oblivion in the garden. But the confrontation accomplished nothing. Hartlow, still holding the stuffed elephant, merely stood in the doorway, announced proudly, "Marianne's gone to London"—and here the smile deepened—"gone off to London in lace and roses she's gone, in lace and roses." Clutching the elephant to him, he announced that he was sleepy and was going to his own couch, which he did. Jenny removed his boots, still mud-encrusted from the walk to Eden Castle earlier that morning, loosened his shirt, and sat with him until sleep overtook him.

There was one other interruption that night, from a sweating, angry Dan Trigg, who informed them that his prize horse, Daybreak, had just returned to the barn, hungry, thirsty, its sides bleeding, clearly abused. Tied onto the saddle was a drunken Russell Locke, passed out cold, a note pinned to his back from the publican at The Hanging Man, listing the amount of his bill for a solid night and day of food and drink, mostly drink, and that he would send a man on the morrow for payment in full.

Dan Trigg, a good man, glared down at Dolly and Jenny. "The bastard never went near Exeter," he cursed. "He left it all for his father." Then shaking his head as though doubting that such a scoundrel could exist, he added, "I've locked him in my barn for the night." Seeing the blood-splotched aprons of the two women, he added kindly, "You don't need him here. Let him sleep off the demon on a pile of manure." He stayed a moment longer to inquire after Marianne, thanked God aloud upon the news of her survival, then quickly bobbed his head and left.

Dolly and Jenny exchanged a quick look, a tacit admittance of the disintegration which surrounded them. Wordlessly they each took up the vigil on their respective patients, Jenny dragging the stool close to the placidly sleeping Hartlow, Dolly returning to the small bedroom at the back of the cottage.

She felt old beyond her years, a nocturnal hag with a broken head who looked down on Marianne. There she saw the traces of something new, the thinnest of moisture escaping from the corners of the girl's eyes, salt brine of repressed pain and humiliation.

The sight was almost more than Dolly could bear. She longed to lift her into her arms, but knew she would only cause greater pain. She thought again of the man who had watched the proceedings of the morning from his high, safe window clad in a white nightshirt, a grave mistake of nature. If there was any justice in Heaven, he would be required to pay for the havoc he had wrought.

If there was any justice in Heaven. . . .

The body mended; it was young and had no choice. The spirit was another matter.

For days Dolly and Jenny watched her, hoping to catch some glimpse of the spirited young girl they had known before. But there was nothing. Even old Ragland kept his promise and always took time from his busy schedule overseeing the excavation of the secret staircase to make daily trips down the steep cliff walk. Usually he appeared at the Locke cottage shortly after dusk with an urgent inquiry, "Any change?"

But Jenny was always forced to reply with a mournful shake of her head. The only comfort that she could pass on to Ragland was the meager comfort that Dolly gave to her. "When she is able to sit up, we're certain it will make a difference."

It didn't. Three weeks after the Public Whipping, Marianne was sitting up. But she was as silent as ever, her eyes down as though suffering fresh pain and humiliation.

On September 3, a month after the terrible ordeal, she was walking with a slight limp, moving in a spiritless path which never took her farther than the garden in one direction and the low front door in the other.

Thoughtful neighbors came daily in loving attempts to coax her out of her silence. Mrs. Wotten brought hot spice buns, once Marianne's favorites; they were not acknowledged and were eaten by others. And old Bob Duncan brought his fiddle, thinking music might make a difference. But nothing worked. In fact people seemed to terrify her and at the first sound of a knock she always moved rapidly back to her small room where Jenny found her sitting on the edge of the bed, her hands trembling and folded tightly in her lap.

When after two months, there still was no discernible change, when her silence seemed to vary little from that of poor demented Hartlow, when Dolly soberly expressed the opinion that if she did not rejoin the living soon, the death of her spirit might become permanent, they held a council.

"New airs," was Dolly's prescription.

"Where?" Jenny asked. "She has no money. Bath or Weymouth would be nice, but—"

Ragland sat to one side of the table, listening to the two old women. Through the opened door he could see Marianne, sitting on the edge of the bed, the same position and attitude, head down. He looked away in a spirit of disgust born of frustration. Frankly he was getting a little weary of it all, his daily trips down the side of the cliff, the smelly little cottage, old Hartlow, lost forever, his once strong and familiar features replaced, apparently for all time, by a grinning clown face. And the girl. No difference really. A living zombie. No, someone had to do something. He'd left matters to the women long enough. Now it was time for a wise, superior male voice.

He sat up straighter at the table and with authority smoothed back his hair, a gesture he'd picked up from Thomas Eden. "What of her sister Jane?" he asked quietly, as though he'd had the solution in his back pocket all the while. "I hear she's married well. If you ask me, I'd say it's time for the sister to come to the aid of her unfortunate family."

Both Dolly and Jenny looked up. Clearly the idea had never occurred to them before. Dolly smiled broadly. "My Lord, I never even gave Jane a thought—"

"We'd have to write first," Jenny warned.

"Then write!" scolded Ragland. "Do something. None of us can go like this for much longer." Again he looked back into the small bedroom, thinking perhaps that a discussion of her future might make a difference to Marianne.

It didn't. If she heard anything at all, she gave no indication of it and continued to sit on the edge of the bed, listlessly rubbing her right arm, a peculiar gesture that seemed to soothe her.

Jenny had another doubt and voiced it. "Is she strong enough to make the journey to London?"

Dolly, who had warmed instantly to the idea, put her fears to rest. "There's nothing wrong with her. I've told you that. She's healed, and miraculously too. She's almost as good as new."

"Then write the letter," Ragland commanded. "Let Jane tend to her for a while. If London fails to revive her, then there's no hope for her. None at all."

By the following afternoon, the letter had been written and posted. Immediately Dolly and Jenny turned to sewing a simple wardrobe for the girl. And when by mid-November no reply had been received from Jane in London, they decided to send her anyway. Another two weeks and the roads would be impassable with winter snows.

Ragland convinced the two old women of the prudence of this course of action and took it upon himself to raise a small purse among the sympathetic neighbors.

The night before the scheduled departure, he sat with Marianne at the table and told her in plain language what was ahead of her and where they were sending her. Midway through his speech, the girl stood up and walked slowly to her room. There she closed and, for the first time, locked the door behind her.

Old Ragland was left with his mouth open. Jenny brooded. "It's not going to work." Dolly still felt confident. "She'll come around in time."

Privately Ragland sided with Jenny. Publicly he soothed, "She'll be fine. London is a proper medicine. I assure you, she'll be fine."

He glanced back at the closed and locked door. Oh, Jesus, but he was weary of the whole thing. And how he looked forward to the morrow when he could say good riddance to the corpselike young girl who had survived and yet not survived Thomas Eden's barbaric punishment. . . .

The miracle that was the Exeter Stagecoach carried six passengers inside and six outside, with up to two tons of luggage. Seven miles an hour was the average speed, and the journey to London took about thirty-six hours, allowing for pauses at the toll gates, short stops for rest and refreshment, and for the fact that passengers had to walk up all hills and sometimes down as well. The inside travelers considered themselves quite superior to the outside, who paid only half fare; no outside passenger could change to an inside seat without the consent of one person at least of those already within, and then had to sit next to that person.

The coach left Exeter from the Church Inn in Newgate Street and, taking the usual route by Honiton, Sherborne, Salisbury, Reading, and Maidenhead, it reached its terminus at the White Bear in Piccadilly Circus in the early hours of the morning.

Ragland stood in the push and crowd of people, trying to keep track of his young charge and her one valise, trying to shield her from the cold drizzle which had obscured the light of day and had turned Newgate Street into one vast, muddy slough.

A most unpleasant duty, his, seeing Marianne off, making sure she took her proper seat on the outside of the coach, that she understood the meaning of the address printed primly in Dolly's handwriting tucked inside her purse. Also he had to make certain that she understood the values of the small bag of coins which Dolly and Jenny had pinned to her underpetticoat near her waist, the generous sum of two guineas, raised by friends for the purpose of this journey.

As the porters were still loading the luggage, there was nothing to do but wait for the stagemaster's call to board. Ragland bent over, trying to get a glimpse of the pale face, trying as everyone had tried for the last three months to find a meaning in it.

He leaned closer, feeling a chill from the wet drizzle. "Marianne?" he suggested kindly, "would you care to wait inside the Inn? It may be a while."

She looked up at him as though seeing him for the first

time. "If you wish," she murmured, without inflection or expression.

Wearily Ragland took her by the arm and steered her through the crowds of people. He noticed, as she walked ahead, the slight limp which still plagued her. That, and a faint numbness in her right arm, were the only visible traces of her ordeal at the whipping oak. The rest of the wounds, under Dolly's and Jenny's care, had healed. Her back still bore long, puckering, still reddish scars and would, according to Dolly, for as long as she lived.

As Ragland pushed open the door of the Inn, he noticed that Marianne was looking at him like a child searching for further instructions. "There," he said, hastily pointing toward a small table by the window where they could sit comfortably and still keep an eye on the coach and the wet cold day. Politely he drew back the chair for her and watched as she sat, gingerly, out of habit, holding her back a distance from the slats. Ragland spied several bits of straw caught in the coarse fabric of her shawl, mute reminders of her unceremonious ride across Exmoor to Exeter in the back of a sheep cart.

Quickly Ragland removed the straw and hid it in the pocket of his coat. It had been the only available means of transportation, as both Dolly and Jenny had doubted seriously Marianne's ability or strength to sit a horse for the long ride to Exeter.

Again Ragland looked across the table at her. Nothing moved in her face. She simply sat there, her eyes fixed on the rough wooden windowsill, her hands folded primly in her lap, her lips slightly open.

A persistent voice close by brought Ragland back to the moment. A serving girl with a rouged face was asking what was his pleasure. "You cain't sit withut' orderin'." She grinned. "Rules of the maister."

Distractedly Ragland nodded. He considered asking Marianne if she had a preference, but knew he would get no response. Finally he ordered, "Two wassails, hot and strong."

The girl bobbed her head prettily and departed, leaving him alone again with the ever-silent Marianne, who sat staring blankly out the window of the Inn, her eyes obviously not focused on anything beyond the raindrops which shed in rivulets through an accumulation of coal dust.

"Marianne?" he spoke softly, feeling the time had come to deliver himself of all the last minute advice which had been heaped upon him by Dolly and Jenny and the score of neighbors who had contributed to the small purse pinned to her waist. "It's for the best," he began, reaching for one small gloved hand resting lifeless upon the table.

"Now, when you reach London, you are to go immediately to your sister's house. The address is in your purse. Do you remember?"

Finally she dragged her eyes away from the window and to his face. Still there was no movement or light in her expression.

"In your purse," he repeated, louder this time, searching her eyes for a sign of comprehension. He moved on without it. "There is coin if you need it, but use it sparingly. Do you understand?"

Her eyelashes were gray-black, long and curled. Motionless. "Marianne?" he scolded. "Do you hear me?"

The serving girl reappeared, bearing two mugs of steaming wassail. She placed the cups on the table and eyed Marianne while Ragland fished for the coins in his pocket.

"Wish it was me going to London Town," she said, grinning. "I'd smile me pleasure for you right enough. Your daughter here looks like she's agoin' to a hangin'." Again she giggled prettily and slipped the coins into her apron. "Her own," she added, turning back to the busy commerce of the Inn.

Ragland ignored her, but received her words. She was right. The pale countenance across the table did resemble a victim on her way to her own execution.

Uncomfortable with this perception, Ragland lowered his head, lifted his mug, and ordered gruffly, "Drink! It'll keep you warm."

At the clear command, Marianne lifted the mug and drank, as Ragland knew she would, never once inquiring what it was or what effect it would have on her.

His annoyance increasing, he looked quickly out at the crowd gathered by the waiting stage. If only he could find one kindly-looking face, one trustworthy set of eyes. He'd pay him out of his own pocket to keep an eye on the girl. He searched for such a face for several minutes. At least it relieved him of the necessity of looking at her. But in the pushing crowd it was impossible to separate the passengers from those who were merely seeing the coach off. Almost overcome by his responsibilities, he ordered Marianne to finish her drink and he did the same and quickly guided her back through the crowds and out into the cold rain, which was falling harder.

Finally, when he thought the stagemaster's cry would never come, it came, a hoarse bellowing for "Passengers only, step forward and show their tickets." A line formed and Ragland and Marianne fell in at the rear. Looking at her out of the corner of his eye, she reminded him of an animal going down to drink, or a child, looking in fright out a window, something ponderous in her mind, clutching her valise as though it were a lifeline.

The line moved slowly forward. In order to relieve his eyes of her, he concentrated on the boarding passengers, there, just getting aboard, clearly a lady, swathed in rich brown furs, the hem of her velvet gown mud-splotched, and with her, two maids in gray, each bobbing nervously from side to side in loyal attention to her Ladyship's comfort. The three together filled one side of the interior of the coach.

Ragland felt in his pocket for Marianne's certificate of boarding. The villagers had only been able to raise sufficient coin for an outside passage. But when he had purchased the ticket, the gentleman had informed him that if the interior was not full, she might ride there.

As he saw three dandies in brocade waistcoats and freshly set wigs climb into the other side of the interior, he feared that Marianne would have to follow the instructions printed on the certificate—one outside passage to London.

He glanced up at the dark, glowering sky. No sign of respite. Clearly the rain had set in. Again he looked over at the silent girl, trying for the last time to cut through the frozen image. "Marianne, are you certain you understand?"

She did not look at him.

"Jane's address," he persisted. "Where is it?"

She was concentrating on a small black and white dog which was scrambling across the muddy road, tail between his legs, trying to avoid being run down by the thick commerce of wagons traveling in all directions.

"Marianne!" he almost shouted.

The dog safely across, she looked up at Ragland, her eyes mysteriously flat, almost hard, as though he were the villain, he alone responsible for everything. Ragland had not expected such an expression, particularly not after all he'd done on the girl's behalf, not the least of which was the miserable trip that morning across the moors driving a sheep cart and an ancient horse from Eden stables, to say nothing of the coins which he had generously donated on her behalf from his own pocket.

No! He had not expected such an expression at all, although he was grateful for it, for it enabled him to grab her roughly by the shoulder beneath the several layers of garments, and certainly enabled him not to dwell on the scars beneath the layered garments, scars he'd seen once when she was asleep, and he'd come upon Dolly nursing them with applications of oil. It was true. He'd seen worse whipping scars, but never on so small a back.

He felt a wave of embarrassment and this too helped him to hand her over to a burly red-haired porter who without so much as looking at Marianne, lifted her up by the waist to the upper level and into the hands of a black-amoor who roughly placed her in the center of the seat, facing backward, between two men, one a fleshy, ruddy-faced farmer, and an old man, completly enshrouded by his gray cape, peering out with bloodshot eyes at all that was going on.

Wedged between these two, like a thin volume, sat Marianne, the valise in her lap, her bonnet wet and askew from the rough ascent, her face gone suddenly white as though for the first time she realized where she was and what was ahead of her.

In a surge of guilt, Ragland stepped up to the high wheel and shouted, "Are you all right, child?"

The flat-faced farmer looked at him with dull eyes. He was shined, fairly neat; he touched the scarf at his neck, stretching his throat muscles. He half-held up his hands in a gesture which Ragland was unable to interpret. Perhaps it meant he was not to worry. Yes, that was it. He was telling Ragland not to worry. He would look after her.

Ragland's relief knew no bounds. He smiled his gratitude and shouted up, "Thank you, sir," and carefully avoided Marianne's eyes.

All passengers were aboard now, the luggage secured.

A porter ran up at the last minute and thrust a bouquet of red roses through the interior window; a discreet white-gloved hand received them and whisked them inside. The stamp and crush of feet around the enormous coach had turned the road into a deplorable condition. Curious crowds had come from everywhere to see the departure of the grand coach on its way to London Town. Adding to the confusion was a large herd of sheep now being driven down Newgate by a farmer and two dogs. Their bleating only added to the din and postponed the departure of the coach.

The coachmaster shouted angrily at the farmer while the man did his best to corral the frightened animals and keep them moving. Ragland watched it all, a carnival, and thought that Marianne certainly had enough to keep her eyes busy. But when he looked up, he was shocked to discover that those penetrating blue eyes were fixed square-ly on him. The intensity of her stare rendered him mo-mentarily useless.

Sternly he shook his head, drew himself up, and raised a hand in farewell, although the gesture carried with it a touch of defense, as though he had privately said, "No more!"

Through it all she watched him, never taking her eyes off him. When the sheep cleared and the stagecoach started forward, she raised her head, leaned forward, and said something—at least her lips moved—and her face bore the expression of a thought.

But Ragland couldn't hear. Everyone about him was shouting, a small crowd running a few steps through the mud after the coach, dogs barking, children screaming in excitement. So he had no idea what her final words were.

Probably not important. At least this was how he com-forted himself as the stage rumbled down the street, its giant wheels struggling with the holes and deep ruts, the passengers atop swaying dangerously from side to side.

Marianne's face was a small white circle, her body lost in the press and push of the farmer and the old man. Without warning, old Ragland felt tears. In this strained moment he admitted honestly to himself what he had never been able to admit during all the days of hectic planning and preparation. They were sending her to her end. She would never survive. If a future in Mortemouth held little for her, London held less. It was like throwing a wounded lamb to tigers.

The coach was out of sight, having turned the corner for the road to Honiton. Ragland stepped gingerly through the mud back to the pavement in front of Church Inn. He was soaked through, his slippers scarcely recognizable as slippers. His hands were trembling and the ominous tears still pressed close behind his eyes.

No need to hurry back. The cart was waiting for him at the edge of town, the horse safely pastured with a friend. Lord Eden was sequestered with the captain of a French merchant ship, setting up buys for his new hobby. The secret tunnel and staircase were nearing completion, all was going well there, so no need to hurry back. All that would greet him would be the excited questions of Dolly and Jenny: "Did she get safely off?" "Was she pretty?" "Did she speak and what did she say?" It would be an endless interrogation in answer to which he could lie and be kind, or tell the truth and be cruel. For the truth, as he had always known it, was that they had just sent her to her end.

If she survived the coach ride, she would be deposited thirty-six hours from now in Piccadilly Circus, that cesspool for highwaymen, cutthroats, and thieves, would be deposited alone in the early hours of the morning with no sense of direction, no idea where to find the small outlying community of Bloomsbury on the very edge of London, alone, without the wit of knowing how and of whom to inquire, undoubtedly in panic revealing the purse of coin to the wrong eyes, knowing nothing of London and its ways.

Ragland shivered in the steady downpour. He felt a little mad, as though the events of the morning had taken a toll of his own senses. He was getting too old for feeling. It was a luxury the aged could ill-afford.

Increasing his step, he pressed his hand inside his wet shirt against a roll of flesh. In a last attempt to rid himself of her image, he prayed, "God be with her," though it was less a prayer than an angry command. . . .

The Banqueting Hall, the most magnificent room in Eden Castle, measured thirty-six feet high, with finely arched and complex saddle-topped ceiling, sixty-eight feet

long and thirty-four feet wide. Built in the fourteenth
century, but within the twelfth century curtain wall, it
was richly decorated with a fine series of Brussels tapestries. The sixteenth-century screen at the end of the Hall
retained its original painted decoration. The three low-
hanging pewter chandeliers were ablaze with one hundred
candles each, casting shimmering light on the elegantly
carved oak table where Thomas Eden sat alone, in a
mauve-velvet dressing gown, picking at cold mutton.

On the plate next to him were the remains of Captain
Girard's dinner, a hard-driving oaf who had eaten with his
fingers and then filled the air with French gibberish. It
seemed to Thomas that every time money had been discussed, the man had lapsed into his native tongue. Not the
Parisian French at which Thomas was fairly skilled, but a
rural, provincial, unintelligible tongue with strains of
Flemish and German mixed in.

It occurred to Thomas that perhaps for future negotia-
tions he should travel to London where, so he had heard,
the French population was increasing as Frenchmen ran
to escape the coming bloodbath. Perhaps in the future he
should be more selective in his choice of "business partners," try to find one at least more compatible with his
own sensibilities.

Well, no matter. He had accomplished his purpose, the
bargain made, dinner over, the foreign rascal on his way
back to his ship under the protection of night, Thomas
now sat awaiting a final visitor, this last caller not as
important as Captain Girard, but a man about whom
Thomas was most curious.

He stretched backward in his chair, reaching up toward
the mahogany beams overhead. A bit of port would suit
him well, help to ward off the chill of the vast room
which persisted in spite of the enormous fire ablaze at one
end.

With a snap of his fingers he summoned the serving
girl who stood at the edge of the shadows. Without looking at her he ordered her to clear the table and bring him
a bottle of port.

"And two glasses," he called, still not looking at her.

Alone, Thomas stood up and stretched. He felt impatient. And bored. He missed Ragland, though he knew
the old man had gone on an important journey that day.

His stablemaster had reported the absence of a horse and sheep cart and even the identity of the small baggage which had ridden in the back of the cart.

Standing directly before the fire, Thomas stopped, his face glazed. He was mildly hurt that Ragland had not told him where he was going and why. He would have been willing to pay the girl's passage. He was most grateful to Heaven that God had permitted her to survive. How many nightmares he had suffered since that hot August morning!

Still she invited it on herself. Unless insubordination were nipped in the bud, not a peer of the realm would be safe. England performed as the greatest civilization the world had ever known because everyone born had a place and the wisdom to stay in it. If it were otherwise, the nation would dissolve into chaos.

Satisfied with his thoughts, he shifted his gaze from the fire to the ornate screen depicting thirteenth-century knights on their way to battle, a glorious reproduction with banners flying, horses neighing on their hind legs, the very excitement and fervor of the moment captured in rich and highly polished wood.

He turned slowly and looked over his shoulder. The entire room pleased him immensely, the only room in the castle in which he felt the full, pleasant, and reassuring weight of his birth and breeding. He deserved it. If on occasion he behaved like an ordinary mortal, God forgive him. The whipping had been severe, but the girl had survived and all the staff had been vividly reminded of how the machine must work.

He started pacing and again stopped. His eyes lifted to the high rain-soaked windows. So! The girl had survived and was now on her way to London. For the best. He never wanted to see her again. Let her find her destiny in London. The people were like children really, in constant need of a strong paternal hand.

Softly he laughed aloud, then moved quickly back to the bottle of port at the end of the table, poured himself a glass, and sipped. Good. Fine vintage, warming, rich-bodied. After a long silence during which time his thoughts repeatedly dwelt on a white, upturned, enraged face, he sipped steadily, eyed the bottle, and counseled himself moderation. There still was business to attend to. Later, in the privacy of his chamber, he would obliterate his thoughts with several such bottles. It was his cursed loneliness more than anything else. He should have married. But whom? Twenty years ago, the "eligible and suitable" girls reminded him of frozen fish, dressed, degutted, and laid out in dead splendor. Now at forty, it was too late. Those eligible fish were gone and all that remained were the beasts, the thin sticks that their proper families could not even pay to get rid of.

No, he'd remain a bachelor, at least until sixty. Then he would wed some thin-lipped parson's daughter, as his grandfather had done, impregnate her once so the line might continue, then go back to his actresses and music hall entertainers, the warm ones who knew what to do, what to expect. They made him laugh.

Thinking on his loneliness seemed to make it worse and, as comfort, he reached again for the port, refilled his glass, and was lifting it to his lips when the serving girl reappeared in the arched doorway with the message, "The gentleman, sir, he's come."

Ah, distraction. Thank God. "Show him in," Thomas said quickly.

The girl bobbed her head and disappeared. Thomas's mind, still working in all directions, found her pleasing, some quality that he'd failed to notice the first time. Quickly he called after her, "Don't go to bed yet. Bring the gentleman in and leave us, but wait outside in the hall."

She looked back at him, a surprise on her face which was quickly replaced with blank, bland obedience. "Yes, milord," she said, curtsying.

He took a deep gulp of port for fortification and assumed a position by the fireplace, a pose designed to impress upon anyone who entered the power of the Lord of the Castle.

A moment later a man appeared in the doorway, a large man with a small head, drenched from the rain, clutching in his hands a well-worn, soft-brimmed tricornered hat. He bobbed his head in deference and stood unmoving, as though fearful or perhaps intimidated by both the room and the man standing before the fire.

Thomas smiled. He enjoyed intimidating people, particularly this rascal. "Come in," he ordered. "Closer to the fire. You're soaked through."

The man obeyed, stepped carefully down into the room, and proceeded to the fire, never once taking his eyes off Thomas. As he approached, Thomas drew back to the table, a subtle movement designed to keep distance between them. He poured a second glass of port and left it there. "If you want it," he said.

Again the man nodded, his eyes darting this way and that, as though the room were full of unseen hazards. He trailed after Thomas to the table, quickly lifted the glass, and drained it. The strong liquid caused him a moment's discomfort, his eyes bulging in an obvious attempt to keep from coughing.

Still amused, Thomas sat at the table opposite where the man stood. He waited for the seizure to pass, then spoke. "You are—" He hesitated as though he were struggling for a name, although he had been aware of both man and name for several months.

The man stood as though at attention, his crude, coarsely woven garments still glistening and rain-soaked. "Locke," he pronounced slowly. "Russell Locke."

He seemed proud of it for some reason although for the world Thomas couldn't understand why. He had a large mouth, both literally and figuratively. In every pub from The Hanging Man to the Pig and Whistle, he'd been announcing to one and all that Thomas Eden owed him a debt, that if it wasn't for him, Thomas Eden would be in Plymouth now, standing trial.

The smile on Thomas's face faltered. "Yes, Russell Locke," he agreed. He leaned back in the chair, warming to the game. "I've heard of you. My 'ears' have heard of you. They bring me reports."

For the first time, Locke smiled. "Out of respect, milord. I thought they might. That's why I talked so much. I didn't know any other way."

"To do what?" Thomas inquired, clearly baiting.

Locke faltered under that steady gaze. "To—reach you," he stammered. "to"—the smile widened as apparently more appropriate words crossed his mind—"to gain an audience."

To gain an audience! How pretty! Thomas leaned forward in his chair and sipped in order to keep from smiling. "I am not the Pope, Locke," he scolded.

"Begging your pardon, milord, but to us you are," Locke replied earnestly.

Thomas looked up, surprised. Not bad for a country man. He'd learned manners and diplomacy from somewhere. Too bad his sister had not availed herself of the same tutor.

"Well, then," Thomas said sharply, annoyed at the persistence of the girl to enter his thoughts, "what precisely is it that you've been telling everyone? Since I'm involved, I feel I have a right to know."

Locke couldn't have agreed more. He stepped forward, bobbing his head furiously. "Oh, indeed, milord," he concurred. "You are the only one. I would have come directly here, but—" He broke off. His face reddened.

"But what?" Thomas urged.

Again the man ducked his head as though to offer a final obsequiousness. "I thought it best to wait for word from you. Then I knew you would be willing to listen."

Thomas studied this last remark. The man might look foolish, but he was not foolish. On double guard, Thomas pushed his glass aside. No more port until later. The bumpkin had completely captured his attention. He ordered, "Then talk," carefully on guard, for he knew the rumors of this man's cooperation with the excise men in Exeter.

Russell talked. Clearly he was a man who needed only an invitation and having received it, the floodgates opened. "I am a poor man, milord," he began, still standing at attention, his eyes focused somewhere above Thomas' head, as though the speech had been carefully rehearsed and direct eye contact would shake his concentration.

He cleared his throat and began again. "I am a poor man, milord, a simple man. I've never seen a room like this." And with that he gestured stiffly to the left, still clutching the hat. "I'm not likely to see one again. My mother's dead, God rest her soul. My father's a fisherman in Mortemouth. In hire to you, he is, when he's up to working, which isn't often now—"

Thomas listened, fascinated by the nerve of the man. A family history no less. He'd heard about Hartlow Locke, but wanted to force the son to state it. "Why isn't he up to working now?" Thomas probed. "My fishing vessels leave every morning with the tide. Why isn't he aboard?"

There was a sternness in his voice which he did nothing to relieve. He enjoyed the confusion washing across Locke's face.

"He's—well, he's poorly," Russell stammered.

"He's taken leave of his senses, you mean," snapped Thomas. "I've heard he sits in his garden all day like an old woman. Is that correct?" There was an overtone of cruelty in his voice, a clear attempt to insult both father and son.

But it didn't work. Russell merely bobbed his head in eager agreement. "Right, milord. He's a weak man, always has been. Jenny Toppinger cares for him. Otherwise I'd a' shipped him off to Bedlam long ago."

Thomas stared sharply at the flat face before him. Ship him off to Bedlam! That London pit of hell for the deranged and mad? He'd visited it on several occasions. It was good entertainment for a Sunday afternoon. But it was a death hole, a living charnel house.

He stood slowly up, a twinge of guilt causing him mild discomfort. Hartlow Locke's derangement dated from August the third of this year, the very morning that—

"Go on," Thomas ordered, reaching for more port in spite of his resolution.

Locke waited obediently until the glass was filled, placed his own empty one stealthily on the edge of the table. If he wanted it refilled, Thomas did not oblige. Locke took the slight with good grace and went on. "As I was saying, milord, I've learned from an early age to fend for myself. There was no one else. It was either learn the ways of the world and survive, or not learn them and perish." He delivered this last with great flourish, as though he'd worked long hours on that well-turned phrase.

Already Thomas was bored. He knew, had always known the nature of the man's mission. What he did not know was the price. Locke rambled on in a passionate discourse on the ways of a hard world, Thomas wandered distractedly down to the screen, finding constant nourishment in the frozen parade of crusading knights. The man was saying something now about rot in the grist mill, mildew on the corn, and a man having to eat.

Enough! Thomas strode back to the table and slammed down the empty glass. "How long have you known the excise men in Exeter?" he demanded, cutting immediately to the heart of the matter.

To his surprise, Locke made the leap with him, without so much as blinking. "Five years, milord," he replied.

"And what do they pay you?"

"For rumors, only a few shillings. For names and places, three guineas."

Thomas continued to stare up at him. "And what is it you want from me?"

Locke grinned. "I want nothing, milord. I rather thought it was the other way around."

Thomas was astonished. Was that a threat? Didn't the stupid oaf know that he had no bargaining power, that if Thomas so desired, Locke would never make it home tonight, that at the very edge of Eden cliff he could meet with a most unfortunate accident? Was it a family of fools?

He turned away, fearful of where his rage might lead him. He already carried a weight of guilt because of the Locke family. He would not be lured into adding to it. "How much do you know?" he demanded, weary of the confrontation, wanting only to be rid of the man.

Again Locke grinned. "Precisely what you know, milord. No more, no less."

Thomas didn't know whether to believe him or not. Apparently Russell saw the indecision in his face and took steps to remove it. "A French sea captain was here earlier this evening," he began, his rehearsed text clearly put aside. "Captain Girard by name, I believe. A bargain was reached between the two of you, a weekly delivery scheduled—"

He smiled, and it was the wide smile of a victor. "The goods will be picked up five miles off the coast by your fishing vessels, then deposited in the tunnel, later to be brought up the newly constructed staircase for safe storage beneath the castle." The grin broadened. "Your fishermen will not bother to mend their nets now. What they are catching does not require nets."

He drew a deep breath and for the first time dared to place the crushed hat on the edge of the table.

Thomas listened, impressed, as the man described in complete detail the entire operation.

"You have, milord, approximately fifty men working

for you, far too many in my opinion. Twenty could do the job as well, eliminating the hazard of too many loose tongues, and also increasing the profit of yourself. Further, if it were my operation, I'd eliminate Ragland. His eyes are asleep half the time, and the excise men have a talent for moving swiftly and silently."

Thomas sat down, then stood up again. He paced before the fire, realizing for the first time that the bumpkin had a brain inside that small head, a brain that perhaps Thomas could use. "Go on," he urged. "Speak until you're finished."

With admirable daring, Locke reached for the bottle of port and served himself. This time he sipped as he had seen Thomas do. "I've finished, milord," he added, baring his teeth as he savored the drink. "I believe it's your turn."

Thomas stared at the man. He was everything he couldn't bear in a human being, cunning, scheming, basically weak, but parading in a mantle of false strength, yet informed, stupid enough to push too far, and smart enough to know he could get away with it. A man could resent and avoid evil on his own plane. But this man was from another plane, a thin, blown edge of misery.

Thomas brought his hands together. "At what occupation are you presently engaged, Mr. Locke?" he asked politely.

"None, milord. I'm free until my grave."

Thomas almost smiled. My God, the man was incredible. "And the condition of your family? Are you a free agent, or do you have dependents?"

"Free, milord, as always, free to follow the most promising wind."

Thomas pushed further. "Your father will not require—"

"My father is dead," Locke replied without blinking. "To all intent and purposes, that is." He sipped again and moved down the table in a gesture of alliance with Thomas, who stood before the fire. "He's as good as dead is what I'm saying, milord. He needs his linens changed every four hours, like a babe, would take a nipple if it were offered to him. His manhood is over. He now has a nanny."

There was something cold and objective in this dismissal.
Then Thomas drew himself up in preparation for deliver-
ence of that other encumbrance. "And your sister?" he
asked.

Their eyes met, man to man. "I have only one sister,
milord. Her name is Jane and she's made a life for herself
in London. With her husband."

So! If the father was dead, the younger sister who had
survived the whipping oak was worse than dead. The dead
leave a memory. The girl had left nothing.

Thomas' pleasure and displeasure met head-on in a
painful collision. Simultaneously Locke had damaged and
enhanced his value to Thomas. Obviously there would be
no reminder of guilt coming from that eager face.

Slowly he walked back to the table. There was one other
matter. "Let's speak of loyalty," he demanded. "What
proof have I of your loyalty?"

With his back turned to Russell, he could not at first
see the man's reaction to this direct and important question. He heard footsteps moving toward him, again the
measured, solid tread of one who knows precisely what
he is about.

Locke stood even with him now, his body giving off a
musty, rain-soaked odor. "You take greater risk, milord,
in not trusting my loyalty. Within the last three months
I have had ample opportunity to bring you down. But for
what purpose? To what end?" With satisfying subservience
he added, "You are my Lord. I want only to serve you."

And yourself, Thomas thought bitterly, walking quickly
away from the man's unappetizing odor. His eyes became
fixed as he considered his options. He could dismiss the
man and upon the instant send his guardsmen in deadly
pursuit. It would be several days before Locke's body,
then unrecognizable, washed ashore.

Or—

Slowly he turned back to the eagerly waiting man.
"You'll find lodging in the Servants' Hall," he announced.
"There will be a purse for you in the morning. Buy
clothes, clean ones, and bathe. If asked, you were hired to
assist Ragland, and that you will do for several weeks.
Later we will talk—of other matters."

He paused for breath, to see what reactions his words

were having on the man. None that he could see, except for the furiously blinking eyes in the blank face. The man was without expression.

Thomas went on. "Further, you are not to seek me out again unless I summon you. You are to have no further traffic with your family, and you are to stay out of public houses. Is that clear?"

Still the man gave no indication that he had either heard or perceived what was being said to him. He stared back, his fingers twitching curiously.

In a final warning Thomas concluded, "You are on trial, Locke. Your every move will be recorded and reported. If you use your head, it could ultimately be profitable. If not, I beg you to remember the whipping oak."

Something stirred in the face staring back at him, a tightness around the jaw as though memory were nudging him. It lasted only a moment, then was gone. The ever-present grin spread across his face again. "Not to worry, milord," he soothed. "I know when and whom to obey. Now I belong to you."

He lowered his head again and stepped backward. Still holding his hat in his hand, he bowed from the waist. Then, quickly, he left the Banqueting Hall.

Thomas had not expected so quick and final an exit. He stared at the empty archway. A viper had threatened him, and instead of chopping off his head, he'd taken him into his household.

He reached for his glass, refilled it, and damned it. He spied Locke's used glass, still sitting at the edge of the table, recalled the audacity of the man. Suddenly he scooped up the piece of crystal and hurled it into the fire.

He felt trapped, felt as though his castle walls had been breached. He began walking about, considerably agitated. Perhaps it wasn't too late. Perhaps he should summon the guardsmen.

No, he'd give him a chance. He would not, could not, bring further destruction down on that family. The father had not survived, the girl would not survive—

He should have married. . . . Ragland had sleeping eyes. . . . Off to London in the back of a sheep cart. . . . The excise men moved swiftly and silently. . . . If Locke were . . .

He found no connection in his thoughts. Filling the glass again, he drained it and noticed the bottle empty, as empty as himself, and as cold.

He sat down heavily at the table, clasped his hands together, and sighed. He would have to be vigilant.

The sound of light footsteps at the door roused him and, hiding his face from the intruder, he pretended to be drinking.

The servant girl asked timidly, "Is that all, milord?"

"All? Yes," said Thomas.

"Can I go to bed, milord?"

He turned slowly, apologetically, "I fear I shall sleep badly," he mourned.

A look of servile pity crossed her face. "Then shall I stay, milord?"

"Only if you wish—"

Without further communication, the girl closed and bolted the door behind her.

Thomas watched, fascinated, as she stood before the fireplace and slowly removed her outer garments. Half-closing his eyes, as he always did at the threat of passion, he asked quietly, "Did you know the man who was just here?"

"No, milord."

"Are you a virgin?"

A moment's pause. "No, milord."

"Would you like a drop of port from my glass? I'm afraid the bottle's gone."

"No, milord."

What an agreeable creature she was, he thought. Agreeable and dull. She was naked now save for a thin white shift, and moving toward him. The impressive abruptness of her movements was such that at every step the lines of her knees and the upper part of her legs were distinctly visible under the shift, and the question involuntarily arose in his mind as to where the center of the undulating body started.

She stood before him, a subtle smile on her face. "May I help you to sleep, milord?"

It was so simple. Why could not all encounters, all life simple? Thomas pondered the quetsion, remembering ture, terrible even in memory of another face, im away.

nutes later, the act completed without memory

or sensation, Thomas heard the girl say goodnight and watched, without objection, as she left the room . . .

In summer, along the edge of North Devon's coast, grew sea purslane and gladdon, rosy honey-scented thrift, and dog violets with the bluest of blossoms, which her father said were the exact color of her eyes.

It was there that Marianne sent her thoughts, away from the rocking, miserable wetness of the coach carrying her through a black afternoon to an unknown destination. She sent her mind back to the sea cliffs of her birth, the salt spray, the pebble ridges and shingle, the only world that brought her true nourishment, and from which she had been banished.

What she had said to Ragland in the final moments before her departure was "Take care of my father." But she knew he had not heard, had in fact refused to hear.

Without warning the coach bounced sharply to the left. A pain erupted and spread over her back, culminating in her right shoulder. Lowering her head to wait out the discomfort, she drew the rain-soaked shawl more closely about her, as though fearful that eyes could penetrate through to the scars on her back.

The old man on her right, sitting beneath his gray cape like a poisonous mushroom, grumbled and cursed the day, the rain, his age, everything. The fleshy farmer on her left was better enduring the ordeal with the help of a flask which seemed bottomless. In a way she was grateful to both men, for she was so tightly wedged between them that she did not have to waste her energy struggling for balance. The coach could swerve and veer as much as it pleased. As long as they remained steady, she remained steady.

Behind her, facing the opposite direction, sat two women and a child who were not faring so well. Their cries for mercy penetrated the gloom, and the child, a young boy of about six, set up a continuous howl of objection to the rough cold wet ride.

But Marianne, a master at screening out the intolerable, sent all her energy and imagination back to the warm sandy ground of her coastal home, to other days when she had been free to run with the wind along the beaches, gathering bouquets of wild flowers for her father's dinner table.

Without warning she suffered a pain in her throat as she recalled the last glimpse she had had of her father, sitting helpless, childlike, soiled, in their garden, his eyes focused on a loosened button on his shirt. Dolly Wisdom had hurried her along, scolding, "Pay him no mind. He'll be as good as new ever you know it."

No more thoughts. There were so few places that she could, with prudence, send her mind, that she had learned, since that hot August morning, simply to let the mind sleep. She knew that the impression she made was one of dull-wittedness. But it was safer in the long run.

Ahead through the black rainy evening, she saw lights, and the bobbing of lanterns. A sharp cry of "Salisbury!" brought her back to the cold night. The lights were coming closer, a scattered arrangement of low cottages and shops, the horses slowing down on the slippery road. There were runners alongside the coach, men and boys shouting up at the passengers, trying to entice them into various pubs and inns, promising warms fires and dry linens and roasted meat and ale.

All about her, in the other passengers, Marianne felt a sharp sense of expectation, although for herself it was a matter of indifference. She had no intention of leaving the coach. It was too great a risk. Why become warm and dry when there was a whole night of misery yet ahead? She would remain in her seat and endure the rain and cold, both more palatable in the long run than the warmth of a pub where, relaxed, people might ask questions. She could not endure that.

The coachmaster cried out to the horses in a thick gutteral voice. The coach turned sharply to the right down a road which resembled a stream. Most of the runners had fallen back, unable to keep pace. Straight ahead, she saw four lanterns held aloft by porters, guiding the coach close to the front door of The Haunch of Venison.

Before the inn door, the coach came to a halt. Scarcely had it stopped than the two women and child behind her spilled to the ground. The women clutched their rain-soaked skirts, and ran as fast as the mud would permit to the door of the inn, dragging the still-weeping child behind them.

The two men on either side of her followed suit, the farmer leaping to ground in one fluid jump, then running

for the shelter of the inn, the old man climbing laboriously
down, wasting his precious breath on curses. Below her
she saw the porters assisting the lady out of the coach.
She looked warm and dry and serene, her head erect
among her furs, tiny rounds of gold bracelets over her
gloved arms. Marianne watched, fascinated, as she approached the inn, everyone falling back to make way.
Bringing up the rear of the procession were the two maids
and three dandies, mincing their way across the puddles,
their brocade knee breeches twisted from the rough ride,
their smooth pink hands adjusting and holding on to their
combed white wigs.

Only the porters remained, unharnessing the horses in
preparation for fresh ones. Even the coachmaster had tak-
en refuge in the inn, whose diamond-shaped panes of window glass were fogged over by the heat and push of
customers, a warm refuge of laughing, shouting voices, the
good smell of roast meat drifting out onto the rain-swept
air. Coming from somewhere in the recesses of the inn,
she heard a fiddle in the high, sliding screech of a jig.

Marianne watched it all, then let her head drop forward.
There was nothing for her there, nothing at all. Still, the
fuss and bustle were disturbing. She could not help but
listen and watch. In her position high upon the coach, she
received stares and pointed looks of inquiry. She could not
rid herself of the feeling of shame, and yet each time she
experienced it, she always asked herself with injured surprise, "What have I to be ashamed of?" Since there was
no ready answer, she felt her nerves being strained tighter
and tighter.

Quickly she lifted her head, allowed herself to take some
of the space vacated by the two men. Three gentlemen in
black cloaks passed her by. She tried to draw deep breath,
but rain ran in at the corners of her mouth.

*Where was her father standing? There! What was in his
hand?*

No! Again she dragged her mind back, like a disobedient child. Another gentleman in a heavy overcoat stepped
between her and the flickering light coming from the inn.
Putting his hand to the beak of his hat, he bowed to her
and asked if there was anything she wanted. Could he be
of service to her?

The man looking up at her, the direct question, the

earnest inquiry, took a dreadful toll. She gazed at him without answering.

Tear the dress, Jack, a clean tear—

The gentleman, his face creased with concern, asked again, "May I be of help? You can't sit here for an hour. You're frozen."

At that moment the wind, as if surmounting all obstacles, sent a sheet of rain flying into her face. The horses whinnied.

"Did you hear me?" the gentleman shouted above the wind. "You must come inside for a while."

She gave no answer, but saw the concern in his face and was frightened by it. When he lifted a leg to the step as though in preparation to mount the coach, she drew quickly to the far side.

Be quick, Jack—

Hearing above the wind and rain the sound of the whip whistling upward into the air, she cried out and at the sound of the cry, the man retreated, leaving her alone on her high place.

Through her fear and the rain, she saw the gentleman at the door of the inn, talking with the coachmaster. She saw him point in her direction, saw the coachmaster, pint in hand, shake his head. An unpleasant sensation gripped her as she watched them talking. They knew! They knew who she was and what had happened. They knew of the scars on her back, had been among the witnesses who had seen her stripped and bound, had perhaps been standing close enough to hear her prayers.

Her agitation was constant. Surely they would tell the others. Everyone in the inn would come out to look at her. She doubled over, hiding her face in the folds of her wet dress, trying to prepare her mind to bear what was upon her. Come spring, she would gather dog violets. Come spring, she would—

They were watching her.

Come spring, she would walk along the headlands and talk to the sapphire sea and wave at Lundy, sitting in the ocean like a sentinel at the Gates of the West.

They still were watching her. They knew! She buried her face deeper in her lap.

The whip had not yet come down. Perhaps Thomas Eden had reconsidered. The mere thought of that one name was nameless medicine, causing her thoughts to cease as she channeled a mesmerizing hate outward, a hate so exalting, so ennobling, that she found she was again capable of lifting her head, a reviving hate that warmed her as surely as though she were sitting before a fire, a hate-filled harbor, a safe hate, a hate beyond mortification and disgust, a redeeming, healing consciousness of hate, canceling all new spheres of liability to pain, converting her within the instant into a statue, sitting upright, a divine hate, feeding her, a hate without qualification or appointment, without authority or opposition, an intentional hate, like a true religion without complexity or resolution, a hate that was pure joy.

She stared back at the men at the door, her mind weary of all images, all illusions. She assumed an air of fully comprehending everything, yet responding to nothing. She watched without interest as the gentleman and the coach-master disappeared into the warmth of the inn. One consolatory reflection occurred to her—that she would inevitably make Thomas Eden as wretched as he had made her, that she would profit from his misery, that she would carefully catalogue and itemize each step of his suffering, and when, in the opinion of a compassionate and weak world, he had suffered enough, she would find unpardonable happiness in increasing his agony.

The intensity and nature of her thoughts warmed her. With conscious intention, without knowing how it would come about, she plotted a future, then clung to it, sitting rigidly up, feeling nothing of her present or past discomfort, all safely obliterated in her healing, sealing hate for Thomas Eden.

So complete was her passage into the future that she was scarcely aware of the gentleman, who reemerged from the inn, carrying a warm blanket and steaming mug in his hand. Carefully he approached her, swung the blanket up onto the coach, placed the mug on the seat, then climbed up beside her. "Miss," he began softly, "my name is William Beckford. Billy if you wish. I mean you no harm. Please let me cover you."

Her eyes stared straight head into the gloomy view, not so much as blinking as he arranged the covering over her, then placed the mug in her cold hands.

"Drink it," he urged kindly. "It will warm you."

But she was no longer cold. With her characteristic decision, without explanation or apology, she simply ceased to be and was a husk, dreaming of delights to come, the irrestible attraction of revenge, the sweetness that would mark the destruction of the man. . . .

Forty hours later—the schedule had been upset by a lame horse—in a dark cold wetness of early morning, the coach rumbled into Piccadilly. As the roads converged on the capital, they became crowded with every kind of vehicle and by travelers walking, carrying packs; adding to the confusion were droves of animals—bullocks, sheep, and pigs—all on their way to the slaughter pens of Smithfield.

Throughout the entire journey from Salisbury, Marianne had not moved except for the walks uphill where she had slipped away to relieve herself. As the coach drew up in front of the White Bear, she looked at the commerce and bustle of the street. In spite of her stern self-control, her face was pale and her lips were quivering, more dead than alive.

Mr. Beckford was waiting to help her down. "Is there anyone to meet you?" he asked kindly.

She shook her head and drew cautiously away. "Let me fetch you a cab," he insisted. "Surely you have an address, someone expecting you?"

When again she failed to respond, he gently took her purse from her and with murmurs of apology, he opened it, withdrawing the piece of paper on which Dolly Wisdom had printed her sister's address.

"Do you know this place?" he asked.

She began to cough and shiver. Mr. Beckford led her slowly to the side of the road, sheltered her from the push of people, and called out to the first passing hired chaise. Because of the crowds the driver could not bring the carriage to the pavement so Mr. Beckford guided her to the center of the road, assisted her into the seat, and closed the door after her.

She saw him hand the paper to the driver, then take some coins from his own pocket and hand them over. Marianne had intended to thank him, but the spasms of cold swept over her in continuous shudders.

As the small black chaise started forward, she saw the

gentleman put his hand to his forehead in a gesture of good luck. She tried to lift her arm in belated acknowledgment of his thoughtfulness. But her sufferings, growing steadily more intense, did their work. There was not a position in which she was not in pain, not a part of her body that did not ache and cause her agony.

As the cab rolled through the night, carrying her away from the bustle of Piccadilly, she saw a lamp now and then burning in a window, an incredible congestion of houses and shops, all piled atop one another, one street after another, thick habitation, all the people in the world, or so it seemed after the space of North Devon.

She should have thanked the gentleman. Now there were other problems. Where was she going? What would she find there? Wouldn't everyone know what had happened? Wouldn't her punishment be common knowledge? How could she endure their stares and endless pryings?

Without warning all disguises were thrown off. She looked frantically about at the strange night, then pressed her head back against the cushion. As she felt the threat of tears, she shut her eyes and conjured up, by dint of will, a rocky sea cliff adorned with sea lavender and strawberry clover.

She held the images sternly before her closed eyes, then wrapped her arms around her shivering body and let the carriage do with her what it would. . . .

Jane Locke was a practical woman. It was this sense of practicality that caused her to resent the need to relight the lamps and candles at four thirty in the morning when they had only just been extinguished an hour earlier, caused her to deeply resent having to drag herself out of a warm bed and leave the side of her sleeping William. She drew her dressing gown around her in preparation for hurrying down the stairs to quiet the halfwitted cries of Millie, her young maid, who had answered the bellcord a few moments earlier.

Jane adjusted the wick of the table lamp. The flame sprang too high, leaping dangerously near the sleeve of her robe. She jumped back, cursing softly. William stirred, looked sleepily up at the light. "What in hell—" he muttered, lifting the pillow, then squashing it down again, his eyes briefly opening.

"Go back to sleep," Jane soothed. "It's probably just one of the gentlemen come back in search of a lost glove." She stood still to see if William had obeyed her. Thoughtfully she shielded the light with her hand until she saw that he had returned peacefully to his sleep. In spite of the apparent emergency at the front door, she lingered, staring down on him, this handsome bright man who had rescued her from the trials and degradation of service and had set her up in her own fashionable two-story house in Bloomsbury just off Southampton Row.

William Pitch was the successful editor of a paper *The Bloomsbury Gazetteer*. All that he asked of her was that she run his house smoothly and provide him with an attractive and safe place to bring his wide assortment of unique and occasionally infamous friends each night.

It was a good arrangement, and while Jane might have preferred that marriage be included in the bargain, she was confident that would come later.

She was a tall, full-breasted woman, and though her skin was still young at twenty-four and her hair black, there could be seen coming, early in her life, the design that was to be the weatherbeaten grain of her face, an undocumented record of time. Four years ago she had fled the stifling provinciality of her home in Mortemouth, and had also fled the painful competition of a more attractive, pampered, and far wittier younger half-sister. During her first year in London she had endured backbreaking labor in service at Lady Groveton's grand palace off Regency Park, the endless chores of underhouse parlor maid, unendurable for someone who could both read and write, and who knew the ways of the world and was hoping to find her place in it. Then one night, in the company of a friend, in the back room of The Mitten and the Mermaid, she had met William Pitch.

She had been smart enough to know what he wanted of her and smart enough not to turn down any of his requests. She knew that he had been attracted by her unsophisticated good looks and knew also that he had been equally attracted by her obvious efficiency, her ability to manage a household.

So it was a good life, though a mildly scandalous one. But here in London, she was above scandal. Each evening her salon was a gallery of the brightest faces in London, gentlemen who could safely bring their mistresses for a discreet evening's relaxation. She possessed a closetful of lovely gowns, had two women in service to her, and counted lords and ladies and authors and artists among her acquaintances. If William was in no hurry to make their personal arrangements permanent, she was smart enough not to rush him. It would all come in time. All she really wanted now was a gay life away from the old hurts and poverty of Mortemouth, from the constant and unfair competition of her younger sister.

Thinking on all this, her face became set, as though in the passing of a moment another year had crept over her. She drew the light farther away from the bed where William lay sleeping. Millie was still at it, a continuous howl for "Miss Jane! Miss Jane!" She scolded herself for even thinking about the past. It always depressed her. She tightened the cord of her dressing gown and hurried toward the top of the stairs.

The lamp threw a weak light ahead of her and, halfway down the stairs, joined the faint illumination from Millie's lamp. Jane also noticed a flickering candle held by Sarah Gibbons, the stern, reliable cook and housekeeper who'd been in service to her during her three years with William. Both women, in a state of considerable agitation, hovered over something in the open doorway.

"Good Lord," Millie gasped. "Come and look." She stepped back, but Sarah's portly rump still blocked Jane's view. For some peculiar reason, she thought it might be a dead animal, although such explanation made no sense.

Millie, a thin girl with a strident voice, talked on, waving her lamp excitedly through the air. "He just drove off," she exclaimed, "just drew up and drove off. Sarah saw it, too. Ask Sarah if you don't believe me."

Still annoyed at the waste of candle and lamp, Jane pushed the gibbering girl aside and drew even with the door. Sarah straightened up painfully. A sharp wind suddenly extinguished her candle, leaving the door darkened save for Jane's lamp.

"What is it?" she demanded. "Almost dawn it is, and the two of you standing about like—"

As she spoke, she lowered the lamp to the front stoop, still nursing the curious but macabre idea that someone had left a dead animal on her doorstep.

At first the faint illumination from the lamp caught nothing but the vague outline of a wet lump, a curled heaped something resembling a pile of discarded clothes. Sarah, all her quiet self-reserve intact, continued to reach down, her long white nightdress blowing backward with the wind. From her bent-over position, she looked up at Jane. "It's a girl, Miss Locke," she announced calmly. "Half-dead she is."

Jane scowled at the pointed "Miss Locke." Sarah knew all too well that she preferred to be called Mrs. Pitch, even if it wasn't true. Quickly she handed Sarah the lamp and called for Millie to assist her. Reaching down gingerly to avoid brushing her rose-velvet robe against the wet muddy figure, together the two women dragged the limp girl into the entry hall. The body stretched out in the process, revealing hands, two thin white arms, a thoroughly drenched head of long fair hair, and a crude brown rain-soaked dress.

Millie, still suffering from an almost hysterical excitement, ran back for the valise. Jane lifted the frozen shoulders and turned the figure over.

Sarah gasped and wheezed, "Lord have mercy, it's no more than a child."

Jane held the lamp lower, her hand suddenly trembling. The recognition was instantaneous, reminding her of the unanswered letter from Dolly Wisdom upstairs on her bureau; a letter which it had been Jane's intention to leave unanswered, finding the nerve and nature of the request almost more than she could bear.

Jane turned away in anger, taking the light with her, her pulse racing. What right did they have to do this? She was sorry about her father, about the humiliation suffered by her brother, poor dear Russell, who had wanted so to come with her. It had been her intention to send for Russell as soon as she legally became Mrs. Pitch. But this? This "child" as Sarah had called her—

Her breath caught in her throat as her thoughts came in rambling fragments. She knew that both Sarah and Millie were watching her, waiting for her reaction, for orders. She also knew, though the thought gave her a start, that if it weren't for the two women's watching her, she'd drag the wet baggage back out onto the pavement and leave it where she'd found it and close and lock her door against its threat forever.

But she knew further that if she were to become the future Mrs. Pitch, she must behave with a degree of civility and decorum in front of the servants. While she knew all this, she was capable of replying to Millie's whispered question of "Do you know her, Miss Locke?" with a calm, contained, "I've never seen her before in my life."

Sarah's voice cut in. "If you don't know her, Miss Locke, why did she come here?" The voice probed on. "Millie said the cabbie gave her a piece of paper. With this address."

Jane continued to stare down at the small figure. She felt defeated. The fact was that the girl was here, apparently half-dead, but here. Jane could not keep either her presence or her identity a secret. That knowledge added to an already great burden of fury.

There *was* one difference, though, and major one at that. Now it was Marianne who was alone, Marianne on foreign territory, Marianne without the nourishment of everyone's love, Marianne the outcast. Jane stared down at the long-lashed eyelids as if she had become belatedly aware of the safety of her own position. Here the girl would be totally dependent upon *her.*

She smiled warmly at Sarah's puzzled face. "I was wrong," she began. "I do know her. She's my sister."

Sarah's bewilderment increased. "Your—what?"

"My sister," Jane repeated, as though it were a common fact that everyone should have known. She smiled graciously. "My half-sister, really. We had different mothers."

While both Sarah and Millie struggled to digest this information, Jane bent over to examine more closely the still face. Her distress was diminishing. She could easily play the role of gracious older sister, all the while keeping the girl in her place. Upon close examination, she saw that certain changes had taken place. The child-face was gone, replaced by something older, pale and drawn. The nails on the fingers, once so smooth and pink and polished, were now jagged and quite dirty. And there were scars on her wrists, rough bands of flesh, souvenirs no doubt of the whipping oak. For one bewildering moment Jane felt something like pity stir within her. How painful it must have been!

"Well, enough," she said, quickly dismissing the puzzling emotion. "Here, both of you, help me with her."

"Where do you want her?" Sarah asked, still looking about suspiciously.

"For tonight, we'll put her in the small storeroom off the pantry. There's a couch there. She'll be warm."

"The storeroom?" Sarah parroted.

"Just for tonight," Jane snapped. "We certainly can't carry her upstairs, and I have no intention of disturbing William."

She thrust the lamp into Millie's hand. With no effort, the two women lifted the girl and carried her back through the labyrinth of rooms, Millie leading the way with the bobbing lamp, opening doors for them, still gasping softly, "My Lord, oh, My Lord!"

It was a windowless cell lined on one side with sacks of flour and sugar, a barrel of oil for the lamps, and an assortment of cast-off furniture. The storeroom was at the rear of the house behind the kitchen. The couch, banished from the drawing room two years ago, when Jane had redecorated in the Chinese fashion, was a lumpy green velvet brocade vomiting its horsehair stuffing at one end. They placed her there. Jane stood back breathless, brushing bits of mud off her robe, her face calm, having come to terms with her new guest.

Sarah continued to look intently at her as though questioning her about everything. Shocked, she scolded, "You can't leave her here, Miss Locke. It's not fit for an animal."

"I said it was only temporary," Jane replied.

The girl on the couch was beginning to stir. One small white hand lifted, bobbed uselessly through the air, then fell back against the couch.

"Leave me alone with her," Jane ordered. "Millie, fetch me one of your nightgowns. Sarah, bring us a bottle of brandy and a blanket. Then both of you go to bed. I'll see to her."

Millie deposited the lamp on the floor and left immediately to do as she had been told. Sarah lingered, her plain English face seeing more. "What do you intend to do with her, Miss Locke?" she inquired casually.

"Do with her?" asked Jane. "I don't understand."

Sarah looked down on the small figure. "What I mean is," she added, "why did she come here?"

Jane stared at the woman, feeling a slight hostility toward her subtle probings. It occurred to her to tell her the truth. Perhaps it would remove the great sympathetic cow eyes, would help to inform Sarah that they were taking in an exile with no place to go.

Coldly, Jane ordered, "Bring the lamp closer, Sarah." As the woman did as she was told, Jane began to unbutton the wet dress, then the undergarments, carefully pulling them back to reveal thin white shoulders. She pushed the girl toward the wall and slowly drew the dress away from her back.

Sarah gasped. The sight proved almost too much even for Jane. It was far worse than she had expected, the crisscrossing of long angry scars, the grisly script of the whipping oak.

The lamp bobbed in Sarah's trembling hand. "God have mercy," she prayed. "What caused it?"

"Disobedience," Jane said without hesitation. "And impudence. She was in service and forgot her place."

Jane averted her eyes from the scarred back and took in the confusion of Sarah's face. It had worked. The sympathy was receding, and was replaced by a look of stern discipline. "So," Sarah said, "she has been sent to you."

Jane nodded, pleased. "To *us*," she corrected. "We must help her to know who she is and where she belongs."

Obviously the task appealed to Sarah. "Well, I could certainly use help around here. There's no mistake about that."

Jane smiled. God bless the woman. She was a pain on occasion, but she was quick, so quick.

Jane stepped back from the couch, feeling a delightful sense of repose. "Then as soon as she is able, Sarah, I'll turn her over to you, for your guidance."

The woman nodded in agreement, her eyes still lingering on the specifics of the scarred back. "It seems a bit harsh, don't it?" she said falteringly.

Jane moved in with a final defense. "I was told," she began, her voice even, "that she threatened Lord Eden's life, caused him considerable pain."

Sarah's eyes grew wide with horror. Following that, her

face relaxed into complete understanding. "Well, it's clear what she needs. A stern hand, that's what."

Jane nodded in blissful agreement. At that moment Millie returned, carrying a white nightshirt. As she caught sight of the mutilated back, she cried out, a soft expulsion of air, as though she were feeling the whip herself.

Sarah hushed her, then warned, "That's what happens to headstrong girls who don't know how to obey orders. Keep it in mind and remember it next time you talk back."

The girl, horrified, retreated to the door, her hand clamped over her mouth. Then she turned and ran, obviously for the safety of her own bedroom.

Jane shared a good smile with Sarah. "A lesson witnessed," she intoned, "is a lesson learned."

Sarah smiled in complete agreement.

Abruptly, Marianne groaned. Her head twisted upon the couch as she fell over onto her back. Both women moved closer, fascinated. The dark blue eyes fluttered open. Looking about at the mysterious surroundings, she tried to lift herself, but lacking the strength, she fell back again onto the couch. Aware of her unbuttoned garments, her hands struggled to rejoin the wet fabric, her eyes darting from Jane to Sarah.

Jane stepped close to the couch, her voice soothing. "You're safe here, Marianne. No need to be afraid."

What sweet revenge! How different she was! The lovely charming child with golden hair had been miraculously transformed into a scarred, thin, haunted waif with sunken eyes and terror as a constant companion.

Thoughtfully, Jane urged, "Sarah, you go on to bed. Leave her to me."

The woman, whose face now bore a splintered expression, half-sympathy, half-condemnation, complied. She drew up an empty crate beside the couch and placed the lamp on it. Shaking her head as though the mysteries of the world amazed her, she left the room.

Marianne began to shiver visibly. Her head rolled from side to side, a soft mysterious "No" escaping from her lips.

Jane, feeling refreshed and clearheaded in spite of the fact that she'd had no sleep, bent over and began forcibly to remove the wet garments. Thoughts continued to tumble about in her mind. But every time Marianne protested "No" to the wet garments which were being stripped from her body, Jane responded with a firm, half-angry, wholly authoritative "Yes!"

In a blaze of morning sun, which belied the ferocity of the night's storm, William Pitch sat at his breakfast table and deftly cracked the top off his boiled egg.

"Whipped, you say?" he inquired, without looking at his sleepy-eyed Jane across the table. "Publicly?" He scooped up the warm yellow yolk and slid it into his mouth. "A bit barbaric, isn't it?"

Jane sipped coffee. The night had been long and clearly she was exhausted. "She deserved it, William," she sighed wearily. "I can assure you of that. She was an impossible child."

As William spread butter on toast, he detected a tone in Jane's voice which interested him. Jealously perhaps, or resentment, No matter. Either might prove interesting. As his common-law wife spilled out the specifics of her late-night visitor, William only half-listened. Of greater interest to him was what was not being said.

At thirty-eight, possessor of one of the quickest wits and brightest minds in London, he took pride in his ability to "read" people. Indeed, his very survival and his present high position were both direct results of his uncanny ability to hear not what people were saying, but what they were thinking, always of far greater importance.

Abandoned at birth by a whore of a mother and a highly respected barrister father, he had been raised in a foundling home, had grown accustomed throughout his childhood to receiving anonymous packets of guineas from a nameless solicitor. When he had come of age, a final packet had arrived in the rich sum of five thousand guineas. Clearly someone had felt that he had performed his duty.

William had taken the money, a poor gift in comparison to his own native born intelligence, had gone up to Oxford, and had come down with highest honors, his wit and ability to turn a phrase rivaling the dying Dr. Johnson's. With the money remaining after his education, he had purchased a small, declining newspaper called *The Bloomsbury Gazetteer*. In ten short years, he had turned it into the "Mind of London." The "B.G." as it was affectionately referred to in literary circles, was well on its way to becoming the pace-setter, the trendmaker, informant to Monarch and commoner alike.

A tall, lean slightly driven man with fair sandy hair, William Pitch was keenly aware of who he was. With the fury of a fanatic, he had hunted down his own disqualification, had discovered his father to be a wheezing, asthmatic old man, not worthy of his attention, either his love or his outrage. He had found his mother in a pauper's grave. Now he channeled all of his considerable energy and intelligence into his newspaper, living scandalously with a country girl because it pleased him to do so, pleased his friends as well, fellows grown jaded and numb by the constant availability of all of London's pleasures. He ran an open house, one of the most notorious salons in London, feeling that the great embarrassment of the past might mend a little if he provided a pleasurable place for others. He asked little of Jane but that she keep his household books in order, manage his small staff efficiently, come to his bed whenever he ordered her to do so, and look pretty and receptive and hospitable every evening from ten until three in the morning, so that his friends, weary of commerce and politics, of titles and wives, might know the unparalleled joy of total relaxation in a free and easy environment.

As he watched Jane, still talking, soft wisps of dark hair curling prettily around her neck, he realized anew how fond he was of her, and how much he hoped that her foolish ideas of marriage did not spoil their good realtionship. He was willing to give her everything he had save his name, and how could he possibly give that away when it wasn't even his, but rather the construct of a nurse in the foundling home who had plucked him out of a basket on the steps of a *pitch* black night while mourning the premature death of her brother, *William,* who had hanged himself that morning in debtors' prison.

William Pitch he had been named and he would not share that with anyone. He stood eternally straight before the embarrassment of the past, and now concentrated on the soft white line of Jane's breast, heaving excitedly beneath the edge of her rose velvet robe.

"William, you're not listening," she accused him, falling back in her chair, sulking, drawing her robe about her, hiding the breast.

But she was wrong, and he told her as much. "I heard everything, Jane, dear," he said. And he had and now gave it back to her, the whole, slightly melodramatic account of the younger sister crossing her master—"Good for the girl," had been his first thought—then being led to the whipping oak and flogged in sight of friends and neighbors and her poor father, a sorrowful, maudlin tale, the girl herself being deposited on his doorstep only the night before, now apparently *his* responsibility. He recited the whole tale for her, yet felt that something was amiss, withheld by Jane, something to do with her bone-dry eyes, which apparently had resisted all the tragic overtones of her own tale, something too to do with the hard little line around her lips, a line which he had never seen before, some weight from her past, still wreaking havoc.

"Where is she now?" he inquired casually, noting the reflection of sun on the silver coffee urn as he refilled both their cups.

"In the storeroom," she replied, still sulking as though angry with him for having heard all.

He looked up, both amused and shocked. "Where did you say?"

"The storeroom," she repeated defensively. "I couldn't very well drag her up the stairs last night, William. Millie was hysterical and Sarah and I couldn't do it alone."

The enigma was beginning to fascinate him. "So you deposited her in the storeroom," he repeated.

Jane nodded. "It suits her well. I'll move her later." Hastily she added, "But not upstairs. She'll be in service here, with your permission, of course. She'll sleep with Millie."

William smiled at the pretty face, reeking falsification. After ten minutes of solid talk, Jane had not come near the truth even once. This younger half-sister had settled with precise fury on her brain. What a marvelous entertainment it might be! He imagined wagers being made all over London on which Locke sister would emerge victorious. In the bored affluence of London society, vast wagers had been made on lesser matters. Human beings hunted such minor sport persistently. Something in their natures demanded it.

"May I see her?" he asked. Never bet on a horserace without first inspecting both animals. He knew intimately

Jane's dark buxom good looks and commonsense ways. But what of the young girl with courage enough to bring her knee up into the balls of a peer of the realm and who had suffered and survived a public whipping because of it? What of her?

Jane looked as though her expression had been tightly stitched onto her face. "Not now," she replied calmly. "She's quite undone, a drowned rat, really. You wouldn't find her to your liking." She stood as though the matter were closed. "She may stay then?" she asked with monstrous kindness.

"Of course," William murmured. "You didn't think I'd turn her out, did you? She's earned a safe harbor and we shall give her one."

Jane smiled her gratitude. He had never seen her so distraught, yet so eager to hide it. Sad! She was losing her country ways. Perhaps the younger sister had arrived just in time. William needed honesty about him. His life, both past and present, was rife with lies and liars.

Jane yawned prettily, throwing her false face into her first true expression. "If you'll excuse me, William" she smiled. "The night was long."

He agreed, though with a wave of his hand called her to him for a moment. Sweet Jane. He *was* fond of her. The storeroom could be filled with a dozen drowned sisters, and he felt certain he would still choose Jane, in spite of her new and unappealing habit of deception.

As she drew near to his side, he encircled her waist and pulled her close, tenderly pressing his face into her breasts.

"William," she protested, halfheartedly. "Sarah and Millie are about. What will they—"

Grinning, he pulled her down onto his lap and thrust his hands between her legs. She gave him only a token struggle, all the while giggling and nuzzling his neck.

The best of both worlds, he thought, still exploring her legs. He knew that all he had to do was lift her in his arms and carry her up to his bed, and in spite of her fatigue, he would find her receptive. Clearly the best of both worlds, a female, part-whore, part-wife, but neither, really. No obligation, no legal entanglements, a "gentleman's agreement" to live together as long as each made the other happy.

Quickly he released her, feeling himself become aroused

and not wishing to go through the laborious process of stockings and knee britches twice in one morning.

Freed, she looked inquiringly at him. "You made me hungry," she pouted.

He feigned sympathy. "Poor Jane. I'll come home early."

She smiled. Leaning across the table, she said earnestly, "I do love you, William. I love you so much."

"And I, you," he concurred, hoping her pronouncement would stop there. It did. She seemed to be looking about at the attractive dining room, the silver gleaming on the table, the rich hues of Persian carpet beneath her feet, the polished mahogany furniture. "How sinful we are," she laughed prettily. "Breakfasting at noon and making love over boiled eggs."

Delighted, William smiled. "It's our secret," he said. "For God's sake don't let the world know how happy we are, or else an edict will be forthcoming for the immediate restoration of our misery. Nothing is more unforgivable in this world than happiness."

"Then it's our secret," she complied. She moved to the door. There she turned back, her thoughts obviously taking an unpleasant direction. "I'm sorry about my sister, William," she apologized. "I promise she shall not disturb you. I didn't give them permission to send her, but"—she lifted her arms vaguely into the air—"they sent her anyway."

He started to tell her that she was behaving unbecomingly, but he could not help saying something utterly different. "We all have an inclination for cruel spectacles," he said. "It will be interesting to observe the victim of one close at hand."

"I don't understand—"

"Your sister has endured what most of us experience in our nightmares. We must watch her, see how the human soul copes with the reality of cruelty."

A look of alarm crossed Jane's face. "Well, if you're going to spend your time watching her, I'll send her packing this very instant."

"Careful," he said pointing toward the door behind him which led to the kitchen and perhaps Sarah's eager ears.

As though aware that she had said too much, Jane drew the robe tightly about her. "I'm tired," she said, "I'm going to bed."

"You do that," he agreed. Remain there if you wish. I'll come home early, and we'll take tea in the bedroom."

He listened to her step on the stairs, an indelible shadow of the woman herself. He waited until in the upper recesses of the house he heard a door close.

Based on the experience of three years, he knew she would require about fifteen minutes before falling asleep. Dropping back into his chair, sipping cold coffee, his whole face bore the rigidity of the dead. Did this unexpected guest bode ill or good? He preferred Jane lighthearted and emptyheaded. If this new presence upset her, it was only a matter of time before both he and his household would be upset as well. He wouldn't abide that.

There was nothing to do but see for himself. He checked his watch. There was time. It was shortly before twelve. He had an appointment at one. With a slight bend to the head, he passed quickly by the garden and proceeded quietly through the hallway which led to the kitchen and the rooms beyond. From the door he saw Sarah busily working at the sink, a colander of potatoes at her elbow. Millie was nowhere in sight, off on errands probably, or sleeping in some quiet corner of the house.

"Good morning," he said, trying not to startle the woman.

She whirled about, her plain, middle-aged face agape. "Oh, I'm sorry, Mr. Pitch. I didn't hear you. More coffee?"

He shook his head. "No, thank you, Sarah."

"More toast?" she offered, drying her hands on the hem of her apron, ready to spring into action at the first hint of his command.

"No, no," he assured her. He had hoped not to find her here. She would undoubtedly tell Jane and there would be new trouble. Well, so be it. It *was* his house.

"I've come to see our new guest," he announced.

Still rubbing her hands, she shook her head. "Arrived in the dead of night, she did. Half-dead herself," she murmured.

He listened closely to see if he could detect sympathy in the woman. He couldn't. She might as well have been discussing the delivery of a load of coal. No wonder Jane was so fatigued. Obviously she had already aroused the whole house against her sister.

Sarah lifted an impassive hand toward the corridor

which led to the storeroom. "In there, I imagine, at least that's where Miss Locke left her last night. Not a peep have I heard. Miss Locke ordered me to stay away." She shrugged lightly, then turned back to scrubbing her potatoes. "Not much to see, Mr. Pitch," she called over her shoulders. "But help yourself."

The storeroom was situated at the end of the service corridor. To the left was the door which led down to the cellar and his admirable assortment of wines. To the right was the door which led out to the garden.

He paused before the storeroom, feeling a curious excitement, followed immediately by irritation. His heart, what was left of it after the cultivation and domination of his mind, always went out to creatures alone and forsaken. Still he preferred to surround himself with wholeness. Whole people were so uncomplicated. Before this morning, he had assumed that Jane was whole.

Thus, William tabulated precisely the capabilities of his emotions, then reached for the doorknob. It didn't turn in his hand. He tried again. Locked! My God, his beautiful monstrous Jane had locked her in. In a growing sense of excitement mingled with anger, he shouted. "Sarah, it's locked, bring the key."

Denied easy access, he felt his curiosity vault. He would see the other side of the cell if he had to break down the door.

Sarah was at his elbow, bewildered, "Locked? Why locked?"

"Do you have the key?"

She looked foolishly about at the floor as though the sought-after object might be there.

The expression irritated William. "The key, Sarah."

Her confusion mounted. "I don't—" Then the light broke. She ran back into the kitchen and returned, key in hand. "It's an extra, Mr. Pitch. Miss Locke must have—"

Quickly he took it from her and was in the process of inserting it, when he stopped. "That's all, Sarah. You may go."

William waited until she had disappeared into the kitchen. Slowly he opened the door. The small interior room was dark. He saw a lamp burning low on an upturned crate. He saw the couch, the familiar discard from the parlor, surrounded by a confusion of barrels and sacks, half-undone, measures protruding. Then he saw the young woman, her arms half-flung off the cushions. Her legs were spread as in a dance, the thin coverlet thrown back. She was asleep. At least her eyes were closed.

Out of delicacy, William kept the door between them, not wanting to startle her into a sudden state of wakefulness. Gazing down on her, he was dumfounded. What was there here to alarm Jane? Beneath the thin coverlet, he saw a child's body, or an old woman's. He thought of Jane's luscious ripe warmth and the mystery only deepened.

A spasm of waking moved over her and she opened her eyes. Instantly he tried to retreat, but it was too late. She'd seen him. Her hands drew the coverlet about her. But her eyes held steady, wide-open, though darkly encircled, like two pieces of coal. The longer she watched him, he saw her expression change from submission to a level, unbending gaze of strength, as though he were nothing more than a passing amusement, an expression he'd never seen in Jane's eyes or those of any other female.

Feeling foolish, clinging to the door, he stepped from behind it and said, "Good morning."

There was no reply, although in truth he didn't expect one. She lay as though she knew that she had to submit herself to a period of observation, but it mattered little to her who was doing the observing.

Feeling the tension, William stepped closer. Surrounding the coal-black circles were two spheres of pristine blue. They stared back at him as if the whole fabric of sleep had begun to decompose. They moved from his face into a slow, expressionless inspection of the small storeroom.

Stepping still closer to the couch until he was looking directly down on her, he asked softly, "Do you know where you are?"

If she did, she gave no indication of it, but instead continued to stare up at him. Her lips, thin and bloodless, had not so much as moved, as though she had not yet been instructed in the art of speech. He had never been so closely observed, yet so bereft of the ability to read the thoughts of the observer.

"You're in London," he began softly, "in Bloomsbury in my house off Southampton Row. Your sister, Jane is here. My name is William Pitch." He felt as though he were reciting a soliloquy to a post. He wondered briefly if the indifference was feigned or real?

As though to add to his confusion, she yawned and turned on her side.

In some frustration, he carefully dragged up a wooden box and sat. "Marianne, is it?" he inquired, thinking perhaps that the matter of names would make a difference.

It didn't. He noticed a few feet away a heap of ruined garments, stiffened from drying, and beside them a valise, thinly packed, equally as soiled and mud-splattered. Seeing the scant belongings, he felt again the melancholy of the abandoned. "Did you sleep well?" he asked, and followed it quickly with, "Would you like coffee?" He followed that with, "Are you feeling ill?" then, "You're not frightened, are you?"

Slowly she turned her head to the barrage of questions. Still no response. The sensuality in her eyes alarmed him, perhaps the same expression that had outraged his Lordship. Well, no matter. It was over, and she was here. Jane had been right. Let her regain her strength, then put her into service.

As he stood up, he looked back down on her and wondered if the public whipping had come before or after his Lordship had had his way. Of course there was the remote possibility that she was still a virgin. But he doubted it seriously. The eyes certainly were not virginal, nor the body in spite of its childlike quality. Quickly he steered away from such thoughts. She'd endured enough. *"Honi soit qui mal y pense"* and his thoughts *were* growing dangerously evil. Enough time wasted. He had work awaiting him, the translation from German to English of that greatest of all eighteenth-century minds, Immanuel Kant. His English readers were fascinated by the German. Too bad they didn't take his teachings to heart.

At the door he stopped again and looked back. She was wearing him out. The abandoned right hand, somehow older and wiser than the rest of her body, lifted, hung suspended in midair. Then, as though it were a great weight, she moved it carefully and placed it on the couch beside her.

He stepped further back and stared at her through the open door. Beyond him in the kitchen he heard a suspicious silence, Sarah listening, just out of view.

"Sarah," he called. "Bring her coffee."

Still he looked at her. There *was* something, a curious inability to break away from that gaze, as though behind her eyes were powerful magnets. There was something else, an unreasonable feeling of shame welling up within him as though *he* had been the one who had punished her.

Annoyed, he pulled away from her gaze and walked hurriedly through the kitchen, throwing back over his shoulder a vague order for Sarah to "See to her." At the front door of his house, he waited. Then, like a man who for too long had forgotten to breathe, he stepped out into the crisp cold early December air, and welcomed the sight of carriages and commerce, wholly welcomed a rational and responding world filled with rational and responding people.

Abruptly he reversed that last thought. Responding perhaps, but rational? What he had found in the storeroom was not so great a mystery. The world was exposed every day to such incidents. The "carnivals" at Tyburn Hill were still the most popular entertainments in town, nothing more satisfying than the circus of a public hanging. Misfortune held a deadly attraction for all. And there were more exciting pleasures to come, the sketches he'd seen recently, secretly smuggled in from France, a sharpened blade suspended high in the air over the victim's head, instant decapitation, new pinnacles of enjoyment for Sunday picnics.

But still, without a doubt, the most interesting of all, rather simple really, yet enormously satisfying, the sight of a woman, stripped and bound and flogged to the very brink of her life.

He shuddered slightly and lifted his head as though for breath. Dear God, he'd never understand men. Never!

As though to flee his inability to understand, he stepped quickly, resignedly, onto the crowded pavement. . . .

Grumbling to herself, Sarah hastily prepared a tray. She used the chipped kitchenware and filled a bowl with lukewarm porridge left over from her own breakfast. She fetched the coffee pot from the dining room and shook it sternly. There was a faint slosh in the bottom. Enough.

They had no right. Millie off at midmorning to care for an ailing aunt in Brighton, Miss Locke upstairs asleep,

Mr. Pitch gone to his office, and who, guess who, gets saddled with the new "guest."

She slammed the cup minus saucer down on the tray and regretted anew her hasty decision three years ago to leave the service of Lady Groveton. Proper people, those, with her a part of a proper household. Suddenly in the tension of the morning, feeling a fatigue from the splintered night's sleep, all the resentment which she usually kept carefully concealed, rose within her.

She didn't like what she was becoming, a common woman, as common as the woman she now worked for. She missed the Grand Palace off Regency Park where fine carriages came up to the door with sweet gentle horses, when a person knew what was expected of her and was justly and graciously praised when she did her job well.

In increasing moodiness, she looked down at her worn black dress, smudged and bespotted with food. Her depression complete, she sat heavily on the kitchen chair. For a few extra guineas she'd allowed her world to go topsy-turvy. Here she was, living in a scandalous house, the two of them not even wed, serving meals at all hours to the rabble he called his friends. Just last evening, hadn't she been forced to serve a blackamoor, a savage with a thick gold chain around his neck and bare nipples?

She shuddered involuntarily. She was not a dumb woman. She knew what she had done. It was simply a matter of greed. Her own! For a few extra guineas she had sold her soul, and now she was forced to serve whores and blackamoors, scoundrels and discards from the whipping post. She bent her head even lower, tears increasing, so involved in her own misery that she scarcely heard a soft, faltering step behind her.

Not until she felt the pressure of a hand on her shoulder did Sarah whirl around, embarrassed, and look up. The girl, lost in the folds of the nightshirt, smiled at her, her face full of recognition, not for the woman herself, but for her state of misery.

"Don't cry," she soothed.

So great was Sarah's astonishment that she couldn't speak. She could only watch in a kind of paralysis as with shaking hands the girl took the chipped cup from her grasp, filled it with coffee, and offered it to her.

That done, the girl fetched another cup from the sideboard, filled it, and sat opposite Sarah at the table. Her long, mussed hair hung down beside her face as she warmed her hands on the hot coffee. "Once," she began, speaking to her cup, "when I was a child, I stepped, barefoot, down on a rake. I cried then like you're crying now." Slowly she looked about at the kitchen floor as though searching for something. "Where's your rake?" she inquired earnestly, though a smile played about the corners of her mouth.

Slowly recovering, Sarah wiped her eyes on the hem of her apron. She sat up straight in the chair, still dabbing at the corners of her eyes, trying to present at least a facade of decorum and dignity. Speech was beyond her.

Meanwhile the girl concentrated on her coffee and was now eyeing the bowl of porridge on the tray.

With a slight movement away from the table, Sarah said, rather gruffly, "Go ahead. It's yours," and watched fascinated as the girl reached for it eagerly. A few minutes later the spoon was scraping the bottom of the bowl.

Apparently it was Marianne's turn for embarrassment. With a shy smile she looked down at the empty bowl. "The last time I ate was in my father's house."

Sarah continued to watch and began to feel uneasy in the expanding silence. Someone should speak. She cleared her throat. "Did you—sleep well?" she faltered, appalled at how silly it sounded.

But apparently it did not sound silly to Marianne. She nodded eagerly. "I must have. I remember nothing." She looked at Sarah as though seeking her help. "The last thing I remember is the coach—and the rain—" She paused, then added, "and the cold."

Sarah listened carefully, her eyes fixed on the girl. She still resembled a drowned rat, dried now. Sarah noticed that she was looking at the kitchen, as though trying to determine precisely where she was.

But at the moment that it occurred to Sarah to tell her, the girl looked up again and asked directly, "Who was that man?"

Since Sarah had been eavesdropping, she was certain that Mr. Pitch had identified himself. Still, perhaps the girl had been half-awake. "William Pitch," she said, wondering precisely how far she should go in her definition of Wiliam Pitch. A new approach occurred to her. "Your sister, Jane, is here, too."

Obviously this last piece of news meant less than nothing to the girl. Or if it did hold meaning, she carefully masked it. "I'm in London?" she asked as though amazed.

"Now where did you think you'd be?" Sarah replied, amused.

Shyly, she asked Sarah a peculiar question. "Do you know who I am?"

Sarah nodded. "You're Miss Locke's sister come to visit." She might have said more but didn't. No need. In an attempt to put her at ease, she added, "Your name is Marianne."

The girl seemed pleased. She folded her hands on the table and fell silent.

In a few scant moments she had made a good impression on Sarah who, in spite of herself, began to like her. There was a simplicity about her, a stern harbored quality, yet a sweetness. Clearly whatever she had endured had taken a toll, but she had not been defeated by it.

"My name is Sarah," she said, for some reason wanting the girl to know.

"Sarah," Marianne repeated. Without warning the radiance of a smile cut through the tension of her face. Lightly she added, "I won't ask why you were crying. It would only make you cry more. Someday, when it's no longer worth your tears, will you tell me?"

Sarah nodded. Merely thinking anew on her misery, she felt her lips tremble. But the girl was right. Perhaps later.

Marianne stood up. She looked down at the nightshirt as though amazed. "Wherever did I get this?" she asked as though seeing it for the first time.

Sarah smiled. "It's Millie's, the girl who works here. All your things were quite ruined, I'm afraid. We had to—" She was going to say something else, but the expression had frozen on Marianne's face.

"Who undressed me?" she asked, her voice cold.

Then it was clear. Her scarred back. Although Sarah had seen it, she now denied it. "Your sister," she replied, rising from the chair, carrying the empty dishes to the sink. In an attempt to change the subject, Sarah asked, "Are you still hungry?" and looked over her shoulder where the girl leaned heavily against the table as though suffering new weakness. "Here," Sarah said, hurrying to her side. "You'd better sit." As she put her arm around the girl's shoulder to assist her to a chair, she was amazed at the thinness.

Marianne gave in to her support and confessed to feeling weak. Safely seated, she folded her hands in her lap, head down, as though some unbearable memory were moving over her.

Sarah watched, feeling herself moved. Apparently the girl's life now was one long effort to hold herself in check. Having known her for less than ten minutes, Sarah was nonetheless convinced that the punishment had been too severe. These lords of the provinces were little more than feudal chieftains, lacking the civility and sense of justice with which London was blessed.

Within the moment, the girl's mood vanished. She looked up. "All my things were ruined?" she asked.

Sarah nodded. "At least for now. We must wash and dry—"

"Then I'd better get to work," Marianne said, leaving the chair, as though eager to restore herself. "I can't go about looking like this. Will you help me?"

Although she had several hours of her own chores yet ahead of her, Sarah agreed readily to help, her fancy galloping in all directions, to the delicacy and obvious breeding of this younger sister compared to the one sleeping upstairs.

For the better part of the afternoon the two women worked together, washing Marianne's meager collection of three dresses, stretching a dark blue muslin over a bush in the garden for the rays of the December sun to dry it. Marianne explored every nook and cranny of the garden, identifying each shrub and flower, spilling out to Sarah the specifics of the garden she'd left at home. Sarah noticed that there were still those occasions when she ventured too close to some forbidden subject and the light vanished from her face. But soon it passed and she'd moved on to some safer subject, her good spirits increasing, her laughter contagious.

About midafternoon Sarah boiled a large tub of water, filled her own bowl and pitcher, and gave Marianne complete access to her own room across from the kitchen. Since the matter of the girl's permanent quarters was still up in the air, Sarah had no choice. Not that she minded.

Marianne said thank you and hugged her lightly in passing. The brief embrace, so quick and spontaneous, left Sarah breathless. She couldn't remember the last time someone had touched her in affection. She turned back into the kitchen, taking the sweet sensation with her.

A short time later Marianne emerged, obviously scrubbed, the long hair pulled back and tied becomingly at the nape of her neck, the blue gown falling in soft folds from the tiny circle of her waist, a vision compared to the wreck of early morning. She stood in the doorway as though awaiting Sarah's inspection.

Sarah approved, and was amazed at the transformation. She was even more amazed at the broader transformation of her own thoughts. Some practical instinct was already telling her that this house would never be the same.

"You look lovely," she said with a smile.

"Not lovely," corrected Marianne, modestly, "but clean at least. Now it's my turn to help you." She filled the sink with the remaining hot water and began immediately to plunge the dishes into it. Sarah started to stop her, then changed her mind. Quite obviously it was Miss Locke's intention to make a servant of the girl. How sad for Miss Locke that the girl had already assumed that role, thus denying her the pleasure of intimidation.

As she moved in and out of the kitchen, bringing Marianne more dishes, she was amazed at her efficiency. Unlike Millie, who had to be told everything, Marianne seemed to know without question the location of each utensil. She said nothing as she worked. There were times when her eyes became sad, but for the most part she reminded Sarah of someone who had spied the target and was taking careful aim.

It was after five when Sarah heard the first telltale pressure of footsteps on the staircase. She looked up from the sink where she was scraping carrots. Marianne sat at the table, folding linen, a job which Sarah had insisted upon after seeing the girl lean weakly over the pan of hot water. Sarah started to say something, then changed her mind, for Marianne too had looked up, her face suddenly grave, a small but recognizable apprehension spreading through her eyes.

"No need," Sarah soothed, keeping her voice down. "No need—"

The footsteps were moving through the dining room.

Sarah saw Marianne straighten herself as though she knew she would need all her wits about her.

Then the kitchen door opened and Jane appeared, dressed in a lovely gown of dark sapphire green, her hair hidden beneath an overlarge wig, a strand of pearls about her neck. Sarah thought wryly, "In her battle clothes, she is, come to do battle."

From her viewpoint at the sideboard she watched carefully as Jane glanced briefly at the girl, averted her eyes, then looked back again. But whatever was forming in her head never had a chance to materialize. Marianne was on her feet. She rushed to Jane, embraced her warmly. "How good to see you!" she exclaimed, kissing the startled woman lightly on both cheeks. Then she stood back as though really seeing her for the first time. "And how beautiful you are," she added, her left hand not quite touching the green silk, as though she didn't want to spoil it.

Clearly flustered by this warm greeting, Jane blushed. Obviously she'd expected something altogether different.

Marianne backed away, her face suddenly sober, her voice low, rich, and seemingly sincere. "I can never thank you enough, Jane," she began "for your hospitality and kindness." Her voice was a precise and harmonious blend of proper chords. "I had no right to descend on you like I did last night, unannounced, unexpected. It was not my idea, but Dolly's. You remember Dolly, don't you, a mistress of everyone's business." She laughed softly. "You might have thrown me out. Yet you received me with love, and I'm very grateful."

Still disarmed, Jane watched, the same glazed effect in her eyes as Sarah felt in her own, as though both were watching a skillful actress. Marianne was now saying something about the misfortune that had descended on their family, the words coming faster and faster, almost as though she were afraid to stop talking.

She moved gracefully about the table, bringing Jane up to date on the last few hours, as though she had a right to know, heaping praise on Sarah for her assistance and promising finally, "I'll be no trouble, Jane. I'll work in the kitchen and earn my keep, and strive only to see that you regret neither your kindness nor your generosity."

Jane appeared dumbfounded, her eyes still searching for something threatening and finding nothing. Even after

Marianne had stopped talking, Jane continued to stare at her, as though there were another knowledge deep within her, a knowledge that did not match in the least the specifics of this new apparition. In spite of Jane's elegant gown and powdered wig, she looked limp, tattered somehow.

Finally, as though she knew she must behave well, she murmured, "I'm glad to see you've recovered. You were quite senseless last night."

Marianne smiled. "It was a wretched ride, in a pouring rain all the way. Only the grace of God and the thought of seeing your face again saw me through it."

Jane's small gray eyes looked beyond Marianne to the opened storeroom door. Almost pouting, she said to Sarah, "I see you found a key."

Sarah, who had been watching the confrontation, decided this was not the moment to bring William Pitch into the awkward matter. She took full blame upon her own shoulders. "Yes, Miss Locke," she said. "I heard her awake and thought she might be hungry." She looked at Marianne, hoping the girl would not refute the story. She didn't, though it seemed to Sarah that her strength was dwindling. Marianne grasped the back of the chair, apparently uncertain whether she should sit or continue to stand. Then, as though it were her kitchen, she invited warmly, "Come, sit, Jane. Let's chat while I work. We've so much to catch up on." It was a clever ruse, still playing the servant, though free now to sit as though her strength were ebbing.

Sarah watched, incredulously, as Jane obeyed, hesitating a moment, then sweeping forward and taking the chair opposite Marianne where she now sat folding linens.

Sarah knew that she ought to turn to her own chores, but the fascination was too great, the two sisters sitting in a state of apparent calm, but a calm as suspect as that which precedes a summer storm.

As she worked, Marianne looked admiringly at the woman opposite her. Again she repeated, "How lovely you are. And how successful your husband must be. I can only assume that nothing but good fortune has smiled on you since the day you arrived in London."

The key word "husband" caused a slight tremor in Jane's face. She looked down, then readily agreed. "He is. Just the most successful editor in London."

Marianne continued to play her part skillfully. "I look

forward to meeting him. I really do. And how fortunate he is to have found you."

Again, confusion covered Jane's face. Torn between wanting to accept the generous words and clearly suspicious of them, she was reduced to the nervous gesture of fingering her pearls. She seemed incapable of taking the lead and was at the complete mercy of the self-possessed Marianne.

As the girl's hands moved skillfully in and out between the folds of linen, her tongue seemed to be keeping pace with her fingers. "I love your house," she was saying now. "It's charming, what I've seen of it. What a pleasure it will be to help Sarah keep it neat and in order. Believe me, there's nothing so grand in all of Mortemouth. You must feel like a princess."

Poor Jane could only nod.

"And you're not to bother about me," Marianne said. "I can sleep anywhere."

Jane blushed. "The storeroom was only temporary," she apologized. "You were quite soaked and mud-covered. If you wish, you may take Millie's room next to Sarah's. When she returns, we'll find somewhere else."

Marianne smiled, the light of true gratitude in her face for the vague arrangements. Again she left her chair and hugged her sister. "I'm so proud of you and have so much to learn from you."

The tableau held, the two sisters locked in close embrace. Finally, as though she didn't want to embarrass her further, Marianne took her seat again.

All this unexpected love seemed to have an infectious result on Jane. For the first time since she'd entered the kitchen, she smiled, her stern mood somewhat undermined. "We'll go shopping tomorrow if you wish," she suggested, almost shyly. "You need everything."

Marianne agreed. "What fun it will be to go together. Like old times," and commenced folding linen again, keeping her eyes down.

Jane watched her closely. As far as Sarah could tell, there was one enormous unresolved question on her mind. Was the girl to be a guest or a servant? Apparently there was no plausible solution at hand. Jane dismissed the dilemma with a light "Then I'll leave you in Sarah's hands."

Marianne appeared the picture of gratitude. "She's been

most kind. I don't know what I would have done without her."

Now Jane stood up, still in search of a battle. "We entertain guests every evening, Marianne," she said, too sweetly. "But nothing shall be expected of you tonight. You must rest and regain your strength from your horrible ordeal. How dreadful it must have been for you."

Sarah saw Marianne's hands freeze in their activity. She looked suddenly smaller somehow, less contained, as though an arrow had found its target.

Jane spied the weakness and with the instinct of a predator moved closer. "I shan't ask you any questions now. But later we must talk. You must tell me everything. Perhaps I can help you to see your mistakes."

The hands were still frozen atop a damask cloth. Sarah, in a surge of pity, came to her rescue. "You must excuse us now, Miss Locke, if tea is to be on time."

Jane nodded good-naturedly, the decision obviously resolved in her mind. A servant, clearly. The girl was to be a servant. She drew herself up, fully restored. "We'll take tea in the parlor, Sarah. William is due shortly. You might allow Marianne to serve so that she can meet him. But don't work her too hard in the beginning. She's gone through a dreadful ordeal. We must give her time, all the time she needs to forget."

"And with you there every step of the way, forcing her to remember," Sarah thought angrily, still unable to take her eyes off the bowed head. "She's outworked me this afternoon, Miss Locke. I think she has enough strength for both of us."

The clearly shifting loyalty displeased Jane. At the door she frowned. "I'm counting on you Sarah, to teach her what obviously in the past she has failed to learn, which indeed has brought her to her present unhappy state. Wouldn't you agree, Marianne?"

Sarah watched with aching heart as Marianne tried to withstand the onslaught. Her hands were trembling perceptibly, her face a deep red. But incredibly she managed to lift her eyes, managed the warmest of smiles. "You're right, Jane," she murmured, almost breathless with effort. "I have known misfortune and I am here to learn at your feet."

Jane listened, a look of supreme pleasure on her face. "There, you see, Sarah?" She smiled. "She's willing to mend her ways, but we must help her." Then she made a ridiculous effort, sweeping the gown about her as she turned, calling back regally over her shoulder, "Tea at five thirty, Sarah, in the parlor. Don't forget."

Sarah waited for the footsteps to diminish, then she went back to where Marianne sat at the table. Perspiration was visible on her forehead although the sun was going down and the room was cool. "Pay her no mind," she whispered. "Someday I'll tell you of the success she's made of her life."

Still Marianne did not move or respond. A powerful spell seemed to have descended over her and Sarah had not the faintest idea how to go about dispelling it.

"Would you like to go to Millie's room and lie down?" she offered kindly.

But there was no response, and weary with futile effort Sarah turned back to the preparation of tea. A few moments later she heard movement behind her, saw Marianne push forward in her chair and move quickly down the narrow hall and out into the garden.

Sarah followed after as far as the door. The clouds had finally won their day-long battle with the sun, and beyond the garden the rows of houses were sinking in a gray light. Higher up on the hill toward the British Museum Library a veil of smoke from evening fires had drawn a charcoal curtain across the sky. The shouts of children at play came to her from lower down Great Russell Street.

Where is she? Sarah wondered. She searched every shadow.

At the back of the garden she saw her, silhoutted against the sky, her head down, as though weeping, or at prayer. . . .

In truth, it was neither. She simply had felt the need for air. Unable to find it in Sarah's kitchen, Marianne had taken momentary refuge in the garden. She thought she had slipped out unobtrusively. But then she spied Sarah at the back door, watching her.

No matter. The woman was kind, clearly suffering from some private agony which Marianne could only guess at.

She could think of a hundred worse companions than Sarah Gibbons.

She walked further back to the very edge of the garden. Beyond the wall she could see the towers and chimneys of the city, could hear the rattle of carriages on cobblestones, a vendor shouting for all to try his chestnuts, a thousand voices and noises, or so it seemed to one who was accustomed to the rhythm of waves slapping against a beach and the plaintive screech of gulls swooping low at eventide.

She adjusted her eyes to the dimness of the evening light and looked back toward the handsome red brick house. Sarah had gone back to her duties and Marianne was blessedly alone, left to recover, to assess, to speculate.

Her random thoughts, gathering momentum, ascended from the general to the specific. She was here, having successfully completed a journey which at times she thought would kill her. But she had survived, and she had every intention of surviving further.

She paced softly at the back of the garden, the cool air reviving her, the dampness of sweat on her forehead feeling like ice, clearing her brain. Poor Jane. Not changed really. Oh, a lovely gown to be sure and undoubtedly a closetful of them upstairs. But the same, uncertain, encumbered.

She lifted her head to the night sky. She still had her wits, her intelligence, her sense of justice, all fed and made doubly strong by an unquenchable need for revenge. There lay her escape route. Of course the particulars had to be worked out, but that, too, was part of her strength, her absolute faith that Fate would arrange itself on her behalf.

For now she would have to be satisfied with a borrowed bed, kitchen duties, and the subtle assaults of her sister. It wasn't the most glorious present, but it was better than the past and the future would compensate for both. Her thoughts so occupied her that for several minutes all the street sounds were blotted from her ears. She heard only the gentle lapping of waves on a beach, saw a cliff path which led up to a black grille inside a castle gate. Through the gate into the inner courtyard, she saw—

Abruptly she closed her eyes. Her mind made a frantic retreat away from the image. A short time later, restored, she looked blackly about her. Half-turning, she caught sight of the red brick house. Why was she standing here in a cold, damp garden when she should be preparing herself for tea?

For it was her intention, as it had been since early that morning, when she'd first seen him bending over her, to have tea this evening with William Pitch. . . .

Most women, William reflected, were diminished by service. But Marianne, his mistress' half-sister, was clearly an exception. He noticed that the girl, encumbered with a large tea tray, looked so excessively at home in the elegant front parlor, fashionably done in chinoiserie, that she made Jane, lounging uselessly to one side in a red lacquered chair, seem like her visitor.

William was surprised to see her up and about. She'd appeared quite pale only that morning, without spirit or will, and certainly without speech. He smiled at catching Voltaire with his aphorisms awry. *"We employ speech only to conceal our thoughts."* Not true, for William was certain now, as he had been earlier that morning, that behind the silent facade was a mind teeming with something.

Leaning back on the couch, he watched her, foregoing for the moment his twin amusement of watching Jane watching her. Brushed and combed, her long fair hair falling prettily down her back in obvious ignorance of the fashion of the day, dressed with utter simplicity in a dark blue country gown that had seen better days, she moved with ease and grace through the rather garish room decorated with Chinese wallpaper, a peasant scene with waterwheels and oxen and almond-eyed workers.

William looked about him, masking his distaste. Jane had talked him into it, this overpowering confusion of red and black and jade green. For himself, he would have felt much more at home with the delicacy of English rose, plain, but substantial English furnishings. But chinoiserie was the style, and they *would* be stylish, if nothing else.

Again he shifted on the couch, mildly puzzled by the feeling of unrest which had plagued him all afternoon. He demanded order in his house. But the atmosphere of his front parlor this evening was not ordered. It was charged with muted tension.

Jane had said nothing all the while that Marianne had been in the room. Prior to that she'd been a talking machine, informing William in a burst that she was certain her younger half-sister had reformed, was truly repentant.

Repentant! Masking a smile, William took the teacup now being offered him by Marianne. As she turned away, he tried in vain to find something in that self-contained exterior that spoke of repentance. As she stood half-turned from his scrutiny, he saw a blush on her cheeks, as though she knew he was watching her, aware with conscious knowledge that she was an object worthy of scrutiny.

A fragment from his day's work at translating Kant entered his mind. *Sapere Aude!* Dare to know. Have the courage to use your own intelligence.

That was it! Precisely and succinctly her entire personality defined by a remote German. *Sapere Aude.* Dare to know. He looked up to see her lightly touching the Orrery on the table, his newest toy, a tiny model of the solar system, duplicating with clockwork the orbits of the earth and moon around the sun, an expensive toy which had brought him pleasure in its rosewood case with inlaid ivory.

"Do you know what that is, Marianne?" he asked quietly.

Quickly Jane looked up from her tea. Her eyes darted nervously to Marianne, whose fingers were lightly assisting the movement of the sun. "Don't touch it," Jane ordered. "It's quite delicate and easily broken."

Marianne looked up at the reprimand, but did not immediately do as she was told.

William interceded. "Nonsense," he said to Jane. "She can't hurt it. It's there to be enjoyed." He was aware of Jane's displeasure, but at the moment was more fascinated with Marianne's pleasure.

"It's the solar system," he instructed gently. "The Heavens reduced to rational order. Here the earth"—and he pointed to a small pewter ball—"and there the moon, and there"—he pointed to the large brass orb—"the sun."

Clearly she was fascinated, one hand extended as though in a desire to touch, the other hand withheld, as though to warn the child in her who went incautiously about.

Before such an enraptured audience, William had no choice but to elaborate. He shifted the Orrery close to her. "You see," he expounded, "all three are in constant revolution, each moving about the other, the entire mystery of the universe performing with clockwork predictability which human reason can reduce to a few simple equations."

Her face furrowed as she leaned still closer. Her eyes, normally blue, burned almost blue-black. William waited to see if she would say anything, but she didn't. He realized that he had yet to hear her say a word.

Jane scolded him lightly. "William, your tea is getting cold," a slight condescension in her voice as though to convey to him that he was wasting his explanation on the dull-witted girl.

"Then I'll have it warmed," he said over his shoulder, and turned immediately back to the subject at hand. He liked Marianne's attention. The Orrery had been in the front parlor for over three weeks. With the exception of himself, no one had paid it the slightest mind.

"You see this empty place here?" he asked, pointing toward the green enameled surface.

Marianne nodded.

"A few years ago, a man named Herschel discovered a new planet there, Uranus, the first planet discovered since ancient times. With that, the diameter of the known solar system doubled, and man, correspondingly, shrank."

She took it all in, and leaned still closer, the better to study the empty place where he was pointing.

Behind them, Jane laughed. "For heaven sakes, William —the child can scarcely read or write and you're filling her head with thoughts of the solar system."

For the first time Marianne looked across the room toward Jane. William thought he saw a tightening of the skin stretched smooth across her forehead. He hoped that she would speak. But she didn't. The spasm passed, the point of ambush evaded.

Mysteriously weary, William withdrew to the couch. It was difficult to sustain enthusiasm in the face of such silence. Perhaps Jane was right. Perhaps the child's ordeal had rendered her simpleminded. At any rate it was none of his concern.

As he sank back onto the couch, he patted Jane on the knee, mending broken bridges. "She showed an interest," he explained. "I thought—"

Jane laughed. "You're too kind, William. And you love to preach. You should have been a minister."

"Oh, of course," he agreed sarcastically and rested his head against the cushion, disliking the sense of a battlefield which had invaded his parlor.

At that moment Sarah appeared in the doorway, her eagle eyes taking in everything. Apparently finding nothing to object to, she drew herself up and delivered herself of her message. "There's a tradesman at the back door, Miss Locke. He requires payment. Will you come?"

Jane objected. "Now? Why so late?"

"He was here earlier," Sarah replied, "but you were sleeping and I didn't want to disturb you."

William chuckled. "The wages of laziness, my dear. Go. Pay the man off. It's your job." He had not intended his voice to be so stern. Without arguing, Jane stood up, cast only a brief glance at Marianne, who stood silently at attention near the door. Then apparently convinced that all was well, she swept out of the door, followed immediately by Sarah.

The two remaining in the room did not move. William knew that he was staring at her, saw her blush.

"Would you care to take a seat?" he asked, curiously annoyed.

She shook her head, indicating that she did not wish to take a seat.

A most awkward position, he thought, his annoyance increasing. Was she guest or servant? How should he treat her, and why didn't she speak? For several minutes, he sat, silent, now and then adjusting his waistcoat, shifting the garter below his knee. Too tight. Everything seemed too tight. The simple wig on his head was crushing his brain, the jacket was binding him across the shoulders, his knee trousers were cutting off the circulation from his knees down.

In an attempt to rid himself of this mysterious discomfort, he stood up and commenced pacing lightly. Suddenly he could stand it no more. "For God's sake," he ordered, "either sit down or leave the room."

Instantly he regretted it. He was a firm believer in the virtues of reason and humane regard. She slipped quietly into a near straightbacked chair and sat, her hands folded primly in her lap.

Incredibly, he wanted to punish her for having so slyly brought him to such a state of agitation. He turned away in order to bring himself to a semblance of self-control. He looked back at her. "Do you think you will be happy in

London?" he inquired, deciding to force her into speech with a direct question.

She looked up at him with utmost gravity. "Why shouldn't I be?"

Although pleased at her capacity to respond, he found the response itself incomplete, almost disagreeable. "Well, I'd say that would be up to you. Wouldn't you agree?"

Again she looked up calmly. "Not necessarily."

He glanced across the room at her. Where had she acquired such exalted airs? "Why not necessarily?" he demanded.

She gave him a momentary and none too friendly glance. "One's happiness generally depends upon the reasonableness of those around him, unless of course, one has the good fortune to occupy a position of such power that reason is unimportant." She continued to sit in the chair, in a position of perfect self-containment, while he was the one who paced restlessly about like some nervous student.

At least she could talk. Oh, God, how she could talk. "Why," he asked, "should the role of reasonableness be so exalted?" He wanted to drive her into a corner, wanted to remove the peculiar privilege which resided on her face.

"It isn't exalted," she replied flatly, "for those who think they possess it."

He leaned forward. "Do you possess it?" he asked bluntly.

"I try," she replied. "I don't always succeed." She looked down, fell into a vague arrangement of her skirt. Without looking up, she asked, "Do you?"

William maintained an ominous silence. *She* was testing him.

Where in the hell was Jane? He was weary of the confrontation. The talking Marianne was worse that the silent one. Clearly she was one of those deviations by which man thinks to reconstruct himself. In fact, looking at her again, he saw a masculine quality in spite of her delicacy and small frame, a confidence, those areas of manhood in which no woman should have a legitimate foothold. He thought with a smile of the havoc she could wreak among his fellows—political liberals, self-serving, yet broadminded wits or halfwits who would take her as a lamb until they felt her lion's claws.

In spite of the nature of his thoughts, he smiled again

at the image. If only Hogarth were still alive. He would sketch her in that likeness, the face of a lamb, the claws of a lion. And God help the man who lacked the wit and intelligence to leave her alone.

He gazed with sharp attention at her downcast eyes. He had hoped she would be a pretty, romantically pitiful bauble to add to his salon. But as bad luck would have it, while she was pretty, she certainly was not agreeable. Finally, this was completed by a sense of wounded pride. He had hoped to dazzle her. In truth he had bored her.

Glancing at her now, he noticed a change in her face. She raised her eyes to him, an expression no longer contained and arrogant, but faltering, as though in humility.

He felt himself taken aback, and was in no way prepared for the words she spoke. "Thank you for telling me about the heavens." Her eyes moved rapidly across the Orrery. She left her chair and stood over the machine.

William followed and stood opposite her, both gazing down at the miniature solar system. The beautiful head opposite him lifted. She said softly, "I'd like to go there someday. Wouldn't you?"

His mind felt momentarily disengaged. Where?" he asked.

"Uranus," she said, "in a flying machine. To the shores of Uranus—assuming, of course, that they have shores."

William laughed. In response to what she had said, he felt happy and restored. She *was* a female, her head filled with foolish notions, a child upon whom the world had placed no burdens save one, a scarred back and accompanying memories.

Apparently she was not upset by his laugh. In fact she seemed pleased by it, as though the restoration of his good humor had been her precise aim. "Why not?" she asked prettily. "Why not a flying machine? We are capable of everything."

William shook his head. "Not quite," he corrected. "Almost, but not quite. Where would we find wings?"

Smiling as though at her own stupidity, she offered timidly, "We could make them. We could study the birds and make ours like theirs. They could teach us."

There was something so open and earnest in her face, a quality that William had never seen in a face before, male or female, an absolute confidence in dreams.

"If you say so," he conceded softly, standing very near to her, feeling himself deprived of all breath. There was a pleasant scent about her, like wind or sea breeze, and her eyes were holding him. He tried to glance away, knowing that he should. The whole room seemed suddenly to fill with her fragrance. When he glanced back at her face, he saw that she was pale, as though she too were experiencing the same discomfort. He had never, never desired anything in his life as much as he now desired the touch, the feel, the sensation of that one hand.

Then from the door came, "Three shillings for a decent piece of lamb! Can you imagine! No telling where—" Jane stopped short. William could just see her face over the dark blue shoulder. Jane laughed nervously. "Still instructing her in the movement of the heavens, William? Will you never give up?"

He moved away, coming back to common sense, feigning a disinterested involvement. "More accurately, she was instructing me."

At the same time, he saw Marianne hurry to the door, her face down. She murmured something about Sarah needing her, and within the instant, she was gone, the room painfully empty, as though a throng had left instead of one. . . .

Eden Castle
North Devon

$\mathcal{W}$HENEVER his mind turned upon such things—and it was not often, for Thomas Eden was basically a very sanguine person—it struck him that during the last few weeks, he had been, if not happy, at least content.

On a brisk cold mid-December morning, standing on the central staircase, looking out over the inner courtyard, wearing only a loose-fitting white shirt and riding breeches, his hair in an almost barbaric state of disarray, he watched as Russell Locke put the magnificent horse through her paces.

Amid cries and shouts from the watching guardsmen, Locke raced her this way and that, a sagacious beast specially trained by Locke himself for special work. A beautiful swift animal, she handled like a dream and could turn on a sixpence.

Thomas' fingers twitched over the thin whip which he held in his hands. How he would like to ride her, as Locke was riding her, around and around the whipping oak, the maneuver clearly designed to display her speed and agility. Abruptly, in a rush and sudden break, Locke stopped the animal directly in front of Thomas.

"Watch this!" he shouted. Thomas stepped closer, long-

ing to touch her, to feel the sweat of her mane, the whites
of her eyes glaring at him as though she were aware of her
own intelligence. Quickly Locke reined her to the left,
slowed her to a sedate gallop at the end of the courtyard.

Then Locke shouted, "Whoa!" As if on opposite command, the horse shot forward in a burst of speed, heading
for the castle gate. Thomas laughed, delighted.

"Incredible!" he shouted while horse and rider were still
a distance away. "You've done a magnificent job, Locke."
The compliment had been earned. It had been Locke who
had worked with the animal for only two weeks, teaching
her to respond to orthodox words of command, but in re-
verse, so that if a revenue man happened upon a horse
laden with contraband and ordered the rider to halt, the
obedient fellow might shout "Whoa!" and the horse would
gallop safely off into the night.

It had been Locke's idea, the only way to escape if
caught hands down with illegal goods. Thomas had not
thought it possible to train an animal in so short a time.
But here was the proof standing before him, her monstrous
sides heaving with exertion.

"Let me try her," Thomas said eagerly, stepping up to
take the reins.

"I'm not certain, milord," Locke said hesitantly. "She
knows my voice, my hand—"

"And she can learn mine," Thomas insisted.

Begrudgingly, Locke slipped from the saddle. "Give her
her head, milord," he instructed, "until right before the
command. Then pull sharply up. She'll know."

Beside himself with excitement, Thomas nodded to the
instructions. As Locke held the stirrups steady, Thomas
swung his leg up and over, enjoying the sensation of her
massive sides. He took the reins from Locke's hand and
led the animal in a slow walk to the end of the courtyard.
She was a beauty, a chestnut brown with rippling muscles
and a good sense of herself.

He tightened his grip on the reins. The cold wind off
the sea blew against him. He looked over at Locke, who
had been joined by several of the groomsmen. They all
stared eagerly toward Thomas, clearly awaiting the master
to perform.

Then perform he would! He wrapped the reins about his
hand and with sudden strength brought the heels of his

boots down against the horse's sides. She shot forward in a burst of speed, her mane in the wind slapping against his hand. He raced her the length of the courtyard, then back, slowing her to a gallop. He could feel the tension and imagined her weighted down with packs of smuggled goods, the night dark, but her feet sure as she picked her way across the cliff top.

He was midyard now, the horse prancing at a steady pace. Suddenly he imagined other hooves behind him. The excise men. Closing his eyes, Thomas imagined that above the howl of the wind, he heard a voice ordering him to stop. Being an obedient fellow, he shouted to the horse, "Whoa!" Upon the command, the horse shot forward, no steady acceleration, but moving within the instant from a gallop to breakneck speed. The whipping oak passed by, a blur of black. Yawning directly ahead was the castle gate. Sharply, Thomas jerked back on the reins. As the bit cut into her tongue, the horse raised up on her hind legs. Thomas gripped at the leather in his hands, doing more damage to prevent his fall. He saw Locke start, alarmed, down the steps. Then she was steady again, white puffs of smoke exploding from her nostrils, shaking her mammoth head as though to tell him that he could let up.

Laughing heartily, he bowed to the thin applause coming from the guardsmen on the steps.

"Quite a trick, milord," one of the men shouted at him. "A topsyturvy animal if ever I saw one."

Thomas smiled and nodded. He guided the animal back along the wall, passed the charnel house. A nauseating odor filled his nostrils in spite of the nine-foot thickness of the Norman walls. The horse too shied away. It was only with the greatest of strength that he kept her from bolting back to the center of the courtyard.

Locke grinned as he drew near. "That's how I trained her, milord." He pointed to the charnel house. "I told her if she didn't behave, she'd get thrown down the death well."

Several of the young grooms snickered. Thomas stared down at Locke. Peculiar attitude for a man whose sister had endured the place. Then he remembered, as far as Locke was concerned, that his sister was dead. Thomas wondered briefly, was she?

As he dismounted and handed the reins to a groom, he asked, "What's her name?"

Locke thought a moment, obviously on the spot. Then, shyly, he ventured, "Brandy?"

In spite of the impudence Thomas laughed. The fellow was quick. And shrewd. He saw him shivering in the biting cold mid-December wind. He *had* done a good job.

Thomas himself shivered, his shirt wet with perspiration from his recent exertion. "Come along, Locke," he ordered. "We'll have brandy and toast—Brandy."

Obviously Locke had not been expecting so great a gift. His face flushed twin circles of red rising on both cheeks.

Thomas turned the horse over to the groomsmen and led the way up the steps with certain misgivings. He was not accustomed to drinking with his men, except Ragland, whose encroaching age had somehow neutered him, made him neither man nor woman, servant or equal. But Locke was a different matter, a man who might become accustomed to such privilege.

Still, Thomas was wise enough to know how to use the "user," and in the lonely stretches of his life and the North Devon coast, a man sometimes had to take his company where he could find it.

"This way, Locke," he ordered, leading the way through the entrance hall, avoiding the arched doors which led to the Banqueting Hall, choosing instead the narrow stone staircase which led down to the dungeon and the new secret stairway.

On the long climb down, he looked back once at Locke. The man seemed disappointed, as though he'd looked forward to the fire and rich furnishings of the Banqueting Hall. Clearly it was no treat for him to return to the cold damp hole where he'd spent the better part of the last month.

A short time later, Thomas stepped down into the vast subterranean storeroom, now only partially filled with the latest delivery—kegs of French brandy, French lace, and tobacco. And there, in a high stack, wrapped in newsprint, were canisters of China tea.

Two wall torches flickered opposite each other on the walls. Directly ahead was the narrow opening of the staircase which led down to the floor of the beach.

At last, completed! Thomas surveyed the room with open pleasure. Locke stood a respectful distance behind, maintaining silence. There was no further need for delay.

The goods were here, with the promise of more on their way. The horse was in the stable, trained and ready.

Expertly, Thomas uncorked a new keg. With Locke's help, they tilted it forward and filled two mugs, a few precious drops splattering onto the stone floor. Thomas lifted his mug in silent toast and Locke did likewise.

"I see no reason," Thomas said, stepping through and around the goods of his storeroom, "why we can't start tonight."

"Nor I, milord," Locke concurred.

"Who will ride?"

"I will," Locke said. "At first. We'll need more horses."

"Then get them."

"I have, milord. Their training is not completed as yet. I plan to have at least a dozen."

Thomas looked up from his brandy. The man was being very generous with a purse that was not his. Apparently Locke saw the look and moved to dispel it. "Quick distribution is the key, milord," he said. "Receive the goods and disperse them as rapidly as possible. All this is pleasing to look at," he added, gesturing to the storeroom, "but it makes you very vulnerable."

Thomas agreed and was on the verge of saying as much when suddenly he heard a low rumbling. Alarmed, he glanced toward the narrow opening which led down to the ocean. A small cloud of dust filtered up. "What in the hell was that?" he demanded.

Locke semed unperturbed. "The earth is soft and loose beneath the stone, milord. The passage below requires buttressing."

"Then do it, for God's sake!" Thomas exploded, "or the whole bloody thing will cave in."

Locke sipped at the brandy. "It was your command, milord, to finish the tunnel as rapidly as possible." He smiled. "The men will bring in timbers next week. It will not collapse. I can promise you that."

Again Thomas glanced toward the opening. Perhaps he was right. The rumbling had ceased. Almost childlike, he glanced back at Locke. "Will they ever find us out?" He smiled.

Locke grinned. "All of Eden Point would have to collapse first. Either that or they would have to become moles."

Thomas laughed. "I've heard you call them ferrets and rats."

"But not moles."

No, Thomas agreed. Again he paced off his storeroom, pleased with what he saw, but wishing he felt more at ease with Locke. Why was the man standing so stiffly, so obsequiously? "Sit," Thomas ordered, and obediently the man sat on an upturned keg, his back still rigid.

Thomas discovered that the only way he could converse with him was not to look at him. "You'll be a rich man, Locke, by the end of the year," he said, gesturing toward the goods.

"And you'll be richer, milord."

Thomas shook his head. "I'm not doing it for the money," he corrected.

"Then why?"

The direct question caught him off guard and seemed an impertinence. Thomas felt absolutely no compulsion to answer. Annoyed, he looked about. Where was Ragland? Spending all his time as always down at the Locke cottage, trying to converse with the senseless, drooling father! At least he felt at ease with Ragland.

He drained the brandy to the bottom of the mug, disheartened by his inability to speak and move with ease. The barrier could not be crossed. It was too great. God, how he longed for human companionship. Then, doubly weary, both of his loneliness and the silent man sitting upright behind him, he wheeled about and dismissed him. "Get on with your business, Locke," he ordered. "I'm certain those dozen horses are costing a pretty penny. Be about training them, so they and you can earn your keep."

"Very well, milord." With no visible objection, Locke placed the mug on a keg and stood up. "Will you be coming, milord?" he asked from the bottom of the steps.

"In a minute. Go along with you."

Thomas listened to the echo of boots striking stone until it diminished and was silent.

Alone in his storeroom, he sat heavily on a keg. If only *he* could meet the French ships out in the channel. If only *he* could train the horses, if only *he* could ride them through the night, dispersing goods, collecting coin.

In this agitated state of mind, he poured himself another brandy. He stared despondently at the stone floor.

Under the influence of this temporary absence of thought, he saw an image of Locke's sister.

He bent wearily over, massaging his forehead. Then, as though to banish the image from his mind, he stood up and moved rapidly down the long line of tea canisters wrapped in newsprint. As he was counting them, his eye fell on the fragment of a headline, English newsprint, "BASTILLE FALLS." Distracted, he unwrapped the single canister and flattened the newsprint on the floor. In the flickering light of the lantern, he read:

"Early in the morning of the Fourteenth of July a mob forced its way into the Bastille and seized a large stock of muskets and guns. All the morning till past noon parleys took place with Governor de Launey. By treachery or mistake, de Launey fired on the crowd outside—"

Thomas' eye stopped. Back he went to reread the key words: "By treachery or mistake."

A knowing smile crossed his face. Hell gate had been opened "By treachery or mistake." He continued to read. ". . . de Launey fired on the crowd outside, whose leaders bore white flags. His action gave the signal for general assault. Guns were brought up; there was a cannonade. The citizens' militia fought with reckless valour and after two hours' struggle, the fortress surrendered. It was immediately sacked and, stone by stone, its demolition began. De Launey was murdered and his bleeding head raised aloft on a pike."

Feeling envious, Thomas reread the account, hearing the shouts of the mob, de Launey murdered, passions unfettered, something to believe in. He looked up at the newspaper's masthead: *The Bloomsbury Gazetteer*. The date: 1789. Over two years old!

With a wave of humor, he raised up from reading. Passions unfettered indeed. Passions dead now. Over two years old! The Bastille had fallen and he hadn't even known about it. Well, what matter? He crushed the newsprint and hurled it to one side. Thank God for English common sense, the dignified orderly change wrought by their own revolution a hundred years ago.

Yet it was this very English common sense that was now killing him. The silence in the storeroom was oppressive. He felt like a mole, burrowing in the earth when, as a man, he should be standing upright in the light of day.

What was he doing here? What in the name of God was he—

Raising up in anger, he shouted, "By God!" at the confinement of stone walls. He approached the lantern and seized it. He struggled up the narrow stone stairs, bumping his head several times against the low ceiling, the odor of burning oil from the bobbing lantern filling his nostrils, joining the smell of dust lingering from the threatened cave-in below. But the most powerful strangulation came from a world of no options, no challenges.

A moment later he slammed the door on the steps behind him. "Locke!" he shouted in a desperate echoing voice.

"I will ride tonight!"

London
Late Spring
1791

A man of intelligence and vision like William Pitch knew precisely what was happening. He didn't like it, but what could one man do?

By late spring of 1791, the liberal toasts to the Fourteenth of July and the new French Constitution came fewer and farther between. The eloquent and able Count de Mirabeau was dead, the zealots at the wheel. As the rumblings increased, even the poet Wordsworth crept back to Cockermouth after having penned, as tribute to the Revolution, "Bliss was it in that dawn to be alive."

Unfortunately the bliss had not materialized. Louis and his Hapsburg Queen stood in ineffectual silhouette against the spreading fires. William also knew precisely the meaning behind men like Danton, Robespierre, Marot and Carnot. He knew further that France was rapidly becoming a nation in arms and that it was only a matter of time before England would either have to confront those arms or bow before them.

He had heard, in city coffeehouses, frequented by politicians and men of letters, the angry and overheated talk, a small English liberal leaven amid the solid English conservative mass. Dangerous radical workingmen's clubs were springing up in principal towns, generally under mid-

dle-class leadership. According to William's sources, they
kept a close correspondence with the Jacobins in Paris.
These agitators formed a small but vociferous minority of
the British public and William knew that eventually the
government would have to take drastic action against them.

William knew all of this and a great deal more. What he
did not know, and what was now causing him great pain,
was which side was right. The people or the government?
Never before had he considered himself an equivocator.
His editorials had power because of the weight of his
conviction. Now? He simply didn't know. And because
of his dilemma, he had refrained altogether from taking
a firm editorial stand, and his paper was foundering, his
staff outraged.

Such was the chaos within William himself as he walked
home on a calm spring evening after a most difficult day.
The air was fresh with budding lilacs along Southampton
Row, a pleasantly rural street with great empty fields inter-
spersed among a few tentative shops. Climbing a slight
hill, he could just see the British Museum Library straight
ahead, standing eloquently in the spring dusk with its
huddle of sheds and sidings that reflected the last rays of
afternoon sun. Perhaps the world yet was full of promise,
with a few quiet hours in which a man could coax a
semblance of peace. Certainly this moment held promise,
this brief respite of a mile which stretched between his
offices and his home, a kind of no-man's land in which
he could recover from the rigors of the day, the peculiar
sensation that he had, somehow, overreached himself, that
he had not really progressed very far from that abandoned
lump of disinherited flesh which had been left on the steps
of the foundling home.

At the corner of Great Russell Street, he stopped. A
cow in the pasture nearby lowed mournfully, her udders
full to bursting. She needed relief, as he needed relief.
Even his salon was no longer the gay, witty diverting place
it once had been. Now it was an angry arena for the discussion of politics, men, friends once, shouting angrily
across the room, taking the government's side, then the
French side, the women retreating, perplexed, into a kind
of dull stupor.

The cow cried out again, a low prolonged moan, begging for relief. Standing in the early dusk, William felt like

crying out. What was ahead of him this night? What had he yet to contend with before he could slip into the tossing interval he now called sleep? Then he remembered. The Masquerade at the Pantheon on Oxford Road. A post-Lenten ball. In the past, it had always been an occasion for great celebration, a joyous evening of music and dancing, and the fun of disguise.

Now he knew precisely what it would be, a lifeless occasion, a government agent behind every mask, the peers keeping to themselves, right on one side, left on the other, in an angry and suspicious atmosphere.

He cursed beneath his breath. The cow persisted in its misery. Why didn't someone come?

Ahead by about a hundred yards, he spied his house, usually a welcome sight, the proverbial Englishman's fortress against the onslaught of weather and a changing world. Even that was no longer true. Jane had changed, had grown suspicious and irrational. Their arguments over the status of the younger sister had long since passed the point of productivity. Determined to make her a servant, Jane had succeeded, and the girl, showing few signs of the will that had first attracted William, had succumbed, as though willing to submit to anything as long as there was peace. He had seen her only rarely during the last few months, some instinct warning him to keep away, that first evening's excitement over the Orrery still a potent memory.

The girl's constant companion was Sarah Gibbons, and she seemed content with the scullery and the severely plain, high-necked dresses with which Jane had provided her. Millie, having stayed on with her ailing aunt in Brighton, had now been replaced entirely by the curious younger half-sister who went efficiently about her chores.

Still looking ahead to his house, he saw someone sweeping the front stoop. He looked more closely and smiled. Perhaps in thinking about her he had caused her to materialize. There she was, a small distant figure clothed in black, expertly wielding a broom, bending her ruined back over the chore at hand so that he might have a clean threshold to cross. Curious! He had never seen her sweeping at this hour before. Suddenly he felt a peculiar surge of gratitude. He paid her nothing at Jane's insistence, yet the girl worked hard from morning to night on his behalf. He watched her a moment longer, then quickly reached

out and plucked a half a dozen ripe lilac plumes from a
bush, a very handsome and instantaneous bouquet which
he hid, schoolboy fashion, behind his back.

Apparently engrossed in the task at hand, she gave no
indication that she was aware of his approach. As he drew
nearer, his foot cracked a twig. She turned sharply, a
guarded expression on her face at first, then a smile that
was ready and winning, but at the same time uncertain.

He found such uncertainty touching, mirroring his own,
and crossed directly over to her, his boots striking harshly
on the pavement. Lifting a hand to his forehead in a kind
of salute, he produced the lilacs and handed them to her.

She glanced over her shoulder toward the house as
though she'd learned to live with prying eyes. She looked
at the lilacs longingly, but something prevented her from
taking them. It was only after he thrust them at her a
second time that she accepted them. "I'll arrange them for
the dining room," she murmured.

"No," he scolded. "They're for you. For your room, or
Millie's, or whoever—" He shook his head and looked
heavenward as though seeking Divine guidance in the
awesome task of keeping his staff in order.

Again she smiled, as though understanding his dilemma.
"The room's mine now," she said, sniffing the flowers.
"Millie's not coming back."

"And good riddance," he said.

The flowers fascinated her so that she hardly seemed to
hear his small jab. Still clutching the broom in one hand,
she looked uneasily about, as though uncertain just what
she should do next.

Curious, he felt embarrassed himself, standing on his
own stoop, a man renowned for his wit and efficiency of
conversation now tongue-tied.

"So!" he said finally, foolishly, as though some great matter had just been resolved.

She looked timidly up at him, her normally blue eyes
mysteriously taking on the violet hue of the lilacs. Then,
as though she too felt the need for conversation, she
asked, "How did France misbehave today, Mr. Pitch?"
There was a lightness in her tone which belied the weight
of the question.

He smiled indulgently. "And what do you know of
France?"

She laid her broom aside as though he had challenged her. She proceeded to rearrange the lilacs, speaking softly, almost apologetically. "I know that their revolution as a few men conceived it is not going well." Briefly she raised her eyes as though to monitor his reaction. "They lack a Cromwell," she said, frowning at the lilacs. "I know that Robespierre will try to become one, but he'll fail, and that sooner or later English lilacs will die for no one will have the time to plant or cultivate them." For the first time she smiled directly at him. "Except the women," she added pointedly. "It seems we always have time for such occupations."

His mouth was open, but he could do little to alter his foolish expression. It was as though she were stirring for the first time from a long sleep.

"And what else do you know?" he prodded.

She hesitated. "I know that the editor of *The Bloomsbury Gazetteer* has weakened his position by refusing to take a firm stand, that his enemies may find him vulnerable now and try to take the lead in controlling opinion."

"What in the—" He stepped back, impressed by the precision of her thoughts and the incisiveness of her attack on him.

Quickly she reassured him. "I only speak because you ask me to, Mr. Pitch. I can remain silent just as easily. Whatever you wish—" She gave a shrug, then bent over and placed the lilacs on the step.

As she reached for the broom, he protested, "No, leave it."

She obeyed without question and stood almost primly before him, her hands empty of all encumbrances, as though she were accustomed to speaking her mind, accustomed to people listening.

Still astonished, he continued to shake his head. She was like a very skillful actress whose repertoire included a variety of roles, all of which she was capable of playing simultaneously to the confusion of her audience.

He asked, "Where did you learn of Cromwell, and where Robespierre?"

Something in the orange dusk caught her eye and fancy, a bird perhaps, he didn't bother to look. But she did, speaking only as an afterthought, as though the greatest fascination of the moment flew above her. "I learned of

Cromwell from my teacher," she said vaguely. "And I learned of Robespierre from you."

"From—me?"

"From your paper," she corrected. Having lost interest in the sky, her smile was quick. "It's always in the parlor, and it's not such a long walk from the kitchen to the parlor." She shook her head, the grim chuckle of a person who in truth found no humor in what she was saying. "I always read it if I can get to it before Sarah does. I'm afraid she finds it appropriate only for cleaning out coals and wrapping fish bone."

It occurred to him to promise her a clean newspaper all her own from now on, but in the astonishment of the moment he had another question and felt a keen compulsion to ask it. "This—teacher," he began, "the one who told you of Cromwell. Your father?"

All traces of humor left her face. "No," she said, moving away from him a few steps, averting her face. She continued to walk as though it were now her intention to walk away from him and the question.

He followed a respectful distance behind her almost to the end of the fence. Just when he was of the opinion that perhaps he should retract the question, she turned to him, the smile again on her face, not quite as dazzling as before.

"Not my father," she said. "An old woman. Named Jenny. Jenny Toppinger." She looked straight at him as though intensely proud. "Jenny lived in Bath when she was younger and taught the children of the court whose parents had come to take the waters. The Duke of Salisbury tried to buy her once, as a permanent tutor to his children." Again she had a firm grip on her feelings and proceeded with all the lightness and gaiety of a child. "But do you know what she told him?" It was a rhetorical queston, requiring no answer and he gave none. "She told him that goats and horses could be bought and sold, but that he diminished himself by asking such a question of another human being." She laughed openly. "He wanted her more than ever then. But he didn't get her." The light of pride shone in her eyes as she added. "I did. For nothing."

"And she was right," William agreed, "and you obviously were very fortunate."

She looked at him as though she doubted what he had

said. But the doubt passed and she proceeded to walk slowly down the pavement. He followed after her, amazed at the transformation. It seemed as though that by removing herself physically from the broom and dusty stoop, she was removing herself emotionally from the mentality of a servant. Except for the severely high-necked black dress, she might have been a privileged young lady out for an evening's stroll, merely filling an idle interval between tea and dinner.

As they passed the end of his property, he drew even with her, walked as an equal. "So it was this Jenny who told you of Cromwell," he prodded.

She nodded, stooping to pick a yellow buttercup from the edge of a field. She looked at everything with the keenest interest, and when she seemed disinclined to speak further, he probed more deeply, feeling a bit more relaxed, his own worries of the day dissipated in her endless surprises. "And what did your Jenny say of Cromwell?" he asked, his hands locked behind him, his eyes focused on the shiny black toe of his boot and the small gray slipper which occasionally was visible beneath the hem of her dress.

She quickened her step and walked ahead of him and talked back to him. "She said he was good," she began, as though it were something he should have known. "She said there had to come a shift in power between the crown and the people." She spoke spontaneously, as though her thoughts had been bottled up too long. "But it's different, what's happening in France. Don't you agree? There the people have known true oppression, while the liberties of the ordinary Englishman are well understood and have often been asserted." She was walking backward, her face alive with excitement. Clutched in her hand was the single yellow buttercup which she used now and then as a baton to stress a point. "Of course, we can't lay claim to equality," she went on. "But the lack is not a very serious grievance. The classes mingle together, don't they, and transition from one class to another is, if not easy, at least possible and quite often achieved."

He stopped walking, the better to listen, the better to study her, the smile, the toss of her hands, the wide eyes, the fair hair pulled loosely back, yet glistening about her face, the absorption, the skill of perception, yet effusive, yet gentle.

William did well to speak at all, so great was his fascination. "And—what of France?" he managed to say. "If you were the editor of the *Gazetteer,* what stand would you take?"

She blushed becomingly at his outrageous proposal, then fell instantly into the challenge. She continued walking, but more slowly, obviously treating the complex question with all seriousness. "England's revolution was entirely a domestic affair," she pondered, as though thinking aloud. "France's will not be. They'll probably involve everyone before they are done. Still—" She broke off, deep in thought. He found himself leaning close, waiting expectantly. "Still," she concluded, "I'd back the people."

"Even though it means war?"

"Oh, there'll always be war, William. Surely you know that. Men love it too much ever to do without it for long."

The fact that she'd addressed him with great familiarity was not lost on him. "Then you are suggesting," he called ahead to her, "that we simply rush into every bloody conflict that—"

"No!" She stopped and walked back to him. "I simply mean that the cause must be weighed, the impulse examined."

"And the French cause is—"

"Just? Yes." There was no margin in her opinion. She spoke firmly, without fear of contradiction.

When she seemed disinclined to speak further, he again began to shake his head. The quietness of the evening, the distant bird calls in the willows and oaks lining the fields, the sweet, refreshing certainty of her manner moved him deeply. She was standing less than two feet from him, the expression of her eyes vivid before him. He felt a peculiar draining of his strength, as though his brief walk and talk with her had sapped his vitality. Yet, paradoxically at the same time he felt alive and refreshed. She was remarkable, and it was wrong of Jane to keep her confined to the Scullery and the constant companionship of Sarah Gibbons.

An idea occurred to him. The Masquerade at the Pantheon tonight. Why not? She'd had no recreation since she'd arrived over six months ago. Her excursions had been limited to running errands down to the shops for Sarah. The rest of the time she had been confined to the rear of the house, engaged in the endless tasks of maintenance. Yet all the while, incredibly, behind the still eyes, the mind had been working, racing Sarah for the paper, personality and intelligence held intact by some dint of will.

She was off again, gathering more buttercups, stooping and bending as her fingers searched for the prettiest.

"Marianne?" he called out. She looked up from the edge of the pasture, an air of indifference about her, as though he were simply a distraction. "Come," he called. She obeyed, lingering a moment longer for three more blossoms.

As she drew near, she extended the flowers to him. "For you," she said with a smile.

He shook his head. "You keep them. They become you."

For an instant she looked distressed, and he was sorry he had not accepted her gift. Still, there were other more pressing matters. "Marianne," he began, aware that she was standing before him. It was difficult, very difficult, to concentrate under such a relentless gaze.

"There's a Masquerade tonight," he began, "at the Pantheon." He felt restless. Perhaps he shouldn't. But he did. "Would you like to come?"

She looked up at him as though he had struck her. She said in a voice not suitable for a child because it was controlled with terror. "No. I couldn't."

"Why not?"

She looked flustered, a discernible redness in her cheeks. "I don't want to," she murmured.

"Why?" he persisted, astonished at her reaction.

"It's not my place," she whispered, and would have turned away altogether. But he reached out and restrained her, his hand on her arm.

"Not your place?" he parroted. "You who just gave me a lecture on the merits of English equality?"

He had intended it as a joke. But as she pulled away from him, he saw that she had taken the reprimand seriously. Clutching the buttercups in her hand, she tried to move past him on the pavement, clearly seeking refuge in the company of her broom.

In some exasperation he blocked her passage. "It's only a dance," he explained.

She tried to pass him on the other side. "I did not give you a lecture," she said sternly. "You asked for my opinion. I gave it."

"I'm sorry," he said, smiling, though still blocking her path. "Now I *am* asking for a lecture, a complete explication of why you will not—"

"Please let me pass, Mr. Pitch," she begged, suddenly formal, her manner revealing new tension.

Finally he stepped aside. It had not been his intention to add to her distress. He had thought the Masquerade would please her. Oviously it had not.

She passed quickly by him, her head down. To his surprise, when she was only a few feet beyond him, she stopped. Without looking at him, she asked softly, "If I went to the Masquerade, who would I be?"

Encouraged, he drew near to her. Close, this time, so close he could see her long-lashed eyelids, see the movement of her shoulders as she breathed. "Yourself?" he ventured tentatively.

She looked up as though at last he had said something that appealed to her. "A serving girl?" she repeated, clearly warming to the notion.

"Why not?" He smiled. "I have a black mask that would suit your dress." He stepped closer and took her hand.

She permitted it only a moment. "Jane?" she asked, as though certain he would understand the problems inherent in the name.

He did. Still he said confidently, "She won't object. She worries about you."

The idea had taken hold in her mind. He could see that.

And it had clearly taken hold in his, the beauty and absurdity of a desire that was in flower, a simple desire, the excuse of a dance, a legitimate reason to raise his hand and touch hers in the simple complexity of a minuet.

"Then it's setled?" he asked eagerly.

Her disress was still real. "Will you stay with me?" she whispered.

Considering that this was his only wish, he agreed readily. "I shall be at your side all evening." She looked like a child who had lost her way home, an image in complete opposition to the brilliant discursive woman of a few moments earlier.

"No further talk, then," he said, wanting only to banish all uncertainty from her mind. "You'll have a good time, I promise you. And you've earned it." Lightly, almost paternally, he rested his arm on her shoulder, a supportive gesture, or at least he tried to make it so.

She permitted the contact, indeed gave into it. Slowly they walked back down the pavement in the gathering dusk toward the red brick house, she moving easily beside him, he thoroughly enjoying the closeness, the rich promise of the evening ahead.

As they drew even with the stoop, she bent over and placed the buttercups alongside the lilacs, then reached again for her broom.

"No," he protested. "No more. Not tonight."

But she insisted. "You'd better go in first," she suggested.

"Why?" He was bewildered by the rapid change in her personality, one minute faltering and weak, the next firm and in control. She was sweeping, in spite of his orders. "Put it down, Marianne."

But she refused. "You'd better go in first," she said again.

In some anger, he demanded again, "Why?" Still not looking at him, she said quietly, "At the window, Jane's watching us from the window."

Quickly he looked over his shoulder toward the fluttering curtains at the parlor window. He saw the white disk of a face, then it disappeared.

He looked back toward Marianne. He saw a faint smile on her lips, the serene muscular unit of someone who has set a goal for herself and achieved it. . . .

As a good general always rides at the head of his troops, Thomas Eden, Thirteenth Baron and Fifth Earl of Eden Castle, in the six months comprising winter and spring of the year 1791, consistently rode at the head of his small band of smugglers.

Clothed in anonymous black and wearing a hooded cloak, he led them to adventure and enterprise along the rugged North Devon coast, overseeing the delivery of the booty himself and collecting the price minus excise from farmers and fishermen who failed to recognize in the grim, sweaty visage and black-gloved hand the Lord himself, Peer of the Realm.

Never had he felt so alive. And in time, the dozen or so trusted fellows with whom he rode and with whom he shared the majority of the profits came to look upon him as their "equal," merely a workingman doing his best to survive the heavyhanded and corrupt taxation of a government that was flirting with war.

Now, from the serene standpoint of a successful man, Thomas looked out the window of his private carriage at the passing London streets. Opposite him, old Ragland dozed, his snores rising. Next to Ragland sat a very dandified Russell Locke, looking quite the macaroni in his new crimson brocade waistcoat and matching knee britches, continuously patting the oversized white wig on his head. He had been poised on the edge of his seat since they had entered London, his sense of excitement amounting almost to hysteria.

Thomas smiled, watching him. It would be good for the lad to taste the pleasures of London. He had a full purse and healthy appetites. A fortnight in the cosmopolitan city might polish some of the rough edges, make him a more suitable companion when they returned to Eden. Thomas had to look to such things. Ragland was getting old. He could not survive many more damp cold Devon winters. Thomas required reliable male companionship, and among the bumpkins of Mortemouth, Russell Locke seemed the most likely candidate for the job. Hadn't he been a loyal associate in their smuggling enterprise, displaying a willingness to strict obedience, yet advancing his own ideas when he felt they were sound?

With the keen eye of a professional judge of men, Thomas had acquired the habit of listening to him, even when he had proposed their present journey to London for the purposes of making new French contacts. As Russell had respectfully pointed out, Captain Girard's weekly deliveries were dispersed within a matter of days. Beyond Wednesday of every week the men and their horses had been idle. It made sense to Thomas, although he loathed the thought of a journey to London. Still, Locke had made his point. London Town would be teeming with Frenchmen; refugees escaping the madmen who ran Paris, rich refugees most of them, who perhaps would be eager to double, triple his supply of goods.

The journey had been planned and undertaken, and as a reward for fathering the idea he'd invited young Locke to go with him, and Ragland to look after him, for there still were moments when the young man displayed the most inept of habits, wearing his country ways as though they were a shield of honor instead of an embarrassment of low birth.

As his coachman guided his carriage onto Oxford Road, Thomas felt a surge of excitement himself. My God, how long was it since he'd last been here? He felt changed. The slight paunch was gone, the belly lean and hard from his constant exercise, his shoulders strong from hoisting the kegs of brandy, his face weathered and rugged from constant exposure to the bracing North Devon winds. At the inn in Salisbury, stopping for a meal, he'd caught an inadvertent glimpse of himself in a window glass and had been incredibly pleased with what he had seen. He glanced across the bobbling carriage at the excitement on Locke's face. In a way he envied him, discovering London for the first time.

"Oxford Street," Thomas said, in the manner of a guide. But Locke scarcely lifted his eyes from the street outside, the throngs of people, a few uniforms here and there, a steady procession of carriages, his hand, rough and calloused, clutching at the window.

In front of the Pantheon their carriage stalled to a halt in the rush of traffic, a hopeless bottleneck. The sudden cessation of movement jarred Ragland awake. He sat up with a start, his old eyes as searching as Russell's young ones.

"Welcome to London," Thomas greeted him, feeling in remarkably good spirits.

The old man blinked and drew back from the late afternoon sun, his hands reaching out to steady himself. "Where are—"

"We're almost there," Thomas reassured him. "After that nap, you'll be fit to dance half the night."

Ragland snorted at the suggestion. "Getting too old," he muttered, and fell back into the corner of the carriage, his eyes gazing dully at the traffic beyond the small window.

Russell's head bobbed from side to side as he tried to take it all in. He read, faltering, the white banner stretched between the colonnades of the Pantheon. "Post-Lenten Masquerade."

"Quite a revelry," Thomas said. "Drinking and debauchery from dusk until dawn. Perhaps a bit heady for your first night in London, but if you wish—"

Russell looked directly at him. "I must see my sister first, milord but later, with your permission—"

Thomas felt a surge of annoyance. Which sister, he wondered, the one who was living in questionable circumstances with some gentleman in Bloomsbury, or the one who—

The carriage started forward again, moving at a snail's pace through the clogged road. Thomas leaned back against the cushions. Not much farther, thank God. He was sick to death of the two faces across the way. Let them go and do as they wished. As for himself, he would dispatch his business here as quickly as possible and herd both of them back to Eden where they belonged.

Amazed by the rapid plunge in his good spirits, he leaned out the window and shouted at his coachman, "Can't you go faster?"

The man yelled something in return, but Thomas couldn't hear. Locke, apparently impervious to the state of Thomas' spirits, continued to bob from side to side, one roughened hand continuously stroking his satin brocade knee britches, a coarse gesture which served to annoy Thomas further. See his sister! What right did he have to fill his purse with Thomas' riches, clothe himself with garments purchased from those riches, ride in Thomas' carriage, then announce calmly that he first had to see his sister?

Thomas closed his eyes to blot the dull bobbing head from his vision. A few minutes later the carriage rattled to a halt. They were here at last, at the end of Oxford Road before the elegant Tudor house that was his London residence. The house had been built by his grandfather, lived in by his father, and avoided by Thomas. It was staffed by people he scarcely knew, but who all too eagerly accepted the generous yearly allowance he sent them. Again that feeling of regret at having left Eden washed over him. No matter how much he might rail against its seclusion, it was still the safest place on earth.

Quickly he alighted from the carriage as though he were trying to leave his disillusionment behind. The source of his annoyance, Russell Locke, merely followed after him, engaged in endless conceits, adjusting the ill-fitting wig, then straightening the tight knee britches.

As Thomas strode angrily through the sturdy Tudor arch, a strange man bowed low. The butler? How was he to know? Inside, he looked back over his shoulder. Ragland was helping the two coachmen with the luggage while Locke was still preening this way and that, clearly impervious to the labor going on around him.

Thomas shouted, "Help with the luggage!" and finally the young man did as he was told, not putting his back to it, however, merely lifting a corner of a trunk gingerly as though afraid of soiling his new feathers.

Thomas had seen enough. As he turned to take refuge in his second-floor chambers, he saw a staff of four women standing before him. Garbed in black, their faces tight with nervousness, they looked as though they were in mourning.

He was in no mood for introductions. Weary and parched, he merely ordered, "Brandy upstairs." He took the steps three at a time, confounded by the mantle of misery which had dropped like lead about him.

He took refuge in the small drawing room, a sparsely furnished, almost mean room. Years ago, following the deaths of his parents and brother, he'd moved the most valuable furnishings out to Eden. All that remained were tattered remnants from his grandfather's day, a few threadbare tapestries, two fairly decent carved wooden chests, and a scattered arrangement of uncomfortable furniture.

He shed his cloak and sank into one of the miserable confinements. The room was stuffy. Obviously the staff of ghouls had not aired it.

Still wrestling with his mysterious misery, he looked ruefully about him. The trouble with any journey was that sooner or later one reached one's destination. Then what? He lifted his hands and pressed them against his eyes, seeing in the self-imposed blindness the clean, windswept rugged headlands of Eden Point.

There was nothing to do but complete his business as quickly as possible and pack the lot of them back to Eden where they belonged, where a man could stand by his

window and hear nothing but the cries of sea gulls and the
rustle of wind.

There was a soft knock on the door. A moment later
Ragland appeared, carrying a tray with a bottle of brandy
and one glass. "To help you recover, milord," he smiled
and placed the tray on one of the carved tables.

The implication that there was something wrong with
him only infuriated him further. "I am not ill," he snapped.
"I have no need for recovery." He reached quickly for the
bottle, poured himself a glass, and downed it in a swallow.

Ragland watched him with a tolerant look, as though to
say they had ridden out a number of crises over the years
and they could ride out this one as well.

Thomas saw the look and resented it. "What are you
standing about for?" he raged.

Wearily Ragland asked, "Shall I sit, milord?"

"Do what you wish." Thomas waved him away and returned to the window. The street was clogged with carriages and foot traffic, the center of attention seeming to
be the Pantheon down the street.

Thomas extended his empty glass in midair, clearly sig-
naling Ragland to fill it. The old man obeyed. "You're out
of sorts, milord, fatigued no doubt. Why don't you lie—"

But Thomas would hear none of it. Still staring down
at the street, his eyes leveled, he asked, "Where's Locke?"

Ragland hesitated. "I took the liberty, milord, of giving
him a few free hours. He has an obligation—"

"To me," Thomas interrupted, confronting the old man.
"He has an obligation to me. That is his one, his only obligation."

Ragland disagreed politely. "He has a sister—"

"In ill-favor," Thomas cut in again, "or have you forgotten?"

Ragland moved closer to the anger. "Not forgotten,
milord. But Russell's not come to see that one. It's the
other one, sir."

When Thomas saw his calm face and heard his reassur-
ances, he turned back to the window. When would he learn
not to reveal himself so pitifully?

"You take some time, too, Ragland," he urged, keeping
his face turned away from the old man. "Go and do what
you wish. If you're fool enough to think that Paradise"—

and he gestured toward the clogged street below—"then go and join them."

Behind him he heard the clink of the bottle as Ragland returned it to the tray. "I'll stay if you wish," he heard him mutter.

"I don't wish," Thomas said.

"What will you do, milord?"

"I'll attend to my interests as rapidly as possible, so that within the week we can leave."

"As you wish, milord."

"Go on," Thomas scolded. "Leave me be."

There was a moment's silence from Ragland as though he were debating with himself whether he should stay or go. Then Thomas heard the door opening, then closing, then silence save for the constant procession of carriages rattling by on the street below.

He continued to stand gloomily by the window, staring down. There was no reason for him to stay here in miserable seclusion. He had friends, many of them, who would greet him warmly, the fellows at White's who would delight in filling his ear with the latest scandal. On the strength of his name alone, he could, within the hour if he wished, collect dinner invitations to the finest houses in London. He could do all this and more, if he chose.

But he didn't choose. Instead he dragged a chair close to the window, retrieved the bottle of brandy from the table, discarded the glass and, cradling the full bottle, he sank heavily into the chair.

He felt small and insignificant in the bustle of London. The brandy helped. At least it numbed. Still, in his present state of mind, all his defeats, both large and small, paraded before his memory: his inability to run the estates at Eden Point; his failure to wed; his failure thus far to produce a legitimate heir; his past debauchery; his present illegal smuggling enterprise; his wealth (even that somehow seemed a failure); his temper, which in the past had led him to ignoble behavior; the public whipping of a—

He lifted the bottle and drank with such force that the residue trickled down on either side of his mouth. He wiped the waste with the back of his hand, his brain blurring, not yet numb enough.

He drank again. When would it come, the blessed paralysis? Outside he heard a small band of street musicians,

heading for the Pantheon, the annual Post-Lenten Masquerade. A series of invisible shudders wrinkled his face.
He felt like something caged. He looked angrily at the
diminishing light. My God, didn't they have enough sense
to bring him a lamp?

He tipped the bottle again. Useless! The numbness
would not come. He wished he were back in his underground storeroom. He would dive headlong into a keg of
brandy and drink or drown. It mattered little either way.

Then he remembered the purpose of this torturous trip,
that the storeroom was empty, that last week's cargo had
been delivered within forty-eight hours, that he was here
to make new contacts, clog the entire Bristol Channel if
necessary with French vessels, all loaded with contraband.

He couldn't very well make contacts sitting here gazing
out over the city. All of London, at least all of London that
mattered, would be congregated in one place tonight, French
emigrés mixing and blending with English aristocracy, the
gallery filled with commoners, all looking with rapture
down on the festivities.

How he loathed even the thought of it. But it *was* the
place to be. With luck he could find what he had come
looking for and tomorrow be on his way back to Eden
Point. If Locke and Ragland wanted to stay, let them.
They were not his responsibility.

He stood, reeling for a moment, a belated but pleasant
effect of the brandy. He must eat something, if the lunatics
lurking outside the door had thought to prepare a meal.
Then he would dress and while the others went about their
pleasure, he would go about his business.

A second thought stopped him. A Masquerade! He'd
brought no costume save for the insanities of current fashion. What could he—

An idea occurred to him, brilliant in its simplicity. He
would go as himself, a smuggler. He would wear the
costume he wore on his night rides, his boots and riding
breeches, black shirt and full-hooded cape. Masked and
thus obscured, he could navigate the threats and hazards of
the Post-Lenten Masquerade as easily as in the past he had
navigated the cliffs and jagged terrain of his North Devon
coast.

The idea burst to full bloom in his mind. Smiling at the
picture in his imagination, he shouted at the invisible pres-

ences outside the door, "Light, and food!" the tensions releasing themselves in a scurry of footsteps. At least they
had good ears.

Unfortunately the new mood did not last. The meal,
poorly cooked and sloppily served, sent him into a new
rage as he shouted at the women to leave the room. With
Ragland gone, he had to dress himself, a tedious process.
The footman, having been sent to fetch a mask, returned
with a cheap cardboard sample, oversized, which covered
three quarters of his face.

Looking less like a smuggler than a blackamoor, Thomas
drew the long cloak about him, new anger at the annoy-
ances welling up inside him. The world was indefensible,
had always been indefensible, and his loathing for it sprang
up afresh, so that he hunched his shoulders against the fair,
calm May evening as though it were December sleet and
set off toward the Pantheon.

Sarah Gibbons was not blind. Neither was she deaf and
dumb. Months earlier she had seen the proverbial handwriting on the wall, the subtle but muted attraction that
Marianne held for William Pitch, the deep silences of the
older sister as she sought more and more to keep the girl
confined, almost a prisoner in the recesses of the house.
Easier to confine the rays of sun or the scattering of stars.

In the back garden now, hanging wash, she heard the
whish of Marianne's broom. The girl *was* diligent, performing her duties with admirable dispatch, a very pleasant
companion for Sarah, certainly preferable to the simpleminded Millie.

As she reached up to the line, she heard another sound
over the broom, a man's voice. She froze, listening. It was
Mr. Pitch. Torn between wanting to hear and the guilt of
eavesdropping, she continued to hang the linen, hearing
only a soft hum of voices. Clearly Marianne had abandoned
her broom. As well as Sarah could tell, the two of them
were walking down the pavement now; she could just see
Mr. Pitch's head over the top of the hedge. A few minutes
later, unable to bear the weight of her curiosity, Sarah
abandoned the wash and took refuge behind the thick
hedge. She heard the girl talking, like a man she was talking, of politics and war.

As they passed beyond her range of hearing, she looked

back toward the house. Pray God Miss Locke wasn't watching. The girl had better be careful or she'd find herself on the way back to Eden Point. Frustrated over her inability to hear, Sarah followed after them to the end of the hedge, then had to content herself with merely seeing them through the foliage, walking and talking quite easily together.

A moment later she saw them turn and start back toward the house. She really shouldn't be listening. It was certainly none of her business. On this note of morality she was about to turn away when the hum of voices became words again and she heard Mr. Pitch invite Marianne to the Masquerade at the Pantheon. Sarah held still, scarcely breathing. Good Lord, she hoped the girl had better sense. And she did. Silently Sarah applauded Marianne's instantaneous refusal. Then the burden of guilt was too much. What if they saw her, listening behind the hedge? What if Miss Locke saw her? Quickly she slipped away and fled the garden and returned to her kitchen, her heart beating too fast with the excitement of the moment.

At least the girl had good sense. She knew where she belonged. Such an evening would be a calamity. She was surprised that Mr. Pitch had even considered the notion. Secure in her sense of everyone in his place, Sarah hurled herself into kitchen chores.

A short time later Marianne appeared in the doorway, her arms filled with flowers, her face as set and determined as Sarah had ever seen it. "Sarah, I have a favor." She smiled. "Will you assist me with the creation of a ball gown?"

Sarah gaped. "A what?"

"It won't be very difficult," Marianne assured her. "Mr. Pitch has invited me to the Masquerade. I'm going as myself, a serving girl, but I thought that we might—"

As she launched forth into her description of a gown, Sarah could only shake her head. Her instincts told her to put a close to the discussion immediately. But there was something so touching about Marianne's enthusiasm, something equally as interesting about the angry voices coming from the parlor, that Sarah nodded and sent her for the sewing box.

To the background of a violent argument which broke out between Mr. Pitch and Miss Locke, Sarah and Marianne fell to work on one of her plain black serving dresses.

They turned under the high-necked collar and at Marianne's suggestion unbuttoned a half a dozen buttons to reveal a provocative yet tasteful portion of breast.

From the parlor, Mr. Pitch shouted, "This is my house and you are under my command." Miss Locke said something but it was inaudible, muffled in sobs. Sarah glanced up at Marianne, who was standing on a crate in the middle of the kitchen, examining closely the amount of cleavage revealed by the unbuttoned bodice. If she was even aware of the battle in the parlor, she gave no indication of it. Sarah shook her head. The girl was incorrigible. And irresistible.

Sarah turned her attention back to the "ball gown." Something was missing. Hurriedly she went into her room, fetched three of her best white silk petticoats, and nipped them in at the waist to accommodate Marianne's slight figure and to give the black skirt a bit of a flare.

Marianne was delighted. "Oh, Sarah, how perfect!" she exclaimed, to the unhappy sounds of Jane weeping. Then they looped up the hem of the black gown at eight-inch intervals, stitched it, and attached a sprig of lilac at each loop, the effect lovely and graceful, the pale purple and green standing out beautifully against the black gown, revealing the white petticoats beneath.

As the battleground moved upstairs, as the entire house shook with two ominous crashes as though a chair had been hurled and a chair returned, Marianne, still standing on the upturned crate, preening in Sarah's own peer glass, serenely suggested the lowering of two additional buttons on her bodice. Sarah objected to the full cleavage. "It's indecent," she scoffed.

"Nonsense," countered Marianne. "It's the loveliest part of the female body. If I had my way, we would wear nothing at all above our waists."

Sarah gasped, feigning a bit more indignation than she actually felt, and suggested a compromise. They left the buttons undone but inserted a small nosegay of lilacs into the hollow between her breasts.

Shortly before nine o'clock the two combatants from upstairs came down. Mr. Pitch was dressed as a Scottish Highlander, his eyes stern and angry behind his mask. Jane was dressed unbecomingly as a haymaid, in plain brown and carrying a delicate rake, her white mask not large enough to cover her eyes, swollen from weeping.

Sarah took a final look at Marianne. She was lovely, although she was certain she would need more than looks to see her through this evening. Marianne hopped down from the crate and hugged Sarah in passing. "Thank you," she whispered, "for everything."

Sarah watched from the door as the three of them, all keeping a safe distance apart, trailed down the front walk toward the waiting carriage, Marianne bringing up the rear, stealing a mischievous glance back at Sarah and waving gaily with her plain black mask.

Sarah smiled and waved back. The girl *was* impossible. As the carriage pulled away, the clock on the mantle in the salon chimed half past nine. Sarah felt an almost unbelievable weariness. She was not by nature designed for such dramatic goings-on. After the tumultuous afternoon and early evening, all she wanted was an interval of peace. To that end she fixed herself a cup of tea and liberally laced it with whiskey from the cut-glass decanter in the dining room. No guilt. She'd earned it. Thank Jesus, the house was quiet, thank Jesus the salon would be empty this night. She needed a respite. The events of late afternoon had been quite enough, thank you.

She sipped her tea, savoring its hot spiked goodness. She didn't know whether to pity Marianne or feel happy for her. She missed her, of that she was certain. Over the last few months she'd formed quite an affection for the young girl of mercurial moods.

But Sarah understood. It had only been within the last few weeks that the child had permitted her to view her back, to rub soothing camphor oil on the still-red, angry-looking scars. Sarah, almost undone with compassion, had welcomed the girl's trust and had treated her nightly in the back room, her fingers following one by one the ten avenues of scarred flesh. She had longed to ask Marianne about the ordeal, but she had refrained. In truth, what could Marianne say that the flesh of her back had not already revealed?

Scattered about her on the kitchen table were the remnants of the evening's effort: dying lilacs, dead buttercups, black thread, a piece of lace, scissors. Wearily she shook her head. Well, she'd done the best she could. A ball gown! She chuckled softly.

The front bell rang, a jarring sound, startling her out of her reverie. Alarmed, she looked sharply up. "Who in the —" The ring came again, someone pulling the bell cord with insistence. Cautiously she stood, reaching for the lamp and a pair of scissors. A woman alone in this remote area of London couldn't be too careful, although it occurred to her that the late night caller was probably one of Mr. Pitch's drunken friends, seeking the warmth and plenty of the nightly salon. Couldn't he see the house dark, the lamps extinguished?

Angry, Sarah strode through the darkened front rooms, holding the lamp aloft, the scissors clutched out of sight in the pocket of her apron. As she approached the door, the bell cord rang still a third time. Sharply she called out, "Who is there?"

Receiving no answer, she placed the lamp on the table and cautiously opened the door. On the other side, in the skittering light of the streetlamp, she saw a young man standing stiffly before her, foolishly bewigged and garbed in shiny satin, the features of his face obscured in shadow.

He remained silent. She tightened her grip on the scissors, ready to do battle with the dandy whoever he was. Then in a flat rural voice, he mumbled, "Miss Jane Locke, please."

"Out," Sarah snapped. "All out, for the evening."

This information seemed to displease him. As he stepped closer to the door, Sarah warned, "Be off with you now. You've no business here. The salon is closed."

"Miss Jane Locke," he repeated again, his voice rising. He moved forward as though he intended to enter, invitation or no.

Quickly Sarah slammed and bolted the door, her heart racing. Merciful heavens, what was the world coming to when a single woman could not sit in safety within the confines of her own kitchen? Hurriedly she went to the broad front window of the parlor, leaving the lamp behind, peering in darkness out at the front stoop. There she saw him, standing in some confusion, a large man, really, with a small head. He was turning aimlessly on the walk. Finally he let himself out of the gate. He stopped beneath the streetlamp. His dandified garments caught the reflection of the light. She saw him glance back toward the house, then begrudgingly start off toward Southampton Row.

Gone! Thank God. She hurried back to the door and tested the latch. Secured. Whoever he was, good riddance. There were public houses aplenty in London. Within the hour he would undoubtedly find solace in one of them. It was none of her concern.

The matter resolved, she retrieved the lamp and made her way back to the kitchen. Her back ached from stitching the hem of Marianne's dress. The nip of whiskey had given her a slight headache. No reason to wait up. It would be dawn at least before they returned. She was confident that she would hear all about it.

Her normally stern head filled with all sorts of romantic conjecture, she set about tidying up the kitchen, returning the crate to the storeroom, her eye falling on the low couch where the poor child had been so rudely deposited that first night. No need to dwell on it. That episode was closed and she had the strong feeling that another was beginning.

The kitchen in order, she poured herself another cup of tea and sat relaxed, waiting. Just as she was beginning to doze off, the bell cord rang again. This time, startled almost out of her wits, she clutched at her breast to still her heart and glared angrily in the direction of the rude noise.

Back again? Well, she wouldn't have it. She just wouldn't have it. She left the chair in a fury, determined to give the rascal a piece of her mind. But midway through the darkened dining room, she stopped. Perhaps it would be wiser simply to ignore him. Certainly safer. These were depraved times, all sorts of madmen disguised as gentlemen roaming the lanes and roads.

Still, she was curious and tiptoed stealthily into the entrance hall, taking up her vigil once again by the broad front window. From that angle she saw a different figure, this one stooped in a short cape, an old man, or so he appeared. He pulled the bell cord once again, waiting. In the splash of light from the streetlamp, she saw his unruly white hair, wigless, sticking out in puffs about his face. He threw one quick glance backward over his shoulder, then appeared to hurry off into the night as though someone were chasing him.

Bewildered, she watched as long as she could until he

disappeared at the corner of the road. Still annoyed, she straightened her back from bending over the window. Apparently Mr. Pitch had failed to send the word around that his salon would be closed this evening.

Incredibly weary from the events of the day and the distraction of the evening, she made her way back to the kitchen and took a final look around. Her one and only true domain. She took up the lamp and carried it down the long corridor to the back of the house and there secured and double-checked both latch and bolt. Standing in the dark, she felt as though she had lived a long, long time and now only wished that age had endowed her with a selective memory or perhaps given her something to remember.

But for the most part she was grateful that she'd been able to pick her own way through life, unfettered by highs or lows. And although it had been a little like watching a cavalcade of the dead, still she was safe, had not had to "endure" like others she could think of.

A carriage rattled by on the road. She listened. When she had decided, not without some arguing, whether to sleep or wait, she went into her room, extinguished the lamp, and settled down to wait.

Too late, Marianne realized she'd made a terrible mistake.

Sitting opposite the two in the carriage in her silly arrangement of sewn-on lilacs, she realized that she had made a dreadful error. When would she learn not to manipulate circumstances or individuals?

Ruefully she glanced out the window at the increase of shops along Southampton Row. Perhaps she should at least pretend that she was having a good time. But only one glance at William's stern face changed her mind.

Regretfully she thought of the premeditated break in her routine, deliberately postponing the sweeping of the front walk from noon until four o'clock. No one passed the walk at noon except tradesmen and farmers on their way to London, and an occasional child guiding his hoop down the road.

But at four o'clock, she knew that would be different, William's customary arrival for tea, a chance to see him outside the confines of the house and well beyond her sister's all-seeing eyes.

Guiltily she looked up at Jane's eyes, red and swollen behind her mask. Again she refocused her attention on the passing street outside the carriage window, noticing an increase in the traffic, carriages on either side providing her with fleeting glances of other passengers, laughing, talking, excited to be abroad, while all around her the mood resembled that of a funeral cortege.

Still, she didn't have the courage to penetrate the gloom, and continued to sit on her side, watching the "Highlander" staring out one window, the "haymaid" out the other.

In all the months she'd been in London, she'd never traveled this far from Bloomsbury. She tried to amuse herself with the strangeness of it all, there the huge tower of a church which rose into the night sky, unlovely but reassuring. The streets were lined on either side with uninterrupted shops, liveries, butchers, tobacconists, confectioneries, public houses, each proclaimed by a neat wooden sign, lamps still burning in many of the windows in spite of the late hour.

"Do they never close?" she asked, more to herself than a direct question.

"Not as long as there is someone who will buy," William said. She looked at him, grateful for his effort.

"How does the poor customer decide which one to do business with?" she asked, preferring the sound of voices to the sound of silence.

"The one who offers the best bargain wins the greatest number of buyers," William replied, apparently willing to pursue the stupid conversation as far as necessary.

She noticed Jane look sharply at William, as though he'd broken a rule by speaking. "No need to fill her head with nonsense," she snapped. "She has no money to seek bargains of any kind."

The comment had obviously given her a great deal of pleasure. She looked back out at the street and Marianne saw a slight smile behind the mask.

William fell silent. Marianne felt as though they were all thrashing about in their places, yet remaining perfectly still. She was in the process of ruining the evening for both of them, and for that she was profoundly sorry.

Gathering her courage about her, she leaned up and

lightly touched Jane's hand. "I'm sorry," she murmured. "I shouldn't have come."

"Nonsense," muttered William under his breath, but loud enough to be heard.

Marianne went on, speaking only to Jane. 'If you wish, I can always go back. It's not that important."

Without looking at her, Jane replied, "You're here now. It's too late to go back." She looked at her with just a bit of nastiness. "All I ask of you is that you behave."

Marianne felt a surge of anger at the implication, as though she were nothing more than an unruly child, accustomed to dragging herself and her family into embarrassing and humiliating situations.

Painfully, she realized the truth of her thoughts. She leaned back in the carriage, and although she was staring out the window, she saw nothing except the specifics of her own misery.

Apparently Jane spotted her unexpected weakness. Pleased, she advised, "Stay close to me this evening. Between William and myself, it should go well enough."

Marianne nodded, scarcely hearing this latest humiliation. Then William was leaning forward, as though bodily to come between the two women. "It will go well, I assure you both." A look of anger shadowed his face. His eyes moved over the facades of the buildings as though searching for one worthy of comment.

"Piccadilly!" he announced, his tone clearly trying to distract.

As William pointed out several landmarks, Marianne tried to appear fascinated, all the while aware of Jane's eyes on her, watching, *watching*. Small memories, like unidentified prehistoric ruins, surfaced in her mind; Jane standing for hours in the corner of the parlor of her father's cottage. Her offense? Marianne couldn't remember. Jane being denied supper, creeping off to bed. Her offense? Marianne couldn't remember. Jane crying herself to sleep at night. The source of her sorrow? Marianne wasn't certain.

As the full weight of Jane's miserable childhood washed over her, Marianne again put out her hand. After a moment, as though uncertain what to do, Jane took it, her head moving perceptibly with the broken arc of two instincts, recoil and advance, so that the head rocked timidly and aggressively at the same time.

"I said not to worry," Jane soothed, still apparently perplexed by Marianne's show of feeling. Kindly, Jane added, "I'll look after you." The words were so sweet and welcome that Marianne smiled and breathed a sigh of relief.

William recognized the reconciliation and the three of them smiled behind their masks, Marianne almost jubilant for the first time that evening.

William launched forth into his role as guide again, directing them into the turn which led to Oxford Road, pointing out and identifying the grand building just up ahead.

"The Pantheon!" he announced proudly, as though he'd had something to do with it. "The new winter Ranelagh. Built by James Wyatt, it was."

Marianne nodded excitedly to everything, still grasping Jane's hand as though fearful of letting go, the small gesture of need working miracles on the tall "haymaid," who looked almost with pride at her younger half-sister.

Jane whispered, "Wyatt sometimes comes to our salon. When he isn't drunk he's very amusing. Which isn't often."

Both girls giggled softly. William said defensively, "Drunk or not, his work is an improvement on that of the Adam brothers, you'll have to agree."

The carriage pulled up directly in front of the brightly lit building. Through the central arch Marianne caught a glimpse of a long avenue of glittering chandeliers. The steps were filled with people in masquerade, everyone laughing and chattering. In the distance she heard the strains of a minuet.

As the coachman opened the door and William stepped out, she caught sight of a young man in an artist's smock with a jaunty beret on his head running toward them. With him, reluctantly following, was a tall, black-clad smuggler. The artist was calling William's name over and over again.

At that moment it occurred to her that she would have to meet people. How would she be introduced? And how identified? Still grasping Jane's hand, she climbed trembling out of the carriage, wishing with all her heart that she were back at Eden Point, running along the cliffs with only the sea gulls for company.

Apparently Jane saw her discomfort and tried to soothe

her. "No need. The past is over, no matter what you've done."

The words, in reality softly spoken, seemed to thunder and echo about the pavement. *No matter what you've done.*

The strange man in the artist's smock was upon them, warmly grasping William's arm. Surely he had heard the words *No matter what you've done.*

Marianne pulled away from the encounter. Taking Jane with her, she whispered, "Let's walk ahead." She stumbled going up the steps, and the only warmth she felt was her hand where Jane grasped it.

Pushing his way through the throngs of people and carriages outside the Pantheon, Thomas Eden, his mask dangling uselessly from his finger, prayed to his God that he should not see anyone he knew.

Unfortunately, at that moment a sharp "Thomas, Thomas Eden!" cut through the din of voices. He stopped, cursing his God and himself for not adjusting his mask before he'd left his house.

Trapped! He turned slowly and saw over the bobbing wigs a young man rushing excitedly toward him. Unhappily, the fellow had the advantage. He *was* masked and wearing an artist's smock, a beret perched aside his head, wigless, like Thomas, revealing a luxuriant head of flowing black hair.

"Thomas Eden?" he shouted again as though uncertain of the identification. He was standing directly before Thomas, his hand extended, grinning. "It *is!*" he exclaimed. "How good to see you!"

Thomas wished that he could return the sentiment, but he was at a loss.

The young man continued to grin. "Would it help if I removed the mask?" he offered.

Thomas nodded, keeping his annoyance in admirable check. "It might," he conceded. "As it is, you have the clear advantage."

The black eyes sparkled, but the mask remained in place. "You took me to the cliff at Eden Point once and threatened to push me over if I didn't give you the blue agate you so desperately wanted."

The fog in Thomas's brain, caused partly by brandy

and his own unhappy state, lifted. Smiling in spite of himself, he announced, "Beckford. Billy Beckford."

Apparently right on the nose. As the young man stripped off his mask, Thomas saw the fair skin, slightly protruding nose, and almost feminine eyes of the little boy who had visited Eden Castle many times in the company of his father, the former Lord Mayor of London and one of Thomas's father's closest friends and hunting companions. As he returned the handshake, both men made their way out of the push of traffic to a relatively quiet place, close to one of the outlying colonnades.

Billy, still looking boyish, shook his head continuously in disbelief. "I thought it was you. But I wasn't certain. My God, it's been years."

With no choice but to be reasonably pleasant, Thomas obliged. "Not that many, please. And I wouldn't have pushed you over the cliff. I hope you know that."

Billy smiled. "I know it now, but I didn't then. You were an imposing figure to a boy of six."

"A fake, I can assure you," Thomas said, with proper repentance, his mind still sorting out the memory, the almost twelve years' difference between them, his father's insistence that he be nice to the little boy. Thomas looked more closely at the face out of the past. Billy still looked the little boy, although by rapid calculation Thomas estimated his age as approaching thirty.

There was that awkward silence, that painful interval when old friends meet and find the passage of years unbridgeable.

Billy spoke first, slightly subdued as though he too were suddenly aware of all that had happened. "Those were good days," he commented nostalgically. "Our fathers the best of friends."

"Indeed," Thomas concurred.

"Have you married?" Billy asked.

"No. And you?"

"Good heavens, no." Billy looked out over the crowd of faces, all masked, his normally high spirits still intact. "I'm to meet someone." He laughed. "Quite a challenge, wouldn't you say?"

Thomas agreed, then added, "Well, you recognized me."

"Only because you were unmasked," Billy said with a smile.

As again Billy searched the crowds, Thomas continued to search through the past. He remembered that after Billy's father had died, Billy had inherited a fine house and estate called Fonthill in a particularly beautiful part of Wiltshire. On trips with his father from London back to North Devon, Thomas had always viewed Fonthill as a kind of halfway house, a lovely classical estate situated close by a little L-shaped lake, a pleasant place to spend a fortnight. Their fathers used to say laughingly that between Beckford land and Eden land they could hunt almost uninterrupted on their private estates all the way from London to the Bristol Channel.

Now *they* were the inheritors, the two of them, and although the land mass had dwindled under the unbearable pressure of taxation, Thomas knew that Billy had inherited nearly a million guineas per year, derived mainly from sugar plantations in Jamaica. Nothing to compare to Thomas' wealth, but adequate nonetheless.

Peculiarly, Thomas now warmed to the chance encounter. Perhaps it might be profitable after all. Surely Billy knew people. As the young man continued to search the crowd, Thomas offered his assistance. "Who is it that you're looking for?" he inquired. "Perhaps I can help. I'm afraid that Eden does not enjoy the same close proximity to London as Fonthill, but still I know a few people."

Billy turned his attention away from the crowd and back to Thomas, something sparking his enthusiasm anew. His fingers moved rapidly in and out of the little empty hollows of the palette which he held in his hand. "Thomas," he began, leaning close, as though to share a secret, "you wouldn't believe what I'm doing at Fonthill. I'm leveling the whole thing and starting again, more than a house this time, an abbey with a tower higher than Salisbury, higher than Antwerp even." The more he talked, the more excited he became and the faster went the fingers in and out of the empty palette.

Thomas indulged him with a smile, although in truth he thought the project absurd and a waste. Fonthill was elegant, grand enough to entertain over five hundred guests. He couldn't imagine why Billy wanted more. He said as much. "I remember Fonthill with pleasure. I hate to think of its destruction."

But Billy's excitement could not be subdued. "That old

palace with tertian fevers with its small doors and mean casements," he said, shuddering dismally. "No, it's no longer adequate. A man must have a tower, don't you think, Thomas?" Not waiting for a reply, he rushed on. "And I intend to have one, the grandest in all of England." Without pausing for breath, he inquired earnestly, "Have you read my book, Thomas?"

Book? Did the romantic dabbler write as well? Thomas murmured his apologies. "The pleasure has not been mine."

"Then I shall send a copy around," Billy offered. "It's quite a good story," he added immodestly "an Arabian tale called *Vathek* in which the hero builds for himself an immense tower of fifteen hundred steps. You see, Thomas" —and he leaned close, clearly instructing—"a tower is something special, not only to be viewed with awe from below, but also to provide the widest possible outlook from the top."

Thomas saw something in the slightly glazed yet boyish eyes that alarmed him. He'd heard rumors that the boy was mad.

Billy rushed on, undaunted, his eyes fixed on some indefinite spot on the pavement, a peculiar downward vision for a man obsessed by towers. "On the Grand Tour, Thomas, I found much that excited my mind. Have you ever seen the tower of Antwerp Cathedral at night, rising in a huge mass above the lower galleries while the light of heaven twinkles through the interstices of the pinnacles?" As he talked, he raised his arms upward, upward, re-creating at least for himself the impressive edifice, his face aglow with memory. With his arms still extended straight up into the air, he looked back at Thomas, a soft smile on his face. "That's what I intend to replace Fonthill with, just the grandest abbey in all of England."

Faced with such passion, deranged or not, Thomas had no choice but to concur. He asked hesitantly, "An abbey, Billy? A practicing abbey?"

"Oh, no, of course not," Billy corrected. "Only the appearance of an abbey, like those of Alcobaca and Batalha in Portugal."

"Then a Folly," Thomas commented meanly, but feeling that he must do something to bring the young man to his senses. He thought of the fashionable Follies springing up all over England, those spurious insincerities, reproductions of Greek and Chinese temples, Gothic ruins where no building had ever stood before, artificial grottoes and waterfalls in the most unlikely places, expensive and foolish vanities.

But apparently this description did not apply to Billy. In fact, quite the contrary, for now he bragged, "Yes, exactly, but the greatest Folly of them all."

Thomas looked closely at the face from his youth. Inside he heard the strains of the first minuet. He'd come on business. Now for the first time he slipped the mask over his face clearly taking refuge behind it, hoping to signal to Billy that they must push on. He'd heard enough about towers, real or imagined. Perhaps the young man wasn't truly mad. Some smuggled, others built towers. Ultimately both received and gave pleasure.

He took the young man's arm, almost a paternal gesture. "Shall we join the festivities?" he invited.

But Billy declined. "I must wait here for Mr. Wyatt," he said. Then, as though fearful that Thomas had missed the name, Billy repeated it with elaboration. "Jamie Wyatt, the premier architect, you know." He stood back and opened his arms to encompass the Pantheon. "This is his. Just think, Thomas, Jamie Wyatt building my tower. There will be nothing like it, nothing like it in all the world."

Thomas felt a compulsion to separate himself from the young man. If he wasn't deranged, he was on the verge of it, and Thomas didn't know how to respond. But as he tried to move away, Billy blocked his path. "Stay with me, Thomas," he begged softly. "I need your good judgment and companionship. We were lost and now found. Let us nourish our friendship."

There was romantic melancholy in his face, his pleading. For the first time Thomas saw clearly the little six-year-old boy standing on the edge of Eden Cliff, handing over his blue agate in return for the gift of acceptance.

Apparently Billy saw the hesitancy on Thomas' face. "I know people " he offered slyly. "Whatever has brought you out of your isolation on Eden Point, I know people who can satisfy you, amuse you, serve you."

In a way Thomas felt sorry for him. How many blue agates had he given away in search of acceptance?

As though to make good his word, Billy began glancing feverishly at the dwindling crowd. A late carriage pulled up at the curb. As the footman swung open the door, a man and two ladies alighted. Only the man was unmasked. As Billy rushed forward in a burst of recognition, Thomas assumed that the great architect, James Wyatt, had arrived. Planning to make his escape in the rush of greetings, Thomas adjusted his mask and started slowly toward the brightly lit central arch. The constant din of voices, the pressure of an old acquaintance turned slightly batty, had left him mildly undone. He was not a talking man, and as always London required of a man that he be able and willing to talk.

He looked back at the party gathered at the edge of the pavement. The man—James Wyatt, he assumed—who had fallen into the clutches of Billy Beckford wore the masquerade of a Scottish Highlander, his kilts hanging foolishly over white knee stockings. The ladies with him were simply disguised, one as a haymaid wielding her delicate rake as though she intended to use it on present company, and the other, slight, looking timid in her serving girl garb done up in ridiculous flounces with flowers attached to the hem of her skirt.

Feeling estranged and mildly repulsed by the pitiful efforts of the privileged class to look common, Thomas considered the unforgivable rudeness of simply walking away from the lot of them, in spite of Billy's urgent plea for him to come and join them.

But he couldn't quite bring himself to do that. He was what he was for better or worse, and while he might ride with his men and don common clothes and lift a glass in a country pub, he was still Lord Thomas Eden.

Burdened with this bothersome sense of himself, he walked slowly toward the curb.

As he drew near, Billy babbled on about the glories of the evening and the great sport of masquerade, clutching the gentleman by the arm and reaching out as though to similarly ensnare Thomas. The serving girl, Thomas noticed, suddenly withdrew, reaching out for the haymaid and fairly dragging her up the steps and into the ballroom where the first minuet was now taking place.

Emptyheaded highborn ladies, Thomas brooded. They'd come to dance and see and be seen. They could not waste their time in conversation standing on the pavement in front of the Pantheon.

He noticed that the Scottish Highlander looked perturbed by their sudden departure. But there was precious little he could do about it, for Billy still had a rigid grip on his arm and was steering him toward Thomas. Like ships at sea, thought Thomas wryly, lost in a fog. Collision was inevitable.

"Thomas Eden," Billy pronounced, a charming flattery in his voice, "William Pitch."

The collision complete, it seemed to Thomas that the Highlander hesitated before extending his hand. Then he did, and Thomas took it, surprised at the identification. He'd expected to be shaking hands with James Wyatt.

"*Editor* Pitch," Billy intoned. "Just about the finest, most liberal mind in London, Thomas, if you're interested."

Thomas wasn't interested. He was not a great reader of newsprint. He had no need of it on Eden Point, where a man could read of all truly important matters in the comings and goings of the tide and the movement of the stars.

Now it was *his* turn, and Billy did himself proud with a simple, straightforward, irrefutable "Lord Eden, if you please, William. A name as old as England."

Thomas liked the sound. In spite of the changing times, the title was his, had become his through a long, backward-stretching line reaching across the years to the tenth century. Continuity! The grace of continuity! That was what legislation and all the personal freedom in the world could never duplicate. Ten Bastilles could fall and the rabble would still be lacking this gift, this privilege, this grace of continuity, this "Lord."

Apparently impressed, William Pitch shook his hand, his eyes behind his mask alert yet calm.

Thomas appreciated such a look and gestured toward the central arch through which the two ladies had just disappeared. "I apologize," he said with a smile, "for frightening off your companions."

Pitch glanced over his shoulder in the same direction, then gracefully accepted the apology. "No need. A respite was in order both for them and me."

Billy beamed, then his face fell. "Two for you, and none for us. Not fair," he protested in mock hurt.

"Take them both," Pitch smiled, bowing low.

Evidently interested, Billy asked, "Who are they? Anyone?"

But Pitch merely wagged a finger. "Don't defeat the purpose of this insanity, please. I should hate to think that we all dressed like fools for nothing."

The three shared a genuine laugh as though newly aware of their ridiculous apparel. Thomas felt himself beginning to relax. Seeing Billy again *was* good. The boy was daft but harmless. And as far as he could tell, there was nothing in Pitch to censor or condemn.

Billy and Pitch were talking to each other, not necessarily private matters, but beyond the reach of Thomas' familiarity. From the conversation he surmised that Pitch held a salon each evening, that Billy had frequented it on occasion, that they were discussing mutual friends.

During this interim Thomas scanned the front of the Pantheon. The crowds had dwindled, the revelers all inside. His eye fell on the shadow cast by one of the colonnades. He saw, or thought he saw, Pitch's two ladies watching them.

His attention was drawn back to the curbside conversation by William Pitch, who said quietly, "I'm sorry, Lord Eden, I can't place you. Do you sit in the House of Lords?"

Thomas looked at him, surprised. It was a peculiarly probing question for an acquaintance of less than five minutes. "No," he replied curtly.

"You *do* have a seat there," the man went on.

Annoyance rising, Thomas said, "I have a seat, but I don't sit in it."

"Why?" The interrogation continued, the man clearly overstepping his bounds.

In an attempt to alter the direction of the conversation, Thomas threw the question back at him. "Why do you ask, sir?"

Without hesitation Pitch replied, "Because now more than ever we need men of substance, understanding, and wisdom in Parliament."

Thomas laughed. "Then that's why I don't sit, sir, because I have none of those admirable qualities."

Billy joined in his amusement. "He's right, you know, William. The villain almost pushed me off a cliff once. We both were boys and I probably deserved it. Still I can't see Thomas in the House of Lords in spite of his right to be there. Devonians have their own peculiar way of managing things." He leaned closer to both men. "It's the Celt in them, you know," he whispered. "They still put water-pots by their chimneys to catch the smokewitches."

Thomas was grateful to Billy for his attempt at levity. Unfortunately it had not served the purpose of diversion at all. If anything, Pitch seemed stirred to even greater interest. "Devon, you say?" he asked, displaying an intense restlessness.

Again Billy served as Thomas' mouthpiece. "North Devon," he announced. "All of it as a matter of fact, or most of it. Sinfully rich, he is, William. My father used to say of Eden lands that between the herring below and the sheep above, all that was lacking for complete supremacy was control of the heavens."

Thomas listened to the drivel, but did not comment on it, still fascinated by the change which had come over William Pitch. The restlessness expanded to uncomfortable nervousness. Twice Thomas saw him glance sharply over his shoulder toward the massive arch of the Pantheon.

"If you gentlemen will excuse me," Pitch muttered, backing away.

But Billy would hear none of it. "Wait, William," he called, taking a final glance at the street, empty of all carriages. "Perhaps he isn't coming," he said mournfully.

"Who?" Pitch asked.

"Wyatt," Billy said. "James Wyatt was to have met me here."

Still moving away, Pitch called back, "Jamie Wyatt is probably facedown on a table at White's."

Billy looked shocked. "Drunk?"

Pitch shrugged. "Whatever. At any rate, you would never find him here."

"Why?"

Several feet away, walking backward, Pitch called, "He never enters one of his own buildings. He's not certain the roof will hold."

Thomas smiled. Whatever had caused the man's distress, he obviously had not lost his sense of humor. Pitch called out to Billy, "If you want to see Wyatt, come by to my house tomorrow evening. Now, if you'll both excuse—"

But again Billy called after him, "Wait! We'll go with you."

In spite of the mask, Thomas thought he saw a stern objection in Pitch's face. Thomas tried to restrain Billy but to no avail. The artist's smock eluded him as Billy started up the stairs, shouting back at Thomas, "Come along. While the others dance, I'll tell you more of my tower."

Not a very exciting promise, but what could Thomas do? Both men were waiting for him at the top of the steps, Pitch ensnared again, Thomas partially ensnared. Between them, like a questionable bridge, stood Billy Beckford.

Thomas bent his head forward, perturbed. If companionship was a cultivated task, it was one that he preferred not to cultivate.

Slowly he climbed the steps, head down, catching sight of his smuggling clothes, wishing that he were astride his horse, galloping at top speed along the dangerous headlands of his North Devon home.

The Grand Ballroom inside the Pantheon was a dazzle of light. Twenty gigantic chandeliers, each bearing at least a thousand candles, stretched in a blinding line down the center of the promenade while on both sides were arrangements of tables covered with white linen that seemed to reflect the light and heighten the illumination.

Beside the Grand Archway the three men stopped. Thomas looked out at the scene before him. Since it was the fashion, spilling over from the turbulence in France, to deny heritage and birth, most of the guests had come garbed in peasant's apparel, hundreds of woodcocks, hay wains, blacksmiths, and shepherdesses, all dancing the stately minuet, while in the gallery above stood the lower classes, dressed for the gala occasion in their best, their church finery, their festival-day clothes.

Apparently Billy made the same speculation. He laughed aloud. "Here's an upside-down world for you, William." He shook his head, as though he longed to flee back to the good sense of building towers which served no purpose. "Please make sense out of it for your readers," he added, "all of us, in next week's editorial."

But Pitch, Thomas observed, was not thinking about next week's editorial. He was casting an urgent glance over the tables, clearly looking for his ladies.

Thomas had had enough. If Billy had forgotten his manners, he hadn't. "Come along, Billy," he said, grasping the young man by the arm in an attempt to steer him away from William Pitch. "Let's find our own amusement. Mr. Pitch has his hands full enough."

But Billy was adamant and he had a good memory. "He offered us his ladies, Thomas," he protested. "Where could we possibly find our own?"

Bristling at the insistent youth, Thomas walked ahead alone. "Then if you'll excuse me—"

But Pitch moved alongside him. His manner had changed again. He sounded almost insistent that Thomas join his party. "I beg you, Lord Eden. No need to take your leave. Tables are scarce, I see. As long as we're here, let's enter into the spirit of the evening. Let's forget our names and questionable positions. Let's keep our masks firmly in place and pretend that beyond that arch the world is in the hands of men of goodwill."

Apparently the fantasy held great appeal for Billy. While Thomas was less enthusiastic, he was not altogether opposed. Pitch interested him. And it was true, there were no available tables and the suggestion of anonymity was a good one.

"I thank you, Mr. Pitch," Thomas said. Then, laughing, he corrected himself. "Or is it Angus?"

Pitch bowed low. "Angus, sir, if you please."

"And I'm Artist," Billy chimed in. "All artists, rolled into one. And Thomas here is Smuggler." He laughed openly. "Angus, Artist, and Smuggler," he pronounced.

The three of them started toward the left side of the room, Pitch leading the way, his head bobbing from side to side in search of his ladies.

There was boisterous laughter all about. To one side, Thomas saw a "highwayman" pull a "milkmaid" down onto his lap, his black-gloved hand probing beneath her tightly laced bodice while a small circle of shepherds and sailors and assorted ruffians urged him on. Thomas watched, amused at the mock protestations coming from the lady, who quite possibly had dreamed all her life of being ravaged by a highwayman.

He hurried to catch up, seeing countless similar scenes, the frivolity and lasciviousness of a society weary of war and the threat of war. Ahead, he saw a hangman stop Billy and attempt to drop a noose over the jaunty beret. Thomas watched as Billy struggled loose, a portion of his boyish enthusiasm diminished as he scowled at the black-hooded fellow.

"Close call, that!" Thomas shouted, enjoying it all in spite of himself.

Glancing ahead, he saw that Pitch had found his ladies, seated at a dark table near the far side of the hall, a little spot of gloom in the midst of all the swirl and color. He saw Pitch whisper something to the haymaid, who sat, still holding her toy rake at a defensive angle.

Watching the exchange, Thomas saw that the haymaid seemed very agitated. Pitch was doing his best to soothe her, while in a chair pressed to the far wall sat the serving girl, her feet primly on the floor, her small head rigid.

"Not very promising," Thomas whispered to Billy while they were still a distance away. "Do you know who they are?"

But if Billy heard, he didn't answer, still keeping a wary eye on the hangman, who seemed to be stalking him. He leaned close to Thomas. "We must keep everything in hand, mustn't we, Thomas?"

Seeing the young man's distress, Thomas laughed and put his arm around him, feeling real affection. "A good smuggler knows how to avoid the noose, Billy. Stay close beside me."

They stood before the table, Pitch's nervousness increasing as he made the false introductions. "Artist and Smuggler," he announced, "meet Haymaid and Serving Girl."

Thomas bowed low with a swirl of his cape, his eyes rapidly assessing the haymaid, then moving on to the serving girl. The latter looked very young, a girl almost, in her low-necked black frock with white petticoats and lilacs, her head a crown of fair hair hanging loose down her back. The most striking feature of her masked face was the unusual size of her prominent eyes, which formed an odd but pleasing contrast to her small mouth. She was a beauty, of that he was certain, in spite of the mask.

"Sirs," she murmured, ducking her head slightly, a becoming gesture which apparently caught Billy's eye as well, for he quickly arranged a chair close beside her.

Thomas took a chair on the far side of the table next to Pitch. Let Billy have her. Clearly she was young, more suitable for Billy. Since the haymaid seemed to belong to Pitch, Thomas decided to go it alone. Seated and resigned, he took himself out of the feeble conversation and became merely a witness, amused at Pitch's pitiful efforts to put his small party of strangers at ease. The haymaid, with her slightly anemic-looking face and curiously reddened eyes, was doing nothing to help, and Billy and the serving girl had not exchanged a word beyond the formal introduction.

Thomas looked longingly back up the aisle to where the highwayman was increasing his assault on the milkmaid, holding her a prisoner in his lap, her screams punctuated by laughter, everyone's but her own, her bodice almost completely undone, the black-gloved hand still probing. A new minuet was forming on the floor, groups of eight taking their place, right feet poised, arms raised, the orchestra in the gallery above tuning their instruments.

In an attempt to break the mysterious gloom which seemed to have settled on their table alone, Thomas leaned forward and proposed, "Billy, the serving girl wants to dance. Shall you take her to the floor or shall I?"

As though jarred to his senses, Billy got to his feet, bowed low, and extended his hand. But the girl demurred, shook her head, and pushed firmly back into her chair.

Somewhat embarrassed, Billy glared at Thomas, shrugged his shoulders, and sat down again.

Thomas stood. "What was it you said, Angus, about the spirit of the occasion?" As the man looked up rather blankly, Thomas strode around the table to where the girl sat and announced, "It's been my experience with serving girls that you don't invite them, you order them." He took the girl's hand and lifted her bodily out of the chair. A slight though genuine cry escaped the lips of the haymaid. Even Pitch offered a mild protestation, but in the heat of the moment Thomas ignored them both. Sensing no real objection from the girl, he led her toward the promenade, where the music was just starting. Near the center of the hall, he found an empty place, arranged the girl opposite him, stopped to catch his breath then, heels together, he bent his knees.

As the dance commenced, he was relieved to see that she wasn't very good at it, for neither was he. He was aware of an almost continuous blush behind her mask as they met, separated, bowed, and dipped. She was graceful though, her slight figure swaying pleasantly to the stately music, the lilacs on her hem beginning to wilt, their delicate odor pleasing as they came together. For some reason she did not strike him as being the pampered daughter of nobility. The other ladies about him clearly were at ease, even in their disguises. This one wasn't.

Still, he was enjoying himself, clearly enjoying the grace of the shy creature opposite him. Perhaps she wasn't such a child after all, for in turns, when their hands met high in the air, he observed a woman's body. "Are you enjoying yourself?" he asked in a moment of closeness.

"I am," she replied, "although I apologize for not being very good."

"You're excellent," he praised her, cursing the next step, which took her away from him. When they drew near again, he tried to put her more at ease. "We can't really be held responsible, you know," he said with a smile. "A smuggler and a serving girl are not generally skilled in the art of minuet."

She returned his smile, though she seemed to be taking it all seriously. At the next turn, feeling sorry for her, he asked, "Would you rather sit down?"

But her answer was quick. "Oh, no."

The composure with which she met the situation set his mind at rest and they concluded the dance, Thomas completely forgetting the foolishness of his bent-knee position. Whoever she was, she was most charming, her hair whirling about her as she turned, her face, what he could see of it, flushing becomingly each time their hands touched. How sweetly she smiled out at him now and then, and how gracefully she did the formal figures with her tiny feet.

As they prepared for the final figure, he approached her in a playful mood and instead of merely taking her hand, quickly slipped his arm around her waist and pulled her to him in rapid turn. Clearly caught off guard, she pressed her head against his chest, and for a moment depended entirely, deliciously, upon his support.

The music ended. He held her a second longer, then quickly released her. She stepped back and looked at him with serious but inquiring eyes.

"I apologize," he murmured, "but it's quite in character for a smuggler."

"And equally in character for a serving girl," she replied, completely in possession of herself.

Delighted, Thomas grew bolder. "Then shall we stay for another?"

A strong voice came from behind them. "This one is mine." As William Pitch stepped in front of Thomas, taking his place, he smiled apologetically, "I'm sorry, Smuggler. Billy has the haymaid, and I'm afraid you're left with the empty table." As the music started again, he added over his shoulder, "There's refreshment there now. Help yourself."

Turning away, Thomas noticed that the serving girl smiled as pleasantly at Pitch as she'd smiled at him. A pretty coquette, obviously only recently come of age. Apparently she would respond to anything masculine. Thomas continued to watch her. The girl was flirting with both of them, her eyes behind the mask apologizing to Thomas and appealing to Pitch.

Thomas smiled and shook his head. What a vixen! Disillusioned and warm, he returned to the table and a tall decanter of wine, three glasses half-filled, two empty. He filled a glass and sat in the shadows, watching the merriment around him. He spied Billy and the haymaid, executing the complex steps as though both were eager for the ordeal to be over. As Thomas dabbed at his forehead with his handkerchief, his eyes moved back to the couple at the center of the room. The young girl was laughing openly with William Pitch, a gift she apparently had not seen fit to bestow on Thomas.

As he sat, he remembered his main purpose for coming. What chance did he have of meeting prospective contacts here? There wasn't a masked face in the room with a serious thought behind it. As the frenzy of laughter rose around him, he caught sight of the highwayman with the milkmaid, her bodice completely undone, revealing bare breasts, struggling with new seriousness to remove herself from the arms that held her tight. They passed directly in front of Thomas, the maid whimpering, her hands trying pitifully to cover herself from the eyes of those who crowded about her. The scene had taken an ugly turn. Thomas considered going to the lady's aid, then changed his mind. Perhaps it was only his imagination.

The little parade proceeded on to the end of the hall and disappeared out into the gardens, the lady begging to be released, her pleas falling on deaf ears.

Several minutes later the air was rent with a terrible piercing scream. The dancers stopped, all heads turned. Instead of focusing on the assault which was taking place in the gardens, Thomas caught himself staring at the young serving girl, who had halted in her step. She gazed as though terrified in the direction of the continuous scream. He saw Pitch try to comfort her, then suddenly she pulled away and bolted, running in the opposite direction the full length of the ballroom and disappearing finally through the central arch which led to the street.

Thomas was on his feet, his attention divided between the disappearance of the girl and the apparent paralysis of William Pitch, who seemed disinclined to follow after her.

As several gentlemen started out into the garden, William Pitch among them, the music sputtered forward and resumed. But Thomas' interest lay in the other direction and he pushed his way through the gaping faces who were struggling for a firsthand glimpse of the unfortunate lady in distress in the darkness of the gardens.

Strange, Thomas thought, that Pitch had let her go, though thank God he had, for Thomas longed to find her and provide her with the protection she so obviously needed. Behind him he heard new shouts of outrage as the tragedy apparently was being played out in full. Even the footmen in the waiting carriages pressed close through the central arch, forgetting their places and clogging the ballroom.

Outside on the pavement, welcoming the cool night air, Thomas stopped and looked eagerly in both directions. Not a sign of her. He stopped a passing coachman and demanded, "A lady, a young lady, have you seen her? She ran out only—"

"No, Guv'ner, not me," the man protested, pulling away as though he might be held responsible. "What's goin' on in there? Sounds like—"

But Thomas rushed on, directly out into the street, his eyes searching each shadow. Nowhere in sight. She'd simply disappeared. Across the way he saw an old woman peddling violets. He crossed quickly, shouting at her while he was still a distance away. "Have you seen a young lady, she—"

Coming upon her sharply and looking down into two

white ovals of sightless eyes, he stopped. She'd seen nothing, neither that evening nor any other evening. As the smell of soiled linen wafted up about him, her bony fingers extended a bouquet of violets. Her moist sunken eyes expressed a deep but tranquil sorrow. "Posies, sir," she croaked. "Only a ha'penny."

Quickly he fished through his pockets and gave her a coin, then backed away, his eyes searching the empty street again. At the far end of Oxford Road he saw a slight figure climb into a cab. The horse started forward and the carriage disappeared around the corner. Gone.

He stared at the emptiness. It might have been she, but how imprudent of her to travel the London streets alone at night. He considered following after her, but dismissed that foolish idea. He wasn't even certain that it was she, and if it was, let her go. In spite of her youth, he had the feeling that she could take care of herself. Standing alone in the middle of the street, he looked back at the glittering entrance to the Pantheon.

If the place held little appeal for him earlier, it held none for him now. As for Billy, he would look him up tomorrow at his club, perhaps invite him to dinner, make his contacts there in the sedate, businesslike atmosphere of an all-male establishment. What in God's name could men of goodwill hope to accomplish with women about? Vain and coquettish one minute, grieved and frightened the next, the extremes of the species deprived them of all depth, dignity, and sincerity. Their only appeal was in their base desires, which they never admitted to, yet which hardly ever left them.

Standing alone on the darkened pavement, Thomas felt incredibly weary. He took a final glance in both directions. No sight of her. Gone.

Slowly he started walking toward his house. A strange evening! He walked heavily, his hands laced behind his back. The pavement here, midway between the confusion of the Pantheon and the dark refuge of his house, was quiet. The only sound was the rhythmical tap of his boots striking the pavement.

And then—

Which individual sense responded first, he was unable to say, but suddenly he smelled dying lilacs, and at the same time he heard breathing, and an infinitesimal passage of time after that, his eyes fell on a small figure sitting on a stoop, her head buried in her lap, hair falling in a cascade around her face, her mask lying on the pavement beside her.

Oh, high fine hand of Heaven, he thought, as stepping forward, he stood looking down on the bent head, sensing her wretchedness as clearly as though it were his own. He knelt before her, his hands moving uselessly about, as though they were awaiting direction from his mind on the manner in which they were to offer solace.

If she was startled by his presence, she gave no indication of it. She wasn't weeping. She was sitting quietly, her face hidden by her hands, as though in fear that the horror of the "milkmaid" would follow after her and engulf her.

Thomas longed to soothe her, but, lacking words, kept quiet and let his presence speak for itself. She was stirring, though her face was still concealed. Thomas stood up and stepped away, not wanting to prohibit any movement on her part. Still he watched her closely, saw in the faint light a double shadow as though she were multiplying. Thinking perhaps that she was ready to speak, he inquired, "Are you well?" and was not answered.

Then he saw emerge from the darkness, as she lifted her face, the light of her eyes, the luminosity in them developing until, by the intensity of their double regard their eyes met. They gazed at each other, as if that gaze had power to avert what they both dreaded. Although Thomas fought the image, he saw the body of another woman suddenly attach itself to that staring face, a body whipped and bleeding, her arms bound to the whipping oak.

Unable to turn away, incapable of speech, experiencing a sensation unlike any he had ever known, Thomas stepped back. The muscles in his face alive, he thought, "It is not possible," feeling that if he turned away, she would disappear and take him with her and they both would melt back into their mutual memories. He closed his eyes and the blindness only caused the sensation to increase while the girl, Marianne Locke, for he remembered her name, seemed protected by knowing *him* in advance, perhaps having known him all evening, in spite of his mask.

As he opened his eyes again, he said, "Ah," with the

slightly shuddering automatism of the last gasp in a body struck at the moment of its final breath.

Marianne sat quietly in the front parlor, reading the latest edition of *The Bloomsbury Gazetteer,* awaiting the entrance of her sister, Jane, who had finally insisted on speaking to her about the "problem at hand."

The parlor windows were opened at midafternoon and the room was filled with May fragrance, predominantly lilacs, reminding Marianne of that night, safely in the past.

What *she* knew and what no one else knew was that she had recognized him instantaneously. There was not a mask in all of England capable of hiding the man behind the face.

She gazed beyond William's newsprint toward the Orrery, the golden orb of the sun ticking its way around the cosmos. She smiled as she recalled the moment of recognition. She had merely stood up and murmured, "Excuse me, sir," and had hurriedly made her way back to the Pantheon, where her sister was waiting. The man in the artist's smock had summoned their carriage and, leaving William behind, the two women had gone home, passing slowly down Oxford Road, passing the tall smuggler, who had continued to stand, as shocked as though he had seen the dead.

As far as she was concerned, it was over. But the house had buzzed about her for almost a week, William and Jane whispering, then falling silent as she entered the room. Even Sarah had taken to looking at her as though she'd grown an extra head.

William's editorial was before her again, the words fairly leaping off the page in anger.

Future schemers of Masquerade Balls should beware. When a company dresses as peasants, they have a tendency to perform as peasants, as witnessed by the brutal episode which took place in the gardens of the Pantheon between Lord and Lady Haldane, respectively disguised as a highwayman and a milkmaid, his Lordship choosing this propitious moment to punish his wayward wife, attacking her brutally whilst a company of drunken fellows cheered him on, a scene worthy of Rome in all its decadence—

The smile of detached amusement faded from Marianne's face. It *had* been unspeakable and terrifying, the woman's screams punctuating the delicacy of the minuet. She had not intended to bolt. It was just that she had felt forces loosed that she couldn't control, like an ambush in waiting.

Quickly she lifted the newsprint where she found William quoting Diderot:

"Certainly there are barbarians," stated Diderot in his play *Le Fils Naturel*,—When won't there be? But the time of barbarism is past, the century has become enlightened. Reason has grown more refined."

Fortunately the great French writer was not present at last week's Pantheon Ball. There he would have found little to substantiate his high expectations for mankind. The company was filled with peasants disguised as peasants, peers of the realm too busy or too disinterested to sit in their inherited seats of Parliament and assist with the running of this country from which they derived so many benefits, an upper class clearly turning their backs on their responsibilities, yet grabbing with both hands all their privileges of passage and class.

Such a society cannot last. It's only a matter of time before the vacuum is filled with "world pain," the self-serving interests of the few destroying all. Our peasant disguises clearly reveal our peasant mentalities. Such a society does not deserve to stand. In the name of Justice, the people will take over and make of it what they will. In the very act of Revolution, Justice will be served. . . .

Marianne stared at the newsprint athough she had ceased reading. So! He'd at last taken a stand of sorts. It lacked true conviction, but that would come later. Slowly she rose, feeling a surge of emotion for the man behind the words. Incapable of giving herself warning, she'd already fallen a little in love with him. Yet, pacing restlessly about the parlor, she found herself diminished by such a thought. She would not return Jane's goodness with that deception. And in spite of all, Jane had been good to her.

She listened, hearing Jane's step on the stairs. She returned to the chair and tried to make herself receptive to the "problem at hand," whatever it may be. Behind her and across the hall, she saw Sarah listening from the dining room. The whole house had been a collection of ears for the last few days, everybody eavesdropping.

The footsteps were outside the door, the soft rustle of taffeta halting suddenly, as though the wearer felt the need to draw a deep breath. Still Marianne waited, head down, wishing she could bridge the gulf between herself and her sister, establish a mutually beneficial atmosphere of trust and understanding.

Jane entered the room. Marianne's heart sank. She recognized Jane's "battle clothes," a state of overdress, her wig freshly set, a dot of artificial color on her cheeks, and the gown, a rich red wine color, elegant for midnight, but at midafternoon ridiculous and clearly deceptive. Whatever wish that Marianne might have had for a relationship of trust and honesty with her sister vanished. The costume itself was powerful enough to force both of them into roles, actresses playing parts.

Jane paused in the doorway, clearly making an entrance. Her lower lip drooped a little, her mouth looked bored and sulky. She hunched her shoulders most unbecomingly. She looked at Marianne, then bobbed her head stiffly and with a sigh sank down on the couch and piled two small pillows to one side.

Since she seemed to be awaiting a comment, Marianne obliged. "You look lovely," she lied, the deception underway.

Jane dismissed the compliment. "It's such a chore, dressing four or five times a day." She shook her head. "William doesn't understand. If he had his way, I'd change clothes every hour, as proper ladies do, or so he says." She giggled. Instead of demure, she looked silly.

There was a pause during which Marianne tried to think of a suitable reply and, failing, the silence expanded. She couldn't quite bring herself to believe that William cared how often Jane or anyone else changed their garments. But she kept quiet, her curiosity mounting.

Jane asked, "Would you like tea?"

Marianne sat up, confused. Was this an order for her to go and fetch it, or an invitation for her to partake of it? Half-rising from the chair, she murmured something about only being a moment.

Quickly Jane ordered her back in the chair. "Sarah will bring it," she said. "I didn't mean for you—" She broke off nervously. "I mean, you are—" Apparently Jane was suffering from a degree of confusion of her own. She pointed to the bell on the small table near Marianne. "Ring, please," she ordered.

Marianne did as she was told, hearing the familiar little tinkle that in the past either she or Sarah had responded to immediately. Sarah appeared instantly. She listened, eyes down, while Jane ordered tea, high tea, no less, requesting an arrangement of caraway cakes and cucumber and cress sandwiches, a company ritual usually and an extra chore as Marianne knew from experience.

She started to protest, for Sarah's sake, but again held her tongue. The theatrical had to run its course, complete with costumes and set pieces and, apparently, high tea.

When Sarah was out of earshot, Jane asked, "Do you get along well with Sarah?"

Without hesitation, Marianne replied truthfully, "Oh, yes, She's a remarkable woman. I don't know what I'd do without her."

Jane seemed to digest the words as again she leaned back listlessly into the cushions. "You're the first one," she murmured.

"The first one what?" asked Marianne.

"To get along with Sarah. She's driven away seven maids since I've been here." Her eyes focused downward as her voice followed suit. "I think she'd like to drive me away as well."

Marianne smiled. "Nonsense. She's very fond of you."

"But you know how to handle her," Jane said, almost in a pout.

"I don't handle her at all," Marianne protested. "We work well together. I try to do my share. Generally she does more than hers." It seemed a foolish, almost witless conversation. Marianne sat back and tried to relax, still bewildered.

Jane made no further attempt to explain anything. She sank deep into the couch, with her head lying on a cushion and her eyes half-closed. Once or twice she raised her eyelids and pronounced a few ironical words, some jest at the expense of provincial people, although, watching her, Marianne saw clearly the Jane of her childhood, the fisherman's daughter, tall, slightly awkward and gangling, perennially unhappy.

A short time later, Sarah returned with the tea tray. She put it almost crossly on the table near Jane, who waited until she had left before she made any move to serve. Then she poured herself a cup of tea and sipped at it, selected an arrangement of small sandwiches and cakes on a plate. Finally, in a cordial tone she told Marianne to serve herself.

Apparently Jane saw her hesitancy and spoke in a clear command. "Take a cup," she ordered. "I want to see how you handle the service."

Her bewilderment mounting, as though she were being tested, Marianne did as she was told, lifted the silver urn, filled the empty cup, and sat down in her chair.

"Cakes?" Janes asked, still watching her closely.

"No, thank you," murmured Marianne, wondering if she'd passed or failed.

Jane returned the plate to the tray, licked the granules of sugar clinging to her fingers, then lay back on the couch like a woman preparing for a nap. She smoothed out the cushions, put them under her outstretched arms, and seemed to take stock of the room around her. She asked, "Do you find this a pleasing room, Marianne?"

The direct yet rather senseless question caught her off guard. Again she wondered, the truth or a lie? In truth she found the Chinese decor gaudy. "It's very different," she replied safely, "from what I'm accustomed to."

Apparently Jane extracted from the simple statement only what she needed. "Yes," she concurred, "I doubt if there's room like this in all of North Devon."

Marianne thought of the small cottage in Mortemouth where the only "decor" was a handful of heather gathered from the moors. The thought did damage to her, reminding her of her father, the happy days she'd known before she'd been put into service in Eden Castle.

Foundering under the weight of recollection, she asked Jane softly, "Do you ever miss home?"

Jane laughed. "No," she concluded firmly. "Why should I?"

It was an unanswerable question. She watched as Jane

poured herself another cup of tea. After an icy moment, Jane spoke again, almost dully. "I've worked all my life to get where I am," she said, studying the shimmering surface of tea. "It's not been easy, and perhaps you don't think it's very much, but—"

Quickly Marianne protested. "I think you've done very well," she soothed. "And more than that, I'm grateful to you for your kindness to me when I sorely needed it." She lowered her head, speaking truthfully for the first time. "I don't know what I would have done, where I would have gone, if you—"

She broke off. Apparently something she had said had struck Jane as well.

"You're my sister," Jane said kindly, as though nothing more needed to be said. The simplicity of the sentiment moved Marianne and she responded with the warmest of smiles. For a moment the meeting was what she had hoped it would be, a simple trusting encounter of two sisters, free of bitterness, almost free of past wounds.

The silence held, the only sounds in the room being those of distant carriages at the bottom of Southampton Row and the soft ticking of the Orrery spinning around in its limited cosmos.

Abruptly Jane stood up and walked a little around the couch. "Do you like it here?" she asked.

An easy question, since there obviously was no place else for her to go. "Yes."

"Are you comfortable with us? With Mr. Pitch and myself?"

Not so easy, this one. Perhaps she enjoyed too greatly talking and being with William Pitch. Still she answered, "Yes."

As though with sudden resolve, Jane straightened her shoulders, lifted her head, the elaborate wig slipping backward in the process. "Then we have decided," she began, "William and myself, that you should move out of the servants' quarters and into one of the rooms upstairs." She made a ceremonious and almost comic little bow as though the matter were over and done with.

But it wasn't closed. Marianne sat up on the edge of her chair, even more bewildered. "W-why?" she stammered.

"Because you don't belong in the servants' quarters," Jane replied. "You're my sister and I think you've served your penance. It's quite an embarrassment, you know, when people ask who you are."

Marianne was curious to know who had been asking after her. "I'm afraid that I don't understand," she said falteringly.

Jane sat on the couch again. "There's nothing to understand," she pronounced primly. "There's a bedchamber at the end of the second-floor corridor. Quite comfortable it is. It's yours."

It was at best a joyless gift. Marianne knew the room well, having cleaned it often after it had been occupied by one of William's late-night guests who had lifted a glass too many. It was a pleasant room, lovely rich mahogany furnishings, a small but exquisite Persian carpet covering a portion of the hardwood floor, delicate French porcelain pitcher and bowl on the water stand, a high window giving a lovely view out onto the gardens. In her mind's eye, Marianne saw clearly the room, but couldn't quite see herself in it.

"Has my work here been unsatisfactory, Jane?" she asked, thinking that perhaps another serving maid was waiting to take her place.

"Of course not," came the reply. Apparently Jane had reached the limit of her endurance. "Oh, for heaven sake, Marianne!" she exclaimed. "Why must you make everything so difficult? Are you that fond of the room off the kitchen? Am I to interpret your hesitancy as a sign that you prefer Sarah's company to ours?"

Before Marianne could answer, Jane stood up as though to close the subject. "You will move your belongings up to the second floor immediately. I shall tell Sarah. She'll have to make do until I can interview a replacement." She looked back at Marianne. "And leave the serving dresses," she ordered. "You can't wear those hideous things."

"I have nothing else," protested Marianne.

Jane pondered the problem. "I'll place one of my gowns in your room. You'll have to hem it, but it will do for tonight. Then, tomorrow, we shall buy others."

Still Marianne sat, aware that she should be making sounds of gratitude. But she couldn't. The scheme held little appeal for her.

"Well, then," Jane concluded, apparently interpreting

Marianne's silence as grateful consent. "You must get moved, and I must go out briefly. We'll expect you at dinner, in your rightful place."

"Jane?"

"No more questions. It's late and I really must be—"

"But I would like to understand—"

"There's nothing to understand. Your position as a serving girl in this house is not suitable."

"It was suitable for over seven months."

Jane looked around sharply from the door. Both remained silent, one in dismay, the other in anger. "If it makes you feel better," she offered, "you can visit Sarah now and then in the kitchen."

There was something patronizing in her voice. Marianne felt a surge of anger. "How am I to know," she began, "that one day you won't come to me and tell me that *this* is unsatisfactory, that for some reason I shall have to vacate the second-floor room and move back to the kitchen?"

As though sensing her anger and pleased by it, Jane smiled sweetly. "Well, I've never heard such a fuss." After making an unabashed scrutiny of Marianne from head to foot, she softened. "We don't lead such a despicable life," she said with a smile. "I think, knowing you, that you might enjoy it." She swept out into the hall and returned a moment later, parasol and gloves in hand. "Has it ever occurred to you," she began, speaking as though to a child, "that it's your future we're thinking of? Neither William nor I am prepared to support you all your life."

For the first time Marianne thought she saw the light of a reason. The move up was merely the first step in a move out. As Jane's sister, and William's houseguest, she would be easily identifiable as "eligible." The nightly salon was to become a marriage market, or worse, a place of procurement where, if she was lucky, she would catch the eye and purse of a rich Londoner. More alarming than this, she saw that Jane had no qualms about the arrangement, apparently void of moral distress.

As though to confirm her terrible suspicions, Jane rhapsodized, "Here in London everything is possible. A pretty face and a quick wit can conquer almost anything." She smiled sweetly. "Be ready for dinner at eight," she ordered. "Take your pick of my gowns. I have enough for both. Now I really must be going."

As though all were resolved, she hurried to the front door and out of it, leaving Marianne sitting in a benumbed, angry state. A moment later, she heard a carriage draw up in front of the house, then pull away.

Marianne sat motionless. Every passing second had its own note, every memory its own ring. Then someone was speaking to her.

"Marianne? Are you all right?"

She looked up at the insistent voice, found Sarah's concerned face. The woman was kneeling before her. "You look like a ghost," she scolded.

Marianne leaned forward and embraced the woman, more than embraced her, hugged her close as though clinging to life itself.

Sarah responded stiffly but admirably, claiming that she'd miss her company in the kitchen, but it was the right thing to do.

Marianne separated herself from the embrace. Hoping for an ally and finding none, she stood. "It seems I'm to become a lady, Sarah," she said with a smile, helping the woman to her feet.

"Not become," Sarah scolded. "You are. The only one in this house as far as I'm concerned." Then she became businesslike. "We have work to do. It'll take more than hemming to make one of her dresses suitable for you. Then I'll help you with your things." Again Sarah confirmed the truth in her heart. "Oh, yes, it's right. In fact it should have come that first night. Putting you in the storeroom like that—" And she shook her head as though belatedly shocked. "Well, it's proper now. You're in your rightful place and—"

She had been talking in feverish haste, and was suddenly silent with a questioning look at Marianne. "You're—pleased, aren't you?"

Slowly Marianne nodded, although her face showed neither surprise nor joy. She wandered toward the back of the house, Sarah following eagerly after her, bobbing from one side to the other, spilling out plans and schemes.

Still, there was something in Marianne which gnawed like self-contempt. As she packed her few belongings, in

preparation for leaving the servant world, she felt crushed
and humiliated, like a servant.

Thomas Eden sat lost in thought at a table placed near
the window of White's Tavern, once a chocolate house,
now a gambling inn. He was awaiting the arrival of a
coach which should have come some time ago; it was
already an hour late.

Billy Beckford, who had accompanied him here, as he
had accompanied him everyplace for the last week, like
a scavenger over a corpse, was engaged in a raucous game
of dice at the center of the crowded, smokefilled room.
While White's was large, it could not begin to accommodate the hordes of gentlemen, laughing and shouting, the
constant rattle of dice, the thick white candles burning on
double standards around the walls.

Very tired and mildly hung over, Thomas crossed his
arms on the table and laid his head upon them. The
warmth of the early summer sun, still hot at the beginning
of dusk, began to strike the surface of the scarred oak
table. A pleasant lassitude enveloped his nerves, and his
thoughts began to run riot as a sick man's will, gradually
taking on strange forms and colors.

*Eden Castle . . . the girl . . . another drink . . . the need
to return . . . the compulsion to stay . . . William Pitch's
house in Bloomsbury . . . tired . . . constantly drunk or
on the verge of it. . . .*

He pressed his eyes closed and wished that he might
doze. Ragland and Locke must be almost to Salisbury by
now. He had put them on the coach and ordered them
home early this morning. While thus far he had been un-
successful with new French contacts, someone must at
least keep their one and only appointment wih Captain
Girard in North Devon. Ragland and Locke could handle
it, would be there in plenty-of time the next day to clear
the fishing fleet and form a small armada at the mouth
of the channel. Ragland and Locke could also handle the
disbursements. Besides, they were both a nuiseance to him
here, loaded with the freight of their own various involve-
ments, Ragland scolding Thomas, *scolding* him if one
could imagine, to leave the girl be.

And Locke was gloomy after his first night on the
town, when he had gone on a fruitless hunt for his sister

and had been set upon by thieves and relieved of everything save one pair of white silk stockings. He'd wandered through the London streets, a small cut on his forehead. God alone knows what would have become of him if Ragland hadn't happened upon him, given him the protection of his cloak, and seen him home. A week ago that had been. The night of the Masquerade—

Dangerous territory, there. He had not expected to see her again. But having seen her even so briefly had reminded him of the "unfinished" nature of the entire episode, a sun setting but not falling, a meal prepared but not eaten.

He heard indistinct sounds from the street, horses trotting, the noise of heavy wheels, mysterious and agitated conversations close by. Slowly he looked up.

But the carriage drawing up outside was not the one he was waiting for. A bewigged gentleman, slightly unsteady on his feet, stepped out and began to make his way to the door. He was carrying beneath his arm a large, tightly rolled sheet of blue paper. Then a very excited Billy Beckford was at Thomas' side, whispering, "It's Wyatt, Thomas. Come and meet him. See his plans for the tower. I need your counsel."

But Thomas shook his head. "Later, perhaps, not now. I'm waiting for—"

A petulance surfaced on Billy's face. "You're really carrying the whole thing too far, Thomas, if you want my opinion. Ragland was right. Leave her be."

Then the lecture was over and Billy was pushing his way through the crowd in an attempt to join the bewigged gentleman at the door, who was engulfed in admirers, men extending their hands, bowing in deference to the lion of English architecture.

Thomas watched it all with slightly raised head, the annoyance of Billy's advice still in his ear. The counsel of the entire world, it seemed, was leave her be. No matter. He was accustomed to keeping his own counsel. He wasn't obsessed, as Ragland had accused him of being. He was simply a man who liked to see a thing through to its natural conclusion. Once he'd had her, that was all he wanted. And knowing where she was, and waiting for the one person who could make it all possible, he felt relief in his burning brain.

Perhaps in the months since the whipping oak she'd learned a form of obedience. It must be very disagreeable for her to endure the humiliation of service in her sister's house. He merely wanted to see her again, to take what had been rightfully his on that hot afternoon last summer, and then write "the end" to the whole episode. Tomorrow evening, at the latest, he would be on his way back to Eden Point, his mind clear, the fever in his brain eased.

He straightened himself with the decision of a strong and healthy man who makes an easy goal. He called for one of the boys to bring an ale. The evening would be long, though promising.

Of course, there wasn't a chance in a million that she was still a virgin, and that was sad. He was certain she had been a virgin that day she had defied him. But now, after seven months in London, it simply was not possible. Well, so much the better. At least this way she knew what to expect. Rather sadly, he remembered her day on the whipping oak. So unnecessary, all so unnecessary.

Then there was a mug of ale before him on the table and he drank it eagerly, as though trying to quench the fever in his brain as well as the desert in his throat. Over the raised mug he saw Billy in close conversation with James Wyatt, the two men bent over the large blue piece of paper which earlier had been rolled beneath Wyatt's arm.

A greasy smell of burned sausages pervaded the air, a crackling of small explosions. The spit in the enormous fireplace was too near the flame. Still, he saw men reaching in with bare fingers and extracting the burned pieces of meat and popping them gingerly into their mouths.

Beyond the smudged window the evening brooded a menacing red, smoke escaping from chimneys, forming halos around the church spires, the glow of the setting sun lingering more pallidly, as if in fear that no one had seen its beauty. Beyond him was the city, with roof upon roof, chimney upon chimney, cut into a deep evening blue perspective. Feeling quite reflective, like a man with victory close at hand, he cast his gaze even farther and shuddered at the thought that every stone, every beam, every tile, everything he now saw in a swift glance was formed with toil during long hours by human brains and human hands. Yet, impressive as it was, it did not begin to compare with nature's hand which alone had wrought his coast, his head-lands, his ocean, his cliffs, his seabirds, his fortress, his Eden.

He realized with a wave of humor that he was home-sick. A small pang of doubt again. Perhaps he should have returned in the coach with Ragland and Locke and ignored the girl. But it was his pride. No one must have a hold on him, no matter how insignificant. It was to break that hold that Fate had brought him to this point, their paths crossing again.

Just then he looked up. Beyond the window a carriage was drawing up to the pavement. He waited, peering close. Then a smile broadened on his face. Quickly he drained his mug, adjusted his jacket, dropped a coin on the table, and started for the door.

Billy called after him, "Thomas, wait, come this way!"

"Not now!" he shouted back. "I'll see you later."

"At Pitch's?" Billy cried, as though fearful of losing all contact.

Thomas nodded, "With luck, yes. At William Pitch's."

A dazzling grin spread across Billy's face as though a brilliant idea had just occurred to him. He lifted his mug into the air and cried, full-voiced, "A thousand guineas says you won't make it to her bed this night."

Within the instant the intoxication of the wager spread. Incredulously Thomas saw the crowd of gentlemen push close to Billy, apparently not overly concerned about odds or the parties involved, their hands already fishing for the proper amount to contribute to the wager.

At the door Thomas watched the madness, gravely at first. Then, confident of success, the spirit of the moment flamed up inside him. "You're on!" he shouted. He lifted his purse from his belt and, holding it high above his head, shouted again, "You're all on!"

It was only a thousand-guinea wager, small by White's standards, but fascinating and appealing nonetheless be-cause it involved a woman and conquest. As the gamblers pushed closer about Billy, seeking details and odds, Thomas hurled his full purse toward them and ordered Billy, "Keep books for me. I'll be too busy myself."

Billy caught the purse and bowed low, then turned im-mediately to his audience, filling them in. The details,

Thomas was certain, would be distorted beyond recognition before the night was over.

No matter. He glanced quickly through the door. The carriage was still waiting at the pavement, and within it sat his guarantee for a successful evening. What harm would there be in returning to Eden Castle tomorrow several thousand guineas richer?

Behind him the wagers were mounting, the laughter raucous as the specifics of Billy's tale reached their ears. As Thomas started out the door, he noticed that even James Wyatt was drawing forth his purse, the money being collected on the large sheet of blue paper, the proposed tower momentarily forgotten in the excitement of the gamble.

On the pavement at last, Thomas stood for a moment, his eyes focused on the discreetly drawn curtains at the carriage window. He stepped forward and knocked lightly on the door. A well-tended hand lifted the curtain and the door opened.

As he stepped into the recesses of the carriage, he saw a woman, overdressed, in a taffeta gown, a ridiculously high powdered wig perched precariously on her head. If she knew how foolish she looked, she gave no indication of it. With a smile Thomas settled in the seat opposite her, amused and confident in the knowledge that for a rich man there was always a way.

With a tap of her parasol on the floor of the carriage, they started forward. Once under way, she smiled stiffly. "Lord Eden? Am I correct?"

He bobbed his head, a little regretful of the betrayal which would shortly be plotted within the confines of the carriage. Still, through his own experience of life, he had come to the conclusion that in this world everyone must look to himself.

So thinking, and relieving himself of any responsibility; remembering the rich purse which would be waiting for him at White's tomorrow and the satisfaction of the encounter itself, the conquest which had been postponed far too long as it was, he leaned forward and extended his hand.

"Miss Jane Locke? Am I correct?" he inquired.

William Pitch stood in the dim evening light of his small office, staring out at the street beyond. It was congested with early evening traffic. But he saw nothing, and felt the combined weight of France and England on his shoulders.

There were certain poisons that could not be contained, certain ingredients of mind and soul that, by their very nature, grew and spread. And the news, now creeping across the channel from France, spoke of such a contamination, this Robespierre, all the more dangerous because he was masquerading as a savior, the one force in muted alliance with the lesser spirits of Danton and Marot who could lead France out of her agony and into the dawn of true independence.

Slowly William's face darkened. The whole thing had death written on it. He could sense it. Yet England slumbered, and awakened only long enough to applaud the "glorious movement," that "nation of courageous men," "the greatest revolution in the history of the world."

Wearily William turned away from the window. The small office was empty now, his colleagues scurrying to the comfort of their homes, impervious to the fact that shortly a new reality would alter the comfort of their homes. No, there was no way to contain it. France was fated to undergo every form of revolutionary experience, France the crucible in which all the modern elements of revolution would be put to the test.

He stared blankly at the rapidly darkening room, sparsely furnished with four desks and a copy table, a low-ceilinged room in which, supposedly, thoughts were organized, then printed for the digestion and edification of any thinking Englishman. He felt again a menacing dip of his spirits. What difference did it make? What reason the effort when half of England couldn't read and the other half read only what amused them? What difference any of it?

He felt tired and overexcited at the same time. He didn't want to think any more about what was going to happen. Pitt had just announced that he believed in fifteen years of peace for Europe. Nonintervention was his policy. Good God, couldn't he see? Couldn't he—

He sat heavily on the corner of his desk, noticing the inkstains on his fingers, the results of a laborious editorial, a too-shrill alarm trying to jar England out of her self-indulgent lethargy. The trouble was the men who ruled England had never been hungry, had never felt a boot on the back of their neck, had never known brutality and terror save that which they inflicted on others. The world, like a good hunting hound, could always be replaced if something happened to it.

Scars, he thought darkly, should be the prime prerequisite of all public leaders. They enabled a man to think on eternity. He smiled, both annoyed and amused by the incoherency of his thoughts. If that were the case, the young girl now living in his house should be Prime Minister. But she wasn't. Quite the contrary. She was, at this very moment, being set up as a sacrifice.

Abruptly William stood. Well, he would have no hand in this latest fiasco, and he'd told Billy Beckford as much when the young man had come around, acting as the go-between for Thomas Eden. He'd also told him that it was his advice to Lord Eden to leave the girl alone. She'd suffered enough at his hands.

But they wouldn't. William knew they wouldn't. Everyplace he looked he saw compromise, deceit, betrayal. It deserved to go, the whole bloody thing, in a great ball of fire.

As though something had been settled, he took out his watch and tilted it toward the fading light outside. Half past seven. Dinner at eight. His salon would be filled by ten, a large portion of all the wit, energy, and power of London congregated under his simple beams. This would be a particularly "exciting" evening, for Billy Beckford had promised him the company of Lord Thomas Eden.

William's heart accelerated in anger. He paced the length of the room, his mind moving ahead. For one second his rage surfaced and he reached blindly for an inkwell and hurled it across the room. With a crash it struck the far wall, and black stain spread and slid, enlarging itself as it ran down the surface of the wall. At the moment there wasn't a hell of a lot he could do about the madmen in France. But here there was an arena over which he had absolute authority.

The awareness of this power blazed out with a vividness that contrasted brutally with the twilight's quiet melancholy. He had once envisioned himself saving worlds. Since that was impossible and perhaps even scarcely worth the effort, he would have to settle for the salvation of a young serving girl.

Quickly he adjusted himself to the evening ahead. He looked out the window and saw dusk struggling into night. He must hurry. He must hurry!

The "serving girl" stood before the peer glass in the upper bedroom, wearing an expression of perfect benevolence. Her placid eyes smiled at the image in the mirror.

Not bad for a hasty job. The trouble was she felt "dressed up," felt restrained in the pale blue gown. Still Sarah had worked miracles, had nipped here, as she had put it, and stitched there, narrowing the waist until now it clung to Marianne like new skin.

Again Marianne glanced in the mirror. She turned to check the height of the softly rolled collar. Sarah had assured her that it was high enough, the one scar that crept across the back of her neck now hidden in white ruffle. She took another last look, then slipped into a chair and sat gazing out the window at dusk falling.

Softly she leaned her head forward and closed her eyes. Whatever went on in Jane's house, it was not Marianne's place to disapprove. The only area over which she had absolute control was her own life and conduct. She would look to that and ignore the rest. But what was she supposed to do? What did William and Jane expect of her? What role did they want her to play now?

She heard a soft knock at the door. Sarah, she imagined. The knock sounded again and she thought it strange, Sarah going so formal with her. Their rooms downstairs had always been opened one to the other.

When the knock sounded a third time, she retreated to the shadows by the window, determined not to reply. If Sarah wished to enter, let her enter of her own volition. Besides, this room did not belong to Marianne. It was not her place to say who could and could not enter.

The knock came again and she saw the door opening, caught only a glimpse of a shoulder silhouetted by the lamplight coming from the hall beyond. Still it was enough for her to see that it was not Sarah. A familiar deep voice which stirred her called softly, "Marianne? Are you here?"

Although the nature of his presence only compounded her confusion, she was pleased to see him and called out from the shadows, "Over here, William."

His head swiveled in that direction, his eyes searching through the semidarkness, finding her at last, then glancing back out into the hall like a trespasser. The lamplight caught his face and she saw a weary visage, an expression which mirrored her own feelings.

"Are you looking for Jane?" she asked, knowing somehow that he wasn't, but feeling a need all the same to deflate the silence.

He shook his head, his hands shoved into his pockets, still looking uncomfortable. Slowly she moved out of the shadows in an attempt to put him at ease. "She went out," she added. "Jane, I mean. Some time ago. She didn't say where."

He nodded, as though he knew this. "I just wanted to see," he began, then hesitated. "I just wanted to see if you were settled."

"Settled, yes," she said with a smile. "I'm afraid however that I understand nothing."

He turned toward her eagerly, as though at last having something definite to respond to. "Aren't you comfortable here?" he inquired earnestly.

"This isn't my room," she said.

"Neither is the one downstairs near the kitchen," he replied as though willing to engage her in a debate on so trivial a matter.

"No," she agreed, "but I felt at home there."

"And you don't here?" Quietly he closed the door behind him, mindlessly pursuing the matter of her comfort. "If the room doesn't please you, we can always find another. It's no great thing. All we want is—"

Again he hesitated, then stopped altogether. Mystified, she looked at him. He was as changed as she was, both of them drowning in a pool of lies and subterfuge.

"What is expected of me, William?" she asked.

He looked at her as though he had not understood the simple question. "What is expected—" he repeated. "I don't understand. What do you mean, what is expected of you?" There was a slight rancor in his voice. "No need to make things more difficult than they are," he went on. "Jane simply felt that—" Again the mind and the tongue apparently broke down simultaneously. Embarrassed, he tried to change the subject. "You look—very nice," he said, with great formality.

"It's Jane's," she replied.

"Yes, but you wear it well."

Again the muddle of mismatched purposes threatened to overwhelm them. They stood as though confronting each other. Their eyes met, and in his, she read shame mingled with bitterness. This look touched a chord in her. She offered him comfort and an apology. "I'm sorry, William," she began, "for upsetting your household. It was wrong of them to send me here. I shouldn't have—"

He was at her side, sternly scolding, "Nonsense. It's where you belong." His voice grew determined. "And nothing will be expected of you, I promise you that. You are my guest, and as such I offer you my hospitality, my table, and my protection."

She found the latter offering strange, but said nothing, concentrating now on his closeness, his shadow falling across her face, his hand lifting toward her.

They stood without moving, only half aware of background noises in the house and the street beyond, the clink of china coming from downstairs the clatter of carriages passing by on Southampton Row, evening birds in the garden.

His hand was on her arm, exerting soft pressure, and she found herself leaning forward, and in some miraculous way, his arms were around her, drawing her closer. They came wordlessly to the embrace, a spontaneous closeness, his hand pressing her head against his heart, an amazing tangle of sensations, leaving her with a feeling of beatitude, akin to tears.

She'd never known such closeness, such warmth, yet responded admirably by nestling closer, her eyes shut. She felt weak and pleasantly vulnerable within his embrace. If ony she could remain thus for the rest of her life.

But she couldn't, and apparently neither could he. Abruptly he stepped back, looking like a man breaking in half, his face contorted, glistening with perspiration. "I'll leave you now," he murmured. At the door he turned again, a glint of anger in his eyes. "Nothing is expected of you tonight," he promised. "Nothing." And with that he left the room, closing the door firmly behind him.

She stood alone. The peer glass caught her image and she saw the woman standing there, in her fine blue gown. Suddenly her hand moved rapidly forward and extinguished the lamp. She didn't want to see the woman. Sitting now in darkness, she would have given all she possessed, life itself, to be released from this new feeling, for in that one brief, innocent embrace, the worst had been confirmed. The awareness of this "worst" caused a strangulation in her throat until finally she leaned over and pressed her brow against the table, horrified at the impact of her discovery, the realization of her capacity to love, the realization of betrayal, of returning Jane's goodness with treachery.

Slowly into these thoughts crept a note of comfort. Perhaps she'd only imagined it. Perhaps William had only intended to offer comfort, as a father soothes a frightened child, by simply taking her in his arms and holding her, for that was all that happened. Nothing more.

In that case the burden of the future would be upon her, to stay away from him until she could rid or cure herself of these feelings.

Hazards within and without. A new room, a new role, new gown, new feelings. At the very moment that she laid herself gratuitously upon such a mountain of guilt and shame, trying to free herself from these new feelings, she heard herself whispering "William" as though the man were still with her, as he *was* with her in memory, as she knew, despairingly, he would always be, for an interval which merely encompassed the rest of her life.

He had held women before, hundreds of them, highborn and lowborn, fragrant and soiled. He had wooed and courted, bought and bartered, traded and dealt. He had won them gambling, had slipped them out from beneath the watchful eyes of husbands, had risked duels, had taken them by force and whimsy, had soothed and assaulted, caressed and struck and, finally over the years, finding nothing new or surprising in the shape and biology of the female body, nothing stimulating in sustained sexual variety, he had at last taken a simple mistress, a goodhearted, uncomplicated country girl, who looked after his table and his bed, satisfying all his needs.

But now—

William sat in the dark in his private bedroom. The window was opened, the night air fragrant. Overwarm, he stood up, tore off his coat, and hurled it into a far corner.

He felt reduced somehow, adolescent. He paced, realizing with a wave of remorse that had he stayed a moment longer in the room with her, he himself would have been guilty of the assault from which he had vowed to protect her.

Abruptly he stretched out across his bed, trying to make his feelings blind to his memory. Yet, and here was the puzzle, he had not intended to touch her. He had been merely indignant at the plot which was being perpetrated against her, had felt it his duty to make her aware of his protection, like a father to a child.

He groaned at this self-deception, and rolled restlessly onto his back. Protection! He was no better than Thomas Eden, perhaps worse. At least there was something honest in Eden's plot, the need, like thirst, to avenge an old humiliation.

His thoughts shifted back to the bedroom down the hall, to the young girl sitting stiffly by the window, scarred, unaware of the game presently being planned by her sister. Before this night was over, if he didn't intervene, she would be scarred again, in deeper and more subtle ways than those acquired at the whipping oak.

Again he tossed on the bed, unable to separate his feelings of desire from his more admirable inclination to protect. He'd thought he was beyond such agony. Part of his misery now was simply the tacit realization that he could still be moved, stirred, that apparently as long as a man lived, he would, at unexpected moments, always be plagued by such discomfort.

Yet, and this too was a puzzle, she was scarcely a woman, more of a child, but endowed with a sweetness, a deceptive simplicity, beneath which he was certain dwelt incredible richness. The man who finally took her would be justly rewarded. But that man must not be himself or Thomas Eden. In both cases she deserved better.

Out of these thoughts he felt a kind of ease slip over him, not satisfaction, but merely the feeling that she was beyond him, that she must be protected. The drumming in his head subsided. He lay, face downward, both hands pressed beneath his body in a peculiarly twisted position, thinking that once he saw her safely through this night, he should go away for a while, recover as it were, France maybe, to see firsthand the madness running rampant in that country, see, out of curiosity if it matched his own,

his alarming digression back to the emotional stability of
a fifteen-year-old boy.

Weariness crept over him as though he had fought and
won a battle, as indeed he had. To the best of his memory, it was the first time in his life that he had ever denied
himself a woman. Any woman. Before tonight, all his body
had to do was signal and a campaign had been launched.

Now he would sleep. At least he had that small comfort.
But a soft knock at the door signaled that even that was
to be put off. He turned his head slightly so that he could
see, but kept quiet. The door opened and he heard a faint
call of "William, are you awake?"

Dear God, he'd never been more awake, but for Jane,
standing silhouetted in the door, fresh from her Judas role,
he feigned sleep.

She called again, "William?"

He considered summoning her to the bed, stripping her,
and using her for a substitute. But he couldn't bring himself to do it. For one thing, it wouldn't work. Jane, a most
generous mistress for over three years, had given him access to every portion of her body. He knew it as intimately
as he knew his own. In total darkness he would be able to
pick Jane out of a hundred women. She was both predictable and reliable, twin features which in the past had made
their relationship a comfort. But not now.

So he let her go, heard her call softly a third time,
"William?" and receiving no answer, saw her close the
door quietly behind her.

He lay, wondering, what had been the bargain? What
arrangement had she made with Thomas Eden? At what
precise hour was he to appear? When would he be given
access to the staircase which led to the second floor? On
what pretense would she lure the "prize" up before him?

His face became resolved. Stealthily he left his bed and
moved across the room to the locked cabinet on the far
wall. In this dark, he felt on the ledge until his fingers
found the key. Not requiring illumination of any kind, he
unlocked the cabinet and reached for the black leather
case resting on the second shelf. He pushed the clasp to
one side and lifted the lid, and his hand went forward as
though his fingertips were eyes, closing firmly about one
of the smooth, cool dueling pistols. The weapon felt strange
in his hand. A handsome set they were, never used, al-

though twice they had made it as far as Lincoln's Inn Field on cold, foggy mornings where only at the last minute reason had intervened, the outraged gentleman of the moment settling on a less severe, less permanent, judgment.

Still he knew them to be effective, knew himself to be an adequate marksman, having put himself through long hours of target practice in the empty fields beyond Bloomsbury when he had been a youth and the possession of dueling pistols and the skill to use them had been necessary for a man's survival.

He studied the weapon in his hand and felt slightly melodramatic. Surely it would never come to this. Thomas Eden was arrogant, but he wouldn't risk his life for a sixteen-year-old girl.

Restored by this commonsense attitude, he continued to fondle the weapon, coming to enjoy the feel of it in his hand. Just in case Eden was not as intelligent as he thought, the weapon might be an effective deterrent.

Finding considerable relief in the decision, he returned the case to the cabinet, minus one pistol. He placed the pistol on the table, allowed his hand to linger on it. What was she doing now? What thinking? Could she guess at what was ahead of her? Did she fear the man? Hate him?

All was silent in his room. There were no answers. He would protect her. Nothing more. He would see her safely through this night, then hopefully Thomas Eden would return to North Devon and leave her alone and, within the fortnight, William would take a fast coach to Dover and pray for a high summer wind which would swiftly push the channel packet to Calais.

Tentative plans made, he stretched out on the bed. Dinner soon. Then his salon would be opened.

For now, he was blessedly alone. The hours that remained to him belonged to that silent partner whose realm started just where logical thought ended.

Quietly Jane closed the door behind her. He was sleeping. Good! She would not have to tell him where she had been, in whose impressive company she'd passed the last several hours, riding with him, with *him* in the carriage well beyond the city, Lord Eden himself, in whose awesome shadow she'd passed all her childhood, never dreaming even in her wildest imagination that one miraculous day, she would be arranging for him to have a victory that it was only within her power to give him.

Still breathless from the excitement of it all, she stared at the closed door beyond which William lay sleeping. Of course, he wouldn't approve, so it was just as well he knew nothing of it. Slowly she let her eyes move down the corridor to the closed door beyond which the "victory" sat waiting.

Jane felt a surge of the old jealousy. She tried putting herself in Marianne's place, not as a woman who had survived unspeakable brutality, but as a mistress, lying beside Lord Eden night after night. If she were in her sister's place, no "arrangement" would have to be made at all. If she had been her sister back on Eden Point, she would have gratified his desires instantly, remembering from her childhood the several young women who had suddenly appeared in new gowns with heavy purses, the fortunate ones who had been summoned to the top of the cliff and who thereafter always seemed to be provided for.

It was very difficult for Jane to imagine anyone with good sense turning their back on such treasure. But perhaps it was not too late. Lord Eden's appetites now ran to her sister, and if Jane could help him to satisfy that appetite, then surely some of the riches would spill into her lap. Marianne *had* caused him grief. Now she simply had a debt to pay, a delightful debt at that, for the man in middle years had grown handsome and assertive, lean and hard, a fine specimen, resembling in no way the slightly paunchy Lord Eden of earlier years who had on occasion deigned to walk the cobblestones of Mortemouth, dispensing shillings and smiles.

Innocently Jane smiled. She had only the highest of motives, offering her sister a second chance, making it possible perhaps for her to be set up in an elegant London house all her own, her own coach and four, a complete staff at her disposal, coin enough to purchase the finest of French gowns, and even when he tired of her, as he surely would, still she would be handsomely set up for life.

These unlimited possibilities produced a kind of shock in her. "Marianne is the quick one," she'd heard her father say hundreds of times. As she approached the closed door down the corridor, she still was struggling to understand the behavior of this "quick" sister. One thing she understood. Marianne must suspect her of nothing and must trust her completely. For the duration of the evening she must put aside all the old hurts and jealousies, must open her arms to this sister who had caused her such grief, must trick her with unabashed love, must bring her to the point where she would follow her willingly to the—

She stopped. Slaughter was the word that had entered her mind. But that wasn't true. It wasn't slaughter. It was rebirth in a new life, rich beyond her comprehension. Lord Eden's mistress!

"Oh, God," she thought, leaning against the wall outside Marianne's door. "If only it had been me."

She slipped past the oil lamp burning in the niche beside the door. She lifted it from its place, knocked softly, and called, lovingly, sweetly, "Marianne?"

"Marianne? Are you there?"

"Bring the *other* carriage!" Thomas shouted angrily down from the second-floor window of his house on Oxford Road.

It was almost midnight, a close June evening made doubly close by the steady drinking which Thomas had indulged in since the late hours of afternoon. Starting at White's and continuing in his own sitting room, a glass had never been far from his hand.

Still, he wasn't drunk, and certainly he was more in control of his senses than the large, fleshy simpleton who stood on the pavement below with a hired chaise at hand.

The man—what was his name?—stared up blankly, lantern aloft. "Other carriage, milord?" he repeated, parrotlike.

"In the coach house," Thomas called back, trying to rein in his anger. It simply served no purpose to lose one's temper with these people. They were beyond comprehension. He reached quickly into his purse for coin. He tossed several onto the pavement below. As his man scrambled for them, he called out, "Send the chaise on its way, and I'll double what you hold in your hand if the carriage is ready within the hour."

Ah, at last the man understood. The clear language of coin. Thomas smiled as he watched the hired chaise pull away, amused at his man running now as though something were pursuing him down the narrow alley in the direction of the coach house.

The street was empty, dark. A few carriages passed now and then, linkboys with flaring torches running ahead to light the way. For a moment the whole earth seemed to be heaving and rolling. Thomas felt giddy. He stepped back from the window and sank heavily into a chair. "A hired chaise!" he thought ruefully. Oh, yes, he could see himself approaching William Pitch's house in a hired chaise.

Quickly he sat up. What time? Timing was all. His watch said it lacked ten minutes of midnight. The Locke woman had proposed two thirty. It seemed late to him, everyone with sense long gone to bed. But she had assured him otherwise. The salon only reached its peak at two. The girl would be weary, she had further assured him, having been up since dawn. She would see her to the upstairs bedroom shortly before two. Then a quarter of an hour more for her to disrobe and fall sleepily into bed. Then, at two thirty Thomas was to appear where she would greet him and slip him the key to the upstairs bedroom. Beyond that he was on his own, she had said, blushing profusely. How different these two sisters! The one called Jane was that sort of character which is often met with in England; very lively without much wit. Her fault was speaking too much. And the other one—

Reflexively Thomas reached out for the half-filled bottle on the table. No! Enough! He wanted to be alert tonight. Now it was much more than a simple conquest. There was a sizeable wager in the bargain as well.

He sat up, resting his head in his hands. The mix of wine and brandy had left a bad taste in his mouth. The heat of the day had taken a toll of his garments. He smelled foul, a mingling odor of body sweat and dayold linen. With amusement he wondered if he should go to the trouble of bathing for her. The wenches that his men took after a night's ride never seemed to object. Why powder and fuss for this one who was no better than a haystack frolic?

It was decided. He would go stubble-chinned, wigless, in the plain dark brown jacket that had seen him through two days.

His mind could not refrain from throwing one or two more thoughts into the bargain—the first, a curious one, that if he were a woman, it would matter little what the man wore or how he smelled, and second, what hell it must be to be a woman, born for the worst, and early on receiving it.

In spite of his earlier resolve, he reached for the bottle and tipped it upward. He should have gone back with Ragland and Locke. He should be there this night when his fishing boats met Girard in the middle of the channel. He should be where he was needed instead of here in London, waiting out the long hours of a foolish night.

Sharply he slammed his fist against the table. What had possessed him? What was she to him to cause such a fever?

Below him on the street he heard the rattling approach of a carriage, the flat-faced hefty man—what *was* his name?—on the reins. "Bit dusty, milord," he called up. "The horses already abed, but here you are, ready and waiting."

Thomas bobbed his head in scant acknowledgement. He stood a moment longer, peering down as though into a void. The truth was, he wanted her. With desire that was pain, he wanted her. Straining against this want, he shouted down at the waiting carriage, "I'm coming."

With all due haste, with the promise of relief, he left the room and entered the darkened corridor. He took the steps running, then abruptly stopped.

He was Lord Thomas Eden. While he might feel like a rake and a schoolboy, he must cling even to the slenderest thread of what he truly was.

With that resolve he continued the rest of the way down the stairs, with dignity, trying with all his might to digest the grotesque intermixture of human agony and absurdity that was the state of manhood.

As though he were in hiding, William Pitch stood beside his magnificent escritoire of black oak and watched his salon. At two in the morning the downstairs rooms of his house were filled with ladies and gentlemen, all amorous and coquettish, stray hands and pouting lips, little better than a public house, a place for assignations.

He wondered sadly when and how it had changed. What had happened to that "nest of singing birds," the manner in which Dr. Johnson had once described a good salon? William himself remembered the London salons of two

decades back, when as a young man of twenty, fresh down
from Oxford, he had mingled in other salons of a most
rarified air: Hogarth, holding forth on a plush settee; Dr.
Johnson and his shadow, Boswell, playing off each other
in perfect concert on the discourses of Diderot and the
tasteless excesses of Rousseau; an Olympian atmosphere
wherein a young man could feel himself treading with the
gods, picking up their snippets for his own nourishment.

Now? Nothing. All dead except Boswell, the flat tip of
his inquisitive nose reddened with excess, his pursed lips
with their delightful sense of relish grown thin and blue,
his ears grown thick and clogged with the wax of age.

William stared out and around his escritoire, feeling like
a trespasser in his own house. Now he made do with fools
like young Billy Beckford there in close huddle with James
Wyatt, whose nose was beginning to resemble Boswell's,
and those blasted blueprints which Billy carried everywhere, his fabulous tower which one day soon would rise
from the Downs of Wiltshire.

A soft explosion of contempt left William's lips. Mind,
he would never enter such a tower. The shaking hands of
Wyatt could scarcely hold a glass, let alone construct a
tower.

Still in hiding, William closed his eyes and wished the
rooms of his house were empty. His feelings from earlier
in the evening were still with him. From where he stood,
just inside the drawing room, he could see clearly across
the entrance hall to the blue flounce of a gown where she
sat alone in the dining room, where she'd been alone almost the whole evening except for a few introductions
from Jane, who had dragged people back and forth, introducing them to her "beloved sister."

Apparently Marianne had shut off all facets of light
within her personality, for no one had seemed compelled
to sit and chat, and sooner or later all had drifted back into
the clogged society of the front rooms, leaving her as
alone as ever.

He longed to go to her side, to reassure her that there
was not a wit or personality in the crowded rooms worthy
of her attention, but he dared not. Their earlier and extraordinary closeness had taken a toll.

Laughter rose about him. A gentleman stumbled at the
edge of the Persian carpet. Two ladies shouted coarse jokes,

glasses in hand, as the man struggled to right himself; shrieks of laughter, a hand knocking against the sun of the Orrery, throwing it out of kilter, the ribald mirth growing, couples strolling upstairs, carnal cravings in their gestures, rakes like racehorses, getting ready for the grandest of Grand Nationals. And Jane, swirling in and between it all, the country girl turned Queen Bee, keeping her sharp eye on each new member who entered the front door.

At the height of the battle, William felt a silence close around him. The only comfort he could find anywhere was in the hem of that blue gown sitting alone in the dining room.

Annoyed, he looked up, hearing music coming from the far corner of the room, a tune by Rameau, delicate against the background of coarse laughter. He saw that a couple had opened his French music box. Several others pressed close to the music, as though in search of a dance. He saw a bewigged woman in a yellow gown bare her teeth like a vixen, as though ready to bite and snarl. She seized a gentleman roughly by the arm as though she wanted a partner for dance. The gentleman bowed low, his mouth brushing the front of her dress.

The sally was applauded by shouts and laughter from the rest of the company, which rose in volume as the lady put her arms around the gentleman in simulated affection and caressed him tenderly.

William watched. It must end. It could not go on. As a full-scale and raucous dance erupted in the drawing room, his eyes returned to the hem of the blue gown. Purity there, and honesty, twin virtues he missed terribly. And Jane, the ringleader in Judas gown passing by him with scarcely an acknowledgment of his presence, moving in a rush toward that temple of innocence, that fragment of blue hem.

Still William watched from his hiding place as Jane bent low over the seated figure as though whispering in her ear. The two women appeared finally in the arched doorway, Jane's arm protectively about Marianne's shoulders, holding the girl in fondest embrace, leading her toward the bottom of the steps.

He saw Marianne say something, a beautiful face in spite of her apparent fatigue and rejection of the evening, looking weary unto death and somewhat frightened by the bawdy shouts coming from the drawing room. She cast only a furtive glance over the "dance," her eyes, in the process, falling on William where he stood in the corner. There they stayed for a moment, a curious brief expression, almost an apology, as though she thought she had failed.

Oh, good Lord, how he longed to go to her. But he could not and took some relief in the realization that upstairs in the privacy of her room she would at least be out of harm's way. He wondered what had happened to Jane's plan. Perhaps his Lordship had found better sport. Perhaps it had never been his intention to appear.

In which case all was well. Still, as a precaution, he called up the steps after the retreating figure, "Lock your door!"

Both women swiveled around in his direction, Marianne halfway up the steps, Jane watching from the entrance hall.

"Yes, do," agreed Jane. "It's a lively gathering tonight," she added, gesturing toward the room where a minuet was being performed with all the grace and dignity of a polka.

Marianne nodded, again casting her eyes in clear discomfort over the whirling figures. William thought, "She must have worn that expression the morning of her ordeal, afraid yet defiant, as though something within her refused to recognize fear."

A moment later she disappeared down the long corridor at the top of the stairs, fairly running, or so it seemed to William, toward the fortress of her room.

Jane turned back to him, deftly adjusting her wig. "She's worn through," she said pitiably. "Not herself at all. Too much excitement for one day." She smiled tenderly. "She needs sleep, don't you agree?"

But before William could answer, and with what seemed unseemly haste, she grasped his arm, scolding lightly, "Do you mean to lurk all evening at your own salon? People are talking. Let's make our guests feel at home."

Before he could protest, she dragged him out from behind the escritoire and thrust him forward into the crowded room.

It mattered little. Marianne was safe, all guests arrived and indulging wholeheartedly in the pursuits of their mindless pleasures. The plan had obviously gone awry, thank God. As he approached his company, it was his one great hope that he would never lay eyes on Thomas Eden again.

As a female hand reached out and drew him close for the dance, he thought again of his torment and renewed his decision to leave for France within the fortnight. As the woman drew him yet closer, he threw off his inertia as if he had just awakened from a deep sleep. The girl was safe, at least for the night, no further need for him to behave like a stray hero from Rousseu's blue-befogged quill.

The woman sidled closer. He'd never seen her before in his life and would never see her again. But for now she was here and available and nameless. As she lifted a glass to his lips, he drank. Why not enjoy? It was his house, his wine and brandy. The lamplight caught her face and he saw before him a fleshy visage with damp locks of hair sticking in wisps on the brow, painted cheeks and yellowed teeth.

In spite of all, he buried his face in her neck with biting teeth, his hands covering both her breasts while behind him the company roared their approval.

In that damp darkness beneath hair and flesh, the woman's body straining toward him, he closed his eyes and thought again with old pride and new regret how much he missed Hogarth, how much Boswell and Johnson, the Olympian slopes where once Gods had tread.

Simultaneously and very skillfully playing the triple roles of hostess, coquette, and betrayer, Jane kept a sharp eye on the door. As Lord Eden himself had pointed out, timing was all.

Standing in the archway at an appropriate site for seeing the front door in one direction and the drawing room in the opposite, Jane watched with mixed feelings as William took a woman in his arms, bent her almost backward as though in the throes of uncontrollable ardor, his face hidden in her neck, the crowd laughing in obvious relief that their host had at last come out of hiding.

The smile on her face was fixed as William actually kissed the woman, clearly a kiss lacking warmth and fullness, merely a theatrical for the amusement of his guests. She had not the slightest idea what had possessed him earlier, the sullenness with which he had eaten a silent dinner, head down, an embarrassment with Marianne sitting at table with them for the first time.

Perhaps it had been wrong of her to force the girl into

their society with such rapidity. Well, it had to be done. It would have been an impossibility to arrange anything under Sarah's eagle eye. If Lord Eden's desires were to be fulfilled, the girl had to be brought out of the kitchen and placed in the greater freedom of the house.

Quickly she looked out toward the street, thinking she had heard a carriage. Nothing. The street was dark, empty. Stealthily she moved her hand to the small pocket tucked in the folds of her gown, and felt the cool substance of a key. She glanced toward the staircase, recalling William's curious warning to Marianne. "Lock your door."

Hurriedly she looked back toward the street. Where was he? Now was the perfect moment, the company laughing heartily, their attention focused on some new activity taking place on the couch, the hall and staircase deserted.

Weary from the suspense of waiting, she leaned against the wall beside the door. In the drawing room beyond, the ribald mirth increased, almost a continuous din. Then she heard something on the street, a carriage rattling to a stop. She hurried forward to open the door before he rang the bell. Peering out into the night, she saw the torches held by the linkboys, saw the coachman and at last the man himself.

He stood on the walkway, adjusting his jacket. Then he was moving up the walk and through the door, sweeping past her, a rough stubble of beard visible on his chin, his eyes rapidly assessing the empty entrance hall.

Foregoing the decency of a greeting, he looked at her as though she were merely a piece of furniture, his eyes cold, businesslike, one hand extended, his voice demanding, "The key, please, and directions."

Quickly she produced the key and handed it to him. "Up the stairs," she whispered, feeling her pulse racing. "Last chamber on the left. She's been retired for—"

But Lord Eden didn't even wait to hear. He strode across the hall as though he owned it, taking the steps two at a time, a roughness in his dress, a foul odor even, a man marching on a plan without ceremony.

She watched until he disappeared at the top of the stairs, then rushed forward as though belatedly to stop him. For the first time the realization of what shortly would transpire penetrated. No match. The girl would be run to

ground. Lord Eden had come to collect a debt, and he
would be paid.

Suffering a curious pang of regret, she turned toward
the company in the drawing room as though she were beseeching them to help. But at that moment a male voice
called gleefully for her to "come and watch."

As she glanced into the crowded room, she saw a woman standing atop the black laquered table, just slipping out
of her gown, standing with great pride before the predominantly male company in her chemise, wagers rising,
sums and odds called out on the probability of her stripping entirely, the woman herself enjoying her notoriety.

Chief among the encouragers, she saw William, sitting
on the edge of the couch, thoroughly enjoying himself. Between the certain knowledge of what was about to take
place upstairs, and the almost totally nude female preening
like a peacock on the table, Jane foundered.

She wanted, had always wanted respectability. Not this.
Well, it was beyond her now. Having set the wheels in
motion, she was powerless to stop them. On the morning
she would court respectability. On the morning she would
pick up the pieces of her sister and pack her back to North
Devon. She did not belong here, had no place here, was
certainly not Jane's responsibility. Then she would speak
to William about their evening salons. They both had their
reputations to consider.

Having thus gratified her need for respectability, she
turned her back on the staircase and the quiet corridor
beyond, and confronted the woman who had just thrown
her loosened corset to the eager, outstretched male hands.

Oh, how complicated and difficult life was sometimes.
How many complex games one had to play! How many
gambles come to nothing, she thought, and yet one must
keep going.

Fatigued and suffering a drowsy headache, yet still feeling the warmth of her sister's apparently genuine affection,
Marianne stood by the table, in the light of a single lamp,
preparing for bed.

Carefully, so as not to damage it, she slipped the blue
gown from her shoulders and placed it gently over a chair.
She gave a little smile as it occurred to her that she would
have to accustom herself to the agony of "dressing up."

Quickly she unfastened the cutting band around her breasts, reveling in the new freedom, stretching luxuriously. A sudden spasm in her back caught her breath and caused her to lean against the table in order to wait out the discomfort. In the interim one hand slipped tentatively around to her back, felt the beginning of the scars, the once torn flesh improperly rejoined.

No! That was over. She did not have the heart or desire to dwell on it further. She slipped from her chemise and stood naked, searching for her small valise, which Sarah had carried up for her that afternoon, in which she had packed her belongings, including her nightdress.

Nowhere in sight. She stood in an uneasy silence. Down below she heard the hearty laughter of the company and felt regret at her inability to take her place among them. Perhaps in time she would come to feel greater ease in society. She hoped so. Obviously it meant a great deal to Jane, and she owed Jane much.

Now there was a more immediate problem. Her brow contracted as again she searched the room for the valise. Just as she bent over the wardrobe, she stopped. Outside the door. Had she heard something? The floor cracking under the pressure of a foot? It sounded again very distinctly in her ears, but it did not seem to come from any definite direction. Instinctively she reached down and picked up the chemise where she had dropped it on the floor.

Perhaps it was Jane, belatedly realizing that she needed night garments. But at that moment the sound outside the door faded. Certainly she had imagined it, although she could measure her own pulse by the very velocity of the beating of her heart. She searched the room again in vain for her valise, then sat down on the near chair, still clasping the chemise to her with no certain knowledge of why she was alarmed.

Again! Listen! A slight sound, a tiny crack. She sat as though bound to the chair, stubbornly disputing with herself the fact of danger. After all, the door was locked. A drunken fellow, perhaps, wandering far afield of the gaiety below?

All this she was thinking when softly, unmistakably, she heard a key in the lock. She felt a flood of relief, recalling that only Jane had a key. In this frame of mind, she was on her feet as the door swung open, her mouth already forming words, then catching suddenly in her throat as the nightmare himself stood before her.

Recognition was instantaneous, as though she had expected him, the smuggler from the Masquerade, her memory of him eternalized by the hieroglyphics of the past. Quickly she moved away, placing the chair and table between them, as though those simple objects would be her sole protection.

He said nothing, but closed the door behind him, his eyes in the dim light never leaving her face.

From round about her in anguish, she heard her own voice whisper, "What do you want?" Although she expected him to reply, he didn't.

She saw in his hesitancy to approach a breach in his armor. He seemed almost shy. "Lady," he began huskily, "I—"

Again he faltered, but still he stared at her as though unable to turn his eyes away.

It seemed to her an age had elapsed since he had entered her room. Cautiously she lowered herself into the chair, afraid that sudden movement on her part would rouse him out of his stupor, remind him of his mission.

Still he stood as though in a state of suspended animation, his hands hanging limp at his sides, his breathing regular and heavy, like an awkward young man who had simply come to compete for modest favors.

She sat in the chair, still clutching the chemise to her, her voice dropping almost into dissolution as she whispered, "Sir, I do not desire your company. Please leave—"

At last he stirred, stepped toward her. "Madame, you owe me—" he pronounced, and stopped short of her by several feet, but still so close she could see the stubble of beard on his face.

The dark misery of her nightmare was borne again in her mind. She thought with sorrow of her good name, her father's ruination, the dying of something within her, the separation from all she had known and loved. Two feelings, terror and anger, wedded somewhere back again and rose crying within her. "I owe you nothing," she said, "and intend to pay nothing."

In the face of her defiance he seemed to soften, certainly not abandoning his intent, but merely postponing it for an interval of amusement. He stepped closer until there was only the table between them, his eyes making careful inventory of her bare shoulders. Incredibly, she saw him smile. "We danced well together," he said. "Remember?"

"I did not know your identity, sir," she replied, longing to rid herself of his eyes, but knowing if she looked away first all was lost.

"I think you did," he contradicted. "I think you knew precisely who I was."

"That's not true," she countered, pressing the chemise closer.

He leaned heavily across the table. "Why do you find me such disagreeable company?" he asked, almost plaintively.

Without hesitation she replied, "You cause fear, sir."

"It is not my intention," he protested. "I wish only to be obeyed."

"According to whose whims, sir?"

"My own. The only ones that matter to me."

He moved sluggishly, almost unwillingly, as though he were aware of the defeat of words. He stepped back from the table, assessing the small room and her presence in it.

She turned in the chair, very stealthily, the better to secure the protection of the chemise.

At the faint movement he turned on her and asked in a quite normal voice, as though he genuinely wanted to know. "Are you happy here?"

"I have no choice," she said.

"Don't you miss your home?"

"Very much."

"Then why don't you return?"

"There are those who think it best that I stay here."

He looked at her intently, a peculiar strength on his face. Then he was moving toward her as though angry at the words, at the postponement of his desire.

Before she could protest or move away, he lifted her roughly to her feet and kissed her with disproportionate strength, as though she were a male of equal power to his who had to be subdued. In the crush of his arms, her fear vaulted. Rage howled within her as she tried to free her hands. She prayed quickly and felt herself little more than a shadow. When the crude embrace ended, she pulled forcibly away, transfigured by her terror, her fate clearly before her. There was no escape, for he blocked her passage to the door. A scream against the din coming from below would be useless. Run to ground at last, she turned her back on him, doubled up, and collapsed to her knees. She felt already dead, aware of the silence coming from behind her. Yet she knew that it would soon be over, that he would lift her up and have his way, and that if there was any life left in her she would be obliged to snuff it out, for she could not live with herself and the weight of memory and sensation.

Then she heard running from outside the hall, heard voices shouting, a terrible commotion. Bent over on herself, her head down, she heard the door pushed violently open. What she heard then sounded like a single volley of thunder in her ears, a resounding explosion that shattered glass somewhere. She held to her knees, her face hidden. She wanted darkness in her mind, to throw a shadow over what she was powerless to alter. If this was the last reckoning, she wanted no part of it.

Behind her and over the din of approaching voices she heard a man give a terse, sharp order. "Get her out of here." She felt something being dropped over her back, a thin coverlet of some sort, heard a woman's voice inquire, "Can you stand? You must! Hurry!"

She thought it a curious question. Of course she could stand. But once up, she felt her knees buckling and would have fallen altogether had it not been for the strong support of arms about her shoulders. "Please, Marianne, you must," the woman urged again. Was it Jane? She couldn't tell. Her only choice was to obey the support of arms and face whatever calamity had occurred in the room behind her.

Erect, she looked back at the tableau, Thomas Eden lying on the floor a few feet away, motionless, sprawled on his back, his legs in the curious position of a man running, a dark pool growing and spreading beneath his shoulder, the material of his coat torn away and still smoldering.

Marianne could not relinquish the sight. Her mind and reason urged her to turn away, but still she stared.

Then the man's voice again, clearly angry this time, "Get her out of here!"

As they hurried out the door, she caught only a brief

glimpse of William. She saw his eyes but at first did not recognize him. In the hurried passage she saw the pistol still in his hand, smelled the burning powder, his hand grasping it as though at the first provocation he intended to use it again.

Outside in the hall they encountered a very white-faced Sarah in her nightcap. Behind her, just coming up the stairs, were the guests, their faces flustered with excitement at the sound of the shot, mauling and pushing, still chattering as though on their way to a new diversion.

Sarah whispered almost hysterically, "I couldn't turn them back, Miss Locke. I tried, but I—"

Quickly Marianne felt herself being passed from hand to hand. As Jane relinquished her support, Sarah took it up. "Take her to the room at the end of the hall," Jane hissed. "Stay with her and lock the door."

They were moving again, Sarah urging her to "Come along. It's all well now."

A foolish sentiment, Marianne thought, wishing only that she could still her body, the spasms increasing, causing her teeth to knock together.

In front of the specified door, Sarah stopped only long enough to jerk it open, then fairly pushed Marianne inside. Quickly she bolted it behind them, and in the darkness guided Marianne to a bed, a bare feather mattress without covering.

In spite of all attempts to control herself, Marianne was emitting little choking sobs, not weeping, for there were no tears, but just the spasms again, inhibiting her breathing.

"Be still," Sarah soothed.

How Marianne wished she might have obliged. She heard a woman's cry, heard the scuffling of a thousand feet, heard repeated shouts for "Physician!" In close concert with what reached her ears was the memory, the image of the man lying bleeding, William still clutching the pistol.

Sarah left her side only once, long enough to light a lamp, then she dragged a heavy chair into position in front of the door. The voices from down the hall persisted, turmoil beyond the human capacity to endure. Sarah bent over and pulled the coverlet into place. The spasms were ever increasing, Marianne's tongue growing thick, her temples throbbing. She was unable to control any part of her body, and as the palsy increased, Sarah hoisted herself up on the edge of the bed and pressed her hands against Marianne's shoulders in an attempt to hold her steady on the bed.

In her final moments of consciousness, Marianne saw that the woman's eyes were streaming with tears. But because of the wrinkles, they couldn't flow down. They spread out, crisscrossed, and formed a smooth gloss on the worn face.

"Try to breathe deeply," Sarah begged.

It was a foolish request, for at that moment Marianne discovered that she couldn't breathe at all. Something was crushing her, and almost blithely she lost consciousness, seeing the last scene in her mind, the light clouds over the North Devon coast, the fresh, life-giving sea air.

Then she saw nothing.

It was difficult for William to say precisely when he knew that his house had been invaded. At the moment that Marianne had been sent up to bed, he had dared to relax, had joined his fellows in the frivolity of the evening.

Then he caught sight of Jane standing in the archway of the drawing room, her attention splintered between the room itself and the staircase. He thought how kind of her, how attractive this new sisterly concern. A while later the woman on the lacquered table removed her chemise, and in the moment of admiring silence he thought he heard a distant outcry.

Something happened. What? An instinct, although he was not a man given to following his instincts. Whatever, he felt a compulsion to move, seeing something else in Jane's face, a pathetic figure, still cowering in the archway, her eyes frightened as she scanned the staircase and beyond. Then he knew that a plan had been constructed and was being carried out.

He ran, ascending the steps as though they were a mountain to be scaled, feeling so certain of the tragedy that he stopped off first in his room, his hand reaching almost disdainfully for the pistol, cocking it even as he overtook the hall. He burst through the door and took one clear look, his eyes confirming the worst, the girl, humiliated and terrified on her knees, her head bowed, the man just stepping toward her, his face peculiarly grim for an amorous encounter.

He lifted the pistol, saw Eden's furtive glance in his direction, then he saw nothing else, felt nothing except the pressure of his finger on the trigger, his eyes almost closed against the thunderous explosion, his fury not even abated as he saw the man spin about under the impact of the shot, coming down on the table with all his weight, his eyes wide open, staring where the lamp fluttered. Then he fell backward onto the floor, motionless, blood spreading from where the ball had heavily grazed the flesh of his shoulder and shattered the pier glass beyond. Fired at such close range, the shot had seared through the flesh and left it smoldering.

He had not intended to shoot, yet there was the man sprawled on the floor, bleeding. And there, Marianne, still on her knees, her scarred back clearly visible, more terrible than he had ever imagined.

As he started toward her to offer comfort, Jane arrived white-faced, looking truly repentant. "Cover her," he ordered, stepping back. "And get her out of here."

The girl was scarcely able to stand, but with Jane's support she managed. She took one horrified look at the man lying unconscious at her feet. No sooner had they left the room than the company arrived, laughing and chattering at first, then falling into a shocked silence at the sight of the man bleeding on the floor.

A physician arrived in good haste and stopped the flow of blood and suggested that prior to surgery it would be best to move Lord Eden to his own lodgings. A few of the company obliged. Together with the watchmen, who had come running at the sound of the shot, they carried him down the stairs and out into the night. There was talk of a duel, illegal in the absence of seconds. But William put a stop to that. With admirable control he informed both the watchmen and the company that the man was a trespasser, that the victim of his illegal advances lay in the room beyond if they cared to look.

No one did, although from the mutterings around him he could tell that their sympathies were with the wounded man. As he was trying to clear his house of all traffic, he heard, coming from the end of the hall, a woman's cry for help. Quickly he called down the stairs for the physician, a heavyset man in a black coat who viewed the goings-on with comforting objectivity. As they rushed to the small room at the end of the hall, he was aware of the man panting heavily. Inside the door, he leaned against the wall for breath. Then, seeing the girl on the bed, her tongue slung sideways, he rushed into action, compressed her tongue and administered three sharp blows to her face. He lifted her head and forced a dram down her throat.

"A seizure," was the physician's diagnosis.

"Annihilation of a soul," thought William.

"Cold compresses throughout the night," was the physician's prescription.

"A place of refuge and peace," was William's.

Jane and Sarah stayed with her while William saw the physician out, treading carefully over the stream of blood on the stairs. From the front door he saw Billy Beckford just climbing into the carriage after Lord Eden, who appeared to be sitting up now. Other carriages were rapidly departing, the evening over, the company requiring a few hours' sleep so that on the morning their tongues could wag.

William closed his door and locked it, extinguished all lamps and candles, and went into his study off the drawing room to sit through the night, what was left of it. It was almost dawn. He stared at the blackness ribbed with faint light. Slowly he lowered his head into his hands as though bodily to contain and support the agitation of his brain.

It would be all over London by twelve noon, the coffee-houses and steakhouses buzzing with the excitement of a major scandal, the story itself undergoing a thousand changes in the telling, emerging by nightfall more fiction than fact.

He groaned, dragged back to his involvement, his irrationality which had triggered the whole melancholy evening. He sat in a fixed stillness, obliterated, as a drop of water is made anonymous by the pond into which it has fallen. My God, the scene had been a farce, a theatrical worthy of the Drury Lane, to be followed by a pantomime. "No oranges on the spikes, please. The actors did their best."

Unable to lift his gaze from the spreading light of dawn at his feet, and unable to turn away from the spreading light in his mind, he reared back, his legs slanting as though to brace himself from a fall.

Marianne. Always Marianne. There his thoughts commenced and ended. Then he must leave. It was as simple as that. He must on the morrow, in spite of wagging tongues, put his affairs in order, delegate authority at his office so that the *Gazetteer* would continue in spite of his absence, see his solicitor for liquidation of certain assets, leave a household account for the care and protection of Jane and Marianne. Then, within a fortnight, he would book passage on the packet from Dover to Calais, and hope to recover from his madness in the madness that now was France. He would send editorials back by courier. At least he would keep his hand in.

In the suffused light of dawn, he stared at his hands. They were like ghosts in the semidarkness of the room, not belonging to him at all. That finger capable of pulling a trigger? Never!

Softly into the silence, coming from upstairs, he heard a faint moan.

He bowed his head and whispered hoarsely, "Leave me in peace. . . ."

It seemed inconceivable to Thomas that a single ball wildly fired and grazing the fleshy part of his right shoulder should cause such agony.

Yet there was the truth of it. He'd never experienced such pain, his shoulder, his arm, indeed the right side of his entire body feeling as though it were aflame, someone holding a torch to him.

Although he had not lost consciousness before in his entire life, on this night he passed senseless three times and was always brought back to new pain by Billy Beckford bending over him, forcing brandy down him while the old surgeon, a thin sharp zealot of a man with hands as cold as winter, continued to cauterize the wound, his fingers red with Thomas's blood.

At dawn, lying on his bed in the upper chamber of his lodgings on Oxford Road, he awakened for the third time, bleary-eyed, still half-conscious, and tried to raise his head. His throat felt dry, his ears rang, yet he was aware enough to see that in his absence from the living someone had stripped him and now he lay, in full view of the company in the room, Billy and the thin-eyed surgeon and there in the corner, two old women he'd never seen before, their eyes glittering with all that there was to see.

"Get them out of here," he mumbled, his misery rising, sinking back into the pillows, which were drenched with his sweat. Billy was there again, his face creased with concern, offering more brandy and whispered advice. "You must lie still, Thomas. Let the surgeon finish."

"And when will that be?" Thomas whispered. "I can take little more."

The surgeon looked up from his work. "Only the dressing remains, Lord Eden," he said, his voice as thin and hard as his fingers. "But you must lie still." Again he felt hands upon him, felt his shoulder being encased in bandage, up and under, an endless wrapping, drawing his arm tighter and tighter to his body.

With his eyes closed, Thomas felt compelled to ask, "Is it serious?"

Billy was there again, good lad, soothing him. "It might have been, Thomas. It tore the flesh. You've lost a great deal of blood. But the bone is intact and you should be as good as new."

Still not looking, Thomas felt two heavy objects being wedged against his shoulder. He looked down, his vision blurred. "What in hell—"

"Sandbags," the surgeon explained crisply, "to hold you rigid."

"Do I have a choice?" Thomas said sulkily.

"No," the man replied, his voice without margin, wiping his hands on the already bloodied sheet.

Thomas looked weakly about. His bed resembled a butcher's floor. "Cleanse me," he whispered weakly. "It's barbaric to ask a man to lie in his own blood."

Billy made a motion toward the door, then hesitated. Apologetically he whispered, "I must recall the women, Thomas. They were here for that—"

"Then call them," Thomas snapped. He moaned, "Oh, my God."

For the next few minutes he shut his eyes to the indignity, the disgrace, of feeling his body handled like a sack of potatoes. Billy and the surgeon lifted him unceremoniously into the air while the old women stripped off the linens and replaced them with fresh ones. The drastic movement caused fresh agony. He felt his eyes fill with tears as the throbbing in his arm erupted into a drumbeat.

Never in his life had he suffered so. He longed for Rag-

land, and old Dolly Wisdom. And for one crumbling moment he wanted his mother, more than life itself, that stern
handsome visage whom he had scarcely known.

Finally the change was completed, the bed clean. He felt
the surgeon return the sandbags to his shoulder, anchoring
him, pinning him like a specimen. Thomas decided that he
despised the man, despised all of them for humbling him.
Only Billy had the kind sense to whisper thoughtfully, "Are
you better now, Thomas? More comfortable?" During this
inquiry Thomas felt his cool hand on his brow.

Weakly he reached up and grasped Billy by the wrist.
"Don't leave me," he whispered. "Sit with me. Please."

Billy assured him that he had no intention of leaving,
but he would stay with him as long as he desired. Thus
reassured, Thomas lay back on the fresh pillow and
listened halfheartedly to the continuous murmurs in the
room.

Eventually the chamber cleared. He heard the surgeon
giving last-minute advice to Billy. Beyond the heavy drapes
he saw the first crack of dawn. The night was over, a
senseless, futile night.

Looking up, he saw Billy sink into a chair close beside
the bed. It occurred to him that the thoughtful thing would
be to dismiss him, send him to his lodgings for a respite
of sleep. But he couldn't bring himself to do that. He
wanted company, and with an obstinate egoism he ignored
Billy's fatigue and turned his head restlessly on the pillow
as though in the throes of fresh agony.

Billy's reaction was gratifying. Quickly he leaned forward and reached for the mug of brandy on the table.
"Drink, Thomas," he urged. "The surgeon recommended
a high state of intoxication for three days."

"Damn the surgeon," Thomas muttered. "All the brandy
in the world won't—" He closed his eyes unhappily. It
felt as though the sandbags were digging into the fresh
wound. He longed to shift his position but could not. "Oh,
my God," he moaned aloud, his head tossing restlessly,
his hand clutching at air.

As though to distract him, Billy leaned forward and
clutched at the wobbling hand. "Thomas," he began softly,
"will there be a redress of grievances? It's your right, you
know. You were fired upon without provocation."

The suggestion entered Thomas's mind very stealthily. Redress of grievances had not occurred to him. He thought again of William Pitch's unexpected appearance in the room. Redress of grievances? Not likely. Instead of building towers, Billy should acquaint himself with the law. He, Thomas, had been the trespasser, the girl naked and weeping before him. Unfortunately, there now were laws to protect the likes of her.

Weakly he muttered, "No redress, Billy. One shot is quite enough."

"But you have cause."

"I have no cause, no legitimate one." He looked almost accusingly at Billy. "I wish you had warned me about Pitch."

Billy sank back in the chair, shaking his head. "He's never done—it was so totally out of character—everyone said that he—" Incoherent and clearly puzzled by the irrational act of William Pitch, Billy could do little more than shake his head.

Thomas watched from the confines of his pillow, his eyes heavy, but his mind still alert. It wasn't William Pitch that confounded him. An idiot could determine the cause of his wrathful act. It was the girl. But he didn't want to think about it. Still, regretfully he smiled. "I lost more than blood this night, Billy."

Billy looked up. "I don't understand."

"The wagers at White's. What did they amount to?"

Billy had to think. Vaguely he shook his head. "Several thousand guineas. I have the notes."

"Then I shall have to pay off and take their jeers as well."

Slowly the confession dawned on Billy. "You mean, you never—"

Thomas shook his head.

Clearly Billy was surprised. But after a moment he touched his chin, stretching his throat muscles. "Consider yourself fortunate, Thomas. She's probably diseased."

"No!" The rebuttal was swift and strong. With his eyes closed, Thomas saw the white untouched skin, the expression in her eyes which bespoke complete inexperience. "No," he added more softly. "She's never been touched."

Billy seemed to digest this information. Then, still puzzled, he leaned forward. "May I ask, Thomas, why this particular one?"

"I have no affection for her," Thomas said defensively. "She owed me, owes me still."

A look of shock spread across Billy's face. "And will you try to collect again?"

Thomas thought on this, then murmured, "No." Peculiarly, he felt himself on the verge of tears, felt womanlike. "I was defeated by words, Billy," he said. Abruptly he broke off, unable even to give voice to the one sight which had literally unsexed him, the girl ultimately confronting him with his own handiwork, reminding him that his present small agony was but a trifle compared to her map of torn flesh.

Apparently Billy saw his distress. "Put her out of your mind, Thomas. As soon as you are able to travel, I'll take you home where you belong. We'll stop at Fonthill on the way, and I'll show you the site of my new tower." He took Thomas' hand. "A man must pin his hope to the light of heaven, Thomas. Appetites are whimsical and easily satisfied. A man must give himself to higher causes."

Thomas listened to the rational discourse, somewhat irrationally delivered. Billy's eyes glittered with the light of a fanatic. Feeling totally the invalid, Thomas whispered, "I place myself in your hands, Billy. For the first time in our long relationship, you must take the lead."

It was a gift weakly given but heartily received. Billy began to lavish little attentions on him. As he lifted the brandy again, Thomas protested, "No more. It does no good anyway." When Billy inquired earnestly as to the nature of his pleasure, Thomas thought for a moment, then replied, weakly, "A beefsteak, the smoking, juicy kind we get at Child's."

Billy smiled. "And a flagon of their warm white wine with aromatic spices and pepper and cinnamon?"

Thomas nodded. "And a round of their good cheddar would be nice."

"And a Bath cake?" Billy contributed, "with burnt sugar and almonds?"

The fare planned, the gloom over, Billy left his chair, his own appetite apparently fanned by the description of the banquet. "Then sleep now, Thomas," he urged. "I shall return at one, ladened. We shall feast together and talk of nothing but the future. I am your servant," he added, bowing elegantly from the door.

In spite of his discomfort, Thomas smiled. He *was* hungry and an appetite was a good sign, the body mending itself. "Send the hags away," Thomas called weakly, spying through the opened door the two old women still hovering about. "And tell the others I wish to be disturbed by no one except yourself."

Billy beamed, as though he had only just realized a lifelong ambition, the respect and devotion of Thomas Eden.

Thomas found extreme gratification in such a look and regretted the shabby treatment he'd once given the young man. "One thing more, Billy," he whispered. "Forgive me."

Puzzled, Billy turned back. "For what, Thomas?"

Grave feelings rose within him, a little effusion of love, a new awareness of what had happened this night, the sharp recall of a small, white, scarred, back. "For—everything," Thomas said, and at the last minute, turned his face to the wall.

He heard the door close softly, heard a whispered dismissal as Billy sent the old women on their way, then heard nothing.

A full morning sun was penetrating the crack in the heavy drapes. With his good hand he wiped the embarrassing moisture from his eyes and tried to study the bandages which encased his right shoulder and half his chest. Where the ball had grazed him, he saw a small coin of spreading red.

What were the words she had spoken to him? "You cause fear, sir."

Thomas lay motionless. He might have taken her so easily had he not been duped into words. Yet in a way perhaps her words had saved his life, for if he'd fallen upon her immediately, he would have taken William Pitch's ball in his back and he would not be here now, lying abed in misery.

Not once had the terror in her eyes abated. Yet she had clung to that thin chemise as though it had been the shield of David. And once again she had defeated him.

Restlessly he turned. A pain as from the digging point of

a sharp knife cut down across his shoulder. His head pressed backward into his pillow.

Tears again. His heart ached as his shoulder ached. As he stared into the mist before him, it seemed to him as if the countenance of his Destiny was smiling at him enigmatically and coldly. . . .

Child's, and White's, and MacFarlandes', and every chophouse and coffeehouse between Tower Hill and Hyde Park Corner was abuzz with the excitement which had transpired the night before in the remote rural area of Bloomsbury.

Citizens, genteel and well-bred, devoured the scraps of gossip, then eagerly invented more. On a dull hot June morning, the gallantry usually associated with truth seemed scarcely worth pursuing.

First Citizen: *Two* naked ladies, you say?

Second Citizen: 'Tis what I heard. One stripping willingly in William Pitch's Chinese drawing room. The other stripped unwillingly in Pitch's upstairs bedroom.

First Citizen: Strange connections for Lord Eden. For a man of intelligence, why did he not take the one who stripped willingly?

Second Citizen: My sources tell me a wager had been made.

First Citizen: Foolish business. A gentleman ought never to wager on a woman's floodgates. Who was the lady?

Second Citizen: No lady, sir. A local from Eden Point. As I understand it, Lord Eden had had her publicly whipped within the year.

First Citizen: I do not approve of Public Whippings.

Second Citizen: Nor do I. But it is my understanding that she did him a grievous wrong.

First Citizen: How so?

Second Citizen: She bit him with her teeth, or so I've heard. In a most unfortunate place. Almost took his manhood.

Third Citizen: It was reported to me that she has supernatural powers and has cast a spell over his Lordship.

First Citizen: Nonsense! No such thing is possible. Not in this day and age. And what, pray tell, is William Pitch's interest in the sordid little affair?

Third Citizen: He wants the temptress for himself.

First Citizen: And what of the common woman who keeps his house?

Second Citizen: She's well-stretched by now. He hungers for a virgin.

Fourth Citizen: A common woe. After five children, my wife is like a bucket. I scarcely know when I've entered or departed. And what of the shot? Is Lord Eden mortally wounded?

Second Citizen: His pride, I daresay. They tell me he was lifeless and bleeding profusely as they carried him out.

First Citizen: Scandalous business. These are licentious times. What a price to pay for a cheap diversion!

Second Citizen: And there's the rub. There was no diversion, according to my sources. Lord Eden left as full as he came, save for his spilling blood. His seed is still clogged and intact.

First Citizen: Beyond reason. An indelicate business. Shall we buy the *Gazetteer* and see what Pitch has to say?

Second Citizen: There will be no word from him today. I understand that in his mortification he attempted suicide, turned the pistol on himself, and would have succeeded had it not been for the watchman's quick hand.

First Citizen: There's more to this than meets the eye. Will there be a redress of grievances? Eden has that right, doesn't he?

Second Citizen: 'Tis rumored he will call William Pitch forward unless the German king intercedes.

Third Citizen: Madness interceding in the name of madness? What topsy-turvy times! I miss the Stuarts. No public spirit, less national principle.

First Citizen: A bold and rash way of talking.

Second Citizen: We live in bold and rash times when a peer of the realm is fired upon without provocation by a common scribbler.

Third Citizen: Pitch is more—

First Citizen: Not last evening he wasn't. With the slightest of pressures on his trigger finger, he obliterated his right to the company of decent men. As for the common wench, she should be publicly whipped again on Tyburn Hill.

Second Citizen: 'Tis rumored that she is fair.

First Citizen: Fairness is not the issue. She has dragged down two good men and for that she should be justly punished.

Third Citizen: I heard that the crowd was drunken and that orgies were in progress in every room.

Second Citizen: Ladies celestial and ladies terrestrial.

First Citizen: On their backs, they are all the same. Still, I believe the scandal will be weighed in the balance and found light.

Third Citizen: I think not. When the great names of England are involved, Eden, Beckford, Wyatt, it speaks of deep moral decay. A lamentable story.

First Citizen: *Two* ladies stripped naked, you say?

Second Citizen: Aye, two. One stripped willingly in Pitch's Chinese drawing room, and the other stripped unwillingly in his upper—

In Child's, and White's, and MacFarlandes', from Tower Hill to Hyde Park Corner, it was a glorious day.

Three weeks after the attempted assault, Marianne was still abed, suffering from a mysterious malady that eluded the old physician. She was pale and listless, had no appetite, and seemed to endure a constant fever.

There were no visitors to her room save Sarah, and that good woman crept up the stairs at every opportunity to sit with her and read to her, comfort her in any way possible. William and Jane stayed away.

In such isolation, Marianne had more than enough time to relive the events of that horrible evening. She knew that Lord Eden could not have gained access to her room without help. Someone had betrayed her. Having immediately and easily eliminated William and Sarah, that left Jane. The thought of the betrayal was such pain to her that she could scarcely bear it.

One afternoon in July as Sarah was reading to her from Mr. Shakespeare's sonnets, a soft knock came at the door. Thinking that it was the physician, come on his daily visit, Sarah called out immediately, "Come in."

To Marianne's surprise, Jane appeared, a very different Jane, one she had never seen before. Her head was unwigged, revealing her natural dark hair, streaked with gray. Her dress was mussed as though she had recently slept in it, her face unrouged. In her trembling hands was a mauled handkerchief, twisted hopelessly out of shape.

Sarah stepped back, apparently as shocked by the appearance as Marianne. "Miss Locke," she murmured. "If you'll excuse me, I—"

But Jane would not excuse her and lightly touched her on the arm, her voice hardly audible. "No, Sarah, stay," she begged. "I have to speak to Marianne and I want you to hear what I'm going to say."

On guard, Marianne tried to raise herself up from her pillows. Weakened from her time in bed, she felt herself beginning to tremble, the old seizures returning. Propped up, she watched, bewildered, as Jane commenced walking slowly about the room, her head still down, her fingers twisting in and out of the handkerchief. Twice she stopped and looked at Marianne as though she were about to speak, and twice she looked away, as though lacking words.

Finally she took up a position at the foot of the bed, her face pitifully naked in a direct ray of hot July sun, revealing new lines, as though she had recently undergone some unspeakable crucible.

"This isn't easy," she began at last, then faltered and stopped, her voice catching, as though tears were close to the surface. She lifted her head and drew a deep shuddering breath, then tried again. "Marianne, I want you to know that—" She grasped the foot of the bed. For a moment Marianne feared that she would collapse. "I want you to know," she went on, "that Lord Eden, that—I—am responsible for—what happened."

Out of the corner of her eye, Marianne saw Sarah look away, as though embarrassed. Clearly it was a confession, and while Marianne had no appetite for the details, still she was curious. "Go on," she invited.

Still not looking at her, Jane commenced to speak, in the manner now of a person who wanted to get it over with. "He contacted me after the Masquerade," she whispered. "He did not state his business at the time and I thought, what harm? It was only on our second meeting that he—" Again she stumbled over the words, her eyes closed, as though she didn't want to see. "—that he made his proposal." She turned rapidly away to the window and stared down on the pavement below. "Of course I said no. I told him I would have no part in it. You believe me, don't you?"

For the first time she looked directly at Marianne, her eyes pleading. "Go on," Marianne urged, withholding her belief.

"He threatened me," Jane said, shaking her head as though even now incapable of believing it. "He threatened all of us, said he would see to it that harm befell our father and our brother." Her voice was rising, her manner quite agitated as she paced in small uneven steps between the foot of the bed and the window. "When I continued to say no, he threatened William, said he would bring ruination down upon him." Suddenly she cried out, "My God, what was I to do?" Then came tears, endless tears, the woman herself slumped against the windowsill, her shoulders heaving with the weight of the ordeal and her confession.

From the bed, Marianne watched it all. It had never occurred to her that Lord Eden had practiced intimidation. Yet she knew that it was certainly in character. She looked back toward the window and the miserable woman weeping. Poor Jane. What hell she must have gone through.

In spite of the deluge of tears, Jane now managed a final word. "I tried to—stop him that night," she sobbed. "I tried to—turn him back, but—"

She sank even lower until she was on her knees as though at prayer, a most painful confession, the woman defeated by it.

Marianne continued to stare, moved in spite of herself. She heard Sarah weeping in sympathy. Of course Lord Eden had intimidated her, and worse, threatened William. Why had she not seen it?

Softly she left the bed and went to the window. She knelt beside the weeping Jane and lifted her tear-streaked face. "I believe you," she whispered. "You had no choice." Lovingly she wiped the tears with the hem of her nightdress, her eyes soothing.

The simple act was almost more than Jane could bear. She fell forward into Marianne's arms and Marianne returned the embrace, the two sisters clinging together, Sarah weeping openly at the door.

The reunion was sweet and genuine, both girls hugging and crying, promising each other lasting trust and devotion. As they helped each other to their feet, Jane asked a searching and peculiar question. "Do you—forgive me, Marianne?"

According to her story, there was nothing to forgive. Still Marianne said, "Yes, of course, I forgive you," and again they fell into each other's arms, Marianne feeling at ease and free from pain for the first time in three weeks.

As Jane helped her back to her bed, Sarah suggested tea for all. The two sisters agreed. In fact Marianne felt hungry and said as much and Jane asked Sarah to bring tea and cakes and sandwiches as well.

After Sarah had left the room, Jane arranged the pillows, then sat close beside Marianne on the bed. "It's been such a dreadful time," she mourned.

Marianne agreed. "But now it's over," she said with a smile.

Jane nodded, blissfully, and took her hand and held it as though she intended never to let go.

The weather grew becalmed and sluggish with late summer heat, and the packets were unable to navigate the channel until early September.

On three occasions William said his good-byes and took off eagerly on horseback. On three occasions he was forced to return and pass the days in isolation, moving between two fixed points, his study and his office, as if he were playing only the two important notes of an octave, the low and high.

His salon was closed, had been closed since late June, the distorted stories still flourishing in the summer heat. As for his house, he usually took his meals alone in the study. He'd not seen Marianne to speak to her since that night.

She'd been ill, a curious illness of spirit. Sarah had been in constant attendance, as had Jane. Now she had recuperated and for the first time was up and about.

From the window of his study he watched the two sisters and marveled at the transformation of both. They were

tending the garden, as now they tended everything together. Marianne was still pale, bending gracefully in a
simple yellow gown, the color of her hair, and Jane,
darker, taller, followed after her protectively. He shook
his head, amazed. He felt like a huge animal, watching
them, and while he was pleased with their reconciliation,
he still was bewildered.

He felt pleased for them, Sarah the watchdog, keeping
both of them safe from the wagging tongues of London,
turning away all visitors. Yet, standing in his study, peering out at them through the window on this brisk bright
September morning, he'd never felt so isolated.

He found he could no longer watch them in the garden.
It was time to leave anyway. The wind had risen with the
promise of winter and would stay risen. Within the week
the packets at Dover would move again. His affairs were
in order, had been in order since mid-July. He'd even said
his good-byes three times before and wondered if he should
say them again or simply leave. His packed valises were at
his feet, his horse saddled and ready.

He longed for his first glimpse of the sea, the wind
filling the sails and blowing him away from the emotions
of the last few months. In truth, he had never known such
inner turmoil, his futile attempts at first to set the story
straight, the anxious moments immediately following the
incident as he had waited to see if Lord Eden would demand a redress of grievances. He hadn't, and now, or so
William had heard, he was languishing melodramatically
at Billy Beckford's Wiltshire estate, on his way back to
Eden Point where William fervently prayed he would stay.
For the rest of it, William had passed the days between
two tortures, the repentant woman that he could share,
and the distant ill one that he couldn't.

Off then! No need to say anything. Quickly he reached
for his valises and started toward the door. As bad luck
would have it, Sarah was just emerging from the dining
room, feather duster in hand. She looked at him as though
he were an interloper. Then, spying the valises in his hand,
her normally suspicious face softened.

"Is it to be today, Mr. Pitch?" she asked kindly, standing back a step. "And you not even saying good-bye?"

He nodded. "I've said it so many times before, Sarah."
He smiled. "It seemed useless."

She shook her head. "Wouldn't be right or proper just to leave without our knowing."

Reprimanded, he placed the valises on the floor and went through the entire ordeal again, speaking like an actor from a memorized playscript. "All is in order, Sarah, as I've said before. The household money will come once a month. It won't be much but it should provide adequately for the three of you. I've asked the watchmen to walk here nightly, and all trade accounts will remain opened and in my name."

She nodded to what she already knew. Under the awkward pressure of the moment, he deviated a bit. "I'm very grateful to you, Sarah, for remaining in my house. I know it has not always been easy or pleasant, but your continuing service is greatly appreciated."

She blushed and ducked her head. "I stayed because I wanted to, Mr. Pitch, because I felt I was needed."

"As you were and are."

The personal sentiments seemed to embarrass her. "We'll be just fine, Mr. Pitch," she said. "Look to yourself. It's not a safe world, particularly where you're going."

He laughed softly. "It may be safer than London."

She seemed to agree, the unspoken knowledge of past events passing between them. He tried to change the subject as well as the mood. "I'll be back by Christmas, I promise. If not then, at least by Twelfth-Day, and I shall expect to be greeted by one of your finest sugar cakes."

Again she blushed. Eager to be off, he asked quietly, "Would you please send Jane to me?"

The woman curtsied and turned immediately, as though grateful to be released by him. Briefly he pondered in the abstract on the mysteries of womanhood. Certainly less selfish than the male of the species, they still required a great effort of understanding. Now he felt oddly weary of that effort, and longed for a period of simple, safe, male companionship.

Deep in his own musing, he failed to hear Jane's approach and was aware of her only when she spoke.

"So! You are really abandoning us today," she said, appearing in the doorway.

"Not abandoning you, Jane," he replied, regretful that

over the weeks she'd not come to an acceptance of his leaving. "You'll be well provided for."

She seemed to be holding herself very rigid. "I don't understand, William," she said. "I should think that past events would have demonstrated that we need more than bread on the table. We need your protection."

He found this melodramatic and smiled tolerantly. "I daresay there's not a threat in London that you and Sarah can't handle. You are strong women."

This she protested. "Not strong. Not me, at any rate."

She looked so miserable that he lightly put his arms around her, drawing her close. The affectionate gesture had a disastrous effect. She flung her arms around his neck. "Why must you go?" she said, weeping. "What am I to do?"

He tried to hold her tenderly, all the while making his voice stern. "You'll wait for me," he soothed. "You will run my house and look after your sister, and keep yourself for me alone, and at Christmas I'll bring you a French bonnet."

Still she clung to him, her arms tightly enfolded about his neck. He found the scene touching but embarrassing. "Jane, please," he begged. "I must go. Don't make it any more difficult."

On hearing those words, she relaxed her grip on him, her face stained with tears. She looked quite pathetic as she murmured, "How have I displeased you?"

"You haven't displeased me," he assured her.

"You've not come to my bed in weeks."

He lowered his head, embarrassment rising. "You were always occupied with Marianne."

"Not always. I did her an injustice."

"So you did."

"But it's past now. She trusts me."

"I know, and I'm happy for you."

"But I had not expected to gain her love, and lose yours."

"You've lost nothing, dearest," he soothed.

"Then why are you leaving?"

It seemed a round-robin, a subject with no beginning, no end. Instead of attempting to answer her, he merely smiled and said, "Take care of everything, and most of all, yourself."

Apparently, seeing him reach for his valises and knowing there was nothing she could do to stop him, her misery vaulted. She took one last look at him, then ran sobbing up to her room where he heard the door close and lock.

He stared after her, his face still damp with her tears. He knew what he should do. But instead he quietly picked up his valises, took a final and tortured look about the appointments and beauty of his home. He shook his head. He's worked so hard and he was turning his back on everything.

At the curb, he saw his horse saddled and standing patiently. Then he saw more, saw the quick movement of the yellow gown. Apparently she had slipped out of the garden gate. She looked up at him. He heard nothing but the rapid movement of his heart. Even the sight of her did damage, her hair and gown blending in the blaze of golden sunlight, enchanting.

He moved slowly down the walkway, never lifting his eyes from hers. Nor did she lift her eyes from him. She still looked pale from her illness, the hollow circles about her eyes merely accenting their deep blueness, their terrible earnestness.

Against such weapons he had no choice but to adopt a stern visage. As he drew near his horse and threw the valises over the saddle, he averted his eyes. "I'm happy to see you well," he said with great formality.

She stepped back as he adjusted the heavy straps, anchoring his luggage. "Sarah said you were leaving," she commented, a simple sentence requiring no response. And he gave none.

He tugged twice at the strap, adjusting it beyond the point of necessity, indulging in countless small gestures, trying to keep his mind and hands busy and averted from her presence. When all gestures were no longer creditable, he turned at last, still clinging to the saddle, and found himself impaled on her eyes.

She looked up, assessing the sky. "There should be a good sailing wind at Dover," she said. "My father used to say that a high blue sky always brought promising winds."

"I earnestly hope so," he replied. "I don't think I could return so unceremoniously a fourth time."

She laughed softly. "I'm sorry to admit I didn't even know you had left before."

"You were ill."

She lowered her head, seemed to be suffering a moment's self-consciousness. He lamented the stiffness of this their last meeting. Still, something howled within him. In spite of his powerful efforts to discipline his mind, he saw her again, cringing in darkness, on her knees before her tormentor. He stepped forward as though to summon her attention. "You will be safe," he said firmly. "I've told both Sarah and Jane that no one is to enter the house after dark. The watchmen have been alerted. You are never to go out unescorted. Is that clear? It is my preference that you never go out at all. Jane or Sarah can see to your needs. It would be safer for a while. Do you understand?"

She did not look at him, but kept her face down, her hands lacing nervously in on themselves. When she refused to comment one way or the other on his advice, he stepped still closer and inquired softly, "You're not afraid, are you?"

She answered readily, "No." Then more hesitantly she added, "I'm worried, though."

"Why?"

"I fear I've driven you away."

He scoffed at that. "Nonsense. To leave London is no great loss." He moved back, putting a safer distance between them. "The people of fashion in England are very ill-educated. Conversation is reduced to a system of insipidity."

She stood motionless before him, listening. "I thought it would be different."

"Once it was. Years ago."

For a moment he thought they might pursue a certain train of thought. Then, without warning, she changed the subject, looked up at him, still holding herself rigid as though for fear of miscalculating her words. "I'm very sorry, William, for all the trouble I've caused."

The blame was not hers and he refused to let her bear it. "It was none of your doing."

"I shouldn't have come here."

"Where else would you have gone?"

"Home," she said simply. She raised her head with just a hint of defiance. "I had nothing to run from. I did nothing, caused no offense."

Watching her closely, taking careful inventory of all aspects of her incredible beauty, the alabaster skin, the soft contours of her body beneath the pleasing gown, her face cleansed of paint and pretense, he found her again the loveliest vision in the world. His breath caught in his throat, as wildly he imagined himself scooping her up onto the horse with him, carrying her to Dover, then to France where in spite of the Revolution, surely they could find a remote cottage of peace.

So powerful was this vision that he found himself trembling, the wind pushing at his back, feeling an intimacy for her which precluded their position on the pavement, standing in broad daylight on a public street.

She ceased talking and looked up at him as though aware of his vision. He bent close to her and whispered, "For Christ's sweet sake, come with me."

If she was shocked by his suggestion, she gave no indication of it. She looked almost serene, as though she had known precisely what he would say. There was a glow on her face which she made no attempt to hide. "I've thought on it," she confessed, simply.

His heart was screaming inside his chest. He stepped closer, his hands still safely inactive. He felt the softness of her breasts against his coat. "And?" he prodded, not daring to move too fast or all would be lost.

Still she looked at him, permitting the closeness, even encouraging it as one small hand attached itself to his sleeve, caressed it. At the moment of greatest hope, he suffered the greatest disappointment.

She whispered, "No. I cannot."

"Why?" he persisted, catching the hand on his sleeve and pressing it to his chest.

"I must stay here," she said.

"Why?" he insisted again almost angrily. "There's nothing for you here except threats and dangers."

Gently she corrected him. "And the love of my sister and the care of Sarah. I could not betray them."

He felt a compulsion to inform her, however painful it might be, of Jane's betrayal of her. But of course she knew that now and had apparently forgiven all. Instead, with the face of a man enduring torture, he moved away from her, stood as though ready, indeed eager, to mount his horse.

He heard her voice again. "There are other matters as well, William, which you wouldn't understand. But primarily it is my obligation to Jane. What sort of sister would I be to repay her goodness in this manner? She's suffered enough on my account."

Slowly he looked back at the insanity of her words. He had not thought her so easily duped. With rigid formality he untied the reins from the post and mounted his horse. "Then I wish you well," he said, looking down on her. They gazed, unspeaking, at each other.

"You will return by Christmas?" she asked.

"It is my plan."

"We'll speak again at Christmas. Perhaps—" Quickly she reached out and touched the side of his leg, her face as drawn as his. "Take with you the knowledge that I care deeply for you," she said.

He looked down on her, confounded. It was a curious declaration, about which nothing could be done. They passed a silence, too deeply entangled in emotion to trust themselves to speech. Then, as though releasing him, she withdrew her hand.

There was no reason for him to delay longer. With admirable control he urged the horse forward. Quickly he wrapped the reins about his wrist as though to bind himself to the saddle, every downward hoofbeat protesting his departure.

At the end of Great Russell Street he stopped and looked back. She was still waiting at the curb, still watching, a small yellow figure stirring his misery.

He could watch and wait no longer. The wind rose. Dover beckoned, the white sails of the channel packet billowing. Suddenly he dug his heels into the horse's side with such strength that the animal reared back, neighing his pain. It was a sound which might have come from his own throat as with eyes unfocused he stole a final look at her, there, so distant.

He drove the animal forward, speed increasing, moving at a dangerous pace through the busy commerce of London, feeling worn out, mauled, speed still increasing, the trade houses and shops and carriages a passing blur on either side, still no thought, still nothing, but speed and wind and wrath. . . .

"There it is, Thomas!" Billy shouted eagerly. "Look! Look ahead!"

From the close rocking confines of the sedan chair, Thomas looked and saw nothing but the splattered black and white landscape of the Wiltshire winter. Obviously Billy, riding ahead on horseback, saw more.

Abruptly Thomas felt the sedan chair being unceremoniously dropped to the ground. Oh, God, would he now be forced to tramp across the cold waste? He didn't give a damn about the site for Billy's tower, and had consented to the uncomfortable expedition simply because he felt he was in Billy's debt. The young man had treated him with admirable tenderness during the last few months of his recuperation, had carried him out of the embarrassment of London to the seclusion of Fonthill Splendons in Wiltshire, on the promise that as soon as he was capable of further travel, he would see him home to Eden Point. That had been over four months ago, and if Thomas' shoulder had improved, his spirits hadn't.

"Are you well, Thomas?" Billy called down, trying to rein in his spinning horse, looking closely with a concern that was about to drive Thomas to distraction.

"Why must I walk?" Thomas grumbled. "I can see from here."

"But you can't," Billy protested. "You can't possibly take in the whole vista from that cramped little box. It's medicinal, Thomas," Billy added. "The physician said you need air and movement."

"Damn the physician," Thomas muttered, slowly pulling himself forward, still protecting his arm as though the wound were fresh and bleeding. Standing erect on the cold ground, he shivered and marked the difference between Wiltshire cold and Devon cold. The latter was bracing, truly health-giving, while this cold was merely damp and penetrating. A longing was forming in the back of his mind and he determined to share it with Billy as soon as he had seen and marveled over this blasted site.

Apparently Billy saw the irritation on his face. Quickly he dismounted and handed the reins to one of the waiting porters. "We'll walk together, Thomas," he soothed. "The better for conversation."

Damn conversation, Thomas thought. He was sick to death of Billy's conversation. But he obliged because he was an honorable man and clearly in Billy's debt.

As they started off across the frozen terrain, Billy launched into a monologue that Thomas knew by heart. "A cruciform shape, Thomas, imagine it if you will, the western entrance thirty feet high opening onto a Grand Staircase that leads up to the Octagon Salon. There, under the two hundred and eighty foot tower, where a three hundred foot long south to north range of galleries cross—"

Oh, dear God, how his ears ached, along with his bones. The damnable arm still caused him pain, in spite of Billy's bumbling physician, who claimed it was totally healed. They were pushing up a slight incline, Thomas growing breathless from the exertion, new waves of self-hate washing over him as he realized how soft he had become in his recuperation.

Damn the girl, he thought, his breath causing a stitch in his side as anger joined his emotions. His boots slipped constantly on the frozen footing, his good arm outreaching for balance. He'd been absent from Eden Point for almost seven months, a bleak, painridden, embarrassing, and expensive seven months, expensive in that he'd paid off almost thirty thousand guineas in gambling debts, his remarkable lack of success that night at William Pitch's being common knowledge and public gossip. "His Lordship's desire nipped in the bud," one of the cheap *Tattler* pamphleteers had said. "The North Devon Peer had his wings clipped," said another.

Mortifying!

"For God's sake, Billy, slow down," he panted. "I'm not a well man." He moved toward a fallen log at the top of the incline and sat heavily. With his good hand he drew the collar of his cloak up about his neck while Billy pointed toward the summit of another incline, designating it "the place."

"Can't you just see it, Thomas?" he rushed on. "The most impressive Gothic structure in all of England, in all the word perhaps, people coming from all over to see and marvel."

Relieved of his own misery by the boy's madness, Thomas watched with a self-indulgent smile as Billy ran a distance up the hill, still describing the marvel which would shortly cover the barren site. "Eight years is Wyatt's estimate," Billy was saying. "My birthday gift to the new century. A Christmas unveiling." Breathless, he sat down on the cold fallen log beside Thomas, seeming not to feel the chill at all. "Promise you will come, Thomas. Promise me the pleasure of your company on the night of the Grand Unveiling."

Thomas smiled wearily, feeling old. "I wouldn't dream of missing it, Billy," he said, indulging the boy. "I must confess, though, your eyes are sharper than mine. Where you see Gothic architecture, I see only dead trees, a dim future, and a bleak past."

Concerned, Billy hovered close, smiling pallidly at the remembrance of pain. "You must not look back, Thomas. The incident is over. You must find a new dream."

There was something amusing in the spectacle of youth preaching to age. Still, Thomas could not deny the wisdom of his words. He was too old for dreams. But he was not too old to be homesick.

He sat up on the log, still cradling his arm. "Billy," he began, moving at last to the subject of his heart, "I must return to Eden Point. I've been absent far too long. I hope you understand."

Apparently Billy did, although his face fell into sorrow as he confessed, "I shall miss your company, Thomas. How good it has been to know you were so close."

Thomas had an idea. "Then come with me," he cordially invited. "Why not? Let me return your hospitality. You know Eden Castle well. There are comfortable chambers—"

Billy nodded readily. "When I was young I thought it the grandest castle in all of England, much better than

Warwick, better even than Windsor." He paused. "And yet a rough place." He laughed softly. "My father used to say of Eden Castle that it was the one place on earth where a lord could freely exercise his rights as a man."

Thomas smiled. "So it is and so it has remained." Again he glanced about at the damp cold site. "You're free until spring," he reminded the young man. "Come with me and look after me. I'm afraid I've grown quite accustomed to your company." With a surprise, he realized only at that moment the truth of his words. Even though he was slightly daft, Billy was good company. They had passed many enjoyable evenings together over cards and flagons of wine. He was a good talker with boundless enthusiasm. He helped to fill the blank spaces which more and more were beginning to represent the sum of Thomas' life.

With a shudder he realized that in spite of his desire to return to Eden Castle, he dreaded being alone with only old Ragland for company, and the bumpkin, Russell Locke, to remind him of the girl, the old debt, and the recent failure and humiliation at her hands. Of course he would have to keep the smuggling enterprise quiet. His trust in Billy was great, but not that great. It would be no matter of consequence anyway. At the height of winter the French ships could not navigate the channel. According to his latest communique from Ragland, there hadn't been a delivery in several weeks.

Quite in earnest, he entreated Billy. "Come with me, then. Let's return to the fire at Fonthill and I shall pen a message to be dispatched by one of your couriers. 'His Lordship is returning in the company of his truest friend, the one man who understands him, who smiles at his weaknesses, and speaks cool words to him, his friend who keeps him from being alone.'"

Billy blossomed under the show of affection. He nodded appreciatively to everything Thomas had said, and agreed. "I shall come for a while." As they started up from the log, Billy grasped him by the shoulder, his young face suddenly sobered. "The tower *will* be built, Thomas," he pledged, as though Thomas had refuted him. "Most people, even you, I fear, think me mad. But the tower shall rise—" His face contorted, as though with pain. Fiercely he concluded, "I shall rid myself of this fever. I vow it."

He looked up toward the incline at the place where his dream resided. The moment was so tense that Thomas found himself quite without words. How could he soothe the young man? How could he inform him that it was part of life's bitter potion to live with unrealized schemes and dreams? He felt uncertain under Billy's feverish gaze, remembered his own schemes of the past, how they had gone tragically awry.

Abruptly Thomas strode away from his obsession and urged Billy to do the same. "Of course it shall be built, your tower!" he shouted over his shoulder. "But not now, not this very moment. Come, man, I'm frozen. My arm's throbbing. I've seen the site and I shall not look upon it again until you've a Grand Abbey to show me."

He started down the hill, hopeful that his false enthusiasm would stir Billy to good sense, at least enough so that he would follow after him.

It worked. Billy followed, slowly at first, at last running to catch up, his words spilling out in customary fashion, his excitement rising for the proposed journey. "We'll celebrate Twelfth Night at Eden Castle," he announced, drawing even with Thomas. "I remember the Banqueting Hall as a boy, filled with guests, the fires lit and roaring, a side of beef on the spit."

With some misgivings, Thomas looked ahead to the gloomy isolation of Eden Castle. Times had changed since his father's day. Well, no matter. If necessary, he'd invite all of Mortemouth up for the Festival Day. For his sake as well as Billy's, the Banqueting Hall would be filled again.

The two porters, waiting patiently at the sedan chair, moved into position, alert and at attention. As Billy swung up on his horse, he shouted, "I'll go ahead, Thomas. Hot wassail will be waiting."

Thomas watched as the horse shot forward under Billy's direction, the hooves throwing back frozen particles of grass and soil. There was this to be said for youth. How quickly transitions were made from obsession to sanity, the madness of the spirit passing away imperceptibly.

The porters behind him stamped their feet, apparently frozen from standing on the cold ground. Quickly Thomas crawled inside the chair and drew the fur up around him. Occasionally, at moments like this, looking out into silent realms, he pondered the perplexity of the world, why some men carried, and other men rode, why some served and others commanded.

"Forward!" he shouted, settled at last. The rocking motion started, jouncing him against the sides of the chair, causing his arm to throb.

Eden Castle, he mused with closed eyes. It would be good to be home. With his eyes still closed, he saw the approach across Exmoor, the air changing, the salt breeze brushing the heather, the headlands appearing, then, without warning, the looming presence of Eden Castle, built out of the same rock upon which it sat, the crenellated turrets and towers rising against the blue backdrop of the channel and ocean, a true fortress, bone of his bone, blood of his blood, his roots going as deep as the ocean floor.

He smiled in spite of the rocking journey. Continuity. Always continuity.

Suddenly the porter ahead tripped on the rough terrain. The chair went down with a rough scrape, the man himself sprawled on the ice. Quickly he picked himself up again and, begging his Lordship's pardon, hoisted his end of the weight and started off again at a more prudent pace.

Impressed by the man's devotion, Thomas vowed to reward him upon his arrival at Fonthill. It was a tragedy that all members of the working class did not have the same spirit of duty and devotion.

She had possessed only the thin chemise as a shield of protection.

Oh, sweet Lord, how his arm hurt!

Beneath the chemise, there had been nothing.

Within the fortnight, he would be home.

"You cause fear, sir."

"Faster!" he shouted, longing for Billy's company, Billy's constant flow of words filling the blank spaces and canceling memories.

Her eyes in the lamplight had been—

"Faster!" Thomas shouted again, aware that with undue speed both porters might slip and fall and the sedan chair would go sprawling.

It mattered little. There were too many images in the narrow confinement with him. He leaned forward, trying to protect his arm.

As the porters raced ahead, Thomas sat in confused and unhappy silence. He felt dull and miserable. Holding his throbbing arm, he bent over on himself.

Still peace would not come.

Eden Castle
New Year's Morn
1793

*R*AGLAND stood before the roaring fire in the Servants' Hall below Eden Castle, warming first his backside, then his front. In his hands he held the dispatch which the courier, half-frozen, had brought during the night. The man himself now lay buried under robes on the couch near the far wall, being tended to by God's saint, little Elfie, who apparently had been the only one up to receive him.

Ragland glanced toward the young girl, still hovering over the man.

"Elfie, let him be," Ragland suggested kindly. "You've done enough. Come, fetch yourself a cup of hot tea, then rest."

The girl, probably no more than fifteen, looked with loving eyes at the old man, then instantly obeyed. As she moved toward the kettle, Ragland noticed that she was growing, indeed flowering. She carried her head erect, no longer cowed and frightened. Her hair was black and shiny and hung straight down like a cascade of Whitby jet. True, she had never spoken, perhaps would never speak. But now there was the glimmer of security in her eyes. She would make a fine, diligent woman.

Ragland watched her, deriving enormous pleasure from

her, as he had from the beginning when he'd first found her in a pitiful heap outside the castle gates. It was good for a man's soul to lift something up and set it right again.

As Elfie settled sleepily on her pallet in the corner of the room, Ragland turned his attention back to the parchment in his hands. As he read, there was a heaviness on his face. So! His Lordship was returning in the company of young Beckford. Not that he hadn't expected it. Still, certain hard adjustments would have to be made. He poured himself a cup of steaming tea and settled painfully at the table in an attempt to put his thoughts in order before Dolly and the other servants arrived.

Why was it always the case that Eden Castle ran more smoothly when his Lordship was away? He withdrew his gold watch, a gift from Lord Eden's father, from the pocket of his coat. Seven o'clock! And still the staff were asleep in their beds. *That* would have to change.

So much to do! The chambers must be aired, then rewarmed, the linens sorted, stores replenished, and menus planned. He eyed again the parchment on the table. A Twelfth Night Celebration had been mentioned. Good Heavens! Eden Castle had not seen a Twelfth Night Celebration since the death of Lord Eden's older brother. All festivities had ceased with the arrival of that mournful news.

Ragland tilted the cup one way, then the other, watching the hot amber liquid follow the direction of the cup. The point of his musing was the very hypothetical consideration of how different things might have been if that kind and interested older brother, James, had lived to inherit, instead of Thomas. Ragland smiled at the consideration.

He mused on the whimsical twists of Destiny, then consumed the hot tea in one gulp, burning his throat in the process, but feeling the need of a mild physical discomfort to match the one in his soul.

He glanced about at the quiet room and noticed Elfie sitting on her pallet. As Ragland looked at her, he saw the daughter he had never had and felt within his heart a surge of love which almost canceled his bleak feelings concerning the news of Lord Eden's return.

"So, the fool comes home," he muttered. Still, in a way he was curious to know everything, the condition of his Lordship's health after that scandalous midsummer night's drama in London. The news had reached Eden Castle, brought by the talkative Parson Branscombe, who had been in London at the time and had reported all.

Had his Lordship taken leave of his senses? In some bewilderment, Ragland shook his head. If he lived to be one hundred and fifty, he would never understand the aberrations of the peerage.

In his musing he'd failed to see Elfie rise from her pallet, obviously taking note of his distress. She poured a glass of ale and stood at his elbow, touching him lightly, offering him warmth.

Startled, he looked up. "Bless you," he murmured, taking the mug. She watched him closely, her face alive with adoration. He returned her gaze and tenderly smoothed down the black hair, stroking her as he would a beloved animal. "Do you understand any of it?" he asked, smiling.

Apparently understanding nothing but the smile, she grinned back at him and mimicked his gesture of endearment and smoothed down his tufts of white hair with a tender stroke.

His old eyes filled with emotion at her obvious love. He vowed that he would retire soon to a small cottage down in Mortemouth and take Elfie with him, and find her a good husband, a considerate man who would understand her silences and treat her gently and with dignity.

Wrapped in such glorious visions of the future, he failed to hear the excited step outside the servants' entrance, the crunching of new snow as Dolly Wisdom burst through the high door in her heavy cloak, her fleshy face rosy with cold.

"News, Ragland!" she exclaimed as she waddled heavily down the steps, drawing from the folds of her skirts two well-wrinkled pieces of paper. "A glorious New Year for poor Hartlow," she went on breathlessly. "Word from both his girls! Look!" Again she insisted upon his attention as she stomped on the receiving rug, scattering flakes of crusted snow. Through the high opened door blew gusts of cold air. The drafts swept down the narrow wooden staircase, causing the fire to leap and twist.

"Close the door!" Ragland shouted, and countered with an announcement of his own. "And I too have news!"

Laboriously Dolly pulled herself back up the steps and closed the door, then turned about and took in the room with a single glance, her sharp eyes resting at last on the sleeping courier. "Who is that?" she demanded, apparently offended by the presence of a stranger in her kitchen.

"If you'd been here last night where you belonged," Ragland scolded, "you might have found out then."

Sniffling from the cold, Dolly plodded back down the stairs and placed the letters on the table. She dabbed primly at her nose with a square of linen. "It was New Year's," she explained curtly. "I spent the evening with Jenny and Hartlow. What harm in that?"

Ragland shrugged. He didn't want to pick a fight with Dolly, although he knew that the leisurely comings and goings of the staff must cease or he'd be held responsible. Without another word he thrust the parchment at her.

He gave her a moment, then spoke as she read. "He's arriving on Thursday, the third. As you can see, it gives us all of two days. I suggest, madame, that you summon your sleeping staff and inform them of what's ahead."

She muttered under her breath. "A Twelfth Night Celebration. On such short notice, it's impossible."

Ragland shook his head, amazed that after fifty years in service, Dolly still was capable of such a luxurious word. Impossible was for lords and ladies, never for servants.

"Well, it must be done," he concluded, "so I suggest that we move on the matter. I'll send Jack Spade to the slaughterhouse for beef and pork. I suggest you get your stores in order and—"

Dolly interrupted. "Did he say anything about—" still eyeing the sleeping messenger with a look of disapproval on her face.

"He said nothing to me," Ragland replied. "Elfie let him in and warmed him. There I found him, and in my opinion there he'll stay for the better part of the day."

Dolly turned with a smile to the silent girl sitting wide-eyed on the pallet. "Good girl, Elfie," she said. "Bright girl to take charge like that."

Ragland softened as both he and Dolly stared down on the lovely face. He knew that Dolly shared his affection for the girl, and on this account he remembered the letters which Dolly had triumphantly waved at him from the top of the stairs. He urged her to "Have a cup and sit a while, a minute's quiet before the storm, and tell me your news."

Dolly smiled and thrust the pages at him. "Delivered

last night, they was, by Royal Post. Jenny let me bring them along, knowing you'd be interested."

Slowly he took the well-mussed sheets of paper, adjusted his eyes to the dim light, and commenced reading. Halfway down the page, he looked up. "From Marianne?" he asked incredulously.

"Herself!" pronounced Dolly. "And from Jane. Read!"

Ragland read, first Marianne's rather idyllic letter, speaking of the glories of London, mentioning specific buildings, her desire and effort to become a lady, and mentioning her affection and devotion to her sister, mentioning too the absence of a Mr. Pitch, the presence of a woman named Sarah, mentioning everything except the scandal which had kept all of London abuzz for the better part of the summer. Jane's letter, shorter, more stilted, he devoured quickly, then turned his attention back to Marianne's elegant handwriting, a letter which was truly remarkable in all of its omissions.

Confounded, he looked up. "She doesn't say a word—"

Dolly shrugged, though still beaming. "Perhaps the dreadful rumor was false. Perhaps it was another female—"

Ragland would not even dignify this nonsense with a reply. Parson Branscombe was, if nothing else, an accurate reporter. It had been Marianne's room that had been breached that night, Marianne's good name that had been further sullied. Clearly the omissions had been acts of thoughtfulness, a desire on the girl's part not to disturb Jenny and Dolly and old Hartlow.

Rapidly he pushed the letters away. Nothing very mysterious about it. How was the poor creature to tell her senseless father that Lord Eden was still pursuing her as he would pursue a hare? All at once Ragland stood, his face red as flame. He seized the parchment covered with Lord Eden's arrogant message, crumpled it in his fist, and hurled it into the fire. As the flames devoured it, his face sank into a kind of satisfaction.

Ignoring Dolly's bewildered expression, he strode to the door which led into the sleeping rooms of the staff. He shouted full-voiced, "Get up! Get up, all of you! Lord Eden returns! There's work to be done, so up with you all. Now!"

As his voice resounded in echo about the underground

chambers, Elfie backed into the corner, her eyes wide in apprehension. Dolly tried to shush him, but to no avail as, gathering up his black greatcoat, he swung it around his shoulders, still shouting, "Awake! Awake! His Lordship returns!" his voice tinged with fury, his face fixed as though bespeaking his determination to play his role, at last stumbling up the narrow steps, still shouting, "Awake! Awake! All up and busy. God returns!" taking his cries with him out into the inner courtyard where a light snow was falling. He glanced about the empty courtyard, seeing it not as it was, but as it would be in three days, filled with citizens of Mortemouth dragged up to form the welcoming party, torches blazing, garlands of holly strewn hither, the vast rooms of the castle ablaze with thousands of candles, the combined, inhuman, and backbreaking effort of perhaps one hundred people required to play out the charade, to set the stage, to cater to the whims of one man.

Abruptly Ragland lifted his face to Heaven as though begging for understanding. But the clouds, slate-gray and spilling snow, provided him wih no answer. It had always been thus and it would always be thus.

On that note of weak resolve, he drew the collar of his coat up about his neck and set out, grim-faced, through the snow to the slaughter-house where, under the expert eye of Jack Spade, several animals would be selected for the singular honor of having their throats cut, their intestines ripped out, their carcasses stretched over well-tended fires for the satiation and gratification of Lord Thomas Eden.

An entourage consisting of three carriages and a half a dozen relief horses started out from Fonthill in Wiltshire at eight on the morning of January the third, and traveled the turnpike in a northwesterly direction, heading toward North Devon and Eden Point.

In the last carriage was an arrangement of trunks, Thomas' and Billy's, looked over by four porters, and a case of Billy's best sherry, and wig boxes and boot brushes and all the other personal items required of a gentleman when he went abroad.

In the second carriage rode half a dozen servants, five males, one female, pressed close together in the narrow confines and plainly dressed in coarse woven garments, sharing a single lap robe.

In the lead carriage, quite the largest, with the Beckford coat of arms emblazoned in gold leaf on either side, rode Thomas and Billy, buried under countless fur robes, a large hamper resting on the seat beside Billy, containing repast for the road—jellied grouse and pheasant, fresh Christmas buns, and several bottles of warming port to ward off any chill which crept beneath the fur lap robes.

They were about an hour into the journey and Thomas was in a fine mood. He was going home after a prolonged and painful absence. As he glanced about on either side at the passing winter scene, he thought ahead to the welcoming warmth of Old Ragland and Dolly Wisdom, and all his servants who had tended him for the better part of his life and who loved him well.

"It is my opinion, Billy," he said, rather meditatively, "that a man should never leave his home."

Billy sat up, clearly excited to be abroad. "Then should I have the horses brought about?" he asked, his eyes merry with cold and good humor.

"Only to visit," Thomas amended, "and then only in a home in which he feels comfortable and as welcome as his own."

Billy nodded in ready agreement, his features softening, as though the sight of Thomas wounded, his arm still supported by the leather sling, moved him greatly. "It was an adventurous summer, wasn't it, Thomas?"

Thomas closed his eyes, finding the adjective a weak one. "Disastrous would be a more appropriate description." He rested his head against the velvet cushions and gave himself over to the jogging movements of the carriage. Thank God, he prayed silently, for Billy's presence, or how easy it would be to slip back into memory.

Billy, apparently unaware of the role he should play, asked a direct and rather painful question. "This girl, Thomas, who has brought you to such grief—do you still think of her often?"

On hearing the question, Thomas' instinct was one of annoyance. How dare he be questioned thus? Then the absurdity of the question itself rushed over him, and in spite of himself, he chuckled. "Think on her!" he said with a smile, amazed at Billy's naivete. "One doesn't think on such a woman, Billy. One perhaps covets her, one suffers for her, one obviously makes a fool of himself over her. But think on her? Never!" He laughed and drew the fur robe over his arm.

Incredibly, Billy blushed and ducked his head. For a moment he looked exactly like the young boy whom Thomas had threatened with death over Eden Cliff. "Perhaps I shouldn't have asked," he mused. "It's just that I know so little of—" He broke off, a faint flush showing on the tips of his ears.

An absolutely confounding thought occurred to Thomas, so wild that for an instant he could scarcely find words. He cut through Billy's embarrassment with a direct question. "Have you never—" He stopped and tried again. "Billy, look at me. Are you a virgin?"

Quickly the young man turned away, his face ashen, though the tips of his ears were still blazing "Salisbury ahead," he said distractedly. "Look! You can see the cathedral."

But Thomas didn't give a damn about Salisbury Cathedral. Of interest was the young man opposite him, reddened with embarrassment, twenty-eight years old if he was a day, who had never known the glories and agonies of a woman.

"Billy," he prompted again. "Are you?"

Suddenly Billy turned on him, displaying a temper of his own. "Well, I'm not diseased either, Thomas. You're right. I've kept to myself, but for all my sacrifice, I have a clean body." Again he looked away in an effort to regain control. Without looking back, he said, "My father was diseased, Thomas. Did you know that?"

No, Thomas didn't know, although he wasn't surprised. Still he was amazed at Billy's innocence and astute enough to see how heavily it weighed upon him.

As Billy commenced a firsthand account of the horrors of veneral disease, Thomas watched him closely. The young man wasn't a sodomite, surely. Then what? Impotent? Like Pitt, the Chancellor of the Exchequer? Thomas had heard it bandied about the clubs of London that everytime William Pitt failed to seduce a woman, he slapped another tax on the poor, already overburdened English citizen, that the relief of the latter was wholly dependent upon the relief of the former and for all his expertise in fiscal policy, his male member generally hung at half-mast as becalmed as a clipper in a high summer day.

But Billy impotent? Thomas couldn't bring himself to believe it. Then what? Listening halfheartedly as Billy described the horrors of the "terrible malady," the painful swelling and poisonous discharge, the burning, the screams, hearing all this and seeing the young man grow quite pale, Thomas decided that the father's misfortune had so impressed the son that he had followed a course of total abstinence. Perhaps, Thomas mused, Billy had over the years perfected the art of self-satisfaction, an art which Thomas himself had indulged in at various points in his life, during long confining winters at Eden Point, when his need was so simply biological that he lacked the energy to obtain a partner. It was a relatively easy performance. Still, he didn't like to abuse it. There was a very respectable school of thought which contended that it led to madness. Why run the risk when there was always an obliging serving girl at one's command?

There passed unexpectedly before his eyes a clear and painful image of Marianne Locke. He backed away from those defiant eyes as though he were under assault. A sharp jolting of the carriage cleared his vision and he was well again.

So! That was it. Billy was a self-satisfier. As the young man concluded his graphic description of diseased genitalia, Thomas thought, what a waste! A young boy in the prime of his manhood who had never known the Gates of Heaven!

Gently, feeling his role of father confessor, Thomas suggested with a wry smile, "You are very much wrong in your melancholy, Billy, to shut the door and deprive yourself of your rights and comfort. Who in the performance of a manly part would not be willing to run the risks?"

Billy's eyes grew wide with horror. "Well, not I, Thomas," he pronounced vigorously. "There are other ways."

"Not as rewarding."

"They suit me well enough."

"Billy," Thomas pleaded, "I have known women and I am as well and clean as you."

Billy had no retort for this, and leaned closer to the window.

Still Thomas persisted. "It's only a matter of choosing with care."

"My father thought he had chosen with care," he replied, never taking his eyes off the scene beyond the window.

Thomas gazed mournfully at the young man. He really was a most agreeable companion and had the true manners of a gentleman. Yet in this one all-important area it was sad to see him so misguided and frightened.

Thomas spoke softly with just a hint of amusement. "Your father probably viewed his scars as the offspring of fun and merriment, and now would you make them the parents of *douleur* and care?"

Billy looked sternly at him. "He suffered. He was in agony."

"We are *all* in agony," Thomas replied, then abruptly stopped speaking as though listening to his own sentiment. In spite of this he went on. "Women were given us to enjoy," he philosophized, "and all enjoyment naturally carries with it a risk and a price."

"I'll spend my purse in other ways," muttered Billy. Without warning, he turned toward Thomas with a lecture of his own. "Look at you," he accused. "Look what you've suffered and endured and lost. Your good name has been dragged through the gutter and you've been a participant in a cheap melodrama, forced to humble yourself." He hesitated as though assessing the prudence of going on. "I didn't tell you for fear of upsetting you, but before we left London, I'd heard that Boswell was preparing a pamphlet on you, a scathing indictment—"

Thomas hadn't heard, and stared at the flushed boyish face opposite him. Well, it was a matter of no great concern. Boswell was a toothless dragon. He'd kept the grave waiting long enough. He might possess a certain power in London, but Eden Point was Thomas' kingdom. There he would be safe.

Finally he gave Billy an indulgent smile. "No matter," he soothed.

"If it's no matter, why did you do it?"

"Do what?"

"Pursue the girl to your own detriment?"

Billy leaned back, as though relieved to be out from under the burden of attention. Skillfully he had shifted it to Thomas.

Keeping his voice low as though there were others in the coach with them, he asked, "Did you really whip her, Thomas?"

Thomas shook his head, annoyed by the shift in the conversation. "No, of course not. It was simply my command. Others executed it."

"Why?"

"She disobeyed me, offended my person."

Billy looked eager, as though at last he wanted specific detail. "How offended you, Thomas?"

"She struck me."

A smile crossed Billy's face. "She appeared so slight the night of the Masquerade."

"An adder is small but deadly."

"I'd seen her before, you know," Billy said calmly.

Surprised, Thomas looked up. "Where?"

"On a coach ride from Wiltshire to London, some years ago it was."

Keenly interested, Thomas pressed for more information. "You spoke with her?"

"No, we exchanged no words. She was quite done in. I had no idea it was at your hand."

Anger rising, Thomas repeated himself. "She offended me."

"So you whipped her?"

"No! Thomas protested, losing all patience. "It was—"

"—your command, yes, I know." There was a look of victory in Billy's face which Thomas resented. His shoulder was beginning to distress him. In the strictest of self-disciplines, Thomas reined in his annoyance and closed his eyes, his hand massaging the old injury.

Apparently he managed to produce a suitably pitiful image, for Billy retreated with an apology. "I'm sorry, Thomas. I shouldn't have brought it up. You were lecturing me on a very personal matter."

Thomas took his point. His shoulder felt as though a giant screw were being applied to the scar. In spite of his discomfort, he leaned his head back against the cushion, a smile on his face. "I shall have the girl one day, Billy. And there's the difference between us. I shall have her with full enjoyment and for those few moments, I shall regret nothing."

Incredulously, Billy stared at him. "You'll try again?"

"And again and again if necessary."

Billy shook his head. "I don't understand."

"No, and you never will until you yourself have tasted the fruits."

As the conversation turned back to Billy, he looked sullenly away and took up his vigil on the bleak passing scenery.

'No need to pursue it,' Thomas thought. 'No need to spoil the journey.' But in the last moment before he let it die, he announced calmly, "When we reach Eden Castle, Billy, I shall find you a clean virgin, a goodhearted North Devon girl, a pristine creature washed doubly clean by sea and wind. I'll send her to you in the Queen's Bedchamber where, on fine French silk you may study her, analyze her anatomy, see for yourself the splendid design."

He paused to mark the effect of his words on the face across from him. The young man was listening, more than listening.

"Then," Thomas concluded, "if you still prefer the dark games you play beneath your linens at night, I shall leave you to your fate and never utter another word. Agreed?"

Still no response from Billy. He was looking out the window, but Thomas suspected that he was seeing nothing.

"Agreed?" Thomas prompted again.

Still no answer.

Thomas needed no reply. A tacit consent was there in the boy's eyes. Enough for now.

For almost three hours they rode in silence. On occasion Thomas dozed, and each time he awakened he saw Billy, gazing blankly out of the window, his face flushed.

At last Thomas stretched. He was hungry. Was he mistaken or was that salt air he whiffed? "Food," he ordered, pointing to the hamper beside Billy on the seat. Finally Billy dragged himself out of his reveries and began to dispense the delicacies within the basket. The cold roasted fowl was delicious. Thomas felt barbaric lifting it in his fingers and sucking its bones. Billy followed suit, the two of them passing the bottle of port back and forth, nibbling a good round of cheddar, their spirits rising as their hungers were satisfied.

Later that afternoon, a short time after they had changed horses at Exeter, and left the turnpike far behind, the driver tapped on the carriage top and gave a hearty shout, "Eden Land!"

Thomas raised up in his seat, as he had done as a boy when he had traveled this same route with his father, feeling a sense of excitement at the beauty and desolation of Exmoor, the hooves of the horses thundering over the well-beloved and familiar terrain.

Obviously Billy sensed his excitement and leaned forward with him. "How much farther Thomas?" Billy asked eagerly.

"Not far!" Thomas shouted. "We'll arrive with the dusk."

Billy sat back, drawing the lap robe up around him again, his face struck by a direct ray of late afternoon sun. "Thomas," he whispered, apparently impervious to the blinding rays in his face. "Make sure she is clean."

He said this with such earnestness that Thomas threw back his head and laughed. He was home and he felt all the largess and warmth and security that he'd missed in London. "She shall be pristine," he promised generously. "I'll check her maidenhead myself. You shall be a lover, Billy. It will be my gift to you in partial payment for your hospitality and friendship."

Billy leaned back against the cushions, dreams that had once had no other life than his own imagination living in reality. With a surge of regret, Thomas watched him and wished that all conquests were so easily accomplished.

But no melancholy. He would not permit it. He ached for his first glimpse of Eden Castle, the staff gathered in welcoming along with the citizens of Mortemouth. And old Ragland, sweet God, how he hungered for a glimpse of Ragland's face.

At dusk and on schedule, as the first sight of Eden Castle came into view, silhouetted blackly against the fiery rose of the winter sunset, Thomas felt himself overwhelmed and, feeling an embarrassment of tears, he closed his eyes.

The past was behind him, at least for a while.

Before him was his home.

It was an occasion for general rejoicing. A triumphal arch was erected across the road which led up the steep incline to Eden Castle. The church bell pealed. The Lord of the Castle had come home from his wanderings.

Houses in the village of Mortemouth were gay with flags. The townspeople turned out to welcome him, and rows of servants in the famous blood-red livery of the Eden family filled the inner courtyard, headed by old Ragland, who made a complimentary speech. For the next few days Eden Castle gave itself up to dancing and merriment.

Many villagers felt that perhaps a new reign was beginning with the New Year. Perhaps this Lord, of whom people knew so little, was at last prepared to assume the responsibilities which had been placed on his shoulders by the death of his older brother. Perhaps now, after a dint at smuggling, sowing his oats in London, and taking a pistol ball in the shoulder, he would settle down and have pity on his poorer neighbors and help them to improve their lot.

The Twelfth Night Festival was splendid, the Banqueting Hall doors thrown open to all, citizens coming from as far away as Tintagel to partake of the plenty, eating as much as they could, then stuffing their garments with hard rolls and rounds of cheese and pieces of beef, security against the rising prices and the hard winter yet to come.

There were musicians and jugglers and acrobats, and the vast room was lined with torches and filled with a continuous din of merry shouts, the women and even some of the men wearing holly wreaths on their heads.

Presiding over it all in melodramatic splendor, sitting at a table on a raised platform at the end of the room, was Thomas Eden, wearing a crimson velvet robe, lifting glass after glass to the familiar faces who came singly and in pairs to pay their respects. He was taking enormous delight in showing Billy how a Lord functioned.

"Over there," Thomas whispered, leaning close to Billy. "Look!" With a gently guiding hand he forced Billy's attention toward the far wall, where in the blazing light beneath a torch, two men lifted a woman into the air, one supporting each leg as she lit a straw from the torch and attempted to transfer the flame to a lantern. Their support, shaky at best, grew shakier as their hands inched up beneath her skirts. Giggling, the woman protested, and as one invisible hand struck home, she screamed, though still laughing, and dropped both straw and lantern and fell, protesting, into their waiting arms.

As they carried her off through the throngs of people, Thomas whispered, "They've found a surer flint with sparks aplenty. She'll need no lantern to see her home this night."

Billy watched, his face revealing his excitement. "It differs only slightly from the Masquerades at the Pantheon," he commented as though to disguise his impression. "Here it's better, though," he added. "More honest life."

Remembering the promise he had made to Billy in the carriage, Thomas asked, "Do you see any that hold appeal?"

Again that wonderful adolescent blush spread over Billy's face, heightened by the empty bottles which lay scattered about the table. "I would confess to no one but you, Thomas," he said with a grin, "but I'm afraid they're all far too experienced for me."

Thomas laughed outright and waved for Ragland to bring fresh bottles. "Surely someplace," he went on, "in that mob, there is a female as virginal as yourself. All we must do is find her!"

He settled back, his hand on his chin, assessing the female flesh before him. It was true. They were an experienced lot, eagerly displaying their wares, the look of hard experience about them; either that, or they were pinched and old, the thick complacent wives of tradesmen and fishermen and farmers, their wombs already worn out from childbearing.

In some desperation, Thomas looked about him. Surely there was someone. "What about that one?" he mused, pointing down at a fair-haired girl assisting Dolly Wisdom with a heavy tray filled with mugs of beer. But at that moment the girl glanced directly at him, and he recognized her as one he himself had taken several times.

She waved her kerchief prettily toward him. Billy muttered, "She seems more interested in you than me."

Thomas turned away, still busily assessing the possibilities before him. Ragland appeared, two bottles in hand. Following a discreet distance behind him was his shadow, the simpleminded girl whom he had rescued from outside the castle gates.

Thomas looked at her as she kept to the shadows, a

young, dark-haired beauty, her simple black dress framing white shoulders, well-developed breasts, and tapered waist.

As he assessed her a second time, he called good-naturedly to Ragland, "How your pet has grown! Bring her forward. Let's see how the climate of Eden has done by her."

He watched as with pride the old man motioned the girl forward. At first she seemed too frightened to move of her own volition, but Ragland took her gently by the arm and whispered something to her, then walked with her to the table.

"Elfie, milord," he announced proudly.

The girl ducked her head as though in embarrassment. Thomas nudged Billy, urging his attention. "Would you believe," he announced, "that this flower is the result of Ragland's cultivation? He found her starving and near death—when was it?—and now look. Miracles are still within the realm of possibility. Don't you agree, Billy?"

Billy nodded. Ragland beamed. The girl kept her eyes to the floor, although Thomas noted one small white slender hand nervously fingering her skirt.

"Does she speak, Ragland?" he asked, finding the delicate creature totally alluring.

"No, milord," Ragland replied. "She doesn't speak, but she understands."

Thomas smiled and poured wine around, including a glass for Ragland. "The perfect female, I'd say, wouldn't you, Billy?"

"Thank you, milord," Ragland bowed, responding both to the compliment and the gift of wine.

As the three men drank, the girl stood motionless before them. In some astonishment, Thomas felt himself respond to her presence. Perhaps he shouldn't be so generous. Perhaps he should keep this one for himself. But he was a man of honor and he owed Billy.

Thoughtfully he suggested to Ragland, "Give her a sip of your wine. Make her feel at home."

"She's never partaken, milord."

"Then it's time."

But still the old man refused, and now, as though he'd read Thomas's mind, he placed a protective arm about the girl's waist and drew her backward. "I only permitted her to stay for a while. It's past her bed hour. Be off with you,

Elfie." Obedient to a fault, the girl turned and ran lightly back into the shadows, taking her marvelous and silent beauty with her.

"Where does she sleep, Ragland?" Thomas asked, still feigning an objective interest in the girl.

"In the Servants' Hall, milord. She quite comfortable there."

"I'm sure she is. You are to be commended. It warms the heart to see such fine results from a Christian act."

Ragland beamed and bobbed his head in gratitude. "She's like my own daughter, milord. Quite a joy."

"I'm sure she is," Thomas murmured. "That's all for now. Would you please send Jack Spade to me? And see that every guest leaves with a full belly and a warm heart."

The old man bowed low and departed. Thomas waited until he was safely out of earshot, then looked at Billy. "Well?" he demanded.

To his amazement Billy looked sad. "She seemed so frightened."

"They're always frightened." Thomas laughed. "It's part of their pretense. Does she suit you?"

Still hesitant, Billy said, "She's scarcely grown, little more than a child."

Without offending him, Thomas reminded, "She's sufficient unto your needs. And she may surprise you. So?"

But Billy shook his head and pronounced a firm, "No! Not that one, Thomas. Not tonight. Perhaps later—"

The old dragons of fear were still lurking about. Then Thomas would have to take matters into his own hands. As he spied the block head and flat face of Jack Spade waiting in the shadows at the end of the table, he stood up, as though to dismiss the matter. "You'll regret that decision, Billy, I can assure you."

"So be it," the young man snapped and plunged into the new wine.

Thomas excused himself and started toward the hulk of the man waiting for him, the man who performed most of his unpleasant chores for him, God's most obedient fellow. Such devotion demanded reward, and as Thomas drew near the tall figure, he withdrew his purse from the folds of his robe.

"Jack Spade," he called out in warm greeting. "A pleasant Twelfth Night to you."

As the man beamed, Thomas considered a plan for the evening and shook out enough coin to cover any pangs of conscience Spade might experience, although in truth Thomas knew that no such pain ever plagued commoners. A miraculous breed, the lowborn. Their measure of life was so simple, uncluttered by civilized refinements such as conscience and guilt. They simply marked the seasons and devoted all their energy to staying warm and well-fed. They were neither perturbed by the thinker, nor tortured by the dreamer, nor dwarfed by the poet. Merely step by step, they lived through.

How he envied them. And, laying a hand on Jack Spade's shoulder, he whispered, "I have need of a favor."

As he filled the rough powerful hand with coin, he knew the man was his, no matter how offensive the scheme or brutal the plot.

It was after three in the morning when the last reveler stumbled drunkenly down the cliff walk from Eden Castle, when the porters extinguished the last torch, when the night watchmen lowered the grillwork defenses and secured the castle gates.

The servants, approaching complete exhaustion, retired immediately. The scattered bones and bits of bread and spilled beer and wine would keep until morning. The shambles that was the Banqueting Hall would be awaiting them at dawn, another full day of backbreaking, bone-wearying restoration.

Thomas had sent Billy to the Queen's Bedchamber shortly after one. The young man had been drinking too much, a harmless state generally, but Thomas knew from experience that too much wine could have a devastating effect on a man's ability to perform. On this night of Billy's initiation, he needed all the help he could get.

Thomas paced in his upper bedchamber, listening to the voices outside his window diminish. It had been a good evening, the villagers warm and receptive. Feeling mellow, he stretched out on the bed and wished that Jack Spade were bringing him the prize. He chuckled softly, pondering his susceptibility to young serving girls. At least this one couldn't talk and, recalling his defeat by words in William's Pitch's house, he considered a tongueless woman as the best of all.

Softly he heard the knock he had been waiting for. He drew his robe about him and hurried to the door.

On the other side was the slack-jawed countenance of Jack Spade, and in his arms, lightly bound at wrists and ankles, a muslin gag distorting her pretty face, her dark eyes rolling in terror was Ragland's pet.

The sight offended Thomas and he ordered, "Put her down and untie her. Surely such measures were not necessary."

Spade stepped inside the room and did as he was told, explaining, "Oh, no, milord, it weren't her. At first she was quiet as a lamb. But when she wouldn't come, I had to pick her up and she did make an outcry then, and I was fearing old Ragland—"

As he talked, he withdrew the bondage from her arms and legs and left her standing somewhat wobbly in a plain white nightshirt in the middle of the floor.

"Ragland's the one," Spade whispered. "He fancies her terrible, milord. If he'd known what I done, he'd come after my head." Spade suddenly stopped, as though aware that he was saying too much. He wiped his mouth with the back of his hand and murmured, "I'm sure he don't begrudge her you, though, milord."

Thomas found the man's presence repulsive. "She's not for me. She's for my guest."

Light dawned on Spade's face. He grinned. "A lamb for a lamb, that's what I always say."

As the man rambled on, Thomas kept his eye on the girl. She seemed frozen in her fear, scarcely breathing, her eyes down.

Thomas disliked what he had to do now, but he owed it to Billy, and while he knew it would cause an increase in the girl's terror, he vowed to do it quickly and gently.

Standing before her, he made a quiet request. "Would you please remove your garment?"

When she failed to obey, Jack Spade laughed gruffly. "She's without wits, milord, dumb as my brood sow. You want me to—"

As the man stepped forward with his brute hands, Thomas ordered sternly, "Stay away." Moving with care, Thomas himself unbuttoned the nightshirt and pushed it from her shoulders and watched it fall in a small circle around her feet.

Clinically he assessed the body. It was good, firm, still developing, but full enough to please a man. He stepped to the edge of the bed and motioned for the girl to follow him. When again she either failed to understand or refused to obey, he finally gave Spade permission to lift her bodily and deposit her on the bed.

As Spade restrained her, Thomas turned a deaf ear to her whimpering and pushed up the sleeve of his robe and with his hand began gently to probe inside of her. She was tight, virginal tight. At last his fingers found it, the thin membrane, the maidenhead intact.

He stepped quickly back in an attempt to ease her fear. Such examinations were customary, even for highborn ladies. A man had a right to know what he was getting. Even though he was standing away from her, her objections were growing more pronounced, the long black hair thrashing from side to side on the bed.

Thomas smiled. She may be minus her wits, but a little spirit helped, heightened the game, sweetened the conquest.

"Newborn as the dawn, eh?" Spade said with a grin. "I could a' told you that. Ragland seen to that. Ragland ain't let a man come near her."

With restraint no longer necessary, both men stepped back and watched the girl, her arms attempting to cover her nakedness. She was a female of marvelous beauty. There was her fear, however, and Thomas decided he would have to do something about that. It was his intention to deliver to Billy the perfect gift.

With the view in mind of putting her at greater ease, Thomas dismissed Jack Spade. There was a moment's protest from the mountainous man, as though in spite of his own limited wits he knew he was being dismissed before the sport began. "You sure you can handle her, milord? I'd best stay, just in case—"

"No," Thomas said sternly, ushering him to the door. "Go to your quarters." Thomas's voice softened. The ability to handle servants was an art. "You must be tired," he added in a tone of consideration. "And I'll need you tomorrow in the event my guest wishes to ride."

The man bobbed his head. He glanced over Thomas' shoulder toward the girl lying on the bed. He grinned. "Be sure and don't leave no footprints," he whispered, "or old Ragland will have my hide."

Thomas stepped away from the foul breath and repeated himself. "She's not for my pleasure. She's for my guest."

Again Jack grinned. "I know others who'd serve him better," he offered slyly.

But Thomas shook his head, eager to be free of the man. "Good night then, Spade," and literally pushed the man into the darkened chill corridor and closed the door behind him. He waited a moment, listening for the heavy receding footsteps, then he turned his attention back to the girl on the bed.

In the dim light of fire and lamp, she resembled a lovely statue. As he moved back to the bed, he stopped and retrieved her night garment. "Put it on," he ordered.

As she scrambled to do as she was told, it occurred to him that perhaps she responded best to orders. She sat, covered now, though a little slumped on the edge of the bed. Thomas sat beside her. "Are you warm enough?" he inquired politely.

There was no response. He noticed that she still was trembling, and considered giving her brandy, then decided against it. He recalled Ragland's words, "She's never partaken before." To an untutored system even the smallest sip might produce sleep. He wanted her awake.

"Are you feeling better?" he asked kindly, bending forward so that he might view her face.

Blessedly she nodded, only a faint response but better than nothing. She was so utterly childlike. He lifted her hands and observed their shape and contour, small, though well-defined fingers, roughened and red from her days in the Scullery, but nonetheless graceful.

She permitted the examination, even appeared to be fascinated by it. As he released her hands, she lifted them before her face as though to see for herself what he had discovered. Softly she smiled. Then, with a delicate movement, she lifted *his* hands, spread the fingers apart as he had done to hers, and the smile grew as though she'd mastered a complex game.

Thomas found her completely enchanting. Quickly he stood before her and drew her to her feet. "You'll come with me," he ordered. "You must work this night."

She looked at him as though struggling to comprehend. For a moment he debated whether or not he should offer her a bauble of some sort, or even coin. Why not? Billy would pay handsomely for such a prize on the London market. He retrieved his purse from the table and withdrew one guinea. "It's yours," he said, handing it to her.

She stared at it but did not seem to know that she was to take it. Thomas placed it on the edge of the table. "If you do well," he said, "you may come for it in the morning."

The girl merely looked at him and drew a deep breath as though confounded by every word and gesture. Again he regretted the game, regretted his involvement in it. Perhaps he should have sent Jack Spade after one of the kitchen whores. But no. He'd promised Billy and he'd keep his word. If the young man failed to respond to this, he was beyond all help.

"Come along with me," he commanded and took her by the hand. He felt it grip his in response, an unspoken bond of trust coming from her to him. His tension increased as he led her down the narrow passage, through the Morning Room, skirting the Great Hall, then fairly running up the flight of stairs which led to the Queen's Bedchamber.

Before the massive carved door he stopped. She was still with him, her fear apparently gone. As he looked down on her in the faint light, she gave him a dazzling, though blank smile. He knocked sharply on the door, then pushed it open.

Positioned about the large room were three lamps burning low. He closed the door behind him, abandoned the girl in the center of the room, raised the lamps, then spied the senseless lump in the middle of the enormous bed, a magnificent bed, constructed on orders of his great-great-grandfather for a state visit from Elizabeth, rivaling the Bed of Ware with its splendid carved columns and damask tapestries. Elizabeth had loved the West Country, where she had felt safe to indulge her various passions away from the clacking tongues of the Court.

With a wave of amusement, Thomas considered the caliber and expertise of passion which would take place in the great bed on this night. Surely Elizabeth would find it wanting. With considerable roughness, he nudged the sleeping lump in the center of the bed. A startled and very sleepy Billy Beckford emerged from the mountain of fur robes.

"Look what I've brought you," Thomas said, trying to

inject a degree of excitement in his voice. Quickly he withdrew a lamp from the table and held it directly in front of the girl. She shied away from the light, but Thomas grasped her hand and drew her back.

Sluggishly Billy rubbed the sleep from his eyes and sat in a childish position on his knees in the bed, looking more boyish than ever in his white nightshirt with high collar and lace trimmed sleeves.

"Well, look!" Thomas urged again, dragging the girl nearer to the bed.

For a moment Billy seemed to be refusing to take an active interest in the prize before him. He continued to rub his eyes and stretch. "What in th—" he muttered, shading his eyes from the lamp.

Thomas felt a cruel disappointment in the yawning, scratching, bleary-eyed young man. Perhaps he didn't know what treasures were contained beneath the white nightdress. Hurriedly he approached the girl and again slipped the garment from her shoulders. There was no protest coming from her. In fact, she had the softest of smiles on her face, as though once the bond of trust had been established between them, nothing could jar it.

Billy stopped yawning. He no longer appeared to be a childish figure of fun. Thomas was no longer annoyed by his lack of response.

"For you, Billy," Thomas murmured. "I promised. Remember?"

Apparently Billy was remembering nothing. He moved, still on his knees, to the edge of the bed, his eyes never leaving the body before him.

Thomas stepped out of the confrontation. The girl endured admirably, permitting Billy to encircle her, turning her head slightly as he passed behind her, a flush on her face as he lightly touched her buttocks.

Standing apart, Thomas noticed that it was Billy who was now trembling. Thomas knew the feeling well, the increase of the pulse, the blood becoming suddenly hot as it raced through the veins, a tightening like a knot in the groin, the entire body aching with a sudden heaviness.

As the unspoken excitement grew, Thomas considered exercising his right as Lord and staying to witness the seduction. But no. Billy needed privacy. Then there was nothing more to stay for, and Thomas slipped quietly to the door.

At that moment, Billy spoke his first words, hushed, aspirate words in a voice that Thomas scarcely recognized. "Is she—clean?" he asked, standing directly before her.

Thomas glanced back. "As clean as the snow falling outside your window," he muttered. Before he left, he saw Billy's hands lifting, like the claws of a small beast, coming furiously up, then stopping short of contact.

Hurriedly Thomas opened the door and closed it behind him. He leaned against it, listening. Nothing. He heard absolutely nothing. Debt paid, he thought. Account closed. As he made his way back through the darkened upper extremities of his castle, he considered summoning Jack Spade again, letting him fetch a willing female. But no. Instead he decided to play Billy's game this night.

As he let himself into his room, he glanced about at the emptiness. Quickly he gulped down a glass of brandy. The heavy desire still coursed through his body. He extinguished the lamp and removed his robe and laid down on his bed.

Amazed by his feelings, he thought again of that other darkened room, that other female, fair as sun, kneeling before him. His painful encounter in that room was no longer repulsive to him. On the contrary, the suspense it produced in his mind now relaxed into an agreeable sensation.

Slowly he turned onto his stomach, as the mussed bed became a woman, not the silent creature who was just here. But the other—

The release was painful and explosive. Then all was quiet except for his blood and pulse and his extravagant enthusiasm for the act he'd just performed in his imagination.

In an attempt to free himself from the grip of the hideous nightmare in which he was being buried alive in some gray crumbling interior, Ragland dragged himself upward from the pillow which had given him no solace and stared about at the dark dawn in his room.

His heart was beating too rapidly. He hugged himself, shivering. The fire was dead. He was tired, yet could not sleep and lay back again on the pillow.

Was it too much to ask, after three days of excruciating

labor, for a peaceful interim of sleep? Apparently it was, for he'd heard movement all night. In an act of generosity, he'd sent the staff directly to their beds. And how had they repaid him? By prowling the night, by punctuating his sleep with distant cries, by tramping back and forth outside the corridor which led to the kitchen, undoubtedly pilfering the stores.

He turned in search of a cool piece of linen. Poor Elfie. He doubted if she'd had a moment's sleep as well. At least he had the defense of the corridor between himself and the disturbances. She, unfortunate girl, had only the pallet in the corner of the kitchen itself.

Come spring, he would retire from a lifetime of service at Eden Castle. He would purchase a small cottage at the edge of Mortemouth. He'd had his eye on such a place, a low white neat cottage with pleasant sunny rooms and a garden. There, Elfie would have her own room. She could tend her flowers and tend him as well and fix his tea in the afternoon and fill the lengthening shadows of his twilight years with the radiance of her beauty and sweet nature. He would find her a husband, a steady, reliable fisherman, and when Ragland went, finally, uncomplainingly, to his grave, he would leave it all to her, to this one bright spot in his otherwise tedious existence.

At the height of his dream, something urged him away from it. It would come in time, but for now there was the harsh reality of the cold January morning.

What would it be today, he wondered? A ride out across the moors? A visit to the sheep farm, an arrogant descent to the cobblestones of Mortemouth, or perhaps this would be the day that Lord Eden showed the young man his smuggling activities.

Whatever, Ragland would be involved. In spite of his sleepless night and pounding head, he would have to serve and function. "Yes, milord. No, milord. Of course, milord."

With utter weariness he fell back onto the pillow, his hands fanning out over the rumpled bed. At the height of his agitation he considered the deeds that he had performed at the command of Lord Eden. The night's Festival rose clearly in his mind, Lord Eden summoning the new wine, then beckoning Elfie to come closer. Ragland had recognized the look in his eye.

No! Quickly he sat up as though under immediate threat.

He would have to get the child out of here. Perhaps he could send her to the village, to Jenny Toppinger. Elfie could stay in Marianne's old room. She'd be no bother. Yes, he'd do it. This very day in fact.

Having settled such a practical decision with dispatch, he permitted himself a moment's relaxation. He prayed briefly, not an extravagant request, merely for divine help in making it through this day.

At the conclusion of the prayer, he waited, as though listening for a response. But he heard nothing, not even the sound of the grate in the kitchen fire, not even old Dolly's footsteps, padding heavily about at her morning chores. At the time when the entire staff should be awakening, he heard nothing, nothing at all.

Except—there *was* something, a faint knock as though a chair had fallen. He listened more closely. A drunken porter, perhaps, stumbling to his bed in the servants' quarters.

Oh, God, but he was tired. If only he could sleep for a moment. He closed his eyes and tried to court a deep and feelingless sleep. But nothing came of it. A half an hour later he was still struggling, navigating back and forth across the rumpled bed like a ship foundering in a storm.

It was no use. He might as well rise and face the day. Perhaps there would be a quiet hour or two this afternoon when he could slip away. On that small note of self-comfort, he rose somewhat unsteadily to his feet and dressed hurriedly against the chill of the morning.

As he stepped out into the corridor, he saw the gray light slipping through the high kitchen windows at the end of the passage. The room itself, normally bustling and warm at this hour of morning, was quiet. He would have to do it all, lay the fire, start tea.

He moved slowly down the corridor, leaning against the wall for support, trying to give his ancient bones time to adjust to the movement and weight of his body. As he stepped inside the room, the sight that greeted his eyes did not disappoint him. It *was* chaos. Soiled platters were everywhere, the partial remains of a side of beef hanging cold on the spit, spilled and congealed cream slipping down the sides of the Buttery. He shook his head. It would take the better part of the day.

Still moving slowly, he went to the woodbox. First, heat.

As he bent over the logs, his eye fell on Elfie's pallet. Empty. Curious. Where would she be about so early in the morning? She loved to walk the headlands, but certainly not in the midst of a snowfall on the coldest of—

Carefully he raised up, bringing a log with him. His eyes were awake, searching the disordered room. Not like her, unless Dolly had invited her to share her bed. Still carrying the log, he moved rapidly toward the corridor along which he'd just passed.

Something drew his attention back into the room, his eyes moving to the high wooden staircase which led up to the courtyard outside. He stopped, peering closer, his attention attracted by something white beneath the stairs, a white smock hanging, or so it seemed.

He blinked, then blinked again, his eyes watering in his desire to see. One step, then two. It *was* something hanging, something white, seen through the treads of the worn wooden steps, something with—

He dropped the log. It clattered to the floor as he ran toward the stairs, toward the something white hanging, a rope clearly visible now, one end tied to the planks of the landing, the other end—

Oh, sweet God! His heart stopped. He brought his hands up to his eyes as though to shield himself, his mouth open, lips working, recognition dawning as he ran, stumbling beneath the opened staircase, and received his first clear glimpse of the something white hanging.

It seemed to him as though the whole room were spinning around, yet his own slight legs were fixed. Still he looked up, his hands reaching toward the something white hanging, then withdrawing in horror. What his hands could not bring themselves to touch, his eyes recorded with painful clarity.

Her head was bent rigidly to one side, the thin neck clearly broken. Her eyes were half-opened, but only the whites were visible. From the right temple trickled a small scar of dried blood which, passing over the cheek, lost itself in the collar of her nightdress. Her teeth had bitten through her lower lip. The rest of her body hung motionless, red splotches of blood appearing beneath the white nightdress, her hands like pink and white flowers limp against her sides, her pale feet so close to him, crusted with blood, while around each ankle were the knotted yet

severed remains of ropes. Tears streaming, Ragland took it
all in. He reached up with one hand as though to comfort
her and felt the flesh still warm. Suddenly he felt pain in
all parts of his body as he lifted his head, howling, both
hands clawing at her as though to pull her down if there
still were time. But her body merely danced grotesquely
in the air. Ragland's howls continued as he fell on his
knees, embracing her legs, aware of footsteps behind him,
an old woman's piercing scream. There were other footsteps, running from all quarters, people closing in, but
none as dear as the something white hanging with blood-
matted, blue-black hair.

A terrible feeling such as he had never known before
came over him. He staggered to his feet and pushed through
the gaping faces. He was in total darkness, yet he found a
knife and, stumbling up the high steps, he fell upon the
knotted rope and slashed away at it until he heard a soft
thud of something hitting the floor.

Again an old woman screamed and called out to him,
but he couldn't hear. Looking down through the planks
of the landing, he saw Elfie crumpled beneath him, the
flower he'd worked so long and hard to cultivate now
dead.

All sound grew faint. He looked at the knife as though
he longed to use it on himself. But he was incapable of
thinking anymore. He closed his eyes. The room began to
shake. He hurled himself toward the door and threw it
open and ran, stumbling out into the snow, still howling,
the snow falling white and silent, the only sounds in his
ears his own screams.

He had no destination, only a need to run, to escape
the outrage in his soul, the memory seared on his eyes of
the abused and battered body, of the something white
hanging.

Thomas slept poorly, a restless night compounded by
unsatisfied desire and too much food. At the first streak
of dawn, he turned feverishly, the bed linens knotted about
his chest. Through one half-opened eye he spied a cold
gray sky spitting snow. He prayed earnestly that no one
disturb him for the better part of the day.

Unfortunately, before the prayer had left his mind, he
heard a knock at the door. "Thomas, let me in, please."

Recognizing Billy's voice, Thomas drew his robe about him. His annoyance at being awakened so early passed. He was eager to hear all. "Coming, Billy," he called out.

"Please, Thomas, hurry."

What a night it must have been. Robed at last, Thomas opened the door. Before he could say a word, Billy pushed passed him, his hands reaching out as though he were being pursued. Nervously he moved to the center of the room, then glanced fearfully back at the still opened door. "Close it, Thomas," he whispered. "Close it and lock it."

Bewildered, Thomas did as he was told. From the door he looked back at the young man. "Billy," he began, "what—"

But the young man fell into the chair and buried his face in his hands, weeping, his slight shoulders heaving under the duress of emotion. "Thomas, I—told you not to bring her," he sobbed. "I told you—I wanted—no part—"

As the sobs increased, Thomas could only stare. Slowly he went to Billy's side and drew a chair close. "What happened, Billy?" he asked softly. "It couldn't be as bad as this. I wanted to give you pleasure, not grief." Up close he saw a scratch on the young face, the blood partially dried, clearly caused by a woman's nails. "Tell me all, Billy," he urged, his concern slipping back into amusement. In his varied and rich experience, he'd received a few such scratches himself. They were honorable battle scars, usually representing a sweet victory.

At the invitation to speak, Billy lifted a tear-streaked face. "I'm—afraid," he faltered, "I'm afraid I hurt her."

At this, Thomas had to turn away to hide a smile. To the virginal Billy, the act must have seemed unspeakably violent. "I assure you," Thomas soothed, "you did not hurt her. The female anatomy is designed for only one purpose, to accommodate the male. She might have given the impression that she was being injured, but I assure you she was not."

"No, Thomas," the young man pleaded. "There was— more, much more." Overcome by emotion, he buried his face in his hands again, the sobs increasing.

Thomas was on the verge of urging Billy to speak again, when outside in the corridor and above the young man's sobs, he heard a peculiar commotion, voices rising, footsteps approaching, prolonged wails of women weeping.

Billy heard it and looked terrified toward the door. "Oh, dear God," he whispered.

Thomas stood, confused.

A loud knock came at the door. A man's voice shouted, "Milord, open up!"

The impudence of the caller was overlooked in the rising mystery. Thomas started toward the door. "Who is—"

Suddenly the door burst opened. Thomas stepped back as though under assault. Out of the corner of his eye he saw Billy scramble to the far corner of the room, his arms shielding his face, as though to ward off blows.

Then his attention was drawn back to the push of people who now crowded into his chamber, staff members all, many weeping openly, led by Dolly Wisdom, her face a distortion of grief and horror. Directly behind her he saw two of the porters. They appeared to be carrying something. He caught only a glimpse of white fabric.

"Milord," Dolly said, weeping. "Begging your pardon. But we felt you should know—"

The poor woman lifted her apron and covered her face. As she stepped to one side a silence filled the room. The porters moved forward with their awkward cargo and gently deposited it at his feet.

Thomas looked down. He felt a peculiar absence of breath. *Sweet God.* He closed his eyes, then opened them. Elfie's body was before him, twisted in a macabre position, the hands, those sweet hands he himself had examined the night before, limp at her sides, the rope still around her neck, and the severed remains of other ropes tied to her ankles, as though she had been restrained in some way, tied like an animal—

He could look no longer. Turning away, he leaned heavily on the table, the atrocity still fresh before his eyes. He felt a sickness in the pit of his stomach. "How—did it happen?"

A man's voice, strong, without margin, answered. "We was hoping, milord, that you might tell us."

He heard Dolly's voice again, strained from weeping. "Ragland found her, milord, this morning he found her, hanged by her own hand. But something happened to her before. Something happened—"

Slowly Thomas raised his eyes to Billy, still cowering in

the corner. "Billy," he shouted, anger rising. "What in the name of God—"

Suddenly the young man bolted from the room. He pushed past the weeping faces and disappeared down the corridor. Several of the watchmen started after him, but Thomas commanded, "No! Leave him to me!"

At the sound of his Lordship's voice, the men retreated. Thomas looked down at the pitiful body at his feet. Such waste. Such a lovely flower. His eyes filled with embarrassing tears. Quickly he turned away. "Where's Ragland?" he murmured. He had to explain to him, had to make him understand what Thomas himself did not understand.

"Gone, milord," Dolly said. "He ran out of the gate this morning, and we've not seen—" Tears overtook her again. She fell silent.

Feeling weak and sick, Thomas looked back at the waiting faces. "I'm very sorry," he said. "And I promise you justice. But first we must find Ragland and give the child a proper burial. Then I assure you that I will—"

Overcome, he could not finish. He bowed his head and heard a slight rustle as the porters lifted her and bore her upward. He heard the scuffle of feet as his staff retreated, the women weeping.

Old Dolly stayed for an apology. "I'm sorry, milord. We felt you should know."

Without looking at her, Thomas nodded. "You were right, Dolly."

The door closed behind him. He stared down at the place where the girl had lain. His head throbbed. The sight of the body was still etched on his memory.

He had brought Billy the perfect gift. He had intended no harm to anyone. Slowly, out of his grief, anger surfaced. He wheeled around, his eyes falling on the corner where Billy had recently taken refuge.

"Billy!" he shouted, his voice echoing about the empty chamber. He ran out the door, his mind reeling under the tragedy of the morning. The young man must be found.

"Billy!"

Three days after Elfie's death, Thomas sat outside the door which led to the chapel. He wondered bleakly if there were any spot on earth where he might avail himself of a moment's peace.

He leaned heavily forward in the chair, still waiting, as he'd been waiting for the last three days for Billy to emerge from his self-imposed ordeal of fasting and atonement. The door had been bolted from the inside. On several occasions Thomas had considered ordering his men to break it down. But it was a priceless piece of carving and thus a high price to pay for a few words with a repentant young man who seemed to suffer from dual natures.

He shivered and drew his cloak about him. He longed for the comfort of a fire and hot food. But his vigil was payment to his staff, whom he knew expected at least the facade of justice. What had happened was deplorable. He must question the foolish young man and, as punishment, send him packing back to Fonthill Splendons. After a period of time, when his staff had settled back in obedience, and old Ragland had returned from God knew where, his relationship with Billy could be resumed.

Thomas rested his head in his hands and tried to make sense out of the tragic incident. Was he himself totally blameless? No! He was not.

At this moment he had a dozen men, led by Russell Locke, searching for Ragland. At his age, the old man was ill-prepared to care for himself. The cold would so easily overtake him. As soon as he was found and brought back and warmed, Thomas would try to explain all.

In a rage, he flew at the carved doors and pounded on them, shouting, "A word, if you will, Billy. I order you to appear."

His shouts were interrupted by the sound of footsteps approaching, a sharp clack of boots moving purposefully up the stairs. As he raised his head, he saw Russell Locke at the far end of the corridor, carrying his heavy riding gloves in his hand, his hair windblown, his face revealing nothing.

"Any word?" Thomas called out while he was still a distance away.

But the young man apparently refused to answer until he'd appeared before Thomas and bowed low. All homage paid, Locke looked directly down on him where he sat in the chair. "A report, milord," he announced proudly.

"Well?"

"A body, sir, was washed up this morning on the beach at Mortemouth."

Thomas sat up. Was there an epidemic of dying? "Ragland?" he asked hoarsely.

"No, milord," Locke replied. "A much younger man, in the uniform of a French sailor."

Thomas fell back into the chair, closing his eyes and lifting them heavenward.

"It's our judgment," Locke went on, "me and the men, I mean, that he fell overboard. The sailor, I mean—"

"Anything else?" Thomas demanded.

Locke shifted his weight from one boot to the other. "Jack Spade claims to have seen old Ragland two nights ago, said he saw him outside his window, said he was going to kill him for fetching up the girl—"

"Then place a guard around Jack Spade," Thomas ordered, though in truth he didn't take the threat seriously. Old Ragland was incapable of killing anyone. "Anything else?" Thomas asked.

The young man ducked his head. "If you'll forgive me for saying so, sir—"

"What?"

Hesitantly, he pointed toward the doors which led to the chapel. "Those hinges, sir, could be easily removed, that is, if you really want—"

Thomas swiveled about, studying the door. There were six large brass hinges, three on either side. It did seem a simple matter to unbolt three of them, then remove one side of the door. Why hadn't he thought of it?

Russell went on, "I mean, sir, if you really want to see inside—"

"Yes," Thomas agreed eagerly. "A sound idea. Be about it if you will."

Locke beamed under his Lordship's praise and produced from the folds of his jacket the necessary tools, a blunt-nosed hammer and wooden wedge.

It took over an hour of steady pounding to loosen the ancient bolts. Thomas stood to one side and watched the perseverance of the young man. Perhaps he shouldn't be so harsh in his judgment of him. He was a good, trusted, and obedient lad, a possible replacement for Ragland, in the event—

With a clatter the last hinge fell to the floor. The door freed, Locke put his shoulder to it and pried it open a sufficient space for one person to pass through.

"Good job," Thomas commended him. "I'll take it from here."

"You sure you—"

"I'm sure. Go along and find yourself a pint of ale. You've earned it."

Thomas watched him down the corridor until he was safely out of sight. He turned his attention back to the crack in the door and the silent chapel beyond. He remembered again the curious expression on Billy's face as he'd first viewed the girl, a blend of anticipation and horror, his deep fear of his father's loathsome infection waging a fierce battle with his newly awakened desire.

"Billy?" Thomas called.

There was no reply.

Thomas eased through the crack in the massive door. The chapel was dark with the smell of burned-down candles, the enclosed musty odor of ancient incense and confession, generations of Eden piety and fear and remorse imbedded in the handsomely carved walls.

He considered returning for the lamp, but decided against it. There were times when clear vision was a state greatly to be avoided. As old Ragland could testify, he thought. He stood at the back of the room, his eyes gradually adjusting to the darkness, seeing the rows of pews, a dozen richly carved, the intricate allegories in the panels on the walls, stories he knew intimately from his childhood; Joseph and his Brethren, David and Goliath, Moses and the Oracles of God.

Without warning, he experienced the intimidation of the room, as though he were still a child, an earnest believer in divine threats, divine punishment.

"Billy?" he called, trying to ignore his feelings. "It's Thomas."

Still no response. As he started down the narrow aisle, he saw the altar, the white marble screen depicting the Passion and Ascension, the raised altarpiece itself, and there, sprawled, facedown, his arms spread, feet together, like a fallen crucifix, he saw a form, neither wood nor marble, merely flesh.

He wondered, what was the point? What was the meaning of earthly existence? Lacking answers, he began moving forward until at last he stood directly over the young man. He bent down and nudged the shoulder. "Billy?" Still receiving no answer, he noticed that the young man was only partially clad, his nightshirt undone and lying loose around his body. As Thomas turned him over, face up, he heard a curious clanking and saw the boy's chest, covered with red welts, rising grooves of self-inflicted punishment, the chain still in his hand, taken, Thomas noticed, from the pulpit where previously it had secured the sixteenth-century German bible.

"Billy," he mourned, viewing the injured flesh, regretting, as he always did in religious matters, the fact that a man could be robbed of his strength by invisible powers.

As he lifted the boy up and cradled him in his arms, he shouted over his shoulder to what he was certain was a congregation of curious servants. "Brandy!" he ordered.

He turned his attention back to the boy in his arms. The sight stabbed Thomas' conscience. He was not guiltless. All the death and injury was his fault, the result of his manipulation. He grew frightened of the vast power in the room.

"Billy?" he urged again, feeling the need for company. "Please, Billy."

Slowly the boy's eyes opened. Thomas saw the hand holding the chain lift weakly as though ready to resume its self-imposed assault on flesh.

"No," Thomas ordered. "Enough." He shook the chain loose and heard it clatter to the floor.

Unarmed, Billy stirred rapidly to consciousness, trying to wrench free from Thomas' arms. "Leave me be," he muttered. "Must die."

"No," Thomas scolded. "You've done enough." He enclosed the boy in his arms, holding him as he would a woman, a faint rocking motion in his body, Billy responding to the closeness, one weak hand reaching up.

Feeling that slight pressure against his chest, Thomas' emotions vaulted. His eyes blurred. No! No interrogation. Whatever had happened in the Queen's Bedchamber would go with Billy to his grave, as obviously the girl had taken it to her grave. It was a tragic incident, but over, and Thomas would carry the lad to his own bed and give himself over to the task of nursing him back to health. They had a common bond now, both bearing visible scars.

Behind him in the corridor he heard a shuffling of feet as the congregation of servants milled about. He heard the respectful voice of Russell Locke. "Brandy, sir," the man murmured and extended a full flask.

But Thomas shook his head and commanded, "Bring it to my chambers." It had occurred to him that a lifeless, scarred Billy would have a much greater effect on the servants than a sputtering, protesting Billy. With some effort, Thomas stood and took the boy with him and permitted the nightshirt to fall opened, revealing the self-flagellation, the boy's features lifeless in Thomas' arms.

Thus he carried him like a fallen warrior back through the chapel and out through the narrow slit in the door, thinking the most unusual thoughts, that sometimes it seemed that life was merely a permission to know death, that every event was simply a trap, ingeniously contrived.

At the sight of the body in Thomas' arm, the servants fell silent. Dolly Wisdom gasped, "Good Lord, Jesus. What next?"

This brief heartfelt expression seemed to set the tone for the others as, moving quickly back with cow eyes and circumflex eyebrows, they cleared a path for Thomas, their heads and necks craning forward for a better look.

A young girl whispered, "He beat hisself."

And a man, "He done his own punishment."

Then a third, "God's hand, that's what done it."

Good, Thomas thought. Obviously they had lost their appetites for interrogation. Hopefully the incident was closed.

The distance from the chapel to Thomas' quarters was about a hundred yards. Most of the servants followed after him the entire distance, keeping a respectful pace behind. As he approached his private door, he heard Dolly Wisdom offer apologetically, "Didn't think he'd do this, milord," she murmured. "Don't serve no purpose."

Thomas looked back and disagreed. "Apparently he thought it did, Dolly."

"I remember him as a boy," she added mournfully. "When he'd come visiting with his father, always dreaming—"

Thomas agreed. "He still is."

Aware that he could no longer support Billy, Thomas motioned for Russell Locke to open the door. From the threshhold he looked back at the servants. "This has been a grim episode for Eden Castle," he said, "and a regrettable way in which to start the New Year. I beseech you to put it from your minds as rapidly as possible, and let us turn our attention to our beloved Ragland. I beg all of you to keep your eyes and ears open, and there will be coin for the one who brings me word of his whereabouts."

Inside the room, Thomas carried Billy to the bed. The boy gave a groan. "Bring me a basin of water and a napkin," Thomas commanded Russell, who had lingered behind. "And leave the brandy. Tell Dolly that some broth would be nice."

Locke nodded and left. Thomas drew a chair close to the bed and sat wearily, his eyes focused on the reviving Billy.

Billy's eyes opened. "Thomas," he groaned.

Quickly Thomas reached out and took the young man's hand. "It's all right, Billy," he soothed. "You must lie still."

In spite of his obvious weakness and discomfort, Billy smiled. "It's my turn now—"

Thomas remembered how Billy had directed the same admonishment to him when he'd taken the shot in his shoulder. "It comes to all men, Billy," he comforted, "the time and need to lie still."

As though memory had come with the return of consciousness, Billy gave a sharp cry. Thomas sat up, alarmed. What balm could he use against memory? "Take ease," he urged, "Rest."

But Billy merely shook his head. "I did not kill her, Thomas. I swear it." The room was silent except for a smothered sob, already grown hoarse. Still Thomas watched, aware that there were scars deeper and more serious than those on Billy's chest. Thomas wondered sharply, what *had* occurred that night three days ago? If asked, how could Billy possibly account for the mutilations on the girl's body? No need to wonder, for Thomas intended never to ask.

He looked back at the stricken face on the pillow. In Billy's clouded eyes appeared something mighty. He lay motionless, his breath barely daring to escape. He gazed upward at the ceiling.

He did not speak.

During the next few weeks, the tales of Ragland's whereabouts grew and spread like rain clouds in a summer squall. The messenger of the moment always told his tale on "good authority," and Thomas listened with dwindling patience and increasing concern.

There were those who held firm to the belief that on the fateful day after Elfie's body had been discovered Ragland had simply walked out into the sea. Others claimed to have heard him swear a lasting vendetta against Eden Castle, and claimed that he was at this moment residing at Penzance, living with a parson who'd taken the old man in.

Thomas had had that rumor checked out, had dispatched half a dozen riders to Cornwall on the explicit orders that they were to personally search every parsonage from here to the coast. They had found nothing.

There were other tales, equally bizarre and improbable. Late-night revelers coming out of The Hanging Man swore they had seen Ragland wandering demented across the moors. And Jack Spade, with the most improbable tale of all, claimed he knew for a fact that Ragland had slipped back into Eden Castle and was at this very moment in hiding, waiting to seek his revenge.

In the cold gray late afternoon light of January thirty-first, Thomas stood at the brink of Eden cliff, wrapped his coat around him, and studied the ever silent face of Billy Beckford, standing dully beside him. He had healed. At least his body had healed. His spirit was still foundering. He was malleable and pliant, agreeable to anything. In fact, Thomas mused, he could order the young man over the side of the cliff and he would surely obey, taking the less than three steps forward, then plunging to a welcome death on the rocks below.

As though alarmed by these thoughts, Thomas took the boy by the arm and guided him backward a few steps. "Not too close, Billy," he warned. Predictably, Billy obeyed.

As Thomas faced directly into the cutting north wind, he wondered how much more he could endure. He had gone to incredible lengths to bring Billy out of his gloom.

They had taken long invigorating rides across the moors. They had walked both the beach and the headlands. Still, nothing that Thomas had shown him seemed to make the slightest difference.

A thought had occurred to him only that morning. There *was* something at Eden Castle that Thomas had not shown him, the remarkable stone passageway leading from the cave on the beach to the stone staircase which led up into the storeroom where the smuggled goods were stored. An incredible sight, in Thomas' opinion. If any scene could jar Billy out of his lethargy, that was surely it.

But Thomas knew he was taking a risk in displaying it. He could count on the allegiance of his men to say nothing. Why should they? To the man, they were enjoying an unprecedented prosperity.

Again he glanced sideways at Billy. What of *his* reaction? Thomas knew that Billy had countless London friends, many in high places. He looked again at the blankly staring young man beside him and thought of the chambers beneath his castle. Then he grabbed his arm. "Come along," he ordered. Without a word of objection, Billy obliged.

Thomas led the way back from the headlands through the castle gates, where the watchmen bowed low and raised the grilles, fairly running now, Billy, still wordless, trotting behind him.

Inside the kitchen they encountered a few servants who froze momentarily at their tasks. Everyone knew where his Lordship was going when he passed this way, and since the Public Whipping of Marianne Locke, everyone knew better than to take notice.

Beyond the kitchen, they descended to the lower level of the castle, the air turning colder, like a crypt. As they approached the first narrow passageway. Thomas reached for the wall torch and lifted it aloft. He glanced back at Billy to see if there was any discernible change of expression.

There was. He looked worried, his eyes moving slowly over the gray stone.

"Prepare yourself for another world, Billy," Thomas warned, "and watch your step," he added. "It's not far, but it's hazardous."

For the first time in three weeks he heard words coming

from the young man. "Thomas," Billy whispered, "where are we—"

So! It had worked. "You'll see," he promised. "You'll see a sight you've never seen before. Only a short distance farther—"

Thomas stepped down into the central chamber. Quickly he hurried around the walls, lighting three additional torches. Then he moved back to the door where he'd abandoned Billy and drew him close to the center where he could look in all directions at the kegs, barrels, and chests.

"Now," Thomas exulted, "do you know where you are?"

From the confusion on his face, Billy did not know. He seemed to be shivering in the damp cold, but there was a flicker of interest in his eyes.

Thomas smiled. They were surrounded by the perfect remedy for chills. He moved toward the kegs of brandy and commenced dragging one forward. Halfway through his effort he stopped, his eyes falling on a strange sight. There against the far wall was a stack of coverlets, mussed, as though someone had recently lain upon them. He started forward for a closer examination when Billy called, "Thomas? Where are you?"

"Coming," he called back, looking again at the curious nest. Perhaps one of his men had decided a guard was needed.

Quickly he returned to the keg and dragged it to the center of the room, stopping to retrieve two sampling cups from atop a barrel. He broke the seal, poured two full cups, and handed one to Billy. "This will warm you," he promised.

Still looking about, Billy took the cup. "What is this place?"

Before Thomas could reply, he stopped again, ears alert. There was a sound coming from the lower staircase.

Thomas heard it, but obviously Billy didn't. "Where did all this come—"

"Shhh!" warned Thomas, hushing him. Both men stood still, Thomas keeping a sharp ear on the staircase to his left. He heard nothing now except the faint creaking of the old support timbers.

Slowly he sipped from his cup. "I thought I heard something," he muttered, keeping his eye on the small black opening.

Growing weary of the mystery Billy sat on a nearby barrel. Thomas glanced at him, one ear still listening. "What do you think?" he said with a smile.

Billy shook his head. "I don't remember this. I thought that as a boy I'd covered every square foot of Eden Castle."

Laughing outright, Thomas drank again. "Of course you don't remember it," he chided, "because it wasn't here." He gestured with his cup. "All this was mere stone, Billy, until a few years back. Then one day I decided—"

There it was again, a discernible footstep. He whirled on the doorway, demanding, "Who is there?"

Thomas was aware of Billy standing beside him.

Alarmed, the boy whispered, "What is it?"

Thomas shook his head, indicating the need for silence. "Listen!" It came again, someone moving in the darkness, just out of sight. A thief, perhaps, someone who'd found the opening in the cove. "Who is there?" he called again.

Still hovering behind him, Billy whispered, "Let's go, Thomas."

At that moment a specter emerged from the doorway. Thomas started forward, then stopped. It was Ragland, or what was left of Ragland. He stood in the doorway, scarcely resembling a man, with his anguished face and distended eyes, his lips blue with cold. There were white patches on his skin. He was covered with filth.

Thomas stepped forward, relieved at finding the old man safe. "Ragland, I—" He stopped as from the folds of the black soiled coat Ragland withdrew a pistol.

Behind him, Thomas heard Billy start to retreat. At the sight of the movement Ragland stepped further into the room, lifted the pistol, and took aim.

"Wait," Thomas soothed. He forced himself to move in front of the pistol, all the while taking note of the glazed look in Ragland's eyes. Thomas saw a derangement in the old face which suggested the futility of speech. Still he had to try. "Ragland," he began softly, "we've been so worried. I've had men out—"

Suddenly the old man interrupted him with a sharp wail. "Damn your men and damn you as well. Do you know what I've lost? Do you even know she's dead?" Tears slipped down the soiled cheeks, but he continued to hold the pistol upright, his finger crooked on the trigger, the weapon pointing directly at Thomas.

Thomas felt death grinning at him, the same feeling he'd suffered the night in William Pitch's house. Quietly, without looking, he warned Billy, "Remain still."

But Ragland heard and stepped closer. His face mysteriously softened. He spoke gently, pleading, "Why? She was nothing to you. There were a hundred others. Why Elfie? She was my only—" Tears overtook him again. Assessing the old man's weakness, Thomas inched forward. His goal was to disarm him as quickly though as gently as possible.

Ragland saw the movement and angrily lifted the pistol higher, aiming it straight at Thomas' heart. "Stay!" he commanded. "Not one step closer, I warn you—"

Thomas obeyed. He glanced over his shoulder at Billy, who stood by the opposite door. Then he turned his attention back to the old man. "Would you like brandy? You must be frozen."

But Ragland cut him off by merely lifting the pistol and steadying his aim. Thomas could see the resolution in his face. "Ragland," he began, "Whatever happened, I'm truly sorry. It was not my intention—"

The old man wept uncontrollably, repeating over and over, "Oh God, oh God, oh God."

Over the weeping, Thomas was aware of a new sound, the pressure of a single step a distance behind him. He'd warned Billy to hold still. He was on the verge of repeating the order when suddenly a shot rang out, coming not from Ragland's weapon, but from the opposite direction. He saw a fireball exploding into old Ragland's chest and sweeping him backward into the narrow staircase. Thomas flattened himself on the floor. He was aware that Ragland's gun had discharged in a reflexive action. This second explosion went wildly up into the ceiling, the small chamber resounding with the echos of shots. The reverberations lashed at Thomas as he raised up and caught a glimpse of Ragland's bleeding chest, the old man fallen in a black and red heap. Behind him Thomas heard the excited voice of Russell Locke. He felt Locke's hands on his shoulders. "Look, milord," the man shouted, pointing up.

Thomas looked upward at the fine silt sifting through

the ceiling. He heard a low distant rumble, growing in intensity, the silt increasing to a steady rain.

Locke shouted, *"Cave-in!"* Thomas felt himself being dragged toward the opposite door where Billy stood ready to bolt. Locke herded them a few steps up the passage. The distant rumbling grew louder. It seemed to be moving closer, the towering stone walls dissolving like breakers, furiously darting sprays of dust which filled their nostrils. Billy crouched on the steps, both arms thrown over his head. Locke shielded Thomas with his own body, the fearful noise still increasing as the frail timbers gave way, releasing a rain of stone, huge wedges falling in the central chamber, the narrow passage warm and close and dust-filled.

Thomas closed his eyes to wait out the endless thunder. The entire ceiling was collapsing. He thought of Ragland, trapped, and raised his head to see if the man had made it to safety. Then he remembered the torn chest and realized in despair that it made no difference.

At last the rumbling subsided, though smoke and dust continued to roll over them in billowing waves. Behind him he heard Billy choking. He glanced backward and saw him stumbling up to the top of the steps.

Locke stood aside. The man's face was covered with white chalky dust. In his hand Thomas saw the pistol which had saved his life. And taken Ragland's.

Apparently Locke saw Thomas' expression. He spoke coldly to the floor. "I've suspected, milord, for some time that Ragland was hiding here," he began. "When the servants told me that you had come down—"

Thomas sensed the man's uneasiness and tried to reassure him. "You saved our lives. I am in your debt."

Clearly relieved, Locke bobbed his head. Thomas looked back into what had been the central storehouse. Now it was a clogged, still smoking mass of fallen boulders, the destruction extending beyond the staircase to the far wall, the wall itself gone, everything buried. Thomas saw in his imagination the old man buried, his frail body crushed, a torn chest the least part of his broken frame.

At the top of the stairs behind him he heard the servants gathering, their voices pinched on a thin edge of hysteria. Somewhere off in the distant recesses of the tunnel he heard a final shattering collapse, the lower timbers giving away. Silence.

Thomas could not move. Softly he slumped forward on the steps. Resting his head on his arms, he was only vaguely aware of the movement at the top of the steps, Russell dispersing the little band of gaping servants as though he knew his Lordship did not wish to be seen in such circumstances. He felt something fragile being born within him. What a trail of death and destruction there had been, starting on the Twelfth Night Celebration and extending here, to the death of his most trusted friend.

A feeling of distress took possession of him as he confronted his own responsibility, his own undeniable and painful part in the tragic sequence of events. With his head bowed, choking on regret and dust, he experienced an intolerable shame. He laid one hand against the cold wall and wished fervently that this last corridor too would collapse.

From the top of the stairs he heard Russell Locke. "Milord, please. It will serve no purpose to—"

In spite of his debt to the man, Thomas shouted, "Leave me be! Escort Mr. Beckford to his room and see to his wants, but leave me be."

There was no reply. Thomas heard footsteps moving away, the man apparently willing to follow his least command. Like Ragland.

Thinking the name caused new grief. Ragland gone, Ragland dead and buried less than thirty feet away, no way even to retrieve the body and give him an honorable burial. Ragland alone, hiding out for days in the tunnel, senseless, waiting to catch Thomas unaware.

A horrible thought occurred to him. The pistol had been pointed at him, not Billy. Ragland must have thought that *he* was the one responsible for—

He stretched upward and hurled himself toward the fallen boulders. Somehow he had to reach Ragland, had to tell him it was Billy who had done damage to the girl. Thomas had not touched her, not once.

He cried out, "Ragland, you must listen! Can you hear?" His eyes moved across the fallen stones, trying to determine where the far staircase had been. "Ragland, listen!" he cried. "It wasn't me. I swear it. Can you hear?"

He lost count of the number of times he cried out, was

aware at last of his throat burning with effort and the
residue of dust. The darkness of the steps was no match
for the darkness in his mind. Everything he touched he destroyed. Everything. *Everything!* Inside his soul the elements were raging. Somewhere the bells were ringing an
alarm, a storm was gathering, the most terrible storm he
had ever known.

Against the wind which had risen in his ear he bowed
his head, more than bowed it, brought it forcibly down
upon the rough sharpness of the boulder.

He fell upon his knees, senseless and thus remained, as
if in prayer.

The five months comprising winter and spring of 1793
were a tumultuous period for the rest of the world as well
as for Eden Castle. The cave-in which had occurred on
that cold January afternoon was repeated in variation
across the English Channel.

Revolution marked the day. The head of Louis XVI was
separated from his body, a grim signal for the official
commencement of the Reign of Terror. Marat was murdered unceremoniously in his bathtub by Citizen Corday.
Thirsting for additional blood, the French then murdered
Queen Marie Antoinette, then the Duke of Orleans, then
the Duchess of Orleans, then the Duke of Everything, the
death machine devouring up to a thousand in one day.

News of this madness reached Eden Castle in the forms
of bulletins which generally fell into the unlikely hands
of Russell Locke, the only hands which were steady enough
to hold the pages and comprehend the bloodbath, and
wonder how long it would be before the insanity reached
England. Not that he ever really felt threatened. God
could not be so merciless as to take from him that which
he had worked so hard to achieve.

There were several subsequent developments after the
cave-in. The very next day, Billy Beckford, stirred to his
senses by the rising horror taking place around him,
summoned his servants and carriages and fled back to mild
Wiltshire. There he buried himself in the plans for his
tower, a paragon of reason and good sense compared to
his unhappy stay at Eden Castle.

Lord Eden lapsed into his deepest and most prolonged
"religious period," wearing black constantly, eating little,

drinking nothing. He spent hours in the chapel, refusing to let anyone rehinge the carved door, slipping in through the crack for long intervals of prayer, emerging white-faced for walks along the headlands, unprotected from the elements except for the simple black jacket which he wore constantly, letting the garments dry on his back after they'd been soaked by rain.

He made few requests. No social traffic passed in or out of the castle gates. He insisted that for what few needs he had, he be attended by one man alone. Russell Locke. And Russell attended him gratefully, relishing every step he took up the scale of authority. He felt old Ragland's mantle settling comfortably on his shoulders.

Still, on occasion, his Lordship's behavior puzzled him. In March, at the coldest point of midwinter, Lord Eden made a curious request, more than a request, he commanded Russell to move his father, the old and now completely mindless Hartlow Locke, up to the safety of Eden Castle. He gave the old man lodgings in the warmth of the servant's kitchen, and demanded nothing of him in return, simply free quarters and board and endless hours in which the old man sat, still clutching the stuffed calico elephant, bearing the scars of countless mendings, the handiwork of Jenny Toppinger, who'd come with him and who assisted Dolly Wisdom with the staff of the castle.

Now, when Russell went below for a cup of tea, it was as though he were still sitting in the kitchen of his childhood cottage. All the familiar faces were there, aged, but otherwise unchanged.

There was one other important alteration to life at Eden. Shortly after the cave-in, Lord Eden called a halt to all smuggling activity. This was a serious blow to the men in the smuggling ring as well as the poor tenants and fishermen up and down the coast, who now had to pay full excise for their simple pleasures or do without. But on this point Lord Eden was adamant. There was no attempt to excavate the cave-in. The door leading down to the underground chamber was boarded and nailed shut. Russell, with the assistance of four other men, dragged a boulder to the mouth of the exterior cave and wedged it tightly into place. The underground cavern became Ragland's crypt. On the specific orders of Lord Eden, it was to remain that way.

With the exception of these changes, life at Eden Castle was placid, the Banqueting Hall and all the great rooms silent and unused. His Lordship moved on a set course which varied not at all and included the walk from his chamber to the chapel, and now and then a longer excursion out onto the headlands, where on occasion he requested that Russell accompany him.

Russell always obeyed, and watched closely for the slightest hint to the substance of his Lordship's thoughts. Generally he found nothing but a pale, drawn face and eyes which appeared to be in perpetual mourning. On one occasion he had confided to Russell that as a child he had seen a drowned man. He had found the body on a summer day, and had not been at all afraid, but at night he had dreamed terrible dreams. He said he'd seen a sea where every wave rolled a dead man to his feet.

He'd concluded the tale of the dream with the soft comment that it was so with him now.

On a dazzling morning in early spring, Russell sat at the table in the servant's kitchen, enjoying a cup of tea, waiting for Dolly and Jenny to prepare the breakfast tray which he customarily delivered to Lord Eden sharply at nine o'clock after his Lordship's morning meditation.

The door at the top of the wooden staircase was open, permitting the sweetest of breezes to waft down and over him, a honey-scented washed sea breeze which had a medicinal effect.

He looked up toward the direction of the breeze. It still was a hazard for his eyes to get past the dark emptiness beneath the steps, the place where the girl had been found hanging. He'd never confessed this to anyone for fear it would make him appear womanlike. He certainly never discussed it openly as did old Dolly, who relived the hideous morning almost daily for the benefit of Jenny Toppinger, who'd had the misfortune to miss the entire event. He'd heard Dolly proclaim that she never looked at the staircase, not even now, months later, without seeing the soiled white nightdress, the poor child's head hanging awkwardly to one side, the tiny feet pointed and dangling.

"God," he muttered, and sent his eyes quickly away to the interior of the room. As he spied his father in the corner, sitting on the stool before a dead fire, his expression changed again. The sight of his father pleased him. The old man's present good fortune was due solely to Russell. Hadn't his Lordship said so time and time again? That he owed Russell a great deal, his life even? He did wish that his father were capable of response. It would have been satisfying to have the old man aware of Russell's accomplishments. But of course Hartlow Locke was aware of nothing, had been aware of nothing since the morning of the Public Whipping.

Dolly was leaning over him, refilling his teacup, scolding him mildly. "What a black look, Russell, on such a glorious morn. You'll chase the sun away if you're not careful."

Russell ignored the rebuke and continued to focus on his father. "Do you think he'll ever speak sense again, Dolly?" he asked.

The old woman raised up and stretched a kink out of her neck. "Not in this life, he won't. His heart's broke and you can't stitch one of them back together with needle and thread." She lifted the teakettle in the air, and again scolded gently. "He's happy enough, though, just sitting there. Sometimes of an afternoon, when just Jenny and me are in the kitchen, we'll hear him laughing and he speaks to her now and then."

"Who?"

"Now, who do you think? Marianne, of course."

Of course. Angrily Russell turned away and lifted his cup and sipped at the hot tea. "Is the tray ready?" he snapped, sending his attention back toward the open doorway atop the kitchen steps.

His breath caught. There, silhouetted before the blaze of morning sun and filling the doorway, he saw the figure of a man. His vision was rendered useless by the explosion of light. It wasn't until he heard Dolly gasp, "Milord, is all well?" that he struggled to his feet. Was he late with the tray? Was the system of bells by which Lord Eden summoned him broken? Had he been so engrossed in his own sense of accomplishment that he'd failed to hear?

"Milord," he murmured, "my apologies."

When Lord Eden failed to respond, Russell suspected the worst, that he was late. He scurried up the steps, got halfway up, then shouted back to Dolly, "The tray. Is the tray ready?" To Lord Eden in a gentler voice he promised, "I'll bring it right along, milord."

At last there were words evolving out of the silhouette.

"No need, Russell," the voice came, as calm as the spring morning.

"But your breakfast, milord."

"I'll breakfast later. I want you to walk with me now. Heaven does not intend for us to pass such a glorious hour imprisoned in stone. Come. We'll walk."

Russell blinked at the voice, deeply registered, like organ music. "Yes, milord," he agreed, and hurried up the steps. He stood back, expecting his Lordship to lead the way. But instead Lord Eden held his ground, his eyes seeing something. He was clothed in black, black boots, black knee trousers, loosely fitting black jacket minus shirt, the bare flesh of his chest showing in a small triangle beneath his chin, his hair growing long and unruly, his whole bearing that of one who has survived excruciating pain.

When he refused to vacate the doorway, Russell inquired, "Are you well, milord? Shall I—"

Slowly Lord Eden lifted his hand and pointed down to the broad oak planks. "Is that the place," he began, "where the girl—"

"It is, milord," Russell quickly confirmed. Below him in the kitchen he heard not a sound.

When apparently he'd looked his fill, he turned rapidly and started off across the cobblestones, setting a fast pace, leaving Russell to catch up. Only once did Lord Eden alter his rapid rate of walking and that was as he drew near the whipping oak. He'd almost passed it by when suddenly he stopped, as though the oak had addressed him.

Russell watched as Lord Eden approached the oak, touched it, encircled it, considered its length and breadth, examined the base where it penetrated the earth.

Standing a short distance away, Russell saw him lift both hands and push back the masses of hair which fell over his eyes. His face appeared to be drained of all color as though from the ravages of sickness. He smiled at the whipping oak, then stepped forward and embraced it.

Russell started forward in concern. "Milord—"

"Stay!" Lord Eden commanded sharply.

Russell obeyed. He watched, bewildered, as his Lordship tightened his grip on the oak, his hands struggling to meet as though ropes were binding him, his legs spread apart, the classic position for punishment.

Russell felt his heart accelerate at the terrifying spectacle. "Please, milord," he begged.

But the man did not respond except to close his eyes. Beyond on the castle walls, Russell was aware of the watchmen staring down on them, their vigil interrupted by the curious sight.

Then Lord Eden stepped away, his face like that of a man witnessing a shipwreck. "My God," he whispered.

He straightened himself, pushed back the unruly hair, and posed a direct question. "Do you think you could survive such an ordeal, Russell?"

Russell hesitated. "I hope, milord, that I never have to put my endurance to that test."

"Your sister did."

"She was disobedient, milord."

"No, she wasn't. She merely imposed her will on mine. Was such an act deserving of this?"

Russell's bewilderment mounted. "I'm afraid I don't understand, milord," he admitted honestly.

Apparently it was a good reply. Lord Eden smiled in agreement. "Nor do I, Russell." Then, as though experiencing a complete change of mood, he straightened his shoulders and walked rapidly past the whipping oak. He led the way through the castle gates and out onto the headlands, moving in an easterly direction to a place where Eden Point softened into crests of broad wooded hills and glens cut square.

Russell struggled after him, his mind still churning with the peculiar events of the morning. It was about half an hour later when he looked up and determined where they were going, to a hidden glen which was accessible only from the top of Eden Point. On three sides it was surrounded by steep cliffs on which trees clung with roots as thick as a man's arm. Down by the water, where the earth had been gradually washed away, their roots stood up, bare and crooked and twisted about one another. It was like an infinite number of serpents which had wanted all at the same time to crawl up out of the pool but had gotten entangled in one another and held fast.

Russell knew the spot. There were old wives in Mortemouth who claimed it was haunted. As Lord Eden started down the steep side, Russell called out anxiously, "Is it safe, milord?"

Lord Eden looked back. "Nothing's safe, Russell. Come along."

Russell hesitated. Then, because he had no choice, he followed after him, although he kept a keen eye on the roots sticking up above the water like a many-armed monster.

Once down at sea level, muddy from the descent and breathless with exertion, Russell stood a distance apart, watching closely as Lord Eden went hurriedly to a nearby thicket. Russell saw him bend over and feel about inside the luxurious green growth as though searching for something.

When a moment later, without hesitation or apology, he raised up, bringing with him a white, gleaming, grinning human skull, Russell retreated.

"Wait!" Lord Eden called out, grinning like the skull. "He's harmless. See?" He thrust the skull close for Russell's inspection, while Russell clung to low-hanging branches, certain beyond any doubt that his Lordship was mad.

"Don't be afraid, Russell," Lord Eden soothed. "This is my friend. Remember? I told you about him, about how I'd found him here when I was a boy. Fully clothed in his flesh he was then, and bloated." He lightly dusted a speck of clinging earth from an eye cavity. "On my word, he looks better now." He held the skull up to the sun and peered closely at it. In apparent seriousness, he inquired, "Do you recognize him?"

Quickly Russell shook his head, still grasping the branches of a nearby tree, ready at the slightest provocation to swing upward to safety. "No, milord," he replied. "I wasn't even in my mothers' womb when—"

"When I was a boy?" Mournfully Lord Eden concurred. "Right you are," he agreed. "Our ages separate us, but our curiosities must bring us together." Again he held the skull upward. "Nohing familiar about him at all?" he asked.

In the rising heat of the morning, insects buzzed close. Russell shook them away and tried to make his face a stone image of interest and cooperation. "A fisherman, perhaps," he offered, "Drowned at sea and washed ashore?"

"He wasn't dressed as a fisherman," Lord Eden said.

A legitimate question occurred to Russell and he asked it. "How do you know it's the same man? Perhaps—"

Adamantly Lord Eden shook his head. "It's the man. I told no one. I buried him myself over there." And he pointed toward the thicket. "He was my friend"—he smiled—"and my nightmare." He took the skull with him and sat heavily on a nearby rock, his face mournful again. "As a child, I came here hoping to find a sea nymph. Instead I found him." He fell into a deep study of the skull as though recognition was on the verge of breaking.

Russell watched and felt himself on the verge of breaking as well. He longed for the cool darkness of the castle, the quiet freedom of his normal mornings. He did not understand what he was doing here, or what possible fascination Lord Eden found in the grinning macabre sight.

Still Lord Eden fondled the skull. Softly he asked, "Are you afraid of death, Russell?"

"I fear I am, milord. Isn't everyone?"

Lord Eden shook his head. "Ragland wasn't. Ragland longed for death. The girl, Elfie, wasn't. She provided it with her own hand. And I don't think your sister is. She's looked it square in the face."

Russell felt a slight annoyance at the reference to his sister. "She's simpleminded," he blurted, forgetting the propriety of a conversation between servant and master, the servant's right to respond only when spoken to. He lowered his head. "I beg your pardon, milord," he muttered.

With admirable largess Lord Eden brushed his apology aside with a firm contradiction. "Not simpleminded, Russell," he said, laughing softly. "You must never deceive yourself on that matter."

Rebuked, Russell lowered his head. "As you say, milord," hoping to conclude the subject.

Unfortunately Lord Eden had other ideas. He laid the skull aside and sat upright on the rock, his face earnest. "Would you have any idea why she won't have me?" he asked, simply, almost childlike.

Russell stared back at him. Was it possible that Lord Eden had spent the entire winter puzzling over such a silly question? "She's scarcely worth your time, milord. There are countless others—"

"But I don't want others," Lord Eden broke in.

To such a forceful confession, Russell could say nothing.

He relaxed his grip on the branches and stood awkwardly at the bottom of the cliff. Dry leaves played about his feet as if to amuse him.

"Pure," Lord Eden mused aloud. "She's pure in God's eyes. The flame of His wrath has not once touched her."

As Russell looked up, he saw Lord Eden stand and hurl the skull, as though in anger, far out into the ocean. It fell with a small pop on a distant breaking wave and disappeared from sight.

Lord Eden walked to the ocean's edge and lifted his face to the sea wind as though deriving actual nourishment from it. Over his shoulder he commanded, "Make preparations to leave for London, Russell. No later than next week. I'm tired of winter and cold and skulls and death. Your sister knows something we don't know, and I think it's time we found out."

As he warmed to the projected journey, he walked back from the water's edge, his face lighter, almost pleasant. "This time, Russell," he announced, "I'll woo her as though she were the finest lady in the realm. I'll court her with gifts, with coin, with grace, whatever is necessary. It should be great sport. Are you game?"

Russell could only gape. His Lordship *was* mad. London! Good God! It was the last place Russell wanted to go. He still remembered all too well the beating he'd received at the hands of city dandies. And had Lord Eden so soon forgotten his own recent humiliation in London?

For once, Russell decided, he must assert his opinion, in the name of good sense and reason. He looked up and met directly the expectant face of his master. "No, milord," he began. "I object. I think it's imprudent for—"

Suddenly Lord Eden lunged forward, both hands extended as though he intended to plant them around Russell's throat and hold on until he'd successfully choked all rebuttal out of him. He stopped himself at the last minute, as though under a severe act of self-discipline.

"Watch yourself, Locke," he ordered, still reining in his anger. "In almost sixty years of service to the Eden family, that nobleman Ragland, whose worthy position you now occupy never once drew a breath in contradiction of his master's orders." He stepped back, jerkily, as though still practicing self-restraint. "I warn you," he muttered, "watch yourself. You occupy your present pleasant position because of your sister and the mutual debts which bind us together. Nothing else. Is that clear?"

Staggered by the rapid change of mood, Russell did well to nod. He retreated a step to increase the distance between them, still keeping a watchful eye on the smoldering countenance of Lord Eden, who was now pacing the sandy beach in short erratic steps as though with difficulty digesting his loss of temper.

"We shall leave within the fortnight!" he shouted at Russell. "So take your objections by the scruff of the neck and throw them to ground." He lifted a trembling hand. "Or I shall do it for you," he threatened.

Quickly Russell hastened to repair the breach. "I have no objection, milord. I live to serve you."

Lord Eden nodded broadly. "You live *because* you serve me," he pronounced pointedly. "I have taken your entire household save two sisters into the security of my castle. I clothe and feed the lot of you. In return I will be obeyed."

Again Russell bobbed his head. "I stand ready to serve," he murmured.

"Then go serve!" thundered Lord Eden. "If you're unfamiliar with the preparations necessary for such a journey, ask Dolly Wisdom for assistance. But go on with you now for I can't stand the sight of you."

Russell scrambled backward, only too pleased to have been dismissed. For several yards up the mud-wet incline, he was unable to get the necessary traction, and for every foot forward he slipped and fell backward. He was aware of Lord Eden watching him. Several minutes later, muddied and breathless, he pulled himself to the summit, his heart beating too rapidly.

At the top, he glanced back at Lord Eden, now diminished by distance, still pacing on the tiny beach, his head bowed, hands locked behind his back, as though trying to walk off the black moods which plagued him.

Russell stared down, inferiority on his brow which seemed to press against his eyes, the eyes themselves mere slits. It was the girl, still the girl, always the girl. As he walked, he shoved his hands in his pockets and kicked angrily at small stones. He resembled a schoolboy who had been publicly humiliated for his slow wits. Always the girl, the curse of his life. It was clear to him now that

Lord Eden had retained his services merely so he could procure the girl for him.

You occupy your present pleasant position because of your sister and the mutual debts which bind us together.

There was the most painful thought of all. In order to escape it, he broke into a run, a lung-bursting sprint into the strong westerly winds of the headlands.

He was nothing, had been born nothing and would remain nothing. The girl. Always the girl.

London
June, 1794

*J*HE British court went into mourning on learning of the execution of Louis the Sixteenth," read Marianne from the June 13 edition of *The Bloomsbury Gazetteer*.

Her audience of two, Jane and Sarah, showed little interest in what she was reading. They concentrated instead on the meager breakfast before them, which consisted of hard bread and weak tea.

Still Marianne read on, in a splash of brilliant morning sun, hoping not only to divert them, but also to let them see that their particular plight had universal implications. The entire world, not just the red brick house on Great Russell Street, was crumbling.

She adjusted the newsprint to the sun, her clear, bell-like voice a curious contradiction to the capsulized version of the horrible events of the last few months.

Sarah interrupted. "Don't need no bloody newspaper to tell me the state of things. I'm the one who takes the two guineas a week and tries to buy food enough for three." She pushed away from the cup of pale tea, her eyes crinkled with worry, her hair growing grayer, or so it seemed to Marianne.

"You do a good job, Sarah," she soothed. "Jane and I would be quite lost without you."

The woman made a harrumphing noise at the tribute. She drew the weak tea and sipped at it. She made a face at the cup. "I've thrown out better than that in the past," she grumbled. "We're going to be starving out soon," she warned. "Exactly half of them guineas go for food tax now, and unless Mr. Pitch—"

Softly Jane groaned, as though the mere sound of the name had reawakened unbearable memories. She covered her face with her hands.

Silence descended on the small kitchen. Marianne looked about. How their lives had changed in the last six months. In order to conserve coal and oil, all three had moved couches into the kitchen, while the rest of the house had been sealed off. Jane had sold most of her clothes for what little she could get for them. In addition, they'd sold a silver service, and two of William's finest paintings from the Italian Renaissance school. Finally, it had been Marianne who'd put a halt to the wholesale auction of William's possessions. First, they had no right, and second, they were realizing only a fraction of the objects' true worth. Better to have credit, Marianne had said, than give away the art that William had spent a lifetime acquiring.

Sarah hadn't seen it that way, nor had Jane at first. But in the beginning the Bloomsbury tradesmen had been only too happy to extend the women unlimited credit. After all, they were living in William Pitch's house and William Pitch was a most solvent man, and surely William Pitch would be home any day now from his escapades in France.

Marianne looked despairingly about. She'd thought all winter that with the coming of summer life would be better. But it wasn't. She recalled how eagerly they all used to await the morning post, confident that William would send word of his impending arrival. But they'd received no word, and during the last few weeks Jane had told them of a persistent nightmare in which she had seen William dead.

In spite of the warm sun, Marianne shivered. Sarah pushed away from the table as though she could no longer endure the lethargy. "There'll be no noon meal," she warned. "And only winter potatoes for evening." She held up a canister of seeds. "The sooner we get these in the ground, the better off we'll be."

Marianne looked up. "I'll do it," she offered, taking the canister, seeing in her mind's eye the weed-clogged garden. It would take at least two days to clear a plot. But Sarah was right. A home supplement of carrots and lettuce, a summer crop of potatoes, would help. Now all credit was closed to them, and at least once a week they had to endure the humiliation of the spunging agents, the men appointed by their creditors to collect their debts.

As she started toward the back door, she looked at Jane, her heart heavy at the sight of the desolate woman. How greatly changed they all were, but most of all Jane. Gone were her lovely gowns and powdered wigs. Now she wore the plain dress of a serving girl, soiled from too many days' wear, her own hair hanging loose, streaks of gray mixed in with the black. Her face seemed to have aged in a like manner, deep erosions appearing on her throat and at the corners of her eyes and mouth.

In addition to the physical disintegration, Marianne had observed an equally devastating disintegration of the spirit. Jane moved through the back rooms of William's house as spiritless as a zombie, following Sarah's directions as best she could, but for the most part assuming the role of an invalid. Her new vulnerability only made her dearer to Marianne.

Almost moved to tears by the sight of her once gay and handsome sister, Marianne went back to the table and gently removed the hands which covered her face. "Come with me," she urged softly. "You can sit in a chair in the sun. The air will do you good."

But Jane merely looked at her, a look of confusion on her face, the almost elemental look of the seriously ill. "I'll help Sarah," she murmured.

At the sink, Sarah grumbled over her shoulder. "Don't need no help."

Jane looked up, as though torn between the two courses of action. Tenderly Marianne resolved the dilemma for her. "Come with me," she urged, lifting her to her feet. "The sun is lovely. I'm sure we'll need no coal this week."

Suddenly fearful, Jane looked about. "The spungers? Will they come again today?"

"No, not today," Marianne replied. "They've already come this week."

"But they'll be back. And it's me they're after." Her fear grew as she looked about the kitchen. "It's my name on the credit. I'm the one. Don't let them take me."

As Jane's fear increased, Marianne wrapped her arms around her, held her as she would a frightened child. "There," she whispered, with a calmness she did not feel. "No one will take you, I promise." The two women stood in close embrace, clinging to each other against the threat of debtor's prison, old Sarah watching, shaking her head.

Marianne continued to hold and soothe, aware that her sister's fear was a very real possibility. Over the last month the spunging agents had grown uglier and more violent. The last two had actually threatened her, clearly ruffians, brutal men hired by creditors who perhaps, under the pressure of inflation, were as financially desperate as themselves.

"Come along," Marianne said almost sternly, disengaging herself from Jane's embrace. "Let's work together as we used to do as children in the garden in Mortemouth." As the image of home flitted across her mind, she felt a new depression of spirit. In her imagination she saw her father and old Jenny Toppinger, and she even thought of her half-brother, Russell, and wondered if he were still playing the dangerous game of smuggling.

She stepped away from Jane, pleased to see that she was quiet. Retrieving the canister of seeds with one hand, she slipped the other about her sister's waist, the two of them moving toward the back door and the warm June sun.

By noon the sun had risen higher and had grown hotter. Several times Marianne leaned heavily on the spade. Her dress was soaked with perspiration and her belly felt cavernous. Sarah had joined her an hour earlier and was following behind her with a rake, breaking up the heavy clods of dirt and pulling to one side the dead weeds. Jane still sat on a small stool, watching the labor with a blank and unresponding face.

"If she's going to eat," muttered Sarah, "she should be out here with the both of us."

"Give her time," Marianne whispered. A salty stream of

sweat slipped into the corner of her eye, momentarily blinding her. The earth beneath her feet appeared suddenly liquid. She looked back at the progress she'd made in three hours. Less than ten feet.

"Are you all right?" Sarah inquired. "Let me do that for a while. You take the rake."

"No, I'm fine," insisted Marianne. "Some water would be good."

Sarah nodded, then turned a critical eye back to Jane. "That's the least she can do." Before Marianne could stop her, she started off across the newly turned soil in a determined path which led to Jane.

Weary, every bone in her body aching, Marianne tried to call after her. But she found she lacked the energy to lift her voice. She felt mildly ill, the unseasonable heat rising about her. The scars on her back seemed to be throbbing individually under the rays of the sun as though each had split and freshly opened. She leaned heavily on the spade, the heat waves drifting up about her, carrying memories of another hot day. How many years would have to pass, she wondered, before she could think on it calmly?

Raising her head, she saw Jane moving docilely toward the back door, apparently registering no protest to Sarah's command. Marianne positioned the spade against the earth, lifted her mud-caked shoe, and pushed with all her might against the rim. The earth gave, the spade moved downward, and at the same time the catch in her back exploded into a thousand fiery fingers. She caught her breath.

Sarah was beside her, gently but firmly removing the spade from her hand, replacing it with the lighter rake. "We need you," the woman scolded. "We need you to read to us and smile for us, for we're no longer capable of either."

Marianne started to protest but knew it was useless. The tools traded, Marianne fell in behind the tall angular woman, admiring the skill and strength with which she manipulated the spade. "I'm afraid we're both going to resemble farm women, Sarah," Marianne joked weakly.

"Won't be nothing new for me," replied the woman. "That's how I was born and that's how I'll die. Your sister's the one that's hurting."

Suddenly, as though in confirmation of her words, there came a blood-chilling scream from the house. Marianne looked sharply at Sarah, then started forward. 'The spungers!' she thought frantically.

She was aware of Sarah moving beside her, both women struggling for footing in the moist soil.

"My God, what is it?" Sarah gasped.

"Hurry!" Marainne urged, fear mounting, clutching the rake as though prepared to use it as a weapon.

While they were still several feet from the back porch, Marianne saw the door swing open, saw Jane appear, her face, of late so somber, now on the verge of exploding with excitement. Still emitting a series of softer screams, she performed a curious little jig up and down, as though she could scarcely contain her joy. In her hand, held aloft over her head like a trophy, Marianne saw a large white envelope.

'Oh, thank God!' she thought. 'It's William. She's had word from William.'

Sarah and Marianne reached the steps at the same time, mutually relieved that the scream had been one of joy. They stood, grinning up at the dancing Jane.

Sarah grew impatient first. "Well, what is it, girl?" she shouted, attempting to make herself heard over the excited squeals.

It had been so long since any of them had had anything to laugh and dance about. For a second Marianne didn't care about the contents of the letter. Jane would share her good news soon enough. For now, it was lovely to stand in the warmth of a June sun, looking up at that laughing face, feeling the deprivation of winter slip from her shoulders.

Then her own curiosity got the best of her. "Jane, please," she begged, shouting as Sarah had done. "What is it? Word from William?"

She thought she detected a slight change in her sister's enraptured face. But no. The radiance was intact, though altered, as Jane ceased her mad little jig and stood breathless, looking down, the white envelope clutched to her breast.

"Well, what is it?" Sarah demanded again. "How long do we have to beg?"

Jane looked very serene, almost saintly. "Just a miracle, Sarah," she replied, sending her eyes heavenward in silent thanks to the source of all miracles.

"Is it William?" Marianne asked again. "Is he—"

Still smiling, Jane began to shake her head back and forth in a negative reply.

Bewildered, Marianne started up the steps. "Then who?"

Jane stopped her with a broad gesture. She commenced to preen on the landing as though it were a small stage. "I was in the kitchen," she began, "fetching your water, as you requested. And suddenly I heard the front bell ring." Here she melodramatically cupped her hand about her ear as though again hearing the bell.

Marianne laughed, thinking that perhaps Jane's natural habitat was the stage of the Drury Lane. "Go on," she urged, placing a restraining hand on Sarah's arm. Sarah's nature and imagination did not include the stage at Drury Lane.

"Well, of course I went to the door and there, standing before me"—she paused for dramatic emphasis—"there was a handsome liveried coachman, all done up in scarlet and gold, and beyond him at the curb, just about the finest coach I've ever seen. The man bowed low like I was Lady Northumberland herself and handed me"—she studied the large white envelope—"this!"

Sarah exhaled a noisy breath and impatiently hurled the spade to the ground. "My God," she muttered. "The woman's daft. I thought it was something."

Sweetly Jane corrected her. "It *is* something, Sarah. Just the answer to all our prayers." With mock grandeur she bowed low and extended the white envelope to Marianne. "It's for you," she said primly.

Marianne stared at the white square being offered her. Jane saw her hesitancy and rushed on. "I took the liberty of opening it," she said with a smile. "With your permission, may I read?"

Sarah muttered, "Some nerve, I'd say."

"Please do," Marianne said, mourning the loss of the brief moment of joy.

Quickly Jane withdrew what was obviously a large, ornate, gilt-trimmed calling card. She lifted the card and her voice as though reciting to the trees:

"LORD THOMAS EDEN of Eden Point, North Devon, requests the honor and privilege of calling on Miss Marianne Locke of Number Sixteen, Great Russell Street. A hasty and affirmative reply satisfying this most urgent need in my soul will be gratefully appreciated.

Your Humble Servant,
THOMAS EDEN"

From the top of the hill beyond Southampton Row, in the little parish church of St. Dunston's, came the sound of church bells. Noon matins. Marianne heard them in a strange way, now so close, now so far away.

Although she had not moved, she felt isolated. She was aware of the other two watching her, Jane still grinning, and old Sarah wearing a less simple expression, her face a safe blank as though withholding her opinion until the first cry of alarm.

Slowly Marianne bowed her head, feeling a fatigue that had nothing to do with her exertion of the morning. She wondered how she should break the news to both women, that none of their problems had been solved. If anything they had increased. As the world was full of predators, now the King of Predators had arrived among them, a man schooled from birth in the art of selfishness and brutality.

As the heat of noon and the moment pressed upon her, she listened again to the bells. Then, because she had nothing to say, she turned and started back toward the freshly turned earth and fallen spade.

Jane called after her. "Wait! You can't just walk away."

Over her shoulder Marianne replied, "I have work to do."

"What of this?" Jane demanded, holding up the letter.

"Save it for winter and we'll use it to start the fire," Marianne said, bending over and retrieving the spade.

She just had enough time to arrange the spade for the first penetration when Jane reached her side. "I don't understand," she demanded. "Do you know how humiliating this must have been for him? To send a formal card to—" She hesitated. Marianne looked up, interested in the coming description.

Jane's voice and manner softened. "It's simply a request to see you again," she pleaded. "My God, he's paying you formal court. Doesn't that mean anything?"

Marianne pushed the spade forward. "Should it?" Beyond Jane's inquiring face, she saw Sarah. Surely she would be an ally.

Jane stared angrily. "You have no right, you know. Lord Eden could be of great assistance to us."

Shocked, Marianne looked up. "In return for what?" she asked pointedly. "Lord Eden is not known for his charitable acts. A bargain would have to be struck. In return for what?" she repeated.

Jane did not hesitate. "In return for hospitality, for a place of ease and relaxation, for—" She faltered.

Marianne urged gently, "Go on."

Forced into a corner, Jane retaliated. Quickly she walked behind Marianne as though to relieve herself of the weight of those eyes. "Well, sweet Lord," she exclaimed. "What is it that you've got that is so precious? Did God create a new and better mold when He made you? I sometimes think that He did from the way you behave." She reemerged in Marianne's view after completing the little half-circle. Although Marianne felt her face burning, she met her sister's gaze straight on, listened as Jane leaned close. "If a dog comes to your door and he's hungry, what does a Christian woman do? She feeds him. If a man, suffering from a much greater hunger, comes to your door, would you do less for the man than you would for the dog?"

Marianne listened incredulously to the nonsense. "Then obviously I'm not a Christian," she murmured, and again positioned the spade against the earth.

Jane announced patly, "You really have no right, you know."

"No right to what?" Marianne asked. "To chart my own destiny?"

Jane spoke on, her voice level. She still held the large white card in her hand. "It's not just your destiny involved here. Mine and Sarah's as well are at stake." She moved closer to Marianne. "Have you so soon forgotten? Have you so successfully blotted that cold rainy night from your mind?"

Alarmed, Marianne looked up. She hadn't expected this. Still, Jane went on as though delivering a rehearsed speech. Behind her, she saw Sarah move to a closer position, obviously the better to hear.

"It is not possible," Jane was saying, "that you've already forgotten the manner in which Sarah and I took you into this house, against Mr. Pitch's wishes, forgotten how we nursed and fed you when you had no place else to go, forgotten how you came to us an outcast, a source of embarrassment both to your family and friends—"

While the words were falling heavily enough on Marianne's ears, Jane seemed to be the one more acutely suffering. Her face appeared pale, the eyes sunken, battered, deep lines etched on either side of her mouth.

She rushed on, as though eager to rid herself of the destructive forces within her. "So we took you in," she concluded, "and gave you shelter because we understood, as you must now understand. You literally hold our futures in your hand, as we held yours in ours that night."

She stepped closer, her eyes beseeching. "How would it do lasting harm to your soul to courteously receive Lord Eden? Clearly he has formed an attachment for you in spite of—" She broke off, apparently unable to find the proper words to describe the past. "How would it harm you," she went on, "to delicately inform him of our plight? In the past I've exchanged words with him and found him to be a most admirable and decent man, even a generous one. To receive him and enlist his aid is no great crime. We cannot go on like this."

Her voice broke. She turned partially away, betraying tears close to the surface. "Look at us," she begged. "No better than field women, trying with no help from God to keep body and soul together." The voice broke again. The tears came. "What are we to do but throw ourselves on his mercy? What alternatives are left?" She shook her head and made a futile attempt to brush the tears away. "You know as well as I that we'll receive no word from William. He's gone and left us to tend to our own survival. What will become of us? What's ahead for us? Where's the hope?"

Grief and fear overtook her. She stood sobbing openly. Sarah turned away as though embarrassed by the outburst.

She retrieved the rake and commenced going over ground that had already been smoothed, leaving Marianne to deal with this unexpected turn, the sight of her sister sobbing, the white card fallen to the ground beween them like an insurmountable obstacle.

Marianne gazed at the fallen card, then dismissed the notion that she could explain herself to the two waiting women. As she lifted a foot to the rim of the spade, she said, "I'm sorry. I cannot."

At those brief and softly spoken words, Jane ran sobbing into the house, the skirts of her patched dress flying out behind her, her hands covering her face as though in abject despair.

With a vigor she did not feel, Marianne plunged the spade into the earth, feeling the blade cutting through the tendrils of grass, lifting the earth in dark moist clumps and depositing it heavily to one side, her memories, her sense of debt and responsibility, pressing against her like an intolerable burden.

She was aware of Sarah working diligently behind her. The two women worked in backbreaking silence until mid-afternoon. In the course of their labors, the white, engraved, gilt-edged calling card was buried in earth, swallowed up for compost for the growing season.

Shortly after three the two women stood back to assess the small, irregularly shaped garden plot. Marianne had seen better. Oh, Lord, had she seen better! She recalled her father's geometrically shaped plot of earth behind their cottage in Mortemouth, a marvel of even rows where the vegetables had grown like jewels, in the days before—

"It isn't much," she commented weakly, to halt the thought before it gained momentum.

Sarah made a wry face. She started toward the back door, muttering, "We will be destitute long before the seeds rise."

Marianne held her position, her eyes focused on the newly turned earth. So! Sarah's safe neutral expression was neither safe nor neutral. As though the realization were intolerable, Marianne fell lightly onto her knees in the dirt. There was not a muscle, bone, nerve in her body that did not ache. She made an attempt to stand, but at that moment she felt a prickly sensation in the hairs on her arms. She felt helpless against the forces around her.

She shook her head twice as though to drive away the frightening sensation, then looked up at the blazing sun.

Paris

August, 1794

$\mathcal{B}$EYOND his mounting excitement at meeting Thomas Paine, William Pitch remembered everything. In one of those crystalline moments of pure recall of which poets speak so lyrically, he remembered, literally, everything.

Now, lying on the pavement before the Assembly, in a hot splash of August sun, he knew that the warm liquid drenching his body was his own blood, knew further that the dismembered limb lying to one side was his own right arm. He knew all this and looked up with glazed eyes at the crowd which pushed around him, and saw nothing save an image of himself, earlier that morning, sitting excitedly in his room at White's Hotel, having coffee, his portmanteau packed, passage booked on the next day's packet crossing the channel. His excitement doubled as he thought of his secret meeting with Citizen Paine, now in ill-health from fever and temporarily released from Luxembourg Prison on behalf of the generous intervention of the American minister, James Monroe.

Then, following the completion of his business with Paine, he planned a hasty exit out of the bloodbath that was Paris, heading toward the channel and the packet that

would take him back to England, to the red brick house
on Great Russell Street, and the woman who had occupied
his thoughts since his departure over a year ago, with a
fever amounting almost to an obsession. Of late, he saw
her image everywhere—the fair hair, the lovely innocent
face. It would serve no purpose to postpone his declaration
of love any longer. He could better serve the Revolution
in England and at the same time serve himself.

In this state of excitement he consumed his morning
coffee, settled his accounts with the concierge, and started
off on foot for the Assembly, the appointed place of his
meeting with Paine. The whole affair had been arranged
by Monsieur Lanthenas, Paine's translator and the only
man who'd been in contact with the "Infamous Incendiary"
during his wretched seven months' imprisonment. The purpose of the meeting was for Pitch to receive portions of
Paine's great manuscript and spirit them out of France
where the revolutionary fires were burning higher and
more out of control every day.

On his excited walk that morning, Pitch purposefully
avoided the Place de la Revolution. He was weary of the
sounds of the tumbrils rattling through the streets, the
shouts of the mob. Worst of all, only last month, had been
Robespierre, that complex leader shot in the mouth, then
dragged speechless, with shattered jaw and bloodstained
cravat, like a broken wax doll splashed with red paint, to
the guillotine.

Lying on the pavement before the Assembly, William
pulled himself out of his memories long enough to face
the reality of the shattered stump which now served as his
right arm. Working over him were two Frenchmen, surgeons, he assumed, trying to staunch the flow of blood.
Weakly, as he turned his head, he saw a cordon of gendarmes, trying to hold back the crowd. Then, kneeling
close beside him, his eyes brought into watery focus the
image of a man. He was dressed in simple black.

This man leaned close and whispered, "Remain silent,
Monsieur. Don't speak!"

In spite of the burning agony which had invaded the
right side of his body, William understood. As an Englishman, he was an alien and therefore subject to prison.
Thomas Paine, obviously fearful that William's physical

agony would interfere with his normally flawless French, had counseled silence.

William obeyed and closed his eyes and in an attempt to endure the ever-increasing agony, gave his mind over again to memory, to an almost clinical reconstruction of the events which had brought him to this fearful point.

He had enjoyed his walk that morning, Paris lovely in August ripeness. He remembered recalling Mary Wollstonecraft's account of Parisian life only a few months after the King's execution: "The whole mode of life here tends to render the people frivolous. They play before me like motes in a sunbeam, enjoying the passing ray."

So they played before William that morning, the lovely ladies, buoyed up as though by animal spirits, strolling the avenues, unconcerned with the various tragedies being played out such a short distance away at the Place de la Revolution, the death carts never silent.

No, he decided that morning that he'd had enough. England loomed large in his thoughts as a haven of sanity, and he was hungry for both the haven and the condition thereof.

Then, at noon as he approached the broad pavement leading to the Assembly, he spied a large crowd, mostly curiosity-seekers come to see Citizen Thomas Paine after he'd presented his petition of release to the Convention. William mingled with the crowd for several moments, making his way to the front, so that he might join Paine's entourage as he emerged from the Assembly.

There, according to Monsieur Lanthenas' plan, William was to blend with Paine's associates and take his place in an appointed carriage, and go with them, unnoticed, to Number 63, Rue de Faubourg St. Denis, Paine's country home, a safe rural retreat.

All went well at first. At precisely twelve noon, William looked up and caught his first glimpse of the man himself, emerging from the Assembly, the pestilence of Luxembourg having clearly taken its toll, though at fifty-three, the face was still thoughtful, alert, full of maturity and character.

Standing at the front of the crowd, William took careful note of the high forehead and bold nose, the unpowdered hair still dark in spite of his long imprisonment, soft with a reddish tinge. But it was the man's eyes which held him enthralled. They had in them the muse of fire. The reason for this careful recording was that William knew of England's interest in her infamous son, that along the Strand and in the Temple, Thomas Paine's friends and enemies were legion and all would read with interest a physical accounting of the man himself.

William filled his eye before moving ahead to join the entourage. Then, at the exact moment of stepping forward, he heard strange movement behind him, someone pushing forward with great speed, a confusion of footsteps, then a telltale odor, the harsh, acrid smell of a firing cap.

He averted his eyes from Thomas Paine, who stood exposed at the top of the broad steps, and glanced over his shoulder. He saw a man behind him, a gleaming light in his eyes, like a fanatic. Then he saw the pistol, a small and rather elegant dueling pistol, raised and pointed directly at Thomas Paine. His mind produced a single word. Assassin! Then his eye determined the angle of the pistol aimed straight at Paine, and William's relationship to that unfired ball. And his last lucid thought? That if he moved now, at the exact moment the finger was tightening against the trigger, he might block the ball with his right arm, *block it,* as though his arm were made of something other than flesh and bone, a harder substance off which the ball would ricochet and fall, useless, to the pavement.

This he did. At the precise moment of the explosion, he felt the impact of the closely fired shot spin him about, like a child's top, his right arm exploding along with the gun, his mad spiral spewing blood, the crowd screaming, until at last he fell where he now lay, that macabre object still lying only a few feet away, his arm, the burned remains of the sleeve of a dark gray jacket which he had so excitedly donned that morning.

"Mon Dieu," he groaned.

Paine was beside him, bending low, his face creased with concern and gratitude. In French he again commanded him to lie still and remain silent.

The burning agony was spreading over his entire body. He heard Paine speak to the surgeons, telling them enough, that they could finish their work at his house in St. Denis. With forceful command, William heard him summon four men and order them to lift and transport him to a waiting carriage.

A gendarme stepped forward, apparently convinced that he and his men were to take custody of William.

Again Paine interceded. Still clutching his temporary release from the Assembly, he held it upward and warned sternly in French, "This represents safe passage for me and my associates. I would not advise—" William heard the voice soften, as though wiser tactics had entered his mind. "The man is wounded," Paine whispered. "Perhaps mortally. Fate may wish to question him first."

Confronted with such simplicity of manner, the gendarmes backed away and permitted the men to lift William and carry him to the curb, through the curious crowd to the waiting carriage.

William felt himself being placed on cushions in a half-sitting position, the stump of his arm bound rigidly to his side, still showing blood. Paine and the surgeons crawled in after him.

For the first time Paine spoke to him in English, though his voice was low. "Fate will have no questions for you," he said with a smile. "Only reward." Those eyes, which earlier had burned with the muse of fire, looked glazed. "I owe you my life," he said, "and as payment I shall personally see to it that death does not claim you. Rest now."

William lifted his head as the carriage pulled away from the curb. The last thing he saw was the crowd. They had become like children again, frivolous and gay. Men, and women, too, were tossing something up into the air, laughing as it came down, then hurling it up again, a summer game of leisure played with an air of exhilaration.

He tried to clear his vision, the better to see. Then he saw too clearly. "Oh, God," he moaned again and felt himself disfigured by pain and horror. As the object of the summer game flew up once again into the air, he recognized the hand, the grey sleeve, the fingers still arched and stiff as if it were suffering from some elaborate denial.

Apparently Thomas Paine saw the grisly scene. He leaned quickly out of the window and shouted at the driver, "Hurry! Get us out of this place!"

With a curious fragrance of lilacs filling the carriage, canceling the odor of seared flesh, with Thomas Paine's steady hand resting lightly on his forehead, William, in his dream, slipped back across the channel, yielding to images of her, her face, her sweetness.

"Marianne," he murmured.

London
August, 1794

TOWARD noon, in the middle of the hottest August that London had known for three decades, Thomas Eden sat at the second-floor window of his house on Oxford Road, searching in vain for a breath of air.

It was an uneasy summer, with regiments of uniforms filling London's streets, bright, brash, earnest young men who'd missed out on the war with the American colonies, but who had come of age in time for the hostilities with France.

In the two months that Thomas had been in London, he had the habit of keeping a constant vigil at his upstairs window. The activity in Oxford Road below fascinated him, the constant comings and goings, the carriages rattling past, hundreds of little street dramas played out before him daily.

He was learning to be a patient man. He shunned all social traffic, had not once been to his club or any of his favorite coffee or chop houses. He had no intention of going. He was here for one purpose alone, and until he realized the accomplishment of that purpose, he would wait and merely witness the lives of others

In two months he had sent around eight different calling cards to the house on Great Russell Street. So far he'd received no response. After each delivery his footman had explained how one of two women always answered the bell, plain, common women, according to the footman, who had received the card, then politely closed the door.

He had sent eight cards. He was prepared to send eighty if necessary. His system had to be cleansed of the girl, and if this was the only way to accomplish it, then he was prepared to wait, even though at times the waiting seemed capable of killing him.

Before him on the airless windowsill was last week's edition of *The Bloomsbury Gazetteer*. In an effort to distract himself from his boredom, he glanced at the front page to an article concerning one Dr. James Graham who prescribed "bathing in earth" as a new way of preserving health and constancy.

Bathing in earth? Thomas lifted the paper and read with interest;

> Dr. James Graham lectures nightly in his large house in Pall Mall, decorated with a pagan gilt sun and splendid interior furnishings. Possessor of a commanding figure, an imposing manner and a persuasive voice, he is currently lecturing on "How to Restore Health and Vigor by Means of Electricity." Large crowds of people are in attendance, each paying two guineas. Attention is rapt. At the end of each lecture, the Goddess of Health appears, a beautifully proportioned young woman, unveiled, who stands regally for the perusion and approval of the admiring audience. . . .

Thomas blinked at the small newsprint. The Goddess of Health. What a splendid spectacle that must be. Quickly he read on.

> Following the lecture, couples may avail themselves of Dr. Graham's Celestial Bed, a marvel which stands on four glass legs and by means of which the most perfect children can be begotten. Also, according to Dr. Graham, the wondrous bed is designed to cure all coldness and hesitancy on the part of reluctant females, and instill the male with increased efficiency of performance. Charges per night for the use of

The Celestial Bed are five hundred guineas. Included in this price are three bottles of Dr. Graham's "Elixir of Life," and appropriate items of stimulation which lead to fulfillment.

Thomas looked down, unseeing, into the street below. "Appropriate items of stimulation which lead to fulfillment." "Designed to cure coldness and hesitancy on the part of reluctant females."

His breathing increased. He felt an uncomfortable ache spread through his body. Dear God, how long could she hold out? How long could he? He looked again at the accompanying illustration of the Celestial Bed.

Abruptly he strode away from the window as though to leave the thought behind. He could not try force again. Or deceit. Too much had happened. His own wound for one thing. He had no reason to believe that William Pitch had become any less protective of the female in his house during the passage of time. He did not wish to repeat his last fateful encounter with the man. Then, too, lodged permanently in the back of his mind were the tragic events which had taken place during the winter at Eden Castle, the result of male force and male insistence.

Thomas shuddered in the August heat, the memories coming in sequence, each more hideous than the one before. No force, and preferably no deceit! He would adhere to his noble vow, to court her honestly, to win her trust, at least long enough to conquer her and perhaps learn her secrets.

On that note of resolve he turned slowly back to the window, the *Gazetteer* still spread out on the sill, the magnificent Celestial Bed holding enormous fascination. Almost stealthily, as though someone were watching, he reached down and carefully tore the front page from the rest of the paper. He folded the clipping and inserted it into the pocket of his shirt. "Goddess of Health!" What a spectacle that must be!

As he was turning away from the newspaper, his eye fell on a small box of print near the bottom of the third page. "In the absence of Mr. William Pitch," the article began.

Thomas took a step toward the cool interior of his chambers. He stopped. "In the absence of Mr. William

Pitch." Slowly the words penetrated. Quickly he whirled back and grabbed up the newsprint. His eyes fairly raced over the small passage. "In the absence of Mr. William Pitch who is at present in France, the Gazetteer is being edited by Mr. Ferrill Temple, a graduate of—"

Again Thomas read over the opening line. "In the absence of Mr. William Pitch who is at present in France—"

Suddenly he ran to the door and flung it open. "Locke!" he shouted. "Locke? Where are you?"

A few minutes later Russell Locke appeared, stiff in his London finery. His eyes were bloodshot and bleary. Obviously he'd been dozing at his post at the top of the stairs, his customary position on Thomas' command in order to protect him from the large and nameless London staff. In return for his loyalty, Thomas gave him his freedom every evening, where, apparently, he roamed the London streets, indulging in every vice that the coins in his purse could buy.

"Move quickly!" Thomas shouted at the figure coming at a slow pace. Thomas turned back into his chamber, pacing rapidly. Pitch gone! In France. The house unguarded. The women vulnerable. He couldn't believe it. His noble vow to court her openly lay in a shambles about his feet.

He pursued his thoughts with something of the obstinate egoism peculiar to obsessed persons. How long had Pitch been absent? Was his household in good condition or disarray? Had he appointed a new watchdog? Was this the reason that he had not received a response? The females, with the innate sense of the prey, knew better than to signal their vulnerability.

In a burst of impatience for answers, he again shouted, "Locke, where in the devil are—"

The young man slipped inside the chamber, running his fingers through his mussed hair. He appeared to be half-asleep and very embarrassed at finding himself in such disarray before his master.

"I hope that for all your present pain at least you enjoyed yourself," Thomas scolded.

"I did," Locke confessed, a flush spread across his cheeks.

"What was her name?" Thomas asked slyly, "or did you bother to find out?"

"Oh, yes, sir," murmured Locke, repeatedly rubbing the side of his head as though that empty globe were on the verge of exploding. "Elizabeth Parker," he replied. "A young one, yet ripe, only seventeen, from Shropshire, or so she said."

Seventeen, Thomas marveled. As young as— His thoughts moved in painful progress to Marianne Locke. Angrily he snapped, "I hope you have the good sense to wear armor, Locke. It is not my intention to take a diseased servant back to Eden Castle."

The young man looked up, alarmed. "She was only seventeen, milord."

"It matters little whether she was seven, seventeen, or seventy," railed Thomas. "Some females are born unchastened. They are virulent carriers. It's their only device for seeking revenge on the poor unwitting male. They take delight in our agony, and I would hate for you to learn the need for protection the hard way."

After his brief tirade, his thoughts went to Billy Beckford, who merely feared the dread disease, and others who actually suffered it. It was rumored about London that the old man, Boswell, kept to his privacy because repeated attacks of the disease had now affected his brain, and he addressed his servants as animals—"Mr. Pig" and "Miss Peacock"—and required that they answer with the noise of their breed.

Truly, Thomas thought, it was man's scourge, as was woman herself. A short interval later, he ralied, reconciling the conflict within him, the moral lecture and the carnal interest.

"Locke," he began, pacing. "I want you to arrange a meeting for me."

"Yes, milord."

"I want it to be a discreet arrangement, one unknown to any save for myself and the party involved."

"Yes, milord."

"There are others living in the house where I shall shortly send you. They too must know nothing."

"Yes, milord."

The dully delivered refrain was beginning to get on

Thomas' nerves. He shouted, "Do you know what I'm asking?

"Yes, milord."

In despair, Thomas turned away to the writing bureau and scribbled a brief message. He moved back to the gaping young man. "You are to take this to the house on Great Russell Street. You are to station yourself outside in an obscure fashion and wait for the single appearance of your sister, Miss Jane Locke. Is that clear?"

Apparently it wasn't, for the young man suddenly stood at attention. His eyes focused sharply on the folded note before him. "For the single appearance of—Miss Jane Locke, milord? Not the—"

"The single appearance," Thomas repeated as though communicating with a dimwitted child. "Do you understand?"

Quickly the young man shook his head. "I thought it was the other, milord. I thought it was—Marianne."

Thomas, never long on patience, found himself totally drained of that rare quality. Something about the flat, dull, dissipated face querying him on such a personal matter sent him into a rage. "What you think or don't think is a matter of monumental unconcern!" he shouted. "All you must do is follow orders, deliver the note, and bring the reply back to me." Almost pitiably, he inquired, "Is that asking too much?"

Locke shook his head, but the expression on his face was still one of bewilderment. In spite of this he tucked the note inside his coat and bobbed his head in respectful obedience and departed the room.

Thomas slumped heavily on the bed, his hands hanging limply between his legs. The room was stiflingly hot. Not a breeze anywhere. He lifted his head, longing for the sweet cool air of North Devon.

His long confinement in his London house was beginning to take a toll. He was a man designed by nature for uninhibited vistas. He could not wait much longer. If the girl persisted in her stubbornness, then other plans would have to be devised.

He walked back to the window. Perhaps the note would work. Perhaps Miss Jane Locke would agree to meet with him and shed some light on why his suit had thus far been ignored. His thoughts moved steadily toward the red

brick house on Great Russell Street. "In the absence of
Mr. William Pitch—" If he'd known two months ago
that the guard dog was gone. . . . No! He must conduct
himself differently now. He had no appetite for violence.
There wasn't a fly in the world that couldn't be trapped
with honey.

The dark mood improved with the thoughts of joy to
come. Perhaps within the week it would all be over, his
appetite and obsession satisfied, the girl conquered, her
gifts enjoyed for a short period of time, then returned,
slightly used but none the worse for wear. Then Thomas
would return to Eden Point and set himself to the dull
but necessary task of finding a wife, the plump daughter
of Lord Salisbury perhaps, an emptyheaded, vain, blue-
blooded girl who could work at her needlepoint during
the day and share his bed at night and give him sons, at
least a son, an heir to Eden Castle and lands. Then, having fulfilled his responsibilities to his ancestors, the rest
of Thomas' life would be his own. Perhaps he might travel
to America, visit the spot where his brother was buried,
see the foolish experiment in democracy for himself.

The woman, Jane Locke, had in the past seemed reasonable. Maybe she could offer her advice. Working together,
unencumbered by the presence of William Pitch, perhaps
the two of them could—

His thoughts stopped. But nothing forced, nothing violent. That approach did not work. Patience. Patience.

Again he settled comfortably in his chair like the prudent traveler who knows that the long journey is not
achieved with hasty steps.

With every passing day, her isolation grew more complete. Cut off by her own principles from all society with
Jane and Sarah, Marianne had taken to sitting alone in
William's small study, considerably altered now, some of
his furniture and many of his books having been sold for
food.

She sat there now on a hot afternoon near the middle
of August, on an upturned keg near the window, pondering
all the various aspects of her dilemma, at a loss to know
how to solve any of them.

Behind her in the house, she heard nothing. Sarah was
probably sleeping. It had become her habit to nap in the

afternoon, or at least that was her claim. Of late their normally pleasant chatting sessions had dissolved into heated arguments of guilt and recrimination.

Slowly Marianne shifted her position on the uncomfortable keg. How often she had tried to make them understand. How often she had failed. And the worst scenes had been those which had always occurred immediately following the arrival of one of the large engraved calling cards. Then Marianne's own apprehension had increased and rendered her as incoherent as those around her. And the exchange of words had grown harsher and Marianne's distress had grown deeper. And the three of them had simply moved away from one another to remote corners of the house to contemplate their plight.

She rested her head on the windowsill. During the last few days, a thought had occurred to her that perhaps she should just leave, should take one of William's last paintings, sell it for what she could, and buy passage back to North Devon. The three of them could not go on like this. The house was becoming a tomb, the air heavy with blame, as though she alone were standing in the path which led to their survival.

Perhaps she was. Perhaps she was being selfish. How would it hurt her to receive Lord Eden for one night, welcome him into the drawing room, converse with him, appraise him of their plight, and accept his offer of help? How would it hurt? At that her head fell heavily forward against the windowsill.

It was a simple matter. If forced to give herself to him, she would take her life immediately afterward. But would that be any great loss?

Outside in the hall, she heard a footstep. A few seconds later she heard the front door open, then close. Quickly she drew back from the window and watched as Jane hurried down the front walk. The third time in as many days. Always at midafternoon she'd excuse herself, go to her room, reappear in remnants of old finery, and leave the house.

Marianne returned to the window and watched as Jane disappeared into the commerce of Southampton Row. A curious routine. Perhaps she went to do business with their creditors. Their threats were certainly real enough, the spunging agents now bullying them twice, sometimes three times a week. Tonight Marianne must ask her. Tonight the silence would have to be broken. If there were new threats, Marianne had a right to know.

Without warning, in her imagination she saw Lord Eden's face before her as he'd appeared that night in the upper bedroom, a gaunt, lean, arrogant face. Her heart sank to a new level of misery. Now, again, he was out there, somewhere, laying claim to her person.

Weary with fear and beyond tears, she laid her head on the windowsill and gazed sideways at the splash of sun on green trees. One hand slipped from her lap and hung awkwardly at her side. Once as a child she'd seen a heifer on the way to slaughter, dragging and squealing, protesting its death.

She wanted darkness in her mind, to throw a shadow over what she was powerless to alter.

She whispered, "Papa?"

"Then it's settled," Lord Eden said, leaning up in his chair, as though making preparation to leave.

Demurely Jane shook her head. It *was* all settled, but she wished to detain him as long as possible. It was very pleasant sitting in a public coffeehouse with Lord Thomas Eden, although she might have preferred a more popular coffeehouse, one on the Strand, where they could be seen by important people instead of this small, rather drab one, less than three blocks from the house on Great Russell Street, frequented only by tradespeople in the neighborhood. Still, there was benefit even there. Several of her most urgent creditors, seeing her here for these last three afternoons in the company of Lord Thomas Eden, had bobbed their heads in extreme politeness, sensing in her companionship with one of the richest men in England quick payment plus interest of their outstanding accounts.

Now, in answer to Lord Eden's impatient expression, she smiled. "What I mean to say, Lord Eden, is simply this. That where Marianne is concerned, things are rarely settled once and for all."

The impatience on his face slid rapidly into anger. "A bargain is a bargain," he reminded her curtly.

"I agree," she said with a smile. "And you have my word that I'll do everything in my power to see it through.

Still, as you so well know, she does have a mind of her own."

Yes, she could see clearly that he knew that. She watched, fascinated, as this powerful man settled uneasily back into his chair, his eyes brooding over the possibility of his scheme failing. 'Let him worry for a minute,' she thought, enjoying her position at the table.

Beyond the window, she saw her half-brother, Russell, waiting like a common lackey beside Lord Eden's coach. Only *she* had been invited to table. Over the last three days as they'd hatched their complicated scheme, she'd come to realize the true meaning of the word miracle. A brilliant idea had evolved between them, a business deal, really, entailing the exchange of money for services.

Lord Eden leaned forward. "I want no violence," he reminded her, as he'd reminded her daily. "I want the girl to clearly understand that I mean her no harm."

Jane smiled. "I understand," she murmured, not absolutely certain that she did. Still, in a very real sense she had to give Marianne credit. Her ploy of constant rejection had been most effective, causing an increase in the man's hunger almost to the point of obsession. "As I said," Jane repeated, "my sister loves me very much and owes me a great deal. I think, under the circumstances, she will behave in a favorable manner."

Lord Eden seemed to draw a sigh of relief. Again he leaned forward as though to leave. "Then tonight?" he inquired, gathering up his hat.

"If all is ready with you," she agreed. "Your part is far more complicated than mine." She giggled prettily. "All I have to do is play the actress. But you must—"

Quickly he cut her off. "All is ready."

Again she looked out at her brother pacing in the hot August sun. "Will Russell be there?"

Lord Eden shook his head. "He'll wait in the carriage in case I need him. She'd recognize him in the house."

"Of course," she agreed. Rather primly she reached for her bonnet. "The demand will be four hundred guineas. I believe we agreed to that."

"We did," he said, rather snappishly.

Coyly, Jane looked out of the window, her hand still on the open brim of her bonnet. "A few in advance would be helpful," she whispered. "Since I intend to tell them that I sold one of my rings, I should have a few coins to show for it. Don't you agree?"

For one tense moment she couldn't tell if Lord Eden agreed or not. He simply stared at her, his face a blank, as though he were trying to identify something in her. Quietly, almost sorrowfully, he reached into his pocket and withdrew the very generous sum of ten guineas and dropped them into her bonnet. He leaned forward. "Tell me, Miss Locke, do you have no regret over what you are doing?"

The blunt question caught her off guard. She forestalled answering by busying herself with the transfer of guineas from her bonnet to her purse. Then: "Regrets, Lord Eden?" she parroted. "I'm afraid I don't understand. My sister is very fortunate to have won your attention. I must confess in all charity that I don't comprehend your interest in her. She's a mere child, stubborn, pampered, favored from birth by our father." She blushed modestly. "I cannot even imagine such a self-centered creature pleasing any man. But your tastes are your own. And as Marianne's sister, and your servant, I'm merely performing a service in bringing you together."

Thus she concluded her little speech, pleased by the sound of it, doubly pleased with the smile which softened Lord Eden's tense features.

There the conversation ended. He stared at her a moment longer, then abruptly stood up, his manner all business. "With your permission, Miss Locke, I'll leave first as always. Until tonight, then?"

With that, he bowed low, a courtly gesture which pleased her immensely. With a slight inclining of her head, she acknowledged his departure. She sat at the table and watched him reappear on the pavement beyond the window, fascinated by the skillful way in which her brother flung open the carriage door for him, then signaled the footman, then crawled in after him.

Alone at last, she felt an incredible weariness. So much had fallen on her shoulders, so much she had already done and so much she had yet to do. Still, for the first time since she could remember, the world looked bright with promise.

On that happy note, she stood up, adjusted her bonnet over her wig, and retucked the tattered edges of her sleeves. Day after tomorrow at the latest she would burn this gown along with all her other worn ones and replace her entire wardrobe with rose taffeta and lilac brocade.

Feeling quite her old self again, she lifted her purse, stopped to enjoy the new weight of coin. How could her sister be so stupid as to turn her back on such wealth? Out on the pavement she moved rapidly through the streets, heading toward the trade shops, her mind running through the glories of the evening meal—the finest roast of beef in all of London, tender fresh asparagus from the greengrocer's, and strawberries, of course strawberries. And a bottle of imported wine, two perhaps so that Marianne could drink heartily and feel relaxed and pliable.

Without warning she heard in her mind Lord Eden's last peculiar question: "Do you have no regrets over what you are doing?"

Her step slowed as she puzzled the question. Regrets? Why should she regret anything? In time, pampered with luxury, Marianne would undoubtedly fall to her knees in thanks. That she was for the moment blinded and embittered by the man's earlier cruel efforts to win her attention was indeed understandable. But if she were blind now, it was Jane's responsibility to see for her.

She felt a surge of excitement. So much to do. She must hurry. If the scheme was to work, all would have to be ready at the proper time.

Again came the nagging question. Why should she regret anything? All she wanted was happiness. For all. Was that a crime, a reason for regret?

She answered both questions with a resounding no! She glanced at a clock in a shop window. Five o'clock. The scheme must commence promptly at nine.

She must hurry! She must hurry!

In a surge of happiness, Marianne looked about at the heavily laden table and the smiling women on either side of her. It was like old times. Better than old times. Marianne sensed a feeling of genuine love which she'd never felt before. All cares were forgotten in the moment of plenty, the kitchen table set with finery, William's Sèvres china and French crystal and silver gleaming and the single dazzling candelabrum. And Jane, her cheeks rouged, presiding over her party like the benefactress that she was. Marianne took it all in, remembering her grim mood of the afternoon. How wrong it had been of her to suspect Jane of anything but the kindest of intentions.

She turned to Jane as though to apologize for her doubts. "I'm not quite certain how you managed," she said, "but I assure you both Sarah and I are very grateful."

Jane dismissed the expression of gratitude. "I told you," she scolded lightly, busying herself with uncorking the wine. "I had a few baubles tucked away. Gifts from William." Her face darkened. "I didn't like the idea of selling them, but—" The mood lifted. "After all, we can't eat pearls and I've no place to wear them, so—"

She leaned in toward the bottle, forcing the cork out with a loud pop. Marianne felt her heart torn by her sister's obvious sacrifice. Someday she would make it up to her, she vowed.

Her attention was drawn to Sarah, standing over the spit, the roast browning beautifully, the odor overwhelmingly good. "If you don't hurry," Marianne joked, "I swear we shall eat it raw."

Sarah smiled and continued to turn the spit. "Not long now," she promised.

Jane poured herself a glass of wine, sipped it, and obviously approved. As she filled the remaining glasses, she said, "I have the strongest feelings of confidence about the future. The worst that could happen has happened. From now on the world will treat us with greater kindness."

Marianne took the glass offered her and felt a stray doubt. She wished she could share Jane's enthusiasm. There were still the tradesmen, the burgeoning debts. She was tempted to ask if the sale of the "baubles" had provided enough to pay off the creditors. But she changed her mind. There would be time for questions later. For now, they were together again.

Sarah joined them at the table, glass in hand. As Jane raised her glass in toast, Marianne listened with head down. "The past is over," Jane began softly. "Our mistreatment of one another a thing of yesterday. Understanding is the order of the new day. Our voices shall be so sweet and tender they could only come from heaven. And if one falters and falls, the other two exist only to lift her up and comfort her."

Carefully Marianne listened to her sister's voice, extraordinarily musical and sincere. As the three lifted their glasses, Marianne kept her eyes down, for fear the stinging tears of joy would spill over and become visible.

"Yes," she murmured. Unfortunately the tears pushed forward until she could no longer contain them. Without being aware how it happened, she found herself in Jane's arms, the two sisters clinging to each other. Marianne was aware of Sarah sniffling behind them, but she did not want the embrace to end.

"My goodness," Sarah grumbled. "A body would think you'd just found each other after a long separation."

Marianne smiled. "We have."

Jane concurred. "We have indeed. And I vow openly in the presence of both of you that nothing, nothing shall ever come between us again."

Then, with a stored-up hunger which stretched over the last seven months, they fell heartily to eating, Sarah slicing off generous ruby-red portions of beef, the emerald green of fresh asparagus decorating each plate, tiny perfectly browned new potatoes resting to one side.

Marianne and Jane chatted excitedly of their childhoods, regaling old Sarah with accounts of some of the eccentric characters who were their neighbors in Mortemouth, one story leading to another, and on occasion both girls talking at once, dissolving into giggles as they recalled old Pensy Morgan, whose wife regularly kicked him out of bed. The old man took to sleeping in his fishing boat until one night it tore loose from its mooring and old Pensy awakened in the middle of the Bristol Channel. And Floss Woodie, who regularly put a kettle of water on the hearth to keep the smoke ghosts away, and all the myths and legend and folklore, the unlucky birds which both Jane and Marianne confessed, as children, to being terrified of, the cuckoo, and the raven and, worst of all, the magpie.

"There was a poem," Jane exclaimed excitedly. "Remember? Designed to keep us safe." She giggled. "Good heavens, I said it so often, I thought I'd never forget it."

Marianne took a deep sip of wine and sat up, ready to help. "I remember it. It starts:

Clean birds by seven,
unclean by two—

She faltered. She glanced toward the ceiling as though for help, started the rhyme again as Jane quickly refilled her glass. "No more," she groaned. "I'm getting light-headed."

Sarah remarked with a grin, "If you ask me, you're both lightheaded."

"Nonsense," slurred Jane. "Just warm, that's all. Isn't that right, Marianne?"

Marianne agreed, then closed her eyes, searching for the lost rhyme.

"Clean birds by seven—" she began.

"Or was it eight?" Jane interrupted, giggling.

"No," Marianne said sternly. Again she drank deep of the wine, then lifted her glass as though in a premature toast to her success.

> Clean birds by seven,
> Unclean by twos,
> The dove in the heavens—

Suddenly Jane interrupted her gleefully with the concluding line, "—is the one I choose."

Both girls fell back in their chairs, laughing. "Sweet Lord," Marianne gasped. "I used to say that over and over. Yet everyplace I looked, there were always magpies."

Nodding in agreement, Jane grasped at her throat as though unable to breathe. "And remember that a snake, even though chopped into pieces, cannot die before sundown."

Marianne leaned close, ready to contribute. "Except an adder," she corrected, "which may be charmed to death by drawing a circle around it with an ash rod."

Sarah shook her head. "And I thought Shropshire was superstitious."

Jane looked at her askance. "Is it said in Shropshire that May kittens should not be kept as they attract snakes into the house?"

"Or," contributed Marianne," that if blankets are washed in May, one runs the risk of washing away one of the family?"

"Or," Jane said, her eyes growing wide, "that if one waits in a church porch at midnight on Midsummer's eve and then peeps through the keyhole of the church door, all those who are to die in the course of the year will be seen walking into the church through the opposite doorway?"

Sarah shivered. "Lord have mercy!"

Both girls burst out in renewed laughter at Sarah's alarm. "Now you know," Jane gasped, "why we behave as we do."

Graciously Sarah played the simpleton, although again she scolded lightly. "It's not the tales as much as the wine, if you ask me."

As Jane reached forward to refill all glasses, Marianne tried to object. "Oh, please no," she begged. "I've never consumed so much."

"Then it's time you did," said Jane, filling the glass anyway. "No harm in it. Our heads have been heavy for too long. It's time they enjoyed a moment of lightness."

Because Marianne did not want to spoil the party, and because in truth she was enjoying herself, she lifted the filled glass and drank heartily, welcoming the tingling sensation in her throat, the pleasurable lassitude extending down into her limbs. "I may never be able to get up from this chair," she slurred, her head bobbing disjointedly.

Jane appeared to be in the same condition, although she stood, weaving a bit, and suggested to Sarah, "Coffee and strawberries in the drawing room? Let's make it a true party, like those we used to have."

Sarah nodded. Jane extended a hand to Marianne. "Come," she urged. "On your feet. We'll walk together and sing as we go."

Marianne pushed back from the table, tried to stand, failed, then tried again. Not until Jane slipped a supportive arm around her waist was the simple feat of standing accomplished. "There," Jane commended. "Now, again how did the poem go?"

Everywhere Marianne looked she saw two of everything —two Janes, two cluttered tables, two approaching doorways. She discovered that she could manipulate better with her eyes closed. Thus she leaned heavily against Jane and began to recite full-voiced, though slightly slurred,

> "Clean birds by seven,
> Unclean by twos,

The dove in the heavens,
Is the one I choose."

Jane took up the refrain, giving it a little melody as she chanted. Bobbing and weaving, the two girls made it through the dining room and across the entrance hall where the clock was striking a quarter to nine.

At the drawing room door, Marianne stopped. It was good seeing the attractive room opened and well lit instead of shrouded in dust covers. "Oh, Jane," she murmured, "what a lovely evening it is."

Jane smiled and led her to the comfortable chair opposite the couch and next to the table where William's Orrery rested. Marianne looked in wonderment at the tiny golden sun circling the earth. Apparently Jane had thought of everything. The miraculous machine had been wound and was working perfectly. As she settled into the chair, she repeated, "What a marvelous evening!"

"It is," Jane concurred, sitting opposite her on the couch. "And just the beginning of many that we'll share. Ours is no ordinary fate. Together, I promise, we'll know greater heights."

Marianne blinked at the sudden somberness in her sister's voice. She found the words peculiar, "Ours is no ordinary fate." She leaned forward, ready to pursue the subject, when Sarah appeared with a tray ladened with coffee and cups and a bowl of fresh strawberries.

"No room," groaned Jane at the sight of the fruit. She pushed backward against the couch as though to loosen her bodice.

"Then coffee," ordered Sarah, "for both of you."

Jane looked saddened. "You really are a spoil sport, Sarah. Let us enjoy ourselves."

But Sarah insisted that they both take a demitasse of black coffee. Marianne attempted to sit up straight, trying to demonstrate that she was not inebriated, merely relaxed and happy. She took the small cup and sipped, her eyes moving back to the Orrery, to memories of her first night in this room.

Quickly she looked about for fear her memories would cast a gloom on Jane's festive mood. But at that moment, Jane too seemed pensive. Marianne saw her turn stiffly and glance toward the window.

The clock struck nine. The sound seemed to provoke in Jane an even greater agitation. She sat rigidly up on the edge of the couch, her eyes glancing continuously over her shoulder.

Marianne could not bear to see such distress. "What is it?" she asked softly.

Jane made a discernible effort to control herself. She laughed and reached for her coffee cup. "It's this room," she said with a shudder. "I'm accustomed to seeing it filled with people. It seems unnatural empty." She bowed her head over her cup.

The three women sat in silence. A light, warm, August breeze blew in through the open window, causing the lamps to dance in eerie shadow across the corridor walls. Marianne felt it clearly, the tension expanding. Jane started to her feet once, then apparently changed her mind. Her head swiveled constantly about at each small noise.

Marianne searched her mind for words of comfort and found nothing but the most mundane thoughts. The wine was still at work in her system. She closed her eyes. In a minute she would speak. In a minute she would leave her chair and go and sit close beside Jane and take her hand and reassure her with sisterly affection.

It was while her eyes were closed, her head resting, that she heard the first small disturbance, scarcely more than the crack of a floorboard, coming from the passageway outside the door. At first she did not look up, and the only sound was the delicate chink of Sarah's spoon against the bowl of strawberries, that, and the sound of her own breathing.

Suddenly she heard it again, the sound as of a heavy footstep. Alarmed, she opened her eyes. She looked at Jane who, curiously, was not looking toward the disturbance, but rather staring almost mournfully at her.

"Did you hear—" Marianne began. But that was as far as she got, for suddenly the front door was flung open with a resounding crack. Sarah screamed, and in the next instant two men rushed into the room, dressed in black with black gloves, their faces obscured by flat, low, crushed, black tricorns.

Marianne tried to rise. The two ruffians moved quickly toward Jane, who continued to sit, white-faced, on the couch. Horrified, Marianne watched as they grabbed Jane

roughly by the arms and lifted her violently to her feet.
Jane was struggling now, her head flung backward in terror, the men twisting her arms behind her in an attempt
to subdue her, the whole room filled with nightmare sounds,
Sarah screaming continuously, Jane struggling against the
brute strength, one of the men shouting out that they were
spunging agents.

"Ladies pay their debts," the other grinned, "or else it's
debtors' prison. If you have four hundred guineas, we shall
pass on and not bother you."

"Oh, sweet God," Jane moaned, her eyes showing white,
her body struggling against her captors. "Please, I beg
you—"

Marianne started forward. She tried to wrest her sister
loose from their grip. "Please," she begged, "leave her be."

But the men merely looked at her as though she were
invisible, and turned their attention back to the struggling,
terrified Jane.

There was one single piercing cry. Marianne looked up
to see a set of black gloved hands holding Jane rigidly
while the other hands ripped the wig from her head.

"No need for such finery in the spunging house," the
man said. In further indignity, one agent held her firm
while the other commenced to unbutton the front of her
gown.

Jane's screams rose louder. Feverishly Marianne glanced
about for a weapon and found nothing. Again she hurled
herself at the men, who were now pulling the gown from
her sister's body, Jane crying pitiably, "Help me, oh, dear
God, help me!" As they dragged her roughly into the entrance hall, Marianne started after them, her head light,
knees weak, the never-ending cries for help ringing in her
ears. She saw Sarah flattened against the far wall, paralyzed
with terror. She took another step and fell and feared she
would lose consciousness. The ruffians turned and watched
her, still holding their prey between them, stripped to her
chemise, her hair outflung as she continued to struggle
futilely against their hands.

The nightmare increasing, Marianne saw one of them
withdraw a length of rope and twist Jane's arms painfully
behind her, her sister's fate sealed with her bondage, her
face scarcely recognizable in its contortions.

How great seemed the distance from the drawing room

to the entrance hall. It occurred to Marianne that she'd been running forever, and finally her breath went and she came to a halt, unable to move further. The bonds were being twisted about Jane's ankles now, tears streaming down her face, her plea for help a demented refrain, "Please, dear God. Please, no. Please, no. Please—"

From her collapse in the entrance hall Marianne looked toward the open doorway through which the men had dragged Jane. Her own eyes were glazed, her wretchedness beyond description. She looked up slowly. Then her head jerked rigidly forward as though it had been snapped by a noose. There, before her, filling the doorway, she saw the figure of a man. In spite of her semiconscious state, recognition was instantaneous. She knew every feature, every line, the stance of the body, the voice. All stood directly over her now, kindly offering her a hand.

"Milady," he said. "I was passing by and heard the disturbance—"

Marianne stared at the face. In the distance she heard her sister's screams, increasing as though the worst were yet to come. Struggling to keep back tears and memory, Marianne pulled herself to her knees, her hands so cold she could scarcely feel them.

As from a great distance, her sister cried out, "Oh, God, Marianne. Help me!"

On her knees before the man, Marianne begged, "Please, milord. I fear they will kill her."

Thomas Eden seemed to hesitate as though he were doing his best to appear a reasonable man. "They're spunging agents," he said gently. "I have no right to interfere with a lawful arrest."

Slowly Marianne lifted her face to him. Her flesh felt frozen, meeting his eyes. An atrocity of words was forming in her mind. "Pay them," she whispered, "and I shall be in your debt."

Their eyes held. Slowly a smile formed on his lips. He extended a hand to her which appeared to be trembling.

Outside the screams had ceased. The silence was even more terrifying. She ignored his hand and whispered fiercely, "Pay them!"

He stood a moment longer, looking down on her, then turned with dispatch and disappeared into the night.

She remained on her knees, her thoughts so intricate that

she could no longer keep them separate. How peculiar, that at the moment of greatest happiness—She was vaguely aware of movement behind her, of Sarah creeping up, still sobbing. A hand rested lightly on her shoulder, as though in comfort.

The old woman wept. "You sold yourself."

Marianne pressed her lips together to keep from crying out. "So I have," she thought. She heard voices on the pavement outside the door, was aware of Sarah collapsed and still weeping in a near chair, heard and recorded everything, but refused to respond. She recognized only one thought as valid, that by dawn it would be over.

A short time later there was movement in the doorway. It was Jane, her arms wrapped protectively about her body, her eyes strangely dry. She exchanged only a brief glance with Marianne, then darted quickly to Sarah's outstretched arms, her face turned away.

Thomas Eden was there, too. In his hand he held a piece of parchment. He preserved a gloomy silence, something in his expression that was shy and ashamed. Then, finally, with a certain haughty distinction, he placed the parchment on the near table and announced, "A clean slate. They should not bother you again."

There was not a sound in the hall or from the world beyond. The rooms and walls, which only moments before had known such dreadful shrieking, now resembled a tomb. In her wretchedness, Marianne waited, still on her knees. She wondered, with a curious wave of objectivity, if the tableau would hold throughout eternity.

She received her answer as, almost politely, Lord Eden held out his hand, clearly bidding her to accompany him.

Trembling, she stood. She gave the two women still intertwined in the closest embrace only a token glance. Sarah was muttering to Jane in a kind of absentminded way. As for Jane herself, she was still clinging to Sarah, her face averted, as though she could not bear to look.

A painful series of thoughts cut through Marianne's despair. Why had the front door been so conveniently left unlocked? Why had Lord Eden just happened to be passing by? What a stroke of good fortune that apparently he'd had the vast amount of four hundred guineas on his person! Perhaps Sarah had been wrong. Perhaps she'd not sold herself as much as she'd been sold as any lamb that goes to the shambles.

"Milady, come," ordered Thomas Eden from the doorway. "A bargain's a bargain."

At the first step, she felt faint, the lingering effects of wine commingling with new terror. As she leaned against the wall, he went to her side and offered her his arm.

She said nothing, but pulled quickly away from his nearness and proceeded under her own power to the doorway. One comforting thought gave her strength, the realization that by dawn it would be over.

Behind her, all remained silent. At the door, the night breeze greeted her. In the spill of light from the entrance hall she saw the walkway, the pavement beyond, and the waiting carriage. A man stood by the open carriage door, a footman sat watching from his high perch. She saw not a sign of the spunging agents.

She went down the walk almost serenely. At the edge of the pavement she looked up at the man waiting. With no great surprise she recognized her half-brother.

"Our father?" she inquired. "Is he well?"

Russell ducked his head. "Well enough," he said with a smile.

She thought he would say more, but he didn't. Instead he placed a firm hand on her elbow, an insistent hand lifting her upward without delicacy or grace into the velvet interior of the coach.

As she settled herself in the far corner, she saw Lord Eden exchange a whispered word with Russell. Then Lord Eden climbed in after her. She saw Russell secure the door and give the signal to the footman. As the carriage lurched forward, she leaned back and stole a final glimpse at the house on Great Russell Street. To her surprise she saw the door closed, the entrance hall darkened, as though within a few short moments the two women had extinguished the lamps and retired.

The suspicion that she had been betrayed continued to press against her. Her present circumstances were almost palatable compared to that painful thought. In spite of her earnest resolve not to feel, she felt that pain with such force that she bowed her head.

Opposite her came a deep, yet soft voice. "Milady, there

is no occasion for you to be afraid. It is not my desire to harm you in any way."

She looked up at him. "I fear no man, milord," she said, struggling to maintain a steadfast gaze.

They looked at each other fixedly, with a spark of defiance in their eyes.

It was as if, at that instant, they both realized that they were worthy adversaries.

Having thus secured his prey, Lord Eden housed her in the very comfortable third-floor apartments which had belonged to his grandmother.

The most spacious chamber in the entire house, it was a matter of subtle architecture and a statement on marital trust as it existed in the sixteenth century when the house had been built, that the grand rooms were marked by only one entrance and exit, a narrow, winding, wooden staircase which could easily be guarded or blocked. Likewise the windows in the rooms themselves were high casements of leaded glass permitting little more than a bird's-eye view of the towers and spires of London. Here the wife of the moment could reside in utter splendor, scarcely aware of the imprisoning nature of her surroundings.

Unfortunately for Thomas Eden, it was not a wife who resided there now, but merely a woman, incredibly lovely and desirable, whom he had purchased fairly and who by rights should be his for as long as she amused him.

But the success of his ruse brought him little satisfaction. Marianne seemed utterly dazed, and within the first week her distress made her seriously unwell. From that first night when he'd led her gently, or so he'd thought, up to the newly aired and redressed apartments, she'd refused everything, had refused his offer of a female servant, claiming that she'd tended herself since she was a child and she was capable of doing it now, had refused the new gowns which he'd ordered sent around, had even refused food and drink, falling at last into a silent misery.

Now, ten days after her imprisonment, seeing her lying lifeless and pale upon the bed, still wearing the wrinkled black gown of her capture, Thomas summoned a physician.

Russell Locke brought the doctor to Thomas' chambers, and Thomas led him the rest of the way up the narrow staircase and through the small doorway which was kept locked and into the bedchamber itself, where the old man grasped melodramatically at his throat and cried out, "Air!"

While Thomas was throwing open the high casement windows, the physician peered down on the pale woman. Slowly, with the effort of age, he bent over and took from his case a small wooden box. Thomas watched as he lifted the lid, revealing a black crawling foam of leeches.

"She must be bled," the old man pronounced.

Marianne drew weakly to one side, protesting, "No—"

The fear in her face alarmed Thomas. Bleeding made no sense. She was already weakened from lack of food. Still, he was at a loss to know how to deal with his unwilling prisoner. But when the physician bared her shoulders and lifted the leeches from the box, she cried out so pitifully that Thomas ordered, "Wait!"

The old man looked over his shoulder, annoyed. Marianne pressed back against the pillow, her face distorted by anguish. Thomas moved to the other side of the bed and drew her attention toward him. "You must eat, then," he ordered.

Given the choice between food and bleeding, Marianne promised weakly, "I'll eat."

Quickly Thomas dismissed the old man, silenced his grumbling with several coins, then shouted down the stairs to the ever-present Russell, "Bring food, and brandy!" He looked back at the woman on the bed. Her misery and reluctance only served to increase his ardor.

But not like that, not lying weak and pale, her usually brilliant eyes lusterless, her hair scattered upon the mussed linen. Obviously she was aware of his gaze. She tried to raise herself and fell weakly back against the pillow.

"Don't," he begged. "Lie still."

She looked directly at him, her eyes distended in what seemed acute fear. That fear caused Thomas' heart to melt. He drew a chair close beside her, thinking her the most beautiful creature he'd ever seen. "Are you so unhappy?" he asked.

In reply to that, she merely shut her eyes. He leaned closer, eager for conversation. "You must know that I'm unhappy, too," he said.

With her eyes still closed, she murmured, "Then I'm sorry for both of us."

"But it doesn't have to be like this."

"I'm your prisoner."

"No, you're my guest."

She opened her eyes, the trace of a smile about her lips. "As a lamb is the guest of the butcher?"

"It is not my intention to slaughter you."

She looked directly at him. "What *is* your intention, milord?"

The direct question caught him off guard. He bowed his head, mindful of his past sins, the offenses he'd already committed against the young face which looked at him without humility. He did not understand the face. All he knew was that he was fascinated by it.

"Compensation?" he offered. "A need to—"

"What?"

For the second time, he was caught off guard by her soft inquiry. "A need to make reparation," he concluded. He felt that his voice had begun to tremble. It was as though he were the one lying weak and helpless and she the figure of command.

Quietly she asked, "How long do you intend to hold me your prisoner, milord?"

"You are not my prisoner," he repeated, feeling anger rising, and trying to control it. "You owe me a debt."

"A debt I will never pay willingly," she replied. "Surely you know that by now."

"In time," he said, sharply.

"Never!"

At that moment a serving woman appeared in the door, bearing a tray. Thomas stood quickly, still hearing the girl's arrogant refusal. "Feed her," he commanded, his anger perilously close to the surface. "Then cleanse and clothe her. If she objects, call for assistance. I want her presentable and sitting upright. We shall dine together this evening in this chamber. Is that clear?"

The serving woman, middle-aged, large-boned, with coarse red hair, bobbed her head, then cast a stern glance at Marianne on the bed. "If she objects, milord—"

"She will not object."

There was silence coming from the bed. Was she weeping? No. She smiled at him. "Are you certain you don't want to stay, milord and witness the sport, for I shall not lift a finger willingly? Nor shall I suffer anyone to come near me." The smile broadened. "It should be a battle to please you, I'm certain, you of all people who take such delight in cruelty."

He saw before him the same stubborn arrogance that she'd first displayed on that hot August morning in Eden Castle. Quickly he turned away from the bed. He shouted at the gaping servant, "Feed her! And make her presentable." Then, as though it were the worse possible epithet he could conceive, he shouted, outraged, "She smells!"

He slammed the door behind him and stood at the top of the narrow staircase. At the bottom of the steps, he saw Russell Locke staring up at him. "What are you gaping at?" he yelled. "Fetch hot water and linens and be prepared to lend a hand." He started down the stairs with such force that the ancient wooden staircase jigged from side to side. "The invalid *will* recuperate!" he shouted back over his shoulder.

He took refuge in his private chambers and slammed the door with resounding force. He went to the table by the window and poured himself a full brandy and drank it all at once and bent over, choking, as the burning liquid fought its way down. He leaned against the table, breathing heavily. By God, no woman would make a jackal of him. She *would* do his bidding.

Below the window, on the cobblestones of Oxford Road, the sun beat mercilessly down. Angrily he thought, 'August again, always August!' If only she were not becoming even more beautiful. What strain had slipped from old Hartlow's cock to make her thus? It was as though he'd gathered the substance of her seed from the North Devon cliffs themselves, beautiful yet hard, capable of defeating a man if a fateful wind happened to blow him against that unbending headland of stone.

Again he poured a glass of brandy and took it with him to his favorite chair by the window. *She* was the one who had forced him to take extreme measures. The ruse that night with the spunging agents had gone well enough. That evening, on her knees before him, he thought he'd seen a new submission in her face. Now he realized bitterly that he'd seen nothing. Apparently she preferred starvation to his presence.

The thought stung, like the beads of sweat rolling down his face into the small cuts where he'd hastily shaved himself that morning. Well, she wouldn't starve, and she would learn to tolerate his presence, and no matter if she didn't he fully intended to collect his debt, perhaps this very evening. Then he'd pack her back to her greedy half-sister and put an end to the whole affair.

Suddenly, coming from the third-floor apartments, he heard a resounding crash. This was followed quickly by the sound of footsteps running. He heard a woman's coarse cry, "For Gawd's sake, help!" Then more footsteps, the corridor outside his door filled with movement.

He sank deeper into his chair and glared unseeing at the open window. There were new screams, sounds above of a tremendous struggle, several loud thumps as though heavy furniture were being overturned.

He closed his eyes. The battle raged on for the better part of the afternoon. At last, approaching five o'clock, all sounds ceased. A soft knock came at the door. Thomas called out, "Come in."

Russell Locke appeared before him. He was soaked from head to foot, a single scratch ran down the left side of his face, and his clothes smelled of beef broth and bath water. But there was a triumphant grin on his face as he announced, "She's ready for your company, milord."

Thomas looked at the mute evidence of the struggle and felt queasy. He had taken a firm vow against all violence and already she had caused him to break that vow. "Later," he muttered, turning away from Russell's grinning face.

"But, milord—" Locke protested.

"I said leave me be!" Thomas shouted.

He waited until he heard the door close, then lifted his glass and drained it. He then set for himself a goal for the night, a rather intricate one; to drink himself senseless, to drink until he was no longer cognizant of who he was, or where he was, or of the young woman or the ominous silence coming from the apartments above him.

But—and here was the fine point of the goal which he set for himself—*not* to drink himself so senseless that he would be unable, under cover of dark, to slip out of St. James's Park and avail himself of the first whore he encountered, some robust, willing female who would endure his embrace, accept his coin, and go on her way.

He accomplished his intricate goal and returned to the house on Oxford Road after midnight, staggering slightly but satiated, his eye combing the darkened high third-floor apartment, like a great blind searchlight of the heart.

Paris
St. Denis
August, 1794

ONLY as the carriage jolted to a halt did William revive and find himself again. For a moment he wished he hadn't. It was so much safer in his unconscious vacuum.

He saw the house, Number 63, Rue de Faubourg St. Denis, a private mansion reportedly to have belonged once to Madame Pompadour. Then he felt movement around him, again felt himself lifted up, his confused gusts of memory still washing over him, the blessed numbness of his stump replaced by agony more pronounced than any he'd ever endured. Around him, there seemed to be as many people as he'd left in front of the Assembly, and leading them all, shouting orders, was the commanding presence of Thomas Paine.

As they carried him from the carriage, he saw through his distorted vision that the house resembled an old mansion farmhouse, enclosed by a wall and gateway from the road. In the courtyard, which was like a farmyard, stocked with fowl—ducks, turkeys, geese—they were greeted by a small group of women. Following the direction of one thick-waisted, gray-haired lady, they carried him through to apartments on the first floor, consisting of three rooms—

the first for wood and water, the next a bedroom, and beyond it a sitting room which led into a garden.

There at Paine's command they placed him on the bed. The women followed behind with basins of water and clean linen. Paine himself cradled William's head and gave him brandy to drink, and as the soothing warmth relaxed him, he thought mournfully that there would be no packet for England on the morrow, no eager return to the house on Great Russell Street, no reunion with the lovely face that had both haunted and sustained him throughout this dreadful year in France.

Then his attention was drawn back to the surgeons, who had resumed work on his arm. New pain shot upward into the back of his head. His eyes watered. Oh, God, death was preferable. He heard a voice, deep and comforting, "Hold to my hand. It can be endured." Something in the voice, so confident, yet easeful, convinced him of his ability to endure, and he did as he was told.

Throughout the entire surgery, William was constantly aware of Paine's presence in the room. Others came and went, but that one face remained fixed.

After everyone in the house had taken their turn at prodding and lifting and shifting him, after the surgeons had sewn the flesh down over the jagged bone of his upper arm and rebound it to his chest, after all had come and looked and given advice and sympathy, and after William himself had raised an enfeebled head and looked, horrified, at his smooth, wingless right side, he was aware then of a soft silence in the room, a sudden emptiness after hours of constant traffic.

"Marianne," he whispered weakly, feeling his head spinning with the effects of brandy and medicine, the shocking event of the day beginning to dawn on him.

Thomas Paine was there again, his own countenance looking none too well, two fiery brick-red spots of fever blazing on his chalk-white cheeks. Gently he spoke. "I don't know your Marianne, Mr. Pitch, but from the number of times you've called her name, I wish I could bring her to you." The man leaned closer, sat on the edge of the bed. "Is she your wife?" he asked.

Peculiarly, William felt an embarrassment of tears. He shook his head. "Not yet, sir. With God's help, perhaps one day." Suddenly he again caught sight of his mutilation. He was a cripple now, a freak. What woman would ever want— As the embarrassing tears increased, he was aware of Paine bending closer, the voice hard.

"Enough, sir. Your tears lack just cause. We are both alive. For that we should be thankful."

Weakly William protested, "One more alive than the other, sir. One whole. One—"

"If it were possible, I would give you my right arm, Mr. Pitch. As it is, all I can give you is my support and lasting gratitude."

William had not intended to force such a sentiment. He had done what he had done willingly, and would do it again if the circumstances required it. Feeling self-anger, he tried to change the subject. "Your papers, sir," he murmured, trying to guide the conversation to less personal matters.

"My papers can wait," Paine replied. "You must regain your health and strength."

William smiled. "As you must."

Paine nodded, returning the smile. "For a blessed interim, the Glorious Revolution will wait. We will be invalids together and concern ourselves with nothing of greater note than the flowers in the garden and perhaps later, playing games such as marbles or battledores."

William closed his eyes. "You have an easy opponent in a one-armed man, sir."

For the second time, Paine looked sternly down on him. "Your value and dignity as a man, Mr. Pitch, did not reside in your arm. Any clerk can hold the pen for you. Here are your riches." Lightly he touched William's forehead. "And those are unscathed, intact as ever, and perhaps tempered and refined by your present crucible."

William listened, his head clearing. He wanted to talk, he wanted to retain the strong presence before him for as long as possible, as defense against those weaker moments when self-pity threatened to overwhelm him. "The Revolution, sir," he began, as objectively as his discomfort would permit. "Is it worth pursuing? I've seen things, as you have, which defy all laws of human decency and conduct. To what end? For what purpose?"

Thomas Paine settled more comfortably on the edge of the bed, as though he had discerned William's need to talk. "All revolutions go poorly in the beginning. By their very nature, they require surgery as radical as that which you have just endured. But as your body will heal, so will the body politic of France." Quietly he shook his head, as though for a moment doubting his own words. "I must confess, though, there have been nights of severe doubt. France seems destined to suffer more than is necessary."

"Why?" William asked, feeling a cessation of discomfort as his mind became engaged in the larger matter.

Paine stood up from the bed and walked a short distance away, his head bowed as though in thought. Wearily he shook his head. "France herself, I fear, is the blame. She breeds idealists, then takes great delight in killing them." He looked back at the bed. "And without idealism, Mr. Pitch, without the strong voices of noble intention, all revolutions will founder in their own blood."

"Then there's no hope?" William asked.

"Oh, there's hope. There's always hope. It will just take France longer. She will suffer more." Paine returned to bed, the fever spots of his cheeks blazing anew. "But think of the difference a Jefferson would have made. What a debt America owes that man! He became their soul and they at least, at the pitch of insanity, had the good sense to listen." He shook his head and again settled wearily on the edge of the bed. "There is no French voice of such stature and wisdom, not now."

"What of your own?"

Thomas Paine laughed, his eyes closed. "I have the misfortune of possessing an English voice, Mr. Pitch, or hadn't you noticed? It is a talent of the French to go conveniently deaf to all accents save their own."

"Then the madness will go on forever?"

"Not forever, Mr. Pitch. Ultimately enough blood will be spilled, enough deceits worked, enough alliances shattered. Then, bloodied and bowed, France will lift her head in search of a leader. Pray God the right man appears."

At the door, William heard soft footsteps and saw the old woman, bearing a tray.

Paine glanced over his shoulder and smiled broadly, "Look—Madame has brought you the elixir of health." And he lifted from the tray a small bouquet of flowers. "August roses," Paine beamed. "I planted them myself two seasons ago, proof that seeds planted in the crucible of winter bear summer blossoms."

He placed the roses on a nearby table. "And healing broth," he added, taking the tray from the old woman and placing it before William. Sternly he commanded, "Take the utensil, Mr. Pitch, in your left hand and feed yourself."

William started to protest but knew it would be useless. Weakly, and with trembling fingers, he lifted the spoon awkwardly, dropped it once, slowly retrieved it, and aimed it for the bowl, spilling some of the hot brew, spilling more as the spoon reached his lips, half-empty.

The woman started forward in assistance, but halted at a signal from Paine. In one of the most tortuous ordeals of his life, William clumsily manipulated the spoon back and forth between his mouth and the bowl, consuming a little, until frustrated, he begged, "No more, please."

"You see?" beamed Paine. "You're still a man." As the woman removed the tray, he added, "You must never think otherwise, or you will do more damage to yourself than the pistol did."

Exhausted, William leaned back upon the pillow. His head was beginning to spin again, the stump of his arm coming to life, the shattered nerve ends awakening. Paine was beside him lifting his head, urging him to drink the brandy.

In a daze, William heard him send the woman away. "I'll sit with him," he whispered, "until his Marianne comes for him again. Go along with you. I'll stay with him until he's safely in his dreams."

William tried to form words of gratitude, but his lips refused to move. Instead he sank back into a blessed blackness, less blessed now, as it was filled with visions of the futility of everything, the futility of the Revolution, the futility of his dreams of Marianne, the futility of his own life, altered so radically on the broad pavement leading up to the Assembly.

Where in God's world was a place for a one-armed man?

Where in God's world?

London
August

SHE could not bear standing on tiptoe any longer, trying to peer out the high window. Looking quickly about, she spied a small three-legged stool and dragged it into position. She climbed aboard, and for the first time during her long confinement, got a clear glimpse of the world beyond. It was glorious, the sun on distant spires, the sound of people moving freely about on the street below.

She stepped down from the stool. By now she knew every inch of the third-floor apartments. Fortunately they were generous chambers, consisting of the large bedroom, a smaller dressing room beyond the arch, and an ample sitting room beyond that. They were sparsely but adequately furnished with old pieces of no real value, but comfortable nonetheless. Recently someone had gone to a great deal of trouble with the new damask wall-hangings, lovely floral designs of lavender and rose, softening the dark wood interior.

She stopped pacing and looked about, as though seeing her "prison" for the first time. It occurred to her that her father's entire cottage at Mortemouth would fit easily inside this one room.

Through the high windows, the sunlight of the late August afternoon fell in two slanting quadrilaterals on the rich rose carpet. She knew so little of her captor. She remembered as though it were a hundred years ago the night of her abduction, remembered the single thought which had brought her comfort, the realization that by dawn it would all be over.

But that was a month ago and still it was not over. Why did he persist in keeping her here? She hadn't seen the man himself in over a week. She'd heard his voice outside the door as he conferred daily with her guards. She saw the never-ending parade of servants, seldom the same one twice in a row, as though he did not want her to form an attachment. And this nameless parade treated her as though she were an inanimate object to be maintained and cared for, but certainly never addressed as a human being.

The isolation could not go on much longer. She commenced pacing again, step by step consuming the light rose spaces. She returned to the window and climbed back onto the stool. "Soon it will be over," she thought, although she knew better, knew that he could hold her a prisoner here as long as he wished, for she was powerless, bereft of allies on the outside, no one to come to her defense.

Outside the door, she heard movement, heard the guard stand, the chair scraping urgently against the wooden landing. Such immediacy of response generally was reserved for only one.

Quickly she left the window and dragged the stool a distance away. She was certain that if he saw her pleasure at standing by the window, he would have the stool removed. She slipped quietly into a straight-backed chair beside the table, facing the door, a guardlike stance of her own.

She heard his voice, a low indistinguishable exchange of some sort, the servant responding, then silence.

Outside the window, darkness steadily thickened. Night soon. Her fears were always greater at night. She heard his voice again, loud and strangely desolate.

"Unlock the door," he commanded.

Every nerve in her body tensed as she heard the key grating in the lock. She saw the heavy door ease open, saw the spill of light from the lamps in the corridor, and realized for the first time how dark the bedchamber had become, how quickly the sun had set.

Then she saw him in outline, standing in the doorway, his powerful figure filling the open space. "Light the lamps," he called over his shoulder. A moment later an old woman entered the room bearing a lighted wick. Marianne never took her eyes off the man in the doorway.

As illumination filled the room, she made an attempt to control her fear. Perhaps at last it *would* be over by dawn. The lamps lit, the old woman glanced toward her and muttered, "Thet's where she always sits, milord. Never says a word."

"That will be all," he said, his voice cold. As she passed by him, he added, "Wait outside."

"Yes, milord."

He closed the door and stepped further into the room, smiling. He was neatly dressed and looked fresh and erect. He stood a few feet from where she sat at the table. "I trust you are well," he inquired with great courtesy, as though the state of her health were a matter of genuine concern to him.

When she failed to respond to his inquiry, he stepped closer. "Are your needs attended to?" he asked, the ludicrous expression of concern still on his face.

"My needs, yes," she replied. "My wants, no."

His face became grave. "All you must do is ask and it shall be granted."

She looked up at him. "My freedom, then. I ask for my freedom."

He looked angry. "Freedom to what?" he asked pointedly. "To return to the house on Great Russell Street, to poverty, to your sister who betrayed you? Freedom to return to Mortemouth, to a senseless father who is looked after by two old women?"

Suddenly she felt a flare of anger. "You are responsible for those harsh conditions, milord," she said, in a voice without margin.

He bowed his head as though he did not want her to speak further. "I did not come here to argue," he murmured, waving his hand in her direction.

She was on the verge of asking him why he had come, then changed her mind. In the silence that followed, she was aware of him staring at her.

When he spoke again, his voice was changed, softer, as though he were making a fresh start. "I'm tired of dining alone," he said, simply, like a small boy about to ask a favor. "With your permission, might I dine here this evening?"

"It is your house, milord," she replied. "You may dine wherever you wish."

He was silent, then asked almost timidly, "Will you—join me?"

"I eat little now."

"You should eat more."

"I have no appetite."

He stepped closer. "Because of me?"

She remained immobile, astounded by his question. Had he no conception of what he had done, was now doing? In despair, she walked to the high window. Beyond she saw dusk falling, saw around a distant tower a flock of dark birds circling with slow, deliberate, wingbeats.

Behind her he waited. "You've not answered my question."

With her face turned away, she murmured, "I find it inconceivable that you should ask."

Again silence descended on the room. When she looked back, she saw him, still standing before the table, his head bowed. He looked bereft.

To her surprise, she found his demeanor almost moving, a giant robbed of his power. "As I said, milord," she added, trying to dispel the curious feeling of sympathy, "it's your house. Dine where you wish."

She saw him moving toward the door. He flung it open and summoned the old serving woman, gave her orders of some sort.

Through the half-opened door, Marianne heard the old woman protest, "Who is to sit guard if I'm—"

"No need for guards," he scolded. "I'm here. Go on with you and be quick about it.

Slowly he turned back into the room. She felt foolish standing unoccupied by the window, felt equally as foolish staring at the lamp. She considered returning to the chair, but such a move would only shorten this distance between them. She did not understand why it had become so quiet. She dragged the stool to a position directly beneath the window and sat, like a child, her knees elevated, her hands primly folded in her lap.

"Are you comfortable?" he asked.

"I beg your pardon?" she inquired, looking up.

"Are you comfortable?"

"Yes," she said.

He did not respond. He took a seat at the table, his position awkward-appearing, placing his folded hands before him, then withdrawing them into his lap. His voice, when he spoke, expressed melancholy. "These chambers belonged to my grandmother," he said, looking about. "She was happiest in London. Hated Eden Point."

His mood required no comment and she gave none. He went on. "With my grandfather, it was just the opposite. He always said he felt excluded and rendered mute by the populace of London. Enormous blocks of piled stone, he called it."

Again he looked about, as though listening to ghost voices. "Do you like London?" he asked.

"I've not seen it, milord," she replied.

"But you've passed time here for several years."

"My movements have been confined," she responded. "I've seen the meadows of Bloomsbury and the towers and spires of the city. From a distance." She glanced briefly up at the high window as though to illustrate her point. "Little else," she concluded.

Almost timidly, he corrected her. "You've seen the Pantheon."

She looked in his direction, remembering that night, her own absurdity with William's lilac pinned to the hem of her servant's gown. "Yes," she concurred.

"We danced together," he went on, his face and voice brightening. "Remember?"

She remembered. "I did not know who you were, milord," she said.

"Would that have made a difference?"

Out of the habit of honesty, she answered, "Yes."

Urgently he leaned forward and placed his hands on the table. "Why?" he demanded.

Again she felt overwhelmed by his apparent insensitivity. She considered reminding him of that hot August morning in the inner courtyard of Eden Castle, then changed her mind.

At that instant she was aware of movement coming from the table, of a chair being pushed back, of footsteps moving toward her. With her eyes down she saw his boots first standing before her, elegant black leather boots polished to a high shine. She held her breath and closed her eyes, and felt the weight of his hand covering hers, heard his voice exceptionally tender, yet hoarse as though bearing the brunt of deep emotion. "I have lost track," he began, "of the number of times that I have prayed for forgiveness for that cruel moment. I have paid a thousand times, and there still is debt."

She listened closely, her eyes focused on his hand, tanned, strong, small black hairs curling atop each knuckle. "I suspect I shall go to my grave owing the debt," he went on, tightening his grip on her hand. "If it were within my power, I would erase every scar from your back and transplant them onto my own, along with the pain you must have suffered—"

His voice broke. He shifted slightly from the awkward stooping position. "Please look at me," he asked, and when she did not, he raised his hand to her face and forced her to see his eyes, which were glittering with emotion.

"Don't," she begged, trying to pull away.

He released her face, but continued to hold her hand. "Say the words that would ease my pain," he requested softly. "Please, Marianne, speak forgiveness."

Again she tried to draw away, but he held her fast. Embarrassed by his closeness, she averted her head. "There is nothing to forgive," she said. "I disobeyed you. It is a punishable offense, and I was punished."

Before he could reply, there came a soft knock at the door. Quickly he turned his back on her and made an effort to arrange his face. "Come in," he called.

She saw a small parade of serving women enter the room, each bearing trays. One quickly covered the large table with a circle of white linen, arranging china and cutlery. The others deposited a platter of roast beef, a round bread, a bottle of wine.

As the women worked, Marianne watched him. He'd taken refuge in the far corner of the room, his back to her, head down, one hand searching for something in his pocket, then finally withdrawing a handkerchief. With the exception of the slight noise the women made as they fussed about the table, there was no sound. Again she felt peculiarly undone by his distress.

One of the women asked timidly, "Shall we stay to serve, milord?" When he either failed to hear or was incapable of response, Marianne took the lead as though it were hers to take. "No, thank you. That will not be necessary. I'll serve. You may go."

She saw indecision in the old eyes looking back at her. All three women glanced from her to Lord Eden, as though seeking confirmation for this new voice of authority. But when he refused to respond, they bobbed their heads and quickly took their leave.

She waited until the door had closed behind them, then sent her attention back to the bowed figure standing in the shadows. In the face of his obvious distress, her fear was subsiding, though she still viewed his presence as potentially threatening. As for pronouncing forgiveness on him, that she could not do.

Finally, when he did look back at her, she saw his hand go to his side as though he were seized with a spasm. His face had gone ashen. She watched carefully as he walked to the table, lifted the decanter, and poured two glasses of wine. From that distance, he extended one to her.

When she did not come, he placed it on the table, lifted his own glass, and drained it. He stared at the empty glass, then sank heavily into the chair. He cast a searching eye in her direction, and in a kind of gruff apology, muttered, "We'll talk no more about it." He gestured to the table and invited, "Come and eat."

She hesitated. Then, because she had denied him once and because in that denial she had felt a kind of power, and because she was hungry, she walked to the chair opposite him and sat.

He bestowed upon her a grateful smile. "Thank you," he said simply. He whispered hoarsely, "I hope I'm not too repulsive to you."

Again Marianne was not inclined to speak or offer consolation. He served her plate generously and served himself as well, and sat now, as though uncertain of himself.

Seeing his uncertainty, she picked up her fork and commenced eating. He followed suit. With the first bite, his mood seemed to lighten. He asked, considerately, "May I

bring you news from home?" Without waiting for her to
reply, he went on, eating and talking. "It's all quite as
you left it, the Point, the Castle, the village. We had a
severe winter, but the tenants forecast a good harvest,
and the herring were running well when I left—"

"News of my father, please?" she interrupted.

Slowly he placed his fork on his plate, took refuge for
a moment behind his napkin. "He's well," he said, melancholy spreading across his face. "He has the protection
of the castle now. Jenny Toppinger and Dolly Wisdom are
there, too. They tend to his needs and see that he is comfortable." Earnestly he looked across at her. "He has my
protection for as long as he lives," he pledged. "I vow it
on my life."

She met his gaze. "I'm grateful."

The simple exchange seemed to take a heavy toll.
Neither fork was lifted again for some moments. Then,
because she felt responsible for this new glumness, she
tried to redirect the conversation along easier lines. "And
old Ragland?" she inquired with a smile. "Is he still as
officious as ever, telling everyone what to do and what will
happen if they don't do it?"

Suddenly a terrible expression cut across his face. He
leaned his elbows on the table. Silence closed around him.
Below on the street, she heard an organ grinder, playing
a forlorn tune.

Seeing the disintegration, she inquired, "Milord?"

He rested his head in his hands and massaged his forehead. "Ragland is dead," he pronounced from behind this
barrier.

Marianne felt cut adrift. "I'm sorry," she murmured. "I
didn't know." Then, "How did he die? He seemed hearty
enough for his age."

It was as if every question, no matter how innocent,
was a new assault. "My fault, as always," he muttered,
"though your brother pulled the actual trigger." With that
beginning, and pouring himself a full glass of wine as
though for fortification, he told her the whole grim story,
leaving nothing out, taking full blame for everything. At
the conclusion of the tale, the lamplight caught his face
and she saw an emaciated visage, devoid of strength. "I
can conceive of no reason," he concluded brokenly, "why
I should continue to draw breath."

Impressed by the depth of his despondency, she sat close to the table. "You were not directly responsible for—"

"I am directly responsible for everything!" he interrupted angrily. "Everything! Within the last few years, I have, wittingly or unwittingly, destroyed more lives than I care to count." He bowed his head even lower. "The most regrettable being your own."

"I am not destroyed, milord," she corrected with a smile. "Look at me."

Slowly he obeyed. She felt a warmth on her cheeks at the intensity of his gaze. His expression was one of disorder, where impulses continued to discharge themselves without rein, a gloomy forest of passions. It was a haunting face. Working an even greater effect on her was his next whispered question, more a plea than a mere inquiry. "What is the source of your strength?"

When she failed to answer, he repeated himself. "The source of your strength, please," he begged.

She tried to return his gaze, but could not. The organ grinder's song floated up to her from afar. She failed to answer him because she could not answer. The source of her strength? What strength? She had never felt weaker in her life.

She was on the verge of confessing this when he stood up. "I'm morbid company tonight, I fear," he apologized. "Every avenue of conversation seems to lead to a grave." He looked back at her. "Please forgive me. I'll leave you now. I'm sorry if I intruded."

As he started toward the door, she called after him, "Milord—"

But he continued across the room and did not speak again until he had reached the door. His voice still carried an inflection of apology. He asked softly, "Would you kindly consider going abroad with me tomorrow through the city? Between the meadows of Bloomsbury and the White Tower there's a great deal to see." Again he lowered his head. In a subdued manner he promised, "I shall conduct myself in a manner befitting a gentleman. I will do nothing to cause you alarm. I swear it." He paused, then inquired, "Did you hear?"

She'd heard. "As your prisoner, milord?" she asked. "Or as your guest?"

In a voice scarcely audible, he replied, "As my guest. As my most honored guest."

"Then I should like that very much."

She'd expected some reply from him, but he gave none. Instead he opened the door and spoke a few words of command to the women outside. She watched in a trance as the women quickly entered the room and cleared away the remains of the half-eaten meal, continued to watch as they hurried down the staircase, and she was still watching when from beyond the door he called back to her, "I pray you sleep well, Marianne. Thank you for your company."

With that, he started down the stairs, leaving the door open. No guard now, no sliding of bolt, nothing but a clear access, a route of escape, the very condition she'd dreamed about for over a month.

She started forward as though she found herself on a path that she'd walked before. All she had to do was pass through the door, down the steps, two flights, right turn through the Great Hall, and straight ahead through the arches to Oxford Road.

Then where? The dead end struck her with a caprice of its own. Back to the house on Great Russell Street to the sister who had twice betrayed her, to Sarah, who perhaps had been an accomplice? Back to North Devon to the empty cottage in Mortemouth? She looked about as the realization dawned on her. She had no place to go. And even if she did—

The second thought was even more unsettling than the first. She retreated back toward the bed and tried to confront the dilemma of freedom.

A curious predicament, when the prison becomes the refuge.

At the bottom of the steps, out of sight on the second-floor landing, Thomas waited with held breath.

He heard everyhing. He was aware of her hesitancy, her slow passage to the door, anther pause, then, miracle of miracles, the prisoner closed her own cell.

By God, what a performance he had given! As he stepped from his hiding place, he again glanced quickly up the steps to the closed door. By God, but he had been skillful! Let any actor at the Drury Lane top that, he thought, grinning, almost laughing openly. The penitent! The upright head bowed with remorse! The crumpled visage! The trembling hands! The half-eaten meal!

He took a last look upward, then moved hurriedly down the corridor toward his own chambers, reviewing the theatrics in his head, relishing it anew as though it were happening all over again.

"These were my grandmother's chambers. She loved London—"

Dear Jesus, from where he had dredged that piece of nonsense, he had no idea. His hag of a grandmother had hated everything, the entire world and everyone in it, had taken voluntary refuge in the high chambers for fear of contamination by the ordinary mortals around whom she was forced to move.

Still, it had made a good story. If his assessment was accurate, and he was certain it was, that had been the turning point, the first delicate assault on her resistance. And of course everything that had followed had been merely brilliant, the reference to North Devon, to the condition of her father, to Thomas' plea for forgiveness. . . .

He stopped outside his door, almost overcome with joy. Oh, dear God, how she had succumbed to that, that pitiful plea for forgiveness. Suddenly he bypassed his door and ran to the top of the stairs which led to the ground floor. He lowered his head the better to see. He called out softly, "Locke? Are you there?"

An old serving woman appeared, her ancient face twisted upward. "Milord?" she inquired.

Still keeping his voice down, "I want to see Russell Locke immediately."

"He's in the kitchen, milord."

"Well, fetch him!"

"Yes, milord."

As he started back toward his chambers, the old woman called out, "Do we sit the door tonight, milord?"

He returned to the top of the steps. "I don't think it will be necessary, old mother," he said with a grin. "The bird is beginning to form an attachment for her cage."

Hurriedly he returned to his chambers and for the first time permitted himself the pleasure of an outright laugh.

He strode about the room exuberantly, lifting his head as though to hear certain fragments of his performance—

I have lost track of the number of times I have prayed for forgiveness. I suspect I shall go to my grave owing the debt.

My God, he had been positively inspired! Still, he moved about the room, always seeing her, her incredible beauty, enhanced by the passing of time, her youthful arrogance not gone, but merely tempered into a kind of awesome pride.

By the window he came to a halt, stopped dead by one thought. What a conquest she would make! What a mistress! What a charming companion! And what a complex of emotions she aroused in him! As he stared, unseeing, down on Oxford Road, he envisioned her, helpless, on the whipping oak, and immediately following this, he saw her helpless beneath him. As he imagined the sweet invasion of that young body, he found stimulation in every aspect of her, her face and hair, her shoulders and breasts, and most curious of all, he imagined her back, the scars for which he was responsible causing the greatest stimulation of all.

Be patient, he counseled himself. He'd made giant strides in one short evening, had coaxed his prey closer with kindness and remorse than he'd ever accomplished with force.

Behind him he heard a knock and called out, "Locke? Is that you?"

The door swung open and the man stood before him, his face uninspired, crumbs of his dinner still clinging to the front of his jacket. My God, how to account for the difference between these two?

There was no accounting, and he had no time for it anyway. Quickly he returned to the table, shuffled through a muss of papers, and retrieved the clipping which only last week he'd torn from *The Bloomsbury Gazetteer*. Hurriedly his eyes scanned the newsprint. "Dr. James Graham and his Celestial Bed." "Designed to cure the most reluctant females."

Thomas pondered the extravagant promise. Perhaps it would work. After a soft and repentant day abroad with her tomorrow, showing her the city as well as his bereft nature, perhaps she would be responsive to the effects of the Celestial Bed. He felt that once she were his, there would be no problem. Her reputation and good name ruined, she would have no choice but to stay with him, as long as she amused him. After that, and because he was an honorable man, he would care for her, would put her back into service at Eden Castle, where she could pass her days in relative security.

But for now he must treat her as the lady she thought she was, must court and woo her, and perhaps, with the help of Dr. Graham's magical bed, conquer her. He looked again at the clipping in his hand, a sad little smile playing about his features. If only she'd been high born. If only Fate had seen fit to let them meet on equal footing.

"Milord," Russell interrupted behind him.

"Yes," he said, stirring himself out of his thoughts. "I have an errand for you." He withdrew a piece of blank paper and scribbled the name and address of Dr. Graham's establishment. He needed to know more, needed to know the details of the bed itself. He must not, under any circumstances, make a fool of himself. His prey was delicate and easily offended. If it was nothing more than a bawdy house, it would not do at all. Therefore he had to speak to the man himself.

Hurriedly, he affixed his name to the note and withdrew from his pocket five guineas. "Go to this address," he commanded Locke. "Find the gentleman whose name is written here and tell him Lord Eden wishes for him to call tonight." He handed over the guineas and added, "If it's too great an inconveniece, tell him he can set his price. But he must come to collect. Is that clear?"

Locke took both the note and the guineas. Apparently he saw only the prefix of doctor. "Is she sick, milord?" he asked.

Incredible how the man could annoy him. "No, she's not sick," he snapped. "Now be off with you. Go straight there and return."

Locke backed up to the door, still eyeing the address on the note. "Am I to walk, milord" he asked slyly. "If it's haste you're after—"

Thomas withdrew another guinea and tossed it toward the man's feet. "Then take a cab," he said. "Just hurry!"

Smiling, Locke scooped up the guinea and bobbed his

head. "I thank you, milord," he said with a grin. "I'm already there."

The messenger under way, Thomas returned to the table and the well-worn clipping concerning Dr. Graham and his bed. He felt a pang of regret. Things had gone so well that evening that perhaps he could have won her affection without deception. But he was wise enough to know that there was a vast difference between the girl feeling sympathy for him and submitting to him. Perhap in the matter of female conquest, there had to be, out of necessity, something unfair about the whole business.

He felt tired and excited all at the same time. He sat heavily in his chair by the window, legs spread, his mind clogged with fragments of his earlier triumph. It was like a fever, an obsession, as strange and as unaccountable as Billy Beckford's tower.

He took refuge in comparatively safe memories of poor Billy. As soon as it was over here, he would pack his possessions back into trunks, his newest possesion, Marianne, at his side, and return to Eden Castle, perhaps stopping off at Fonthill Splendons on the way to display his new toy to Billy.

The thought brought him pleasure. There was not a reason in the world, if the girl behaved herself, why she should not pass the rest of her life in luxury. All he required in return was open access to her bed. He knew countless women who would bargain their souls for such an arrangement. Why was this one different?

There was a flutter at his feet. He noticed that he'd dropped the clipping concerning the magical bed. Slowly he bent to retrieve it, his eyes falling on the illustration of a naked woman designated as the "Goddess of Health," standing beside a magnificent bed. The caption read, "A virgin looks forward to her deflowering."

For a long time, Thomas stared at the picture. For some reason he could not quite see Marianne in the same posture, the same mood. Still, perhaps—

He heard a carriage on the street below and eagerly leaned forward. The carriage rattled past. Of course Locke had not had time even to get there. Pall Mall was a distance away. What if the man refused to come? Why should he? The Eden wealth was known and respected. He was willing to pay anything. Anything!

Thus he passed the next few hours in considerable turbulence, denying himself sleep, brandy, food, focusing all his attention on the street outside the window, coming to know it so well that he could monitor the regular passage of the night watchman.

It was after midnight when, sunk with brooding, he heard a carriage drawing near to the curb, then stop, horses neighing. He heard Locke's voice, slightly high-pitched as though excited. "This way, sir. How good of you!"

Slowly Thomas raised up. Below on the pavement, he saw two figures hurrying toward the front door of his house—Locke's sloping awkward gait, the other man taller, much taller, carrying himself with dignity.

As they disappeared beneath the eaves, Thomas attempted to straighten himself. Under whatever circumstances were necessary, he must have her and be done with it. If the man whose footsteps he now heard on the stairs could help him, then he could name his purse.

He moved quickly about the room, adjusting his person, smoothing back his long hair, turning up the lamps from where they had burned low.

At last there was a knock at the door. "Come in," Thomas called. The door opened and he saw only Locke's face, flushed, his eyes glittering brightly.

"Well?" Thomas demanded. "Where is he?"

Locke crept inside the door and closed it quietly behind him. "He's outside, milord. I just wanted to say"—he stopped, grinning broadly—"well, I ain't never seen anything like it. It was—" He hesitated. "Well, the reason I'm late is—" Incredibly he giggled. "I've never seen such goings-on, milord," he said, still keeping his voice down.

While Thomas was mildly interested in Locke's reaction, he was also aware of the gentleman waiting outside in the corridor. He would receive Locke's impressions later, such as they were. For now, he commanded, "Show the gentleman in, Locke. He did not come to idle his time in my corridor."

Reprimanded, the young man retreated to the door. Thomas felt a degree of nervousness that was wholly unaccountable, not unlike the days of his youth when the vicar had come to Eden Castle.

He stood in the center of the room, continuously making small adjustments to his person, smoothing down his plain dark brown jacket, wondering if perhaps he shouldn't have had his hair dressed, or better, wigged.

Where *was* he?

As his nervousness increased, he continued to focus rigidly on the partially opened door, listening, hearing nothing. He was on the verge of calling for Locke again when suddenly an odor reached his nostrils, an almost sickening sweet odor, like a bower of honeysuckle in late spring after a rain.

He lifted his head and drew another breath of the peculiar fragrance, his eyes fixed on the door, his head inclined as though he were trying to see around it.

Still nothing. Not a sound. He was ready to step forward when he saw a shadow, a slanted outline moving across the spill of light from the lamp in the corridor. The shadow grew in size until Thomas knew that the man himself must be standing directly outside the door.

But still nothing. In some perplexity, Thomas inched forward. "Dr. Graham? Are you there?" he called out.

Without warning the door was flung open and Thomas caught his first glimpse of the most remarkable sight he'd ever seen in his life.

A commanding figure, Dr. James Graham filled the doorway, a sunburst of a man, swathed in golden satin from the tips of his golden and glittering shoes to golden stockings, golden brocade knee pants and elegantly cut coat, a froth of golden lace studded with brilliants at his neck, a high starched gold satin Elizabethan collar extending from the back of his jacket, like the rays of the sun, each extension etched with additional brilliants, the sunburst rising as high as his golden pompadoured wig, laced through with strands of pearls and diamonds.

Before such an apparition, Thomas was speechless. Apparently the resplendent Dr. Graham did not object to the silence, for he now struck a pose, one leg extended and turned slightly to the right, the other rigid, his left hand resting lightly on his hip, the right crooked, upraised, the hand opened, fingers curled gracefully inward, a large ring on each finger, palm spread, as though he were waiting for someone to place something in it.

As he continued to stand, as though aware of himself as spectacle, Thomas' eyes fought their way through the glitter and gold satin to the man's face, which appeared flabby and colorless, as though unaccustomed to exposure. One feature was predominant—the mouth, which was slightly opened, limp, with thick lips, sensuous. The other features were a little heavy, the chin, the nose, and the eyes; into one was set a monocle which shone like a round blind eye.

There was an unearthly quality about him. Thomas had never seen anything like him before, and began to understand Locke's incoherency. When, after several moments, the man still had given no sign of altering his pose, Thomas cleared his throat and considered bowing, although in his entire life he'd bowed to no man save His Royal Highness.

There would be no bow, but someone had to break the silence. "Dr. Graham, I believe."

From out of the flabby face and through the sensuous lips came a deep, sonorous, persuasive voice. "Do you possess a dog?" the voice inquired, the posture and pose as rigid as ever, the one good eye staring straight ahead.

"A—dog?" Thomas faltered. "Not here. No. At Eden Point there are hounds."

"In the presence of a dog," the man intoned, "we find ourselves in the presence of Satan."

For the first time he altered the pose, stepping inside the room, his good eye moving hurriedly about, resembling an oyster in its own juice.

Thomas stepped back as the man stepped forward, a subtle ballet. He considered pursuing the "Dog-as-Satan" thought and decided against it. "No, no dog here," he murmured. In an attempt to recover himself and get to the point of the encounter, he smiled hospitably. "I thank you for coming, Dr. Graham," he said. "I know how—"

Suddenly the man stirred again. The beringed hand lifted and plunged inside the golden jacket and withdrew a small wand, about two feet in length, its shaft golden and studded with amber stones, topped with a golden medallion etched in a circle of faces which, as well as Thomas could tell, resembled mythological creatures. Dr. Graham lifted the wand upward into the air and slowly extended it toward all four corners of the room.

Thomas watched the curious ritual and felt himself torn between fascination and impatience. As the man turned this way and that, the high glittering Elizabethan

collar bobbed with its weight, the brilliants capturing and
reflecting the lamplight, covering the walls with explosions
of smaller light. Something in the man's stern concentration warned Thomas against interruption, so he merely
watched as he lifted the wand upward, pointing it toward
the ceiling.

For some reason the wand seemed to have taken on
dreadful weight. Dr. Graham held it suspended over his
head with both hands, the froth of golden lace at his wrists
quivering with effort. He endured the invisible pressure
for a moment, then quickly he broke away.

Within the moment, he appeared to recover himself.
With a certain haughty and bored distinction he held out
his hand. "I am Dr. James Graham," he pronounced, his
voice impressive in its tone and timbre, although Thomas
thought he discerned a faint Scottish burr.

By way of reply, Thomas murmured, "And I am
Lord—"

"Thomas Eden," the man said with a smile, completing
the introduction for him. He commenced moving about
the room, casting small fireworks on every darkened wall,
a living sun. "I have been aware of you for some time,
Lord Eden," he went on, his magnificent voice trailing
after him. "I have felt your pain. I know the kind of brain
and body you possess, your family and society, the time
in history into which you were born, all this and more."
Near the window he stopped. He looked back at Thomas,
who continued to stand as in a trance near the center of
the room.

Feeling more and more like an awkward schoolboy,
Thomas did well to nod. The fatigue which he'd felt
earlier seemed to be diminishing. Again he was aware of
the peculiar odor, now stronger. Not honeysuckle, he decided. Too sweet. More like—

"Lord Eden?"

He looked up as Dr. Graham summoned his attention,
and saw the man now hovering over his chair, the wand
still in his hand, seeming to explore every corner of the
crushed dark green velour. "You have suffered here recently," Dr. Graham commented, his face heavy with
pity. "You have suffered *here,* yet the source of your
suffering is"—slowly he lifted the wand and pointed it
toward the ceiling—"is there!" he concluded sternly.

Impressed, Thomas nodded. "How did—you—"

But the man merely waved away his half-completed question and again struck a pose by the chair. "When a being is alternating expansion and contraction, he is energy," he announced.

Thomas nodded.

"A completely expanded being is space," Dr. Graham went on, fondling the wand, feeling of the etched mythical faces, like a blind man. "Since expansion is permeative, we can be in the same space with one or more other expanded beings. In fact, it is possible for all the entities in the universe to be one space. Do I make myself clear?"

Before the glittering man and the overpowering odor and the parade of words, Thomas felt dull. "I'm—sorry, Dr. Graham," he murmured.

But the man brushed aside his apology. "No need," he pronounced. "You are an invalid, suffering a terrible disease. I am here to help you."

There was such compassion, such largess and understanding in the man's voice and attitude, that Thomas felt doubly weakened, suffered a slight tremor as though he *were* an invalid. And when Dr. Graham swept majestically around to where he stood and brought his sun and sweet odor with him and put his arm around Thomas' shoulder and said in the richest of voices, "Please relax, Lord Eden, because nothing is secret from me and no one is abandoned," Thomas actually found himself leaning into the man, permitting himself to be guided to a straight chair near the center of the room where he sat heavily, almost regretful when the man's arm departed his shoulder.

He closed his eyes in this new and enjoyable weakness. He could sense the man's presence still before him, like a fire in December. He opened his eyes to the shifting kaleidoscope of sun, to savor in a flash of perception that this was no ordinary mortal standing before him.

"I *am* in pain," he murmured obligingly, hungry for sympathy as well as solution.

"Of course you are," Dr. Graham purred, lifting the wand with the gold medallion and holding it directly before Thomas' eyes. "Do you see these faces?" he inquired.

"I see," murmured Thomas, studying the circular arrangement, spying a Medusa head, a horned image, a sea serpent, and a cyclops.

"Then study them closely and listen as I speak."

Thomas obeyed, although obedience had little to do with it. He wanted nothing else but to sit and listen to the magical voice, study the curious faces which all seemed to be looking at him, and breathe deeply of the sweet odor.

As Dr. Graham spoke, his voice formed individual words and pushed them forward like separate jewels, a necklace of words, settling pleasantly on Thomas' hearing. "Each of us," Dr. Graham began, "is the same kind of being. You, me, the source of your agony above, each is capable of outflowing attention and awareness, and each is capable of withdrawing it. And that is all we need to do—give full permission, loving attention, to absolutely anything that we see in our minds, in our bodies, in the bodies of others."

A discernible peace began to settle over Thomas. The Medusa head was smiling at him.

Graham went on. "Expansion in love is an action that is available to every being in the universe. A willing awareness will take us to paradise and make us free. Nothing else controls our Fate. Whatever you are doing, love yourself for doing it."

Thomas had never heard such words. Now the cyclops was smiling at him.

"And whatever you are thinking, love yourself for thinking it. Love is the only dimension that needs to be changed. If you are not sure how it feels to be loving, love yourself for not being sure of how it feels to be loving. . . ."

The wondrous voice was rising in a crescendo, the jewel-like words exploding all about.

"There is nothing on earth," Dr. Graham proclaimed at fever pitch, "more important than the love which conscious beings feel toward each other. No matter what your spiritual condition is, no matter where you find yourself in the universe, your obligation is always the same, to love, to love openly and freely, with your entire body, to avail yourself of the infinite experience of love, to love, to love with the blessing of the cosmos, the transcendence of the soul, to love, to love, to love—"

As the words beat against Thomas, he bowed his head as though under assault, but what a magnificent assault, a fiery presence of sun and heat standing before him, every mythical creature's face smiling at him, the sweet perfume filling his nostrils, the command still coming, "—to love, to love, to love."

The voice ceased. He was aware of Dr. Graham moving away from him. He mourned the loss, though the message was still with him. "Dear God," he murmured hoarsely.

"God has nothing to do with it," said Dr. Graham, standing a distance away. "Here is the power." And he held up the golden medallion.

Thomas gazed at the remarkable man. "Where do you come from, Dr. Graham?" he asked.

"From the Goddess of Earth," he replied without hesitation. He pocketed the golden wand and Thomas was fearful he was preparing to take his leave. "No, don't go," he begged. "I must talk with you."

But Dr. Graham shook his head. "I have clients waiting," he said wearily. "I must go. The paths are many and dark and my time is limited. Shortly I will be called to rejoin the Goddess of Earth and I must give a good accounting."

Seeing that he could not postpone the man's departure, Thomas stepped forward. "I need your help," he said.

Dr. Graham agreed. "You do indeed."

"The bed," Thomas went on, "The Celestial Bed—"

The man smiled, a most gratifying warmth. "It has been reserved for you for centuries," he intoned. "It was written during the last Ice Age that on tomorrow evening you and the young lady would occupy it—together."

Overcome, Thomas could only stutter. "I—don't—understand—"

"It's not necessary that you understand," Dr. Graham corrected him, lifting his eyes as though to the heavenly host. "All that's necessary is that you love."

The heat from that dazzling voice encompassed him. "Her objections will crumble like sand on a beach," Dr. Graham promised. "Tomorrow evening you will direct your carriage to the rear of my house on Pall Mall, in the company of the young lady, of course. The Goddess of Health will greet you at the door and escort you to the Celestial Chamber. You will be provided with the Elixir of Life, and within moments the Celestial Bed will beckon to both of you. She will disrobe first and unless you move with haste, she will break her own maidenhead to permit you easeful access to the temple of her body."

Thomas clung to the table. "She will not—object?" he begged, still seeking reassurance.

Dr. Graham shook his head as though offended by the question. "The Celestial Bed rests on four Cosmic legs. Their energy source is the center of the universe. No mere human, not even a virgin, has the power to resist. She will be yours tomorrow evening, Lord Eden. I swear it."

In a state of reverence, Thomas still clung heavily to the table. With deep regret he saw the sunburst move toward the door. "Must you go?" he asked.

The voice was sonorous and sad. "The world is a dark place, Lord Eden. My lamp alone can light the way."

"I must see you again," he declared, starting forward.

"And you shall," Dr. Graham soothed. "Tomorrow evening, if you wish, before you enter the Celestial Chamber, you may both partake of my earth bath and lecture, a magical health treatment which restores your limbs to the condition of youth."

"Yes, yes," Thomas replied. "All of it. I must have all of it!"

As the sunburst was slipping out of the door, taking its golden rays, the good doctor called back, "Bring a purse of two thousand guineas, if you will."

Without hesitation, Thomas agreed, "Of course, of course!"

As the last fragment of golden satin faded from his view, Thomas fought back an impulse to run after him. But at the same time he felt an urge to remain silent, to hold himself still, lest the mood break and splinter about him like fragile glass.

"Oh, God," he groaned. Tomorrow night—cosmic legs which derive their strength from the center of the universe!

Hope was set in motion. The young girl sleeping upstairs was on the verge of being completely his. He stared upward at the beamed ceiling as though trying to see through it, directly into her chamber. In what position did she sleep? Clothed or naked?

"On the morrow," a voice soothed. "Be patient until tomorrow!"

She breakfasted alone in her third-floor apartments, though she ate little, her anticipation of the day's events blunted by the residue of nightmares.

Then she dressed herself in a simple pale blue gown, affixed a matching bonnet to her head, still amazed by the open door through which the old serving woman had passed all morning. She paused to study its openness, going back in her mind to the nightmare, hearing in the silence of morning William's cries as she'd heard them all through the night.

Quickly she pushed the outrageous dream away. Night was over. The man was waiting for her downstairs. As for William, he was undoubtedly well, possibly wed to some French lady, his life complete and happy. Otherwise she would surely have heard.

Thus she said good-bye to the fossil of William Pitch that lay in her heart and straightened her shoulders and tightened the pale blue satin streamers of her bonnet and walked slowly down the stairs.

At the bottom of the steps she saw her brother, Russell, outlandishly clad in canary yellow. Beyond him, looking as weary as she felt, she saw Thomas Eden, dressed somberly in dark gray, his eyes heavy from lack of sleep, though lightening as they caught sight of her.

"Milady." He smiled, bowing low. After the bow, she was aware of his eyes making a slow journey over the gown, returning to her face with what appeared to be an expression of gratitude. "A Devon sea lavender come to life," he pronounced. "What a happy choice, that gown. I selected it myself, seeing you in it."

She wished she'd chosen the plain brown one instead. It had suited her mood upon awakening. But she was forced to admit that even she had hopes for the day. The night before, the man's obvious repentance had moved her. Perhaps abroad with him in sunlight, she could talk her way into complete freedom. What she would do with it, or where she would go, she had no idea.

As he extended his hand to her, she sidestepped it and led the way through the arched door to the pavement, where at midmorning the traffic of Oxford Road was bustling. The sights and sound of people walking freely about moved her. She had wanted to walk, and was therefore disappointed when he caught up with her and directed her toward the waiting carriage.

Russell, smiling slyly as though he knew something she didn't held the door for her. She looked up at Thomas.

"Must we ride?" she asked. "After imprisonment, I long for exercise."

She saw a discernible cloud cross his face at her mention of imprisonment. But kindly he explained, "The distances are too great. We'll go from point to point by carriage, then walk about when we get there."

She started again to protest, but decided against it. The day would be long enough as it were. It would not be of benefit to either one of them to start on a note of discord.

Disregarding his offer of help, she reached for the hand support and lifted herself into the carriage's interior. She remembered the night over a month ago when she'd sat in the same corner and had looked despairingly out at the night.

Now she looked over at Lord Eden opposite her. He sat erect, his hair lightly dressed, clean-shaven, his arm resting on the cushioned support. His eyes were open, but appeared to be unseeing. It was precisely the position of the dead.

She saw Russell peering in through the window, awaiting the command. Lord Eden gave it and Russell scurried around and climbed up on the high seat beside the coachman. With a flick of the reins, the carriage lurched forward.

Something about the seating arrangement amused her. "Doesn't my brother usually accompany you inside the carriage?" she inquired politely.

"Not in the presence of a lady," he replied, still not looking at her.

She took the reply for what it was, a foolish attempt to flatter her, and concentrated on the passing sights of Oxford Road, one of the busiest streets in London and, she thought ruefully, surely one of the ugliest. Commercial shops were wedged in between large houses, their little signature boards hanging limp in the airless morn, a few weak displays of late August geraniums looking parched and dried, mostly a gray-black-brown scene, the larger houses appearing prosperous though uninhabited. And there, just ahead, the majestic and slightly pretentious Pantheon. She leaned up for a better look at the now-closed portals. A few old men sat on the great staircase, taking the sun.

Apparently he saw her interest in the building. "It seems a long time ago, doesn't it?" he commented softly.

She looked back at him in the dark interior of the coach.

That evening which had caused her such distress now produced a smile. "You were dressed as a smuggler, I remember," she said.

"I *was* a smuggler," he replied.

"I know."

"And you were dressed as a serving maid," he said.

"I *was* a serving maid," she said with a smile.

"I know," he replied.

The exchange produced an agreeable warmth on both their faces. When she looked out of the window again, the Pantheon was gone, and they were approaching a broad avenue lined on both sides with tall yew trees, a lovely boulevard skirting a broad green park. It was a beautiful vista, like a painting, with people lounging about on the soft green grass, children rolling hoops, and there she saw a small brown and white spotted dog chasing a squirrel.

"If you'd care to stop, we can," he offered kindly. "But there's much to see."

She shook her head. "You're the captain of the day. I'm in your hands."

The expression of such a gift seemed to bewilder him. "It's your pleasure I'm concerned with," he murmured.

She believed him and tried to imagine their relationship without the weight of memory behind it, merely a man and a maid abroad on a lovely sun-drenched morning. It required an effort of some imagining, but she accomplished it. And when, a few moments later, spying a flower stall at the edge of the park, he leaned out and ordered the coachman to stop and quickly left the carriage and returned with an incredibly beautiful bouquet of pale cream-colored roses and presented them to her, she thought that the most remarkable thing about miracles is that they do happen.

"To go with your gown," was his brief, almost self-conscious explanation.

Smiling, she accepted both the flowers and the compliment and nestled her face to the soft velvet petals and sniffed their fragrance. In spite of her unexpected happiness, she warned herself that wisdom should reckon on the unforeseen.

They rode in silence into the heart of the city, then out again, the coachman apparently taking his directions from Russell, who obviously had conferred with Lord Eden. Everyone knew where they were going except Marianne, and she liked it that way.

The past was losing its grip on her. This repentant man sitting opposite her was not the man who had ordered her public whipping, or who had abducted her in the dead of night. She didn't know who this man was, but he was not the same man.

The carriage pulled over to the pavement and came to a halt. Beyond the window, she saw a broad river.

"The Thames," he announced. "Here I thought we would take the air." He leaned forward and pointed, "There's London Bridge, and there"—he gestured behind her—"is Wren's Monument to the Great Fire."

She found herself looking excitedly in both directions, delighted at last with the opportunity to stretch her legs and feel grass beneath her feet. Russell was already at the door. Lord Eden alighted first and strangely this time did not extend his hand in assistance. Carefully she placed the pale creamy roses on the seat, chose one to accompany her, and looked regretfully at the others. "I'm afraid they'll die," she said.

"Then we shall buy more," he promised.

She stepped from the carriage and adjusted her bonnet. While Lord Eden was conferring in private with Russell and the coachman, she turned her attention toward the silvery Thames and the springy bosom of the surrounding hills and fields. The air seemed fresher here, closer to the water, and she thought how long it had been since she'd seen her home at the edge of the water.

She was in the act of starting forward when he came up beside her. He seemed so much taller standing than sitting, quite overpowering, his birth and breeding showing in every angle of his face.

He was silent beside her, his eyes assessing the best approach to London Bridge. When he spoke, he said simply, "Let's go to the river's edge first. It's said that to touch the Thames is to bring one good fortune." Without changing his attitude or voice, he added. "Perhaps the river will be more considerate of you than I have been in the past."

At the approach to the banks of the river, there was a gentle slope which she could have managed easily. Nonetheless, seeing him descend first and extend his hand, this time she accepted it, and felt it lightly close around hers.

It lasted only a moment, then he withdrew a safe distance to the edge of the river and stood with his back to her, staring out at a barge which was being poled against the current by the three bargemen, shirtless, their back muscles glistening in the heat of the day.

He began to speak, a queer little speech, rigid with formality as though he'd taken it word for word from a guide pamphlet. His hand lifted toward the upper river and his voice came out as measured as a schoolboy reciting Beowulf.

"The old town of Cirencester," he began, his brow knitted in the direction in which he was pointing, "known as Corinium in the time of the Romans, is in the Cotswolds. In a field near the town reclines a statue of a bearded old man. By the statue a spring feeds a small stream." He looked quickly over his shoulder, not directly at her, but at a point over the top of her head.

She stiffened to attention and somehow felt as though she were a child again, and old Jenny Toppinger was drilling her on the names and dates of the Monarchs.

"This statue and springs," he went on, sending his attention upriver again, "are in themselves unremarkable, but this little stream, gathering other waters as it flows along, is the accepted source of one of the most famous rivers in the world." Here he spread his arms wide as though to embrace the vision before him. "The Thames," he pronounced, almost reverently.

He looked back at her, as though for her impression. Quickly she bobbed her head, duly impressed.

"The—Thames," he muttered under his breath, searching for the next line. A Eureka light dawned on his face. "Whilst still a gentle river," he went on laboriously, "making its way through some of England's most beautiful lands, it wanders past many places where England's history has unfolded—Windsor, home of the Monarchs, and Runnymede, where King John's Barons saw the signing of the Magna Carta, over five hundred years ago—"

All at once she saw him lift his head, as though the stiff prepared text had become a source of pride.

He repeated, "Over five hundred years ago," and she saw a light in his eyes, a simple pride, available to all Englishmen, the certain knowledge of who they were and the unique richness of their island country. She'd seen it in her father before, had on occasion felt it in herself. She'd thought it was merely the balm the lower classes used to soothe the abrasive effects of poverty. She'd not expected, and was therefore surprised, to find it in one high born.

"It's a lovely river," she murmured, in appreciation of his words and apparent effort, as well as of the mighty river itself. She took a final whiff from the perfect rose which she'd separated from the bouquet and stepped forward to the edge of the water and lightly tossed out the flower; it floated prettily on the water, the tide carrying it gently downward toward the channel.

The gesture seemed to please him. "Once," he began quietly, "I saw the Venetian Ambassadors arrive in a grand barge, bedecked with flowers, the entire river a carpet of flowers. But," he concluded, "it wasn't as lovely as that single blossom tossed by your hand."

She felt herself blushing both from the compliment as well as from the weight of his eyes. They walked easily along the embankment, his hands clasped behind his back, his head bowed. She walked beside him, taking two steps to his one.

Feeling a desire to contribute to the moment, she said, "Jenny Toppinger told me the story of Elizabeth Regina, as a girl, coming down this river to her imprisonment and sitting on the steps of the White Tower, refusing to go in."

He nodded thoughtfully. "Perhaps our greatest Monarch."

"Yes," she agreed. "At least Jenny said so, and Jenny knows everything."

The sun had risen high, almost a position of noon. Gulls swooping over the river attracted her attention. At the end of the promenade there was a small open-air gallery with an arrangement of wooden benches from which one could have an uncluttered view of London Bridge. Beneath the central span, the barge which they had seen earlier was now passing. They watched as the bargemen lowered their long poles, one muscular lad reaching up in a spirit of play as though to grasp the span directly above him. They heard all of the men shout at the bridgemen, an easy sense of fellowship apparent between them.

As the barge slipped out again into the sun, she glanced at Lord Eden and saw the most remarkable expression on his face, an incredible longing, as though if the bargemen had called to him, he would have eagerly swum out and joined them, become one with them, and willingly done his share of work.

"Milord," she said, summoning his attention back to the bank. "You wouldn't like it. Oh, perhaps for a day or two it would be sport, but on the third day your back muscles would ache, the muscles in your arms would swell up, the palms of your hands would be bleeding, the sun would burn, and you'd jump off the barge at the first landing and flee back to Eden Castle."

He laughed, conceding her wisdom, his eyes lingering on her face. The laugh died but his eyes were still there. "You are so beautiful," he whispered.

She walked the short distance to the wooden bench and sat down. Such intimacies did not belong to the day. When she looked up to find him still staring at her, she rose quickly and started off down the embankment, calling over her shoulder, "There's more to London than the river. We must hurry if we're to see it all."

Some moments later she heard his step behind her. "I apologize—" he started.

Quickly she shook her head. Feeling the heat of noon, she loosened her bonnet and removed it. "Where next, milord?" she asked, trying to recapture the tourist mood.

He pointed straight ahead toward a high-rising obelisk. "Wren's Monument?" he inquired. "It's only a short distance. If you like, we can walk."

She nodded, feeling the old formality spring up between them. It was better this way. Hurriedly they made their way back to the carriage, where she saw Russell and the coachman, their legs propped up, enjoying a pipe and a morning's chat. At their approach, both men hopped down and stood at attention. Again she waited while Lord Eden whispered a few words to them. Then he dismissed them and both men climbed aboard the carriage and urged the horses forward.

In alarm, she stepped closer. "Where are they—"

But he merely ordered, "To the Monument," pointing his finger in that direction, then lightly taking her arm in assistance across the cobblestones.

The street they now threaded was so narrow and shut in by shadows that when they came out unexpectedly into the vast sky, she was startled to find the day still light and clear. No words were spoken during the short walk through foot traffic. Once safely on the pavement, he released her arm, though he still walked protectively close to her, stepping forward at each oncoming pedestrian and forcing him or her out into the street in order to make a clear passage for her.

As they crossed Gracechurch Street, he suggested, "Look up!" Following his bidding, she lifted her eyes. It appeared that the tower was swaying.

Quickly she stepped away and closed her eyes. When she looked back the tower was steady again, a single pillar reaching two hundred feet into the air.

They circled it once, Lord Eden launching forth again into his prepared travelogue, more at ease now or so it seemed.

"Designed by the great Christopher Wren," he intoned, "erected to mark the spot where the Great Fire of London broke out in 1656."

Mentally she corrected him, 1666, but said nothing. Jenny had told her about the Great Fire as well. She felt a surge of belated appreciation for her old schoolmistress. Her school had been unorthodox, a low stool by the fire of her father's cottage, but Jenny had taken Marianne's blank female mind and had tried to fill it.

Apparently Lord Eden saw the distance on her face. "Are you well?" he inquired earnestly.

"Very well, milord," she replied. "Just thinking of home."

The confession seemed to bewilder him. "Home?"

"Mortemouth," she replied, and as his bewilderment increased, she led the way to the small door in the base of the pillar, from which several children were now emerging, their faces flushed with exertion, their pretty locks plastered with perspiration against their smooth foreheads.

"Is it quite a climb?" she asked one young boy, a lad of about twelve with black eyes and rosy cheeks.

He grinned. "Not if you do it ever'day, maistress, like we'es do."

"You make the climb every day?" she asked. "Why?"

Without hesitation he replied, "From up thur it's like bein' a bird, a maistress. If you stand thur long enow, you begin to think that all you have to do is leap off and spread yer wings—"

Behind her, she was aware of Lord Eden, listening with tolerance to the boy's fantasies. "And if you could fly, boy," he asked, "where would you go?"

Again, without hesitation, his comrades pushing playfully about him, he announced, "To Amurica, maister."

"And what would you do in America?" Lord Eden demanded.

A younger boy, with mischievous smile, answered for him. "Fight red savages!" He grinned.

"No!" Sternly the older boy corrected him. "I'd be a farmer, maister," he said, with the seriousness of youth.

"Can't you be a farmer in England?" Lord Eden persisted.

"Not with a bloody tyrant on the throne, maister," the boy answered readily. His mood lightened. He turned to Marianne with an offer. "If you and yer father want to go to the top, I'll take you for a ha'penny."

Father! Quickly she averted her face to conceal a smile. She heard Lord Eden shouting angrily, "Be off with you now, all of you! Ruffians, that's what you are! Be grateful I'm a kind man or I'd report your treason."

She heard the boys scrambling off, then turned back to see a flush spread over Lord Eden's face. "They're only children," she soothed.

"Impertinent radicals," he answered, his anger seeming to increase. "The seed of an English Robespierre."

"Children, milord," she soothed again.

He shouted once more at the retreating boys. "America is where you belong. With the other rabble, and good riddance, I say."

As passersby began to stare, she counseled, "Let them be, milord," and guided him into the shaded interior of the monument. Looking up, she saw a narrow turnpike stair running all the way to the top. "Shall we attempt it?" she asked, still trying to soothe his wounded vanity.

Begrudgingly he looked up at the narrow and steep ascent. "Dare we?" he snapped sarcastically, "lest we be tempted to leap like birds?"

Still soothing, she suggested, "Then it will be our obligation to restrain one another." Quickly she tied her bonnet loosely about her neck and let it hang against her back, thus freeing her hands for the ascent. Lifting her skirts, she started upward.

Abruptly she broke into a run, longing to increase the distance between them. A short time later, gasping for breath, she stepped out onto a circular balcony, loosely confined by a single hand railing, while beneath her stretched all of London, all the world, or so it seemed. Her first impulse was to press tightly against the core of the column. But at length, adjusting both her vision and her equilibrium to the extreme height, she dared to ease forward, her eyes sweeping the world in half an arc, the wind blowing her hair and gown backward, the sensation one of pleasure mingled with a degree of fear. By closing her eyes, she easily imagined that she was standing on Eden Point.

Breathing deeply of air, space, and memory, she was not at first aware of the heavy footsteps behind her. When he did emerge beside her, his breathing was so tortured that she was fearful of his collapse.

"Breathe slowly, milord," she suggested, and was amazed when he wasted what little breath he had left on a new burst of anger.

"Why do you insist," he gasped, "upon addressing me by that stupid epithet?"

While he struggled for breath, she struggled for understanding. "What am I to call you, milord, except milord?"

"My Christian name is simple," he snapped, again trying to draw breath. "Easily pronounced and easily recalled. Thomas," he pronounced. "Can you speak it?"

She watched him and loathed his patronization. "Of course I can speak it, milord," she said, "but I don't wish to." She left his side and walked around the column, seeing a different view of London, her mind furiously occupied with his condescension. She closed her eyes and when she opened them, he was standing close beside her.

"Will you forgive me?" he murmured. "I wanted the day to be without events save happy ones."

"No apologies are necessary, milord. It was a harmless incident. The boy meant nothing."

He leaned closer, rested one arm against the pillar. "Look at me, Marianne," he commanded.

Her name sounded strange on his lips, as though he'd addressed her thus for years. When she failed to obey, his hand started forward and lifted her chin. In the close proximity of his face, her vision distorted. She saw the traceries of fine lines around his eyes and at the corners of his mouth, saw the mouth coming closer, felt his hand leave her chin and slip around her neck, catching her hair, the mouth coming still nearer. She closed her eyes as his lips touched hers, lightly, in a subtle testing.

It lasted only a moment, a kiss more tender with protection than violent with passion. At the conclusion, they stared at each other.

Lord Eden stepped away first. "If—I offended you," he stammered.

She considered making comment, then decided against it. Perhaps his wounded pride had been healed. It amounted to nothing more. Moving slowly around the pillar, she led the way down the spiral staircase.

The descent was easier and silent, except at one point, midway down, he stopped for breath. "Did I cause offense?" he asked.

"No, milord," she replied, and turned her attention to the narrow staircase.

She reached bottom first, then looked back and saw him a good ten yards behind her, his face still dark with worry. With her feet once again on earth, the impact of the recent embrace struck her. She should have resisted. In a delayed reaction she felt a blush creep over her cheeks. As he drew even with her, she led the way out onto the sunny pavement where they encountered a small group of sightseers, three gentlemen in elegant dress, all looking up, apparently trying to assess the wisdom of the climb.

As Lord Eden emerged, blinking into the sunlight, one of the young gentlemen called out in high spirits, "Is it worth it, milord?"

Standing to one side, Marianne watched as he struggled for a reply. "It's a hard climb," he said.

"But is it worth it?" another persisted.

Lord Eden looked to Marianne as though for help. Blushing under the weight of so many male eyes, she murmured, "It's a good view if you're not bothered by high places." Quickly she took refuge in adjusting her bonnet. When she looked back the three gentlemen were gone and Lord Eden was watching her.

"Where now, milord?" she asked lightly, trying to break the intensity of his gaze.

They made their way back across Gracechurch Street. He took the lead, walking a step before her. The foot traffic was diminishing and the sun was bobbing in and out between the buildings.

They walked thus for several blocks, not speaking. She lost track of the exact distance. The heat of the day at high noon was rising, but still she found the excursion pleasurable, her eyes feeding themselves on remarkable sights—the dazzling painted murals on the fronts of Guild Halls, a one-legged beggar singing for alms in an appealing voice, a quaint old woman with three small dogs tucked in her arms, a heavy black coalwagon drawn by four white horses. On occasions she forgot she had a guide, and lagged behind to examine a piece of copper in a shop window, a young painter working at his easel, his brush miraculously re-creating the timber-frame house opposite where he sat.

But each time that she struggled to keep up, she saw there was no need, for always he was only a few steps ahead of her, waiting patiently, watching over her protectively, a kind of pleasure on his face.

A few blocks farther and he stopped. Beyond him was a broad avenue, and beyond that, a most magnificent sight.

"St. Paul's," he said simply. "It seems to be Christopher Wren's morning."

She could not take her eyes off the magnificent cathedral before her, without compare, surely, in the whole world, a triumphant arrangement of saucer domes and grouped pillars, the large central dome making a solemn and imposing focus for the whole cathedral. It rose like a miracle on the summit of Ludgate Hill, perfectly proportioned to its site, so exquisitely fitted that the eye could not conceive of an alteration.

"Would you care to go in?" he asked, and apparently took her silence as an affirmative answer. She was aware of his hand on her arm, guiding her closer to the great building, leading her up the broad front steps and through the cathedral doors.

Making the quick transition from light to shadow, her eyes struggled to see. Even after her vision cleared, she knew somehow that she would never see it all. She was aware of small groups of people standing quietly about, looking upward as she was doing into the interior of the dome.

If Lord Eden had prepared a lecture for this particular sight, he withheld it, apparently feeling that the masterpiece spoke for itself.

In the course of the next hour, she examined it all, followed the line of wall rising straight to the lofty elevation of towers, studied the immense windows on either side of the lower aisles, the elegant pillars marching up the center of the nave, and always returning to the dome itself, the work of a magician instead of an architect. If the cathedral had a heart, here it was.

When she was incapable of seeing more, they retreated to one of the pews and sat. He seemed to be maintaining a guarded distance, as though still shaken by his lapse atop the monument.

Without warning he asked, "Do you believe in God?"

She looked at him. "I have no reason not to believe in Him," she replied, knowing that it was a simple answer, but hoping it would suffice.

It didn't. He leaned forward, pursuing the matter. "What in your life gives evidence of His existence?" he asked, something in his face convincing her that he wanted to know.

She replied simply, "*I* give evidence of His existence." She paused. "As you give evidence of His existence."

"I don't understand," he said, leaning back. "I was brought up to believe, and I've certainly passed enough hours in chapel. As a child, I used to fear God, but fear cannot be counted as belief, can it?"

She sensed a distress deeper than what he was revealing. "I think belief comes easier for the poor than it does the rich."

"Why?"

"A poor man has nothing else to turn to," she responded.

He muttered, "Then fortunate is the poor man, for the rich man turns to phantoms for comfort. He is not without anxiety from the moment of his first breath to the occasion of his last." His face grew darker, his eyes staring straight ahead. "His wealth imprisons him," he concluded, "and there is no escape."

She watched him, the downward angle of his head, his hands kneading one another between his legs, his posture slumped as though he were devoid of strength.

Faced with such bleakness, she had no recourse but to lightly touch his arm in comfort. "You stand in harsh judgment of yourself," she suggested. "At the moment I find you good company, considerate and thoughtful."

"Then why did you refuse to acknowledge my suit?" he demanded.

The bluntness of his question took her off guard. "It was my right to do so," she said.

"Without explanation?"

"Did I owe you one, milord?" she asked. "Do I owe you one minute of my life if I do not choose to freely give it?"

Apparently the question was unanswerable. A new weariness in his face, he stood. "Have you looked your fill?" he inquired, the old formality back in place.

"I have, milord," she replied, equally as formal, and led the way to the end of the pew and down the long nave aisle, standing to one side for an orderly procession of schoolboys. Weary of the cross-purposes which seemed constantly to plague them, she stared fixedly at the passing rosy-cheeked boys, then at the first opportunity hurried down the aisle and out the magnificent door where again the heat of the day slapped her in the face and she leaned against a near railing. She was weary of the little games they had played all morning. She wanted to go home. She longed for the cottage in Mortemouth. If she were truly free, perhaps he would grant her this much, a small purse for passage and the gift of her life.

She heard his step behind her. "No more talk of God or the past," he promised. "No more talk of debt or obligation. Let's return to the river. All should be ready."

She yielded to his authority, briefly wondering what was being readied at the river, and at the same time surrendering her dreams of home, at least for now.

The walk back seemed longer and hotter. The foot traffic had tripled. In spite of his interference, she felt herself continuously jostled about, the passing faces forming a bizarre parade before her eyes.

A short time later she whiffed the fresh scent of river

breeze, and as they turned the final corner, leaving stone and mortar behind, she spied the river itself, the embankment and a new sight. There on the soft green where they had earlier strolled was a gold and white striped canopy, a tent shaped like something out of the Arabian Nights, enclosed on three sides, the fourth flap pulled back in open view of the river. Alongside the pavement, she saw his carriage, joined now by two others. At least a half a dozen men in white jackets were hurrying back and forth between the carriages and the canopy, carrying trays covered with white linen.

Puzzled, she looked up at him. But he said nothing and led her across the grass, past the men who halted their labors long enough to bow. Russell came to greet him, his canary yellow suit showing signs of wilting in the sun.

"All is ready, milord," he said.

Still Lord Eden said nothing, but guided her around to the front of the canopy, where inside she saw a table covered with white linen, elegantly set with glittering crystal and silver, a colorful Persian carpet under foot, and at the corners of the canopy itself, four large silver urns filled with cream colored roses, dozens of them, not merely bouquets, but entire gardens of flowers.

Finding it overpowering, she did well to follow his suggestion that she take a seat and refresh herself. He sat opposite her at table as one of the waiters filled their glasses with cool white wine.

"A picnic by the river," he said simply. She almost laughed aloud as she looked around at the bounty, a golden roasted chicken on the table between them, a bowl filled to overflowing with white grapes and peaches, a perfect round of cheddar, and a basketful of white rolls, as buttery and as golden as the sun.

"I trust you are hungry," he said with a smile, seeing her hesitation. She realized that she was and allowed one of the waiters to serve her plate, whereupon all the men disappeared as if by magic, leaving them alone beneath the canopy, the river ahead of them, the heat and noise of the city a safe distance behind them.

He lifted his glass and she followed suit, curious as to the nature of his toast. "To you," he said simply.

She kept still, expecting more, but slowly he lifted his glass to his lips and drank, and she did likewise. As they commenced eating, she found it difficult to keep her eyes off the surroundings. Everywhere she looked was beauty. A gentle breeze blew over them from the river. She felt the anxiety and cross-purposes of the morning slipping away.

By midmeal she felt quite relaxed. "We used to have picnics in Mortemouth," she said laughing, "but they did not resemble this."

"What were they like?" he asked, eating heartily. "Tell me—I want to know."

"We ate herring for the most part," she began, "pickled in brine, and if the catch had been good the day before, my father had cider, and occasionally he would give me a sip." She shook her head "I didn't like it, but I'd always ask for a sip anyway. It made him laugh to see my face."

"Then you did it just to amuse him?"

She nodded, remembering those good moments. The food and wine were beginning to have a mellowing effect on both of them. She watched as he leaned back in his chair, fingering a handful of white grapes.

"Milord," she began tentatively. "What plans do you have for me?"

He looked up from the grapes. "What plans do I have for you?" he repeated. "I have no plans except to give you pleasure."

"Then it would please me greatly, milord, if I might return home."

He sat up. "So soon? We've scarcely begun. There's Westminster—"

"I want to return home to North Devon."

He stared at her as though disbelieving. "Why? What is for you there? I told you your father lives at Eden Castle now, and is safe. I'm certain that your cottage is newly occupied—"

"Then I shall find another," she replied, "and take my father home."

Slowly he stood up. "Have I displeased you?" he demanded.

She hurried to reassure him. "Not displeased me, milord," she said. "It's been a lovely day—"

"And it's not over," he interrupted.

She conceded as much. "But when it is, milord, what then? I can't stay forever in that third-floor apartment, and

I have little desire to return to Great Russell Street. You
have convinced me that I am not your prisoner. Then what
am I?"

He stared at her as though contemplating the question.
In the intensity of his gaze, she sensed that a decision was
being made, that within moments, perhaps, she would
know her fate.

But she was wrong. He merely raised his hand with an
arrogance which seemed to say he owed her no reply and
left the canopy and walked the short distance to the river
where he stood with his back to her.

In his nonanswer, she found cause for alarm. Perhaps it
was his intention that she should go on occupying the third-
floor apartment. Forever! But in what capacity? If she was
not his prisoner, neither was she his guest, and they both
knew that. His mistress then? Certainly he was not so
stupid to believe that she would sacrifice what was left of
her good name for such sinful luxury as now surrounded
her.

Suddenly she sat up on the edge of the chair, seeing a
plan in everything that had happened. His mercurial moods,
his seeming kindness, his curious questions at St. Paul's,
his eagerness to comfort and protect atop the monument,
all part of his plan. She felt within herself a deep melancholy, the grim realization that she had been an unwitting
partner to her own entrapment.

Escape! The single word struck against her brain. With
his back turned and his mind apparently lost in brooding,
she might accomplish it, then once free, throw herself on
the mercy of the city. She was capable of employment and
a good worker. Perhaps in exchange for an honest fortnight's labor, an employer would grant her enough wages
for the journey home. And after that—

Then do it! Now! On that resolve she stood up and took
a final look at the man brooding at the water's edge. Behind her she heard the faint traffic noises coming from the
city.

Moving quickly, she stepped out and around the edge
of the canopy, thinking that perhaps if she could find the
way, she would return to St. Paul's. Surely so grand a
house of God would offer her temporary refuge. Without
a backward look, she increased her speed across the grass
until she was running, aware of several of the white-coated

men watching her, but aware of little else but the need to escape.

She was on the pavement, skirting his carriage. Only a few steps more across the cobblestones and she would be able to blend with the crowds. Looking ahead across the thoroughfare, she failed to perceive the shadow just emerging from behind his carriage. Suddenly she felt one strong hand descend on her arm, saw a flash of brilliant canary yellow. Then Russell was before her, blocking her passage, grinning down on her and at the same time shaking his head. "You'd better think twice, lady," he said, scowling at her.

She struggled as Russell's blank face loomed large above her. "Please," she begged. "Let me go."

But he showed no inclination of doing so and held her pinned against the carriage, a curious expression of good humor on his face.

Coming from the direction of the canopy, she heard a deep, angry voice of authority. "Release her," the voice ordered.

She saw Lord Eden moving toward her with great strides. When at first Russell failed to comply with his command, he seemed to increase his speed until he was standing beside them, his arm upraised as though he intended to knock the fellow aside.

"Release her!" he ordered again.

"She was running away, milord," Russell tried to explain.

"Nonsense," countered Lord Eden. "She was merely bored with this place, as I am, and eager to move on."

In spite of the afternoon heat, Marianne felt herself shivering. Lord Eden placed an arm around her shoulder in simulated affection. "She's merely tired"—he smiled— "and wishes to return to the carriage."

From round about her in anguish, she heard her own voice. "I need no assistance, milord," and pulled away from his arm and up into the carriage, where she saw the dying roses of morning and sank heavily into her customary spot by the window.

She closed her eyes. There was no hope, and thinking thus, she made herself into a nonresponding husk. No longer would she play into his hands so agreeably with smiles and conversations. She would endure the rest of the day in silence.

Without looking, she was aware of him entering the carriage and taking his accustomed seat. As they made their way back into the city, she saw little and took interest in less. It wasn't until a shadow fell across her face that she looked up and saw him sitting directly opposite her, his face lined with concern. "I wish you would have waited," he said mournfully.

She felt repulsed by his presence and turned her eyes out the window and resolutely gave no reply.

"Please, Marianne," he begged.

Still she kept silent, a feeling of abysmal shame mingling with her distress. She could not bring herself to look at him, for she was certain that his face would not contain one angle of truth. She knew now that he would not release her until he was abundantly satisfied. Perhaps not even then.

The silence between them increased. Then softly he spoke the most unexpected words. "If you truly wish to go home, Marianne, then I shall take you there. I've caused you enough unhappiness."

She looked up, unable to believe what she had heard. The rhythm of the carriage sounded like a pulse. He sighed heavily. "I mean it sincerely," he vowed. "I, too, am weary of London. The city extracts a heavy toll. As soon as arrangements can be made, we shall depart together."

She looked at him, still unable to believe. Yet she'd been wrong about one thing. In his face there was the light of truth. Leaning closer, he bowed his head. "Please indulge me for the remainder of the day," he begged, "and I promise you before the week is out we both shall return to North Devon where we belong."

She had never thought it possible to go from such despair to such happiness in so short a time. "I'm most grateful, milord," she murmured, and allowed him to take her hand and lift it to his lips, a harmless gesture, more a sealed bargain than anything else.

Again she leaned back in the seat and began to take note of the passing scenery. She was aware of him still looking at her, almost reverently. Perhaps she'd been wrong about him. Perhaps he merely wanted her companionship and friendship, twin gifts that she was not loath to give, unless he took both for granted.

But he did not seem to be doing that now. In fact, for

the rest of the day he seemed to be making an extraordinary effort to treat her with kindness, subduing his aggressive role in endless considerations.

Dusk found them at the eastern edge of the city. A perfect dome of peacock blue sank into gold amid the blackening trees and the dark violet distances. The glowing blue tint was just deep enough to pick out in points of crystal one or two stars. All that was left of the daylight lay in a golden glitter across the far edge of London.

In spite of her weariness after a long day of touring, she felt an exhilaration. "Thank you, milord," she murmured as the carriage started down the incline which led back into the city.

In the darkness she could scarcely see his face. But she sensed in him a similar attitude of relaxation. "There were rough places," he conceded thoughtfully, "but all in all, a most successful outing."

She agreed and relaxed into the cushioned interior. The night sky outside her window was a dark blue now, relieved here and there by little streamers of clouds jockeying for precedence, like her thoughts. She saw in her imagination the wild beauty of Exmoor, the desolate landscape that was the approach to Eden Point. Then she imagined the sea breeze, the vast headlands bedazzled with wild flowers, the peculiarly lovely fragrance from her childhood of herring and seaweed, of sun-bleached sand and pristine white cottages, like proper old women, lifting their small gardens, like skirts, at the water's edge.

So deeply enthralling were her thoughts that she failed to notice the traffic of the city increasing around them, the carriage moving steadily down strange streets, as though it knew precisely where it was going. She became aware of the two linkboys who had joined them, and a night watchman riding beside them on horseback, and the peculiar music of carriage wheels on cobblestone.

Suddenly she was jarred out of her reverie by the appearance of the strangest house she had ever seen. Along the pavement ran a procession of many large torches, all blazing brightly in the night, the congestion of at least a dozen carriages pushing close to the curb. A short distance from the pavement stood the house itself, a large crowd lined up in disorderly fashion, all leaning toward the front entrance, an imposing white brick structure, every window ablaze with light, and over the door a large pagan gilt sun.

She leaned forward in her seat as the sounds of shouting reached her ear. "Milord," she began, puzzled, and stopped short as on the steps of the house, beneath the pagan sun, a bizarre sight greeted her eyes. A woman had just emerged from the house in a thin diaphanous robe and stood on the steps, her head lifted, as slowly she slipped the robe from her shoulders and stood—

Marianne blinked, certain her eyes had deceived her. The woman stood before the crowd absolutely naked.

She tried again. "Milord, what is—"

Then he too was leaning forward, shouting directions to the coachman in an attempt to lead him through the congestion of traffic.

They pulled into a narrow lane alongside the strange house and continued at a slow pace toward the rear, where they approached a large carriage house with its door open. They came to a halt inside the carriage house, the door closing behind them, the horses whinnying to a halt.

In some alarm she looked about, then remembered the overly grand spectacle which he'd arranged for her at noon alongside the river, and assumed that this was something along that order, a closing extravagance, some excess which was characteristic of him and which perhaps in view of their new ease with each other, she should indulge him.

In that mood, she followed him out of the carriage and into the shadowy interior of the carriage house. She saw Russell, grinning, quickly alight, step up to the door, and knock soundly four times. She noticed a certain jaunty confidence about him, a confidence matched by Lord Eden himself, who stood close beside her, his hand on her waist, pulling her close, closer than she cared to be.

"Milord, what is this place?" she asked, pulling free, yet still held half-suspended by his grasp.

"A fitting end," he said smiling mysteriously.

She was on the verge of questioning him further when the door burst open and two young women identically clad in diaphanous robes appeared as though in procession, the thin folds of their garments concealing nothing. Following a step behind them, she saw the most incredible man she'd ever seen in her life, an imposing male figure clad entirely in dazzling gold, from the gold of his sparkling wig to the giant sunburst which framed his face. In his hand he carried a wand of some sort with a golden medallion attached. He waved this wand in her direction while the seminaked women bowed low as though in ritual obedience.

The whole spectacle was so bizarre that her first inclination was to laugh. She saw Lord Eden move toward the golden man, saw him take a large leather pouch from his inner pocket and hand it to him whereupon the man felt it as though to assess its weight, then tucked it deftly inside the golden coat. He beamed broadly.

As the two men continued to exchange a few words, Marianne sent her attention back to the young women. Their robes, pristine white, seemed to be cut with broad openings in the sleeves so that their hands could move in and out with ease. She blushed to see them caressing their own bodies, their hands beneath the robes fondling their breasts, then following the contours of their bodies down to their hips.

In some fascination, Marianne watched it all, embarrassed, yet curious to know what it meant.

The "Golden Sun" drew near to her, smiled down on her, and thrust the glowing medallion before her eyes. She stared at it, bewildered, uncertain what she should do. She tried to read the medallion itself, but could not. The etched designs resembled rat scratchings.

As he continued to stand before her, she noticed golden sparkles in his eyebrows, golden sparkles on the ridge of his nose, a madman's face or a clown's. Her sense of bewilderment mixed with amusement persisted as she saw the utter seriousness in the faces around her.

Then the Golden Sun removed the medallion from her vision and his own foolish face took its place, peering close. "Do you feel relaxed?" he asked, in a mellifluous, over-cultivated voice.

With all the attention in the carriage house drawn to her, her mind had never been so blank or her tongue less ready to form words. While she was struggling to understand, she saw him nod, as though pleased by her lack of response. Then Lord Eden was beside her again, his arm around her waist. Before she could protest, the two undulating young women opened the door and before her she saw a golden hallway, incredible illumination coming from an invisible source, the gold of the walls blending

with the gold of carpet and ceiling, an enormous sunbeam
leading at a distance to a large round doorway, its surface
inset and sparkling as though with jewels or fire.

A sense of detached curiosity settled over her. The prospect of following the "sunbeam" to the "sun" itself was
irresistible.

Around her waist she felt pressure from Lord Eden's
hand. They were crossing the threshold, treading slowly
down the golden corridor, which was now lined with a half
a dozen maids in similar robes who appeared to have
stepped out of the walls, with fixed smiles on their faces.

She felt an urge to return their smiles, but decided
against it. She stole a sideward glance at Lord Eden. His
face seemed unnaturally flushed. If he saw the nubile
young girls on either side, he gave no indication of it, but
kept his eyes straight ahead.

Abruptly from all about there came the sound of a tremendous organ, an explosion of music. "Milord, what—"
she whispered, looking quickly around her, seeing that
the young girls had fallen in line behind them, two by two,
a smiling procession, their robes pulled back, baring their
bodies completely. At the sight of such nakedness she
quickly averted her eyes. As the thunderous organ music
increased to deafening pitch, she saw the golden sun doors
open, the man himself appearing in the inner room, although she was certain they had left him standing in the
carriage house.

She'd seen enough and started to say as much when the
young women were all about her, separating her from
Lord Eden, forming a circle and leading her forward into
the inner room.

Alarm vaulted. "Milord!" she called out and looked
quickly over her shoulder. He was still behind her, though
being led by the Golden Sun in the opposite direction of
the inner room, a room which she noticed was pristine
white, the walls covered in white velour, the floor white
and soft as a cloud, as though its true surface were a
gigantic pillow.

The young women still hovered about her. A sickeningly
sweet odor filled her nostrils. Their hands caressed her body
as they had caressed their own. She struggled once in an
attempt to move away, but she continuously lost her footing on the soft white surface. As their hands moved over

her and as the sweetish odor increased, she was on the verge of crying out. Suddenly the organ music subsided. The young women withdrew. As they moved silently through the sunburst, the door closed behind them. The white room went totally black. She stood in darkness, her heart beating too fast. "Milord," she whispered. "Are you there?"

Receiving no answer, she pushed backward into a near corner, feeling the floor here grow more solid beneath her feet.

"Milord?" she begged. "Please answer."

A sudden rattling drew her eyes forward. She saw one of the white velour walls beginning to part, saw a blinding white light, and for a moment saw little else. She pressed closer to her safe corner, wondering what had prompted him to bring her to this madhouse.

She lowered her head to wait out the blinding light, then looked up. Before her on a raised platform was an enormous bed, made entirely of white fur, or so it seemed, a monstrous structure, standing on high glass legs and completely surrounded by walls of mirrors, ceilings of mirrors, mirrors everywhere, enlarging and distorting the size of the bed itself. The four posts which extended above the bed were lit by torches of fire, and these four eyes of fires were caught in the reflection of mirrors and amplified and multiplied until it seemed as though the high white surface was caught in a conflagration of flame and light.

As her eyes slowly adjusted to the incredible spectacle, she saw a familiar figure on the far side of the room opposite her.

"Is it you, milord?" she whispered.

When he did not respond, she stepped tentatively away from her safe corner, lifting her skirts slightly, the better to manipulate the soft spongy surface. As her eyes adjusted to the illumination from the torches, she saw that it *was* him, though a strange him, seated calmly at a table of sorts, a low white bench, backless, with a raised shelf before it like a student's desk. As she drew nearer, she noticed that he appeared surprisingly relaxed, a tall decanter of some sort placed before him on the bench out of which he poured himself a glass of amber-colored liquid, drank it down, filled a second glass, and extended it to her.

She watched these insignificant movements, trying to read some sense into them. "Lord Eden," she began, standing a safe distance away. "I must—"

"Not now, Marianne," he scolded her in a curious tone. "Come. Sit down beside me."

As he patted the bench, indicating where she was to sit, she noticed that he had changed his garments, was no longer wearing the gray coat and dark breeches. He was now clothed in a loosely fitting white robe, gathered at the waist by a limply knotted cord, revealing a V-shaped expanse of naked chest covered with tight coils of black hair. Apparently, as they had become separated upon entering the room, he had taken advantage of the moment of blackness to disrobe.

Again she saw him patting the bench beside him, his voice and attitude most peculiar, a foolish grin fixed as though for all time upon his face. "Come, Marianne," he repeated in a husky melodramatic voice. "Come and drink."

"Drink what, milord?" she asked, still wary.

He lifted the decanter as though to display its harmless quality. "A relaxing elixir for the conclusion of a full day, that's all." He urged again, more forcefully, "Come! Sit!"

In view of the enjoyable day and because he had generously offered to take her home, she indulged him and slid along the bench, stopping about two feet from him.

"Closer," he urged. "Here!"

Again she obliged until she was seated close to him, the glass of amber liquid in her hand, the absurdity of the moment almost overwhelming, so that at the last minute she sipped in order to hide a smile.

He seemed very pleased. "Marianne," he murmured, said it twice as though testing its sound in the quiet room, that silly grin still stitched to his face.

She bobbed her head as though confirming her identity and found it difficult to look at him, but found it equally as difficult to look anywhere else in the room.

She sipped, then asked, "What is this place?"

He was drinking more rapidly than she, and once again filled his glass. "This is a place of miracles," he said, gesturing with his glass.

"What kind of miracles?"

He pointed with his glass to the high bed. "You see that?" he whispered, leaning close.

She nodded, finding the question absurd. She would have to be blind not to see it.

"It's attached to the center of the earth as well as the cosmos," he went on, his voice low.

She looked again, wondering if she'd failed to see something the first time. As she lifted her eyes, she was aware of him slyly refilling her glass. "It's a handsome bed, milord, to be sure, but I see no heavenly connection—"

"You can't see it," he scolded. "You must feel it!"

The foolishness he was so soberly speaking caused her a moment of alarm. Perhaps there was something in the air, or in the "elixir" they were drinking.

"I still don't understand, milord," she protested lightly. "What are we—"

He pushed close, so close she could feel his body next to hers. "You're so full of questions, Marianne. Be at ease. There's nothing here to harm you, I promise."

"I am at ease, milord. Just curious."

He lifted her hand and examined it, separating her fingers, studying the palm and thumb, his eyes half-closed. "What a remarkable hand," he whispered.

She looked close. Perhaps she'd overlooked something in this limb which had been attached to her for life.

Still holding her hand before him, he spoke softly, as though to her hand. "Do you remember this morning atop the Monument?" he began, "when you granted me the rare gift of a brief kiss?"

"I remember, milord."

"How did it strike you?" he asked of her hand.

"As kind and protective, not unpleasant."

Slowly he turned on her, the foolish grin spreading. "Not unpleasant? A peculiar way to put it."

She shrugged. "I thought nothing of it at the time. Nor do I now. Your pride had been injured. My response was an offer of comfort. Nothing more."

Suddenly he was on his feet beside her, his arms around her. She was startled by the ease with which he swung her clear of the ground and held her half-suspended, her body crushed against the solid bulk of his chest. "Then comfort me now," he pleaded, hoarsely, burying his face in her neck.

"Milord," she gasped. "Are you mad?" As he loosened his grip, she struggled free and retreated to the far end of the bench. She looked back, aware for the first time of what he had hoped would transpire in this ghastly room.

Gasping for breath and undone by his strength, she announced, "Milord, I would like to leave now. May we go?"

He followed after her. "You—feel nothing?" he inquired.

"What am I supposed to feel?"

He spied her half-empty glass and moved it nearer. "Here," he urged. "Drink some more."

"I don't wish to drink more."

"But you must."

"Why must I?" she demanded, meeting his authority and, in a way, topping it.

Before her small flare of anger, he made a curious retreat. As though bewildered, he shook his head. "Dr. Graham said—"

"And who is Dr. Graham?" she demanded, wondering how long she could blunt his advances. When he failed to answer, she made her own assumptions. "I assume that Dr. Graham is the silly man who led us into this madhouse, and I earnestly hope, milord, that you did not give him too large a purse, for if you did, you are a greater fool than he. But I'm the greatest fool of all for staying here a moment longer."

On that note of resolution she started toward the door. Then he was running after her, the ridiculous white robe flapping opened to reveal bare and bony knees, his feet also bare, a comic figure save for one thing, the expression on his face.

They reached the door simultaneously. He pushed her backward with one hand, the other hand tightening on her arm. There was a confidence in his expression which alarmed her. As she attempted a subtle retreat, he held her fast, his eyes staring down, his voice low. "We came here for a purpose, lady, and now we shall see it through."

Her protest, as he lifted her bodily into his arms was a single sharp cry, her arms flailing out against his face and shoulders, her feet kicking, heart accelerating in horror, her struggle impressive but futile against his strength as he carried her steadily toward the high Celestial Bed and finally dumped her unceremoniously onto its white fur surface. In that instant of freedom, she tried to scramble

away, whereupon he threw himself on top of her, pinning
her arms with one hand, his moving down the front of
her gown, fumbling with the long line of buttons, then
finally ripping the pale blue fabric and peeling it back,
revealing her breasts.

Until that moment it had been a poor humor practiced
upon her. But suddenly it ceased to be a joke and took on
a different aspect, exorcising the memories of all the anguish she'd suffered at his hands. She was aware of a terrible
compelling regret both for herself and him as well. It
seemed blasphemous not to inform him of the thoughts in
her mind.

As his hand continued in its exploration, she ceased
struggling and lay still beneath him. As apparently he
sensed her lack of resistance, he looked down on her as
though mystified, holding his passion in check, giving her
time to speak.

"Milord," she whispered, "you are making love to a dead
woman, for as soon as the act is completed, I shall find the
first means at my disposal for concluding my life."

The threat, delivered as soft as a benediction, hung on
the air between them. He looked intensely down at her,
his hands stilled. The expression on his face ceased into
an angle of pain as slowly he drew backward.

At the first sense of freedom she scrambled upward,
pulling the torn fragments of her gown together and but-
toning the three remaining buttons. She did not at first
comprehend the degree of her fear or the sincerity of her
whispered resolution. But as she caught a glimpse of him
standing a short distance away, she wondered how long
they could torture each other without death being the
natural conclusion, for one or both.

Then she ran from his presence, with what little strength
she had left, intent only on fleeing the place, her hands
shaking as though palsied, aware of him calling after her,
"Marianne, wait! Please, wait!", his voice sounding more
like an animal's wail than a man's.

Still running, she glanced over her shoulder and saw him
following in the white robe, though clutching his other
garments, dropping a boot in his haste.

The corridor was blessedly empty, free of sunburst men
and nubile, half-clad young women. She led the way
through the golden door, beyond which she longed for a

glimpse of the carriage, the means by which she might flee this place.

And there it was, the coachman drowsing aboard the high seat, Lord Eden still in desperate pursuit. Without waiting for assistance or explanation, she flung open the carriage door and took hasty refuge in the far corner, her arms clasping her body in an attempt to hold her gown together, pressing tightly against the cushioned interior as though she were trying to push through the carriage walls.

Outside she heard a splintered exchange, Lord Eden commanding in a shattered voice, "Take us home!"

"Milord, young Locke's inside with the ladies," the coachman protested.

"Damn Locke! Take us home!" Eden exploded.

She was aware of the weight of a foot stepping inside, but saw nothing and responded to nothing. After the first lurch of the carriage, she closed her eyes. Try as she did, she could not stop shaking as she recalled the events, the helplessness of her near fallen state.

Once she heard him whisper, "Marianne, please—"

Rigidly she shook her head, indicating that she had nothing to say, was indeed incapable of speech. In this atmosphere the journey was completed, the sights outside her window growing familiar as the carriage turned into Oxford Road, past the Pantheon, that cursed structure, stopping at last before the high Tudor house, once her prison, although it was difficult to discern that as she alighted from the carriage even before it came to a firm halt, running across the pavement toward the steps, through the entrance hall where a serving woman stopped to gape. She was aware again of his close pursuit only a few steps behind her, still calling out, "Marianne, wait, pray God, wait!" She took the stairs two at a time, lifting the soiled hem of her gown, her eye fixed on the door at the top of the third-floor landing as though it were a safe harbor.

As she pushed through the door she heard his step behind her. As she was in the process of closing it, she felt the weight of his shoulder on the other side, felt the solid oak give as though she were a creature of weightlessness. Against his determined approach, she retreated backward into the room, wondering if the horror were truly over or merely postponed.

He stood in the open doorway, panting for breath, still

clutching his garments to him, the white robe and bare feet looking more absurd than ever. Behind him, struggling up the stairs, she saw several servants, their faces pinched in curiosity. But that was all she saw, for suddenly, reaching backward, he slammed the door with such force that she felt vibrations beneath her feet.

She walked away from him a step or two further, reaching behind her for something solid against which she could buttress her fear. "Milord," she said, "we have nothing to say and I wish to retire." Her bravado almost amused her, trying to face him down.

But apparently it worked, for suddenly he dropped the awkward bundle of clothes, as though her simplicity were one of the most devastating forces he'd ever encountered. As she retreated further back to the bed, clutching the post for support, she saw him commence to pace, a battered, heavily breathing figure, one hand grasping at his hair as though he intended to pull it out, his head shaking back and forth.

He kept up this curious pacing at the heart of the mystery. Out of the slow, measured tread, she heard the beginning of words.

As long as he paced and muttered only, she was safe. She had no quarrel with either pacing or muttering. But then abruptly he stopped and confronted her directly, his face as anguished as she'd ever seen it.

He shouted, "What do you want?" his voice, in spite of its pitch sounding remote, his eyes pleading for sympathy. "I—don't understand," he said, again pacing and shaking his head. "You—seemed willing, earlier. You seemed— receptive, responsive. I treated you with grace and dignity, I concerned myself only with your pleasure, I shared, I gave—" He spoke this in a tone of amazement as though impressed by his own behavior.

She listened carefully, still clutching at the bedpost, hearing the bitter disappointment in his voice, topped only by his massive confusion. "And now, I don't understand!" he shouted, voice rising. "What do you want? How am I to behave toward you? What do you expect of me, what price that I have not paid? Tell me, lady. I want to know. I *demand* to know. Do you intend to enter a convent? To take your virginity with you to the grave? Is it *all* men, or just this man? Then tell me how I am lacking. My earlier

offense to your person has been more than paid by the
agony of my prolonged ordeal. I have suffered as you have
suffered, have scars even to show for it."

"Do you care to see?" he demanded. "In shape and size
they are different from yours, but believe me, lady, the
pain was the same, my blood when spilled the same color
as yours."

It was a desperate monologue, punctuated by the constant and pitiful refrain, "Then tell me, lady, what do you
want? Direct me, guide me, so that our mutual torture
may come to an end."

He approached her now by a single step, his arms outstretched in one last pleading, "What do you want?" he
cried. *"What-do-you-want?"*

In the silence brought on by the cessation of his voice,
she foundered. She could not really say when the word
first occurred to her, that small, incredible word now
forming at the back of her brain, not forming actually,
for the ease with which it surfaced suggested that perhaps
it had been there always, since that hot August morning
she'd survived the whipping oak, not normally a word of
revenge, and in all honesty not now coming as revenge,
fighting its way through the back of her throat and into her
mouth, one word only, reaching her tongue and consciousness simultaneously, enabling her to feel more in command than at any time since Thomas Eden had entered her
life, an amazing word—where *had* it come from—still
moving through her brain, a desperate and perhaps shame-
less solution, but it had the merit of positivity.

When at first she did not respond to his tortured plea of
"What do you want?" he cut the distance between them
by a single step, shouting again, angrily, "What do you
want?"

The word was there now, fully formed, like a long-
awaited infant ready for birth. In reply to his last anguished outburst of "What do you want?" she delivered herself of the word, softly, with that same smile with which
she'd held the horrors of the charnel house at bay.

"Marriage," she said. In the event he'd missed it the
first time, she repeated it, "Marriage, milord."

But he hadn't missed it. He stared, like something dormant, almost crouching before her as though the word had
the power to deliver a fateful blow. He moved back to

the door as if unprotected from the impact of the word.
In a stupor, still gazing at her, he opened the door and
backed out.

She watched him go down the steps, then slowly made
her way across the room and closed the door behind him.
She stood for a long time watching the night sky through
the high casement windows, the clouds brushing the surface of the moon, reminding her of evenings at home in
spring with the lilac burgeoning in the cottage garden.

Boots and carriages clattered on the cobbles. Murmurs
of voices reached her from the street below. Her sense of
detachment, that had never left her since she had given
voice to the simple word, settled in the room. The prospect
of stretching herself on that comfortable-looking bed was
irresistible.

"Suppose he agrees," she thought. "Suppose he doesn't
agree—"

She was too tired to care. She pushed off the tattered
gown, pulled on a soft silk nightdress, and slipped between
cool soothing sheets.

By the count of five, she was asleep.

Marriage!
He took the single word all the way down the stairs with
him, a serious weight accumulating with each step.

Marriage!

Had she lost her senses? That a man in his position
should live with his mistress was not in the least remarkable, but marriage with a member of the lower orders was
unthinkable.

Marriage!

Did she realize the impossibility of what she was asking?
Apparently she didn't. As he entered his chambers, and
as the absurdity of the word washed over him, he laughed
aloud and spoke the word as though to test its absurdity.

"Marriage!"

Looking down, his eyes skimmed over the silly white
robe, his normal garments abandoned—where? Then he
remembered. Upstairs in her chambers.

The absurdity of the entire evening washed over him.
My God, what a fool he'd been! How duped! Two thousand guineas for the privilige of being transformed into an
ass!

As his mind began to grasp the extreme dimensions of his ridiculous behavior, he ripped off the robe and hurled it into a far corner and glared after it as though he longed to attack it further.

He was damned certain of one thing. He would send for his solicitor in the morning and bring charges against the charlatan Graham. He might not recover his purse, but that was of little import. The man must be driven out of town, his "elixir of life" dumped into the gutter where it belonged, his young women put out on the lanes of St. James's Park where they could be recognized for what they were. Whores!

His anger increasing, he flung open the wardrobe door and withdrew a dressing gown. With an anguish bordering on obsession he continued to glare at the white robe in the corner, feeling heat on his face as he saw himself duped, taken in, as easily as a provincial bumpkin.

No matter. He would seek revenge. Before it was over, Dr. James Graham would be quaking in fear beneath his Celestial Bed. The mere thought of the madness caused fresh humiliation, and immediately following this came a new and painful thought. If he turned his solicitor loose on Dr. Graham, the story of the entire evening would spread and he would again be the laughingstock of London.

No, he must tell no one. No one must know beyond himself, and unhappily, her. At the thought of her, his eyes moved upward to the ceiling. His embarrassment was softened by the good memories of the day. Within the moment, he was so moved that his eyes misted. Walking slowly, as though he were in some way injured, he made his way to his chair beside the window, threw open the casements, and on the street below heard the watchman call out the hour of midnight.

Her. Every twilight corner of his life warmed at the thought. A most remarkable her—a gleam of white skin, dark blue eyes beneath flaxen hair, how sweetly she had looked at him at moments, how fearfully atop the Monument. Even when she did not speak a word, her grace and gentle dignity spoke volumes. It had gone so well for them until the foolishness of the evening. Then—

Thinking on it caused new distress. He leaned his head against the sill and saw her face and swimming eyes. It

astonished him to find how rich his life was even in the
memory of her.

Slowly he raised his eyes. Well, then, was he in love?
Since he had no appetite for life without her, he assumed
that he was. "Oh, God," he groaned, again resting his head
heavily upon the sill, the image of her coursing through
him with the whole dread pleasure and pain of love.

But marriage? How would that be possible for a man
of his position? He could see the bans—"Lord Eden mar-
ries fisherman's daughter from Mortemouth." And what
of the line? The only valid claim of the aristocracy was
the purity of blood. No, it would not work. Perhaps
through some genetic quirk she had managed to acquire
a mysterious breeding, but the fact remained. The senseless dribbling old man who had spawned her had also
spawned the idiot Russell and the avaricious Jane. A man
in Thomas' position had to be able to count on more than
genetic whimsy. History was involved, an impressive and
noble line stretching back across the English landscape to
the tenth century. It would move forward one day. He
would see to it, but not through the suspect womb of a
fisherman's daughter, no matter how remarkable and beautiful she was.

He sat musing thus, his body half-turned at the window,
as though at any moment he might climb the steps again
to the third-floor apartments and present his case. But
something prevented him from doing this, some knowledge
based on the strongest experience that she had made her
demand and would settle for nothing less.

In merely thinking on her, his body doubled up in its
desire. With his eyes half-closed, he fantasized, saw himself climbing the steps to her room and overpowering her.

Yet at the conclusion of this fantasy, instead of satisfaction, he faced new torment. He would have to guard her
constantly or else one day, like the pitiable Ragland when
he had discovered Elfie, he would find her hanging from
a beam.

Such an image loosed a chill as sharp as March wind
upon him. He passed over an hour in this state, his thoughts
moving back and forth over possibilities, rejecting them
all. About one o'clock the rattle of a carriage on the cobbles below attracted his attention. He looked down to see
a hired chaise pull close to the pavement. A moment later,

a hulk which he recognized as Russell Locke got out, followed immediately by a young woman who giggled prettily and clung to his arm as though for support. After the chaise had pulled away, both stood on the curb, Locke drawing her close, kissing her.

Thomas drew back a safe distance, but not so far that he couldn't see or hear. What he heard and saw was remarkable. The young girl simpered, "Is this your house, Lord Eden? It's very grand, ain't it?"

And Russell replied in a deep pompous voice, "It's adequate. But come. There's a private chamber where we won't be disturbed by the servants. Come, my lamb."

"Private chambers," thought Thomas angrily.

The young woman giggled again. "You must be very rich, Lord Eden."

Russell, leaning close, drew the girl to him. "You shall be adequately rewarded for your cooperation."

As they started up the steps, the girl laughed modestly and said, "I ain't never done it with a Lord."

Thomas, in his outrage at the impersonation started forward, was ready to stop them before they reached the front door. Half out of the chair, he froze, an idea forming. As the idea took flight, all became quiet. How simple it was, how incredible that it had not occurred to him before, how remarkable, how—

Suddenly he left the window and ran toward the door. No! Not too hasty. Think it through.

Impersonation!

The bogus Locke posing as Lord Eden, the girl believing it all. Then why not an impersonation of his own, a bogus wedding ceremony, vows recited in full, yet empty, no record, nothing committed to paper. But not here, not in London, it wouldn't work here, and not at Eden Point either, where within the close community, registers could be too easily checked and tongues would wag.

Then where? Stumped so soon in the delirium of his brilliant idea, he fell to pacing. He needed a rural retreat, a seat of feudal authority unchallenged by civil servants and such nonsense as laws and parish registers. He needed a hungry or corrupt priest and he needed the authority of elegant surroundings, for she was no fool. A country inn would not serve. He needed—

He stopped and smashed his fist down against the table.

Yes, of course, why hadn't he thought of it before? He needed the isolation, the historical weight, and enclosed elegance of Fonthill Splendons. Further, he needed the innocent, boyish, trustworthy, *due* cooperation of Billy Beckford.

For the second time that long dreary evening, he laughed outright. How could Billy refuse him anything? Hadn't he nursed him back to health after his ordeal with the girl, and then interceded on his behalf with the outraged servants?

Thomas stood in the center of his chambers, his hands clasped before him, head lifted. "Oh, Billy," he moaned softly. "Come to my aid now as you have never come before."

Thus concluding his prayer to some unnamed source, he hurled himself toward his writing bureau, withdrew quill and paper, and feverishly commenced penning a message.

Once, twice, three times during his writing he looked up and laughed aloud, with the exuberance of a plotting schoolboy, his dazzling idea emerging full-blown in his head, the step-by-step deception which, God willing, would convert the source of his obsessive fever into an obliging and submissive "wife."

He laughed again and suddenly clamped a hand over his mouth. Mustn't wake the sleeping household until he was ready for them to be awakened.

For the duration of his writing, he did not utter a sound.

Russell Locke, slightly tipsy from too much negus, yet feeling as alive and exhilarated as he'd ever felt in his life, was just about to mount the first assistant to the "Goddess of Health," a comely lass he'd picked up at Dr. James Graham's pleasure palace. The girl, the picture of cooperation, had willingly stripped for him, a seductive ritual which had shaken Locke to his very toes.

Now she lay before him, clothed only in God's gifts, her legs gracefully apart, one hand cupped about her breast, the other beckoning.

Locke gulped, his lids helf-closed, and was just starting toward the Gates of Paradise when suddenly he heard monstrous shouting.

"Locke? Locke? Are you there? No time to be abed. Locke! Arise!"

Half-suspended over the waiting female, Locke turned angrily toward the closed door of his room. "Damn!" he cursed. He had recognized the voice instantly.

The young girl appeared frightened. "Milord, who is it?" she whispered and began to make feeble attempts to cover her nakedness.

Still half-suspended in a ridiculous position, his bare ass facing the door like a full moon rising, Locke listened, horrified, as the voice drew nearer. Too late, it occurred to him to rise and clothe himself. In the next moment, the door to the small ground-floor chamber burst open and Lord Eden appeared, his face flushed, clasping a parchment in his hand.

Still on his hands and knees, Locke glanced over his shoulder. "Milord," he muttered, trying to rise, the girl beneath him curling herself into a tight knot of embarrassment.

"Milord?" she repeated, glancing accusingly at Locke. "I thought you were—"

Grinning, Lord Eden walked expansively to the side of the couch. "We're all Lords here, lady." He smiled. "Every last one of us." He looked at the stupid Locke. "Some more than others, perhaps, but Lords nonetheless."

Leaving the girl to ponder his words, he turned his attention to Locke. "Up, man!" he ordered. "Prepare yourself for the road. This urgent message by noon tomorrow must be in the hands of Mr. William Beckford of Wiltshire. You know the house. We've stopped there often enough. Now, up!" He swatted Locke's bare bottom with the message itself.

Locke stumbled backward, trying in all modesty to conceal his limp member, which only moments before had been starched and at the ready.

"Wiltshire, milord," he muttered, drawing on trousers, his foot catching on the narrow opening of the knee britches, causing him to perform a little one-legged dance about the room.

"I said Wiltshire, didn't I?" thundered Lord Eden, his good humor apparently heightened by the realization of coitus interruptus.

While Locke hastily dressed, he saw Eden circle the couch, assessing the female flesh there, the girl's apprehension slowly turning into seductive lassitude.

"Damn," cursed Locke beneath his breath. The vulture would probably send him off into the night, then have her for himself.

"I beg your pardon?" Lord Eden inquired, hearing the mutterings.

"Nothing, milord," murmured Locke. As he pulled on his boots, and a heavy jacket as protection against the night chill, he thought again of the endless miles ahead of him and did little to mask his irritation. "How am I to accomplish this midnight flight, milord?" he snapped.

In a burst of generosity, Lord Eden announced, "Any way you wish, Locke. Hire a chaise if you so desire. All I ask is that you be back here by midnight tomorrow."

"Do you require a response, milord?"

Lord Eden looked straight at him, his foolish grin subsiding. "Only an affirmative response," he said. "Mr. Beckford need say nothing but yes."

Dressed, though still angry, Locke looked longingly at the young girl on the couch, who apparently had determined who was Lord Eden and who wasn't, and who at the moment was displaying all her various gifts of nature for the benefit of Lord Eden.

In spite of a vigorous attempt at self-control, Locke mumbled, "Not fair." Then, seeing Lord Eden's stern face before him, he prepared himself for a tongue-lashing.

Instead he felt Lord Eden's arm go almost gently around his shoulders, a totally unexpected gesture of affection. Miracle of miracles, he heard Lord Eden's voice, intimate and close.

"Not fair, Locke?" he queried. "I'm only sending you on a journey which, if successful, will bind us together forever."

Still suspicious, Locke tried to disengage himself from the arm which weighed heavily on his shoulder. "Forever, milord? I don't understand."

Lord Eden leaned closer. "How do you respond to 'Brother-in-law'?"

Locke ducked his head, then quickly looked up. "Brother-in-law?" he repeated incredulously.

Lord Eden nodded. "Yes, Locke. I intend to make Marianne my wife."

It took a moment for the words to penetrate. But when they did, Locke stood back, throwing off his inertia as if he had just awakened from a profound sleep. "Wife?" he repeated, his voice cracking slightly.

Again Lord Eden nodded. "Now go," he urged, planting the letter firmly in Locke's hand. "Clear the way for my wedded bliss that will forever bind together the Eden and Locke families."

Locke was trembling so violently he could scarcely hold the letter in his hand. *Wife!* Dear God, how the word thundered about in his head. Wife! His little sister, his dearest little sister, Lady Eden! Wife! Legal claim to the vast fortune of the Eden family. Wife! Her loyal brother at her side. *Wife!*

So great was his agitation that for a moment he saw nothing and heard nothing. He was aware of Lord Eden shaking him, urging him to make haste.

It was Locke's turn to wear the silly grin. As he tucked the precious letter into his inner pocket for safekeeping, he pointed toward the female on the couch. "You may have her, milord, if you wish." As he flew through the door on his important mission, he glanced back and saw Lord Eden assessing the body before him.

Well, no matter. It was none of his concern. What *was* of concern to him was the long ride ahead, bearing the vital message that would forever alter his life and turn it toward the sun.

On his way out, Russell stopped by the kitchen. The ride would be long and uninterrupted. He would need refreshment. As he was preparing a small knapsack of cheese and rolls, he heard footsteps outside the door, coming from the direction of his chamber.

He looked up, listening. It was Lord Eden's voice. The girl was with him. Russell moved stealthily to the half-opened door, the better to hear.

"Go along with you," Lord Eden was saying. "You're too young for this sort of life. Find yourself a good husband."

Amazed, Russell leaned closer, the better to hear and see. In the dark corridor, he saw Lord Eden put his arm about the girl in a most protective manner, his voice as loving and kind as Russell had ever heard it.

"How old are you?" Lord Eden asked.

"Eighteen, milord," the girl replied.

Sadly, Lord Eden shook his head. "And where's your home?"

"Canterbury, milord. My family is there, my mum and—"

As they passed by the door, Russell leaned further out, the better to see. He could not believe his eyes or ears. Lord Eden turning his back on a piece like that?

At the end of the corridor, Russell saw them stop, saw Lord Eden take his purse from the pocket of his robe and hand her several guineas. "Go home," he counseled kindly. His voice rose. "Don't go back to Dr. Graham's. The man means you no good. Go home to Canterbury where you belong, where you can find an honest lad who will love you decently."

The girl took the money, her voice breaking as though under the pressure of tears. "You're most kind, milord. No one has never talked like that to me."

Lord Eden led her gently to the door and held it open for her. As the girl slipped out into the night, Russell saw him close the door and stand for a moment, as though he too had been moved by the encounter. Russell held steady until he heard his footsteps diminish at the top of the stairs.

Still amazed, he turned back to the preparations of his knapsack. In all the time he'd been with Lord Eden, he'd never seen him behave thus. Something or someone had brought about an incredible change in him. Smiling, Russell closed the knapsack and lifted his head. His sister, of course. Dear little Marianne, who would shortly become Lady Eden.

A constant stream of images, each more glorious than the one before, filled his head as he walked the length of Oxford Road. Finally he spied a hired chaise and waved it close to the pavement, informed the driver, a sturdy lad, of the destination, promised he would be handsomely paid for the long trip, and after a brief discussion concerning fresh horses, the lad agreed.

As Russell climbed into the seat, it occurred to him that perhaps he should make one stop before heading out into open country. He leaned out the window and shouted, "Great Russell Street, driver, if you will."

As the chaise rattled across the darkened cobbles, Russell smiled as he imagined Jane's face when he broke the news. Yes, she must be told, for it was really a matter of much consequence to them both.

Wife! Lady Eden! With what astonishing shrewdness Marianne had brought it off!

There was mild regret that in the past he'd not been more tender toward her. But he would remedy that in the future and become tenderness itself.

His dear little sister, his dear, dear little sister. . . .

It was a somnambulant twenty-four-hour period in the Tudor house on Oxford Road, no one moving.

Thomas slept most of the day. At dusk he took up his vigil at the window. Feeling mellow, he gazed at the street below with its diminishing traffic, his eye on the lookout for Locke's return. Slowly he looked up at the ceiling. His "wife." My God, the thought had the power to stir him. According to one of the serving women, Marianne had been placid all day, as though she too were awaiting news, entertaining herself with a piece of needlework.

Damn! Where was he? Again Thomas leaned far out the window, searching the street below in both directions. The idiot had had plenty of time to make it there and back. Was there a possibility that Billy had said no to the deception?

His disquiet increasing, Thomas thought, he wouldn't dare. He didn't like the plot himself, but what could he do? If it pleased the lady to think of herself as a wife, why not let her? It was not his intention to abuse her or to treat her with anything but respect. His spirit and heart were as large as his fortune. He could and would accommodate her in either capacity, as wife or mistress. But he must have her.

Suddenly on the street below he heard a chaise drawing near. He leaned over. With a shout of delight he feasted his eyes on the dusty, sleep-worn image of Russell Locke. "What's the news?" he called out, scarcely able to contain himself.

Looking up, Locke smiled from the pavement, opened his coat, and revealed a piece of parchment.

"Well, man, speak!" Thomas demanded.

But instead the rascal darted up the steps and disappeared inside the house. A moment later his boots sounded in the corridor.

Thomas was there to greet him. He took the parchment and hurried to the writing bureau, where a lamp burned. Locke stood looking at him and smiling. Thomas read the message written in exceptionally poor penmanship:

My Dearest Thomas,
    If your scheme will bring you happiness, then I offer you my home, my cooperation, my heart, and my loving trust—

Your Servant,
Billy

Thomas couldn't speak.

"Good news, I hope, milord," Locke inquired, still grinning, as though he knew full well that the news was good.

Still moved, Thomas nodded. "The best, Locke, just the very best."

Recovering himself, he reached for another sheet of paper and scribbled three names upon it. "In the morning I want to see these three people in my chambers. Fetch them if you must, but see that they are here."

Locke took the paper and nodded. For the first time Thomas saw his fatigued face and suggested, "Get some rest, Locke. You've earned it. And after a night's sleep, make preparation to close the house. Within the fortnight we must be on our way to Wiltshire."

"And to the wedding?" Locke asked eagerly.

Thomas smiled. "To the wedding." He sat in his chair as he heard Locke leave the room. There was no question in Thomas' mind. He was "marrying" the whole bloody family. Well, no matter. It was a small price to pay.

Curiously, a cloud of depression settled over him. He remained in the chair, gazing fixedly at the floor. Perhaps the deception was too cruel. If she ever found out—

Abruptly he stood. She must never find out. For a moment he cursed the structure of society that kept them apart. He had no objection to a legal ceremony but what would his peers think?

On that note of self-comfort, he bathed and shaved himself and dressed in dark blue brocade. About a half an hour later he climbed the stairs to her apartments, looking forward to seeing her again, as a man dying of thirst spies a natural spring.

Before the closed door, he paused, head down, feeling childlike, remembering how as a child he used to stand before the closed door of his mother's chambers, hearing laughter within, the gleeful high-pitched squeals of his older brother, who always seemed to have gained easy access to the warm loving shelter of maternal arms.

Through his middle-aged eyes silence and sorrow stared into darkness, into something unknown, to heart and mind inconceivable, the willing love of a desired woman.

Dear God, how he needed her!

On that urgent prayer, he lifted a hand, curled it into a gentle fist and, pleadingly, knocked once.

All day long she'd sat on the edge of her bed, waiting, feeling suspense in the quietness of the house, keeping her mind busy and occupying her hands by creating with white thread against a starched blue background a North Devon gull. Now the poor creature, even complete with wings, looked strangely fixed on the stiff needlepoint, the intimation of flight an impossibility.

Weary, her neck aching from her futile effort, she tossed the lifeless square to one side and fell backward across the bed. All during the day and even now at dusk, she felt strangely detached, the same detachment she used to feel as a child when, standing on the headlands on North Devon, she'd watch a storm out in the ocean.

Then, as now, she knew that sooner or later the storm would move inward and descend on her. But for one blessed moment she could hold herself still and imagine a clear-rising morning sun, and real gulls soaring in the glorious freedom of flight.

She heard a soft knock at the door. Alarmed, she sat up. The storm so soon? She was on the verge of calling out when she saw the door open.

His shadow entered first. "Am I intruding?" he asked politely, only his head visible, a clearly groomed, shaved, and brushed head.

She stood beside the bed, her nerves alert to the encounter. "No, milord," she said. "I've passed the day sewing. I'm afraid I have no natural inclination for the needle. I welcome company."

"If I'd known—" he began and entered the room. He loked vaguely about. "Have your needs been attended to?"

She nodded. "They have, milord. I've been well looked after."

He nodded as though pleased that she appeared pleased. Silence. Her eyes never left his face. His scarcely met hers.

In an attempt to break the silence, she stepped toward the table, took a seat, and invited him to do the same.

At first he hesitated, as though the purpose of his visit could best be accomplished standing erect. But at the last minute he seemed to change his mind and with a curious little bow, as though he wanted to do her bidding, took the chair opposite her, drew it out a distance from the table, and sat, his hands interlaced and lightly resting on his lap.

She'd never seen him so uncertain, not even the night before, running down the sunbeam corridor in that ridiculous white robe, clasping his garments to him. Remembering the scene, she ducked her head to hide a smile. When she looked up, he was still sitting, apparently content with the silence.

She noticed his elegant dark blue jacket, white knee stockings, an expanse of white shirtfront, his cheeks almost rosy. "And you, milord?" she asked, finding the silence unpleasant. "Did your day go well?"

He looked up, as though she'd summoned him back from some distant point. "Ah, yes," he replied. "Yes, very well."

She nodded and found something comic in the encounter, the two of them sitting so close, yet their minds running in opposite directions.

Abruptly he was on his feet before the table, a determined though distraught look on his face. "Marianne," he began. "I'm not very good at this, having never done it before in my life—"

She sat up.

"What I'm trying to say is—" His obstinate tongue seemed literally to refuse to obey the dictates of his mind. He was pacing in short steps directly before the table. Everytime he passed the lamp, the displacement of air caused by his movements made the flame leap high.

In an attempt to wait out his hesitancy, Marianne concentrated on the dancing flame. Then he was seated again, this time the chair pulled close to the table. He clasped his hands before him and blurted out a curious recital. "God said He would make all things new. Do you think that's possible?" Before she could even think on what he'd said, he rushed on. "How powerful is the past for you, Marianne? What I'm trying to say is, well, how powerful is the past?"

She perceived the purpose of the question and postponed her answer. Finally she took refuge in the abstract. "The past, for all men, is of vital importance. It affects what they are, what they will become—"

"But *you,*" he asked urgently, leaning closer, apparently seeing through her subterfuge and, in a sense, pinning her with a direct question.

She knew what he wanted her to say. He wanted reassurance that the brutality of that hot August morning had never happened. But it had. True, the memory no longer haunted her. She was capable of sleeping through the night without seeing it re-created in nightmares. Still— "The past goes with me, milord, as it does with all of us." She looked directly at him. "But there is antidote to the past, and that's the future."

He continued to stare at her as though piecing her words together in an attempt to derive their ultimate meaning. Softly, he began to shake his head as though overcome. "I've committed so many heinous deeds in my life," he murmured. "Satan must have fair warning before my death, so he can bank the fires high."

Confronted with such anguish, she had no choice but to offer solace. "You've affected good deeds as well, milord. You've given my father refuge, you've helped my sister, you've taken in my brother—"

Her listing of his good deeds seemed to have a curious effect on him. He shook his head and lifted a hand as though to hush her. "Done for a purpose, lady," he said harshly, leaving the table. "Done with nothing but self-interest in mind, the accomplishment of my own selfish purposes."

She asked a question to which she already knew the answer. "And what was that, milord?"

He looked back at her. "You," he said simply. "The avenues of my kindness to them, I was certain, would lead directly to you."

Blushing, she lowered her head. "It seems as though you were right, milord."

He rushed back to the table. "But not as I want you, not

under duress, not confined to your rooms, not frightened of my very step on the stairs."

With held breath she asked quietly, "Then how, milord? Tell me, so that I may please you, and relieve your suffering."

His face went calm as though as last they had approached the turning point. Slowly he came around the table until he stood at her side. His face, so close, blurred in her vision, but she forced herself to look up, meeting him as an equal.

"Would you—" he began, faltered, cleared his throat, then tried again. "Would you do me the extreme honor of —becoming—my wife?"

Her heart accelerated, then seemed to stop. She remembered, curiously, the dead Cornwellian at the bottom of the pit in the charnel house. This memory caused her to feel an instant's lightheadedness. Peculiar. She'd waited all day, no, longer than that, had waited for years, since her last lucid moment on the whipping oak. Only now that it had come, she felt the same detachment she'd felt all day, as though there was another Marianne and another Thomas Eden in the room.

She looked up at him and saw that he was willing to wait for her reply. His face no longer appeared perplexed or troubled. Rather it seemed as though a bell of silence had sunk over him, that he was held suspended in the quiet land between his question and her response.

It mattered little whether or not he was in a hurry. She fully intended to take all the time she needed. She stood and walked a distance away from the table toward the bed, where her eye fell on her amateur needlework, the dead gull anchored by thousands of knots. She'd believed that she had, over the years, burned out the last vestige of vanity from her consciousness. But in that moment, when her eyes searched his face and the grand contours of the room, she felt herself carried away by personal hunger, the benefit of title by marriage, the triumphant return after her humiliating exile, the temptation of riches, acceptance and entry into the very world which had ordered her punishment. A wave of self-loathing burned itself into her head. The need for revenge was over. If she intended to join her life with this man's, then it had to be free from tyranny, both his and hers. They were both guilty, although not of those deeds of which they accused themselves.

She looked up, surprised to find her thoughts had taken her around the bed and deposited her beneath the high casement windows. Still he was waiting. She thought briefly of William Pitch. If she had gone with him, where would she be now?

Her thoughts, taking such unexpected turns, left her confused. She took a step forward to the window and breathed deeply. "I thank you for the honor, milord," she began, "and if it is your true wish, then I accept."

At first he seemed not to hear, but stood, blinking at her. Slowly he was moving toward her, his arms extended. In the next moment she felt those arms go around her, not with any degree of violence, rather a tender, grateful gesture, drawing her close, his hand pressing her head lightly to his breast, his other hand flattened against the small of her back.

It was a shelter from which she felt no compulsion to run. He towered over her and rested his cheek lightly atop her head. She discovered that she was nearly blind with tears, as though a long battle had come to an end and another was commencing.

It was a prolonged embrace with neither feeling the need for words. It came to an end when, gently, he turned her face and lightly kissed the tears from her eyes, apparently impervious to the ones which glistened on his own cheeks. Moved by the sight, she submitted to the kiss, then moved slowly with him back to the table where he returned her to the chair, as though she were precious cargo.

Taking the chair opposite her, he appeared to become very businesslike. "I've made plans," he began. "We will leave here within a fortnight and travel to Wiltshire, to Fonthill Splendons, the home of William Beckford, whom I believe you know."

She nodded.

"We will be married there and proceed on to Eden Point."

She smiled. "Home."

"Home," he repeated. As his hand went out to her across the table, she took it, and in that moment was contained the promise of enormous possibilities.

As their hands met and enfolded, he whispered fervently, "Marianne, I shall do everything within my power to make you happy."

"And I, you, milord."

His face clouded. "Speak my name," he begged, "my Christian name, as a wife would speak it."

She lowered her head. "Thomas," she murmured. "Again?" he pleaded.

"Thomas."

A dazzling smile broke across his face, as though his pleasure knew no bounds. He lifted her hand to his lips and kissed it, assessed it as though it were a chaste bloom. Suddenly the tenderness in his eyes changed, flared into something more tortured.

"For Christ's sweet sake," he whispered. "I must leave you or else—" As though making a desperate effort at self-control, he walked rapidly to the door.

She watched, fascinated by his apparent illness, incredulous that she should be the cause of it. At the door he stopped and looked back, control returning. "I must ask one favor, Marianne," he began, his voice apologetic.

She looked closer. "What is it, mi—" She stopped, corrected herself. "Thomas," she concluded.

"For a period of time, we must, I'm afraid, keep our union secret."

She started to rise. He moved back to the table, his manner patient but firm, as though he wanted very much for her to listen closely and believe him. "We are," he went on, "breaking all rules of society. Ordinarily your situation in life would prevent our union altogether. But more important, and please understand me, is the disgraceful household of your sister Jane, with which the name of Eden cannot be openly allied."

There were heated protests forming in her brain, but before his calm, authoritative presence, she kept still. Distasteful as it was, she knew he spoke the truth. To openly publish bans on the coming marriage of Miss Marianne Locke, fisherman's daughter, and Lord Thomas Eden, Fifth Earl and Thirteenth Baron of Eden Point, would cause tidal waves of embarrassment and a cacophony of clacking tongues for both of them. She was forced to admit that he was right. Besides, what did it matter? She would know the truth, and he would know it, and perhaps in time—

"And in time," he said, coming closer as though keeping pace with her thoughts, "when everyone comes to see you for what you are, my heart, my breath, my life, then we will inform all the world that this man"—he stood before her, arms outstretched—"and this woman"—gently he clasped her by the shoulders and lifted her upward—"are one," he concluded and bent low over her face, his eyes fading from her vision as once again he kissed her, far different in nature from the first kiss, his lips, his tongue feeding on her mouth, while she, with lost breath, responded, feeling an unprecedented current rising within herself.

With effort he disengaged himself and made a hasty retreat back to the door. He stayed a moment longer to inform her, "You are my dearest possession." Then he was gone, leaving her standing beside the table, the moisture from his kiss still on her lips.

She stared after the closed door. She felt alternately calm, then agitated. At the moment when she needed it most, the comforting sense of detachment deserted her. She longed for company, an objective face with eyes, mouth, and most importantly ears, someone who would listen to her and reassure her.

But there was no one. She was alone. Against this assault of aloneness, she prepared herself for an early bed, and burrowed deeply beneath the linens as though for protection against the doubts in her mind.

Of all her feelings, the most puzzling of all was a peculiar sense of defeat. Why at the moment of triumph should she feel defeated?

The following morning at nine o'clock there was a line of three carriages parked before the pavement in front of the house on Oxford Road. Elegant embossed emblems on on the sides of the carriages identified each—Mr. Roger Maybole, Jewelers; Mr. John Chetwynd, Furriers; and Madame de la Rouchard, Dressmakers.

The transformation had begun. The fisherman's daughter was to disappear and in her place they would conjure up a lady.

Overseeing it all was the glowing Thomas, smiling broadly throughout the confusion, on occasion even directing foot traffic up the stairs to the third-floor apartments. At the same time, he managed to shout a few orders to his own harried staff, commanding them to open and air the Grand Dining Hall, which had been closed since the death of his grandfather, commanding further that it be filled with her favorite roses, the cream-colored blossoms that had so delighted her on their day abroad in the city, and ordering a banquet to be laid for just the two of them that evening, a celebration dinner, though he stopped short of telling them specifically what was being celebrated.

At ten o'clock that evening, Thomas stood in the entrance hall in his best dress blacks, gazing with anticipation up the stairs in the direction of the third-floor apartments. He felt envious. He had not seen her once during the long day while a never-ending stream of tradespeople had had the pleasure of her company. Now, blessedly, his house was empty save for his own staff, who'd worked miracles.

He looked around. It reminded him of the old days of his grandfather, every lamp lit and gleaming, the hundred-candle chandelier in the Grand Dining Hall shimmering above the long table, his grandmother's magnificent French porcelain and crystal laid in a simple setting for two, every cream-colored rose in London affixed in elegant bouquets, the entire house smelling of roses.

Again he looked up the stairs, hearing something. My God, he was like a schoolboy in his eager anticipation, or, more accurately, a "bridegroom." Without warning his heart contracted with sadness, from a feeling of despair at the ruse he would shortly work upon her. Why couldn't Fate have seen fit to plant her in the womb of a duchess, or better, a queen?

No matter. He would have her anyway. He banished the feelings of despair and felt his inside pocket wherein rested a green velvet case. He hoped it would please her, although on closer examination the diamond had suddenly struck him as too large and garish for her delicate beauty.

At the top of the third-floor landing, he heard a door open. He held his position in the center of the entrance hall, amazed at his turbulence of feeling. She must be good for him. Never had he felt his blood race so.

It was while his head was down that he first became

aware of a soft step on the stair, a rustling of silk and a delicate odor, like lavender on a summer morn.

Slowly he raised his head. Before him on the first-floor landing stood an apparition which lent a new dimension to the definition of beauty. In a cloud of pale pink silk she stood, traceries of seed pearls extending from her white breasts to the hem of the gown, around her fair neck a strand of matched pearls, the gown itself exquisitely tailored, following the gentle natural slope of her waist down over hips, then billowing outward, her golden hair done up, a soft spray of ringlets around her forehead, the length of hair knotted and intertwined with additional pearls. And triumphant over all the artifices of dressmaker and jewelers was the magnificent gift of nature, that face, that alabaster skin, those dark lavender eyes profoundly framed with black feather lashes, the mouth partially open, like a morning rosebud, a goddess, a queen, the crown of nature, her unearthly peace and strength intact in spite of her new garb.

Thomas tried to speak and failed. Weakly he reached out for the bannister, unable to take his eyes off her.

It was she who spoke first, her voice wafting down and settling over him like a benediction. "Milord," she smiled. "I trust your silence does not mean displeasure."

"Displeasure?" he murmured incredulously, and extended a trembling hand, beckoning her to come close so that he might test the apparition for its substance.

Unfortunately, as she drew nearer, her beauty merely increased, and he noted features he'd never seen before, a precious inventory promising riches to come—a small black mole at the base of her neck, her shell ears previously covered by her hair, the graceful arch of her throat.

Apparently his silence alarmed her. "Milord, please speak. Do I suit you?"

An expression like pain crossed his face. He lifted her hand to his lips and kissed it. "Milady," he whispered gallantly, "you would please God's angels." Slowly he withdrew the jewel box from his inner coat. "To plight our troth." He smiled, lifted the diamond for her inspection, then placed it on the third finger of her right hand.

He watched her reaction closely; it seemed very subdued. He thought he heard her say, "It's lovely," but he couldn't be certain. She did lift her bare left hand as though wishing that the ring might be transferred to the proper finger. But he was grateful that she said nothing and in an attempt to comfort her, promised that a single gold band to be worn in the privacy of their chamber would ease the nakedness.

There was a moment's silence during which time he thought he saw a blush creep up the sides of her face. To dispel any anxiety she might have concerning the "marriage bed," he took her by the arm and led her toward the Grand Dining Hall, claiming a tremendous appetite, eager to see her face as she beheld the splendid room, the bouquets of roses in her honor.

But as far as he could tell she noticed nothing and took her seat at the end of the table as though she'd been residing in that place of honor all her life.

Before her quiet acceptance, Thomas felt himself sinking into misery. For the first time in his life, he wanted to give happiness to someone. And he seemed incapable of doing it. Was the lack in him or her? And how could he remedy it?

Perhaps he'd know more after he'd made her his "wife." Perhaps in the moment of sublime intimacy, she'd give him the precious gift of her trust and love.

For now, all he could do was be patient and wait, and learn to live with her indifference, which cut into his soul and left it bleeding.

On a crisp cold October morning in 1794, two old crones with bent backs and scruffs of white hair poking out from beneath their tattered kerchiefs stood on the northwest corner of Leicester Square hawking the last of summer's posies. Their gloves were stained and fingerless, their sagging breasts two dead lumps about their waists. They were cold and hungry and toothless, and dreading winter.

"Oye, Posies!" one shouted, lifting a faded clump of violets to a stream of uninterested passersby.

"Roses red for kissing cousins!" shouted the other, her bewhiskered chin thrust forward in defiance.

Nearby a chestnut vendor warmed his hands over red coals. The first crone took note and muttered, "I wish the Devil would set me on fire. That one peddles warmth. We peddle garbage."

" 'Tis out of season," agreed the other. "As true ladies of commerce, we should go with the wind."

"Piss on the wind," said the other. "To a luvverly pub, that's where we should go."

"Not empty-pocketed," scolded the other. "Elves and fairies don't know the likes of us. Come, lift your voice. Cry 'Roses,' cry 'Violets,' cry 'Heaven for a ha'penny.' "

Again they lifted their posies to the crowded intersection. Suddenly one gasped, "Lord, look! What a vision is that?"

The other focused her eyes in the appointed direction. "Good Gawd, 'tis the King?"

The first crone shook her head. "Wrong shape, but look and stop prattling."

Before them, stopped by the traffic of the crowded street, was an entourage of five carriages, clearly trying to make their way to the western edge of the city. For the moment, however, they were hopelessly stalled by the convergence of farm wagons, the congestion made worse by a herd of sheep being driven up Charing Cross.

The first crone stepped close to the pavement and waved her sister to follow her. The dim eyes squinted at the emblazoned coat of arms on the side of the first carriage.

"Ed-den," she read.

The other giggled. "On my soul, 'tis Adam and Eve, and the snake's bringing up the rear."

As the coachman sitting high atop the first carriage waved them away with the tip of his whip, they retreated back to their carts, but continued to peer closely out. Inside the lead carriage bearing the Eden coat of arms and drawn by four black stallions, they saw the figure of a man, warmly wrapped in a dark cloak. Sitting opposite him they saw the pale lovely face of a young girl, the ermine collar of her cape turned up about her neck in protection against the autumn chill.

In the second and third carriages, they saw an assortment of servants, several of the males passing a flask back and forth, obviously electing to ward off the chill in their own way.

Following behind the third carriage, they saw the fourth and fifth, containing no person at all save watchmen, but packed high with trunks and valises, clearly a royal house on the move to winter quarters.

They took it all in, then returned their attention to the lead carriage. In their old faces were hard expressions of longing and question.

The first crone muttered enviously, "Heaven's smiles are fair on some."

The second protested. "Look how they sit, sister, his poor eyes staring like a dead man's, and hers—"

"Shhh," whispered the first. "Now she looks at us. See!"

As the young woman stared in their direction, they lifted their soiled skirts and performed an awkward curtsy, one sticking her finger beneath her chin, smiling toothlessly, the other lifting her sagging breasts as though offering the young girl a tit.

"She's scarce a babe," murmured the second. "Look! Not a track of time on that smooth brow."

"What 'tis, you suppose?" mused the first. "Father and child? Husband and wife?"

"Man and whore," snapped the second.

"No!" objected the first. "No ronyon, that. I know the look of a virgin. She's never known a man's boneless part."

"Then what?" demanded the second. "She's pampered, clearly, a virtuous creature in ermine."

"Quick, look how she stares at us, a pretty child, though saddened and ill at ease."

The first tightened her kerchief about her straggly hair, musing, "One's the cuckold there. Maid or man, I know not. But they do not sit in honesty."

"Look at the hinds in the second carriage," one said. "They've known stinking clothes that fretted in their own grease." Then mournfully she shook her head. "Oye, an arm and a leg I'd give for their bottle."

Suddenly the first one gasped. "By your mercy, she's beckoning to us."

As they started off the pavement, they looked warily up at the coachman with his whip in hand. "Hold your distemper, sir!" cried the first. "Your lady summons us."

The coachman, a brash-looking young man, leaned out and over as though to confirm their claim. At that moment they saw the young girl draw down the window, the trace of a smile on her pretty face. "Your violets are lovely," she called. "May I see them?"

At first the gentleman sitting opposite her seemed to object. The old crones saw his hand move forward, then slowly withdraw.

Quickly they fetched their trays of posies and lifted them high for her inspection. The first crone smiled sweetly. "Are you a princess, milady?" she asked.

The young woman shook her head, laughing. "I'm a woman, same as you."

The second crone snickered. "A shallow likeness, I'd say, save where God divided us and left a hole."

"Shhh!" scolded the first, clearly appalled by her sister's crudeness. To the young woman she smiled, "Are you abroad for long?" she asked, a wheedling tone in her voice.

"Forever, I hope," the young woman replied, closely examining the blossoms before her. "I'm going home."

The gentleman scolded, "Be quick, Marianne. The traffic's clearing."

If the young woman heard him, she gave no indication of it. Rather deliberately she continued her close examination of the flowers.

The first crone, growing brave, whispered, "Are you married to the gentleman, milady? You look not a wife."

A small cloud crossed the pretty face. She stared fixedly at the violets in her hand. "I am won, but not wed," she said.

The old crone sternly shook her head, keeping her voice down. "Be warned, milady. Many a flower vendor started out in a gentleman's bed, then, deflowered, banked the fires of winter with a few wilted posies."

Again the gentleman leaned forward, his voice softened. "Marianne, we must move. May I purchase a bouquet for you?"

She nodded, selecting two. As he handed over a half penny, she urged, "A guinea, Thomas. Give them a guinea."

He hesitated, then reached for his purse and rather stiffly thrust the money into the gnarled upraised hands.

The old crones could scarcely contain their joy. "May heaven send you good fortune," they called after the carriage moving slowly forward now through the clogged street.

"A guinea, sister. Look!" whispered the second crone.

"Come, no more posies today. A toasty afternoon in a toasty pub beside a toasty fire with a pint or two—"

But the first crone continued to stand on the pavement, staring after the entourage. "A kind heart, she has," she murmured.

The second crone joined her. "Aye. A man should run through fire for such a kind heart."

The first crone smiled. "I think he has, sister. He bears the scars of fire."

"Then come," urged the second crone. "Let's drink to their cooling."

But the first seemed loath to leave until the carriages had disappeared. "If she were my daughter," she whispered, "I'd pray for her."

"Come," commanded the second. "We'll pray for both and pity both and lift pints and be happy sisters to balance the world for their rich misery. Then we'll fly to the Gates of Paradise on our own high spirits. God sent her. Let it go at that."

The carriages were gone from sight, though the first crone whispered, "Blessings on your heart." Eagerly she waddled back to the pavement, gathered up her remaining posies, and cried exuberantly, "To the Thameside, sister, there to be senseless and warm by nightfall!"

"Aye, we'll do it," said the other with a grin. "What an errand! Lead the way!"

It was after midnight when the horses, winded from the speed of their unbroken journey, turned off the central turnpike and headed down the narrow lane which led to the elegant isolation of Fonthill Splendons.

Everytime Thomas saw the old place he felt a surge of admiration. True, Eden Castle, with its craggy roughhewn lines rising like a specter out of the cliff walls, suited his personality. Still, it was pleasant to have within one's temporal boundaries the grand classical style of Fonthill.

Immediately upon their arrival, Marianne, clearly fatigued, requested that she be taken to her chambers. As Billy's large staff scurried about making everyone comfortable, the head butler, a stiff-backed, arrogant old man who poignantly reminded Thomas of his beloved Ragland, announced, "Lord Eden, Mr. Beckford will receive you in the library."

As the clock was striking half past one, Thomas found himself being ushered into the large familiar room which he'd known as a boy as a place where the men gathered, relieved of all females. In spite of his own fatigue, he was feeling rather nostalgic. All had gone well thus far, his total conquest of his "bride" only hours away.

He paused in the doorway, assessing the room—the familiar volumes, a wall map charting the course of the sun and moon and stars, an inviting fire in the large marble well, the ornately carved fourteenth-century screen behind which he and Billy had hidden as boys, listening to their fathers solve the problems of Empire.

On the large table at the center of the room, he saw a scattering of blueprints, and behind the table, just emerging from a position of intense concentration, he saw his friend Billy, clad in a luxuriant emerald-green dressing gown, his face changed, a portion of his boyishness gone, his eyes still gleaming with the obsession of his tower, but controlled now, the look of a man who has accepted his madness and is not to be trifled with.

In all sincerity and true affection, Thomas opened his arms. The two men met in warm embrace. Thomas held him at arm's length, amazed at the new maturity he saw before him, realizing all too well the hard-earned nature of that maturity.

Remembering too much and his own heinous involvement in the wicked plot, Thomas again clasped the young man to his heart. "Billy," he murmured. "How well you look!"

Beckford seemed equally moved by the double embrace. He smiled. "So! You're to be a bogus bridegroom, Thomas."

Thomas nodded. "With your help."

"You have it," Beckford assured him. "You will always have it. When my heart feels feeble and fluctuating, I think of you and our friendship, and am immediately made strong."

Thomas felt overcome by the declaration of love. His emotions were brimming. Apparently Billy saw his unease and moved to dispel it. "Brandy, Thomas? It's a long ride from London, and I know you made it unbroken by intervals."

Grateful, Thomas nodded. As Billy moved to the side-

board, Thomas fell into a close examination of the blueprints; one looked down on a monumental cross-shaped
structure, its parts clearly marked in neat draftsman hand;
'A, The Great Western Hall; B, Marbled Corridor, C,
Sanctuary. . . .

Billy drew even with him, extending a glass. "To wedded
bliss." He smiled.

Thomas held up a blueprint. "And to your dream as
well."

Both men sipped. "Have you broken ground yet?" Thomas inquired, gesturing toward the blueprints.

Lovingly Billy stroked the large sheets of paper. "Just
that. It's difficult to keep Wyatt sober. He works one day,
drinks two, and requires three in which to recover."

Thomas laughed. "Well, stay with it, Billy. From what
I see here, it will be the most imposing structure in all of
England."

"I intend to, Thomas," he replied calmly. "It's my life."
Warmly he invited, "Come, sit by the fire. Tell me of
your passion."

Thomas followed after him, seeing mysteriously *her* face
before him, the beautiful contrast he'd witnessed all day
between the small bouquets of violets purchased for a
ransom on a crowded street corner of London, and the
whiteness of her skin.

As they took seats in the chairs flanking the fireplace,
Billy asked, "Is your prey secured for the night? Are my
servants her jailers?"

Thomas objected to his choice of words. "She's not my
prey, Billy, and she requires no jailer."

"Is it true you bought her from her sister?"

The voice and attitude behind the question seemed impudent. "A transaction was made," Thomas snapped. "But
that was a long time ago. She's come around."

"Then why the deception?"

Annoyed at the interrogation, Thomas sat up in the chair.
"My God, man, what am I to do? Marry her publicly? In
Westminster?"

Slowly Billy shook his head. "No, of course not. You
can't do that. But why deceive her, Thomas? A woman of
her birth should have no objections to becoming a mistress."

Wearily Thomas sank back in his chair. "You don't know

the lady, Billy. Believe me. I've passed through hell for her." He lifted his glass and drained it. As he dabbed at the moisture at the corners of his eyes, he muttered, "She has brought my life to a halt. Five years ago I would have said that nothing, and certainly not a woman, would be capable of doing that." He placed the glass on a near table, and smiled wanly. "But there you are. Half a man sits before you. The other half is with her."

A look of honest commiseration crossed Billy's face, followed rapidly by condemnation. "They are fools of the Devil, women. He uses them to distract us and drive us to madness."

The two men stared, unspeaking, into the fire. Softly Billy asked, "What do you expect to find when you mount her?"

"Heaven," Thomas murmured without hesitation.

"And after heaven, when you come down?"

Thomas thought, then closed his eyes. "Does a man have a right to ask for more than heaven?"

Sympathetically Billy shook his head. "Poor Thomas. You *are* imprisoned." Quickly he stood up, fetched the bottle of brandy, and brought it back with him to the fire. "I'm sure you want to know the arrangements I've made."

Thomas looked up, eagerness replacing his melancholy. "I'm grateful, Billy."

"As though God were moving on your side, He sent to the door of my overseer last week an Italian itinerant, a strange fellow, not unschooled, though hungry and wearing the clothes of a beggar." Billy smiled. "With an eye trained for such things, I sensed a rascal. I fed him, stuck a nightcap on his head, put him to bed, and the next morning made a proposition." He lifted his glass as though in toast. "This knave will play your priest for you in the morning. Then my men will escort him to the channel, and on his word, he has promised never to set foot in England again."

Thomas sat up, immensely pleased. "No records then at all?" he asked.

Billy shook his head. "Pray your lady does not require to see them."

Thomas frowned. He'd not thought of that. "It must all be accomplished with great haste," he said. "At her request we'll be proceeding on to Eden Castle immediately following the ceremony."

In mock sorrow, Billy mourned, "Then I shall be robbed of the pleasure of providing you with a conjugal bed?"

"It's her desire," Thomas explained. "She's hungry for home."

"How do you plan to introduce her?"

"We've discussed that as well. As Miss Locke. She knows it cannot be otherwise."

As though confounded, Billy shook his head. "In some matters, she's the spirit of cooperation. In others, the spirit of obstinacy." Again he shook his head. "I fear you've set for yourself a hazardous course, Thomas."

Feeling helpless, Thomas shrugged. "It's the only course, so hazardous or not, I must attempt it."

"Has she forgiven you the whipping oak?"

Soberly Thomas bowed his head. "I don't know. I haven't forgiven myself."

Billy stared at him. Softly he laughed. "You should ally yourself with me, Thomas, and build an impossible tower defying gravity. Believe me, it's much simpler."

Feeling a weariness approaching illness, Thomas pulled himself laboriously from the chair. He looked down on his friend. "If only we were given a choice in our various madnesses." Feeling twice his age, he started toward the door. There he stopped and called back, "I'm grateful for your Italian priest, Billy. But I trust the ritual will be Anglican and not Popish."

Billy laughed. "What difference? It will all be a lie."

He followed after Thomas to the door. "Your customary quarters have been prepared for you. Get a good night's rest. There's red meat waiting for you, to thicken your blood. Perhaps the lady has merely outschemed you, in which case you must be able to perform like the most ardent of bridegrooms."

Thomas laughed heartily in spite of his fatigue at the preposterous idea of a scheming Marianne. "She is innocence itself, Billy."

"And shortly, at least in her own mind, she will become Lady Eden."

An intense look passed between the two men. Thomas disengaged himself and proceeded on through the door.

"Seven o'clock, Billy," he called back. "You shall be my only attendant."

"I'm honored," Billy replied with a slight bow.

A servant was waiting beyond the door with a lamp to escort Thomas to his chambers. At the end of the corridor, Thomas looked back, surprised to find Billy still watching him. In a flare of resentment he realized that he'd allowed his good friend to cast a shadow of depression over him. It was really so unimportant, the whole thing. Surely he wasn't the first man to deceive a woman, and neither would he be the last. Then what was the fuss, the veiled threats, and hints of threats? On the morning she would be his.

Legally, or illegally, it mattered little.

At a quarter past seven on the morning of October the second, 1794, Marianne Locke, dressed in a pale yellow gown with embroidered veil, walked alone through the vast corridors of Fonthill Splendons, following behind the steward who'd been sent to fetch her, coming at last to the small thirteenth-century chapel off the Great Hall. There she was greeted by a priest who spoke broken English and who joined her hand to Thomas Eden's, and under the witnessing eye of William Beckford, a wedding ceremony of some kind took place.

It was not as she had imagined it would be. The chapel was very cold and dark and flowerless, the priest's words scarcely audible, Thomas shy to the point of discomfort, the chapel doors, during the brief ceremony, closed and bolted. Mr. Beckford refused to look at her even, not shy, like Thomas, but somehow discomfited.

Nonetheless, at the conclusion of the dreary fifteen-minute ritual, Marianne believed herself to be Lord Eden's legal wife.

Scarcely had the final words been pronounced than Thomas again turned her over to the custody of the steward, with the stern command that within the hour her luggage was to be packed and loaded on the carriage parked at the front of Fonthill Splendons.

In a way, she was grateful for the frenzied rush. It prevented her from thinking, from coming to any real awareness of what had been done. It wasn't until the trunks had been loaded, she in her traveling clothes sitting in the corner of the carriage, watching Thomas bid Mr. Beckford a hasty but warm farewell, that the magnitude of her situation swept over her. Lady Eden! In secret at least for a while, to be sure. Still, Lady Eden! She shivered in the chill of the cold sunless October morning.

Then Thomas was seated opposite her, apparently incapable of looking directly at her, his head out the window, shouting something to the coachman driving the second carriage. Their entourage had been reduced to two carriages, the remaining three having traveled through the night ahead of his Lordship in order to ready the preparation for their arrival at Eden Castle.

The five miles which stretched between Fonthill and the turnpike were passed in silence. Marianne's own misgivings were lost in Thomas' agitation. With an unprecedented air of concern, he felt compelled to check on everything. Was the luggage atop secured? Were the horses fresh? Was the steward at the rear armed against the threat of highwaymen? Had the axles of the carriage wheel been checked for the rough ride across the moors? All these questions and countless others were shouted out the windows, full-voiced, by Thomas, the coachman responding over the rush of wind.

It wasn't until they approached the turnpike itself that he finally gave up his shouting match and withdrew his head, hair wind-tossed, back into the carriage. Marianne noticed a flush to his cheeks, the results of his exposure to the cold wind. The carriage interior was chilled from the lowered window. Shivering, she suggested, "Milord, might we close the window?"

He looked at her with peculiar detachment as though seeing her for the first time. Apologetically he leaned forward and raised the window. "I'm sorry. I didn't realize—" From beneath the seat he removed a fur lap rug and thoughtfully placed it over her. "Better?" he asked, the flush still on his face.

She nodded, mystified by his new agitation. She asked bluntly, "Do you have any regrets?"

Again he looked at her as though baffled by the question. "Regrets? About what?"

She smiled and shook her head, indicating that perhaps neither the question nor the answer were important. Beneath the lap robe she felt of the small gold band which he'd placed on her finger during the ceremony. If he had already forgotten, perhaps she could forget as well. But she knew she couldn't and whatever the nature of his present facade, she would accept it, and learn to live with it, for marriage in her eyes, even an enforced one, was a matter of utter seriousness, a commitment to the grave.

She heard movement opposite her, saw him bend over and retrieve a second lap rug from beneath the seat, spread it over his legs and lean back comfortably, his head resting against the cushions, his eyes closed.

She watched, amazed at the rapidity with which sleep came, although a few moments later he surprised her by speaking softly, his eyes still closed, "It's a full day of riding we have, Marianne," he murmured. "Make yourself comfortable."

He burrowed deeper beneath the lap rug, turned his face into the comfort of the cushion, and instantly fell asleep.

She looked again at the man opposite her. Sleep transfigured him. If he knew how harmless and impotent and worn he looked, he would never sleep again. She made a quick judgment and tucked the realization away in the back of her mind. He was a mere mortal, nothing more, a strong-willed, selfish mortal, but mortal all the same. The thought pleased her, provided her with a fleeting feeling of what might be called tenderness toward him.

She adjusted her lap rug, curled into her own corner, and gave herself over to the rather violent but rhythmic lullaby of the carriage. Within moments the fatigue and rush of the last few days took their toll and she too fell asleep.

She awakened once to a midafternoon sun and saw him staring at her. But again there was nothing in his eyes to cause alarm, and within the moment she returned to sleep.

The sun was just setting, though enough gold and rose was left in the sky to see as they approached Eden Castle. While they were still about a half a mile distant, the lead carriage stopped and permitted the second carriage to go ahead, a tradition, enabling his Lordship to make a triumphant entry.

Both Thomas and Marianne were awake, had been awake for some time, since they'd entered Exmoor, the peculiar silence within the carriage not as noticeable under the excitement of home. Both windows were down, Marianne luxuriating in the perfume of salt breeze, at times scarcely able to contain her joy. Her eyes hungrily devoured the carpet of purple heather outside the carriage, her senses filled with the sights and sounds and smells of her childhood.

"There it is!" Thomas shouted as, leaning out his window, he caught his first glimpse of the towers of Eden Castle.

From her side, Marianne saw it as well, that fortress which had loomed over her like a gigantic shadow and which was now to be her home.

With boyish enthusiasm, Thomas insisted, "Do you see it? Look! Look! There it is!"

Although she was perfectly capable of seeing it on her side, he insisted that she share his window. Sitting so close to him and sharing his sense of homecoming, Marianne felt for the first time the full impact of the centuries, the ancient fortress dominating the countryside.

In his enthusiasm he took her hand. The worn look of age which she noticed on his face while he slept vanished. It was as though slowly, by degrees, and because of his close proximity to his birthplace, he was assuming once again the mantle, manner, and attitude of *Lord* Eden.

As though in an attempt to curb his mounting excitement, he pressed back in his seat and tried to draw a deep breath. "Every time I return home, I vow never to leave it again," he said, smiling, as though unable to account for his own feelings, "Why is it?" he asked, "that this is the only place in the world where I feel joined with myself, with nature?"

Suddenly there was a great shout from the four watchmen who had ridden out on horseback to escort them through the gates. Marianne gave her full attention to the incredible scene outside the window, the horsemen flanking the carriage, two on each side with torches held high, Thomas shouting good-naturedly to first one, then the other, the carriage swerving into the main gate, both iron grilles being raised with speed, the horses' hooves clattering over the wooden planks, then the sight of the inner courtyard, watchmen holding torches stationed at intervals along the top of the wall, at least seventy-five men, lanterns strung in gay profusion from arch to arch, a dazzling spectacle of light and color, as from each man there arose now a cheer, welcoming his Lordship home.

Through the gate the carriage started a majestic turn around the inner courtyard. At least a hundred people lined their route, villagers from Mortemouth, women tossing bouquets of flowers and autumn leaves into the paths of the horses.

Marianne's head bobbed from one side to the other, trying to take it all in, seeing firsthand a great nobleman's establishment, remembering the days when she too had gone up the hill, flowers in hand, to take her place in the welcome of the moment with the other villagers.

Without warning, not thinking about it, certainly not expecting it, she saw it. At first she tried to drag her eyes away and send them in the opposite direction. But she could not. Her eyes, as though they had minds of their own, stayed focused on the thick black finger of oak rising in the center of the courtyard.

She did not see the man sitting opposite her anymore. With her head turned rigidly in one direction, she was aware of someone taking her hands, pressing them to his breast in urgent concern.

"Marianne, I'm sorry," he whispered quickly. "I should have had it removed. I will tomorrow, I promise."

With all her might she tore her hands away from him and tore her eyes away from the whipping oak. "No," she said, on diminished breath, "leave it." Fiercely she repeated, "Leave it!"

Once more she looked up. The carriage was just coming to a halt before the Great Hall, where the staff was lined up on the bottom step, strangers to her, all strangers except—

"Jenny," she gasped one beloved face at the end of the line. Without waiting for the aid of a steward or the company of Thomas, she was out of the carriage and into the open arms of the old woman who had raised her, who had, as much as anybody, formed her.

In the closeness of the embrace, Marianne broke. How long it had been since she'd sniffed Jenny's peculiar fragrance, a faint mix of cinnamon and lavender. How long it had been since she'd seen that mock-stern old Devonion face crack and break under the pressure of her own vast reserves of love and caring.

Feeling again the familiar contours of the woman's body, Marianne snuggled her face into the soft shoulder and realized how much she'd missed the supportive love of this saint.

"Oh, Jenny," she murmured, holding the woman at arm's length, trying not to cry, but crying anyway. There was another quick embrace as though Jenny herself needed a moment's recovery before she could form words.

Then, "Child," she said, shaking her head, moving back a step as though the better to see. "Let me look at you." She added sternly, "Let me see if I can find the taint of London on you."

Under her close scrutiny, Marianne felt self-conscious. Jenny wasn't the only one assessing her. She was now acutely aware of all eyes on her. The two dozen staff members stood at attention, but their heads and eyes swiveled clearly in her direction. To one side she saw a half dozen waiting stewards, and beyond them, Thomas, one hand still on the carriage door, and beyond him, the now silent villagers and watchmen with torches, the entire spectacle a frozen tableau, all eyes on her.

Under such a weight, Marianne tried to stand erect, to sustain herself with a quick assessment of her own worth. But as the silence expanded, inevitably she remembered that other morning in the inner courtyard.

Remembering all, she lowered her head and struggled for something to cling to. Then she felt a strong arm about her waist, heard Thomas' voice, in answer to Jenny's question about the taint of London, say, "She's quite unchanged, Jenny. It's London that profited from the gift of her presence."

Looking up, Marianne saw the rapid transitions on the faces before her, the traditional mask of reverence which all servants wear for all masters. The women, including Jenny, curtsied low, the men bowed. On the second step, obviously in a position of some authority, she saw her brother Russell, his hair freshly powdered, looking very elegant in a rose brocade suit with lace front.

Russell, grinning broadly, pushed his way through the line of servants to make the traditional welcoming speech. "Milord," he pronounced, bowing low. "We welcome you home and rejoice in your good health and well-being. Eden Castle languishes in your absence, and like God in His

Heaven, nothing is greater cause for celebration than the return of our Lord to his birthplace."

Marianne lowered her head to keep from smiling. Poor Russell. How long it must have taken him to compose his speech. Unfortunately he was not yet finished.

"As the gentle breezes caress the rose," he went on, with approriate gestures, "so we, your staff, welcome you with all the obedience and homage that nature pays to the circling gull, our affections surrounding you like—"

Predictably, Thomas had had enough. "We thank you," he said, interrupting. Then he turned to face the villagers and tenants. He raised his voice to a shout and repeated, "We thank you for this warm welcome. Now you must excuse us. The journey was long and uninterrupted. We hope to be in residence for some time. And it will be our pleasure to see you all personally within the next few weeks."

There was a mild shout of approval and a soft scattering of applause. Marianne thought, how many times before they had heard those empty words. And in the meantime tenant roofs leaked, broken equipment stayed broken. The fishermen and farmers and all their families knew that the next time they saw Lord Eden would be in the departing Procession, the entourage of carriage passing back out of the gates on their way to London or Weymouth or some other pleasure spot.

All speeches over, Marianne felt Thomas' hand on her arm, heard him giving the stewards directions as to the dispersement of the baggage, then heard him announce to Jenny that they would dine alone in his private chambers. Jenny nodded quickly and turned to see to his command.

Marianne called after her. "Wait, Jenny. I'll go with you. I would like to see my father."

But Thomas objected. "Not now. After we've supped, Jenny will bring him to the chambers."

"No, milord," Marianne insisted with gentle firmness. "I want to see him now."

A look of annoyance crossed his face. "It's not necessary, only a delay of a few hours."

"You needn't come, Thomas," she soothed. "You go along. I know the way."

Then he was close at her side, whispering fiercely for

her ears alone. "He's kept in the basement kitchen," he said, as though that explained all.

"I know"— she smiled—"I know the room well."

"It won't do for you to be seen there," he added, his eyes pleading, as though trying to make her understand. She was aware of the departing servants, their heads down, obviously listening. She was also aware of Jenny, waiting a short distance away, her face made rigid by the conflict.

"Miss Locke," she said now, with strange formality. "He's having his supper anyway. Dolly's with him. Let us prepare him and bring him to you."

But Marianne's thoughts had stopped on "Miss Locke." For the first time she wondered how her presence had been explained. With the marriage to be kept a secret, was she viewed as nothing more than one of his passing mistresses? Angry at her belated realization of this problem, she held her ground. "I wish to see him now," she announced to all who cared to hear. "I need no one's assistance, or guidance, or counsel," she added pointedly.

As she hurried off, she heard Thomas' undisguised curse, heard Jenny's ridiculous apology. She was aware of the servants ahead of her parting to give her free passage. Looking neither to the right nor the left, she walked steadily toward the ground-level door which led down into the kitchen of the castle.

As she walked rapidly along the familiar path, head down, she caught sight of the hem of her gown, amber in color, trimmed in soft, dark-brown fur. She remembered that other young girl who'd worn her same skin but quite a different gown, a plain black coarse muslin with white apron. Suddenly she was filled with a ferocious hatred, a burning desire to destroy the elegant gown. Under the duress of such feelings, she flung open the kitchen door and stopped to assess the large room below. It was empty except for two in the far corner beside a low burning fire, an old woman whom she did not at first recognize, and an old man, sitting slumped in a tattered cushioned chair, his head inclining forward on his chest, his hair white and unkempt, his eyes, even from that distance, fixed and blank and staring.

Her heart accelerated painfully, then seemed to stop. She'd known the man in better days. He had been a threat to no one. He'd loved freedom, a pint of ale now and then, a good catch as frequently, the feel of sun on his face, companions at the close of day, a bit of soft-boiled food, warm clothes and a clean bed. What would it have cost the world to have given him these?

As Marianne stared down at the old man, she was aware of the bent, white-haired woman moving as though frightened toward her. Obviously age had dimmed her sight. She stopped at the bottom of the steps, a half-filled bowl of porridge still in her hand. "Who is there?" she called up.

Marianne felt helpless. But such weak despair would serve no one. Out of the habit of discipline, she pushed aside the deep pain of the scene before her, as she begged Dolly Wisdom, "Don't you remember me? Has it been so long?"

There was immediate light on Dolly's face. Quickly she thrust the bowl of porridge behind her, aimed for a near table, and missed. As bowl, porridge, and spoon clattered to the floor, she hurled herself into the embrace.

"Dolly, dear Dolly," murmured Marianne, thinking how blessed she was to have known the love and care of two mothers.

As though embarrassed, Dolly pulled herself free of Marianne's arms and made a feeble attempt at grooming. Her gnarled hands smoothed back the tufts of white hair, then moved down the front of her apron stained with dried porridge. "I wanted to come up," she murmured, "but someone has to stay with him." She indicated the silent old man in the chair by the fire.

Again, Marianne found herself staring at him. Behind her, at the top of the landing, she was aware of a confusion of footsteps, the curious servants no doubt.

Then she was moving past the large serving table cluttered with remnants of meal preparation, the main force of her concentration focused on the man himself.

Quietly she knelt before him, lifted one useless hand to her lips. "Papa?" she whispered. "It's Marianne. I've come home." She felt her voice begin to break and tried to seize control. "Papa, can you hear me?" She looked closely for the slightest hint of recognition and saw nothing. The eyes were glazed, the mouth open, a thin stream of saliva mixed with porridge cutting a path down the side of his chin.

Suddenly she could look at him no longer. As she bowed her head, her eyes caught sight of something yellow, very tattered, soft and plump wedged between the side of the chair and his leg. Gently she pulled it forward.

In this room of faulty recognition, she recognized it instantly, stained and broken beyond repair, like the man himself. It was her childhood toy, the small calico elephant who'd never known a jungle save the flower garden behind her father's cottage.

"I will not go to sleep, Papa, without my elephant. He's beneath the lilacs. Please fetch him for me."

Without warning, her eyes filled. "Papa, I love you," she said, weeping, knowing the words would not be understood, but feeling a need to say them anyway.

Behind her she heard a kind voice. "Marianne, please," Thomas begged. "You're distraught from the journey. You need rest."

She permitted him to lift her to her feet, made no attempt to assign blame, for what good would blame do? She was aware of his command for Jenny to follow shortly and help with "Miss Locke's" luggage. She was aware of little else except their passage through the dark interior of the castle, up the steps, his arms firmly about her, leading her to the suite of rooms in the east wing, now flanked on either side by two serving girls with lamps held aloft.

As they pushed open the door, Thomas led her through into the lovely interior, the warm wood tones and tapestries glowing in the light of the fire, her trunks placed to one side, bowls of fresh flowers everywhere. With a wave of his hand, he dismissed the two girls, told them to wait outside. When the door had closed behind them, he led Marianne to a chair, gently relinquished her to it, then stood, staring down on her. His voice sounded strangely weak. "You may not choose to believe my words," he began, "but my suffering is as great as yours, for I am the cause—"

Quickly she shook her head. If either of them were to survive the ties that now bound them together, they would have to forget the past. When she spoke, she knew she was lying. "I'm only tired, Thomas. Give me a few moments alone and I shall try to live up to your expectations."

"Then I'll leave you, madame," he said courteously. She heard the door close behind him, heard his muffled command to the two young girls not to enter the room until they were summoned, then heard nothing but the diminishing tread of his footstep.

Slowly she looked about her at the grand room. Beyond the bed, she saw two large French doors, solidly glassed with tiny mullioned windows. Beyond that, she saw night.

A few minutes later she heard a soft knock at the door, then a beloved voice, "Marianne? It's me, Jenny. I've come to help."

In a rush of affection, remembering how Jenny's miraculous caress could ease all hurt and banish all fear, Marianne called out,

"Come, Jenny, please. I need you."

At half past eleven, having dined lightly on cold sliced beef and winter salad, Thomas and Marianne sat before the fire in her chambers. They appeared tranquil, though Marianne was learning to suspect the realiability of appearances.

It was true. She felt better. She'd passed a healing interval with Jenny, the two of them chattering over those aspects of the past that were safe and nourishing. Marianne had prepared herself for the wedding bed, had bathed carefully in lavender water, had been grateful when Jenny refrained from making any comment on the scars on her back, had felt extreme gratitude when Jenny refused to question her about anything. Obviously, her new capacity, whatever that was, was unimportant. Marianne was here and they were reunited, and that was all that mattered.

Marianne had brushed free her long hair, had dressed herself in a silk lavender robe, then, after having kissed Jenny lightly on the cheek, had told her that Lord Eden was awaiting her word and would she please inform him that she was ready.

Without question, the dear soul had obeyed. A remarkably short time later, Thomas had appeared, freshly groomed and shaved, Russell following behind with an assortment of servants bearing trays.

They dined alone in silence. The servants cleared away the remains of the meal. Thomas took a pipe from the pocket of his robe, lit it, while she watched in mild fascination, having never seen him smoke before.

Thoughtfully he asked, "The fumes, I trust, will not not bother you?"

Quickly she reassured him. "No, milord. William Pitch enjoyed a pipe. I find the odor pleasing."

She noticed a small tremor on his face at her mention of William Pitch and momentarily regretted it. That, too, was part of the past that needed burying.

They sat before the fire, resembling two statues, content and respective of each other's silences, studying the fire as though it were a captivating theatrical.

"It burns brightly," Thomas commented foolishly.

"It does, milord," she replied, equally as foolish. "What's the wood?"

His brow furrowed as apparently he turned his thoughts sincerely to the empty question. "Oak, I believe. Of course. What else? Good solid English oak."

"We burned some pine when I was a girl," she went on, mindlessly pursuing the subject. "But it has a tendency to pop, particularly if it isn't cured."

He nodded in serious agreement. "It's all in the curing. *All* in the curing."

Silence. The pitifully weak subject was at last exhausted. With a start he inquired, "Are you comfortable here?" motioning to the large chamber.

She followed with her eyes the direction of his hand. "It's very grand," she commented.

"It was my mother's, he said. "She always found it— quite—comfortable."

"And I'm sure I will as well."

The senseless exchange went on, the most mundane and pedestrian sort of idle chatter, punctured by expanding silences.

He asked suddenly, "Would you care for wine? Brandy?"

She shook her head, then on a considerate afterthought, said, "Help yourself, though."

"No, no, I think not."

Although she was too warm already, she leaned forward as though to warm her hands by the fire. She tried to act with a degree of calmness in spite of the agitation she felt within. "Milord," she began, "if you wish—"

Abruptly he cut her off, as though not wanting her to give voice to what he wished. He too leaned forward in his chair, alternately rubbing his hands, then examining them. "You're very fond of Jenny Toppinger, aren't you?" he asked, as calmly as though they'd been discussing the topic all evening.

Bewildered, she nodded, "I am. Very." When he seemed inclined to say nothing further, she added, "She raised me, you know, the one reliable female face from my entire childhood."

He nodded soberly. With an air of largess he said, "You shall have her."

Marianne looked up, not certain she'd heard what he'd said. "I beg your pardon?"

"I said you shall have her. She'll be yours."

Bewilderment mounting, Marianne laughed. "I'm not certain I understand what you mean, milord."

He left the chair as though mildly angry. "I said you shall have her," he repeated, as though for a dense child. "You'll need a woman, so Jenny Toppinger shall be yours."

She watched him, then could no longer restrain from laughing. "Where do I keep her chained, milord?" she asked, amused by his conception of ownership.

It was his turn to look puzzled. Apparently hearing her laugh only served to increase his anger. "What I meant to say was that her duties will entail only looking after you," he snapped. "She will be at your command."

In mock seriousness, Marianne shook her head. "Oh, I don't think that Jenny could function at all under that arrangement. Sweet Heavens, she's spent her life teaching me to look after myself."

"You don't understand," he said, striding back to her chair. "Your position is changed now. You must sever all ties with your friends in the kitchen. A new relationship must be established."

"Why?"

He cast his eyes heavenward, as though seeking Divine Guidance. Marianne gazed into his face. When it seemed he would never answer, she left her chair and walked behind him, suggesting softly, "Milord, I would suggest that we leave my relationships with my friends exactly as they are. They've worked very well. They need no tampering."

In clear anger, he whirled on her, demanding, "Do you have any conception of your elevation? Do you realize the heights to which you have been lifted?" He made a motion toward the room itself and shook his head, as if she were beyond help. But then he seemed to recollect. "It will take time," he said, apparently striving for understanding. "It will be easier if you let me guide you."

Repentant, though still smiling, Marianne said, "Of course, milord. I'm grateful for all your assistance. And I hope that in time you will come to rely upon my assistance as well."

He frowned down on her. "With what? How do I need assistance?"

Somberly she shook her head. "One always needs to rediscover oneself. You are a human being, and as such, you are flawed—"

"How?" he demanded, obviously wanting to know.

"Please, milord," she suggested quietly. "This is not the time nor the occasion," and returned to her chair.

But he merely followed after her, his face in turmoil blended with horrified curiosity, as though stunned by her conception of him as flawed. "No," he said sternly, "I want to hear. Tell me of my flaws. I want to know now."

She heard petulance in his voice, almost a childlike quality. Regretfully she murmured, "I'm sorry I mentioned it, milord. Please, let's not pursue it."

"No," he commanded. "We *will* pursue it. You made an accusation. Now I have a right—"

"It was not an accusation, milord. I merely stated that—"

"—that I was—flawed." The word seemed to come out with difficulty as though even the mere pronouncing of it was painful. "Now, all I'm asking is for you to be specific, tell me—"

She shook her head, finding it difficult to believe the whole silly subject. When she failed to speak, he gave a dry little laugh of derision. "Perhaps you spoke in haste," he said, smiling, providing her with a way out.

"I did not speak in haste, milord."

"Then tell me," he demanded.

She looked directly at him, feeling a small flare of anger of her own. "It is inconceivable to me that you find the news so startling."

"Tell me," he demanded again.

She shook her head.

"Then you refuse?" he asked, his face as gloomy as she'd ever seen it.

"It's not a matter of refusal," she murmured. "It's just that—"

Suddenly he turned and strode toward the door, his head erect, all self-doubt gone. "Then I shall leave you alone, madame," he announced imperiously. "My flaws must be so offensive to you that you cannot form words—"

"Thomas—"

"No, say nothing more, madame. I would not dream of contaminating such a pristine presence with my offensive flaws." The sarcasm in his voice was heavy and she hated it. Still, she could not quite bring herself to believe that he was leaving. "Thomas, I—"

"Sleep well, madame," he said from the door. "I shall corrupt you in no way. In fact, I shall retire to my chambers now to—contemplate my flaws!"

With that, he was gone, taking his angry hurt face with him, slamming the door behind him. She stared, unbelieving, at the closed door. She rejected the idea of following him. Instead she stared glumly into the fire and listened to his heavy tread in the corridor.

She leaned closer to the fire. She had envisioned all sorts of conclusions to the evening, but this was not one of them. She looked quickly over her shoulder, as though perhaps he might have returned.

But he hadn't. She was alone in the grand chamber, perpared for a wedding night and all the turbulence that that entailed. Yet now it was over before it had even begun.

She sat there, listening. She heard the watchman call every hour until three o'clock. Then, she settled back in the chair, choosing to leave the bed empty.

As the watchman cried out four o'clock, her thoughts took a different turn. She was a wife now, and as such, had certain obligations. She must learn to hold her tongue. She sat up, wide awake, not quite comprehending her pensive thoughts. Then what was her goal now? As long as she was here, the only goal that made sense was a good marriage. Under the best of circumstances, considering the distance of birth between them, that would be difficult. Under the worst of circumstances, like now, it would be impossible.

Then perhaps. . . . Suddenly she glanced toward the door, as if the door had spoken to her. She knew the way

to his chambers. She sat a moment longer in silent delibera-
tion, then quickly she left the chair. Twice during the
short passage from chair to door, she stopped, doubt still
plaguing her. Perhaps she shouldn't. Yet someplace beyond the dark corridors, there was a husband brooding,
hurt, alone. And she was alone.

The hint was clear enough. On that final and determined
conviction, she opened the door.

Sleeplessness was a general plague that night. Thomas
too sat brooding in his chambers.

Flawed! Why hadn't she told him? In what way? Her
arrogance galled him.

Flawed! What a cheerless word! Still, perhaps he had
been hasty. There *were* faults, a few of them, but he
thought he kept them well concealed.

Flawed! Her word, not his. Harsher then mere faults,
perhaps incurable. If he offended her, then he would stay
away from her.

So went his thoughts until the early hours of morning.
Still, he could not adjust to the fact that she was so near
and "legally" his. A husband, even in a charade, had
rights.

Outside his window, he heard the watchman cry "Four
o'clock." Without losing too much face, he could always
check on her safety and well-being. After all, that wing
of the castle was far removed and deserted.

Flawed! How the word hurt though.

He rose from the chair, where he'd sat slumped in anger
and self-pity all night.

Flawed! Then so be it. The hunt had been too long and
arduous to surrender now.

Flawed! Perhaps he had too much pride. Then he would
seek to curb his pride and perhaps, in the process, mend
a flaw.

On that note of self-comfort, he flung open the door.

In silence she made her way through the dim corridors,
feeling the chill of damp stone walls. Perhaps she should
have kept to her chambers. Had she taken a wrong turn?
One gray corridor looked exactly like all the rest, and from
her earlier days at Eden Castle, she was not as familiar
with the upper regions as she was the lower. Still another

turn, and then another. God, it was a cold gray place, like a graveyard really. How unhappy a child who passed a youth here!

Suddenly, at the end of the long corridor, she saw a figure. She stopped, silently praying, shivering, a voice she scarcely recognized as her own, calling out, "Who is it?"

He was hurrying toward her, providing her with a sense of relief at his first spoken word. "Marianne?" he called, increasing his speed until he stood directly before her, his face knitted with concern. "I thought I heard something," he lied. "I was coming to check."

"I heard it too," she lied. "The rooms are so far apart."

"You're chilled."

"I thought I was lost."

Their words tumbled out over each other, interrupting, trying to explain their presence in the dark corridor.

Both fell silent. She was aware of him standing close, looking down on her. Quickly he bent over and scooped her up in his arms. She did nothing to resist.

A wife, she thought, shivering again, but not from cold. He was moving with her, carrying her back to his chambers. Once she felt an urge to speak and stilled it. Words had no place here. Let it happen. Let her please him.

He closed the door and lowered her from his arms back to the floor until she was standing before him. To her surprise, he merely looked at her, as though unaware of her readiness, as though still out of long habit, he approached her warily.

The lavender robe she was wearing was joined at two points, with narrow satin ribbons at her throat and waist. Slowly she released the ribbons and pushed the robe backward off her shoulders. Then *she* would be the seducer. Standing before him, she said, "I am your wife, Thomas."

When he still seemed hesitant, staring at her as though in a trance, she stepped close to him and gently lifted his hand to her breast.

Then he moved. He clasped her to him with such force that she lost her balance, and again she felt herself being lifted and carried toward the bed, as at last he took the lead. Nothing like this lack of control had ever attended her in the past. It was not resignation she felt, or alarm, but merely acceptance, calm in the face of his increasing ardor.

He left her for an instant, standing before the bed. Then, his own robe discarded, his arms moved around her and locked under her breasts. His mouth was close against her neck and she understood that she had entirely misjudged him, not only as a lover, but as a man. His grip told her that he was beyond pleading with, that the hours of discourse and conversation and waiting were over.

She was on the bed then, his mouth pressed to her breast. The sensation was one she'd never felt before, like small strands of connecting nerve ends stretching between her nipples and the pit of her stomach. To her surprise, she was kissing him strumpet fashion, using her thighs and fingers like a trained mistress, coaxing her lover into a giving mood.

In truth, he was already clearly in a giving mood, but as though to postpone the sweetness and make it last, he fell to exploring her with his lips and hands, the one seeking her mouth and neck and hair, the other her breasts, back, and thighs. His movements were in leisurely contrast to the frenzied impatience he had shown earlier, and he went about it as though he were assessing what was his in an unhurried way.

Now she was the one suffering terrible impatience. With her eyes closed, she was aware of nothing but his warm firm hands playing contentedly over her loins and buttocks, as though seeking an exact compromise between the assertion of mastery and the act of courtship.

Then, aroused to such a pitch that she felt she could never absorb enough of him, her body opened and with a short reflexive cry, she received him, her body contracting instantly as though to seal that part of him which soothed her emptiness.

It was over in a remarkably short time, the whole ecstatic process of domination and submission, although it was repeated three more times with her active assistance, her curiosity extending now to *his* body, her hands performing acts she'd never dreamed possible, at dawn, the two of them lying spent in each other's arms, a brief interval of an hour's sleep, then passion again, their bodies, with practice fitting neatly together, testing the design, she wriggling back into his embrace, as though this new sensation, in its very newness, had to be repeated in order to make up for all the days she'd lived without it. She ran a hand the length of his firm, muscled back, then drew him close until his head rested on her breasts.

With the first light of dawn, she knelt by his side in bed. "Am I very wicked?" She smiled.

He pulled her down onto her stomach in a playful manner, and, straddling her, commenced to kiss each scar of her back, a gesture which commenced with tenderness and concluded, as all gestures had concluded that night, in passion, as he stretched out atop her and took her again, his hands cupped beneath her breasts, his face buried in her hair.

He rolled to one side, relieving her of his weight. She mourned his absence, then merely followed after him, settling into his arms, content in her realization that his capacity to comfort her would be there when she awakened.

A wife! What a splendid designation! She drew him closer until their bodies were touching at all points, as though to save time, after an interval of rest, they might, effortlessly, become reengaged.

He smiled at her approvingly and tucked her head beneath his chin, and in that warm cocoon she fell instantly asleep.

Generally a man or woman charts his or her birth from the day he or she slips from the mother's womb. But Thomas and Marianne listed a new date of birth, or at best, rebirth, that incredible interval of five days, during which time neither felt the slightest compulsion to leave the chambers, for fear a fever of desire would overwhelm them and they would be too far removed from bed to satisfy it. So for five days, Jenny Toppinger was the only one summoned to their chambers to bring food, to take care of their physical needs, to ask no questions, and to close the door softly behind her.

On the morning of the sixth day, as Marianne stirred sluggishly, every bone aching after a night as delirious as any they'd ever spent, in a muss of bed linens and with her eyes still closed, her hands fanned out in search of his body, always so reliable and rewardingly there.

Finding nothing but a warm indentation, she opened

her eyes in a moment of panic. She saw him standing in
his robe in the center of the room, apparently preoccupied
in some mysterious way with the far blank wall. His hair
was tangled and there was a stubble of beard on his chin.
The faint scents of hair, clothing, skin, and human breath
came to her across the room, all characteristic and familiar
and highly evocative.

She did not stir further, but froze in order to enjoy an
assessment of him. How well now she knew him, this
Thomas, this younger son, for in the intervals between
lovemaking they'd talked intimately, compulsively, a five-
day marathon.

Now, what *was* he doing? She pushed back the pillow
in order to see him more clearly, as with seeming haste he
approached the far wall and lightly knocked against it, his
hands flattened on the wood panels, standing back as though
to assess the wall in relationship to the chimneypiece.

Suddenly, without glancing toward the bed, he ran from
the room, leaving the door open. Totally bewildered, she
sat up, clutching the linens to her, and listened closely as
she followed the progress of his footsteps around the
corner and into the Morning Room where, coming from
that side of the wall, she heard similar knocking.

A few moments later he returned, obviously quite excited, trailing a length of twine in his hands, measuring
a distance along the floor to the far wall.

Tired of her bewilderment, she asked softly, "Thomas,
what *are* you doing?"

At the sound of her voice, he whirled about, an apology
on his lips. "Did I disturb you? I'm sorry."

She shook her head and again assessed him, standing
beside the bed now. "I was awake," she said, "but what
are you doing?"

Before he replied, his hand moved, uninhibited, to her
breast. "We must be up today," he said softly, the movement of his hand arousing feelings within her that made
that proposal seem absurd.

"Why?" she asked.

"Because there will be construction going on in here,"
he said, the pressure from his fingertips increasing.

"What kind of construction?" she asked, wondering how
long she could merely endure.

He moved closer, applying both hands to her breasts, the

same caressing motions. "Because," he whispered, "I never want you farther away from me than that door." With a bob of his head, he motioned toward the far wall.

"There's no door there," she said, smiling. It could not go on much longer.

"There will be," he replied, becoming quite breathless. "And beyond the door will be your new chambers, the finest in all of England."

Her aching increased. "Your mother's apartments are—"

"—too far away," he interrupted. "We'll both stay there, however, until the work is done here."

"Live in the same room?" she asked, smiling. "It's wicked, even for man and wife."

"It's necessary. A man cannot survive without his—"

Suddenly there was a soft knock at the door. They heard Jenny call out, "Milord, breakfast—"

Thomas looked first at the door, then at Marianne. "Shall we surprise them all?" he whispered.

Regretfully she nodded.

He called out, "Jenny, we'll take breakfast in the dining hall."

There was a moment's pause as apparently the woman adjusted to his change of plans. "Very well, milord."

"And send a serving girl," he added.

Marianne sat up. "For what?"

"To assist you."

Lightly she scolded him. "I need no assistance, Thomas. I just need clothes." Quickly she ran to the door and called for Jenny to bring certain pieces of apparel.

A short time later, Jenny returned followed by two young girls. She handed the clothes through the door, then two pitchers of steaming lavender water and fresh linen. Robed now, Marianne received them all, received as well the lowered eyes and slightly embarrassed expression on Jenny's face.

Marianne longed to reassure her of the propriety of their passion, the moral and legal privileges of every husband and wife. But she caught herself in time and after Jenny had left, she turned back to Thomas, who was already shaving.

"I'm afraid she thinks I've fallen into hell," she said sadly.

He looked up, razor in hand. "Who?"

"Jenny."

He dismissed it with a wave of his hand. "You are no longer concerned with what the servants think."

"Jenny is not my servant."

He looked at her as though trying to understand her. Shrugging, he turned back to the mirror. With his chin upraised, his voice sounded distorted. "I'm afraid you'll find it difficult pleasing everyone, Marianne. The servants as well as the tenants are accustomed to our peculiar behavior. They almost expect it of us. Your only responsibility now is to please yourself." He turned and smiled at her. "And me, which you do beautifully."

She accepted the compliment and felt there was something else she should say, but decided against it. She could make peace with Jenny later, when the marriage was publicly announced. Her own conscience was at rest, and that was all that mattered.

Thomas dressed quickly while she was still bathing. He settled comfortably into a chair to watch her. Throughout the entire process she was aware of him watching her, was equally aware of her own feelings. If she did not clothe herself soon, she knew they would be back in bed and have it all to do over again.

Quickly she slipped into a pale green gown, her fingers joining the many buttons up the front. She brushed and knotted her hair and at last stood to face him, who throughout the whole long process had never taken his eyes off her.

At the center of the room they met for a kiss. Playfully he commanded, "Close your eyes and turn around."

When equally as playful she demanded "Why?" he ordered her with mock sternness to do as he said and she obeyed. In the next minute she felt his hands around her throat, felt a cool circle drop lightly around her neck.

He guided her to the pier glass, where she saw an elegant strand of matched emeralds encircling her neck and heard his explanation, "They belonged to my mother."

They were beautiful and she thanked him with a warm kiss, all the time wishing that such things meant as much to her as they did to him. She knew him well enough now to predict the exact pattern of his behavior on such occasions, as though he must seal her allegiance with a gift.

Somehow in their life together, she must teach him the joy of love freely given.

Still, "Thank you, Thomas," she murmured and received a gift far greater than the emeralds about her neck, received his smile, the light on his face suggesting that he had never known such happiness.

This gift she accepted willingly and drew herself up and took his arm. A sense of completeness stole over her and she surrendered to it with a gratitude that she could not have expressed in words.

It did not take Eden Castle long to decide that the presence of someone in authority had arrived and was now essential to the well-being of all at Eden Point.

A curious kind of democracy settled over the grand old fortress, which in the past had known the reassuring division of master and servant. Now at all hours of the day, "Miss Locke," or Lady Eden as she was always being called by some of the younger staff members, could be found in the servants' kitchen, planning the menu, having a cup of tea with Jenny and Dolly, or simply sitting quietly with her father before the fire.

As Thomas had predicted, by December Marianne's sister Jane and her serving woman, Sarah, had arrived to take their places in his household. There had been no word from William Pitch, and the allotted money had been exhausted altogether. So they had closed the house on Russell Street and had taken refuge in the plenty of Eden Point.

Of course the problems were complex. Where was one to put the sister of one's mistress? Certainly not in the servants' quarters. Likewise, Marianne had thoughtfully decided that the winter's dampness in the lower confines of the castle was hard on her father and Jenny and Dolly, thus the three of them had been moved up to first-floor guestrooms.

All during the winter months, Thomas occupied himself with the construction of the new chambers next to his own and tried to move with comparative ease through the fireworks of equality that burst about him. He could endure anything as long as he had her to himself at night. The fever, instead of healing with intimacy, had only increased. When he was away from her, as he was frequently now, he found it unendurable. The ambitious and

expensive chambers, to be merely the grandest in all of
England, seemed to require more and more of his attention
as master artisans arrived from London to do the wood-
carving and marble work. If, at night, he found himself
at table, surrounded by a covey of Lockes, as indeed he
did, for they ate communally now, he endured it all, the
chattering, simpering Jane, the arrogant Russell, the silent,
staring Hartlow, all made palatable by the presence of his
sun and moon, Marianne, upon whom he was becoming
increasingly dependent, not just for solace at night, but
for the entire new order, the smooth-running, beautifully
functioning castle itself.

"It's merely chaos," she had scolded him. "Let me turn
my hand to it and see what I can do."

He'd agreed, feeling it would give her some occupation
while he was busy with the workmen and artisans. And,
indeed, she had turned her hand.

For many years, no Lord of Eden had thought it worth-
while to take much personal interest in his own properties.
The estates were merely a source of revenue and since it
was a very rich and extensive inheritance, all seemed well
and no questions were asked.

But "Miss Locke" had looked around her and decided
to ask questions. A simple person herself, she quickly won
the confidence of the simple folks living round about.
Many of them had dismal tales to tell—of long neglect of
land and buildings, of the absence of any kind of capital
improvement and, as a result, the continuing use of inadequate methods. Evictions were not unknown, even
though the tenant might have fallen on evil days more
through his landlord's fault than his own. Because there
seemed to be no one else to do it, Marianne set about the
work that was crying to be done.

Thomas was keenly aware of her remarkable progress,
of the ease with which she fitted into her new position in
the countryside. Day after day, all during that winter, when
weather permitted she could be seen riding about the
estates on horseback. Thomas gave her a free hand so
that she could plan improvements as she saw fit, ordering
new gates to be made, arranging for fences to be mended
and hedgerows planted, selling a field here and buying a
plot of land there.

She developed a strong business capacity, which in a

very short time showed results in the increased productivity of the estates. She instigated what she called "Thursday Afternoon Tenant Day," and during this time she received any tenant, any fisherman or villager, who had a complaint of any nature, from a sick child to a broken piece of equipment to a boat in need of repairs. To the best of her ability she satisfied them all, taking in her arms a colicky child, signing over notes for repairs, reassuring everyone that if it were at all possible, something would be done.

On a Thursday afternoon in late April, concealed within a near doorway, Thomas watched her, sitting in her straight-backed chair behind a desk as she received a line of tenants, treating each of them to the warmth of her smile. He saw her now send Jane, whom she had enlisted in her cause for hot tea, not for herself, but for a faltering aged woman who was winded by the long climb up Eden Point.

Thomas watched it all, falling even more deeply in love with her, wondering again how he'd been so fortunate to acquire this jewel, more of an aristocrat than his blue-blooded friends who had consistently shunned him in his new alliance with the "fisherman's daughter."

Now he felt impatience as he saw the woman, Sarah, usher new tenants through the central arch, the line stretching almost to the door. It was midafternoon and Marianne had been "receiving" since early morning. The only trouble with her new involvement was that it robbed him of her company. Then, too, on this particular afternoon, he had greater cause for impatience. The new chambers were completed and she had yet to see them. The last of the workmen had left the day before, and Jenny and Dolly were at this very minute filling the urns with her favorite roses.

As he watched her lean forward in concern toward the tenant of the moment, he saw her small straight back clad in simple, almost servantlike navy blue, her long hair done up in a knot as though she were aware of her youthful appearance and taking all means necessary to counteract it. She looked pale, he decided as well, and why not? She had hurled herself into a man's job, outworking the servants on occasions, but still coming to him at night in his mother's chambers, as happily and as giving as though she'd done nothing but lie abed all day, as his mother had done, holding court with an army of servants, to satisfy her slightest whim.

Softly he shook his head, still unable to comprehend her, the source of her energy and tirelessness. She was more his wife than any wife he had ever dreamed of possessing, and one day he would find the courage within himself to rectify the farce he'd performed on her at Fonthill Splendons. Not that a legal ceremony required courage, but the thought of telling her, of seeing the hurt on her face, *that* was the demand of courage, and he couldn't meet it now, not yet, not when her obvious contentment was still so new, so precious to him.

In his deep contemplation of her, he realized belatedly that he'd stepped too far out from his concealment in the doorway. With a rapid turn of her head, as though she'd sensed him long before she'd seen him, her face brightened, though her cheeks were still pale. She called out, "Thomas, come! Meet the people who make you rich."

For a moment the old aristocratic bonds pinched at him. Never in its long history had a Lord of Eden Castle sat openly at table in the Great Hall and "received" his tenants. Tenants were not objects to be received. One received guests of equality and played the gracious host. But tenants were merely unseen faces who tilled the soil and ran the nets and earned their keep by showing profit for the estates.

Seeing his hesitancy, she called again, "Thomas, come, they're friends, really. They wish us well."

Friends! He didn't give a damn whether they were friends or not. But then he did, seeing the pleading in her eyes, an embarrassment really, as though in his hesitancy she was afraid he might injure the feelings of the blank-faced old woman standing before her at the table, holding a small basket in her hands.

Reluctantly he emerged from the doorway, his feelings slightly assuaged by the deferential bows now being offered him by the other tenants in line. A few of the men swiftly removed their hats, seeing the appearance of his Lord-ship. He gave a slight nod to all and drew close to Mari-anne, who looked extremely pleased with herself.

"Sit down, Thomas," she invited, "if you're not busy," indicating a vacant chair beside her.

Again he hesitated, possessing absolutely no appetite for

what she was doing. For the first time he noticed a foul
odor in the Hall, a nauseating blend of cow manure and
body sweat. He had no quarrel with these people as long as
they stayed in their place and afforded him the right to
stay in his. "I think not," he said, ignoring both her invitation and the vacant chair. "I wanted to see when you
might be finished here."

"Oh, I'm afraid not for quite a while," she replied, as
though it would have been pleasant to have him at her
side, but certainly not necessary.

She turned her attention back to the old woman standing before her. She reached across the table and received
the gnarled hand. "You're Mrs. Gavin," she said softly.
"I remember you when I was little. You brought us
gingerbread once. I've never forgotten it, and I've never
tasted better."

A radiant smile broke out on the worn old face. "Aye,
and I remembered your appetite for gingerbread, and I
brun' you some to give you welcome."

Thomas noted the joy on Marianne's face as, within the
instant, she skirted the table and fell into a warm embrace
with the old woman, as grateful for the gift of gingerbread
as though it were a priceless jewel. Behind the warm
embrace, he noticed the selfconscious though pleased
smiles on all the faces who watched, a maudlin scene
really, overemotional and unnecessary.

Feeling excluded, Thomas turned and, without a word,
strode across the Great Hall. Marianne called after him.
Without looking at her, he called back, "Later, when
you're not busy." As he reached the far door, he slackened
his pace and stole a glance at her, pleased by the hurt expression in her face. Beyond the door, in the loneliness of
the passage, his pleasure diminished. Perhaps he should
have stayed. But what a waste! Her so-called Christian
concern would come to nothing but further bilking of his
purse. The lower classes of tenants were notoriously ex-
ploitive. Give them a pence and they would demand a
guinea. He paid overseers to listen to their endless com-
plaints. It was not Marianne's job, and he would tell her
so this very night.

He went through the passage with the assurance born
of an easy conscience. As he started up the steps, he passed
Jane and Jenny Toppinger coming down. Jane, as unrouged

and simple-appearing as he'd ever seen her, curtsied stiffly and extended him an invitation. "We're having tea in the dining hall, Lord Eden," she said, smiling. "Won't you join us?"

He'd attended their teas before and had marveled how the lot of them could instantly convert that grand room into a chattering cottage kitchen. "No, thank you," he said, almost archly. "I will have tea in the new chambers. Jenny, would you fetch it for me?" he added, ignoring the look of familiarity on Jane's face.

Indelicately Jane argued. "Lord Eden, if Jenny's having tea herself, how can she bring it to you? How much simpler if you'd just—"

Mildly he exploded. "Damn it, I want tea alone in the new chambers. Is that clear?"

Jenny was already scurrying down the corridor. Jane stayed a moment longer, as though trying to assess her position of authority as Marianne's sister. Apparently a stray wisp of wisdom intervened. She turned and lifted her skirts and scurried after Jenny.

"Damn it!" he muttered. Was he never to know peace and the order of servants who knew their place? His gaze followed after the retreating women. Yes, he'd have to talk with Marianne that very evening. Certain adjustments would have to be made. Although he'd planned a private celebration in honor of her new chambers, at some point he'd have to lay down the law. No more Thursday-afternoon tenant receptions, no more easeful coming and going of her family. There were adequate apartments near the kitchen. Thanks to his generosity, they were all fed, clothed, and housed. Surely his Christian duty did not entail socializing with them as well.

On that bleak note he trudged wearily up the stairs, nearly colliding with two serving girls in the process of moving her clothes from the old chambers to the new. In spite of the weight of gowns and hatboxes, they bowed low and gave him passage. As he was just starting down the corridor, he heard a cry, sharp, like an alarm. As he turned toward the sound of distress, the two young girls flattened themselves against the wall. He froze, waiting for the cry to come again. Then it did, old Jenny, or so he guessed, her voice splitting the solemn quiet of the upper corridor.

"Lord Eden!" she cried, "Come quick. Marianne—"

Then he was running, past the frightened girls, taking the steps downward three at a time, Jenny crying out again, just out of sight on the first-floor landing. He saw her finally, a handkerchief pressed to her mouth, her eyes wide in alarm. She was pointing toward the Great Hall, where, beyond the door, he saw a cluster of people—Jane, Sarah, Dolly—bent over a fallen figure.

Quickly he pushed his way through the frightened tenants, where at that moment Jane had loosened the collar about Marianne's throat while Sarah, praying aloud, tried to warm her hands.

"Move back!" he shouted. As the crowd obeyed, he shouted again in greater anger for the stewards to clear the room. As the tenants shuffled out the door, he knelt in concern beside the extremely pale and lifeless figure on the floor. "What happened?" he demanded as he lifted her in his arms, alarmed by the dead weight of her body, cradling her close so that her head rested against his chest.

When no one moved to answer him right away, he demanded again, "I asked what happened?" glaring at the little semicircle of faces as though they were responsible.

Dolly Wisdom found her tongue and nerve first. "Milord," she sniffled, "she was returning to her chair and simply fell to the floor."

Again the foul odor of retreating tenants filled his nostrils. "The damned place smells diseased," he cursed. "Air it!" He carried her back through the Hall, commanding only Jenny Toppinger to follow after him, but aware a few moments later of the entire female parade trailing behind him up the stairs.

She looked pale, so terribly pale, her mouth opened slightly, the dark blue eyes usually so alive closed as though in death. Suddenly he felt terror at her stillness.

"Hurry!" he shouted, increasing his step, uncaring anymore who followed so long as they might help. Once in the new chambers, he placed her gently on the handsome bed of carved rosewood, elegantly canopied with purple velvet brocade. Within the moment, the women closed in and took custody of her. He retreated back to the door, helpless to penetrate the feminine circle, not really wanting to, so long as they revived her and gave her back to him, whole and restored.

For an agonizing time, he had to content himself with pacing in his own chambers. He imagined the worst, that she had contracted some dread incurable tenant disease, a fever perhaps, or worse, pox. As his despair grew, he tried to listen to the voices coming from the other room. But he heard little, a splash of water, the woman, Jane, quickly departing, then returning with a bottle of salts clutched in her hand. But there were no words at all, causing his terror to increase. He sank into a chair, feeling unwell himself. It was as if something of his soul had flowed into her and now he was sharing her illness.

What was taking them so long? Why couldn't they give him a word at least? Surely he had never suffered so much. In an attempt to ease that suffering, he moved to the near window. Beyond the balcony was the inner courtyard, grey and ominous in the early evening light. A few tenants were still straggling toward the gate. Then, the whipping oak. His eyes moved passed it and came back. The burden was so heavy he did not think he could bear it. If anything happened to her, he would have himself bound to it and lashed to death, an easy parting compared to life without her.

Softly into his devastation he heard a voice, Jenny, saying, "You may go in."

He turned eagerly. "Is she—"

But the woman merely bobbed her head and retreated, joining the other women in the corridor, giving him access to her room.

She was in bed, her long hair loosed about her face, a strong smell of oil of clove hanging on the air, her eyes still closed, her face as pale as the linen upon which she lay. He approached her hesitantly, still fearful. Had they summoned him to view her corpse? Where was life? The grand chamber which he'd hoped to share with her now resembled a burial vault, the urns of roses funeral flowers.

Then there was life, her eyes opened, the beauty of a smile on her lips. "Thomas," she whispered, and lifted a hand and drew him close.

He responded not with words, for he was beyond speech. She drew him closer and kissed him. "Poor Thomas," she murmured. "You look so frightened."

"And why shouldn't I be?" he responded with mock gruffness. "I leave you one minute fawning over gingerbread, and the next minute—" He broke off as though he had no desire to describe the scene of her collapsed on the floor.

She laughed softly. "It was not the gingerbread that made me ill, Thomas—"

He sat on the bed beside her, still clasping her hand. He considered speaking to her about certain alterations in the running of the castle. But he decided against it. She seemed to be looking about her, aware for the first time of where she was.

He watched her carefully for the least sign of pleasure as her eyes moved slowly over the white marble fireplace, the tapestries, the magnificent wood carved panels, the urns filled with roses. Instead of pleasure, he thought he saw exhaustion on her face. After her limited inspection from the bed, her eyes closed and she drew the velvet brocade coverlet closer to her chin.

When she seemed disinclined to make comment, he leaned over her, prompting, "Do you like it?"

With her eyes closed, she said, "It's far too grand, Thomas."

"Why don't you let me be the judge of that?"

"There are so many others who get by on so much less."

"I'm not concerned with the others."

Her eyes opened. "You should be. Your world would collapse without them."

Feeling minor disappointment, he stood up from the bed. "My world collapsed today *because* of them," he said pointedly.

She looked at him as though unable to comprehend what he was saying. "Thomas, this has nothing to do with the tenants."

"How can you say that?" he scolded. "They reek of disease and filth, and you receive them as though they were—"

Smiling, she motioned him back to the bed. Without a word, she took his hand and guided it beneath the coverlet, under her nightdress until it was resting, palm down, on her bare stomach. "There is the problem," she said playfully.

He felt of her flesh, warm beneath the covers, exploring a bit on his own as long as he was there, fondling the curvature of her hips. "I don't understand—"

"By Jenny's estimate, it should be an October child."

He said nothing. He looked at her as though his ears had deceived him.

"I hope you are not displeased, milord," she said, smiling. "I shall lose my figure and become lumpen and misshapen, but—"

Awareness dawned. His hand lightened on the precious area where beneath her flesh a part of him was growing. "A—child?" he repeated, as though wanting confirmation.

She nodded. Quickly he withdrew his hand as though her abdomen had become suddenly hot. "Are you—well?" he asked, concerned. "Is there any—"

"I'm well, milord, and in excellent hands. Jenny has delivered every baby in Mortemouth for the last twenty-five years."

"A baby," he thought again, still stirred. A son, the continuity of line, the best of Marianne, the best of himself. Tenderly he enclosed her in his arms and lifted her to him as the thought kept him fascinated.

"Come, Thomas," she invited, a slightly wicked glint in her eye. "Come, lie beside me."

Immediately he rejected the idea. "It wouldn't be safe," he said, rising from the bed.

"Nonsense," she scoffed. "The seed is anchored. We need pay it no mind for long months. Please—" she whispered again, turning back the coverlet. "I want you."

But again he refused. "No. For your own sake, no."

She raised up on her elbows, defiant. "I will not be denied you, Thomas, for seven long months."

"And I will run no risk," he replied firmly, "that will deny me you for the rest of my life." As long as the subject had been launched, he thought he might as well complete it. "You must cease all your activities, Marianne."

She sat up straight in bed, but he continued anyway despite the look of shock on her face. "I forbid you to leave these chambers without either myself or Jenny at your side. There will be no more long rides across the moors, no more visitations from the tenants. We shall take our meals here so that you might avoid the steps, and, on fair days, I shall carry you out to the headlands, so that you might take the air and sun. Beyond that, there will be no activity except that which I personally approve of—"

Throughout his little speech, he was aware of the change

on her face, from mild annoyance and surprise to what appeared to be rage. Suddenly, without a word, she threw back the covers and left the bed, padding barefoot across the floor toward the outer door.

"Marianne?" he called sharply after her. "Where are you going?"

She turned angrily back, appearing childlike in her long white nightdress. "I've been a prisoner once, milord," she said, her voice even. "I have no intention of becoming one again."

As she flung open the door, he ran after her and caught up with her in the corridor. Angrily he picked her up and carried her back into the room, enduring her screams and calls for help. Twice he placed her on the bed and twice she scrambled free. The third time, as he overtook her in the hall, he saw Jenny hurrying toward them, apparently alarmed by the screams. When Marianne saw her, she cried aloud, quite melodramatically, as though for her life, "Jenny, help me! Please help me!"

Embarrassed, Thomas released her and watched, helpless, as she ran into the old woman's arms. He stepped aside as the two women made their way back to her chambers, Jenny's arm protectively around her shoulder, her sharp eyes looking accusingly at Thomas. He started after them into the room only to have the door slammed in his face. In a rage, he considered breaking it in. But instead he retreated, weary and confused.

He paced outside her door, trying hard to understand and understanding nothing. It was merely her well-being that he had in mind, hers and the child's. She was not strong enough for childbirth. She must rest and preserve all the strength at her disposal. Why couldn't she understand this?

Bewildered, he continued to pace. A few moments later, Jenny appeared. She looked at him, only a token glance, started to pass him by, then stopped, head down. "I beg your pardon, milord. A word if I may?" she asked softly.

Without waiting for his permission, she spoke. "When Marianne was a child, she took to wandering out of the back garden against my express orders. Two or three times every day, I would have to stop my work and go and fetch her wandering about the quay, or up on the headlands. And everytime I brought her back, I spanked her, each time a little harder." For the first time she looked up at him. "I broke two rods on her and drew blood, but each time she would be gone again. Finally I gave up, turned her over to God. If harm befell her, so be it. I was doing more damage in an attempt to keep her safe."

She stepped away from him. "She's wandered ever since, milord, and always returned safely, and the only harm that has ever befallen her is what you inflicted on her."

He looked away.

"I mean no offense, milord," she murmured quickly. "But she's healthy, and the babe secure, and not even you possess a rod strong enough to make her obey."

Almost plaintively he asked, "Then what do I do?"

She smiled wearily and shrugged. "Do as I did. Turn her over to God. He's the only One who can even come close to handling her."

She went off down the corridor, leaving him alone to try to fathom the new silence coming from behind the closed doors.

Quietly he knocked and, receiving no reply, went in. She was back in bed, staring up at the canopy overhead, eyes open. If she was aware of his presence in the room, she gave no indication of it.

He crept close, uncertain of her response to him, not wanting to anger her again. Clinging to the bedpost, he said softly, "Jenny tells me you were an obstinate child."

No response.

"She said you ran away repeatedly against her express orders."

Still no response.

"She said she broke two rods on you."

Still not so much as a glimmer of response.

"She said that even I do not possess a rod strong enough to force you to obey."

With tenderness, she smiled at him. "She's mistaken about that, milord."

He looked at her intently, in an attempt to read both her smile and her words. If the message was muddled before, it wasn't now as she laid back the coverlet, again inviting him into the warmth of her bed.

Disbelieving, he shook his head, and with a laugh, sent his eyes heavenward, as though to the only Source rumored to understand her. As he sat down on the bed and commenced pulling off his boots, he thought that perhaps it would suffice merely to lie beside her, to hold her, to talk of their coming child. Surely in the name of good sense, he thought, and out of respect for her condition, she would expect nothing of him except his presence and his pledge of devotion. But he was wrong.

On a hot mid-August morning, Marianne stood naked before the pier glass in her chambers, appalled by the reflection that stared back at her.

The legs were the same as always and the shoulders and neck and head. It was the middle, the grotesquely misshapen middle, from her swollen breasts to the pumpkinlike protuberance of her lower belly.

"Oh, God, Jenny," she mourned, cupping her arms beneath the heavy weight. "I fear you've miscalculated this time. By October, I'll explode."

Behind her, Jenny scolded her for her immodesty. "Clothe yourself, Marianne. His Lordship is waiting to walk."

"Clothe myself! In what?" exclaimed Marianne. "There's not a bolt of cloth in all of England large enough to cover this." Again she ran her hand over her rounded belly, the awful weight affecting her posture, pulling her forward.

"Enough!" Jenny snapped, clearly embarrassed. "Here, hold on to my arm." As she held out giant bloomers, Marianne did as she was told, laboriously lifting one leg, then the other. From the wardrobe, Jenny fetched chemise and gown, both loose-fitting, but beautifully finished with petit-point lace and hundreds of tiny tucks starting at her breasts and falling downward in a graceful accordion pleat.

Marianne had never seen them before. As Jenny fumbled with the buttons at the back of her neck, she admired the pale pink silk so laboriously fashioned. "Did you have a hand in this, Jenny?" she asked softly.

" 'Twas nothing," Jenny scoffed, the buttons secure, her hands smoothing, adjusting the fall of the fabric.

Marianne knew better. The garment represented hours of work. The private effort of love both pleased and moved her. She turned abruptly and embraced the old woman, as much of an embrace as her protruding stomach would allow.

"You mustn't waste your time on such vanities," she scolded lightly.

"I didn't view it as a waste of time," Jenny replied, clearly pleased with herself and her work. "You have a position to maintain now."

Marianne scoffed at that. "I'm the same as always," she said, studying her reflection in the glass. The mirror assured her that she was not. But while the body was inflated, she noticed that her face had taken on a cast and color that she'd never seen before, as though she were enjoying an excess of vitality that warmed her blood. Without tempting fate too much, she thought that she was happier than she'd ever been in her life, surrounded by family and friends, secure in Thomas' love. Occasionally she was at a loss to draw any connection whatsoever between the man as she had first known him and the man she had married.

Again she patted her bulging stomach, admirably concealed by the tiny tucks of pink silk. Still, by pressing her hand close to her groin, she could feel him kicking, the Fourteenth Baron and Sixth Earl of Eden Castle, floating in her womb, drawing nourishment from her body.

Overcome with happiness, she gripped the edges of the pier glass with a force that alarmed Jenny. "What is it, Marianne?" she asked sharply, moving around, the better to see her face.

Smiling, Marianne closed her eyes and rested her forehead against the glass. "Nothing," she soothed. More urgently, she grasped Jenny's hand.

"The child is well, isn't he, Jenny?"

Jenny laughed. "The child is well, though it's a bit premature to call it a he."

Reassured, Marianne said confidently, "It's a he," she said, smiling. "God would not dare send Thomas a daughter. Not at first anyway."

There was a knock at her door, and Thomas' voice. "Are you ready? The sun will be high and hot today. If you insist upon walking, let's do it early."

She took a final look in the mirror. The bulge was still there in spite of the lovely gown. But it was a precious bulge. On that note of comfort, she again thanked Jenny for the dress and hurried as fast as her new girth would permit to the door where, on the other side, she found Thomas, looking preoccupied but almost sinfully handsome in his black walking coat and high black boots.

"You'll need a shawl," he ordered, stepping back to give her passage.

"In August, Thomas, of course not," she countered, taking his arm and pressing lightly against him, their child literally between them.

Obviously Thomas was aware of the pressure and momentarily disarmed by it. With old Jenny still watching, he could do little but step away. "I don't know why you insist upon walking," he scolded, escorting her to the door.

"Because it's healthy for all of us," Marianne said. She saw the parting look of helplessness that passed between Jenny and Thomas, then she took the lead down the corridor, hearing Thomas call for her to wait at the top of the stairs. She obeyed, then again took his arm for the descent.

Laboriously she made her way down the steps, feeling his arm around her, carefully supporting her. At the first floor, he stopped, insisting that she catch her breath.

His manner seemed unnecessarily sharp, something on his face which spoke of more than concern.

"Do our excursions so displease you, milord?" she asked.

"Not displease," he replied, "I question the wisdom of going abroad for your sake."

"With you beside me, what could befall me?"

"Jenny says the birth could be difficult."

"Then all the more reason to gain as much strength as possible," she countered. She saw him about to say something else, but apparently he changed his mind. He took her arm again and escorted her down the outer steps and into the blaze of sun of the inner courtyard.

She noticed his subtle movements as they passed the whipping oak, placing himself between her and the sight of it, choosing that opportunity to sternly tell her, "—not the village today. The path is too steep. If you insist on this madness, you'll have to content yourself with the headlands."

She nodded, still puzzled by his peculiar behavior. She'd

looked forward to the village, but decided against arguing with him. The headlands would do nicely.

As they approached the gate, she watched Thomas awkwardly exchange greetings with the watchmen. He knew them all by name. Why didn't he address them by name? Then blessedly the clanking of the twin grates prohibited all speech. Once they were raised, he hurried her through, his head lowered, his arm again protectively about her.

An incredible thought occurred to her. "Milord," she asked, "do I embarrass you?"

"Of course not," he snapped, still moving her hastily forward as though in protective custody.

Once beyond the gate and the gaping eyes of the watchmen, he released her somewhat, though he maintained a firm grip on her arm.

Still, she felt she might have struck on something important. Perhaps he believed that a woman in her condition was not to be seen in public. To carry a child was a temporary embarrassment. Finally she laughed, "Oh, Thomas, how ridiculous you are. If I embarrass you, I'm sorry. But those men back there, they all have families. They've seen a woman swell."

On the safe level path that led to the headlands, he released her arm and walked a step or two ahead. "You don't embarrass me, Marianne," he said almost wearily. He stopped and confronted her. "But there's a vast difference between their common women and you."

"Not all all, Thomas," she said.

As though hurt, he murmured, "You can't believe that."

"But I do. Those common women, as you call them, received their husbands in love, the same as I did."

Abruptly he turned and walked on down the path, the sea wind beginning to ruffle his hair, his head down, apparently in deep gloom.

For the length of the headland, he walked about ten feet ahead of her, saying nothing, turning now and then to glance at her over his shoulder. She'd never seen him so preoccupied and wondered if perhaps it wasn't something deeper, more serious than simply being abroad with a bulging woman.

At the exact point where the land curved to follow the channel, there was a bench, placed there by Thomas for her enjoyment. It was to this spot that he led her, still refusing to look directly at her. He placed her on the bench and then moved quickly away as though he desired a distance between them.

She was becoming alarmed by his remote manner. "Thomas, what is it?" she asked bluntly, feeling the wind blow her words backward.

When he failed to reply, she asked, "Do I displease you so?"

He looked at her, a pained expression on his face. Then he was beside her, taking her hands in his. "Not displease, Marianne. Never displeasure," he said with apparent earnestness.

"Then what?"

For the first time since they'd left the castle, he smiled. Averting his eyes from her, he appeared to gaze far out into the channel. Wearily he shook his head. "I've suffered anxieties of late," he began.

"Over what?"

"You."

She looked surprised. "Why me?"

An intense flush spread over his face. "If anything should happen—"

"Thomas, nothing is going to happen. Nature is a grand design, almost foolproof, and I shall be none the worse for wear. I promise you."

But when she saw how alarmed he really was, she took his face between her hands and kissed him lightly. "Isn't there anything I can do to reassure you?"

His face seemed to pale. "Yes," he said.

"Then tell me," she begged, ready to do anything to put his mind at ease.

He hesitated, an indescribable expression on his face. "Marry me—again," he said.

She stared at him. "Marry you—again?"

"Why not?" he said, defensively. "It's not all that unusual. Renewal of vows. It happens."

She tried to conceal her bewilderment, which was rapidly growing into amusement. "But, Thomas, our vows are not a year old. I shouldn't think they would need—"

"How can it harm?" he interrupted. He rose and left her side as though physical movement might help express his case. A few steps away, he stopped and looked back. "I see nothing out of order with the suggestion. Our vows, the first ones, were made in Wiltshire. They should be made in Devon."

"Why?"

He stammered, stopped, tried a fresh start. "Because it's fitting," he blurted.

"Are vows spoken in Wiltshire less binding than those spoken in Devon?"

"No, of course not," he snapped and again turned his back on her.

Lacking understanding, she was aware of his frustration, but helpless to do anything about it. She looked down at her protruding belly and quietly laughed. "I'm afraid I'd make a peculiar-appearing bride," she said.

As though on a note of hope, he turned eagerly. "No one need see but Parson Branscombe and the witnesses."

Pointedly she asked, "Then even the second marriage would be a secret?"

He said nothing.

The wind on the headlands seemed to be increasing in force. It took their words and their silence and blew them away, but left intact the awkward cross-purpose through which they were presently struggling.

She rose heavily and bowed her head into the wind and went to his side. "A renewal of vows," she chided him gently. "My vows need no renewal, Thomas. I'm more your wife now than I was on that cold October morning at Fonthill." She ran her hand lightly across his chest, her fingers stopping at the opening of his shirt for a tender examination of flesh. "Then," she went on, "I had great misgivings. Now I have none."

She was standing close to him, her face raised, wanting very much for him to kiss her. Instead he moved away and whispered petulantly, "We didn't even have a wedding feast."

Wearily she shook her head. "And how could we have one now with the second ceremony performed in secret?"

They stared at each other across the blowing wind. Suddenly he seized her arm. "If I make the arrangements, will you speak your vows again with me?"

"Sir," she protested softly, "I see no reason—"

"Then see no reason," he replied. "Humor me. Grant my request."

Suddenly the child within her throbbed. A sharp pain

started in her lower stomach and shot upward into her breasts. She clung to his arm.

Angrily he scooped her up. "I told you," he scolded. "This is not good for you."

For a few minutes she had to endure his anger until the spasm passed. As she felt herself being carried back over the headlands, she insisted, "It was nothing, Thomas. I swear it. Your son has set his own timetable. That's all. Please. Let me walk."

Begrudgingly he put her down as though he knew that she would have her way. He continued to lend her a supportive arm and carefully monitored each step as they walked back toward the castle.

They walked in silence. She wondered if the foolishness of the second marriage had been forgotten. But unfortunately it hadn't. As the castle gate came into view and the path became even, he released her and walked alone, his eyes downcast as if speaking words printed on the smooth cobblestones. "We shall repeat our vows within the week," he said, as sternly as though he were issuing a command.

A rebuttal was on her lips, but her attention was drawn to the open castle gates and beyond, where a small black carriage was just rattling to a halt. "Milord," she murmured, her eye still fixed on the carriage. "I believe we have a guest."

Thomas squinted ahead, apparently trying to make out the identity of the carriage and the unannounced caller. Quickly he increased his step. He called to the watchman at the gate. "Who is it?"

The man shook his head. "He refused to give his name, milord," he replied. "Said he was a friend of—Miss Locke's."

Marianne saw the confusion on the poor man's face. Then her attention was drawn back to the carriage, standing before the Great Hall, no sign of life yet, the horses stamping at the ground.

As they passed beneath the gate, Thomas muttered, "It's a hired chaise. The guards are getting careless. It should have been stopped for identification."

Moving ahead of him, Marianne kept her eyes focused on the small black carriage. She saw now, just coming out of the Great Hall, her brother Russell in the company of three stewards. She saw several watchmen near the wall move forward. At the angle at which she stood, the whipping oak was blocking her view. Quickly she moved to one side, still keeping her eye on the carriage.

The door was opening. The coachman jumped down from his high seat and extended a hand into the chaise. A moment later, a man awkwardly emerged, his upper torso falling heavily against the door as though lacking support for the short descent to the ground.

Marianne stopped. She tried to draw deep breath and couldn't. In spite of the distance, she recognized him. She stood rigid, remembering the last time she'd seen him, on the sun-drenched pavement of Great Russell Street.

Then she was moving toward him as fast as her bulky body would permit, her sole desire to see him closer. He. Her excitement increased as now he turned in her direction. His body seemed peculiarly off-center, one arm hidden behind him. *Or gone.*

"Oh, William," she whispered, an angry flush spread over her face at the sight of him mutilated. There was a look of shock on his face now as apparently he struggled to digest the changed state of *her* person. The two of them met at last in a warm, though limited embrace, her hand moving instantly to his tucked sleeve, where beneath the roughness of fabric she felt a short protruding stump.

She was aware of nothing and no one save him, the face, the warmth, the tenderness of William Pitch. It was as though time had not passed at all.

He stepped away from her, his face struggling for control, his eyes focused darkly on something over her shoulder. "Lord Eden," he said softly.

She'd forgotten about Thomas and now quickly brushed the tears from her eyes. She took his arm and led him forward. "Milord," she said, "you remember William Pitch, I believe."

Closely she watched Thomas' face. At first she thought she saw anger, the memory of bad blood between them, the near tragedy of that night in the second-floor bedroom still a fresh wound. Then blessedly his face seemed to relax. Curiosity, perhaps compassion, replaced the anger as his eye fell on the absence of Wlliam's right arm.

"Welcome, Mr. Pitch"—he smiled—"to Eden Castle."

William took the extended hand with his left, a stiff

movement which seemed to cause him embarrassment. "Milord," he said, "I apologize for my unannounced arrival. If it's an inconvenience, I shall leave immediately." He faltered, looked briefly about, his eye stopping on Marianne. With utmost speed, his vision moved back to Thomas. "I came to extend my greetings and best wishes, and—" Again he faltered. He seemed weakened, unsure of himself. Marianne noticed his left hand trembling violently and stepped closer as though to assist him.

But a moment later he continued speaking. "I've just returned from France, milord," he went on, "and in my absence I seem to have lost the only family I ever knew."

With admirable grace, Thomas replied, "If I can assist you in finding that family, sir, I'll be most happy to do so."

William bowed his head. "I was told they came here, milord."

Marianne looked closely at his face, now an emaciated visage, with damp locks sticking in wisps on the brow. She wondered, mournfully, how many more times in her life she would have to say good-bye to him. The one on the pavement had been hard enough. She stepped forward, and in essence told him good-bye again. "Jane is here, William," she said. "And Sarah is with her."

Their eyes met and held, as though the good-bye had been confirmed. How she longed to speak with him in private, to explain. Then she heard herself asking Russell to fetch Jane quickly, as though her sister's presence were required on many counts.

There was a terrible silence about the company. Thomas appeared tired, William stood awkwardly at the center of attention, his eyes periodically inspecting the inner courtyard, staying rigidly away from Marianne. To fill the painful interim, she said, "You will stay, of course, William. There's so much we want to hear about. I'm afraid that news reaches us very slowly here at Eden."

"It is not my desire to intrude."

"I assure you, it will be no intrusion," she replied. "Will it, Thomas?"

Apparently the direct question stirred him out of his lethargy. In a rather pointed gesture, he placed his arm around Marianne and drew her close. "No intrusion at all, Mr. Pitch. I meant what I said before—you are welcome here for as long as you wish to stay. And Marianne is right. You must give us news from the continent. The only wayfarers here are the gulls, and they are scarcely equipped to bring us news."

Inside the shelter of his arm, Marianne felt peculiarly weak. Beneath her gown she felt another pain, sharper than the one before. But fortunately no one noticed, for at that moment Jane appeared at the top of the steps, her face a contortion of joy, then agony, as seeing his mutilation, she burst into tears and ran down the steps and embraced him.

Marianne noticed William's face as he received her, his one arm holding her close, though his face was scowling into her hair, his eyes suddenly hard as though to shield himself.

Sarah appeared through the same door, the hem of her apron pressed against her mouth. Marianne was grateful that the woman kept her sobs to herself. One such scene was enough for all of them.

With the sobbing Jane still clinging to him, William looked desperately about as though for direction.

Marianne, still recovering from the last spasm of pain, suggested weakly, "His trunks, Thomas. Have the stewards take his trunks."

As the trunks were being lowered from the top of the chaise, William singled out one large carton and ordered the stewards to hand it to him.

The men obeyed. It was only at the last minute that both stewards realized that William was incapable of taking it. Marianne noticed a flair of anger at his helplessness. Sharply he ordered the stewards to give it to Marianne.

"A gift," he explained, still not looking at her. "I have little of value left, but you admired it once. I hope it will give you pleasure in your new life."

As the steward placed the carton near her feet, Marianne asked him to open it for her. The lid was scarcely raised, the first layer of straw removed when she knew what it was. The tiny golden orb of the sun caught the reflection from the real sun, momentarily causing her eyes to blur. The Orrery. How much pleasure it had given her once.

As Thomas bent over in examination of the small globe, Marianne found William's eyes and forced them to stay with hers. In that instant she was transported back to the front parlor in Bloomsbury, a hideous time, made palatable by the kindness of the man who had taken the effort to explain the heavens to her.

"Thank you, William," she said simply. In spite of her increasing weakness, she issued a spate of orders, sending the stewards with the trunks to second-floor chambers, asking Russell to send Dolly Wisdom to her so they might plan a banquet for the evening befitting the arrival of an old and dear friend.

If Thomas had any objections, he did not voice them aloud. As the company scattered, she waited by the chaise to see each of them on his or her appointed task. Jane had regained enough control to take full command of William, and was leading him up the stairs. The grooms came for the weary horses and led them off to the stables. Russell took the coachman to the kitchen for lodgings and refreshment, and ultimately there were only two standing in the courtyard.

"Thank you for receiving him," she said to Thomas, who stood a distance away.

"He's no threat to me now," he said, as though with genuine compassion for the man who once had leveled a pistol at him. "He looks quite pathetic. I look forward to hearing where he left his arm."

He looked pointedly at her. "And you, milady?" he asked softly. "What is he to you?"

She waited, taking care with her answer. "He was kind to me," she said simply.

Apparently the answer sufficed. Gently Thomas put his arm around her shoulder and drew her close. "Then I shall be kind to him," he promised.

Jenny appeared at the top of the steps, looking in Marianne's direction. "Dolly is with your father," she called out. "Will you entrust me with the menu?"

Marianne laughed. "I'll do more than that, Jenny. I'll let you arrange it." She turned back to Thomas. "What are your plans, milord?" she asked, moving toward the steps.

He followed after her, keeping his voice low. "I would like to speak further with you on the subject we briefly discussed on our walk."

Delicately she begged off. "Not now, milord. I think I shall follow your good advice and retire to my chambers. Perhaps later, before dinner this evening."

She could tell he wasn't happy with the postponement,

but since it was his suggestion that she get more rest, he couldn't very well refute it. "Then until later," he said with a slight bow.

At the top of the steps, Jenny waited, looking down. Behind Marianne, Thomas stood, looking up.

At that instant, bowing her head to the expanse of steps before her, she knew she faced an incredibly difficult task, and that was to manipulate the steep stairs without giving either of them the slightest indication that she was suffering pain as intense as any she had ever experienced in her life. . . .

"I'm afraid it was neither courageous nor noble," said William, sitting at table, appearing more relaxed than before. "I saw the pistol aimed at Paine and without thinking stepped in front of it."

Marianne sat at the far end of the table, listening intently, praying that the discomfort would hold off a bit longer. During the afternoon, lying flat on her back, the spasms had subsided. Reassured by Jenny's infallible prediction of an October child, she viewed them merely as false labor, or perhaps the weight of the child himself.

She scanned lovingly the table in the Banqueting Hall, enjoying the muddle of aristocracy and democracy that she suspected annoyed Thomas. Jane was there, red-eyed, clinging to William's every word, and next her brother Russell, and nearest to her, Jenny, who'd protested vigorously when Marianne had invited her, but who nonetheless appeared sharply at ten o'clock in her best black dress with blue trim.

During the heavy meal, William had kept them fascinated with stories of the Revolution, of the little Corsican named Bonaparte, upon whom at first the Revolution had pinned such hopes. Only now, after the last course of strawberries and cream and several bottles of wine, had he apparently relaxed enough to speak of his own misfortune.

From her end of the table, Marianne focused on Thomas' face, highlighted by candlelight and a new kind of excitement. He had been enthralled all evening by William's stories, the two men relaxing into a fellowship that she would not have dared to predict earlier that morning.

Now Thomas leaned forward in an obvious desire to

hear more concerning the shooting itself. "This Paine?" he asked. "You say he's an Englishman?"

William gave him an amazed look. "The greatest of Englishmen, milord. A true son of liberty. He has given much to all causes of freedom, both here and in America." Again he shook his head in disbelief. "I cannot believe you do not know the name," he murmured.

Thomas laughed. "On the morning, Mr. Pitch, I shall take you abroad and show you the isolation of my little kingdom. News travels from London to Exeter and there it stops. If we want it, we must go and fetch it."

Something in William's face suggested to Marianne that such isolation appealed. "You are truly fortunate, milord, to let in only that part of the world that pleases you."

Quickly Thomas motioned for the steward to refill William's glass as well as his own. Then again, he moved his chair closer. "Now tell us about your remarkable Mr. Thomas Paine, if you will. Obviously he owes you much, his life for a start."

William drank and shook his head. "He owes me nothing, milord. Quite the contrary, I suspect we all bear a debt to him."

Thomas moved still closer. "Then tell us of Robespierre and the Terror. The newspapers were full of it the last time I was in London. Surely the accounts were exaggerated."

Again William shook his head, his left hand massaging the stump of his arm in a peculiar gesture which Marianne had noticed before, a self-comforting motion, like a child in a rocking chair. He glanced across the scattering of female company and declined to speak further. "With your forgiveness, milord, the atrocities are not suitable for mixed company."

Quickly Marianne spoke up. "Then let the squeamish leave. Dinner is over. I long to hear it all.'"

Thomas smiled his approval and waited patiently to see if anyone chose to leave. Apparently none did. "Now, speak, Mr. Pitch. Your audience has been forewarned."

Again William hesitated, drank deep of the wine. Clearly the pain of his experience was still too close.

But he spoke anyway, slowly at first, his words seeming to slip out independent of his eyes, which were focused on his wineglass as his fingers rolled the stem about, tip-ping the red claret close to one edge, then the other. "The victims were transported in tumbrils," he began, "small cartlike devices of varying sizes. At first there were only two or three beheadings a week. Later the number grew to two or three hundred, the tumbrils rattling day and night between Luxembourg and the Place de la Revolution."

Marianne noticed the claret slipping closer and closer to the edge. Still the voice spoke on, its quiet intensity holding enthralled all those about the table.

"Great wagonloads of hay were brought in from the country," he said "to soak up the blood. But still it was not unusual to pass couples with blood-moist shoes, as gay as though they were on holiday, having just come from viewing the death machine and the rivers of blood."

His voice became strangely low. "And when the death machine could not kill them fast enough," he went on, the wineglass tilting back and forth like a metronome, "the terrorists devised new sport, leading the victims to the banks of the Seine, stripping them and binding them together, one man, one woman, tying lead weights to their feet, and drowning them in the river."

Someone, old Jenny, murmured, "Dear God." Jane turned away in her chair.

"Once," he went on, his voice strangely rising, "I saw a citizen grab a baby from a mother as she was dragged to the guillotine. At first I though it was an honorable gesture, the man intending to save the child. But when a cry of disapproval arose from the crowd, he tossed the child up into the air and a soldier speared it with his sword." His voice fell to a whisper. "The child, held aloft and squirming, screamed for minutes before it died."

Suddenly the wine spilled. The red stain spread across white linen. In a voice peculiar in its breathlessness, Thomas angrily demanded, "And this in the name of liberty?"

Abruptly William closed his eyes. He shook his head. "I don't know, milord," he admitted. "It's an abuse of liberty, but the very word dictator abuses liberty as well." He opened his eyes. "What does one do with a profound horror of tyranny?"

Without hesitation, Thomas replied, "One does not slaughter women and children, for then any revolution is no more than the destruction of a lesser crime by a greater."

Again William debated with something less than whole-hearted conviction. "Not in the beginning it wasn't."

"What it was in the beginning is unimportant," Thomas argued.

"The cause was good, the King a tyrant."

"And what of the terrorists on the Committees?" demanded Thomas. Marianne had never seen him so roused. Yet in spite of his excitement, she detected something else as well, a kind of enjoyment, as though he'd been too long removed from good male companionship and the events of the world.

He went on, speaking of the hypocrisy of the Revolutionists, the elusive target of perfectibility, and she was surprised to discover that apparently William did not object, as though perhaps he'd waited a long time for someone to speak aloud the doubts that had grown in the darkness of his heart.

As the two persisted with their discourse, the others at table began to drift away, first Russell, clearly seeking out more suitable companionship where drink flowed unencumbered by dialogue. Then Jane and Sarah took their leave with a nod to Marianne as though to remind her that in London, in the days of their Grand Salon, when the men spoke politics, the women departed to private chambers.

Marianne returned their nod but held her seat. Then only four remained, Thomas and William, their chairs drawn close together at the far end of the table, the claret passing freely between them, and Jenny and Marianne at the other. Jenny clearly was waiting for permission to leave. Marianne granted it with a whispered, "Run along, Jenny, if you wish. You must be tired."

"Shall I see you to bed?" Jenny whispered thoughtfully.

Marianne shook her head. "I can manage. Go along now."

As Jenny left the table, neither man so much as looked up, both totally unaware that with the exception of Marianne they were now alone.

She leaned back in her chair, enjoying the moment, listening to the once bitter enemies rail at each other in heated though friendly discourse. She found herself studying first one, then the other, their differences, which were not nearly so great as their similarities, both well-constructed men, Thomas, the larger, more rugged, peculiarly less polished in spite of his high birth, William, his fine mind partially dulled by the crucible he had endured, looking physically diminished by the absence of his arm, certainly not the same confident, self-assured man she'd known in London, but still sensitive, and now suffering from the failure of his philosophy that one man can make a difference in any enterprise.

As she listened to the debate, this seemed to be the main thrust of their differences, William pleading emptily for the importance of one man; Thomas rather cynically placing full responsibility on something he called "movements of history" against which one man was impotent.

Quietly recording it all, Marianne's eyes moved from one face to the other, loving both in different ways, wishing with bemused irony that nature had seen fit to combine both men in the skin of one man. After one speech during which William had waxed particularly eloquent concerning justice, Thomas smiled indulgently and remarked, "Too much virtue, too often proclaimed, my friend, can become a bore, a smokescreen as it were to conceal the true acts of so-called virtuous men." Again he leaned forward and dragged his chair after him, less than a foot separating the two men now. "For example," he went on, as though about to make a point. "Tell me of Robespierre's suicide. What became of his virtue when he lifted the pistol and—"

William interjected strongly. "Oh, you're wrong, Eden. Robespierre did not commit suicide. I can attest to it."

As once again the discourse shot forward, Marianne closed her eyes, her hands resting against her baby, who seemed to have grown quiet. The small of her back ached from the awesome weight. She considered retiring, having convinced herself the Revolution would be under discussion until the early hours of the morning. But the thought of climbing the three flights of stairs, unaided, discouraged her. Perhaps she should have had Jenny wait. As the pain in her back persisted, she shifted in the chair in an attempt to straighten her spine. She felt peculiarly breathless, unable to draw enough air into her lungs.

Still the men talked on, apparently impervious to her. Perhaps she should try to navigate the stairs. The discomfort was increasing, her lungs crying for air that she could not give them. Perhaps she would encounter a steward or a serving maid in the corridor who would be kind enough to assist her. It wasn't that far and the pain not that severe. It had been worse this afternoon. All that plagued her now was the ache in her back and this strange breathlessness.

Slowly she moved forward to the edge of the chair so as not to disturb the two men at the end of the table. Placing her palms flat on the table for maximum support, she pushed forward. Suddenly she felt a single pain, as sharp as any she'd ever felt before. Beneath her gown she felt a rush of warm water. Still clinging to the table in a half-raised position, she managed one cry, "Thomas!" The last thing she saw was his surprised face, looking up at her, his mouth opened in speech, the expression in his eyes sending a chill through her as he shouted in what sounded like anger, "No! Not yet. I beg you—"

As she slipped to her knees, she heard chairs scraping, heard both men running toward her. But beyond that she saw nothing and was conscious of nothing except the pain and Thomas' pale face grieving over her, the look of anger still in his eyes as though somehow she had inconvenienced him.

Off in the distance, she heard a man shouting for Jenny. In those long moments when her vision cleared, she found herself on the floor, half beneath the table, William bent over her in concern, Thomas continuing to stare down on her, the look of anger gone now, replaced by something else. Surely not regret, though his mouth was partially open, his face drained of all color, as repeatedly he sought William's reassurance, "It's not coming, is it?" he begged. "It's not due for over a month. Is this merely—"

Jenny was bending over her, asking foolish questions which she could not answer, her attention, what little she could muster, still focused on Thomas. She felt irritated by his curious stubbornness to accept the fact that birth was imminent. Had she so totally misunderstood him? She had thought he had wanted the child as much as she.

Fresh waves of pain consumed her and she was conscious of nothing but the upheaval within her, a flurry of footsteps, hands lifting her.

Through it all she could make out nothing but a man's voice stridently protesting.

A bastard!

The word had haunted Thomas throughout Marianne's confinement. Now, during the long agonizing days of her labor, the word surfaced in his mind with such terrifying regularity that the corridor outside her chamber where he paced became a Gethsemane.

A bastard!

Repeatedly he tried to enter her chambers and repeatedly a solid phalanx of women kept him out. When he thought he could endure no more, he took refuge in the chapel where, on his knees in an attempt at prayer, the word continuously assaulted his mind.

A bastard!

His firstborn, no line of succession. To add to his torture was his last glimpse of Marianne as they had carried her from table up to her chambers, panting and perspiring, a countenance pitiful to behold.

Now, on the third day, on his knees before the carved altarpiece, the sound of her screams still resounding in his ears, he buried his face in his hands and wept. He was deserving of no mercy, so why bother asking for it? How proud he had been of the staged marriage! What a coup! Then, when indeed she had become his wife in every sense save the legal one, he'd lacked the courage to inform her of the deception for fear of losing her.

Prostrate on the floor before the altar, he rubbed his eyes, trying to stop the flow of tears. His hand brushed across the stubble of beard. He felt weak, yet he could not take food or drink, had taken neither for three days as the attention of the entire castle focused on the upper chamber and the woman enduring agony in order to bring forth—

A bastard!

Suddenly he ground his forehead into the cold stone floor. Her labor was going poorly. Jenny had told him that. Her small stature made her ill-equipped for birth. Her suffering was acute and apparently there was nothing anyone could do but wait and watch. She had endured with admirable courage until today when the screams had started again.

Hearing them in memory, a thought occurred to him.

What if she were to die? He stared unseeing at the altar-piece, his vision distorted by the sideward angle, Christ on the cross, the spikes piercing His feet and hands, yet on His face a benign, almost tranquil expression.

Angrily Thomas averted his face. The poet-woodcarver had lied. One did not endure intense suffering with tranquility. One railed against it, resisted it, sought ways to defy it, but one did not smile at it.

From a distance, he heard the sound of agony again, heard footsteps running, an old woman crying for assistance. Quickly he sat up and clamped his hands over his ears. It could not go on much longer. As the distant cries increased, he laced both arms over his head as though to ward off physical blows and wept openly.

A bastard! The word was darkly etched upon his conscience. Of course if the child survived and was female, it would not matter so much. But a son—

He heard footsteps at the back of the chapel. Without looking up, he heard William Pitch's voice, soothing, "Milord, Jenny tells me it will be over soon. You must look to yourself. Your wife will need you to comfort her. Won't you come with me?"

With his head down, Thomas was aware of the man standing directly before him. Suddenly his self-hatred consumed him. He raised a ravaged face to William. His voice was almost contemptuous. "The lady is not my wife, sir, and she is at present enduring to bring forth a bastard."

In spite of the dim light of the chapel he saw clearly the stunned disbelief on William's face. "But—there was a ceremony," he stammered, "or so I heard in London. At Fonthill."

Thomas lifted his head as though in a last degrading agony. "A sham, sir, a fake ceremony, performed at my insistence by an Italian itinerant."

Pitch's face was before him like a huge condemning moon, disbelief giving way to anger, anger to outrage. Thomas watched him, in a spasm of expectation, watched hopefully the man's good left arm trembling at his side, still watching as Pitch stammered his outrage, the hand lifting now, high into the air, Thomas never taking his eyes off it, the fingers curling into a fist, the blow delivered at last to the side of Thomas' head, a stunning blow which sent him reeling backward, causing him to strike his forehead on the iron grillwork which separated the smiling Christ from suffering humanity.

Thomas lay stunned, tasting blood. His forehead was burning. Yet he experienced the peace of punishment and cursed the Revolution that had taken the man's good right arm and prevented him from beating him senseless.

Then he heard nothing except angry retreating footsteps, the ringing in his ears amplified though still inadequate to cancel out the piercing screams of the woman who had yet to be told that for all her great effort, she was bringing forth a bastard.

On the evening of the fourth day, with Jenny presiding over the canal of birth, and five women including Jane, Sarah, and Dolly Wisdom holding Marianne rigidly down on her bed, she pushed a son from her womb, an indignant, angry, squawling infant whose lung power spoke of persistent life in spite of the difficult birth.

If there was no question concerning the son's survival, there was considerable question concerning Marianne's as, at the exact moment of birth, she went limp upon the bed, the five women stepping quickly back as they no longer had anything to restrain.

Quickly Jenny cut and tied the cord and thrust the screaming infant into Sarah's arms, then pushed the gaping women aside and held a potion of ammonia near Marianne's face. Slowly she stirred, her eyes opening, breath resuming, though labored. Checking once again on the well-being of the infant, Jenny gave the women orders for cleaning up and, bone-tired and still trembling from the long ordeal, the old woman went in search of Lord Eden.

She found him in the chapel, where she knew he'd passed the last four days. Stopping at the door and spying his bent, prostrate figure, she shook her head, certain after years of presiding over the ritual of birth that the ordeal was more difficult for men than for women.

Still, it was over for both of them and she had joyful news which would shortly cancel any lasting effects of agony. "Milord," she whispered, striving for his attention.

When he did not stir from his crouched position in the front pew, she walked to his side. "Milord," she spoke again, then stopped short, seeing his face, as ravaged and

as bloodstained as the one she'd just left. There appeared
to be a small wound on his forehead.

She knelt beside him, confident that her news would
revive him. "Milord, you have a son, a beautiful child with
fair hair and dark eyes. Won't you come with me? Your
wife is well but spent. She would—"

He stirred. The news, instead of bringing him comfort,
only seemed to add to his distress. Sharply he arose from
the pew with such force that he knocked her backward.
As he ran from the chapel, she cried after him, "Milord,
wait—"

But he didn't wait. As Jenny struggled to recover from
the blow which he'd loosed upon her, she heard his footsteps, not moving toward his wife's chambers, but instead
taking the stairs downward with great speed.

She ran out into the corridor, hearing three floors below
a slamming of doors, the alarmed cry of one of the stewards. Running to a slit window, she saw him stumbling
across the inner courtyard, heading toward the stables.

Confused, she clung to the window at a loss to explain his
behavior. Had he understood what she had said? In her
own weary excitement, had she somehow failed to make
the message clear, to convince him that the danger was
over, that all was well?

Suddenly she saw a horse dart from the stable, a rider
clinging to its back, a groom running uselessly after it, the
horse and rider accelerating to top speed, approaching the
closed grillwork of the gate as though impervious to the
fact that impalement was imminent.

She muffled a scream as, at the last second, the guards
drew up the grille. Without breaking speed, the horse and
rider clattered beneath the gate and disappeared into the
night.

She stood a moment longer, watching the confusion of
torches in the courtyard below as the watchmen on the
walls hurried to the gate, apparently in search of an explanation.

Behind her she heard Jane's urgent voice, "You'd better
come, Jenny," she begged. "There's still bleeding. We can't
stop it."

Jenny closed her eyes. She understood exactly nothing.
"Jenny, please!" Jane urged. "Come quick, she's—"

Jenny drew a deep breath, straightened her shoulders,

and looked about her. Men! She would never understand them. A useless breed, really, not fit to rule the world. Cowardly! Self-important! Selfish! Did his Lordship really think that his escape into the night would change anything here? The facts remained that now he had a son and heir, and perhaps a dying wife.

With the characteristic strength of one who was needed to keep things going, she proceeded down the corridor with Jane following behind her, her head erect, ready to meet and cope with the next ordeal.

Whatever that may be.

Two weeks after the difficult birth, Marianne was still abed, weak from loss of blood, her physical condition made worse by the anxiety she suffered over Thomas's mysterious disappearance.

On a bright September morning, as Jenny bathed her, she felt a surge of annoyance, more than the mere helplessness and isolation of an invalid. Why was it that Jenny refused to look at her, and why was it that no one but Jenny ever came to her room? Repeatedly she'd asked for William's company, and had been denied it. She knew that William was still in the castle, for Jane had told her so, in the days when Jane had visited her, although that had been over a week ago.

It had been the same length of time since she had seen Sarah, who used to take such delight in bathing her son and placing him on her nipple. And Dolly and all the rest of them, where were they? And why did no one bring her news of the search parties which reportedly were out looking for Thomas? And why did her son still lie in his crib, unnamed, unchristened? And when would she regain enough strength simply to lift her hand without it requiring major effort? And—and this question hurt the most—where was Thomas? Why had he deserted her?

Suddenly annoyed by Jenny's fluttering attentions, Marianne found enough strength to hurl the small washbasin across the room. As Jenny stepped back, washcloth in hand, Marianne saw a mixed expression on her face, anguish, then pity, then the most annoying of all, understanding.

Embarrassed by her childish behavior, and unable to

control her emotions, Marianne turned her face to the pillow and wept. "I'm—sorry, Jenny."

Then Jenny was there, holding her, smoothing back her hair, telling her again as she had told her every day for the last two weeks about the peculiarities of men and their responses to childbirth, the frustration of their helplessness, how she'd seen many men run away, and every one of them had returned.

Once, several days ago, when Marianne had been too weak to lift her head, she'd been willing, even eager, to believe it.

Not now. Thomas was no ordinary man, no fisherman from Mortemouth or tenant of Eden Point. He was Lord Eden, Peer of the Realm, in need of an heir and she had given him one. Then why?

For a few minutes, Marianne let Jenny talk, let her believe that her words of comfort were being received and understood. But when she released her to the pillow again, Marianne felt a death of her spirit as acutely as she'd ever felt it before.

As though in an attempt to revive that obviously flagging spirit, Jenny placed the baby in her arms. Marianne bared her breast and gave him her nipple, and as the child began hungrily to suck, she closed her eyes to the sensation, which was not unpleasurable, her loneliness mounting until she was no longer able to hold back the tears.

It was late that evening when she was awakened out of a light sleep by a loud disturbance in the corridor outside her door. Several women were protesting something, their protests apparently falling on deaf ears.

She held still in the bed. Some instinct told her that this was not Jenny approaching. At the exact instant she turned her head on the pillow, the door burst open.

Admittedly the room was dimly lit, only two lamps burning. Still, it wasn't the lack of illumination that hampered her recognition. It was the man himself, or more accurately the condition of the man.

As he came to a sudden halt in the doorway, she saw Jenny hovering alarmed outside. "Milord," Jenny begged, "Cleanse yourself first. I beg you."

Without looking to the right or to the left, Thomas reached out for the door and slammed it behind him, isolating himself in the room with her.

At first she thought he was drunk. As he continued to stand before the door, unmoving, she decided he was ill as well, and incredibly filthy, his eyes glittering strangely from behind a growth of several weeks' beard, his clothes scarcely recognizable and foul-smelling, his hair tangled and unkempt.

"Thomas?" she ventured weakly, raising herself on one elbow, bewildered by his strange condition, yet thanking God that he had safely returned.

He continued to stare at her, his eyes swollen from lack of sleep, his face scratched as though he'd run through brambles. There was a tension about his stillness.

Her alarm increasing, she threw back the covers and swung her legs over the bed. "Milord, please," she murmured. "Come closer so that I—"

"Keep your place, lady," he ordered. His voice was as changed as his appearance, without inflection, a ghost voice.

Sitting aside the bed, shivering, trying to understand, she said, "I've missed you. I've been worried. Where were you?"

Suddenly he stirred. His head lifted. The light from the near lamp caught his features. His voice was as cold now, as though she were his enemy. "Lady, I owe you no explanation."

He moved toward her, stopping short of the bed by several feet, but still close enough for her to detect his foul odor, see something in his face that frightened her. She drew back into bed and pulled the covers up. "I want no explanation, milord," she said. "I'm only grateful for your safety."

Suddenly he grew expansive. He looked about the room as though seeing it for the first time. "You live in considerable luxury, lady," he said, "compared to my recent habitation."

"I did not ask for the chamber, milord. You provided me with it."

He pointed a stained finger at her. "But you did not turn it down, did you?"

"For fear of offending you, no."

"Offending me?" he parroted.

She watched him closely. Something was terribly wrong. When the light fell just right so that she could see his face, she wished not to see it. When shadows enveloped him, she longed to see more clearly, confident that sight would enhance understanding.

Roughly he dragged a chair across the floor and positioned it near the bed. Wearily he stretched out in it, extending his legs, deliberately raising one dung-encrusted boot for her inspection. "You asked where I've been, lady?" he inquired. "I've been in every barnyard from here to St. Ives. I've ridden three horses to ground and drunk myself senseless every night. I've washed with pigs, slept with horses, dined with gypsies, and smiled at ladies." He pushed back the unruly hair from his eyes. "What do you say to that?"

She said nothing, was capable of saying nothing.

He leaned forward now. "Whores all, madame, under the guise of ladies. Like all females."

"I am not a whore, milord," she whispered. "I am your wife."

"Wife?" Suddenly he leaned back in the chair, a look of agony on his face. "Wife?" he mourned. "Is that what you think?"

She placed a hand over her lips to keep from crying out. "I was led to believe so, milord."

"Then you were misled, lady." He pushed himself from the chair and stood directly over her, one soiled hand on her face, forcing her to look at him. "You said your vows before an Italian itinerant. The ceremony was a sham." He faltered and briefly looked away. "I—had no choice, I thought, I—" When he looked back, his eyes were pleading with her. "Your understanding, lady. Is it too much to—" But before she could answer, his face stiffened. Defenses in place, he repeated, "An Italian itinerant, lady, gone now from the face of this earth."

She closed her eyes, her sense of horror overpowering. "Once, milord," she gasped, "you convinced me of your love."

The infant in the crib on the far side of the bed whimpered. Thomas raised his eyes in that direction as though aware for the first time of the existence of the child. As he stared toward the crib, she cried out. Helpless, she watched him scoop up the child as a bear scoops up a lamb.

"A pretty bastard," he commented. "What do you call him?"

Marianne shook her head, her hands covering her face,

still trying to keep back the sobs, which were dry and burning in her throat.

"No name?" Thomas scolded. "A true bastard then."

He placed the infant back in the crib. The child's whimpering grew into shrieks. Thomas looked down into the crib. "A true complainer as well." He cursed. "The fisherman's blood within him, no doubt."

She watched with a strange listlessness, convinced that she was going mad. There was nothing about the man that she recognized, no angle of his face, no tone of voice. It was as though a stranger had invaded her chambers.

When he started back toward her, she cried out again. Before such a cry, he retreated. In spite of her own terror, she saw pain on his face, a death mask of his own.

Someone was knocking violently on the door. The infant was screaming. He stared at her a moment longer. She thought he might say something else. One hand extended toward her as though beseeching. When he lifted his head, she thought she saw tears on his face. Then, as the knocking and the wailing increased, he grabbed for his jacket, his face covered with the peculiar moisture. "Lady, it's best that I leave you," he said.

He ran from the room and burst through the knot of people outside who'd been aroused by her screams. Someone was asking her questions, but she could neither hear nor understand them, so how could she possibly answer them?

Yet her inner mind was curiously calm and at peace. She had no great pain. But she was wet through with sweat, worn and weary. Greedily she drank down a soothing drink that Jenny held to her mouth.

So it was over. She'd have nothing more to do with it. She was a whore, her child a bastard. She had paid, her account was settled.

She lay back on the pillow and remembered all that had happened. Suddenly she grew restless, her hands fumbled under the folds of linen.

"What is it, Marianne?" Jenny asked, concerned.

What was it? For a moment, Marianne couldn't remember. It had come to her mind that something had to be removed. But she had no possessions on earth anymore. She owned nothing, so what needed to be removed?

Then she remembered. She withdrew a hand from beneath the cover. Her bridal ring. She wore that on her finger still. She drew it off and gazed at it. She shut her eyes and held it out to Jenny.

"What am I to do with this?" Jenny asked. As Marianne did not answer, Jenny added, "Shall I keep it for you?"

Marianne shook her head, her eyes tightly closed.

"He's not in his mind, child. Be patient."

She opened her eyes and looked at the ring where it lay in Jenny's hand. It seemed to her that never before had she understood what it betokened. The life that ring had falsely wed her to, that she had loathed at first, had raged at and defied—nonetheless, she had loved it, joyed in it, both in good days and evil.

The room was clearing. She heard a soft rustle of footsteps. The last clear thought that formed in her mind was that surely God would not abandon her, would not hold her responsible for a covenant made for her without her knowledge.

Three weeks later, taking only the dark blue gown she wore on her back and carrying her infant son in her arms, Marianne passed through the Great Hall and stepped out into the bright September sun of the inner courtyard.

She had said her awkward good-byes, all of them that mattered. Her family had elected to remain in the castle, and why not? She didn't blame them. Never had they enjoyed such plenty and security. Only Jenny was going with her, dear, good Jenny who had gone ahead to clear the air in her father's cottage down in Mortemouth.

In the doorway out to the inner courtyard she stopped short. At the bottom of the steps, she saw William Pitch. Several stewards were standing to one side watching her, their faces mirroring the confusion that had swept through the entire castle over the events of the last few weeks. She nodded politely to them, renewed her grip on her sleeping son, and proceeded down the steps, wishing that William were not there, for she'd said her good-byes to him as well.

Only the night before William had told her that at Lord Eden's request, he was taking up temporary residence in the castle. She'd been a little surprised, but in a way it had been predictable. William's crucible in France had taken a terrible toll. In every conversation she'd had with him, he'd made it clear that he was done with life. All he wanted now was a place of peace and isolation away from pitying eyes and a world without hope or solution.

In spite of his new cynicism, there still was a decency to William, an honor that Thomas would not be beyond exploiting. Marianne knew all too well that under pressure Thomas could be eloquent and most persuasive. What a tale of pity he must have woven for William in an attempt to enlist his aid!

She looked with regret at the brilliant man who once had been the "Mind of London." Now he was reduced to the empty role of go-between, a bearer of messages in a hopeless cause.

She thought that everything had been said. As she drew near the bottom step, he moved toward her. His face looked stern though sad. "This isn't necessary, you know," he began. "Lord Eden says you're welcome here for as long as you wish to stay."

She walked past him a few steps, lowering her head from the sun, unaccustomed to its brilliance. From somewhere in the upper regions of the castle she had the sensation of eyes watching her. She straightened her back and adjusted the swaddling blanket around her son. "I don't want to stay, William," she replied, not unkindly. "Now if you'll excuse me, I must hurry. Jenny can't do everything."

But he merely fell in beside her, keeping pace with her across the courtyard. "What will you do?" he asked, peering closely at her face.

She laughed lightly. "I have a son to raise, William. That should occupy about twenty years of my life." Out of the corner of her eye, she saw the whipping oak and increased her step, head down.

"You can't do it alone," he protested.

"I shan't be alone," she replied. "I have Jenny and all my friends in the village."

"Still it isn't necessary."

"You're welcome there yourself, William, if you choose to stay in Devon. I used to enjoy our long chats."

He hurried in front of her, blocking her path. "Please, Marianne. Lord Eden begs you to reconsider."

She looked at his urgent face and discovered with a pang of regret that she felt nothing for him, felt nothing for anyone except the small bundle in her arms. "Let me pass, William."

But he held his ground, clearly playing his role as go-between. "I spent the evening with Lord Eden," he began. "He said he is suffering deep regret, said it was never his intention for you to leave the castle. He said he wishes that you would—"

"He owes me nothing," she whispered fiercely. "Tell him for me that all I wish now is to be left alone in peace. Tell him further that there was feeling once, deep and genuine, but it's gone now without leaving a trace. Tell him that I have fully grasped my situation, and wish, indeed demand, to face it in my own way."

Quickly she sidestepped him and hurried on toward the gate, where the watchmen looked at her with varying degrees of pity and recognition.

William called after her, "Marianne, wait—"

But she had no intention of waiting. Beyond the second grille was freedom, the magical new beginning, a sun sparkling on the turquoise waters of the channel and the shrill scream of gulls exulting in their free-wheeling antics. She had passed through a crucible and with God's help, she had survived. There was nothing in the name of Eden to threaten or harm her anymore.

As she took the gate running, she saw the watchmen bow to her, a thoughtful gesture generously given and generously received. In her brief though false tenure as Lady Eden, she had made friends. She was not alone and she had nothing to fear.

These thoughts passed through her mind like quicksilver as she approached the headland and the narrow path leading down to Mortemouth. Safe beyond the castle gate, she stopped breathless from her sprint. She drew back the blanket and looked lovingly at her son. A fair, sturdy infant. With her help he would grow to fair, sturdy manhood. What fun they could have together exploring the coves and crannies of North Devon! He was all she wanted, all she needed.

Gathering him close to her breast, she hugged him with

such force that he whimpered, stirred in his blanket, and reached one tiny fist up to her face.

"Why Edward?" Jenny laughed, lifting the child from his bath as Marianne put the finishing touches to his christening gown.

"Why not?" replied Marianne, a bit defensively. "Two of our greatest monarchs were Edwards."

"With one rotten apple in between," commented Jenny. As she placed the child, wriggling and fat at three months, on clean linen, she mused, "He doesn't even look very much like an Edward."

Then it was Marianne's turn to laugh. "And how does an Edward look?" she asked, taking over the drying process. "In my opinion, he could be anything he wants to be." Slowly she wrapped the child and carried him to her father's old chair. She drew back the top of her dress and gave him her breast, still full with milk. As the child sucked contentedly, she felt that contentment spread, and looked about her, pleased.

In three short months she and Jenny had worked wonders in the small cottage. She found the low-ceilinged rooms comforting after the vast emptiness of Eden Castle. The walls were freshly whitewashed, neat white curtains hung at the windows. Before December's cold had set in, she and Jenny had turned the garden for spring planting. Jenny had commenced tutoring again, her true love, and while her ten students could pay little, the grateful parents always seemed able to manage a wagonload of firewood, a tub of fresh butter, a line of herring, or a side of pork.

They were surviving, not easily, but come spring with the garden and a few chickens of their own, they could manage very well. What few hardships they had to endure were made palatable in the kindness of the villagers, as, with one accord they had welcomed Marianne and her son back into their midst.

In the narrow kitchen, she heard Jenny emptying the bathwater. In a rush of affection, Marianne wondered what she would do without the woman. Her expert eye saw everything, not only the domestic needs of the cottage, but saw deeper, saw those occasions when Marianne would lapse into a dark depression, thinking on all that had happened, and how helpless she was to alter any of it.

On these occasions, Jenny would lovingly revive her with suggestions for walks to the quay, searching for shells on the beach, taking the child with them and introducing him to the feel of salt spray, the omnipresent and comforting roar of the ocean.

As Jenny appeared in the low doorway, drying her hands on her apron, Marianne studied her. "Jenny," she said, and held out her hand.

Jenny looked mystified at her, though she finished drying her hands and took Marianne's. Neither woman spoke, the light of understanding dawning in Jenny's face. She smiled. "The Lord looks after us," she said. "Our mutual thanks should be to Him."

"They are," said Marianne, "but I will reserve for all time an exceptionally tender place for you."

Jenny's eyes were fastened on Marianne. "You are the daughter I never had," she whispered. "I could more easily abandon my own life than I could abandon you."

Gently she reached over to kiss Marianne on the forehead. Quickly Marianne's arms went around her neck. Even though she was locked in a close and reciprocal embrace, Marianne's thoughts moved heavily to the top of Eden Point, to the pain of betrayal.

Abruptly Jenny disengaged herself and stood back, all business. "We'd best hurry. Parson Branscombe said eight o'clock. We must get this Edward named in the eyes of God."

Marianne glanced down at her son. "He's hungry." She smiled. "You run along and dress. It won't take me long."

As Jenny disappeared into Hartlow's old bedroom, now her own, Marianne leaned back in the chair, closing her eyes against the slight discomfort of her son, drawing on her nipple. The Lord looks after us, Jenny had said. Marianne smiled wryly. It seemed to her that once or twice the Lord had closed His eyes. What was ahead for her, for her bastard son? Jenny was old. She worked hard. There was a limit to physical endurance. How many times had William Pitch been sent down the cliff with a packet of guineas? She'd lost count, but as many times she'd sent him right back up again. She doubted seriously if Thomas' conscience was bothering him, for she knew, based on experience, that he had none, was blessedly bereft of that single sense which so sternly dictates the actions and responses of most people.

Still, the child was growing. What was to become of him? A fisherman in Mortemouth? One of the rough jacks who inhabited The Hanging Man pub? She didn't know, had no idea.

"Come along," she whispered to her son. "Surely you've had enough." A few minutes later the child released her breast and smacked contentedly, his dark eyes, Eden eyes unfortunately, growing heavy with sleep.

Marianne placed him on the couch and dried her breast. She dressed him in the christening gown of white muslin, with a small lace trim taken from Jenny's best shawl. Then she dressed herself in brown muslin which old Mrs. Malvina had given her in exchange for teaching her granddaughter to write her name.

At a quarter to eight, both women left the cottage, inadequately clothed in their shawls against the biting cold December evening. They hurried down the narrow cobblestones, heading toward the Chapel of the Fishermen, a plain one-room stone structure, built in the last century by the fishermen of Mortemouth.

There, at ten minutes after eight, in the presence of a dozen or so villagers, with Parson Branscombe presiding in his best black coat, without benefit to godparents, the child was christened Edward Hartlow Eden.

In the registry of Baptisms of the parish, these words were written:

27 August, 1796
Edward Hartlow Eden, son of
Thomas Eden, Earl of Eden, by
Marianne Locke.

At the conclusion of the brief ceremony, the villagers gathered around to admire the child. There were thoughtful gifts; a warm blanket, freshly washed hand-me-downs from other children now grown too large to wear them, and a delightful stuffed toy puppy.

Marianne received them all with gratitude, embracing the women, allowing the men with their rough hands to self-consciously tweak the child beneath his chin.

The fellowship at the front of the chapel was close and

warm, the candlelight playing off the ruddy faces of the fishermen, Parson Branscombe beaming as though he'd something to do with it.

At one point, when old Mrs. Malvina insisted upon holding the baby, Marianne released him to her and turned away to straighten herself and try to hide the spreading milk stain on her dress. At that moment she saw movement at the rear of the small chapel, in a secluded corner on the back pew where no light fell. She squinted her eyes into the darkness, trying to see who it was who was holding back from the warmth at the front of the room.

Feeling that no one should be excluded on this joyous occasion, she called out, "Won't you join us? It's warm here."

Suddenly the black-hooded figure stood. He held his position for a moment, then quickly slipped out of the door, closing it behind him. The sharp draft made the candles flutter. Marianne stared at the empty darkness at the back of the room. Her heart accelerated.

Jenny was at her side, whispering, "Who was it?"

Slowly Marianne shook her head. "I don't know." She stared a moment longer, her sense of disquiet increasing. She remembered that terrifying night when Thomas had returned and entered her chambers, remembered how he had crushed the boy to him. Behind her, her son was crying at being passed from hand to hand. Urgently she whispered to Jenny, "We must go home now."

Taking their leave as gracefully as possible, Jenny gathered up the small gifts, Marianne retrieved her son and, staying close together, they hurried back through the night toward the safety of their cottage.

The dark evening was all about them, the sea was calm. Constantly Marianne turned her head, searching out each moving shadow, breaking finally into a run at the sight of the cottage itself, windows rosy with the promise of the fire they'd left burning in the fireplace.

Once inside, Marianne locked and bolted the door. Jenny sensed her apprehension. "Do you think it was——"

Marianne shook her head. "I don't know."

The wind was increasing, rattling at the windows. Quickly Jenny took the baby from her and led her to a chair near the fireplace. "You mustn't imagine things," she soothed. "Here, now, Edward's asleep. Let's do the same."

But as she bent to put him in the crib, Marianne sharply protested, "No! Give him to me."

As Jenny did as she was told, Marianne took her son and clasped him to her. Long after Jenny had retired, Marianne continued to sit before the fire, rocking Edward back and forth, shivering in spite of the heat from the blazing logs.

Christmas morning dawned clear and cold, a light scattering of snow over Mortemouth. They had no tree, no gifts, but from somewhere Jenny had begged, borrowed or stolen—Marianne was never quite sure which—a plump tender chicken, and that was now stewing in a pot on the stove, filling the cottage with a delicious odor.

As Jenny puttered about in the kitchen, promising additional surprises, Marianne knelt on the floor by the fire, Edward on his blanket before her. She exulted in his beauty, the way he was filling out. He had a rich bawling voice and clearly a will of his own, and Marianne delighted in both, sensing that perhaps the child was becoming for her a passion and power that should be checked, but she refused to check it.

As he cooed and giggled and kicked his chubby legs in the air, she saw him growing up healthy and strong-willed and intelligent and handsome. "He *will* be good-looking, Jenny, don't you think?" she called out, burying her face in the child's round belly, giggling with him.

Jenny, a dripping spoon in hand, stuck her head around the corner of the kitchen, entering into the spirit of the occasion. "He will leave a wake of broken hearts, I promise you," she said, grinning.

Sobered, Marianne looked up. "I'm not certain I want him to do that." Almost breathlessly, she asked, "Jenny, will you teach him everything you know? He must be schooled. He must be intelligent. I don't want him to stay in Mortemouth."

Jenny laughed. "Shall we start now? You come peel the spuds and I'll give him his figures."

For a moment, both women stared down on the child. He *was* beautiful with his golden hair and dark eyes, evincing even at that tender age a charm of manner as he grinned back at the women, as though pleased with himself.

"Good Lord," grumbled Jenny, returning to the kitchen. "You'd think you were the only mother in the world."

"I am," Marianne smiled, lifting the baby and kissing him. She pressed his smooth face to hers. It felt cool as moonlight, and when she released him her head swam and she was torn between wanting to see him grown and wanting to keep him forever a babe, totally dependent upon her.

Shortly before noon, there was a knock at the door. Marianne stretched out on the blanket with Edward, looked over her shoulder. As Jenny started to the door, Marianne sat up, "See who it is first."

Jenny peered out of the near window, then grinned, "It's Mr. Pitch."

Cautiously Marianne sat up. "Is he alone?"

Jenny looked again. "As far as I can tell."

She opened the door. For a moment, blinded by sunlight, Marianne saw nothing but the outline of the man himself. She went to him and kissed him lightly on the cheek. "Happy Christmas Day, William," she smiled.

He returned her kiss. His face was ruddy with cold, a residue of snow on his boots. "The Devon cold is worse than London." He shivered. "Do you remember there, on occasion, we'd have roses on Christmas Day?"

She remembered. "Come in," she urged, pleased to see him, but concerned with the draft rushing across the floor toward the baby.

As Jenny went to close the door, William stepped back out onto the stoop. Grinning like Father Christmas, he dragged a heavy sled across the threshold. "What's Christmas without gifts?" He smiled. Awkwardly, with his good arm he continued to jockey the bulging sled laden with gifts toward the center of the room.

"Good Lord," Jenny gasped, closing the door, then hurrying back for a closer examination of the various riches. "Look! A goose," she exclaimed, lifting a plucked leg. "And a plum pudding!" Grinning, she lifted the wrapped cake and studied it lovingly. "Dolly's, I bet. She can make them fit for angels."

During this time, Marianne had scooped up the baby and wrapped his blanket around him as protection against the chill. Quietly she sat in the chair and watched both of

them as they pored over the various gifts, foodstuffs for
the most part, luxuries unheard of in the village of Mortemouth. She watched as long as she could, then decided she
had better speak. "We can't accept any of it, William. You
know that. I'm sorry for troubling you, but you must take
them back."

A stunned silence filled the room as she took on the
burden of both William's and Jenny's staring eyes. "For
heaven's sake, why?" Jenny demanded. "I for one know
that Lord Eden had nothing to do with this plum pudding.
This came from Dolly, and—"

"It doesn't matter," Marianne said. "They must all go
back."

William stepped forward. "It's only food, and a few
baubles for him."

"They must go back," she repeated a third time, wanting to close the conversation.

Sternly Jenny scolded her. "You're being very proud
and foolish, Marianne."

Angrily Marianne replied. "I'm doing what I must do
and if you can't understand, I'm sorry."

Jenny stared at her, then mournfully placed the plum
pudding back on the sled and retreated to the kitchen.

Marianne lowered her head, regretful that she'd spoken
so sharply. William was still there, trying to play the
diplomat. He laughed. "If you knew the trouble I had
getting it down the cliff, you wouldn't send it back."

"I'm sorry," she said, "but I didn't ask for it and I don't
need it."

Awkwardly, William shook off his cape and adjusted a
chair close beside hers. "And what about him?" he asked,
motioning toward the baby.

Marianne drew back the blanket and revealed her plump
pink child. "Does he look neglected, William?" She
smiled. "Does he really look as though he needs anything?"

William shook his head. The conversation died. For several long moments he stared into the fire. "I know someone who *does* need something," he said, finally.

Marianne looked at him, clearly understanding the in-
nuendo of his words. The Christmas day which had
dawned with such simple promise turned bleak. Abruptly
she stood up and walked a few steps beyond the fire.
"William, I long for news of my family. If you've come to

tell me about my father, or Dolly, or Jane, you're most welcome to stay. But—"

He followed after her. "You must hear me out, Marianne," he begged. "He is suffering intensely."

"He enjoys suffering."

"Not this kind. He walks about late at night and returns and sits alone in your chamber beside your bed. He talks to the empty room on occasion. I know. I've heard him. He sees no one, answers no correspondence. He's grown quite pale and suffers intensely from the cold."

She stared incredulously at him. "You loathed him once, William. How has he seduced you?"

He stood still, his hand rubbing the stump of his arm. "He hasn't seduced me, Marianne. He has over the last few months revealed large portions of himself to me. I've seen every angle and shade and degree of remorse known to man. I admit, he has blundered brutally and ruthlessly. He has deceived and contrived and inflicted enormous pain. But he has paid, is paying more than either of us can imagine."

She listened to his heartfelt plea. Off in the kitchen, she heard a strained silence, Jenny clearly eavesdropping.

"Please," William begged softly. "He wants an audience with you. He will come here if you give him permission."

Then she was furious. "He wants an audience?" she repeated, amazed. "There will be no audience, not in this life or the next. You may convey that message to him. There—will—be—no—audience!" she repeated, stammering in her rage, "save when I am in my grave and helpless to protest it."

Bewildered, William stepped toward her as though to comfort.

"No," she warned. "Don't come near me."

"Marianne, please—"

"I beg you leave us alone," she said, lifting her head.

When he refused to obey, she took the child and left the room, retreated into her back bedroom where she closed and bolted the door.

Beyond, she heard the murmur of voices as apparently Jenny reappeared. She listened closely, but couldn't hear what they were saying. It didn't matter. Her son was hungry. She sat on the edge of the bed and as Edward nursed, she heard the front door open, heard the sled being dragged out. The cottage grew silent. She looked out the back window. As her eyes grew accustomed to tears, she made out the dim sheen of the withered snow-covered leaves on the path, and the faint light from the sky above the tree tops.

The roll of waves on the strand below the cottage came to her in dull heavy sighs.

On countless occasions that winter, she saw Thomas Eden, hooded, his face obscured, standing a distance away, watching the cottage. When spring came, she saw him even more frequently when she was in the garden with her son, saw him standing across the cobblestones at the edge of the path, always watching, just watching her in a kind of stubborn silence. Each time she saw him, she quickly gathered Edward to her and whisked him into the cottage, where she locked and bolted both doors and did not go outside again until he disappeared.

From December to March, she was visited weekly by someone from the castle, mostly William, but on occasion Jane and Sarah. No matter how skillfully they contrived to make the visits innocent, sooner or later, each in his own way revealed his true role as messenger, filling her ear and bespoiling the air with news of the man she loathed.

In time, and in a rather hard way, she made it clear to all that no one would be welcomed in the cottage so long as a certain name passed his or her lips. By April, the weekly treks down the side of the cliff had stopped altogether, and she now enjoyed an isolation not quite as splendid as she'd hoped it would be.

As always, she found her only comfort in her son, who sat beside her in a blaze of sunlight as she pulled weeds from the long rows of carrots and cabbages in the back garden, laughing at her as she tickled him beneath the chin with a delicate frond of fern, listening to her intently as though he understood every word she spoke lovingly to him. He was growing quite sturdy, reaching out with eager fists to grab handfuls of her long hair, the exact color of his own.

In spite of the ban on the mention of Thomas Eden's name, she still heard of him from various sources, from the gossiping women down on the quay cleaning fish.

"Ready for Bedlam, or so I hear," announced an old woman as, one day, Marianne passed close with Edward, taking the air.

And another, "Jack Spade told my man that Lord Eden parades about in a bedsheet, and the only wagon permitted through the gate is the weekly load of spirits from Exeter."

Quietly Marianne propped her son up on the stone wall, gazing out to sea, listening.

"Jack Spade says it's terrible," another went on. "One night the stewards found him naked at the gate. It took six men to lock him in his chambers."

As the tongues clacked, Marianne bent her head low over her son, feeling ill. Quickly she hurried around the wall and onto the beach. There she placed Edward on clean sand and walked a distance away to the water's edge, to clear her head of the gossip.

Behind her she heard Edward whimpering. Quickly she returned and went down on her knees and lifted the little boy, still crying because sand had spoiled the good bun she had given him for sitting quietly.

Abruptly she was aware of the woman staring at her over the wall. Their faces seemed to say, "There's Thomas Eden's whore and bastard son."

She knelt, frightened for a moment. Then she took the boy in her arms and hurried toward the safety of her cottage, ran quickly, stumbling over the grass tussocks and heaps of earth, anger flaming within her, wondering if she would have to scour the world for a simple place of peace.

It was on a hot August morning and she was working in the garden when the back door of the cottage burst open and she saw Russell standing before her. This was something different. *He* had never come before. His face was pale and sweat-streaked, his boots half-undone, his shirt opened, as though he'd been roused out of a late sleep.

He'd scarcely paused in the doorway when he started toward her, his breath catching as though he'd run without respite. "Madame," he began with strange formality, "I know you don't trust me and there's little love between us, but Mr. Pitch sent me to inform you that Lord Eden's killing himself. He said not to come back without you."

Hurriedly she turned away. He grabbed her arm. "No,

madame," he said sternly. "You have no choice and little time. He'll be dead within the hour."

She tried to pull free. "News of his death does not concern me, Russell."

He held her rigidly. "No matter what sin you charge him with," he begged, "you must come." He renewed his grip on her arm. "You have the choice, lady," he threatened, "of coming with me civilly or I swear I'll drag you up that cliff." She had no choice. In spite of her fear, she tried to maintain a calm demeanor. "I'll come, sir, but expect no grieving from me."

For a moment she thought he was angry enough to strike her. But instead he seemed to manage an effort of self-control, and used his hand to push her roughly toward the door.

Inside, she saw Jenny, curiously unprotesting of the treatment she was receiving. With sinking spirits, she wondered if that strong alliance had finally broken. Behind her, Russell continued to swear, now urging speed. Quickly she lifted Edward from his crib.

"The child stays," Russell ordered.

"He goes with me," she said, confronting him.

Russell wavered, obviousy caught in indecision. "Then bring him." Again he reached out for her arm and dragged her through the door. He set a fast pace. Marianne stumbled to catch up, Edward crying softly. Jenny following behind.

Not once all the way up the steep path did he release his hold on her arm. It she faltered, he merely dragged her after him. She felt the hem of her skirt catching on brambles, felt the increase of wind as they neared the headlands.

Before them stretched the cobbles which led to the gate. She saw the grilles open, the watchmen curiously absent. Suddenly she halted, tried to pull back. "Russell, please, let me go!"

But he was adamant and again dragged her forward, her arm numb where he grasped it.

Then it came to her, a sound in the silence darkly etched on her memory for all time, a singing sound almost, a sharp whistle rising and falling with a snap.

Through the gate now and he released her, as though he knew she were close enough to the horror to be magnetized by it. She stood alone, except for Edward clinging to her. Before her stretched the inner courtyard, curiously empty, though not emptied. She saw scattered knots of watchmen huddled together near the far wall, saw a few familiar faces near the bottom of the steps leading to the Great Hall, saw William, turned away, recognizable only by the absence of his arm, saw Dolly, weeping, and two or three others.

At times when the wind was behind her, she couldn't hear the sound at all. But now the wind was not behind her and she heard it clearly. She clutched at her son and stepped forward to the center of the courtyard, to the whipping oak, where a man hung bound and bleeding.

She appeared from the rear, seeing first only his bared arms, the tendons pulled taut by the hemp about his wrists. Next she saw his head, fallen backward in his agony, eyes closed, mouth half-opened, a stream of blood spilling from his lips.

The whistling stopped. She was partially aware of another man standing to one side, his breath roaring in her ears, a gruff, untutored voice, defying his manhood with tears.

"Milady," this man sobbed. She turned to see Jack Spade standing beside her, whip in hand curiously gentle tears coursing down his face. "Milady," he wept, trying to brush the tears away. "He—threatened my life, said he'd banish me if I didn't do it." His voice grew strangely thin and clear. "I have a wife and nine children." He stepped forward, sobbing openly, pleading with her. "Where would I go? What would I do?"

Before his bewildered grief, she retreated. Her eyes wandered back to the man on the whipping oak. A choking stench met her, fragments of that other hot August morning when *she* had counted the oceanic distance between one and ten.

"How many did he command?" she heard herself ask and recognized neither the voice nor the question.

"Forty," the weeping man said.

She lifted her head as though she were drowning. Something was breaking within her, yet almost clinically she assessed the torn back with scarcely an inch of flesh left whole. She stepped still closer. His hair was grayer than she remembered it, a heavy beard grew on his chin.

Somewhere there was a child crying. Why didn't someone comfort it?

The pain in her breast increased as she drew nearer the whipping oak. The corpse smell was stronger here. At last someone had taken the crying child from her. The man on the whipping oak stirred, his lips moved.

She watched him a moment longer. Slowly she reached for the knife in the sheaf at Jack Spade's waist With one strong slash she cut the ropes that bound him.

She looked up at those watching her. She spoke calmly. "Take him inside."

Jack Spade lifted him in his arms and bore him away.

For over a week, Thomas knew nothing. There was a world where he was, but it bore no resemblance to anything he had seen or heard before. In a fragment of conscious mind, he thought, "I am dead."

But he wasn't dead, it was merely a dark filled with a darker phantom who now and then forced a warm liquid between his lips, an insistent phantom who would not relent until he'd swallowed. Continuously he had the sensation of smothering, of linen clogging nostrils and mouth. But there was little else, and for the most part he found himself tenanted in quiet surroundings, a peculiar sense of completedness, as though the madness into which he'd quietly slipped over the last few months had at last taken possession of him. He felt profoundly grateful for the release from the custom of sanity.

Then one morning he awakened. His body turned about in search of a position of comfort and found none. With one eye opened, he saw that a good angel of certainty made all the surrounding objects stand still. He was set down in this world in his bedchamber, other objects fixed approximately in their right places, his chest of drawers, his bureau, the windows overlooking the courtyard.

On this morning, he heard the good angel giving orders to someone else in the room. "Open the window," she commanded. "The odor here is enough to kill anyone."

"He soils his linens continuously," an older woman complained.

"He can't help it. Just give us air."

"Shall I cleanse him?"

"No, I'll do it. Leave us."

"But you've not had rest for—"

"I said, leave us."

He opened both eyes. The voice sounded weary and angry. He heard footsteps leaving the room, heard the door close, then heard nothing. He had to see for himself. In a futile effort, he tried to raise his head, and for his efforts, it felt as though he'd fallen backward into flames.

He felt hands removing something from his fiery back and heard her voice again, cold and angry. "You would do well to lie still, Thomas."

Again he had the sensation of smothering, his face lying heavily against the linen. The hands were about his head, turning it sideways so he could breathe.

Then he saw her, not the memory of her which had so tortured him during the months away from her, but saw her solid. He tried to speak and thought he had, but her lack of response suggested otherwise. She seemed to be very busy. She appeared at his side, then disappeared, placing strips of something cool across his back. Twice more he thought he'd spoken her name and twice more there was no response. He considered trying to lift himself again, feeling certain that it would displease her and she would be forced to speak.

But now he found he could not move at all, as though his ribs, knees, shoulder blades, were merely a composite memory. In his increasing frustration and discomfort, he groaned. He felt her hands lifted from his back. For a moment he was unable to tell if she was still standing over him or not. Then she was there again, cleansing his wounds, dipping a blood-red cloth into a bowl of blood-red water.

Weakly he let the world fall topsy-turvy from its orbit and slipped back into the permissible madness.

He knew where he was now and knew that she was here and that her hands, like a rope let down from heaven, would sooner or later draw him up out of his abyss of not-being.

Thomas's recuperation was prolonged and agonizing. The forty lashes plus his already weakened condition brought on by Marianne's absence took a toll of his physical resources. It was the middle of September before he was even capable of sitting up alone, a wobbly, wasted, hollow-eyed specimen.

During his recuperation, although Marianne had attended him almost singlehandedly, they had exchanged few words. Words seemed out of place in the smelly, close chambers. All of the energy was being used up by the pain, the network of open lacerations crisscrossing his back.

To all intent and purposes, she had moved back into the castle. At least she had given Jenny orders to temporarily close the cottage in Mortemouth. Her son Edward had been given over to the corporate and loving care of Sarah, Jenny, and Dolly.

Near the middle of September, she raised Thomas to a sitting position for the first time, hovered over him while his bruised body found its center of balance, then wearily stepped back, assessing him. In spite of the fact that over the difficult weeks she'd tried to discipline her heart against all feeling, she felt a peculiar weakness, as though she were the one recovering. As she watched him feebly arrange his nightshirt over his legs, she sank into the chair behind her that on more than one occasion had served as her bed.

He looked diminished, as though his ordeal had shrunken him, although her back and shoulders ached from weeks of lifting him, with Russell's help, out of the filth of his body waste.

As he tried a sudden movement forward, she saw a grimace of pain on his face and warned, "Sit still, Thomas."

He groaned, yet held his head peculiarly erect, an angle she recognized from her own recovery when the neck muscles seemed to control all the nerve endings across the back. She watched him as he experimented with movement and finally settled into a safe position, back straight, head erect, his legs hanging off the side of the bed. "Marianne?" he murmured, as though to confirm her presence, though he was looking straight at her.

"I'm here, Thomas," she reassured him.

"How long will it take before—"

"Before you're well? Several months I would imagine."

He closed his eyes, both hands gripping the side of the bed, as though in fear of falling.

Alarmed, she sat up. "Would you like to lie back again?"

Slowly he shook his head. "God, no," he muttered. "I feel as though my flesh has grown to this bed. Let me have the satisfaction of sitting upright like a man, at least for a minute."

She nodded and rose from her chair. "I warn you against sharp movement, milord. Now if you'll excuse me, I—"

"Marianne—"

She had scarcely made it around the chair on her way to the door when he stopped her. She looked back. "Milord?"

He appeared embarrassed. "Where—I mean—must you go?"

"I was going to fetch your breakfast," she replied, still moving away.

"I'm not hungry."

"You need the strength that food can give you." She was at the door, her hand on the knob.

His protest grew more urgent. "Let it wait, I beg you."

"I'll only be a minute. It's for your own—"

Suddenly he exploded in limited anger "My God, I said let it wait! Can't you see I must speak with you?"

Feeling anger herself, she responded. "And can't you see we have nothing to say?" The door was opened; she stood on the threshold. "Nothing has changed, milord," she said. "Out of some admittedly misplaced sense of duty, I've nursed you back to a semblance of health. But I don't intend to take up permanent residence here. So we need say nothing to each other. Not now, or ever."

As she left the room, she heard him cry after her. "Marianne, wait!" A few steps further, she heard a crash, the noise clearly decipherable. His weakened legs 'had been called upon to perform in a manner in which they could not. She paused a moment and, hearing nothing further, slowly returned to the room.

It was as she had imagined. He had made it as far as her chair, then collapsed across it, in a sprawled kneeling position, faint strips of blood reappearing on his clean nightshirt. She watched him in his agony, his arms struggling to raise his head and torso, a pitiful sight in the face of which she strengthened her resolve.

As his strainings continued, she warned him coldly, "Milord, you are doing further damage to yourself."

He slumped weakly to the floor in a half-prone position, his brow covered with sweat from his effort. "Then why didn't you let me die?" he whispered.

She held her position several feet away. "It's a senseless way to die."

"But you nursed me."

"I owed you that."

The struggle was on again, his weak arms trying to form a base of support for his back, his knuckles white from grasping the sides of her chair.

She watched him, her face without expression, aware of the spreading blood on his back. "Thomas, you're only—"

"I don't give a damn," he muttered, on his knees, clutching at the chair. He appeared breathless from his efforts, yet his eyes were fixed on her. "I propose a business arrangement," he said, trying to draw a deep breath. "Marriage—"

She stared incredulously down on him. "Another farce? Where this time? Is the Italian itinerant back to mumble over us?"

Painfully he shook his head. "No farce this time, I swear it. Here, with bans published all over England."

Wearily she shook her head. "Thomas, in the name of God, what is the point?"

He looked straight at her. "*You* are."

Feeling it to be an unsafe subject, she moved away from it. "And what's the business arrangement?" she asked.

He looked up at her, the effort showing in his face. "I'll give you possession of Eden Castle and Eden Point," he said simply, yet with conviction.

She continued to stare down on him. She felt terribly hard at that moment and she wanted to stay hard. "You know as well as I do, milord, that under English law I can take possession of nothing, not even myself. I'm a woman."

He looked blankly about at the floor. Again his eyes lifted on a note of hope. "Then our son," he suggested. "I will deed it to him. All of it."

"He's a bastard, milord," she coldly reminded him. "Would you put your property in the hands of a bastard?"

He leaned his forehead against the arm of her chair, his

discomfort clearly increasing. "If it's the only way," he whispered, "that I can keep you."

She watched him, having heard clearly all that he'd said. She felt wary, for if nothing else she knew him for his ability to deceive. From now on, in all areas, she would be cautious for both of them.

Complete possession of Eden Castle and Eden Point, an ancient bastion bearing a name as old as England, rich in grazing and farmland on one side, and the entire Atlantic Ocean on the other.

She turned away, aware that he was closely watching, absorbed more by her coming reply than by his own discomfort. Outside the window she saw the September sun rising higher. From her high angle at the third-floor window, she could not see the floor of the inner courtyard and perhaps that was just as well. There were memories there capable of influencing her. She must keep her own counsel now, as objectively, as clinically, as she had ever done before.

He mumbled something to her, but she merely shook her head and went on pacing quietly, her steps slowly devouring the brilliant blues and reds in the Persian carpet beneath her feet. 'How different,' she thought, 'from the bare worn oak planks of the cottage in Mortemouth.' The overriding question which had so plagued her for the past year concerning what would become of her son had perhaps just been answered. With the deed to Eden Castle and Eden Point clutched in his fist, his future was solved. Now there was another question in her mind, equally as urgent. What would become of her under this new arrangement?

Apparently he sensed the question and although his strength was fast waning, he lifted his head. "Lady," he began, softly, "my desire for conquest is gone. You will find me a gentle and malleable companion. I want nothing from you and will place no demands on you. I swear it."

Slowly she came back to the chair on which, as though totally exhausted, he now rested his arms and head. Such inexplicable meekness was new to her. Ever cautious, it occurred to her that it might be a new role, variations on an old masquerade. Still, there was nothing in the drawn white face that spoke of a farce. Baffled by this strange personality, not quite able to bring herself to believe what he was doing on her behalf, she murmured, "I don't understand, milord."

He lifted his face. Slowly his hand fanned out over the dark blue velour cushions of the chair where she'd passed day and night for the past three weeks, his fingers caressing the indentations left by her body, as though his fingertips had eyes and were now feeding themselves on the memories of her presence. "All I know," he whispered hoarsely, "is that when you are here, my life has purpose and balance, the sun and moon move as they should, and my universe is blest with order." Slowly he lowered his head until the side of his face was resting on the cushion. "But when you are gone," he whispered, "I am without compass, without rudder, or anchor—"

It was over. Apparently he was not able to look up again. The avowal of his terrible need had cost him dearly, and cost her as well. The image of the crumpled man at her feet blurred. This was not the moment for incautious emotion.

"Publish the bans," she demanded, "both here and in London."

He nodded in agreement.

London society, weary of the aggressive little Corsican general and the closeted madness of their monarch, clasped the scandal to their breasts with inordinate fever. This was as it used to be, when the days were fair and the parks were filled with prettily gossiping men and women, and the only topic suitable for good digestion at the breakfast table was the latest peccadillos of Lord This and Lady That.

"I find it impossible to believe," proclaimed one gentleman in The Blue Bell and Crown in Holborn. "Look at this!" He spread out the morning edition of *The London Chronicle* for his friends' inspection. There at the bottom of the second page was a cartoon. A lady with ample bosom was sitting spread-legged, skirts drawn up, on the end of the quay, fishing. Her line was tossed far out into the ocean and, at the end of it, foundering, though clearly hooked, was a large fish with Lord Thomas Eden's face.

"Incredible," murmured the second gentleman. "Clearly a breach in the wall."

First Gentleman—"The old world of order and place is disappearing."

Third Gentleman—"Then there's no hope for any of us. First, anarchy abroad, now anarchy at home. Where will it end?"

Second Gentleman—"Apparently in the marriage prison for Eden. Look at this!" He pushed forward for their inspection and enjoyment a second newspaper, another cartoon, a caricature of Eden Castle with over-drawn turrets and towers, and stretching between two predominant towers was a line of wash presided over by a buxom washmaid who was just hanging Lord Eden out to dry.

First Gentleman—"Surely he has been deceived. The lady has cast a spell on him, perhaps?"

Second Gentleman, derisively—"Lady! Daughter of a Mortemouth fisherman, one of William Pitch's whores, or so I've heard."

First Gentleman—"Scandalous! I wouldn't be surprised if HRH relieves Eden of his titles."

Second Gentleman, still derisive—"HRH doesn't know to unbutton his trousers when he makes water. No, the scandal will be permitted, the outrage endured, another chink in the bulwark of civilization."

First Gentleman—"Blessings to God that Milton is dead."

Second Gentleman, bewildered—"Milton? Where is the connection?"

First Gentleman—"Plain as death. England seems to be in the process of forgetting her precedence of teaching other nations how to live."

Second Gentleman—"Point well taken. Regrettable."

Third Gentleman—"How I mourn for Boswell! What fodder he could make of it!"

First Gentleman—"But I can't understand. Why marriage?"

Second Gentleman—"I hear there's a bastard."

Third Gentleman—"There are always bastards. I repeat the question. Why marriage?"

First Gentleman, still stunned—"God forbid. That ancient and honorable name, sullied for all time."

Third Gentleman—"I trust they enjoy each other's company for they shall know none from decent society."

First Gentleman, nodding—"Marriage bans like a death

warrant, eh? Eden Point will become like the far side of
the moon."

Second Gentleman—"Cut off."

First Gentleman—"Adrift."

Second Gentleman—"No responsible person will go
near it."

Third Gentleman—"Tch, tch."

First Gentleman—"The younger Eden was never of the
same stature as the older one killed in the American War.
Something was missing there, has always been missing."

Second Gentleman—"Lacking the genteel character of a
gentleman."

First Gentleman—"But a whore?"

Third Gentleman—"I hear she's fair."

First Gentleman—"A fair whore."

Second Gentleman, making a quick rhyme—

> A fair whore lives at Eden Point,
> Her bastard son she shall anoint,
> With gold and silver of ancient date,
> With Eden atop her as her mate.

First and Third Gentlemen, laughing, applauding—"Very
good, excellently well done!"

Third Gentleman—"Recall that tonight at Clifton's. It
shall please the company."

Second Gentleman—"I shall compose more, an epic to
the dangerous cunning female and the weak beguiled Lord."

First Gentleman—"It has promise."

Third Gentleman, frowning—"Still, it's a regrettable
business. I make one vow. The tongue shall drop from my
mouth before I address that prostitute as Lady Eden."

First Gentleman—"God forbid, yes."

Second Gentleman—"A fisherman's daughter. Not even
of the middle class, although that would be as offensive."

First Gentleman, shaking his head—"How *did* she do
it?"

Third Gentleman, coyly—"Need you ask? How do the
whores in St. James's Park do it?"

First Gentleman, indignant—"I'm sure I wouldn't know."

Third Gentleman, laughing—"Come now. Obviously
you've forgotten. Shall we go and find one? The three of

us can share. If Lord Eden gets a whore, why not all of us?"

First Gentleman, warming to the idea—"Discussing the lust of others has made me feel lustful."

Second Gentleman—"Then let's depart. If our Ladies have lovers and our Lords have whores, debauchery is the rule of the day."

First Gentleman—"We must be wary though, lest our whore connives and fleeces us like the whore who sits on Eden Point."

Second Gentleman, catching the unintended pun—"That's very good. 'The whore who sits on Eden's point!' "

Third Gentleman, laughing heartily, mindlessly repeating —"Very good indeed. The whore who sits on Eden's point. Save *that* for Clifton's. That's a rare jewel."

Laughing uproariously, the three gentlemen left The Blue Bell and Crown.

The cartoons were still spread across the table near their coffee cups. As a young serving girl came to clear the table, her eye fell on the caricatures. Unable to read, she studied the pictures. She bent closer over the cartoon of the buxom young girl reeling in the smiling Lord.

Her eyes were wistful.

Six months after the bans of marriage had been published in Mortemouth, Exeter, Salisbury, London, Norwich, York, and Newcastle-on-Trent, with almost all of England as witness, on a dreary, rainy March afternoon in 1798, attended by a grim-faced castle staff, in the small, dank, private chapel on the second floor of Eden Castle, Marianne Locke, fisherman's daughter from Mortemouth wed Lord Thomas Eden, fifth Earl and Thirteenth Baron of Eden Point. Again!

The ceremony was performed by Parson Branscombe, the pudgy and fulsome local minister. Now, however, he seemed intimidated by his surroundings and said only what had to be said in a voice so low it could scarcely be heard.

The groom wore a plain black suit, and was wigless and still considerably stooped from his experience on the whipping oak. He spoke his vows, apparently did not hear Parson Branscombe's invitation for him to kiss the bride, signed the parish registry, and left immediately in the company of his manservant, Russell Locke, on a day-long ride across the moors in an attempt to regain his strength and dexterity.

The bride wore a simple dark-blue gown and lingered over the certificate of marriage long after the groom had left, making certain that Branscombe affixed his signature in the proper place, that the seal and date were in order, and insisting finally that the certificate itself be kept in the castle vault along with her son's deed of possession to Eden Point.

After the grim ceremony, which boasted neither flowers nor music, the castle staff went back to their various chores. The bride retrieved her handsome two-year-old son from Jenny and took him to her private apartments on the third floor. There she placed him on the soft furl of Persian carpet. As the child amused himself with the interwoven patterns of flowers and buds, Marianne quietly closed the door leading to Thomas' chambers. She stared at the bolt as though she were considering its reinforcement. Then she backed away, leaving the door closed but not locked.

As the twilight came on, she watched her son. She may not have been his father's wife at the time of his birth, but she intended never to let him forget that she was his mother.

She listened. The castle was so quiet. Where was every-one? Jenny might have come and brought her a cup of tea, or a visit from William would have been pleasant. Apparently poor William had taken up permanent residence in the castle, an isolated place where a one-armed man could hide from the world and his disenchantment with it. Where was Jane, who above all knew the importance of that grim little ceremony performed today under the dripping leaks of the chapel?

But they were all absent, and while she knew where they were, huddled about the great fire in the kitchen, gossiping no doubt and sipping tea, she couldn't quite bring herself to go and join them.

In her loneliness, she looked up through the two windows with their bright lattice-figure curtains. The light of late afternoon fell on the brilliant carpet. Little Edward skipped and danced. She watched him closely, deriving nourishment from him as she had since the day of his birth.

She leaned forward in her chair, her loneliness diminish-ing in his exuberance. What does he know? she wondered.

He knows but little of the world as yet. He knows he is small and is going to be big. He knows perhaps that he is two and will soon be three, but he does not know what is meant by a "year." Nor does he know that everything he views within this chamber and for miles beyond is his.

He skipped toward the fireplace. He seemed to consider the fireplace and white marble screen carved with crusading knights as the most important and dignified thing in the room. Now he pointed at it, as though insistent that she see it as well.

She nodded and laughed with him, and the child laughed back, laughed uncontrollably. He was at the age when laughter was still only an utterance of joy, not an appreciation for the ridiculous. In the warmth of his obvious and nonsensical joy, her loneliness disappeared altogether. She slipped to her hands and knees and started toward him and caught him shrieking and propped him on her stomach and laughed with him, not because he was funny, but because it gave her joy to see his bright face.

The wedding feast was a simple repast of cold sliced beef and country soup served in her chambers, with Thomas in his dressing gown, coughing continuously from his exposure to the cold, damp day.

The most animated their faces ever became was when young Edward was brought in by Jenny to say goodnight to his parents. Almost shyly at first, Thomas approached him, clearly ill at ease. But the boy's irrepressible charm won him over, and at the close of the brief interval, Thomas lifted him in his arms and clasped him to his breast with awkward strength.

The boy was taken to bed. Shortly before midnight, Thomas bade her goodnight and closed the door between their chambers.

On April Fourth, she walked with him along the headlands, the brisk cool spring wind blowing back her long skirts as she kept her eye on the man who kept a step or two ahead of her. And said nothing.

On the afternoon of April Twelfth, she went riding with him across the moors as far as The Hanging Man pub. She was aware of the tenants' curious glances as they passed, her stallion, the color of hot chocolate taking the lead as they raced over the stubbly dormant heather.

At the edge of the moor they stopped for a rest. She gazed eastward toward London. No messengers, no wedding gifts, no expressions of good wishes had come from that direction in all the days since their marriage. As she felt the wind sweep over the bleakness, she lifted her head. "Milord," she said, "I suspect that we are quite alone."

He looked at her as though trying to understand the meaning behind her words. Quickly he reined his horse about and bent to adjust a stirrup. "The condition is nothing new to me, lady," he said. "I have no friends and need no enemies. London is a foreign country to me." He smiled at her. "Be advised. There is your kingdom." He pointed back toward Eden Point. "Come!" he shouted, spurring his horse. "A race!"

As he shot forward, she lingered a moment, looking toward London regretfully, not so much for her sake, but for his.

Then she applied a gentle whip to her horse and started after him.

Later that night she lay abed, one lamp burning on the table, her eye fixed on the closed though not locked door between their chambers. She heard a knock and sat up eagerly. "Milord?" she called out.

Thomas appeared, boots off, shirt undone. He stood in the shadows. "I didn't mean to disturb you, milady," he began.

"You didn't."

"I thought I would look in on you. The ride was hard today."

"I'm well, milord."

He nodded. "Then sleep," he murmured and turned to go.

"Milord?"

He looked back. "Yes?"

She hesitated. "You, too, milord. Sleep well."

Again he nodded and closed the door.

She stared at the spot where he had stood, then sank heavily beneath the bed linens and buried her face in the pillow.

In the days and weeks that followed, she busied herself with the design, execution, and planting of formal gardens on the east side of the castle. Thomas attended and assisted her on occasion, but mostly he rode out with Russell, sometimes being gone the entire day, coming home at night, his cheeks ruddy, his previous good health returning.

They continued to treat each other with merciless politeness and formality, "Milord this, and milady that," their true feelings never surfacing except in those intervals when they were alone with their son. Then apparently neither were capable of resisting the life force within the child, and for a pleasant time they laughed and pursued him and almost forgot about their "business arrangement" and the terms of their new life.

During the early days of June, Lord Eden stayed in her chambers each night until late, the two of them sitting like an old married couple, Marianne working needlepoint, which she loathed, but which kept her mind busy, Thomas filling his pipe. Once or twice she saw him looking at her. Generally, a short time later, he would take an urgent leave, bidding her goodnight and closing though not locking the door between them.

One evening near the middle of July, he performed this same ritual, bade her a late goodnight and left her staring at the closed door. In the throes of deepening despair, Marianne hurled her needlepoint to one side, feeling as though she were locked into a kind of double celibacy. Weary and shivering though the evening was warm, she prepared herself for bed and crawled between empty sheets.

Suddenly behind her, the door burst open. She looked over her shoulder. He was standing in the doorway, his dressing gown half undone, his hair mussed as though he'd recently driven his fingers through it.

"Lady," he commanded, his voice stern, "I have decided that I have rights—rights of the marital bed."

Her heart quickened. Slowly she turned beneath the sheets to face him. "I—don't understand, milord."

"How much clearer need I make it? On my word I swear to live within all the terms of our arrangement save this one."

"But, milord—"

"I apologize in advance for any discomfort I may cause you," he went on, standing over her, "but I find I'm incapable of brotherly coexistence."

"Milord, you said—"

"Damn what I said!" he exploded. "It's gone on long enough."

Meekly she lay upon the bed, her fingers, out of sight, already undoing the ties of her nightdress. As he approached her, she was ready. With remarkable speed, he threw back the coverlet and was on her and then into her with one sharp hungry thrust.

As he busied himself with her breasts, she pressed her head gently backward into the pillow, her eyes closed.

At last, at long last.

Eight months and twenty-three days later, in the middle of an early March snowstorm, with Thomas in constant attendance to the displeasure of the females in the castle, Marianne, after an easy labor, gave birth to a red, wriggly, delicate-faced, dark-haired son.

Throughout the short interval of bearable pain, Thomas never left her side, refusing this time to be banished to the chapel. The moment that Jenny cut the cord, he insisted that he hold the child, still wet with birth blood. With Marianne's agreement, they named him James, after his dead brother buried in America.

Marianne, a little amazed at the ease of it all after the four agonizing days spent bringing Edward into the world, endured the cleansing process and realized somewhat belatedly that now she was the mother of two sons. As old Jenny and Sarah fussed over her, she watched Thomas by the window, still cradling the child, a look of soft quizzical love on his face that she'd never seen him give to Edward. In a spasm of weakness, she turned her head to one side and closed her eyes as though suffering a premonition of the future—the eldest son illegitimate, the second, favored son, the legitimate heir.

As she looked back, she saw Thomas begrudgingly relinquish his son to Jenny for the purposes of cleansing. As his eye fell on her, she tried to dispel her gloomy glimpse of the future. Gentle he sat beside her on the bed and lifted her into his arms.

His expression pleased her. Perhaps their tumultuous past was over. Tenderly she fingered his graying beard, which he had cultivated since his illness. "Milord," she suggested, "perhaps we should create our own England, in lieu of the one that fails to recognize us."

For just an instant a cloud marred his brow. Then he laughed. "I'm in agreement, lady, and perfectly willing. What population shall we aim for? Two dozen sons? Three dozen perhaps, and as many daughters to break the hearts of all those who have spurned us?"

Wearily smiling, she shook her head. "Not tonight, milord. Perhaps later—"

He took her hand and pressed it to his lips. She looked at him closely, feeling the need to hear the truth from him. "Do you have any regrets, Thomas?" he asked.

"None."

"Do you miss your London friends?"

"I have no London friends."

"You did once."

"They were not friends."

"And what of Billy Beckford?"

Slowly, without answering, he released her hand and walked to the window. She watched, feeling a depression in his hesitancy. After several moments when he still had not replied, she turned her face to the pillow, feeling peculiarly weak and weeping. Why had she not been wise enough to see what an empty victory it would be? In their union they had cut themselves off entirely from the rest of the world. Suddenly the years stretched ahead like bleak and endless winters. The castle would be their prison, and beyond that, the larger prison of the moors.

"Are you crying, Marianne?" It was Jenny bending over her with her new son.

Before she could reply, Thomas answered for her from the window. "She's tired, Jenny. Leave her be. I'll take my son."

With her eyes half-closed, Marianne saw the exchange, the bewilderment on Jenny's face as she relinquished the infant to Lord Eden and left the room. Marianne saw Thomas fold back the blanket to examine his placidly sleeping son, saw him carry him to the fire where he sat with him, the loneliness on his face increasing as he leaned his head back and closed his eyes.

The room was silent, a peculiar mood, a tomb bearing new life, the only sound the crackling of the fire.

In the manner of true exiles, their exile was never mentioned again. If they did not exist for the world, then the world did not exist for them. For the next year and a half, they hurled themselves into the rearing of their sons, the dominant, willful Edward always seeming to occupy more of their time and energies than the pale, sweet-natured James.

Their only links with the outside world during this period were the weekly dispatches sent down from London from *The Bloomsbury Gazetteer* for the benefit of William Pitch. While he had not as yet relinquished ownership of the once-flourishing paper, he had long since ceded all editorial duties. And while he never exerted any power, still he insisted that he be "kept informed." Pitch was the only one in the castle who seemed to thrive on the exile. If the rest of the world chose to go mad, that was none of his concern. But while he did not particularly care to witness it, he still had a hunger to hear about it, once a week, through the articulate editorials of the *Gazetteer*.

So, generally late on a Saturday afternoon, a rider would appear at the gate, dusty from the road, and the watchmen would grant him immediate entrance, knowing the pattern by now. The small portfolio of news would be delivered to William's chambers—Jane's now as well, though still a marriage had never taken place. And that evening, at table, William would share with them as much as they cared to hear. During this period the *Gazetteer* was full of one particular name, England's newest hero, the greatest naval commander she had ever produced, one Horatio Nelson.

According to William, Nelson could do no wrong. Every encounter he had with the French, while hopeless appearing on the face of it, led to greater glory and greater victory. However, he was paying a price for his notoriety. The conflict seemed to be devouring him a piece at a time.

According to the weekly dispatches, he was wounded at Calvi, on the Corsican coast, and lost the sight of his right eye. Next he distinguished himself at the Battle of Cape St. Vincent by leading a landing party in an attack on the strongly fortified port of Santa Cruz de Tenerife. The attack was a bold gamble and unlike the others, it failed. The British were driven off with heavy losses and Nelson's right arm was badly mangled up to the elbow. The arm had to be cut off in a crude amputation in a pitching boat, and Nelson was invalided home to England in great pain.

After that, William's fascination with the man became an obsession, as though he were trying to chart the progress of his own life against that of a man who had been similarly mutilated. If every issue of the *Gazetteer* did not carry at least one account of Nelson, William flew into a rage and spoke of returning to the editorship, feeling certain that he was needed again.

But his rages were few, for word of the dramatic man and his exploits seemed to be the only nourishment that all of England required. Soon the messenger was given instructions to bring not only the *Gazetteer*, but every pamphlet, every piece of newsprint he could find which bore the name of Nelson. Through this means of communication, Eden Castle was kept well informed of Napoleon's movements, for where Napoleon's fleet was, Nelson was not far behind. When the French fleet set out on an expedition to conquer Egypt, Nelson was at Toulon. When the French escaped under the cover of a storm, Nelson followed it in a long and exciting pursuit, finally cornering the entire fleet in the Bay of Aboukir and totally destroying it. All the papers proclaimed him "the Hero of the Nile." An adoring nation gave him a large sum of money.

One night at table, Marianne noticed a new gravity to William's manner. He had not lifted his eyes during the entire meal. The *Gazetteer* which had been delivered that afternoon was beside him on the table.

Near the end of the mostly silent meal, Marianne sensed something wrong. "I take it the news is not good, William?"

Thomas looked up from his plate. "No Nelson tonight?" He smiled. "I thought something was missing. My digestive tract scarcely knows how to function on a Saturday evening without news of Nelson to aid it."

When William did not immediately respond, Jane smiled and said, "He's in trouble, milord."

Thomas looked at her in mock surprise. "Nelson in trouble? Impossible. God, perhaps, even St. Peter, but never Nelson."

As Jane smiled again, Marianne turned her attention back to William, who seemed to be brooding unnecessarily. "What is it, William?" she urged. "Tell us. We rely upon you to remind us that we do still inhabit this earth."

Suddenly William stood. With his good arm he pushed

the paper toward Marianne. "Read for yourself," he suggested, "then judge for yourself whether or not you want to inhabit this earth."

Bewildered, Marianne picked up the paper and flattened it on the table. Before she could start to read, William spoke again, his head down. "I will never understand this country," he muttered. "Never! The man has given service beyond any reasonable definition of duty. And yet our noble monarch has the audacity, the nerve, to—"

As his outrage overtook him, he ceased talking and channelled all his energy into rapid pacing.

In the interim Marianne glanced down at the paper. The banner read, NELSON CONDEMNED FOR HIS CONDUCT.

At the end of the table, Thomas was urging her to "Read it loud, Marianne. What is it? Has he failed to walk on water?"

William turned on him. "Milord, the jest is not well taken. Such ingratitude is shameful and must be treated as such. Sooner or later this country must face the truth of what she has known all along, that a madman now resides at Windsor, and while he toils in his carrot patch removing his weeds, *he* is the most insidious weed, choking the life breath out of every Englishman."

Marianne looked up, pleased. This was the old William, assuming a steady posture of outrage, speaking the truth as he saw it with conviction.

Thomas, reprimanded and obviously impressed with William's anger, again suggested, "Well, for heaven's sake, read it, Marianne. The exploits of the Royal Farmer have always fascinated me. What could he possibly have done to top his other insanities?"

Quickly Marianne scanned the account. "It seems that HRH has proclaimed a Royal Condemnation of Lord Nelson," she began.

As William cursed, Thomas demanded, "For God's sake, why?"

Marianne tilted the paper closer to the candles. "It seems that there is a woman, milord."

"Isn't there always?"

"Emma Hamilton," she said, ignoring the remark and reading on. "Wife of Sir William Hamilton, British Ambassador to Naples."

Thomas sat up, clearly relishing someone else's scandal.

"Don't tell me. Lady Emma nursed Nelson's wounds, then Nelson nursed hers."

In spite of the somberness at table, Marianne smiled. "Something along those lines, milord." She read on. "Apparently her influence over Nelson is so great that he has disobeyed the King's orders to leave Naples and has been summoned home."

On hearing the foolishness spoken aloud, William exploded again. "Why don't we just pillory him, put him in stocks on Tyburn Hill? Then a grateful nation can parade by and spit on the man who singlehandedly has kept the French madness from our shores." Again he turned angrily away from the table.

Marianne tried to offer him assurance. "I doubt, William, if the entire nation shares George's condemnation. It would be my guess that Nelson would emerge as strong as ever."

"That's not the point," William protested, turning back to her. "The Royal Condemnation is part of history now. What will history say, that England devours her heroes, crowns them with one hand and thrusts a sword in their belly with the other? If Nelson's appetites included the Queen herself, then he should be given her as a small payment for leaving parts of himself scattered about the globe on behalf of England."

Jane smiled nervously. "Perhaps they are very much in love," she murmured, apparently missing the entire point.

Thomas stood now and tried to place a comforting arm about William's shoulder. "It will pass," he soothed. *"You* are probably suffering more than Nelson. What could a Royal Condemnation mean to him? And besides, the Lady Emma has apparently been an effective nurse in the past. Undoubtedly they are at this moment closeted in some secret rendezvous, nursing each other."

But William could not be assuaged. He shrugged off Thomas' arm and looked about at the table as though he were surrounded by idiots and children. Wearily he shook his head. "You don't understand."

Then suddenly the weariness seemed to slip off him. He paced rapidly twice more the length of the table, his hand continuously massaging the stump of his arm, his head down, a tremendous conflict brewing somewhere in his mind. Marianne watched, as did the other two, all sensing a painful decision in the making.

He looked up from his pacing. For just a moment, she saw the same man who had exploded in brilliant and righteous indignation at the foolishness of the Masquerade Ball. "I am going back," he announced.

Jane started forward, her face anguished, clearly wondering if she were on the verge of losing him again.

"I am going back," he repeated with greater conviction. "I'm serving no one here, least of all myself. My God, what time I have wasted!" A smile broke out on his face. "The Royal Farmer had better look up from his carrot patch, for I intend to bombard him with enough verbal shot to make him think he's with Nelson at the pitch of battle."

With that he grabbed for the paper and left the room, the sound of his footsteps reverberating on the stone floors, not measured and remote like a funeral march, but angry, decisive, determined.

A few moments later, Jane murmured her apologies and followed after him.

Thomas sat back in his chair. He drained his wineglass. "Taking it all a bit seriously, isn't he?" he commented.

Marianne leaned forward. "Nelson is more than just a man to him, Thomas. Surely you can understand that."

"He's Jesus Christ to him, that's who he is," Thomas retorted.

"No. William looks at him and says, why not me? He's never really recovered from his time in Paris, you know." She paused, then smiled. "Until now."

Slowly Thomas stood and walked the length of the table. Something in his expression suggested to Marianne that William and his trials were no longer the topic of the evening. He pushed the cutlery to one side and sat on the table, looking down on her. "He needs a woman," he said, resting his hand on her knee.

"Lord Nelson?" She smiled. "Obviously he has one."

"I mean William."

"And he has Jane."

"I repeat, he needs a woman."

His voice was changed, deeper, his gaze intense upon her. "Did you ever love him?" he asked, his hand moving up her leg.

Marianne kept her eyes on his hand. "I thought I did once. He's a gentle man."

"Did you love him?" he insisted.

Finally she looked up at him, past sensations rising vividly in her mind as his hand pressed against her upper leg. "No, milord," she whispered.

For a moment, some controversy seemed to be raging in his head. Then all was resolved as he lifted her to her feet, then into his arms as, nuzzling her neck and ear, he softly pleaded, "Nurse me."

On a fair spring morn, as they were leaving the Great Hall in the company of their two young sons for their daily walk across the headlands, Marianne glanced toward the gate and saw a messenger on horseback. For a moment she thought it was the courier from London bearing *The Bloomsbury Gazetteer*. Then she remembered William's hasty departure three weeks previously, with Jane at his side, on his way to do battle with the King. With Editor Pitch back at his desk, all messengers had stopped.

Then who?

"Milord," Marianne said, pointing toward the gate, where the watchmen were holding the messenger at bay.

She saw Thomas look up and squint into the sun, then slowly rise from his kneeling position before James. "Wait here with the children," he commanded, and Marianne obeyed.

She watched him as he took great strides across the courtyard. His appearance gave her constant pleasure. Nearing fifty, he was still the most intensely attractive man she'd ever known.

These reflections made her blush as she watched him draw near the first grillwork barrier, the watchman shouting something at him now. She saw the gates rising. Apparently the messengers had passed inspection.

In front of Thomas, the horse stopped. The messenger alighted and withdrew from his saddlebag a pamphlet of some sort. From that distance it was imposssible to read Thomas' face or the nature of the message. A moment later she saw him motion for one of the groomsmen to take the horse and rider away for refreshments and respite. The watchmen lowered the grilles. Thomas continued to stand, intently reading the message.

Still she waited in the cool spring morning sun, her
curiosity increasing. Edward, at her side, scuffed annoy-
ingly at the gravel, clearly irritated that his morning outing
was being delayed.

Whatever the nature of the message, it obviously was
quite lengthy and occupying all of Thomas' attention. She
was on the verge of going to him when slowly he started
walking back to her, his head bowed.

While he was still several yards away, she called out,
"Thomas, what is it?"

He did not reply, but simply drew near and placed in
her hands a large pamphlet made of parchment and
rimmed in gold, a crest of some sort on the front, and
bound with a pale lavender ribbon.

"An invitation," he said calmly. "Apparently our exile
is coming to an end."

She tried to read his calm expression and at the same
time read the elegant print. But the sun danced across the
snow white parchment and caused the words to blur,
"From whom?" she asked, bewildered by the sense of
panic within her.

"Beckford," he replied, walking a few steps away. "It
seems that Billy has at last built his tower. There will be
a week-long celebration at Christmas." He turned back.
"As you can see, Lord and Lady Eden have been invited."

At that moment she recognized the panic within her,
for she saw it clearly on his face. The terms of their exile
had been hard but simple. All that had been asked of them
was that they find within themselves all that they required. This they had done and quite successfully. Now
apparently the rest of the world wanted to take a look
at them, to see how they had fared.

In the silent interim, her eyes finally adjusting to the
sun on white parchment, she studied her lengthy invitation,
which included a guest list and a calendar of events, culminating with the grand unveiling of Fonthill Abbey. She
thought grimly, "I can't go through with it." Thomas was
still pacing a distance from her, an expression on his face
which suggested that he shared her fears.

"Read carefully, lady," he suggested now. "All the bad
children are being lumped together."

Puzzled, she looked again at the guest list. Two names
down, after Benjamin West, President of the Royal Acad-

emy, and the satirical poet, Dr. Wolcot, she saw them, incredible titles appearing so primly on the page—Lord Horatio Nelson, followed by Lord and Lady Hamilton.

"Good heavens!" she gasped. "What a company!"

Then apparently his mind was made up. He returned to her side and took the pamphlet from her. "We'll give the messenger food and rest, then send him on his way. I fear that Lord and Lady Eden will be occupied during that time."

On a clear tone of resolve, he stuffed the pamphlet inside his jacket and bent over James, drawing the bonnet about his pink smooth face.

With caution, she asked, "Occupied with what, milord?"

Astonished, he looked up. "You're not suggesting that you want to go, are you?"

She hesitated, trying to organize her thoughts, taking refuge for a moment in Edward's upturned face as he sulkily insisted that they "go see the ocean."

"In a minute," she said, smiling, and released his hand. As Edward amused himself with a fistful of pebbles, she faced Thomas. "I don't *want* to go, milord," she began, "but perhaps we should."

He raised up from bending over James. "Why?" he demanded. "I see no reason for such an occasion. We are contented here. I've said from the beginning that Beckford's tower was insanity—"

"Billy's tower has nothing to do with it," she interrupted.

"Then what?"

Again she paused, frustrated at being asked questions that she could not answer for herself. She yearned, with heart and mind, to be of real service to him, to prove beyond all doubt that she was able to compensate for his exile, when he'd broken all barriers and taken her as his wife. She could not simply continue to satisfy him in bed and give him children. Eden Castle had always had a Lady Eden. If she now was filling the role, then she must fill it properly.

These thoughts and others, the sight of her son playing at her feet, bearing the onus of bastardy, with both his parents in hiding behind the walls of Eden Castle, all this pressed against her.

Finally she said simply, "For their sakes"—she motioned to their sons—"we should go."

Thomas stared at her. "Do you know the risks?"

She nodded.

"I'm not even certain we can count on Billy's good intentions."

"I think we can."

"In society's eyes we have done wrong."

She smiled. "Then we must correct society's vision."

He looked at her as though trying to read the conviction behind her words. He stepped close and lifted her face. "I will not bear silent witness to anyone who hurts or spurns you."

She covered his hand with hers. "With you beside me, I shall feel neither, milord."

He bent close and lightly kissed her. Immediately Edward objected by wriggling between them, still insistent that they proceed with the point of the outing.

As Thomas scooped him up, more to get him out of the way than anything else, he said, "I see no need to make a firm decision now. The messenger will stay until morning. I believe it requires more thought on both our parts."

Marianne nodded, although in truth her mind was already firm in its decision. They would go, of that she was certain. What she was less certain of was what would happen once they arrived. As she followed after Thomas and the boys across the inner courtyard, one thought only interposed between her and peace. By this time next year, she told herself, she would know what her future would be, whether she would be free to venture beyond the boundaries of the moors as Lady Eden, or as Thomas Eden's whore.

For the first time, she realized how safe it had been not knowing.

As the months passed with alarming rapidity, there were so many worries in Marianne's mind that she scarcely knew which one to attend to first. Her wardrobe for one, after years of neglect needed refurbishing, and since she was loath to leave her sons for a trip to London, the dressmakers came to her, bearing bolts of elegant satin and brocade and silk. In the rush of excitement and fittings, she sometimes managed to forget the specifics of the or-

deal ahead of her. But on certain evenings, after the
tradesmen, the fitters, the furriers had retired for the night,
and she was left alone amid the trunks and packing cases,
she stared at the image in the pier glass, looking back at
her, and thought, "How old she looks at twenty-six, how
plain, how undistinguished." In such despairing moments,
she wondered why she had forced him into the decision,
staking everything on a foolish Christmas Masque, sally-
ing forth into the enemy camp without weapons or defense,
a witless maneuver.

On this particular night, the first of December, with the
date of their departure less than two weeks away, she sat
alone in her chambers, listening to Thomas grumble in
the next room. The tailors had now turned their attentions
to him, had convinced him that the comfortable and worn
black jackets he was accustomed to wearing were not suitable for such a grand occasion.

Apparently he was protesting everything from the cut of
the new fashions to the material itself. Listening, she
smiled, hearing in his honest outburst a resentment as
deep as her own. What a big to-do about absolutely nothing! The magnificent wardrobe, the presence of three
lady's maids, the elegant new coiffure, would not alter
her in the slightest.

Suddenly she was too tired to care one way or the other.
As male voices continued to rise and fall in the next
room, she half closed the window on the cold December
air, shrugged herself out of her dressing gown, and slipped
between cool sheets.

She had always survived, would always survive.

It was understandable that Billy Beckford was determined to entertain his guests, particularly his special guest,
the Hero of the Nile, in the grandest manner possible. And
the great attraction was of course to be the Abbey, as it
had now come to be called. James Wyatt, the architect,
was to be of the party and thus needed no extra goad
to persuade him to see to it that the still uncompleted
building was looking its best with no sign of work or workmen when the time came.

But the Abbey was to be kept well in the background
until a grand finale on the last night. Before then, the
guests would find it no hardship to be confined to the

grandeur of Fonthill Splendons and to tours of the demesne, carefully planned so as to keep the new toy as much out of sight as possible—not an easy task.

Very early in the dark hours of a cold snowy mid-December morning, an entourage of three carriages left Eden Castle. In the lead carriage were Lord and Lady Eden, behind them their servants, and in the third carriage their trunks. Late that afternoon the entourage pulled into the private lane which led to the isolation of Fonthill Splendons.

Marianne stared bleakly out of the window, remembering the last time she'd traveled this road, the morning of the false marriage. The same man was sitting opposite her now, yet how they both had changed. Apparently Thomas saw the look on her face and misinterpreted it ."Shall we turn back, lady?" He smiled.

She shook her head. "No, William would never forgive us."

He laughed outright. "I could have sworn that William would have appeared at the castle gate in time to stow away atop the carriage."

Inside her fur muff, Marianne felt her hands trembling. She missed her sons, the warm familiarity of Eden Point. The coming ordeal rose vividly before her mind. Her brain felt disordered. As Thomas, now leaning out of the window, shouted, "There it is!" her heart stopped.

Not knowing what to expect on arrival at a Great House, she was apprehensive to find only servants about her. Neither their host, Billy Beckford, nor any of the guests were in sight. Within moments of their arrival, they had been ushered up to private chambers, the door had been closed, and they were as alone as they had been in the carriage.

Instantly she took it as a bad omen. But Thomas reassured her that it was standard, that the guests and the host always kept well out of sight until the entire company met that night for the first ball. Somewhat reassured, Marianne settled uncomfortably on the edge of a stiff unused bed and watched awkwardly as the maids unpacked her trunks. She longed to help, but with a discreet shake of his head, Thomas told her no. To add to her feeling of isolation, he left their chambers a few moments

later and did not return until it was dark, with brandy on
his breath and a flush of excitement on his face as he
informed her that he'd met Nelson and that Billy sent her
his warmest welcome.

He seemed so at ease, so sure of himself, while she was
not faring well at all. "I don't understand," she complained.

Behind her, Thomas stretched out across the bed as
relaxed as she'd ever seen him. "Understand what?" he
mumbled, looking as though he were tired and on the
verge of sleep.

"What's the point?" she demanded, confronting him at
the foot of the bed. "We go to all of these absurd preparations and travel all this distance to spend the first hours
in compete isolation."

"Only the ladies," he said, smiling sleepily up at her.

"Why the ladies?" she demanded.

"To rest. To prepare for the evening."

"And why not the men?"

Slightly annoyed, he grumbled, "Oh, for God's sake,
Marianne. It's always been like this. I don't know why.
The ladies appear at a certain time."

"Like trained dogs?"

He raised up on his elbows. "Would you have wanted
to go with me to the clubroom?"

"It might have been better than what I did, which was
nothing." Her boredom and nervous tension were taking a
tremendous toll. Before his calm expression, she felt her
anger vault. In a rush of emotion she began to suspect that
only *she* had been isolated, that someplace in the grand
palace the ladies had met in similar fashion as the gentlemen. Only she had been left out, Eden's whore, the fisherman's daughter who undoubtedly still smelled of fish.

Although she was perfectly aware of her foolishness,
there was nothing she could do to control it. As the dangerous feelings increased, she turned away from his smiling
face and took all of her misery with her to a far window-
seat.

She was not aware of him near her until he touched her,
lifted her face revealing tears. "I've never seen you cry
thus," he murmured.

"I've never felt this way," she wept. "I don't want to
stay here, Thomas. Please, let's go home."

Gently he lifted her to her feet and held her close. "You have nothing to be afraid of."

"You don't understand," she cried. "I don't belong."

Quickly he scolded her. "You are my wife."

"In North Devon, perhaps," she replied feverishly. "But not here." Struggling free, she ran to the far side of the room. He started after her when there was a knock on the door, the maids bringing a light supper. Thomas retreated at their intrusion.

They ate in silence, or more accurately, he ate. She touched nothing. A short time later, the maids returned, like executioners, to "prepare her," or so they said. As they led her into the little dressing room off the sitting room, she looked back at Thomas. There was a peculiar expression on his face. Disappointment? Regret?

She was certain of both, and like a prisoner under sentence of death, she submitted to the cleansing and dressing process, confident that within an hour it would make no difference.

Fonthill Splendons was a massive, overgrand palace filled with a network of vast marble corridors, most of them lined with oil portraits of past London officialdom. The grandest of all was a pink marble corridor called the "Avenue of Lord Mayors," a cavernous rosy-tinted hall lined on both sides with bronze busts of all the past Lord Mayors of London.

Down this corridor now, preceded by two pages carrying torches, passed Lord and Lady Eden. The walk had been endless from their chambers on the fourth floor to the lower reception rooms. Marianne, beautifully gowned in white satin cut low in the fashion of the day to reveal her breasts, a single strand of pearls about her neck, her own hair simply done up and curled lightly about her face, shivered as she walked, one hand resting lightly on Thomas', which seemed to be rising higher and higher in the air. Gently she pushed it down to shoulder height. She wished she'd brought her cape and hoped fervently she'd stop shivering before they joined the company—wherever they might be.

The mood from which she had suffered earlier in the day had now diminished. It was still there, though now it had solidified into a kind of numbness. The image of the condemned continuously came to her mind.

The marble corridor was empty save for the fixed and frozen busts of rather pompous-looking gentlemen and, of course, the two young pages who hurried along before them, always keeping a discreet distance in front.

"Are you as well as you look, madame?" whispered Thomas, scarcely moving his lips, keeping his head erect, eyes straight ahead.

"I've never been worse, milord," she whispered back. "It reminds me of a hot August morning when I was a girl—"

Suddenly the hand which supported hers curled tightly around her arm. She knew he disliked any reference to that morning. Now he stopped, the echoing sound of all footsteps ceasing, as the two pages halted, keeping their faces tactfully averted.

He stared sternly down on her. "Then we shall turn about," he said firmly.

But she held her ground. "No, milord. Let's proceed. We've come this far."

Finally he lifted his hand again into the air, she placed her hand atop it, and once again the dreary little procession was moving forward, the two pages walking more slowly now.

There was a sharp turn at the conclusion of the pink marble corridor. Marianne found herself in a massive Rotunda with black and white checkerboard marble floor and gigantic Greek statuary lining the walls, virile young men, naked, in various positions of athletic prowess, their empty marble eyes blank and unseeing in spite of the effort on their chiseled faces.

What a convenient infirmity, Marianne thought. Since the faculty most revealing of terror was the eyes, how marvelous for a while to be without them.

As they crossed the Rotunda, she heard the first signs of life, musical instruments being tuned and, more ominous, the continuous roar of human voices, thousands of voices, or so it seemed. Her hand no longer rested atop Thomas', but now it grasped at it as though that single support were all between her and collapse.

Beyond the Rotunda, they entered another small corridor, two rows of uniformed stewards on both sides, their

eyes as fixed and sightless as the Greek Athletes. Beyond
the corridor was a small reception hall. The music and
voices were overpowering in her ears. She saw Billy
Beckford, standing in the center of a high arched door,
looking out over the most immense ballroom she had ever
seen.

The two pages ran ahead and summoned Billy's attention. He looked over his shoulder in their direction, a
broad grin breaking on his still boyish face. Within the
instant he was upon them, his arms outstretched, grasping
Thomas by the shoulders in clear and uninhibited affection.

"Thomas." He smiled. "I was about to give up—on both
of you."

Then Marianne was the sole recipient of his attention
as he approvingly scanned her from head to toe. "Lady
Eden," he murmured. "If only the heart were visible,
you could see how full mine is now at the sight of you."

It seemed excessive, but she leaned toward him and extended her hand. "Thank heavens, Mr. Beckford, that the
heart is concealed, for mine, I fear, would be a still and
frozen sight."

In concern, he studied her hand. "You *are* cold, lady."

"Not cold, Mr. Beckford. Terrified."

Briefly a sympathetic smile flickered across his face. "I
understand the cause," he said kindly, "but believe me,
there's no reason for it." He stepped closer, pressing her
hand to his breast as though to warm it. "I love Thomas
like a brother. I would do nothing to hurt him. Or you.
Do you believe me?"

She nodded. Beyond the arched door the voices rose, the
delicate peal of female laughter supported by a solid
layer of lower male tones. She was aware of Thomas and
Billy staring at her. In an attempt to shift both their focus
and the conversation, she retrieved her hand. "Mr. Beckford, I look forward to seeing your Abbey. I understand
it's the tallest tower in all of England."

The man beamed. "More than that, lady. It's a miracle,
and on the closing night of the party I shall show it to you
in all its dazzling beauty."

"I shall look forward to it, sir."

"Now," said Mr. Beckford, "as the musicians are about
to start, let me introduce you to the company. How selfish
of me to keep you to myself."

Thomas was beside her again, his hand raised. As Beck-ford moved ahead of them to the doorway, she lifted one trembling hand and placed it over Thomas' and remem-bered almost cruelly the three-room, low-ceilinged cottage in Mortemouth, the place of her birth, her mother dead, her now mad father, her half-brother Russell who served as her husband's manservant, and her half-sister Jane, a common-law wife who had once operated one of the most notorious salons in London. The accumulative weight of her lack of credentials swept over her. After tonight, this blue-blooded bastion would never be the same.

But at the precise moment when she needed a smile, one appeared on her face for all the wrong reasons. As Thomas led her through the doorway, she saw the ballroom for the first time, thronged with elegantly dressed and coiffed ladies and gentlemen, casually chatting.

Billy's voice sounded strangely weak and faraway as he personally took over the duties of introduction. A uni-formed attendant struck the floor twice with his standard. The voices hung for a moment on the air, then diminished as, with one accord, as though all heads, all eyes, were being controlled and manipulated by a common cord, they turned and faced Marianne where she stood at the top of the stairs.

"Ladies and gentlemen," Billy began in his faraway voice. "It gives me great and warm pleasure to introduce Lord and Lady Eden of Eden Point, North Devon."

She stood beside Thomas and felt the weight of their eyes, a weight compounded now by the absolute silence in the vast room. She tried to make out specific faces, but couldn't. Over her head the endless rows of chandeliers only distorted her vision further. Were *they* to do some-thing now? Had the entire party simply come to a halt?

Still no movement, no sound. Even the musicians in the upper gallery had apparently lost interest in their instru-ments and were staring down on her. If she did not move soon, there was a distinct possibility that she would never move again.

Then, movement. Not from her, but from the front row of the gaping company, a woman beautifully gowned in black silk, diamonds around her neck and twisted through her fair hair, stepped forward. She was smiling and approaching the stairs, the most beautiful woman

Marianne had ever seen, something in her face which was unassailable as though she were well aware that she was the only one moving and regretted her isolation, but not enough to cease movement.

She was climbing the steps now, gracefully lifting her gown, her eyes trained only on Marianne, the smile broadening. Like an apparition she came until at last she was standing directly before Marianne, her violet eyes sparkling, her voice a cool caress. "Lady Eden," she smiled. "How I've looked forward to meeting you. My name is Emma Hamilton."

The sense of silent winter which had encompassed Marianne dissolved. In the sincere warmth of that smile, she felt the thaw in all parts of her brain. Then here she was, the notorious Emma, the woman for whom Nelson had disobeyed his King.

"Milady," murmured Marianne, smiling gratefully, taking the hand extended to her. "I was afraid I'd wandered into a graveyard. How reassuring is the light in your eyes."

Emma Hamilton laughed prettily and leaned close in confidence. "Don't let them fool you, my dear. Most of them *are* corpses." Then she turned her attention to Thomas, extending to him the same heartfelt greeting. "I don't know the West Country very well, milord, but I hear your Eden is appropriately named."

Thomas glowed under the compliment. "It is, milady, and we must remedy your lack of knowledge of the place. Eden Castle is always opened to you."

She bowed her head in acceptance of the invitation. Beyond Emma's smooth white shoulder, Marianne saw the company, still gaping. "Milady," she whispered. "What is the order of these affairs? How long must we stand like this? I feel like a prize hog on the block."

Again Emma laughed and drew Marianne close to her. From off the white shoulders, Marianne caught a delicate whiff of perfume. "I'd say you've stood long enough," whispered Emma. "Perhaps it would help if you were aware of the service you are performing for them. Our appearance on these steps will fill the silence of their breakfast tables for months to come." Emma took her arm now and led her a step or two down. "And I assure you, milady," she whispered, "you do not in any way resemble a hog, prize or otherwise."

She took her arm and led her the rest of the way down the steps. As they passed by Billy, standing midway on the stairs, Marianne noticed a warm look pass between the two of them, Billy's eyes seeming to say "Thank you."

Emma was talking again, apparently impervious to the gaping faces. "I tried to seek you out this afternoon, Marianne," she said, softly. "But I was told you were resting. I feared this ordeal for you and felt that if we entered together, it might go easier for you."

Regretfully Marianne shook her head. "I was not resting. In truth I was deciding whether I should stay or leave. Your company would have settled the matter quickly for me."

She felt Emma's arm around her waist now. "Of all the rituals involved in these country house parties," she whispered, "I find the early evening gentleman's hour the most boring of all. Shall we walk tomorrow afernoon?" she proposed then.

Marianne smiled. The woman was irresistible. "I'd like that very much."

Emma leaned closer. "Meet me in the Rotunda at four o'clock. Perhaps we can steal a glance at Billy's miraculous tower."

They were on the floor of the ballroom now. The crowd was still frozen in their attention, mostly old faces, heavily veined, colorless, though there were a few young ones sprinkled here and there. She was aware of Thomas behind her, chatting to Billy, the four of them still set very much apart.

From the front row of the company, Marianne saw two men step forward, one short, middle-aged with graying hair, the buttons on his coat straining to hold back a slight paunch. And the other—

He was unmistakable. He wore a dazzling red uniform with dark blue trim. The front of his chest was covered with gold medallions and ribbons, his hair graying slightly, arranged in a soft pageboy. A black patch covered one eye, and one arm of his coat was pinned neatly up. His face was peculiarly tender and sensitive-appearing, a beautiful transparent English complexion, so fine around the temples that she could see the traceries of blood vessels. Here was Napoleon's nemesis, the Hero of the Nile.

"Dear God," she thought, "if only William were here."

Then Emma was guiding her, not toward the dashing figure of Horatio Nelson, but rather toward the short, squat, uncomfortable-looking little man who stood rigidly at attention beside Nelson, as though trying to match his stature.

"Lord and Lady Eden," Emma said, "I would like you to meet my husband, Lord William Hamiton."

The man stepped forward as though from a receiving line, received Thomas' handshake, and murmured a greeting, then lifted Marianne's hand and pressed it lightly to his lips. "Lady Eden," he said with a smile. "Rumors of your beauty were sadly underrated. I fear that between my wife and yourself, the rest of the unfortunate ladies of the company might as well retire to their chambers."

He seemed gallant and warm, a sadness in his slightly dimmed eyes, a look about him which suggested that the facade must be preserved despite personal humiliation.

"Milord," Marianne said, curtsying to him. "Thank you for your generous words. But the women here need feel no threat from me."

Lord Hamilton countered gallantly. "What they need feel and what they truly feel are quite opposite. Your beauty speaks for itself."

The intensity of his gaze caused a blush to creep up her cheeks. As though she sensed her discomfort, Emma was there again, guiding her to one side until she stood directly before the man himself.

"Lady Eden," Emma said simply, as though she were aware of the inadequacy of words, "Horatio Nelson."

For a moment he only stared down on her. The blush which had commenced with Lord Hamilton grew and spread until she was certain it covered her entire face. What a state of mind God must have enjoyed, she thought, when He created this man, for if ever He created a man in His own image, this was he. And He had succeeded with all parts, from the elegantly slanted forehead to the patrician nose to the firm beautifully molded mouth.

Aware that she was gazing as intently as he, she extended her hand and bowed her head, resting her eyes for a moment on the marble floor. "Milord," she whispered.

As he pressed her hand to his lips, she again thought of

William Pitch. "Milord," she said, "a dear friend of mine sends his highest esteem and very best regards."

Nelson acknowledged the sentiment graciously. "I thank you, milady. We are in need at the present of high esteem and best regards."

She remembered the Royal Condemnation and William's outrage at it. "The times will pass, milord," she continued. "Frequently it has happened in our history that the people lean in one direction and the monarch leans in another."

Suddenly in the small group around her, there was silence as profound as the greater silence emanating from the vast room. Had she said to much? The wrong thing?

Then Lord Nelson gave her a disarming, grateful smile. "Your candor is as refreshing as your beauty, Lady Eden. Please convey my thanks to your dear friend. Support from unknown quarters is perhaps the most rewarding of all."

Then Marianne stepped aside and made way for Thomas, and a moment later the musicians began to play and the company at last dispersed for the first dance. Without knowing precisely how it happened, Marianne found herself in partners with Lord Hamilton, Thomas paired with Emma, Lord Nelson retreating to a far table, surrounded by his aides.

"Don't worry," Emma whispered, as she took her place in the square. "He never dances. Since Cape St. Vincent, his balance is quite off."

Marianne nodded. The music commenced and as the stately configuration evolved, she noticed Emma chatting warmly with Thomas, her face glowing, as though she were quite at ease under the close scrutiny of both husband and lover.

It was well after four in the morning when the music came to an end. Marianne had danced continuously for over five hours, meeting an endless succession of faces, mostly male, occasionally catching glimpses of Thomas watching her, an unmistakable glow of pride on his face. And Emma's presence was everywhere, moving from group to group, settling occasionally next to Nelson and once leaning close and kissing him lightly on the cheek.

For Marianne, the terror was over. If she had not been wholly accepted, neither had she been wholly rejected. In the early hours of the morning, as Thomas escorted her up the steps, she heard Emma call out behind her, "Don't forget our appointment tomorrow, Marianne. While the gentlemen solve the problems of Empire, we shall solve the problems of the gentlemen."

Marianne looked back over her shoulder and saw the elegant woman on the arm of Lord Nelson, Lord Hamilton trailing behind like a dutiful pet. "The Rotunda at four?" she confirmed.

Emma nodded. Lord Nelson and Lord Hamilton bowed to her, then Thomas whisked her away. A single page led them back up to their chambers, a hurried yet quiet walk with the glorious evening still spinning in her head. Inside their rooms, she dimissed her sleepy-eyed servants and sent them off to bed. Thomas closed the door behind them, then leaned against it, his eyes soft in the firelight.

Almost self-consciously she stood in the center of the room. She experienced a surge of enormous emotions, mystifying in their intensity. "Milord," she asked, "is that a look of pleasure or displeasure?"

He smiled and shook his head. "There is not a gentleman in Fonthill who would not eagerly change places with me at this moment."

She closed her eyes and turned away for fear he would misinterpret her tears. Then she felt his hands on her shoulders, felt them moving down her back separating buttons from buttonholes. Methodically, tenderly he undressed her, and at last pulled the singe clasp that held her hair. She stepped out of the circle of clothes and faced him. In a rush, he grasped her to him and carried her to the bed.

She watched him as he shed his clothes. He always looked, she thought, very young when he was on the verge of making love to her. Instantly she resented the quarter of a century that existed between them and prayed that God would see fit to take them at the same time.

The thought of life without him was intolerable.

The next five days were among the most glorious that she had ever known, leisurely afternoon walks with Emma, an intimacy springing up between the two women as though they had known each other forever. There were nightly banquets and masques, and on occasion, when pressed by the company, Lord Nelson held them captivated

with firsthand accounts of battles in faraway places, endless color and light and elegance, and always at night,
the most intense and gratifying love-making she'd ever
shared with Thomas.

On the evening of December 23 as darkness fell, the
guests set out in a fleet of carriages with Nelson in the
lead and were driven in a winding route to Billy's Abbey
through thick snowy woods illuminated by numberless
lamps suspended in the trees and accompanied by a
military band playing solemn airs and marches.

In the second carriage, behind Nelson and Emma, Marianne leaned close to Thomas, feeling the drama in the
cold air, her senses almost numbed from the bombard-
ment of the past few days, yet still alert and ready for
Billy's "miracle."

As the carriages rolled slowly through the snow, the
effect was greatly increased by the continuous rolling of
drums placed about on distant eminences, by the blaze of
lights displayed here and there, sometimes moving, at
others stationary, now gleaming from bright arms and
armor, then darkness being permitted to enshroud all.

Her head bobbing from one window to the other,
Marianne whispered, "I've never seen anything like this
in my life, Thomas."

"Nor will you ever see anything like it again," he said,
clearly as impressed as she. "I believe that Billy has really
done it this time."

Suddenly the woods gave way, and before them on a
high knoll, completely surrounded by blazing torches, she
saw it, the most dazzling structure she'd ever seen, a
gigantic Abbey, its turrets ablaze in the light of torches,
its tower stretching out of sight into the gray clouds overhead, a Gothic wonder with thousands of candles lighting
each mullioned window from inside as though at its heart
there were flames, a rich cluster of abbatial buildings,
buttresses, pinnacles, and fretted spires, towering in all
their pride and marking the ground with deep shadows
that appeared interminable, so far and so wide were they
stretched along.

The appearance, on the arrival of the company, hushed
them into silent admiration. Thomas stepped out and
reached back for Marianne, who could not take her eyes
off the monumental structure, increased now in the splen-

dor of near torches, contrasting with the deep shadows falling on the walls, battlements, and turrets of the edifice. Lights flickered here and there, striking the salient parts of the buttresses and arches of the Great Tower, until they faded into the gloom above.

All about them was the company, still stunned and silent. Ahead of them was Billy, the dreamer of the dream, clearly pleased by the reaction.

"Come!" he shouted, as though not to break the spell but to increase it. "The exterior merely conceals the greater glory of the interior." As the crowd filed passed, Thomas hung back and Marianne with him, both their heads tilted upward, studying the massive spire, which seemed to touch the roots of heaven.

Billy was beside them, an intimacy on his face which Marianne felt was reserved only for Thomas. The young man seemed to sense Thomas' speechlessness. After a moment's pause, he fell into Thomas' arms, clearly overcome.

"Remember the beginning of the dream?" he asked, softly. "I brought you to this very spot where nothing stood but dead trees."

Thomas nodded, obviously remembering. "Those were bleak days," he said quietly. "Both our dreams running far ahead of us."

Thomas drew Marianne close under one arm, Billy close under the other, his eyes glistening. "Let the Fates beware," he smiled, "when an Englishman sets his mind to something." Again he looked up to the height of the tower. "It's magnificent, Billy," he marveled. "Truly magnificent."

Billy beamed. "Benjamin West is going to paint it for me," he announced. He stepped forward, his arm raised, as though somehow they had failed to see and appreciate all of it. "The tower is two hundred and eighty feet, Thomas. Even Wyatt said it couldn't be done, but he did it." He started toward the massive arched doorway, dragging them after him. "Look," he said with a gesture. There, in the thirty-foot-high west doorway, posed for the purpose of contrast, was a dwarf. The contrast was effective. The small man made the doorway appear celestial in proportion.

Marianne took it all in, deeply moved, seeing in the gigantic structure something totally romantic and human.

"It's a perfect tribute, Billy, to the new century. England will be forever in your debt."

Billy smiled, then again he was running ahead of them, trying to gather together his guests, urging them all through the massive doorway past the dwarf, who grinned at them like an imp, as though he knew something they didn't.

Inside, Billy proved true to his word. They were taken on tour up the Great Staircase, through the Octagonal Salon, and beyond to St. Michael's Gallery and the elegantly furnished yellow Damask Drawing room, each chamber containing works of art more magnificent than the one before it.

At some point in the evening, she felt Emma beside her. "If this is a dream, pray God it lasts," she whispered.

Marianne agreed and smiled as she saw Emma take Nelson's arm, who seemed to be regarding it all with silent interest.

The evening culminated in a banquet in the medieval manner, the company all at ease, the gentlemen lifting glass after glass in toast to Billy's accomplishment. In the early hours of the morning, they were driven back to the old palace. Marianne turned in the carriage for a final glimpse of the Great Abbey.

She shook her head, still in awe. "Our sons must see it, Thomas," she said. "They must know the force of a dream and what it can do."

Thomas drew her close and lightly pressed her head against his shoulder. "They shall see it," he promised. "It will stand forever."

Nestling beneath his chin, she thought again of her sons. Suddenly she missed them terribly. "Let's go home tomorrow, milord," she whispered.

He hid his face in her hair.

"Home," he repeated.

It was late in the afternoon before their trunks were packed and loaded on the carriages. Billy came to bid them farewell. He embraced first Thomas, then Marianne. As he held her at arm's length after the embrace, she said, simply, "Thank you, Billy," and hoped that it would suffice and convey the weight of gratitude in her heart.

She saw Emma coming out the broad front doorway.

"You shan't get away without a final kiss," Emma said, coming closer, her arms opened. Marianne fell into them, returning the embrace. Laughing, she murmured, "I've run out of words with which to express my gratitude."

But Emma shushed her quickly. "It's I who should be grateful to you. Don't forget now what we have discussed. We'll take on all of London society next season. You and Lord Eden must come and stay with us. We'll have a glorious time, I promise."

Marianne nodded and returned the invitation. "And you have promised to come to Eden. Convey our farewells to Lord Nelson and your husband and remind both of them that Eden Castle will be honored with their presences."

Again there was a warm embrace. She saw Thomas holding the carriage door for her. Inside the carriage she leaned forward for a final farewell, consciously luxuriating in a tenderness for Billy, for Emma, for Thomas, for herself, like all deep feelings, concealing a melancholy strain.

As the carriage turned into the long driveway leading to the turnpike, she settled back in the seat, watching Thomas watching her. She considered herself fortunate, unlike Emma, to have a husband and lover combined in one man.

"How good," she thought, "how good all of it to belong to a race of men with as many facets as a diamond, kindness and compassion laced with cruelty and intolerance." Suddenly she sensed perceptions so sharp as to be almost unbearable, as though a layer of oblivion had lifted and permitted her one crystalline glimpse of the entire world in all its unlimited possibilities. She closed her eyes.

"Are you tired, Marianne?" Thomas asked gently.

"With joy, milord."

In the dark early hours of the following morning, their carriages rattled over the cobblestones leading to Eden Castle. Hurriedly the sleepy-eyed watchmen drew up the gates. Inside the inner courtyard, the drowsy servants tumbled from their carriage. Across from Marianne, nestled beneath a warm lap robe, Thomas slept. Beyond the carriage window, in the pale moonlight, in a scattering of light snow, she saw the whipping oak.

Quietly she stepped out and dismissed the lingering servants. As the footmen attended to the trunks, she walked slowly across the courtyard, as though drawn to the solid black object. Her joy now, like her terror then, was without understanding. She touched it, felt its cold hard surface beneath her fingers, her feelings pressing in upon her. For one splintered moment she tried to appraise them. She would like to have been able to say to herself, "It's been a good life." But it couldn't be appraised, for it was only an outline. And it wasn't over.

Again she reached out her hand and touched the wood cautiously, as though she were afraid of breaking something. A lantern threw Thomas' shadow, now very black, across the inner courtyard; he walked heavily, with uneven steps, hindered by his fatigue.

He stood directly behind her. "Milady," he said quietly. "Shall I remove it? It should be removed. I offered once before if you remember."

She remembered. But then as now she said, "No." But she did not say it fiercely as before, said it gently, as though merely objecting to the removal of an old friend. "No, milord," she said with a smile, facing him. "Leave it. Between the two of us, we may have need of it again."

Beyond the lantern in the darkness, the footmen continued to unload the trunks. It was late. Come morning, there was so much to attend to; her sons for one, and Eden Castle, and perhaps the spring visitation from Lord Nelson and Emma Hamilton, and the London season, and beyond that the Empire, and the powerful new century. She intended to have a hand in all of it.

She saw Thomas shivering with cold and fatigue. "Come, milord, she urged. "We will look in on our sons before we retire."

And so saying, and reassured that he was behind her, that now he would always be behind her, she led the way up the stairs to the Great Hall, as confident as though she had been designed by nature for such an ascent.

A pulsing romantic saga

Marilyn Harris
Bledding Sorrow

Within a magnificent, spirit-ravaged mansion, on
the eerily beautiful Yorkshire moors, a lovely child-
bride is kept drugged and hidden—forced to submit
to her husband's strange desires . . .

Ann Bledding, young mistress of the manor, dared
to escape with James, the handsome coachman: but
she was destined to re-enact the tortured passions of
an ancient horror too terrible to end—a love too
strong to die!

"A chilling novel, centered around an ancestral estate in
England, a recurring family madness, a ghastly crime
in the 17th Century, reappearing spectres . . . rich prose
and deftly maintained suspense."

Milwaukee Journal

AVON   31971 $1.95

SOR 5-77

AVON PRESENTS THE BEST
IN SPECTACULAR WOMEN'S ROMANCE

Kathleen E. Woodiwiss

The Flame and the Flower	35485/$2.25
The Wolf and the Dove	35477/$2.25
Shanna (large-format)	31641/$3.95

Laurie McBain

Devil's Desire	30650/$1.95
Moonstruck Madness	31385/$1.95

Rosemary Rogers

Sweet Savage Love	28027/$1.95
Dark Fires	23523/$1.95
The Wildest Heart	28035/$1.95
Wicked Loving Lies	30221/$1.95

The achievement of Avon's authors of original romances has been nothing less than a phenomenon—sweeping, passionate, beautifully written adventures that have thrilled millions of readers—the focus of the national media, and a whole new trend in publishing.

Available wherever paperbacks are sold, or direct from Avon Books, Mail Order Dept., 959 Eighth Ave., New York, N. Y. 10019. Includes 25¢ per copy for postage and handling; allow 4-6 weeks for delivery.

Shanna

A woman with surging desires
of the spirit, the flesh,
and the heart . . .

Ruark

A man burning to possess her
in vengeance and
in ecstasy . . .

Shanna

A romance of passion
beyond wildest dreams!

KATHLEEN E. WOODIWISS

The author of the bestselling epics **THE FLAME AND
THE FLOWER** and **THE WOLF AND THE DOVE** has
written a breathtaking saga that moves with rapturous abandon to London, the Caribbean, and Virginia—an unforget-
table novel that will stir the hearts of millions across the
country, throughout the world.

AVON 31641 $3.95

Permanent deluxe edition

SHANNA 4-77

*To her people
she was Sarah Wells.
To her Indian captors
she was . . .*

GHOST FOX

JAMES HOUSTON

AN EPIC NOVEL
OF RAPTURE AND SURVIVAL

"This stunning novel has everything going for it
to capture and hold the reader's imagination: exciting action and drama, convincing characteriza-
tions and ultimately, a very moving love story."
Publishers Weekly

"A powerful, totally convincing book, drumming
with action, tender and moving."
Cosmopolitan

"Impressively realized, appealing . . . an American historical novel of high quality."
Wall Street Journal

 Avon   35733 $1.95

GHOST 2-78